PRAISE FOR THE MARKED TRILOGY

"Exhilarating adventure in an edgy world of angels and demons highlights the opener of Day's Marked trilogy. Dynamic and vibrant, Eve is an impressive protagonist, and her fierce spirit and determination to make the best of her circumstances will keep readers enthralled."
—*Publishers Weekly*

"Day, a.k.a. multitalented author Sylvia Day, explodes onto the urban fantasy scene with a new twist on the Cain and Abel story. It's dark, gritty, and sexy to the max, so readers can be thankful the next chapter in this pulse-pounding series is only a month away!"　　—*RT Book Reviews*

"Great characters and terrific storytelling in a hot-blooded adrenaline ride. A keep-you-up-all-night read."　　　　　　　—Patricia Briggs,
#1 *New York Times* bestselling author

"*Eve of Darkness* is a sizzling, heart-pounding urban fantasy that thrilled and fascinated me from beginning to end. Eve is a smart, spirited heroine I won't soon forget!"　　—Jeri Smith-Ready, award-winning author of
Wicked Game and *Bad to the Bone*

TOR BOOKS BY SYLVIA DAY

Eve of Darkness
Eve of Destruction
Eve of Chaos

THREE
EVES

Sylvia Day

WRITING AS S. J. DAY

TOR

A TOM DOHERTY ASSOCIATES BOOK
NEW YORK

THREE EVES

Eve of Darkness copyright © 2009 by Sylvia Day
Eve of Destruction copyright © 2009 by Sylvia Day
Eve of Chaos copyright © 2009 by Sylvia Day

A Tor Book
Published by Tom Doherty Associates
175 Fifth Avenue
New York, NY 10010

www.tor-forge.com

Tor® is a registered trademark of Macmillan Publishing Group, LLC.

ISBN 978-1-250-30503-9 (trade paperback)

Our books may be purchased in bulk for promotional, educational, or business use. Please contact your local bookseller or the Macmillan Corporate and Premium Sales Department at 1-800-221-7945, extension 5442, or by email at MacmillanSpecialMarkets@macmillan.com.

First Edition: February 2019

Printed in the United States of America

0 9 8 7 6 5 4 3 2 1

CONTENTS

EVE OF DARKNESS

A story doesn't blossom into a published book until it is loved by an editor. A published book doesn't reach enough readers if it isn't championed by its editor. An author doesn't spread her wings fearlessly without the security of a supportive (and patient) editor.

I am grateful to Heather Osborn for her enthusiasm for the Marked series. There is nothing in the world like having an editor whose hopes and dreams for your stories are as limitless as your own.

Thank you, Heather.

ACKNOWLEDGMENTS

The art department at Tor, especially Seth Lerner. Months of work went into the packaging of the Marked series—design tweaks, background changes, multiple cover models. . . . The amount of time and effort that was invested in the covers means a great deal to me.

Melissa Frain at Tor, Nikki Duncan, and Joy Harris for loving this book and prodding me often to hurry up and finish the other two, which kept me motivated while doing so.

Denise McClain for the extremely thoughtful and helpful feedback.

Jordan Summers, Shayla Black, Karin Tabke, and Sasha White for being there for me whenever I needed a caring ear at the other end of the phone line. How blessed I am to have friends like you!

Gary Tabke for answering my questions regarding police procedures. Any errors are entirely mine.

Frauke Spanuth for her brilliant marketing branding and help with German translation.

Tina Trevaskis for honesty and friendship.

And Nikola Tesla for the radio, remote controls, and AC power, none of which I could have lived without while writing this book.

Sin is crouching at your door; it desires to have you but you shall master it.

—THE LORD TO CAIN, GENESIS 4:7

CHAPTER 1

The Devil is in the details.

Evangeline Hollis understood the true gist of that saying now, surrounded as she was by thousands of Satan's minions. Some wore Seattle Seahawks baseball caps, others wore San Diego Chargers jerseys. All bore detailed designs similar to tribal tattoos on their skin that betrayed both what species of cursed being they were and what their rank in Hell's hierarchy was. To her enhanced eyes, it looked like a damn festival for sinners. They were drinking beer, devouring nachos, and waving giant foam fingers.

In reality, the event was a football game in Qualcomm Stadium. The day was classic Southern California perfection—sunny and warm, the eighty-degree temperature balanced by a delightfully cool breeze. Mortals mingled with Infernal beings in blissful ignorance, simply enjoying a bit of afternoon spectator sport. To Eve, the scene was macabre; like watching hungry wolves sunning themselves alongside lambs. Gore, violence, and death were the inevitable result of any interaction between the two.

"Stop thinking about them."

Alec Cain's deep, sensual voice made her shiver inside, but outwardly she shot him a rueful glance over the top of her sunglasses. He was always telling her to ignore their prey when they weren't on the hunt. As if rogue fae, demons, mages, werewolves, dragons, and thousands of variants of the same were easily disregarded.

"There's a woman breastfeeding her child next to an incubus," she muttered.

"Angel." His nickname for her moved over her skin like a tangible caress. Alec's voice could turn driving directions into foreplay. "We're taking the day off, remember?"

She blew out her breath and looked away. At a few inches over six feet, Alec was blessed with a powerful chest and tautly ridged abdomen that were noticeable even through his fitted white tank. He had long, muscular legs presently showcased in knee-length Dickies shorts and biceps so beautifully defined they were coveted by both men and women.

He was her lover . . . occasionally. Like all sweets, Alec was delicious and satisfying, but too much of him caused a sugar crash that left her dazed and reeling. He'd also ruined life as she had known it. Her career aspiration had been interior design, not Infernal bounty hunting.

"If only it was that simple," Eve groused. "How can I go on vacation when I'm surrounded by work? Besides, they stink even when I'm ignoring them."

"All I smell is you," he purred, leaning over to nuzzle his nose against her cheek. "Yum."

"It creeps me out that they're everywhere. I went to McDonald's yesterday and the person serving me at the window was a faery. I couldn't even eat my Big Mac."

"Betcha ate the fries." Pulling down his shades, Alec looked at her with somber eyes. "There's a difference between staying on your toes and paranoia."

"I'm cautious, not a basket case. Until I find a way out of this mark business, I'm making the best of it."

"I'm proud of you."

Eve sighed. Having Alec for a mentor was such a bad idea, and not just because it was the equivalent of a Hollywood casting couch in most Marks' eyes. Never mind that the true "casting couch" was the exchange of sexual favors in return for a position you *wanted*. No one ever wanted the Mark of Cain.

The Marks' hierarchy started at the bottom with the newbies and topped off with Alec, the original and most badass Mark of them all. There was no way to surpass him. There was also no way to work with him. He was the quintessential loner, the very definition of the word. Yet here was Eve, a six-week newbie in the field, perched solidly at the top because he didn't trust anyone else to watch her back. She was important to him.

The other Marks thought working with God's primary enforcer had to be a vacation. While it was true that Infernals didn't mess with Alec unless they had a death wish, it didn't make things any easier. Demons now targeted *her* as a way to get to him. To make things worse, Alec had been marked so long that he'd forgotten what it was like to be new and confused. There were things he expected her to simply "know," and he became frustrated when he realized she didn't.

He squeezed her hand. "What happened to the girl who just wanted to forget about everything for a couple of hours?"

"That was before she was kidnapped and nearly blown to smithereens." Eve stood. "I'll be back. I need to use the little girls' room."

As she stood, Alec caught her wrist. Her brows rose in silent inquiry.

"Angel." He kissed the back of her hand. "When I tell you to stop thinking about them, it's not because I want you to live in a fantasy world.

I just want you to see the good stuff around you. You saw a mother nursing her baby, but you didn't see the miracle of it. You were too busy looking at the demon next to her. Don't give them the power to ruin your day."

Frowning, Eve absorbed his words, then nodded her acceptance. Alec had lived with the mark since the dawn of time and could still see miracles; she could try.

"I'll be right back," she said.

He released her. After inching her way past the other spectators in their aisle, Eve sprinted up the wide cement steps. She still marveled over the speed, strength, and agility that came with the mark burned into her upper arm. She'd always been athletic, but now she was Supergirl. Well . . . she couldn't fly. But she could jump really damn high. She could also see in the dark and bust through dead-bolted doors, talents she'd never anticipated needing or appreciating.

Eve reached the concourse and followed the signs to the nearest restroom. The line protruded just outside the entrance. Luckily, she wasn't desperate. More than anything, she'd just needed to get out of her seat.

So she waited patiently, rocking in her flip-flops with her hands in her pockets. An occasional breeze passed by, ruffling through her ponytail. It carried the mingled scent of evil and rotting souls, a pungent stench that made her stomach roil. It fell somewhere between decomposition and fresh shit, and it amazed her that the Unmarked couldn't smell it.

How had she lived twenty-eight years of her life in complete ignorance? How had Alec lived centuries in complete awareness?

"Mom!" The young boy in front of her was crossing his legs and wiggling madly. "I have to *go!*"

Although the woman looked as if she could be the child's sister, Eve wasn't unduly surprised. Many women in Southern California didn't age. They just became plasticized caricatures of their youthful selves. This one was bleached blonde with a perfect tan, breasts a size too large for her slender frame, and plumped, glossy lips.

The mother looked around.

"Let me go in the boys' bathroom," he begged.

"I can't go in there with you."

"I'll be done in a minute!"

Eve guessed the boy was around six years old. Old enough to pee by himself, but she understood the mother's concern. A child had been killed in a public restroom in nearby Oceanside while his aunt waited outside. The demon who orchestrated that horror had used the oldest trick in the book—pretending to be God.

The harried mother hesitated for a long moment, then gave a jerky nod. "Hurry. You can wash your hands here in the girls' bathroom."

The boy ran past the drinking fountains and ducked into the men's room. Eve offered a commiserating smile to his mom. The line moved incrementally forward. Two teenagers joined in behind her. They were dressed in the predominant fashion of layered tank tops paired with low-rise jeans. Expensive perfume saturated the air around them, which created a welcome relief from the odor of decay. In the stadium, the crowd roared. One of the Chargers' outside linebackers was a werewolf. From the high-frequency praise of the Infernals in the crowd, he'd done something worth cheering about.

"Why is the line so long?" the girl behind her asked.

Eve shrugged, but the woman in front of her replied, "The bathrooms down there—" she pointed to the left with a French manicured nail "—are closed for repairs."

As if on cue, the mark seared into Eve's deltoid began to tingle, then burn. She sighed and abandoned her place. "You can take my spot. I don't have to go that bad."

"Thanks," the teenager replied.

Eve headed to the left, muttering to herself, "Some vacation."

"You were bored anyway, babe," purred a familiar voice.

Glancing to the side, Eve watched as Reed Abel fell into step with her, his mouth curved in a devilish smile that belied the wings and halo he occasionally sported for shock value. He was a *mal'akh,* but there wasn't much angelic about Alec's brother.

"That doesn't mean I wanted to be put to work." Reed was the handler in charge of her assignments, which was just a nasty trick in her opinion. Why God allowed and encouraged dissension between the two brothers was beyond her comprehension.

"We could blow this taco stand," he suggested. "Go have some hot, sweaty fun."

She wasn't touching that invitation with a ten-foot pole. Like his brother, Reed scorched a girl in both good and bad ways. "Are you kidding about the assignment? Do you need me for something more substantial or what?"

"You thought it was substantial enough before." He winked mischievously.

Eve smacked him. "Don't be crude. I refuse to be the latest toy you and your brother fight over. Go find something else to play with."

"I'm not playing with you."

There was something sincere in his tone. She ignored it by necessity, although less circumspect parts of her perked up.

"The bathroom?" she asked instead, when the yellow OUT OF SERVICE sign came into view.

"Yeah." He caught her arm and tugged her closer. "Raguel suggested it was time for an extension of your classroom training. I'll go get Cain."

Raguel was the archangel whose jurisdiction she fell under. He was the bail bondsman, Reed was the dispatcher, and she was the bounty hunter. It was a well-oiled system for most, but her road had been bumpy from the very beginning.

She sniffed the air. The acrid stench of Infernal wrinkled her nose. "You know . . . this is like sending a medical student into brain surgery the day she first reads about it."

"You don't know your own strengths, babe."

She glared. "I know when I'm getting my ass kicked."

"You're batting a thousand so far. This one's a wolf and you're good with them. But be careful anyway."

"Easy for you to say. You're not the one risking your hide."

His lips pressed to her temple in a quick, hard kiss. "Risking yours is enough, trust me."

Skirting the OUT OF SERVICE sign, Eve entered the men's restroom, lamenting the fact that she was wearing her favorite flip-flops. Due to the rigors of her "job," she'd taken to wearing combat boots whenever she left home, but Alec had coaxed her into going casual today. She should have known better.

The harsh ammonia smell of stale urine assaulted her nostrils. Finding her target was easy. He stood in the center of the room, alone. A teenage werewolf who was eerily familiar.

"Remember me?" he asked, smiling.

The boy was tall and thin, his face long and unremarkable. He wore a dirty gray hooded sweatshirt and jeans so low his ass was hanging out. A dark spot moved across his cheek and came to rest on his left cheekbone. His detail—swirls around a diamond shape. Like the mark on her arm, it served a similar purpose to military insignia.

Recognition hit her hard, followed by an immediate chill down her spine. "Shouldn't you be in Northern California with your pack?"

"The Alpha sent me down here to even the score. He thinks Cain needs to learn what it's like to lose someone he loves."

"There was no way to save the Alpha's son," she argued. "Cain doesn't pick and choose his hunts. He follows orders."

"He made a deal. For you. And he broke his promise."

Eve frowned. Alec had never mentioned a deal to her. But that was something she would explore later. There was a more immediate question. "You think you can take me by yourself?"

His smirk turned into a grin. "I brought a friend."

"Great." That was never good.

The large handicapped stall in the back slammed open and something absolutely horrific thundered out. *Holy shit.* An Infernal that large should have reeked for yards. Instead, the only thing Eve smelled was wolf.

The dragon hadn't fully shifted. He still wore his pants and shoes, and dark hair still covered his head. But his mouth was a protruding muzzle of razor-sharp teeth, his eyes were those of a lizard, and all of his visible flesh was covered in gorgeous multihued scales.

"You smell tasty," he rumbled.

She'd heard that Marks smelled sickly sweet to Infernals, which made her laugh inwardly. There was no such thing as a sweet Mark. They were all bitter. "You don't smell like anything."

We failed, she realized with a sinking feeling in her gut. Infernals still had the means to hide themselves in crowds.

"Brilliant, isn't it?" the wolf asked. "Obviously, you didn't wipe out our operation completely."

The dragon roared and it was a fearsome, deafening sound that echoed in the confined space of the bathroom. The mortals couldn't hear it, though, and Eve's eardrums were invincible despite their celestial sensitivity. Another boon granted by the mark. The dragon shoved the wolf aside and stomped closer.

"Guess that's my cue to leave," the kid said. "I'll give the Alpha your regards."

Eve's gaze remained riveted on her opponent. "Yeah, tell him he screwed with the wrong chick."

The wolf laughed and departed. Eve wanted to do the same.

For all her bravado, she was out of her league. If she had been capable of physical reactions to stress, her heart would be hammering and she'd be short of breath. No doubt about it, she was going to be suffering when this confrontation was over, *if* she was still alive. A religious person might pray for Alec to get here soon, but that wasn't an option for Eve. The Almighty did exactly what he wanted and nothing more. The purpose of prayer was to make the supplicant feel like he was doing something. It made Eve feel like she was wasting her breath.

"Where's Cain?" the dragon growled, approaching her with his hulking, lumbering stride. "I smell his stench on you."

"He's watching the game, which is what you should be doing." Eve couldn't risk telling him that Alec was coming. He might just kill her quickly and bail. In his mortal guise, with no odor to betray him, he could slip right past Alec. But if the dragon thought he had time, he might toy with her. Infernals liked to play.

"I need a snack." His voice was so guttural she could hardly understand him. "You'll do."

"Have you tried the nachos?" she suggested, her hands fisting. Deep inside her, power coiled. Hunger and aggression, too. It was base and animalistic, not at all the elegant sort of violence she might have expected God to employ in the destruction of his enemies. The surge was brutal . . . and addicting. "The chips are kind of stale and the cheese is from a can, but it's a lot less dangerous to your health."

He snorted, which shot a burst of fire out of his muzzle. "I've heard about you. You're no threat to me."

"Really?" She tilted her head, frowning in mock confusion. Demons used sarcasm, evasion, and lies to their advantage. Eve did, too. "When's the last time you got an update on me? Does Hell have a newsletter? A chat room? Otherwise, you're probably behind the times."

"You're cocky. And stupid. You think that sting in Upland made you a hero? Hell's branches are like the Hydra, bitch. Cut off one head, we grow back two."

An icy lump settled in Eve's gut. "More to sever," she managed, albeit with a slight tremor.

The dragon held up his hands. As thick, sharp claws grew out of the tips of his fingers, he leered and drool ran from his gaping maw. "You're a baby. Should make you juicy and tender."

"A *baby*?" she scoffed, fighting the urge to step back. "Do you have any idea what I've been through these last six weeks? I have some serious workplace rage."

Eve widened her stance, raised her fists, and took a deep breath. This was going to hurt. "Ready to see for yourself?"

The dragon's chest expanded on an inhale and he altered, his body assuming its natural reptilian appearance. He loomed above her, his head bent on a long graceful neck to accommodate the ceiling. He was a beautiful creature, with iridescent scales and lithe lines. Problem was, that stunning hide was like cement. Any attempt to kick or hit it would only lead to pain. For her, not him.

Their hide has very little vulnerability, Raguel had taught in Dragon 101. *Points of weakness are the webbing between their toes, the joint connecting the forelimbs to the torso, their eyes, and their rectum. The first will not cause mortal wounds, the second and third require proximity that can get you killed, and the fourth . . . well, as the kids say, you do not want to go there.*

Holding out her hand, Eve requested a blade. A sword appeared, hovering in midair, ablaze but for the hilt. Fire. Fire in Hell, fire in Heaven, fire blasting from the dragon's nostrils forcing her to leap backward to avoid being singed.

Pyromaniacs, the lot of 'em.

If she had a choice, she'd prefer her revolver. But she couldn't carry all the time and the Almighty preferred the flame-covered sword. Never let it be said that God didn't have a flair for the dramatic. He knew his strengths, and a bit of flashy intimidation was one of them.

The dragon laughed or chortled or choked . . . whatever. He wasn't impressed. The sound of his amusement gave Eve the willies and she rolled her wrist, using the substantial weight of the blade to limber up. She'd started out being the sorriest swordsman in her class. Now she was passably proficient, getting better every day.

"You missed me," she taunted grimly, wincing when her flip-flops clung to the sticky floor. Stupid footwear choice.

One of the many things she'd learned since getting saddled with this job was that presenting a formidable appearance went a long way toward hiding her deficiencies. Her enemies could smell her fear and they thrived on it. Throwing them for a loop with a little cockiness was sometimes the only way to gain any sort of advantage.

The dragon took a step toward her, his talons gouging into the tile, his weight vibrating the ground beneath them. The barrage of flames had made the room hot, but she didn't sweat. She couldn't; her body was a temple now.

Swinging at her with one short forelimb, the beast roared with terrible intent. He countered her evasive leap with a lash of his tail, which boasted a hard weighty scale on the tip that was used like a mace. It sank deep into the spot she'd occupied before she stumbled out of the way with a yelp. He yanked the appendage free in a shower of ceramic dust.

As she ran past him, he pivoted, his swinging tail ripping several sinks out of the wall. Eve darted around his side and managed to dislodge one of his scales with a hurried thrust of her blade.

He'd demolished the bathroom; she gave him a paper cut.

"Stupid cunt!" the beast bellowed, seemingly oblivious to the water spraying madly from the broken pipes. The depth of hatred and malevolence in the reptilian eyes added to the growing layer of hardness on her soul that was slowly changing her. Permanently.

Eve's fury rose to mask her terror. Infernals such as this guy were for much more advanced Marks. If he hadn't masked his scent and details, she wouldn't be fighting him.

She was in deep shit. And damn it, she was sick of being soaked all the time. Every Infernal she came across doused her with water.

"Reed." Her voice was not her own. Lower and deeper, it was the language of Marks. Known as a "herald," the tone was instinctive and indecipherable to Infernals. "Hurry up. I'm in trouble."

The sensation of a hot summer breeze moved over her—Reed's reply.

Lifting her free arm for balance, Eve began to feint and parry, her torso canted to the side to present a smaller target. She ducked behind her sword when another burst of flame spewed from his nostrils. The back of her hand was charred by the heat and she screamed. The damage would heal in moments, but that didn't prevent the initial agony.

Eve fell back, tripping over broken tiles and sobbing as a sharp piece penetrated the sole of her sandal and dug deep into her heel. Viscous warmth and the resulting slipperiness of her sole betrayed her blood loss. The dragon roared with triumph at the smell of her wounds and snapped at her with his razor-sharp teeth.

She wasn't going to die in a men's bathroom. No way.

"How the mighty have fallen," Alec drawled.

Eve gasped with relief at the sound of his voice. She ducked the beast's lashing tail, then rushed to peer around his body.

Alec lounged against the tiled threshold of the bathroom with both arms crossed. He looked relaxed and slightly bored, but there was a terrible darkness in his eyes when he hazarded a glance at her. She was his only weakness, a vulnerability he struggled to hide.

"Cain," the dragon rumbled, his posture wary.

"Damon? You used to be The Man. A courtier in the court of Asmodeus." Alec made a chastising noise with his tongue. "Now the best you can do is terrorize rookie Marks?"

"Hey," Eve protested. "Compared to the bathroom, I'm doing all right."

The fact that her opponent had his back to her and didn't seem to think that was a danger chafed. What the hell did she have to do to get some respect?

Frustration wiped out her fear and left only angry determination behind. Eve moved to the dragon's left side and leaped the full height of the room, putting the weight of her body behind the downward slash of her blade. She attacked the slender fold where his tiny forelimb attached to his torso and it severed cleanly, the limb splashing onto the floor with a thud. Crimson blood spurted from the newly made hole and mixed with the water spewing from the distorted pipes.

The dragon howled and spun around, knocking Eve to her back. She skidded several feet in the gore-stained lake that covered the decimated tile. He retaliated with a burst of flame. The inferno engulfed her, melting hair and skin from the top of her head down to her feet, boiling her in the flood that washed over and around her. The agony was such that she couldn't voice a sound and when the flames ceased abruptly, she hoped for the relief of death.

But she wasn't going alone.

Fueled by adrenaline and the animosity of a woman completely fed up with her life, Eve vaulted to her feet. She slammed into the beast's neck and belly where she clung to the tips of his scales with one-handed desperation. The impact to her raw, burnt flesh was devastating and she cried out, nearly dropping her sword.

Alec was there before her, one arm banded around the dragon's neck while the other hand gouged at the eyes. The beast flayed and screeched, whipping its neck to and fro in a vain effort to free himself of his attackers.

As Eve plunged the length of her blade through the vulnerable flesh created by the missing forelimb, she felt massive talons tearing into her spine. Her body arched, forcing her weapon the final inch needed to penetrate the dragon's heart.

The beast howled, then exploded in a burst of white-hot embers.

Eve crashed to the ground, paralyzed by her wounds. She lay blinking, gasping, surrounded by the requiem created by the shower from the pipes.

The vibration of footsteps pounding through water assailed her, then Alec was pulling her gingerly into his lap.

"Angel . . ." His hands shook as he tentatively touched her ruined skin. "Don't you dare die on me. You hear me? I just got you back, damn you—"

"Alec." She tried to open her eyes, but the effort required more energy than she possessed. Shivers wracked her abused frame and rattled her teeth. The faint chemical tang of tap water filled her nostrils, as did the scent of ashes, demon, and blood. *Her* blood.

She could finally smell and taste the sweetness of it.

"I'm here." His voice broke. "I-I'm here."

"The Alpha did this."

"What?"

"The Alpha. He wanted . . . his son . . . he tried . . ."

"Shh. Don't talk, angel." A hot tear splashed onto her raw skin. Then another. "Save your strength."

"We missed something in Upland," she whispered, sinking into an encroaching blanket of darkness. The pain was fading, the fear receding. "Go back . . . We missed something . . ."

CHAPTER 2

Six weeks earlier . . .

E ve knew, the moment her eyes met his, that they were going to have a torrid, extremely brief affair.

His shoulder brushed hers as he walked by. The scent of his skin lingered in her nostrils for a delicious moment and she shivered, her blood thrumming with anticipation. She didn't know his name, she didn't know *him*, but the compulsion to take the handsome stranger home with her was powerful and irresistible.

A tiny voice in her mind urged her to use caution, told her to slow down. Think twice. She wasn't a "casual sex" woman, never had been. But one look, and lust had hit her like a freight train.

His face . . . God, his face looked so much like Alec Cain's they could have been brothers. Smooth olive skin, night-black hair, and espresso-brown eyes. Sex incarnate. Though a decade had passed since the night Alec had ruined her for other men, Eve doubted he'd changed much. Men like Alec just got better with age.

The man who'd just passed her carried that same air of dangerous, tightly restrained power. That sense of being barely leashed. The urbane Armani suit that draped his tall, leanly muscled frame only emphasized that primitive quality she hungered for. The animal attraction was intense, quickening her pulse and knotting her stomach.

Her heels tapped a rhythmic staccato upon the golden-veined marble floor. Somewhere deep inside her, alarm bells were ringing. She felt almost as if she were fleeing, as if the sight and smell of a dominant male were something to fear. But parts of her were far from afraid.

The vast lobby of Gadara Tower was congested by business-minded pedestrians. The steady hum of numerous conversations and the industrious whirring of the glass tube elevator motors failed to hide her rapid breathing. Fifty floors above her, a massive skylight allowed natural illumination to flood the atrium. It was that drenching sunlight gleaming on thick, inky strands of hair that first drew her attention to her mystery man. The gentle heat from above combined with the lush vegetation in planters created a slight, sensual humidity.

All together, she was feeling turned on. Hot under the collar. One look at a seductive stranger had incited a dark, unfamiliar sexual urgency. It was riding her hard. Cracking the whip. From the moment she entered Gadara Tower she had felt odd, jittery, as if she drank too much coffee. Never prone to nerves, she didn't feel like herself. She longed to go home and take a hot bath.

Eve's hand flexed, adjusting her perspiration-slick grip on the handle of her leather portfolio. Within the zippered confines rested a dozen of her best drawings; the reason she was here. Raguel Gadara was expanding his real estate empire and she was one of a select few interior designers under consideration. She had poured her heart and soul into her presentation. She'd been certain she would leave the building with the job in the bag. Instead, she cooled her heels in his waiting room for twenty minutes before being informed that Mr. Gadara would have to reschedule. Eve understood the message—*I have the power to select you or not.*

Gadara was about to learn a hard lesson about Eve Hollis: *she* had the power to *accept* and she wouldn't work with a man who played power games. He'd just power-played himself out of the best damn interior designer in the country.

To say that she was horribly disappointed would be an understatement. She had latched on to the opportunity to pitch to Gadara with uncustomary fervor. For weeks now she'd felt excited. Expectant. Like a roller coaster poised on the downward slope, ready to race. Now she felt like she'd rolled back into the station without going anywhere.

The elevators to the parking garage were ahead of her and she quickened her pace. Then she spotted a gray-painted door that bore a Stairs sign.

Compelled to move in that direction, she veered off course, almost as if she were a passenger in her own body, just tagging along for the ride.

The moment her hand wrapped around the door handle, the mystery man was with her, his chest to her back as he propelled her into the airless stairwell. She was spun around with barely tempered brute strength and pinned to the closing door, sealing them in. Her precious portfolio fell to the cement floor and was promptly forgotten.

"Oh!" Her heartbeat stuttered, shifting gears from trepidation to sexual hunger. Her neck arched as the man licked and sucked at her tender throat, his much taller body hunched over hers. The rich, spicy scent of his skin inundated her senses, rushing through her blood like a potent aphrodisiac. Her hands slipped between his jacket and shirt, caressing the straining length of his tautly muscled back. He was hot, his skin burning. Pressed up against her as he was, he was making her sweat.

His left hand engulfed her breast through silk and lace, squeezing and kneading the achingly swollen flesh. His right hand caught the edge of her pinstriped pencil skirt and yanked it upward roughly. A loud tear echoed through the space as the slit in the back gave way under the pressure.

"Slow down," she begged, even as she grew more aroused. "I-I don't normally do things like . . . this."

He ignored her, cupping her thigh and hauling her tighter against him. Eve felt his erection thick and hard against her belly, and she shivered. It had been a long time since her last sexual encounter. Too long. She was primed, and when he reached between her legs, he knew just how ready she was.

"Temptress," he rumbled, his voice deep and aggressive. With a clench of his fist, he tore her thong and dropped the remnants on the floor. He released her long enough to shrug out of his suit jacket. "Unzip me."

The command was undeniable.

Eve fumbled as she worked to unfasten his belt. His strong fingers were rubbing between her legs, sliding through the slickness there. The hand at her breast gentled, his thumb stroking back and forth across her puckered nipple. She whimpered and spread her legs wider, helpless against the hunger.

A monotonous droning noise caught her attention. A quick glance up confirmed her suspicions—a security camera was pointed in their direction, the flashing red light beneath the circular lens confirming that it was fully operational.

Flushing with embarrassment, Eve wondered what she must look like with her knee-length skirt bunched around her waist. A wanton. A slut.

What the hell had gotten into her? She'd never done anything like this before.

But she felt delicious, despite her consternation. The man who reminded her of Alec Cain was pushing all the right buttons. The ones that turned off her inner morality police.

"Hurry," he growled.

Jolting at the sound of his rough voice, Eve resumed her task, somehow managing to tug the belt free and open his trousers. The waistband clung to his lean hips for a moment, then collapsed into a puddle around his ankles. When she lifted the wrinkled tails of his shirt, she discovered he was going commando. He was thick, long, and ready.

"Oh God," she breathed, her body clenching with excitement and heady lust.

"Yes," the man purred, just before he caught her by the backs of her thighs and hefted her with effortless strength. "He knows."

"Condom?" she gasped. Her eyes met his. His gaze was dark and intent, roiling with mysterious secrets and dangerous desires. She began to pant. With hunger. With fear.

"Hush," he crooned, brushing his lips across hers. She felt the muscles in his buttocks and thighs tauten.

Then he thrust deep.

Her cry was both pained and aroused. He gave her no time to think, to move, to fight. He launched into a hard, pounding rhythm and rode her straight into climax. She writhed and sobbed with the pleasure, her body shuddering violently in his arms. He continued to surge into her, over and over again, stroking through her spasms, spurring her into another violent orgasm. And another.

"No more," she begged, pushing weakly at his shoulders. "I can't take any more . . ."

Holding her with one arm beneath her buttocks, he tore at her shirt, scattering the tiny ivory buttons across the floor and down the cement stairs. He bared her shoulder and watched as she came again, the climax arching her body like a tightly strung bow. He lifted his hand and bared his palm, revealing an intricate tattoo in the center. It began to glow, turning into a white-hot brand.

"Bear the Mark of Cain," he growled, pressing his hand against her upper arm and searing her skin. He took her mouth, swallowing her screams, rocking into her, his tempo unfaltering.

Eve's nails dug into the flesh of his back, the mixture of intense pleasure and pain overloading her senses, making her see things that couldn't be real.

Her lover appeared to change, illuminating from within, his clothes falling away to reveal a muscular body and rich golden skin. His dark eyes changed to swirling amber as he threw his head back and roared. His powerful neck corded with strain as he came hard and long. Deep inside her.

It was a nightmare and a wet dream rolled into one, hurling her into an experience that stole her sanity. Huge white feathered wings unfurled from his back and embraced her.

Darkness followed suit, closing swiftly around her.

CHAPTER 3

"Ms. Hollis? Ms. Hollis, can you hear me?"
Eve's eyelids fluttered, then lifted.
"Ms. Hollis?"

She ached all over and felt hot, but she was shivering, as if she had the flu.

Awareness of her surroundings came to her in lapping waves—the male voice calling out to her, the dozen faces that stared down at her, the glass ceiling of Gadara Tower.

She bolted upright, her head whacking into the chin of a rubbernecker. The man cursed and stumbled backward, but her attention was focused on her clothes. As she took note of the crisply ironed length of her skirt, her fingers drifted down the row of tiny white buttons that secured her pale blue shirt.

"What happened?" she asked, her voice hoarse and raw as if she'd been screaming.

"We're not sure."

She turned her head to meet the blue eyes of a uniformed paramedic. Her gaze dropped to his name tag. *Woodbridge.*

"Have you eaten today?" he asked, his arm strong at her back.

Thinking about her morning, she nodded. "Yogurt and coffee."

Woodbridge smiled. "It's two in the afternoon. That's a long time to go with just yogurt. I think your blood sugar dropped. You became light-headed and passed out."

Two Gadara security guards pushed the crowd back and Eve stood with the paramedic's assistance. She wobbled a moment on her heels, was steadied by strong hands, then fingers pushed into her long black hair and gently felt her scalp. "Does it hurt anywhere?"

She hurt everywhere, but she knew what he meant. "No."

"I don't feel a bump, but I'd like to take you to the hospital as a precaution."

"Sure." She held on to his arm as the room tilted.

As she felt the unmistakable trickle of semen down her inner thighs, blood drained from her face. Her dizziness worsened and her empty stomach heaved.

"Wait. I changed my mind," she whispered through parched lips, her right hand lifting to touch her left upper arm. A painful welt could be felt through her shirt sleeve. "I just want to go home."

Eve stared at her computer monitor and felt an odd, vibrating panic well up inside her.

The Mark of Cain. The mark given by God to Cain as protection from harm while he wandered the Earth as punishment for killing his brother, Abel.

She'd been screwed within an inch of her life by a religious zealot.

That was scary enough. But what was even more frightening was the familiarity of the design. She'd seen it before, caressed it with her fingertips, her lips, thought it made the man who bore it even more of a rebel. Alec Cain's tattoo had turned her on and spurred a night of sin that haunted her to this day.

Backing her desk chair away from her computer, Eve stood and left her home office. Every step she took toward the kitchen reminded her of the heated encounter in the stairwell. The soreness between her legs made it impossible to forget the feel of her mystery man moving fiercely inside her.

The breath she exhaled was shaky, as was the rest of her.

How could she explain the pleasure she hadn't wanted to feel? The brand on her arm? The intact condition of her clothing? And the wings . . . Good God, the man had wrapped her in soft, white wings.

"I'm losing my mind."

After she'd showered, Eve stared at the burn on her arm, a one-inch wide triquetra surrounded by a circlet of three serpents, each eating the tail of the snake before it. Unlike most deep burns, the intricate details of the mark were clearly visible. She might have thought the design was exotic and pretty, if she'd actually wanted it. Now it was hidden beneath a bandage and a thick coating of Silvadene burn cream.

The doorbell rang, and Eve hurried toward the living room. She reached into the console table by the door and pulled out her revolver. With quiet deliberation, she unzipped its padded case. She was a single woman living alone in the heart of a metropolis; it made sense to own a registered handgun. And since Eve believed that something worth doing was worth doing well, she maintained a membership at the local gun club and practiced often.

"Evangeline?"

The voice was familiar and dear; it belonged to her next-door neighbor, Mrs. Basso. Eve breathed a sigh of relief, surprised to find that she'd been frightened of something as simple as a visitor. She put the gun away.

Pulling open the door, she found her neighbor waiting for her with a concerned frown and a Tupperware bowl in her hands. Mrs. Basso wore her customary Dockers, dress shirt, and sweater vest. Today her ensemble was comprised of various shades of blue. Pearls decorated her ears, throat, and wrist. She'd been a raving beauty in her youth. Now she had a stately elegance that was marred only by the slight stooping of her shoulders.

"Are you okay?" she asked. "You look tired."

"I'm fine," Eve lied.

Mrs. Basso owned Basso's Ristorante and Grille, a popular Italian restaurant. She and her husband had once operated the establishment together, but with Mr. Basso's passing a year ago she'd begun leasing the business out. This afforded her a steady, reliable income without much work on her part. Because she was alone, Eve checked on her a couple of times a week. When she made a run to the store, she always checked to see if Mrs. Basso needed anything. In return, her neighbor doted on her like a favored grandchild.

"You should get your thyroid checked," Mrs. Basso said.

Eve smiled. "Okay."

Mrs. Basso extended the bowl to her. "I made you some homemade chicken noodle soup. Lots of garlic and a dash of basil. You should eat all of it."

"You didn't have to do that," Eve protested.

"And you don't have to spend your time looking after me," she countered. "But we do it anyway."

Eve accepted the offering. "Come in and eat it with me."

Mrs. Basso shook her head. "Thank you, but a *Buffy the Vampire Slayer* rerun comes on in a few minutes and it's one of my favorites."

"Which season?"

"Six."

"Ahh, the one where Buffy and Spike finally get together."

Mrs. Basso blushed. "That Spike is a hunk. Eat all the soup, you hear?"

Eve laughed. "Of course. Thank you."

"It's the least I can do after all you do for me." With a wave, she moved back down the hall and paused. "There's a new Hugh Jackman movie out next week. He's a hunk, too."

"It's a date."

Mrs. Basso winked and stepped out of view.

Eve stared down the hall for a long time, clinging to the feeling of normalcy. The minute she closed her door it was gone, leaving her with a throbbing in her arm and between her legs, and a desperate need to know what in hell happened to her.

Fetching a spoon from the kitchen, Eve sat on her cream-colored sofa and turned on the television. She watched *Buffy*. A boyfriend had turned her on to the television series in the third season. It was the only thing she remembered about that particular relationship. And that was more than she could say about many of the romances she'd had since Alec Cain. But if she was honest, she hadn't really had a relationship with him either. She'd just been screwed, in more ways than one.

As Buffy and Spike beat the crap out of each other, Eve felt her shoulders and arms tensing to the point of pain. Wild, edgy, aggressive energy pulsed through her veins. Sweat dotted her upper lip and her vision grew fuzzy.

The doorbell rang again and she lurched to her feet. "I ate every drop," she yelled as she moved toward the door. She smiled at the thought of Mrs. Basso following up on her as if she were an errant child.

"Angel."

Eve paused, her steps faltering.

"Open the door."

She retrieved her gun, her hand slipping into the protective case to grip the hilt. Padding quietly to the door, she lifted on tiptoe to peer out the peephole.

For a moment she stood unblinking, unable to believe what—*whom*—she was looking at.

"Come on, angel," he purred, using the pet name only he'd ever used. Evangeline. Eve. *Angel*. "Let me in."

Even through the distorted glass, Alec Cain was breathtaking. Her damned mouth was watering.

Unfortunately, he also closely resembled the man who'd attacked her earlier. Her warning bells were clanging hell for leather. She hadn't listened to them earlier and look where that had gotten her.

Eve backed up silently.

"Angel," he said, softer this time, his voice so clear she knew he had to be resting his forehead against the door. "I know what happened today. You shouldn't be alone. Let me in."

Alec's voice. Hearing it in person, after all these years, stabbed her like a knife. Dark and rich like chocolate, it was decadent. Sinful. It had urged her to relinquish her virginity, an act that was painful for most women, but had been the pinnacle of pleasure for her. She'd fallen head over heels that night. Would have done anything for him, gone anywhere he wanted. *Anything,* if it meant they would be together.

Stupid. Naïve.

Shaking her head, Eve continued to retreat, tears streaming down her cheeks. Her arms were straight and steady, pointing the muzzle directly at the door. She wasn't surprised that he knew what happened to her today. The fact was, Alec always knew. From the beginning, he'd had an uncanny way of knowing what she was thinking and feeling. She was pretty sure that's why he was so damn good in the sack. Before she knew what she wanted, he was giving it to her.

"Eve, listen to me. You can't be alone now. It's not safe."

You're not safe, she thought.

"I'm the closest thing you've got," he retorted, as if he'd read her mind.

No. Go away. She couldn't voice the words. Her throat was too tight.

"I won't, angel. I'm coming in. Keep backing away."

"I-I'll sh-shoot you."

Eve could sense him pause.

Then her door burst open in an explosion of splintered wood and bent locks. Three dead bolts. The kind bullets couldn't break.

Her entire body shook violently, but she held the gun level.

He entered her condominium with casual ease, his steel-toed boots thudding heavily on her polished wood floors.

Alec Cain was tall, dark perfection. He wore black from head to toe, from his fitted T-shirt to his leather pants. His inky locks were a bit too long, caressing his nape and falling over his brow. His full lips were drawn tight with strain. His brown eyes were burning. That intensity had done crazy things to her equilibrium when she was a wild child of eighteen. It did crazy things to her now.

The past decade hadn't aged him at all.

"I told you to go away, Alec."

He tossed his leather jacket and helmet onto her sofa as he passed it. "Are you really going to shoot me if I don't?"

"If you don't turn around and get out of my house, yeah."

Alec could stand stock still and be merely gorgeous, but when he moved, all bets were off. There was a sleek, predatory grace to him that was riveting. A woman couldn't help but wonder if he would be as smooth in bed. Eve knew he was. Sex was an art form to Alec, and he was a master.

"I'm not leaving, angel."

Eve's nostrils flared. Then she squeezed the trigger.

CHAPTER 4

The click of the hammer falling was deafening in the quiet room. Had there been a round in the chamber, Alec would be sporting a steaming hole in his chest.

"You can't hurt me," he said softly.

"Don't underestimate me. I always keep the gun stored on an empty chamber. You won't be so healthy when I squeeze off a live round." She gestured toward the door with a hard jerk of her chin. "Get out, while you're still in one piece."

Her home no longer felt like her own. Alec dominated her living room. The darkness of his clothes was completely at odds with the soft champagne colors she'd decorated with. In an odd twist of fate, she and he matched. She wore a black cotton tank top and matching shorts, her comfort clothes.

"I can't." He turned his back to her and pushed the door closed, the protruding dead bolts fitting into the gaping holes in the decimated jamb. He hooked the slender chain into place (the one piece of security she hadn't bothered with before), then grabbed the wooden chair next to the console table and wedged it under the haphazardly hanging knob.

Locking them in together.

He faced her. "That mark on your arm is going to start messing with you."

The damn thing was already messing with her. It throbbed and burned something fierce. "What is it?"

"Both a blessing and a curse." Alec stepped closer, completely unconcerned with the danger her gun presented. "It's a punishment, a form of penance."

"What-the-fuck-ever. I'm agnostic and you're insane. Take your lunatic bullshit and get out of my house."

"You're going to get sick and need someone here."

"Well, it sure as hell isn't going to be you. I'll call a friend. Someone *reliable*."

Outwardly, the dig didn't appear to affect him, but she sensed it had struck home.

"A friend isn't going to be able to help you, Eve. Especially a woman. Not unless you started swinging both ways, which I really doubt. You like men too much."

"No, I only like *parts* of men."

"You liked *all* of me."

"I was a stupid kid." She snorted. "But I learned my lesson the first time." His challenging smile made her breath catch and she stilled, absorbing what he'd said. "Wait. Are you talking about *sex?*"

Eve's eyes widened and her gaze dropped to his groin. The man was rocked, cocked, and ready to go. Every inch of that hard, muscled frame was edgy with tension and arousal. Sudden fury gave her strength, and her shaking stopped.

"No way, Alec. You're insane if you think I'll let you touch me again. Go find someone else to torment. I'm all stocked up on angst."

The angular lines of his face softened. "Angel—"

"Don't 'angel' me. I'm not your angel. I'm not your *anything*."

"You're everything, which is why I left."

"Shut up." Fire was coursing through her veins, making it hard to think.

Alec studied her intently. "The fever's kicking in. Your cheeks are flushed and you're beginning to sweat. You need to lie down."

"Yeah, that'd be convenient for you, wouldn't it? Disarm me and get me horizontal."

"If I just wanted to get laid, why hit up a woman who holds the grudge from hell? I'm not that hard up."

That smarted, the knowledge that he could crook his finger and have whomever he wanted. She should take comfort knowing she wasn't the only one to chase him. But it just made her jealous and cranky.

"If you know what happened," she bit out, "then you know that man looked like you." Although now that he was here in the flesh, Eve saw the differences between them. No one looked like Alec, although the winged man had been awfully close.

But at this point, she didn't care. She just wanted Alec out of her house. She couldn't deal with him. Not today. God, *not ever.* Never again. Even after all these years, he still drove her crazy.

Sweat dripped down her temple and Eve wiped it away impatiently. "This afternoon pretty much ruined me for men with your coloring. Switching teams actually sounds pretty good at the moment."

"Don't," he said tightly, the muscles in his arms flexing. "I'm barely holding it together as it is. I'd hunt him down now, if you weren't about to be extremely sick. You need me here, more than you need me out there."

Her laughter was harsh and without humor. "You're something I *don't* need in my life, especially now."

Alec rubbed the back of his neck. The pose showed off his well-defined biceps to perfection. It pissed her off that she could still find him so damned attractive.

"I'm sorry, angel."

Somehow, he managed to fill those words with a wealth of regret. But she wasn't buying what he was selling. He was one of those guys who never stayed in one place for long and left broken hearts in his wake. The first time she'd been too young to know better. There was no excuse now.

Perspiration gathered between her breasts and trickled down her chest. Eve rubbed at the wetness through her tank top. "It's been a really crappy day, Alec. I need to go to the doctor in the morning. If you would leave and not come back, I'd be super grateful. I might even forgive you for being crazy. Someday."

A sudden flare of heat spread across her skin and made her dizzy. The room spun and she stumbled. Alec caught her, cradling her violently shivering body down to the floor. He pulled the gun from her lax fingers, and set it down carefully beside him.

"Alec . . ." The smell of his skin, achingly familiar, drugged her already confused senses.

"I'm here, angel," he crooned, pulling her into his embrace.

She clutched at his arm and found the raised mark with her fingertips. Turning her head, Eve saw it. The trinity knot and serpents were just like hers, only his brand had another image in the center. An open eye. His looked like an embossed tattoo, while hers was most definitely a blistering burn.

"Dear God," she gasped, her breathing labored as she felt consciousness slipping from her. "What's going on?"

He brushed strands of her hair away from her face. Her skin tingled where he touched her, goose bumps rising. Everything about the way he looked at her exacerbated her fever. There was nothing in the world like being wanted with a primitive desire. The one thing she'd never doubted was that Alec was madly in lust with her.

"You were drawn to *him* because of me, weren't you?" His lips hovered above hers so that their panting breaths mingled and became one. It was as intimate as sex, that sharing of breaths between them.

She didn't have to answer. He knew. He always knew.

His thumb brushed across her cheekbone. He moved to kiss her, but Eve jerked her head away.

"Damn you," she breathed, her nails digging into his skin.

"We're both damned." He pulled her into his lap and tucked her flushed face into the crook of his neck, where the scent of his skin was so strong.

Against her will, she nuzzled him, rubbing her sweat into his flesh. She felt the urge to crawl inside him, to see what made him tick. Her tongue darted out and tasted him. He shuddered in response, squeezing her tighter. Her wound was on the arm facing away from him and she felt his fingertips move, feather light, over her bandage.

Her voice came as no more than a whisper. "I haven't done anything wrong."

"You're right, angel. You haven't." His lips pressed hard to her damp forehead.

"Then why?"

He exhaled harshly. "Because of me. Because I couldn't resist you."

Eve opened her mouth to reply, but weariness pulled hard at her and she sank into darkness.

CHAPTER 5

The deep rumbling growl of a Harley drew Eve's gaze to the parking lot of the ice-cream shop where she worked after school. It was five in the evening and the day was just starting to end. The horizon was the color of a tangerine tinged with burgundy.

She walked to the end of the counter to catch a glimpse of the Heritage Softail that lounged in front of the Circle K convenience store next door. It was a black and chrome beauty, boasting custom saddlebags and a well-worn seat.

"What I wouldn't give for a bike like that," she whispered, "and the freedom of the road."

Not that she was unhappy with her life, because she wasn't. It was just . . . ordinary.

Sighing, she looked over her shoulder at the clock and silently begged it to tick a little faster. Her shift was over at six. The final football game of the season started at seven fifteen. While her high school was across the street, the field they played on was a few miles away.

"Hey. Are we going to Chad's party after the game?"

Eve glanced at her friend Janice and shrugged. "I'm not sure. Depends if Robert's going or not."

Shaking her head, Janice went back to work wiping off the counters, her long, blonde ponytail swaying with her exertions. "You can't avoid him forever."

"I know. And I know he'll stop talking shit about me when he hooks up with someone else, but in the meantime, I just want to stay out of his way."

Crouching down, Eve opened the doors beneath the display case. She pulled out the glass cleaner and a roll of paper towels.

"He's an asshole," Janice muttered. "I'm glad you didn't screw him."

"Yeah." Eve stood. "Me, too."

She tossed one last longing glance at the Harley and froze. The owner was shoving a paper bag into one of the saddlebags. Then he tossed one leg over the bike and settled into the seat.

Wow.

He was tall, dark, and dangerous. His long legs and fine ass were draped in loose, low-slung blue jeans, his powerful biceps bared by the fitted white tank top he wore. His jaw was square and bold, his lips firm but sensual. Wicked. The lines that bracketed them only emphasized how gorgeous he was.

Completely unaware of her fascination, he turned the key and revved the engine, his black leather boots resting firmly on the asphalt, ready to push the bike back. The anticipation of his departure made her shiver.

Then he turned his head and saw her.

Eve knew the exact moment he became aware of her stare because he stilled, his large frame visibly tensing. The hand on his thigh reached for his sunglasses so he could push them up. As they lifted, they caught the overly long lock of glossy black hair that fell over his brow and took it with them.

Their eyes met. Electricity arced through the space between them. She shivered. The bottle of glass cleaner fell from her nerveless fingers and thudded on the linoleum floor.

"Wow . . ." Janice's voice breathed the awe Eve felt. "He's got to be famous."

Eve didn't break eye contact. She couldn't. "Why?"

"No normal guy is that fucking hot." Janice blew out her breath. "Hey!"

Fingers snapped in front of Eve's face.

"Huh?"

"Stop staring at him. You're going to give him ideas."

"Maybe I want *him* to have ideas."

Janice yanked her around and glared at her with narrowed green eyes. "Evie, no. First off, that guy is way out of your league. Second, he's too old for you. Third, everything about him screams bad news."

The rumble outside stopped and Eve looked back over her shoulder. He stood beside the bike—watching her.

"Listen, Eve. You have the worst luck with guys, worse than me, and that's saying something. But this guy—hunky as he is—is serious trouble. Look at him. Men that look like that . . ." Janice snorted. "I see him, and I see teen pregnancy and welfare."

That's not what Eve saw when she looked at him. She didn't know what it was, but something inside her was so drawn to him that she felt an invisible string pulling her, urging her to close the distance between them.

Hi, she mouthed, trying to smile, but failing. There was nothing to smile about.

*His jaw tensed, his hand fisting at his side. His dark gaze was hot.
Burning. No man had ever looked at her with that level of intensity. As
if nothing in the world existed but her.*

Biting her lower lip, she willed him to come closer. Talk to me.
Come on.

*She saw the nearly imperceptible shake of his head. He yanked his
shades back down, shielding his eyes. He ignored her as he remounted
his bike and restarted the engine. But she knew he still felt her stare.*

He rode away without another glance in her direction.

The feeling of inexplicable loss stayed with Eve for days after he left.

A wet cloth swiping over Eve's skin brought her to a distant awareness.
The whirring ceiling fan blew air across the lingering dampness, cooling
her fevered skin. Her tongue felt thick in her mouth and her hand lifted to
her parched throat. As her forearm crossed her chest, she realized she was
naked and groaned, hating the feeling of helplessness.

"Here." A thickly muscled arm slipped beneath her shoulders and
raised her to meet the edge of a drinking glass. Her lips parted gratefully
and ice water filled her empty stomach, causing her to shiver. Burning hot
outside, freezing cold inside.

Inhaling a spicy exotic scent that was unmistakable, she croaked,
"Alec?"

"In the flesh." He mantled her body, his hip pressed to hers as he sat
on the edge of the bed.

"I-I don't want you to see me . . . l-like this. Go away."

Pressing a kiss to her brow, Alec followed her down to the pillow. Silken
strands of his hair stroked over her hypersensitive skin. Pleasure flowed
through her. Familiar pleasure. Longed-for pleasure. Contradicting her
order to leave, her hand lifted to his thick hair. Her fingers slid deep into
the glossy locks, her palm cupping the back of his head to keep him close.

"I feel like shit," she muttered.

"I know. I'm sorry, angel. Women always take the Change hardest."

"What . . . what change?"

"Hush," he soothed, wiping her forehead with the wet washcloth.
"Sleep now. I'll take care of you."

Her nipples throbbed as if pinched by clamps, the ache boring deep.
Her hands moved to them, covering the puckered tips with her palms. A
large, warm hand surrounded hers, then pulled them away. At eighteen,
she hadn't been this curvy, less than a handful. She was much fuller now,
a fact he seemed to appreciate if the rhythmic kneading of his hand on
her breast was any indication. She whimpered, finding relief in the pressure of his touch.

Her fingers drifted along the length of his side, feeling hot, smooth skin
stretched tight over lean, hard muscles. The image of Alec bare-chested

flashed behind her closed eyelids, followed by heated remembrances of the last time he'd handled her so intimately.

Sick as she was, her body still hungered for him. How the hell could she be horny at a time like this? "Alec . . . What's happening to me?"

"You're becoming like me."

"Oh God." As the burn on her arm heated painfully, she whimpered. "Shoot me now."

"Just a few more days, angel. You're strong. You'll be even stronger when you get through this."

"Few days? How long have I—?"

"Three days."

Three days?

And he was still here.

She fought to stay awake, but she lost the battle and drifted off.

As soon as Eve exited the ice-cream shop to the back alley, she knew he was there. She closed her eyes and sighed, then straightened her shoulders and locked the door.

"What do you want, Robert?" she asked wearily, loose bits of old asphalt crunching beneath her Vans. "I've had a long day and I really want to go home."

Her ex leaned against the hood of his white '67 Mustang, arms and legs crossed. He was arguably the most popular guy at Loara High and it was obvious why. A California blond with blue eyes, he had a great body from both surfing at dawn at Huntington Beach and afternoon football practice. But his looks hadn't been enough to tempt her out of her virginity.

At eighteen, she was the oldest girl she knew who still hadn't had sex. Sometimes the peer pressure was fierce, but mostly she was fine with waiting for more than a quick, painful screw in the back of some guy's car.

"I thought you might want a ride to Jason's party," he said with a half-smile.

Eve shook her head. "Thanks, but I'm not up for it tonight."

Her uniform of bright red shorts and a white polo shirt with "Henry's Ice Cream" embroidered on the breast was irritating her. She wanted nothing more than to toss it in the hamper and watch the latest episode of 90210 in a pair of baggy sweats.

"I've got a cooler in the car and a dime bag," he coaxed. "We can skip the party and drive out to the tracks."

"Give it a rest." She started walking. "I'm not doing it, okay? You broke up with me and told everyone I'm a bad lay. Everyone thinks I put out. We're done."

Leaping to his feet, Robert stepped into her path. "Come on, Evie. I know you're scared, but I'll make it good for you. Other people are starting to talk about how cold you are. Your rep as a hottie is slipping, baby."

"Whatever. Like I care."

His voice lowered and became cajoling. He gripped her upper arms, and rubbed up and down. "A couple beers and a joint, and you'll be nice and relaxed when I pop your cherry. You don't want to be a damn virgin forever."

She opened her mouth to take him down a notch.

"Who said she's still a virgin?"

Eve quivered at the sound of the deep rumbling voice. She knew it was him. Hell on wheels.

"Who the fuck are you?" Robert challenged, pushing Eve to the side.

The sudden illumination of the Harley's headlight gave away his position. "You ready to go, angel?"

The nickname startled her and she hesitated. Then one foot stepped in front of the other. The next thing Eve knew, a helmet was in her hands. She pulled it on quickly, her body instantly reacting to the exotic male scent that permeated the inside of the protective gear. Her nipples peaked hard and tight, her breathing altered.

She wanted him. Like she'd never wanted anything or anybody in her life. All the raging teenage hormones in her body went haywire around him. She'd had heavy petting sessions that hadn't made her this hot, and all she'd done was smell him.

"This is bullshit, Eve," Robert snapped. "We dated for months. You owe me."

Eve flipped him the bird and climbed onto the back of the bike, her arms wrapping around her mystery guy's lean middle. He smelled spicy. Exotic. Delicious. She pressed her nose to his back and breathed him in. Unable to fight the temptation, she stroked her fingertips over his six-pack abs, shivering when tingles spread up her arms and pooled in her breasts, making them swell and ache.

His hand slapped over hers, halting her explorations.

"Hang on," he growled.

The hog rumbled to life and they roared off into the night.

Eve jerked to consciousness.

Desire burned through her veins. She writhed in torment, her head tossing, her limbs flailing, her breasts swollen with the need to be touched and caressed.

The scent of lavender and vanilla filled her nostrils. Reality hit her hard enough to force the breath from her lungs.

Her fabric softener. She turned her head and breathed in the smell. Clean sheets.

She was home. Alone. It had all been a dream.

"Alec . . . ?" She thrashed, her skin so hot and tight she felt as if it might split open.

Her nipples were hard and aching again, but now the flesh between her legs was plump and slick, the brand on her arm burning. Throbbing.

"Alec!" she cried again, with all the strength of a mewling kitten. Her mouth felt as if it were filled with cotton. Her body quaked with hunger and, unable to do otherwise, she spread her legs wide and thrust her hand into the damp curls between her thighs. She'd never been so aroused in her life; the need for sex was more powerful than her need to breathe. Her other hand cupped a swollen breast, squeezing it, praying for relief from her sensual anguish and the goddamn heat. She felt like she was melting from the inside out.

Through her panting breaths she heard the padding of bare feet upon her hardwood floors. The steady, confident stride was familiar and deeply comforting.

Closer. Closer.

The footsteps stopped abruptly in her bedroom doorway.

"Alec." Her fingers parted the tender folds of her sex, exposing her burning flesh to the fan's soft breeze.

"Christ," he whispered, his voice a deep lustful rasp. "Have mercy."

She moved sinuously upon the cool satin sheets of her bed. Were they purple? Or would he be sentimental and choose the white? Much as she wanted to open her eyes and see, she couldn't find the strength to lift her heavy lids.

"Alec." She pushed two fingers inside her, but it wasn't enough to fill the emptiness. She was soaked, desperate. "What's happening to me?"

Her words left her on a sob, hot tears leaking out from the corners of her closed eyes. Her body was no longer her own; the sexual hunger was an alien force, clawing and biting her in its quest for freedom.

Alec. It wanted Alec. And after a decade of starving, it wasn't willing to wait a moment longer to have him.

His breath hissed out between clenched teeth. She heard him step toward her, then the bed dipped slightly as he sat. His hot, open mouth pressed against her calf. "I knew what the Change would do to you."

As his tongue dipped behind her knee, her free hand left her breast and slid into his hair.

His teeth nipped at her inner thigh and she gasped in surprise. "But I didn't know what it would do to *me*."

Grasping her pumping wrist, he stilled her movements and pulled her hand free. She cried out when she felt his tongue licking her fingers, a rough sound of pure male satisfaction filling the air as he tasted her desire. Warm, wet heat engulfed her to the knuckles, then he was sucking in long deep pulls until there was nothing left to consume.

"Damn it." He lunged for the pulsing flesh between her legs, covering it with his open mouth. Eve jerked violently, her senses overloaded with the feel and smell of him. Her heart raced at his nearness and the growling sounds he made as his tongue flicked desperately. Her knees bent and her feet pushed into the mattress, lifting her hips. He rumbled a warning and pinned her down with his large hands. "Stay still."

He held her open with his fingers, nuzzling his lips against her, his hair sweeping across the sensitive skin of her thighs.

She struggled against his hold, but he was too strong and she was too weak. *"Please . . ."*

Alec tilted his head and pushed his tongue through the spasming muscles, the rough texture both soothing and abrading the sensitive tissues. She keened softly at the teasing fullness, nowhere near as thick and long as she needed, but wonderful nevertheless. In and out. Piercing her hard and fast. His groans were animalistic, base and raw, as if he'd gone too long without having her this way. As if he'd missed it.

"Not enough," she breathed, twisting and arching, burning up. Losing her sanity. "It's not *enough*."

Alec's mouth surrounded her, gently suckling. His tongue fluttered in a wicked back-and-forth tease.

As she climaxed hard, she cried out, her legs trembling. The relief was so intense she couldn't catch her breath, every follicle and nerve ending prickling with acute, near-painful pleasure. His lips closed, pressed a soft kiss against her, and then opened again. His approach gentled, and he licked her in a patient, loving rhythm.

Eve reached for his shoulders and found his warm skin covered in soft cotton. She tugged ineffectually at the material. "Naked."

Alec pushed up and the mattress jerked with his violent movements, then he was coming over her. Bare skin to bare skin. He caught her wrists in one hand and pulled them gently over her head.

She found the strength to open her gritty eyes. Dark hair fell around his flushed face. His brown irises were swallowed by his dilated pupils, roiling with violent need.

He pressed his cheek to hers. "Don't hate me for what's happening to you."

Kneeing her legs open, he pushed inside her. A violent shudder coursed the length of his frame. "Angel . . . You're burning me up."

He was so long and hard, built for a woman's pleasure. She knew he would fill her completely, the stretching sensation incredible and addicting.

"Deeper," she coaxed, raising her hips.

The instant he sank to the end of her, the pain eased, leaving only drugging, drowning pleasure behind.

He murmured hoarse praise, clutching her close, beginning to move.

She sobbed, her fever breaking, sweat dripping from every pore and soaking her hair. The bed. Him.

His powerful thighs flexed against hers as he kept her pinned and rode her skillfully. Slow. Rolling his hips. She watched him with heavy lidded eyes, watched him watch her as he pumped into her, his abdomen flexing and rippling with his thrusts. Watched his eyes burn as she writhed and whimpered his name.

Alec was inexhaustible. He would climax with a clenched jaw and deep, stifled groans, but he never softened completely. Her keening cries as she came made him hard again. She could feel him thicken inside her as he rocked in and out. Ready for more.

No other man could compete. He'd ruined her from the very first. No one touched her the way he did. No one looked at her the way he did, studying every nuance of her response and adjusting his movements so she kept coming. And coming. No one had that wickedly dark voice that goaded her. Whispering how she felt to him, how she pleased him, how much he loved to be inside her.

They had sex for hours, moments melding into each other, Alec thrusting between her spread thighs in that lazy, sensual rhythm that said, *Feel that? Feel me? I'm in you. Inside you.*

The room grew dark as the sun set.

Sick as she'd been, she shouldn't have been able to take him, but she grew stronger with every moment that passed, the dull throb of the burn on her arm pumping a wild, edgy power through her veins until she was abandoned. Scratching at his back, biting his neck, spurring him on with her heels in his flexing ass.

Through sheer mulish determination, Eve broke through Alec's steely control, grabbed him by the throat and balls, and rocked his world. As she pleasured him ruthlessly, his guttural cries filled the room, swelling up through the vaulted ceiling of her condominium.

"Getting ready to leave again?" she asked harshly, clinging to his straining, sweat-slicked body with arms made powerful by the energy inside her. "Storing up future memories?"

He grunted and licked the side of her face. "Making up for lost time. You'll cover the future in daily installments."

"You wish." She nipped his ear with sharp teeth, making him curse. "Enjoy the ride while it lasts."

His head lifted, revealing glowing eyes that sent violent shivers down her spine. Resting one hand on the mattress, he drove powerfully into her. Eve was so focused on the pounding of his hips against hers and the impending orgasm that she failed to register the danger until it was too late.

Alec lifted his free hand, revealing the white-hot image of an eye in the center of his palm.

"Oh, hell no!" She shoved at his shoulders.

"Set me as a seal upon thine heart, as a seal upon thine arm—"

He gripped her branded deltoid and burned her anew.

Eve bit out a curse and belted him square in the jaw.

CHAPTER 6

E ve frowned as the Harley rounded the corner of her street and pulled over to the curb several houses up from her own. Her dad would be dozing on the couch now, her mother upstairs in bed reading a romance novel, and her little sister chatting on her private phone line instead of sleeping. It was home and she loved it, but she didn't want to go there now. The thought of being separated from the man in front of her made her feel panicky.

"Did we have to come here right away?" she asked, regretting answering honestly when he'd asked for directions.

As he turned off the engine, she laced her fingers together to keep him close. He was so warm, so solid, so big. Nothing like the boys she went to school with.

He gently pried her fingers open. "Yes, it's better for you, angel."

"Can't we go somewhere else? It's still early."

"No."

"Why? Why did you come tonight if you didn't want to hang out with me?"

She felt him sigh. "I don't 'hang out,' and even if I did, I couldn't hang out with you."

"Because of my age?" God, she was so sick of being treated like a kid.

"Among other reasons."

His head turned slightly and the glimpse of his profile, even under the weak illumination of the streetlights, took her breath away. Her heart thudded in an elevated rhythm, her breathing was quick and shallow. His lean hips were cradled between her spread thighs, her breasts pressed to his back. She knew he felt some of the pull she did or he wouldn't have been waiting for her tonight.

But she wanted to prove it, so Eve shimmied her torso, rubbing her erect nipples against him.

His breath hissed out between clenched teeth. "Get off the bike."

The tone of his voice brooked no argument so she dismounted with a moue. "What's your name?"

There was a long silence while he stared at her with that hot, intense stare. She could tell he was debating whether to tell her or not. Finally, he said, "Alec Cain."

Eve nodded and adjusted the strap of her bag. "Thanks for the ride, Alec."

She set off toward her house and a moment later the hog rumbled to life. Though the urge to look back was nearly overwhelming, her pride was stronger.

She knew if he felt anything like she did when they were together, he would be back.

Eve rested her right hand on the tile and stood with head bent beneath the pummeling water spray of her shower.

Seven days. Seven days of her life gone.

She knew something drastic had happened to her during that short time. The brands on her left arm were completely healed and settled into something that resembled a tribal tattoo. Exactly like Alec's. After nearly a week without food and very little to drink, she should be weak and dehydrated. She was neither. Instead she felt like a million bucks, her foot tapping impatiently on the stone shower floor because she couldn't contain all of the restless energy inside her.

Shutting off the tap, Eve grabbed the fresh towel she'd set atop the lid of her hamper. She dried her skin quickly, then wrapped her wet hair into a turban and padded out to the bedroom.

There was no way to ignore the naked man sprawled facedown across her bed. Alec had chosen the white sheets, a selection that set butterflies loose in her stomach. It made her bed look like a cloud. His dark masculinity upon that backdrop made him look like a fallen angel.

She would never forget the night she lost her virginity. He'd lain beneath her like a wicked fantasy upon white sheets, urging her on with hoarsely voiced encouragements.

Sighing, her gaze moved from his face down the muscular expanse of his back to the dimples just above his perfect ass.

"Have mercy," she whispered, repeating the words he'd used the night before.

Eve tore her gaze away and looked around the room, noting the washcloths on her mahogany nightstand. She imagined what the last week must have been like for him and the intimacy involved in caring for her. The man she couldn't trust to stick around at all had been dependable in her most dire hours. What was the sense in that?

Her jaw clenched. Alec knew exactly what had happened to her a week ago. Then he'd done the exact same thing to her last night. Because of him and the winged mystery man, she was altered. Physically. Mentally. In every way. She could feel the Change like a narcotic slipping through her veins.

Pivoting on her heel, Eve snatched up the short silk robe that hung on the back of the bedroom door and left the room. She went to the kitchen for much-needed food and coffee, knowing she was going to need plenty of both for the confrontation to come.

Alec watched Evangeline Hollis leave the high school parking lot, crossing Euclid Street to reach the Circle K convenience store. His gaze drank in every nuance of her figure—the long, lithe legs, slight but luscious curves, golden California tan, and hair of long black silk. She walked with three other girls, but she didn't fit in. Not because she was Asian, but because she was above them, beyond them. Every delectable inch of her body was ripe with sexual promise and a confidence he admired.

At times he cursed the sudden urge he'd had to grab a bottle of water from the convenience store the day he first saw her. If he'd kept on riding, he wouldn't be in this predicament. But he knew fate and coincidence were mortal concepts. A divine plan was at work, and somehow this angel fit into his. Unfortunately for her.

Wanting to protect her, Alec had fought the compulsion to meet her and fled via Interstate 5 on his way to San Diego. Another city in an endless string of cities he visited in the course of his nomadic life. His bike roared past 1313 Harbor Boulevard: Disneyland—The Happiest Place on Earth.

Then he realized the source of the pull he felt toward her. When she'd mouthed "Hi" with those glossy red lips, he'd felt the first stirrings of connection, something he hadn't experienced in so long he had almost forgotten what it felt like.

Why her? he despaired. *She's so young. Too young.* Centuries *younger than he was.*

But Alec knew the answer. She was his forbidden fruit. Set out to tempt him with what he could never have. One taste and Eve would be his, but the price she'd pay would destroy them both.

Yet, despite knowing the consequences, Alec had found himself exiting the freeway and backtracking to her. Now, two weeks later, he watched her from the shadow of a large tree and ached for the feel of her arching beneath him.

One taste. He was starved for it.

He couldn't forget the feel of her breasts against his back, her curious fingertips drifting across his stomach, the sound of her voice coaxing, Can't we go somewhere?

Yes, he'd wanted to say. Let's go and never come back.

Temptation. God's most oft-used test.

But Alec wasn't going to fail this one. He was leaving today if it killed him. He'd come to see her one last time, then he would go, finding strength in the fact that he'd resisted his own needs in favor of hers.

Alec was about to turn away, finally prepared to get on his hog and leave her behind, when Eve paused on the corner, her head turning in his direction. He stilled. Waiting. Wondering if she saw him.

She arched a brow, staring. Then she blew him a mocking kiss and flipped him off, before turning on her heel and sauntering away.

Eat your heart out, her actions said.

Taunting him. Tempting him. Not understanding that he was afraid for her, *not himself. She* would *pay the price for his infraction. His punishment would come from knowing that he was the cause of hers.*

His jaw clenched so tight his teeth ground together.

Sliding his sunglasses back on, he walked to his bike and hit the road.

Pausing on the threshold between the living room and the hallway, Alec carefully studied the set of Eve's shoulders. She was clad in a blood-red, knee-length silk kimono robe. Her black hair tumbled halfway down her back, the thick strands swaying with the salt-tinged breeze drifting through the open balcony door.

She looked relaxed, her hip leaning into the jamb of the sliding glass door, her hands filled with a steaming cup of coffee as she stared at the ocean view. But he knew her senses were alert, her hearing more acute, her sense of smell inhumanly accurate. When she reached full strength, her speed and stamina would make Olympic athletes weep in envy . . . if she ever moved slowly enough that they could see her. She was a hunter now, a predator.

Tightening the towel he had wrapped around his waist, Alec crossed the vast space, admiring how well she'd done for herself. She had a gleaming new Chrysler 300 in her garage downstairs and she was so close to the beach that her living room balcony hung over the sand.

She was going to hate him for ruining her perfect life.

"Good morning, angel."

Eve spun to face him. Despite hours of hard sex, she looked none the worse for wear. Her dark eyes, almond shaped and framed by thick sooty lashes, were clear and bright. She would heal with remarkable speed now. At least on the outside. As for the inside . . .

He ran a hand through his damp hair. Would she understand when he explained? And even if she did, would it mitigate the fact that he was the reason this had happened to her?

She held up a hand, halting his advance when he was a few feet away. "What am I now?"

"You're a Mark." He spoke calmly, while inside he felt far from it. "You're stronger, faster—"

"Better, stronger, faster?" Her laughter was harsh. "I'm the fucking Bionic Woman? What the hell was that fever I had?"

Alec crossed his arms over his bare chest and decided to take the high road. She had every right to be pissed and confused. "Punishment. Women's sexuality has been used against them since my mom ate the forbidden fruit. Why do you think childbirth is so painful?"

"Are you *insane*? What does childbirth have to do with me?" She made a slashing gesture with her hand. "On second thought, don't tell me. Just explain what I'm being punished for."

"For tempting me."

"I haven't seen you in ten damn years!" she snapped. "You got your rocks off and left."

Eve had never been able to hide anything from him. She was hurt. The knowledge tightened his throat and made him speak gruffly. "I love you."

A visible shudder moved through her. She reached out and gripped the door frame. "Screw you."

"Evangeline—"

"Go to hell."

"My job is to send demons back there. Now it's your job, too."

"You're nuts. You need help." She jerked her chin toward the door. "There are lots of shrinks out there. Go find one. I'll even let you take the Yellow Pages with you. For old time's sake."

"Did he show you his wings, angel?" Alec stepped closer. "Did he spread them wide? Intimidate you with them?"

Her fingers gripping the jamb were white, as were the edges of her lips.

"I bet he made a great show out of the marking, didn't he? How did he say it?" He deepened his voice, then growled, "Bear the Mark of Cain!"

The coffee cup fell from her fingers and shattered on the hardwood floor, coffee exploding outward in a wide splatter. Her knees buckled and Alec lunged forward, catching her.

He carried her to the sofa and sat, cradling her in his lap. Tucking Eve's head under his chin, he rocked her, taking comfort from her embrace even as he gave the same to her.

"What about you tempting me?" she accused, her breath gusting across his throat. "How was I supposed to resist you? A girl my age . . . a guy like you—"

A soft sob escaped her. Alec thrust his hand into her hair and held her tight against him.

That night haunted him. He'd rented a suite, bought every beautifully scented flower he could find at the florist's, and lit the room with a profusion of candles. He took her virginity on white satin sheets covered in rose petals.

"I couldn't have done anything differently," he said softly.

"You knew you weren't going to stay before you seduced me."

He spoke with his lips pressed to the crown of her head. "I tried to spare you any suffering by leaving. I hoped that if we separated, you could still have the same future you would have had before you met me."

Eve struggled out of his embrace, fighting him with such fervor she fell on the floor. "You're an asshole." Rising to her knees, she slapped him.

Alec clenched his jaw and turned the other cheek.

She cursed and pushed to her feet, her robe askew. He stood with her, securing his towel while facing her head on.

"Spare me any suffering," she scoffed, glaring at him. "That's lame, Alec. You have to do better than that."

"What do you want me to say?"

She ran both hands through her hair and growled. "Something that makes sense. Something sincere and believable."

"I'm sorry, angel."

Pausing midstep, Eve gaped at him. "That's it? You're *sorry*?"

"Would it be better to say that I would do it again?"

She looked away. "Don't do that."

"Don't do what?"

"Look at me like that."

"You love me." Alec smiled wryly.

They stared at each other across the few feet that separated them.

"Hate to burst your bubble," she said grimly, "but I have more important things in my life than you. You're expendable."

"Actually, I'm not, but we'll get to that later. In the meantime, you can't ignore what happened last night."

"It doesn't mean what you think it means." She walked past him to the kitchen.

He followed. "It means we're in a lot of shit. It also means getting you out of this mess just got a hell of a lot more complicated."

She grabbed two mugs from her cabinet and changed the subject. "You want to explain the winged man?"

"*Yes,* brother, *would you like to explain me?*"

Eve turned at the sound of the voice she would never forget. He strode in from the balcony as if he owned the place. The man who'd screwed her into unconsciousness in the stairwell. His smile was sensual and slightly cruel, and it made her shiver, not entirely with fear.

Alec snarled and vaulted across the room with a ferocity and speed that frightened her, hitting his brother in the midsection with a brutal tackle. The ensuing scuffle was far from brotherly tussling. It was a fight to the death, and the sounds and sights of the battle did something strange to her. Made her mark burn, made her pulse race. The scent of blood in the air caused a physical reaction that she likened to blood lust. A rough growl rumbled up from her chest.

Alec lifted his brother into the air like a WWE wrestler and smashed him onto her glass-topped coffee table, destroying it. A moment later, he finished off the job by braining his brother with her Waterford crystal candy bowl.

The sickening crunch of a crushing skull should have horrified her, should have made her vomit, and she was in fact stumbling toward her sink to do just that when Alec disappeared.

Vanished into thin air.

One moment he was pushing to his feet, his bare body sheened with sweat and high-velocity blood spatter. The next he was gone.

Eve paused, unblinking, her body's natural response seized by shock. Her gaze dropped to the dead man on the floor.

Then she spun to the sink and wanted to retch, but her body wouldn't cooperate.

"Oh my God," she gasped, hanging on to the curved granite edge to remain standing. As her mark sizzled within her skin, a sharp sound escaped from her throat.

"Yeah, that's where he went," came a dry voice from the living room. The corpse on the floor rose to its feet, its disfigured head restoring before her very eyes, the dent slowly filling like a balloon. Wings sprouted from the man's back and he shook them out, testing each side with a quick flap before retracting them.

"Cain never learns," he said, winking at her, once again looking like the Armani-clad businessman from Gadara Tower.

"I'm insane," she gasped. "Certifiable."

Alec's brother laughed. "Don't get your panties in a twist, babe. He'll be back, and in one piece, too."

"You're dead," Eve muttered, "and I'm going to pass out."

"You're too healthy for that. All the physical reactions you used to have to stress won't happen anymore."

"*What* the hell are you?"

He smiled, the arrogant curve of his lips a faint echo of Alec's.

Brothers.

She could see it now. All the hints of Alec that had drawn her to him the other day *were* Alec. His blood. His genes. His traits. But all the warmth and love that shone in Alec's dark eyes were absent from this man's. His gaze was filled simply with mischief and male appreciation.

Somehow that was easier to bear right now.

"I'm the guy who fucked you into three screaming orgasms, babe."

"I see asshole runs in your family." The full reality of talking to a stranger she'd screwed in a public place, *on camera,* a stranger who happened to be Alec's brother, and had *wings,* and had been a *corpse* a minute ago, hit her hard and she leaned heavily on her countertop. "I could use a good bout of unconsciousness right about now."

"Reed," he said more softly, his leer fading into something more sincere. "My name is Reed, Evangeline."

"What did you do to me?"

"Did Alec tell you that you're marked now?" Reed settled onto a bar-stool and picked an apple from the fruit bowl. "Damned to hunt the scourge of the earth and make the world safer for everyone?"

"I got the damned part. *Who's* doing the damning is a bit murky."

"Let's just say you should reconsider being an agnostic."

Eve turned on the faucet and splashed water over her face. "Christ . . . Shit!" she hissed, as her mark burned.

He grinned. "You're getting warmer."

"Ha-ha." Forcing herself to act normal, she retrieved one of the mugs she'd set out earlier and filled it with steaming coffee. "Why now? It's been ten years."

"The wheels of justice turn just as slowly up there as they do down here."

"How does Alec fit into all of this?" She shot a worried glance over her shoulder. "Is he okay?"

"He's fine. It's not the first time he's killed me. As for how he fits . . ." Reed shrugged. "He could have spared you if he'd kept his dick in his pants."

Grabbing creamer out of the fridge, Eve poured a liberal splash into her mug. "I understand that part. Is he under some sort of vow of celibacy?" She liked the thought of that.

Reed laughed. "That's rich."

Scowling, she returned the creamer to its spot in the fridge door and shut it with more force than necessary.

"Sweetheart, your name may be Eve, but in this lusty tale, you play the apple. 'Look, but don't touch.'" Reed took a hearty bite of the Red Delicious in his hand.

"That's sick. Who tortures people like that?"

"Free will," he said, chewing with obvious relish. "You always get a choice, but sometimes it's obvious which choice you're supposed to make. If you decide to do your own thing, you pay the consequences." Reed licked his lips. "If Alec had made the right choice, you'd be married now with two kids. Happy as a clam."

Eve stared into her coffee and wondered what that life would have been like.

"So what's the mark for?" she asked finally.

Studying Reed over the rim of her mug, Eve noted that his hair was much shorter than Alec's, his lips thinner, the air about him more intense. Unlike Alec's grungy attire, Reed's garments were perfectly tailored. To-day he sported fitted gray slacks and a black dress shirt, worn open at the collar and rolled up at the sleeves.

"Well, the mark has several uses. It originally put you in line for a hear-ing. The court docket is full and it's important to get penciled in as soon as possible."

"A hearing?"

"Everyone gets a hearing, babe." His smile affected her; there was no getting around it. Fact was, it wasn't just his similarities to Alec that were attractive. "Alec's contribution to the mark waived the hearing and acts as somewhat of a plea bargain. Instead of arguing your case, you get to earn your indulgences in the field."

"Why doesn't that sound as if he did me a favor?"

Reed shrugged. "Depends on how you look at it. It was the only way to guarantee that he would be with you all the time. If you'd gone to trial, you would have been assigned to whichever position was next in the queue that you were best qualified for. Not all positions require mentors and not all positions are in the field." His gaze narrowed as he considered her. "This way, he's certain to be with you."

"And what am I supposed to do in the field?"

"Hunt demons, feral fey, rogue interdimensional beings, warlocks, and various other nasties. You're going to have to work for absolution just as Alec has been doing for centuries."

"Centuries?" She was in lust with a man who was *centuries* old? Eve set her coffee down before she dropped it again. "He's immortal?"

"Almost. Marks heal quickly, so it takes a lot to kill one. There's no time limit on how long you have to prove your worth, and the whole 'sevenfold vengeance' protection has a way of scaring off most hazards to your health."

"Sevenfold vengeance?"

"It's mentioned in the book of Genesis. 'And the Lord said unto him, therefore whosoever slayeth Cain, vengeance shall be taken on him sevenfold. And the Lord set a mark upon Cain, lest any finding him should kill him.' You've got the mark. You get the protection."

"How bad is that? The sevenfold stuff."

"Whatever the demon does to the Mark, they get the same in return. Seven times over."

Eve's brows rose. "That could be bad, I take it."

"Usually so. As I said, it works as a deterrent most of the time. Only the most evil, wretched, and insane creatures don't care."

"Lovely."

He stood and rounded the kitchen island. There was no mistaking the change in his focus.

She lifted her chin. He caged her in with the counter at her back. "In addition to learning how to kill and dealing with a fear of all things evil, you've got Alec to manage, and your feelings about what happened to you because of his lust." He held up the half-eaten apple between them. "Then there are the apples."

She arched a brow, hoping to hide how her body responded to his nearness. Her senses remembered him—his smell, the power and heat of his large frame, the near brutality of his passion. The orgasms he'd wrung from her body.

"The apples?" she asked softly, focusing on his lips as they curved into a feral smile.

Reed ran the bitten side of the apple from the hollow of her throat down to her cleavage. Shivering, Eve reached behind her and gripped the edge of the counter. He lowered his head slowly, watching her, giving her time to pull away. His tongue touched her skin and slid up the trail he'd made in a long, slow glide. His teeth nipped at her chin, then he moved to take her mouth. She turned her head away.

His warm chuckle filled the electrically charged air between them. Then he changed tactics, sliding his hand into her robe and cupping her breast. As his fingers found her nipple and pinched roughly, his tongue slid along the shell of her ear. "Apples, baby. Temptations. The exercising of your free will."

Reed's hips pressed against hers, his knees bending so that the hard ridge of his cock notched into the softness of her sex. He thrust gently, nudging her. She gasped, but kept her hands on the counter. Her body was so tightly strung the slightest provocation had her ready to tear off her clothes. Anytime. Anywhere.

"I wondered," he breathed, his lips to her ear, "what you had that twisted Cain up in knots." His other hand cupped her ass and urged her to rock into him as he tugged and rolled her nipple, sending shockwaves down to the aching flesh between her legs. "Now I know."

"Back off."

His tongue thrust into her ear and her knees buckled. "Hottest, tightest fuck I've ever had. Your slick pussy sucking on my cock. And those sounds you make . . . those little whimpers . . ." He growled. "I want to take you right now. Hard and deep. Pound my dick into you and watch you come until you can't take any more." His hand on her ass slid lower, lifting her leg to anchor it onto his hip. His thrusts grew bolder, more fervent, his chest rising and falling with his harsh breathing. "You're a predator now, Eve. And predators like to fuck."

"Back off!" Eve's hands went to his shoulders and pushed. He flew across the room and landed in a heap on her living room rug.

"Oh my God," she breathed. The damn mark seared her skin anew and made her dizzy.

Reed threw his head back and laughed, rising to his feet with an easy grace. "See? You're beginning to catch on already."

He reached down and adjusted himself, drawing her attention to the obvious wet spot on his pants where she'd been rubbing against him. "Watch out for the apples, babe."

With a rakish wink, he disappeared—vanished—just as Alec had, and a moment later Alec was back. Still naked, but minus the blood, his handsome face marred by a fierce scowl.

Eve picked up the apple and threw it at him.

CHAPTER 7

Alec caught the apple and crushed it into a juicy pulp with his fist.
He was a successful hunter because of his patience. Unlike most Marks, his goal wasn't quantity but quality. Infernals were like all parasitic organisms. They learned, adapted, mutated. As they survived repeated attempts on their lives, they grew stronger and more formidable.

When Alec was summoned to make a kill, he was prepared to wait for days, weeks, months, or even years to strike. Long, protracted battles were wearisome and drew too much attention. He preferred a quick assassination, and he bided his time until that opportunity presented itself.

That was why he was frustrated by his inability to be patient with Abel. His brother was like fingernails on a chalkboard. Alec couldn't ignore him or forgive him. The grudge he carried was too deeply ingrained.

With a quick stride, he moved to the kitchen and opened the trash compactor. He unclenched his fist, releasing the destroyed apple to thud to the bottom of the lined basket. Sticky juice coated his fingers and he watched, detached, as it dripped. Drop after drop.

Eve made a small noise and he glanced at her. She stood nearby, flushed and bright eyed. Aroused.

Alec growled low in his throat. "Stay away from him."

Her chin lifted. She looked prepared to argue, then she turned around and lifted to her tiptoes, pulling open a cupboard and reaching for a bottle of Baileys Irish Cream.

"If you're looking for a buzz," he bit out, "you won't get one there."

She paused midmovement.

"Your body doesn't process alcohol—or any mind-altering substance—the same way it used to."

Her hand fell as a fist into the counter. She faced him, her sloe eyes narrowing with flaring anger. "Are you saying I can't get high?"

"You can orgasm from here to eternity," he said roughly. "That high enough for you?"

"Fuck."

"I'm happy to oblige."

"Oh, shut up!" she snapped. "This is entirely *your* fault."

"Is that all you've got?" he taunted, his blood hot and his temper high. He'd been punished for killing his brother *again,* which left Alec spoiling for a fight. Or a hard, raw screw. Since the latter was what had gotten Eve in trouble in the first place, he would be better off settling for the former. "Your life just blew up in your face and 'shut up' is the best you can do?"

Her fists clenched, and he felt a surge of satisfaction. If she was pissed off at him, she wouldn't be thinking about Abel.

"I don't know," she retorted. "I'm feeling like a superhero. I might be able to kick your naked ass. Maybe we'd both feel better if I did."

Alec laughed and moved to the sink to wash his hands. "You can say that after watching me kill a man? You've got balls, angel. Thank God, 'cause you'll need 'em."

"Don't make light of this, Alec."

Turning off the tap, he crossed over to her. His hips pinned her to the cupboard while his wet hands caressed her cheeks. "I'm not."

"I feel like I've lost my mind."

"You haven't lost anything. You're still the same smart, sexy woman I remember."

"I wasn't a woman then," she grumbled.

He smoothed her eyebrows and followed the curve of her cheekbones. "You gonna argue with me about that, too?"

Eve sighed and rested her cheek into his palm. "You killed him."

"Yeah."

"Explain that to me." Her dark eyes gazed up at him with a mixture of revulsion and wary fascination. "He said it wasn't the first time."

"'Am I my brother's keeper?'" he recited softly.

Eve blinked up at him, a frown marring the beauty of her face. "You're going to quote scripture at a time like . . ."

As her voice faded, Alec watched her confusion turn into a slowly dawning comprehension. She had never been able to hide anything from him, but she'd have to learn to don a poker face now. Infernals would take advantage of any perceived weakness.

"The Mark of Cain," she whispered. "Alec *Cain.*"

"I know it sounds fantastical," he began tightly.

"I believe you." She made an impatient gesture with her hand and barked a little laugh. "I'm not even all that surprised. Not after the last week.

"Seven full days. Shit . . . I suppose that's not a coincidence."

"There's no such thing as coincidence."

"What's going on?" Her hand covered the spot on her arm where the mark rested. "What does this mean?"

"It's a calling, angel. A—"

"I thought it was a punishment."

"It serves that purpose, too."

The way she bit her lower lip was an added sign of her distress, but the inner core of steel that had first attracted him to her did not fail. "Killing demons and fairies? Look at me, Alec. Do I look like I can do that?"

"You're capable of anything that needs to be done. Far more so than most Marks."

"*Most* Marks?" Her eyes widened. "There are *more*?"

"Thousands."

"Jesus . . . Ow, damn it! This thing keeps burning."

"Because you're taking the Lord's name in vain. You'll have to get over that."

Her mouth took on a mulish cast. "This is bullshit. Why me? *Why*?"

He exhaled harshly, his breath ruffling the hair atop her head. There was no way to deny his culpability in her downfall. But he wasn't going to keep pointing it out.

"After my father was created," he said instead, "the angels were commanded to prostrate before him, because he was created in the image of the Lord."

Eve snorted. "God's not at all full of himself, is he?"

"Watch it," Alec warned, shaking her a little. "That mouth is going to get you in trouble."

"That's not the only troublesome part of me."

"Some of the angels refused, insisting they were superior to man—"

"I have a tendency to agree with them."

"Those who opposed God's will were banished from the heavens. They fell to earth, where they mated with man and produced nephilim—half-angels who felt animosity toward the Lord. My family began to lose its position in the food chain."

"So God drafted you?"

He laughed softly, humorlessly. "He said sin crouched at our door and it was my duty to master it. If I did well, I would be forgiven the death of my brother. If I didn't, the Infernals would kill me."

"Why doesn't anyone know this part of the story?"

"It's in the Bible, angel. The order of events is a bit skewed, but it's mentioned."

"So you had no choice."

"We are always given a choice. It was my brother Seth who urged me to accept the offer. Since I had . . . *experience,* it made sense. In the end, I was grateful to be given a purpose. I'm good at what I do."

"You have *another* brother?" She was clearly horrified by the thought.

"Thirty-two of them, and twenty-three sisters. Not all are still here on earth. Many have already ascended."

"Oh, jeez . . ." She winced. "Your poor mother."

"You have to consider that without television, radio, and sporting events, sex was the best form of entertainment there was."

"I'd abstain, if it saved me from birthing that many kids."

"No, you wouldn't," he teased, achingly aware of her simmering state of arousal. Beneath Eve's fear and confusion Alec scented the underlying spice of pure desire. Combined with the salt-tinged sea breeze coming through the open sliding glass door, it was potent and alluring. Eve, by nature, was a sexual creature. That proclivity would be enhanced now.

"Go back to your explanation," she said. "You started killing the nephilim?"

"Yes, which angered Sammael."

"Sammael?"

"Satan."

"Oh, gotcha."

"As the nephilim began to interbreed with other nephilim and the fallen, Sammael trained their offspring, instilling in them a hatred for everything but him. I couldn't handle the job alone. There were too many to kill, too many variations and mutations."

"So God started marking other people?"

"Sinners. Giving them a chance to work off their offenses."

"I'm not a sinner. And the whole setup is totally jacked. There are millions of religious zealots around the world who kill in his name every day, but why use them, right? That would make too much sense. Better to draft unwilling suckers like me. That's more fun. Put the screws to them, watch them squirm."

"Evangeline . . ." Alec's stomach knotted. "You don't have to like Him, but you're going to have to respect His power."

"What more can he do to me?" She pushed him away.

He briefly considered resisting, then thought his state of undress might give him an advantage. He was a hunter by nature, a predator. He knew he would have to approach her with caution. He would have to maneuver skillfully, bending and adjusting as necessary in order to keep Eve close. She would have to see him coming, because surprising her with a pounce would shatter her trust further, and she needed to trust him. Otherwise he had no hope of keeping her alive.

As if she sensed his intent, Eve shot him an arch glance and tightened the belt on her robe. "You went to see him like that? With it all hanging out?"

He shrugged. "It's not as if I had a choice."

"I can't do this, Alec. You got me into this, you get me out of it."

"I'm trying."

"Try harder." She gave a little growl, like a pissed-off kitten. "Listen. I can't watch horror movies. I get freaked out just walking alone through parking garages. Being the Bionic Woman isn't going to change the fact that I don't have it in my programming to kill things."

"This is coming from the woman who met me at the door with a loaded gun?"

"Self-defense is a different story," she argued, turning her back to him and guzzling her neglected coffee.

"He wouldn't have marked you if you couldn't handle it."

Eve choked and glared at him over her shoulder. "We're talking about the god who promised Moses he'd go to heaven if he worked like a dog and ruined his life, then at the last minute reneged on the deal."

Alec's jaw clenched as he linked his fingers behind his back. "I'm starting to think He picked you not because of *me,* but because of *you.* You've got a lot to learn."

"Whatever. Your brother said I could have a trial. I want one."

"It's too late for that."

A terrible stillness gripped her. "Because of what you did?"

He nodded, hating the unfamiliar feeling of dread weighting his gut. Eve had to trust him, implicitly. And now she had every reason not to. The battlefield was not a place to doubt the person watching your back. "I can't help you if I'm on the other side of the world. I had to do what I did to stay with you."

Eve walked away, departing the kitchen and heading down the hallway to her bedroom.

He followed. "Where are you going?"

"You're not my favorite person right now."

"Angel . . ."

Eve spun about in a flurry of ebony hair and blood-red silk. The movement was agile and inherently graceful. Sensual.

"I *will* get you out of this," he said, struggling against his body's reaction to the sight of her. He was so hard it hurt.

Her gaze dropped and her lips parted on a silent gasp. She pointed viciously at his erection. "Put that thing away! It's gotten me into enough trouble as it is."

She entered her room and slammed the door.

"My gear is in there," he called after her, smiling.

A heartbeat later his jeans and shirt flew into the hall and hit him square in the chest.

"You prefer me to go commando?" he asked.

"Shut up and get dressed." But there was a hitch in her voice that told him she wasn't unaffected by the idea.

"We're not done talking."

"Give it a rest, okay?"

He moved to the guest room, his bare feet on the polished hardwood creating a mournful tempo. The extra bedroom bore the same sparse modern styling of the master bedroom and was nearly equal in size. Massive slabs of polished, lacquered pine hung from metal tracks on the ceiling and acted as doors for the floor-to-ceiling closets that occupied the entire right wall. The matching wood floor was littered with several fluffy white rugs cut in irregular shapes. A built-in system of shelves decorated the bottom half of the rear wall, while the top half was covered in black-and-white photos in silver frames.

The bed was to the left. It sat low to the ground and was quite large. A California king, Alec guessed. It was covered with a chocolate satin duvet and cream pillows with brown and rust-colored trim.

The sight of the perfectly made bed both lured and depressed him. He was exhausted. While Eve's body had been changing and storing up energy, his had been drained by worry, guilt, and lack of sleep. If he had a choice, he'd be curled up with her, not fighting the urge to crash. Alone.

He was tired of being alone. Which added to the whole fucked-up situation he found himself in.

His desire to do what was best for Eve—get her life back—was in direct opposition to his long-held need to cease wandering. His mentorship gave him the opportunity, for the first time, to prove that he could play well with others.

Finally, after centuries of nomadic living, he'd been assigned to a home base. Through his mentorship of Eve, he could learn what he needed to know to achieve his ambitions. If he absorbed all the layers of the mark system well enough, he had a shot at pleading his case for stability. He could teach others to perform as well in the field as he did . . . if he had a cadre of handlers and Marks at his disposal.

It had been his long-held dream that one day he would convince Jehovah that by running his own firm he'd be more productive. Everyone knew that expansion of the mark system was long overdue. He wanted to be the one to step into play when a new firm was created. No one had the field experience that he did.

As usual, the choices given to him were damned if he did, damned if he didn't. He needed Eve to get ahead. But he wasn't what *she* needed.

His eyes went gritty with exhaustion.

"Don't do this to me," he bit out, glancing skyward. "You know damn well it's not a good time for me to fall asleep."

But his wishes were ignored, as usual. He was due for a punishment because of killing Abel, and Jehovah had kept the method of chastisement on retainer. Benching him in the heat of the game was an easy and effective way of putting him in his place—behind the curve.

Alec collapsed face-first into the mattress and lost consciousness despite his best efforts.

When he awoke a few hours later, his anger surged as if it had been simmering throughout his forced nap. Through the open doorway to the hall, the cries of seagulls and the sound of waves crashing against the beach reminded him of a thousand other awakenings. Too many days of his life all the same, blending seamlessly and unremarkably into each other. He wanted a different life, one he shared with someone. He wanted Eve, but he couldn't have her.

He would have to find a way to free her, then let her go. Again. He had no idea where he would find the strength to walk away a second time, but he'd do it. Even if it killed him.

"Eve!" he shouted, running his hands through his hair before pushing to his feet.

She was gone. He sensed it. Her absence from the house left a chilling void. It was also life threatening. An untrained Mark was a susceptible and irresistible target for Infernals.

Cursing under his breath, Alec yanked on his clothes and raced out of the house.

Taking a deep breath, Eve pushed open her car door and stepped into the Southern California sunshine.

She paused a moment to run her hands over her Knott's Berry Farm T-shirt. If she'd turned her brain on, instead of running on instinct, she would have found something more suitable to wear to church than sweatpants and a faded T-shirt. Although she didn't believe in organized religion, she respected the beliefs of those who did. But she hadn't planned to come here.

Her gaze moved over the roof of her car to the contemporary, almost-southwestern style of the new Catholic church. In her opinion, it looked more modern Christian than old-world Catholic, but what the hell did she know?

Which was exactly why she was here. She never tackled any project without exhaustive research first. As a child, her Southern Baptist parents had exposed her to religion, but her recollection of those early Bible classes was weak at best.

Eve rounded her car and crossed the massive parking lot, heading toward the carved wooden doors that protected the interior. There were a few vehicles near the front. Some had religious stickers or emblems on the back, but for the most part there were no outward indicators of devotion. The sort of devotion that could drive someone to visit church in the middle of a workweek.

Gripping the handle, she pulled open the door and entered the cool, quiet interior. Like the outside, the inside had a clean minimalist design. The ceiling arched thirty-plus feet above the center of the worship hall and boasted exposed wooden beams in an intricate pattern. Straight ahead, a bronzed statue of the Crucifixion protruded from the wall and shimmered under the glare of a massive spotlight. Eve shivered at the sight, finding the depiction of eternal torment creepy rather than inspiring.

As always, she paused within the threshold, searching inwardly for any sense of awe or contentment. So many people described a sense of home-coming when they entered a house of God. She felt no different than she would entering a convenience store.

The low drone of voices off to her right turned her attention toward a recess filled with a life-size statue of the Virgin Mary and a profusion of lit votives. Two people knelt there, a woman and her child, their heads bent in prayer.

"Can I help you?"

The warm huskiness of the masculine voice froze her in place. The timbre was that of a phone sex operator, which put it seriously out of its element in a church.

Curious, Eve pivoted to face the source.

She was startled to discover a portly balding man in a priest collar. "Hi," she managed through her stupefaction.

"Hello," he replied.

Not the same voice. She frowned.

"I'm Father Simmons. This is Father Riesgo." The priest gestured behind her and Eve canted her body to see whom he referred to.

She almost gaped, but caught herself in time. "Father."

Younger than Father Simmons by a good two decades, Father Riesgo looked so fish-out-of-water in the collar that it seemed more of a costume than anything else. His features were rugged and blunt, his green eyes extraordinary, his cheek marred by a scar she guessed came courtesy of a knife blade. With his dark hair slicked back in a short tail, he seemed more renegade than missionary.

"Hello." He smiled, revealing perfect white teeth. "How can I help you?"

"I need a Bible."

Both priests blinked, as if taken aback. She inwardly kicked herself for being an idiot. So her father didn't own a Bible and her mother's was written in kanji. She should have headed to the bookstore, not driven around aimlessly until she found a church in which to give her moronic tendencies free rein.

Father Simmons set his hand on Father Riesgo's shoulder and said, "I will begin preparations."

As odd as her day had been so far, the fact that she'd been left to the care of Father Riesgo was not inconsequential. Perhaps they thought she was a nut who might require some muscle to get rid of. Eve couldn't decide if that was funny or sad.

Riesgo nodded and waited until the other priest had moved out of earshot. Then he returned his attention to Eve and studied her for a long moment. "What's your name?"

She winced and extended her hand. "Sorry. Evangeline Hollis."

"Ms. Hollis. It's a pleasure to meet you." His grip was strong and bold, like the rest of him. He gestured to the nearest pew, but she shook her head. "Okay," he agreed, in that sinful voice. "Are you a member of this parish?"

"To be honest, Father, I'm not even Catholic."

"Why come here, then? To St. Mary's?"

She hesitated a moment, reluctant to display any further stupidity. Riesgo was the kind of man one approached without facetiousness. His green eyes seemed to take in everything with a laserlike intensity, and the set of his square jaw warned against subterfuge. But in the end, Eve went with the truth simply because that was her nature. "I'm not sure. I'd like to refresh my memory about some biblical stories, particularly the one about Cain and Abel, and I realized I don't own a Bible. This building just happened to cross my path at the wrong time."

"Perhaps it wasn't wrong."

Eve took a tentative sidestep toward the door.

Riesgo stepped as well, keeping abreast of her. "We offer classes, Ms. Hollis. The Rite of Christian Initiation. We would love to have you participate. For many, the Bible is a journey that needs a guide. I wouldn't want you to feel lost or overwhelmed."

"I appreciate the offer, but I'm not interested in joining the church. I just need a research source."

Riesgo's smile returned. "Walmart sells Bibles. They're priced around five dollars, I believe."

"Of course." She mentally kicked herself. "I should have thought of that. Thank you."

Eve continued to edge her way toward the door.

Father Riesgo kept pace, grinning. "Ms. Hollis?"

"Yes?"

He reached into his pocket and held a business card out to her. "If you have any questions, please feel free to contact us here."

"You're too kind." She accepted the card only in the name of politeness. "There are churches closer to me, so I doubt I'll be bothering you again."

Father Riesgo was disconcerting by nature, but when his focus narrowed, the intensity was arresting. He wasn't handsome by standard definition, but charisma . . . he had it in spades. Combined with the husky voice, he probably lured a ton of women to mass.

"Hmm . . ." His skeptical hum made her slightly defensive.

"I have a bad sense of direction."

He shook his head. "I don't think so. You're looking for answers, and your search brought you here. Would you mind waiting a moment? I have something for you."

"I'm in a hurry," she demurred, fearing a long lecture and hard sell ahead of her.

"A minute only. I'll be quick."

He set off at a lope down the center aisle. She watched in fascination, absently noting that the severity of his black garb did nothing to detract from the grace with which he moved.

"Go," she ordered herself.

Eve retreated toward the door. She figured if she made it to the parking lot before he came back, her escape was meant to be.

There was a padlocked tithing box on the wall near the exit. She dropped his business card into the slot and reached for the door handle.

Her hand had barely made contact with the cool metal when Riesgo reappeared at the end of the aisle with a dark red bag in his hand. Her often lamentable curiosity kicked in with a vengeance. The priest looked both excited and impassioned, making it impossible for her to turn away.

He reached her in no time and began to speak in a rush. "Last week, I was compelled to buy this—" he reached into the bag and withdrew a book "—although I didn't know why. My sister owns a Bible that's been passed down in my family for generations and my mother is no longer with us."

Eve accepted the proffered Bible with tentative hands. It was covered in satin-soft burgundy leather and trimmed with ornate, feminine embroidery of floral vines and colorful butterflies. Such craftsmanship was costly. She stared at it in confusion.

"It's yours," he said.

Her stunned gaze lifted to meet his. "I can't accept this!"

"I bought it for you."

"No, you didn't."

"Yes," his eyes twinkled, "I did."

"You're nuts."

"I believe in miracles."

She thrust it at him. "Take it back."

"No."

"I'm going to drop it," she threatened.

"I don't think you can."

"Watch me."

"Borrow it," he suggested.

"Huh?"

"You need a Bible. I have one. Borrow it. When you're done, bring it back."

Her nose wrinkled.

His arms crossed, making it clear he wasn't budging.

"You're wrong about me," she said. "I'm not a lost soul looking to be found."

She'd already been found. That was the problem.

"Fine," he countered easily. "Do your research and bring it back. The Good Book should get some use, not sit in a bag in a desk drawer."

When Eve stepped out of the church a few minutes later, she couldn't believe she had the Bible in her hand. Frustrated by the bizarre twists that were marring the once steady course of her life, she paused on the sidewalk at the edge of the parking lot and groaned.

"I don't like this," she said aloud, figuring the proximity to the church couldn't hurt her chances of being heard by someone upstairs.

A drop of water hit her cheek. Then another splattered on the end of her nose. Frowning, she looked up at the cloudless blue sky. A droplet hit her smack in the eye and stung.

"Ow! Damn it."

High pitched chortling turned her gaze back to the church. She rubbed her eyes and searched for the source. Just as her vision cleared, a stream of liquid hit her dead center on the forehead.

Eve jumped back and swiped the back of her hand across her face. Her gaze lifted to the archway above her.

"Ha-ha!" cried a gleeful voice.

Her eyes widened when she found the source, then narrowed defensively when she realized the water spraying her was urine.

Gargoyle urine.

The little cement beast was about the size of a gallon of milk. He sported tiny wings and a broad grin. Dancing with joy, he hopped from foot to foot in a frenetic circle that should have toppled him to the ground.

"Joey marked the Mark! Joey marked the Mark!" he chanted, pissing all the while.

"Holy shit," she breathed, pinching herself.

A sharp whack to the back of her head knocked the bag from her hands and confirmed that she wasn't having a nightmare.

"Shame on you!"

Clutching her skull, Eve turned to face her attacker—a stooped elderly woman brandishing a very heavy handbag.

"It's not what you think," Eve complained, rubbing at a rapidly swelling knot.

"Whack her again, Granny," suggested the angelic-looking heathen at her side.

"Beat it!" the woman ordered with a menacing shake of her bag.

Eve debated the merits of laughing . . . or bawling. "Give me a break, lady."

"Sinner," the heathen child said.

"I am *not* a sinner! This is not my fault."

A large, warm hand touched Eve's shoulder, then the dropped bag came into her line of vision. "Here."

Father Riesgo. The voice was unmistakable.

Eve glanced at the archway behind them. The gargoyle was gone. The Gothic creature had been out of place on the modern exterior of the church.

"Father," the purse-wielding woman greeted sweetly.

"I see you've met Ms. Hollis." He glanced at Eve. "Don't give up on her yet, Mrs. Bradley. I have high hopes."

Accepting the bag, Eve stepped away in a rush. "Thanks. Bye."

As she hurried to her car, she ignored the fulminating glare from

Mrs. Bradley that was burning a hole in the back of her head. But she couldn't shake the feeling that she was being watched by a darker, more malevolent force.

The sensation scared the hell out of her.

After sliding into the driver's seat, Eve locked the doors and released the breath she hadn't realized she was holding.

"I'm getting out of this," she promised whoever might be listening. She reached into her purse and withdrew the hand wipes her mother, a retired nurse, insisted she carry.

After she scrubbed her face and hands, Eve turned the ignition. Then she drove around the block, looking for "Joey." She had no idea what she'd do when she found him, but damned if she'd let herself get pissed on and not track the little shit down.

CHAPTER 8

An hour of fruitless searching later, Eve parked her car in her assigned spot in her condominium complex's parking garage. With her hands wrapped around the steering wheel, she refused to look at the empty space where Alec's Harley had been when she left. He might be gone for five minutes or five years or forever.

The first time they made love, he'd disappeared before she awoke. She'd waited in their hotel room all morning. Tired. Sore. Madly, stupidly in love. She had believed he intended to come back for her. No man could hold a woman as he'd held her and not return.

In the end, she'd left only when the maid told her she would have to pay for another night if she didn't vacate.

Days of waiting and hoping and heartbreak followed. Weeks passed, then years. She wanted to kick herself for being in the same spot, feeling the same pain ten years later. Smart people learned from their mistakes; they didn't keep making the same ones.

A sudden rapping on her car window jolted her out of her musings. Frightened, she looked out the window and found Mrs. Basso leaning over with a frown.

"Eve? Are you okay?"

Her tense shoulders sagged with relief. She pushed open the door. "You scared me."

"You're jumpy today." Mrs. Basso held mail and keys in her frail hands. The mailboxes were all located on the ground floor, just a few feet away from the parking garage.

Climbing out of her car, Eve managed a reassuring smile. "I have a lot on my mind."

"I bet part of it is six foot two and around two hundred pounds."

Eve blinked.

"He was looking for you," Mrs. Basso said. "Seemed really concerned that you were gone."

"Did he say where he was going?" *Or if he'd be back?*

"No. He had a duffel bag with him though. Don't fret. If he's got a brain, he'll be back. You're worth it."

Touching Mrs. Basso's shoulder gently, Eve kissed her wrinkled cheek. "Thank you."

"Come on, I'll walk up with you."

Depressed by the prospect of returning to her empty condo, Eve briefly considered heading to her parents' place but didn't think she could deal with her mother at the moment. Some days, her mom's quirkiness was just what the doctor ordered. Most days, however, it drove her nuts. Since she was already on the edge of insanity, she thought it best to keep her distance for now.

Eve shook her head. "I think I need to walk a bit and clear my mind."

"I would feel better if you came upstairs. You've had a rough week."

Eve laughed softly, without humor. She wished she could explain. Part of her believed her friend would understand. "I won't be gone long. Just a few minutes."

Mrs. Basso sighed. "Okay. We still on for the movies?"

"You betcha."

She watched Mrs. Basso head to the elevators, then left the building through the garage's pedestrian gate.

It was a beautiful day and the number of sunbathers on the beach gave her a feeling of security. Too many witnesses. Which was both good and bad. The exposure that kept her safe also exposed her when she most wished to be private.

As she walked the length of the beach, she kept her head down to discourage interaction. She was too busy thinking to be interested in casual conversation. If she wanted out of this mark business, she'd need something of value to bargain with.

The wind whipped loose strands of her hair across her face and throat. Her heightened senses magnified the sensation until it was almost unbearable. Not in an uncomfortable way, just alien. Disconcerting.

She'd always controlled every aspect of her life, even as a kid. Her mom, a native of Japan, was an eclectic mix of old-world Bushido and 1970s hippy nonchalance, and her Alabama-native dad was so mellow, she wondered if he was awake half the time. A twenty-year employee of the phone company, Darrel Hollis's normal tone of voice was that of a terminally bored telephone operator. In response to her parents' loving indifference, Eve had become self-reliant and responsible to an extreme degree. Everything had its place and could be neatly compartmentalized. Interior design fit beautifully within that structured way of thinking. Assassinating monsters for God didn't.

"Hey, baby."

The catcall drifted across the breeze along with a vile stench. As her nose wrinkled in protest, her head turned to find the heckler. Some were

easily ignored, others bolder. She needed to know which class of annoyance this guy was.

She found him sitting in the sand on a black towel, his legs stretched
out before him, propped up by canted arms. He was fair haired and blue
eyed, and sported arms sleeved in tattoos. His face bore a foreign cast,
and his irises were hard and glittered like sapphires. He wore only makeshift shorts cut off crudely below the knee and a leer that made her skin
crawl.

"Come sit with me," he cajoled in a gutturally accented voice. He patted the spot next to him in a gesture that was anything but inviting. An
indigo teardrop stained the skin at the corner of his eye, distinguishing
him as a felon. She was about to look away when he flicked his tongue at
her in a lewd gesture.

"Jesus!" she cried, stumbling backward into the lapping water. She was
so horrified by the impossibly long and slender forked appendage that had
slithered out of his mouth, she barely registered the mark burning her deltoid in chastisement.

A red slash appeared across the demon's face and he hissed like the
snake his tongue resembled. *"Du Miststück!"* he spat.

She had no idea what that meant, but it didn't sound good.

As he leaped to his feet, Eve sidestepped to avoid him. "Stay away
from me."

"Make me."

The menacing tone with which the words were spoken made her hackles rise. It also sent a surge of heat and animosity through her veins.
"Christ, you're a real piece of work."

His head jerked to the side as if struck, and when he looked at her
again, his eyes were unnatural. Brilliant and intensely, inhumanly blue.
He lunged. She shrieked and pivoted to run, crashing into something warm
and rock-hard.

"Leave her alone," a dark voice warned. Masculine arms wrapped
around her and Eve struggled briefly before absorbing the familiar scent
of his skin into her lungs. It was heaven compared to the stench in the air
and she gulped with relief.

"Reed." Her hands fisted in his expensive dress shirt.

"You can't intercede," her tormenter said smugly.

"You'd risk the wrath of your brethren for her?" Reed asked.

"She cut me first."

"I did no—" Eve began, only to find her face pressed brutally into
Reed's chest. She briefly considered biting him, but her overactive libido
kicked in with a vengeance, mingling with the hair-trigger aggressiveness
pumping from the throbbing mark. It was like PMS multiplied by a million.

"She was toying with you," Reed drawled. "Assuming you were big
enough to take it."

"Is *she* big enough to take it?"

"Can you take *me*?" Reed retorted. "You're not in the queue; I'm not barred from stepping in."

A stream of unintelligible words that sounded German poured from her antagonist, and Eve wrenched free to face him. She could feel the evil radiating off him, and his tattoos writhed sinuously over his unmoving skin, as if they were alive.

Wondering if she was the only one aware of the man, her gaze surveyed the area around them. The proliferation of beachgoers hadn't diminished, yet no one paid any attention to the tense scene taking place in their midst.

Reed's hand settled at the small of her back, giving her much-needed support in a madly spinning world.

"Go away," Reed said. "Let's just forget this happened."

"I won't forget." The man crossed his arms. "We'll meet again," he told Eve.

"You cross that line," Reed warned, "and you'll start a war none of us wants."

"*You* don't want it."

Eve's gaze shot back and forth between the two bristling men, trying to grasp the undercurrent arcing between them. They were doing some kind of manly staring thing, then the blond sank back onto his towel and sprawled in a pose so relaxed it was clearly meant to insult.

You're no threat to me, his posture said.

Reed exhaled slowly and carefully, deliberately stemming his rising ire. Backing down from a challenge wasn't in his nature, but he didn't have a choice. Any offensive move on his part would put the blame for this unauthorized confrontation firmly on his shoulders. He didn't need any more heat right now, not after the upbraiding he'd endured for his most recent fight with Cain.

Cain the hero. Cain the fearless. Cain the invincible. No matter how often he broke the rules, Cain always emerged unscathed, his reputation strengthened by his sheer audacity.

Now Cain had been given his heart's desire and Reed's sampling of her charms was rebuked, his protestations of her willingness disregarded. *He,* who had always toed the line without question, had rarely been given anything he truly desired.

Hands off Evangeline, he'd been told.

Tightening his jaw, Reed reached for Eve's elbow and pulled her away. Damned if he would toe the line in this. If he had to reap his own rewards, he'd start with her.

"What the hell is going on?" Eve queried on a hiss of breath.

"A major fuck-up," he snapped. "Where's Cain?"

"Sleeping. And why do you two have different names? It's confusing."

"Eventually, you will have to change names, too. It looks suspicious if you don't die."

"Screw that."

He led her up the beach. At the last minute, he directed her toward the patio of a Mexican restaurant and cantina. Festive music blared from hidden speakers and the spice-laden scent of food teased his nostrils. He heard Eve's stomach growl and shook his head. "You haven't eaten?"

"I haven't thought about it. By the way, I don't have any cash and the patio is closed to noncustomers."

He shot her an arch glance. "I don't expect my dates to pay when they're with me."

"This is a date?"

"It is now."

"I'm not feeling it. Not after that creep on the beach."

"He was a Nix," Reed corrected. "And you need to watch your mouth. If I hadn't shown up when I did, you'd be dead right now."

"I didn't say anything!" Eve sank into the plastic patio chair he pulled out for her. Their table was in the corner formed by two Plexiglas panels. It afforded them a view of the beach while shielding their food from the ocean breeze and sand.

"You used the Lord's name," he explained, taking the chair opposite her. "It's a weapon against demons. Rarely deadly but always painful."

"How the hell was I supposed to know that? He was heckling me. If he'd left me alone, none of that would have happened."

"You're ripe for the picking. An untried, clueless Mark. I could kill Cain for falling asleep on the job." He snorted. "Irresponsible, as usual."

"What's a Nix?"

He noticed she chose to ignore the dig about Cain, and he smiled inwardly. The first time he saw her, Eve had been dressed for business. Her unbound hair had been the only hint of softness about her. Her "look but don't touch" air had stirred him, but it was the moment their eyes met that his interest went beyond merely pissing off Cain. Whoever said Asian women were shy and reserved had been smoking something at the time.

"A water demon." Reed gestured to a waiter. "The Nix used to be concentrated in Europe, but they've since spread to most coastal cities."

"He didn't look like a demon," she muttered.

"What does a demon look like?"

"Not like that. Aside from the freaky tattoos, he reminded me of a ski instructor, like he should be wearing a turtleneck and sitting near a stone fireplace at a lodge."

"You've got a vivid imagination." His mouth curved. "But those weren't tattoos. They were *details*—markings that tell us about his affiliations and his status within those affiliations."

"Like gang markings?"

"Exactly. Even in Hell there's a hierarchy and it's constantly under threat by warring factions. Infernals most likely passed on the practice of marking symbols into flesh to mortals." Reed looked at the approaching waiter, a young Latino wearing Oakley shades, hoop earings, and an El Gordito apron tied around his jeans-covered hips. "Two Modelos," he ordered.

"And two shots of tequila," Eve added.

"That's not going—"

"To get me buzzed? I don't care." She managed a brief smile at the waiter. "And a taco plate, please. With lots of salsa. The hot kind."

"Make that two," Reed said.

Eve waited until they were alone again before speaking. "The guy's *details* were moving. Writhing."

"He was trying to intimidate you." And it hadn't worked well, something Reed noted and admired. "Infernals can move them at will, and only others of their kind and Marks can see the show."

"That's why no one paid much attention to him on the beach?"

"Exactly. Some Infernals prefer to keep their details as visible as possible, especially if they're higher ranking. Others prefer to keep them out of sight to maintain a low profile. They can't remove them, but they can put them in places no one wants to look." He shrugged elegantly. "Pointless, really, because they stink so bad you can smell them coming. And when their number's up, it's up. Hidden details or not, once they're in the queue, it's only a matter of time."

"Is that what that smell was? It reeked like a sewer."

"Rotting soul. You can't miss it."

Her eyes widened with such horror, Reed felt a sharp tinge of sympathy . . . even as he appreciated how her inevitable resentment would create a rift between her and Cain.

Eve leaned forward, resting her forearms on the table and staring at him with a grimly determined gaze. "How do I get out of this gig?"

"There's no way—"

"I don't believe that. There has to be a way."

Leaning back, he settled more comfortably into his chair. "Why?"

"Because I feel like a victim, that's why." Her jaw hardened. "And I'm not the type to take it lying down."

"A victim." He stilled at that.

"Wouldn't you feel the same in my shoes?" she challenged.

Maybe. *Probably.*

"You've been placed in a position of power," he prevaricated, "and given the tools to change the world and make it safer for others. Can't you view this as a blessing rather than a curse?"

"The Mark of Cain is a blessing? You're slick, but not *that* slick. And I'm not stupid."

"Slick?"

The waiter returned with a tray bearing two bottles of beer, two shot glasses, and chips and salsa. Eve sat back to make room. Reed continued to watch her, smiling.

"The clothes. The cockiness." An impatient hand gesture encompassed him from head to toe. "Slick."

"Style and confidence, babe. I happen to like both qualities." His voice lowered. "So do you."

She shook her head, but the look in her eyes gave proof to his statement.

Reed reached over and caught her hand. Her fingers were long and slender, her skin soft as silk. That would change. Wield a weapon often enough and it left its mark with roughened flesh. "You don't have to admit it."

"I won't."

He bared her wrist, then lowered his head. As his lips parted and his tongue stroked across her vein, Eve watched in helpless fascination. He could smell her growing arousal and knew she'd be hot and wet. Her recently acquired hyperactive sex drive was a godsend to his plan to have her again, no pun intended. Restraint was difficult the first few years. The heightened senses and fluctuating emotions were killer until one learned to control or ignore them. The best and fastest way to release all that tension was with long, hard sex. Reed was determined to be the man Eve turned to as a pressure valve.

Straightening, he kept his gaze locked with hers. He reached for the salt with one hand, slowly stroking across her palm with the thumb of the other.

"Where is this going?" Her normally clipped tone was softened by hoarseness.

"To bed."

"Not with me."

He smiled and sprinkled salt over her damp skin. Picking up a shot glass, Reed licked her wrist and tossed back the tequila.

Eve handed him a slice of lime. "You're not here to get laid."

"How can you be sure?" He bit into the tart pulp with relish.

"You're the type who likes to be chased, not do the chasing."

"You don't know me as well as you think. But that'll change."

"I told you, I want out." With an offhand toast, Eve downed her shot and chased it with a long swig of the beer. She growled. "Okay. This sucks. It's like drinking water."

"You can't bargain with God, Eve."

"You can bargain with anyone, as long as you have something they want that they can't get anywhere else." She turned her head, her gaze moving to the strip of street visible from her position.

His glance followed hers. Sport-utility vehicles traveled alongside luxury sports cars. Joggers and in-line skaters weaved in and around each other.

"Are some of those people . . . *Infernals*?" she asked.

"Certainly."

She glanced back at him. "They coexist peacefully with the rest of us?"

"If you call living with greed, depression, murder, and lies 'peaceful.'" Reed tipped his bottle back and drank deeply. "Complete destruction of humanity isn't the goal. They need mortals for entertainment."

"Lovely." She exhaled sharply. "You mentioned a queue?"

"There comes a point when an Infernal crosses the line one too many times."

"They have to cross a line first?"

"We're not vigilantes," he said, chuckling. "We can't go around whacking the bad guys for the hell of it. There's a balance to everything. A yin and a yang, if you will. Orders have to come down. Once that happens, all bets are off."

"And then what?"

"The Mark nearest in location who has the necessary skills is dispatched to take them out."

"Who makes that call? God?"

"The Lord assigns Cain directly. The seraphim manage everyone else."

Her lips pursed and he could practically see her curiosity. When she finally said, "Tell me how it works," Reed's answering smile was indulgent.

"Relating it to the human judicial system might make it easier to understand. Every sinner has a trial in absentia and the Lord presides over every case. Christ acts as the public defender. Clear so far?"

"I watch *Law & Order*."

"Okay, good. If there's a conviction, one of the seraphim send the order down to a firm to hunt the Infernal."

"A firm?"

"Think of it as the bail bond agency. An archangel becomes responsible for bringing them in—like a bail bondsman. They don't actually do any hunting. The Marks do the dirty work and they collect a bounty, just as a bounty hunter would, only in this case the prize is indulgences. Earn enough and you'll work off your penance."

"Bring them in? As in dead or alive?"

"Dead."

"Blood-and-gore-dead? Or some kind of magical-dead?"

"There's nothing magic about it." He set his hand atop hers, trying to offer what little comfort he could. "Sometimes it's dirty, sometimes it's not. You'll learn the difference. Training is intense and thorough."

"Training in Infernal hunting?" She shook her head. "No thanks."

"Some Marks think the work is glamorous."

"My idea of glamour is drinking champagne and wearing a little black dress."

Reed's mouth curved. "Can't wait to see it."

"How do I get out?"

"Of the dress? I'll help with that."

"Jeez. Not the dress. This bounty-hunting gig."

"Not possible."

"Bullshit. I want to talk to someone else."

His smile turned into a grin. "My superior?"

"Sure. Why not?"

"You'll meet him soon enough. In the meantime, class should begin shortly. You'll be notified when it's time."

"Class?" Eve stared across the table at Reed and hated the fact that she didn't have a buzz, yet felt light-headed anyway.

Her gaze moved beyond his shoulder. She straightened. "Heads up. We've got company."

Reed didn't even flinch. "About time he showed up."

"What the hell are you doing here?" Alec barked, stopping at their table.

"Waiting for you," she replied, kicking out a chair for him.

Alec caught the back and dropped into the seat. He looked at Reed. "What do you want?"

"Good morning to you, too."

"I want to know how to get rid of the mark," Eve said.

"I haven't figured it out yet," Alec said grimly, "but I'm working on it."

"It's impossible," Reed scoffed.

"Listen." She crossed her arms. "I don't subscribe to the 'impossible' school of thought. Anything is possible. We just have to figure out how."

"You don't even know what's involved with the job yet, babe."

"She's not your *babe*," Alec snapped.

Reed smiled.

Eve glared at both of them. "I know I'm not about to get pissed on and provoked every day of my life. I have a job I love, a home I worked damned hard for, and a life that suits me, even if it's not perfect. I don't want to hunt demons and nasties."

"Pissed *off*," Reed corrected.

"What?"

"You said 'pissed *on* and provoked' not 'pissed *off* and provoked.'"

"I know what I said! And I meant what I said. I was out running errands while Alec was napping and ran across a gargoyle with a rotten sense of humor and a large bladder."

Alec froze. "A gargoyle?"

"What did it look like?" Reed asked.

"Like a gargoyle," she said dryly. "Made of gray stone or cement, small wings, big mouth. This one was kind of cute, with a face like an Ewok."

"No," Alec said. "What did its *details* look like?"

She frowned. "It didn't have any."

"It had to have some kind of designator," Reed argued. "They're marked just like you are."

"Then he hid his details up his ass or something, because I saw every inch of him, even the bottom of his feet. He was bouncing around, spinning circles, and laughing like an idiot."

"Maybe your sight isn't working yet," Alec suggested. "They can't hide their details in body cavities. On the buttocks, genitalia, or even under their hair, yes. But it has to be on the skin."

"I'm telling you, this guy had nothing on him," she insisted. "And I know my 'sight' is working, because I saw the jerk on the beach's details just fine."

"Jerk on the . . ." Alec scowled. "You ran into something else?"

"You can see why taking a nap was a great idea," Reed drawled.

"Screw you." Alec looked fit to kill again. "That was probably your idea."

"Not this time. I was too busy keeping your girl alive."

"You can't even keep *yourself* alive."

Eve stood.

The brothers barked in unison, "Where are you going?"

"Away from you two. I'll take my food to go, then you can fight over which one of you will pay."

"Sit down, angel."

Alec's voice arrested her, the tone of command undeniable. This was a different side of Alec. Even more delicious than the others.

Damned libido.

Angry with her unruly desires, Eve plopped back into her seat.

"Tell me everything that happened," Alec said. "Every detail."

When she finished, the two men exchanged glances.

"What?" Eve asked.

"The tengu went after you," Reed said. "He shouldn't have."

"Tengu?"

"The demon you thought was a gargoyle."

"I feel like the kid in school who has Kick Me taped to her back," she muttered. She looked at Alec. His unwritten sign said Don't Mess with Me. If she had to wear any sign, that was the one she wanted.

"We have to find him." Alec's fingers drummed atop the plastic table.

The server returned with their food and they all waited while the plates were set down. Alec ordered the same meal, then watched Eve closely as she began to eat.

"Why do we need to find him?" Eve asked between bites of her first taco.

"We need to know who he's affiliated with."

"By his details?"

"Yes."

"Fine."

A smile tugged at the corner of Alec's mouth. "You sound grumpy."

"Neither of you believe me. That thing was completely gray from head to toe. Not a speck of color or design on him."

"Your senses probably didn't kick in until you ran across the Nix on the beach," Reed pointed out, wiping his mouth with a paper napkin. "They fluctuate quite a bit for the first couple of weeks."

"A Nix?" Alec swore.

"Is that bad?" Eve glanced back and forth between the two.

"Hell yeah, that's bad. And I bet you riled him up with that mouth of yours."

"There's nothing wrong with my mouth."

Both men's gazes dropped to her lips. They tingled in response. She cleared her throat.

"And the tengu is bad, too?" she asked in order to break the sudden tension.

"Any demon is bad," Reed answered. "But as far as pests go, a tengu is a mosquito and a Nix is a rat. Our resources are strapped, so the tengu fall fairly low on the scale. We don't hunt them as actively as we do some other Infernals."

"We're going to hunt this one," Alec said grimly.

"I'm going, too." Eve wiped off her fingers. "If that thing had details, I want to see them."

"It definitely had details, babe." Reed picked up his beer. "There's no doubt about that."

"Says you," she corrected. She looked at Alec. "What do you intend to do when you find him?"

Alec shrugged. "Shake him down and see what kind of information falls out."

"Unless he has hidden talents, it doesn't seem like a fair fight. He was small."

"It's the demon he works for that concerns me. The tengu are lesser demons who lack initiative and ambition. It's out of character to risk bringing attention to himself. They like to cause trouble, but only indirectly."

"It's not going to be dangerous, is it?"

His gaze softened. "You'll just point him out and get out of the way."

"I can do that." Eve picked up her fork, scooped up some rice, and tried to concentrate on eating. It wasn't as easy as she would have wished.

She was too exhilarated, a response she found more disturbing than exciting.

"Now . . ." Alec's voice was laden with frustration. "Tell me what happened with the Nix."

CHAPTER 9

As Eve unlocked her front door, she took a moment to appreciate the speed with which it had been replaced. But when she stepped inside her condo, admiration gave way to trepidation.

Someone was inside her home.

Alec sensed her hesitation. He caught her arm and pulled her back, taking a defensive position in front of her. Then he sniffed the air and shot her a questioning glance.

She sighed. She didn't need an enhanced sense of smell to recognize the scents of curry and freshly steamed rice. "It's my mother."

An odd look passed over his handsome features. Shock and wariness, perhaps. Then a dawning wonder.

It was the worst possible time for Miyoko Hollis to be visiting. She would view Alec's presence in Eve's house with more significance than Eve was presently prepared to give him. And he knew it, if the sudden mischievous grin he wore was any indication.

"Evie-san?" her mother called out.

"Yeah, it's me, Mom." Eve narrowed her eyes at Alec. She hoped like hell her father wasn't here, because if he was and if he'd seen Alec's belongings in her bedroom, he'd expect there to be a ring on her finger. Despite her traditional Japanese upbringing, Miyoko actually had less old-fashioned views of courtship.

"Behave," Eve admonished.

"Of course." But the gleam in Alec's eyes belied the promise.

Her mother's head peeked out from around the support pillar that anchored the end of the island. The same thick, inky black hair she'd passed on to Eve was permed into tight, short corkscrews that made her look as young as her daughter.

"Oh, hello," her mother greeted, her face brightening at the sight of Alec. She appreciated a good-looking man as much as the next woman.

The rest of Miyoko's four-foot eleven-inch frame appeared, revealing an apron that protected a lime-colored sweater tank and multihued skirt. A tiny, diamond-encrusted cross decorated her neck. The Hollises were Christian—Southern Baptist, to be precise, although they attended the occasional festival at the Orange County Buddhist Church for the food and entertainment. Eve had been baptized as a child, but broke free in junior high, refusing to accompany her family to any further church events. It was still a point of contention between her and the rest of the family. They didn't understand her renouncement of organized religion, but then, they'd never tried to.

Eve made the introductions, her gaze darting to the end of the couch where two suitcases waited with feigned innocuousness.

"Where's Dad?

"Fishing with his buddies again, near Acapulco."

Damn.

Her mother was a caregiver by nature. When her husband was away, she needed someone to fuss over. Since Eve's sister, Sophia, lived in Kentucky, Eve was the recipient of that fussing.

The whole day had been hell. Now, her mother and Alec were in her house at the same time. Eve cringed inwardly.

"A pleasure to meet you, Mrs. Hollis," Alec greeted her.

"Please. Call me Miyoko."

"*Konichiwa,* Miyoko-san." He bowed.

Eve watched startled pleasure pass over her mother's face, but Alec's charm wouldn't be enough to make up for his bad-boy exterior. The slightly overlong hair, worn jeans, ripped physique, and scuffed biker boots made him unacceptable from the get-go. Her mother had impossible-to-meet standards for her daughters' suitors. Reed's exterior would be closer to passing muster, but his arrogance would never make the cut. In all of Eve's years of dating, she had yet to meet a man her mother approved of for longer than five minutes.

"It smells wonderful in here," Alec praised.

"Japanese curry." Her mother beamed. "Have you tried it before?"

"Yes. It's one of my favorites."

For a moment, Eve was startled by the statement. Then she considered how long Alec had been living and how far he'd traveled.

"I made two flavors," her mother said, returning to the kitchen where onions, carrots, and potatoes were in various stages of being peeled and cut. "Hot and mild."

"Why mild?" Eve asked, going to the fridge for a can of soda. She lifted one up to her guests in silent query. They both nodded, so Eve pulled out three and kicked the door closed.

"I invited Mrs. Basso to have dinner with us. Poor dear. I can't imagine living alone."

"I'm glad she accepted." Eve set the sodas on the counter and opened the dishwasher. It was empty.

"You shouldn't live out of the dishwasher," Miyoko admonished. "I put the dishes away for you."

"You didn't have to do that. I can take care of myself."

"I don't mind."

Maybe her mother didn't mind, Eve thought, but she'd never let Eve forget that she'd done it.

Eve turned to the cupboard that held her glasses and found Alec there before her, pulling them down. He handed her one, then pushed the other two—one at a time—under the fridge's ice dispenser.

She watched with a mixture of horror and pleasure. This was the man who'd taken her virginity ten years ago. It seemed impossible that he was in her home, moving around as if he'd lived with her the whole time.

Their gazes met and held.

"How long are you visiting, Alec?" her mother asked.

"Actually, business has brought me into the area indefinitely," Alec replied, setting both ice-filled glasses in front of Eve, and taking the empty one from her hand.

"Oh?" Wariness crept into Miyoko's tone. "What do you do?"

"I'm a headhunter."

"For what company?"

Alec smiled. "For Meggido Industries. We specialize in disaster avoidance."

"How interesting." Her mom's eyes lit up.

As her mother reassessed Alec, Eve could practically see the wheels turning in her head. It wouldn't go well if Miyoko researched Alec's company and found it to be a fraud.

"How did you meet Evangeline?"

"It was years ago, when she was in—"

"—college," Eve interjected, before gulping down her soda.

Miyoko paused in the act of scooping up vegetables. She frowned. Alec rested his hip against the counter and smiled.

"I need a shower." Eve set her empty glass on the counter.

"Don't leave that there," her mother scolded.

"It's my house, Mom." But she picked up the cup and carried it to the sink.

"Can I help with anything?" Alec asked as Eve left the room.

"Would you mind cutting the onions?" Miyoko asked. "They make me cry."

As she traversed the length of the hallway, Eve forced herself to shake off the feeling of being invaded. Her mother had obviously been in her house for a while. The washing machine was running and the air smelled like floor cleaner, which made her wonder how long Alec had been out looking for her.

You're lucky you're not dead, he'd said when she finished telling him about the Nix.

She couldn't imagine living a life where a walk on the beach was a death wish waiting to be fulfilled. Even church wasn't sacred. Nothing was safe. A shiver moved through her.

After a very hot, very long shower, Eve felt slightly better. She pulled on a merlot velour jogging suit and left her hair down to dry naturally. When she exited to the hallway, she ran into Alec as he was stepping out of the guest bedroom. He had changed into a button-down shirt and loose slacks. He looked respectable and edible. She stared.

The corner of his mouth lifted. "I have many sides that you haven't yet seen, angel."

"Not *my* fault."

"No." He stepped closer. "It isn't."

The scent of his skin intoxicated her. "I'm becoming a nymphomaniac."

"I'm available."

"For how long?" she challenged. "I keep wondering when I'm going to look around and find you gone."

"I'll be with you until we find a way to free you."

"So you're temporary."

"Do you *want* permanent?" His gaze was hot.

Eve debated that question for a long moment, then offered a weak shrug. She didn't know what the hell she wanted. A week ago she would have said a successful career, a loving husband, two kids, and a dog. Normal. Comfortable.

"My mom is planning on staying the night," she said instead.

He nodded, but his intensity didn't diminish. "I noticed. I offered to find a hotel, but she absolutely refused the guest room. She says the futon in your office is fine."

Eve sighed. "She doesn't like sleeping in a big bed without my dad. She doesn't even pull out the futon, she sleeps on it like a couch."

"A wife after my own heart."

"I can't see you ever getting married."

"Just because it didn't work the first time, doesn't mean it won't ever work."

She stilled.

"I told you," he murmured, watching her with heavy-lidded eyes. "There's a lot you don't know about me."

"I never got the chance to learn."

"You have one now."

Eve leaned back against the wall. Alec moved in, stepping closer and caging her with one hand beside her head. Memories of their recent night together flooded her mind. The desperate consuming lust. The gnawing hunger. The skill and passion with which he slaked both.

With only centimeters between them, she could feel the heat of his skin and if she listened with her new hearing, she could make out the steadily increasing beat of his heart.

"Your heart is starting to race," she whispered.

"Because I'm with you. Sex is one of the rare times when we're capable of experiencing the full force of our physical responses."

"We're not having sex."

"In my head we are."

Eve's lower lip quivered. It would be so easy to turn to him for comfort and support, but that was what had landed her in trouble in the first place. And when she managed to shed the mark, he would leave along with it.

That didn't stop her from wanting him. Badly.

Her stomach growled, breaking the moment.

"I cannot believe I'm hungry already," she whispered, grateful for the intrusion, however embarrassing. "Those taco plates usually fill me up all day."

"Your body is going through some pretty drastic changes. It requires fuel to manage it all."

"Will my system revert when I'm . . . free?"

Alec sighed, his breath flowing across her lips like a feather-light kiss. "I don't know, angel. I've never met a former Mark."

"Really?" She bit her lower lip.

"Really." He pressed his temple to hers. She could sense his sexual hunger in the underlying tension of his powerful frame.

"I'll find a way," she promised, as much to herself as to him.

"I'll help you."

The doorbell rang, and they broke apart. She looked away first.

"What about the gargoyle?" she asked, as they moved into the living room.

"We'll catch up with him tomorrow." Alec noted her questioning glance and explained, "He can't go far. Tengu draw their energy from the inhabitants of the building they decorate. They stir feelings of anxiety and unhappiness, and feed off of them. Straying too far is like starving."

"That's fascinating."

"All Infernals have their preferences and vulnerabilities. The Nix have to stay near water, as do kappas. Trolls live near woods. When you start your classes, you'll learn the vagaries of each branch. Knowledge is power. Exploiting a weakness can save your life."

Eve reached for the doorknob. "How many branches are there?"

"A few hundred. But each has subdivisions that can number into the thousands."

"Oh my G—" She caught herself.

"Watch it."

She growled. "I'm trying."

Pulling open the door, Eve felt her mood improving when she found Mrs. Basso on her doorstep. Tonight her neighbor wore olive slacks with a matching sweater vest and emerald necklace. A loose white blouse kept the ensemble feminine and casual.

Eve hugged her.

"You look gorgeous," Mrs. Basso said.

"So do you," she returned. Then she introduced her to Alec.

Mrs. Basso held a brown paper bag and a bottle of Chianti in her hands. Eve offered to take both from her, but she declined with a curious blush staining her cheeks.

"Evie-san!" her mother called out. "Can you set the table?"

"Yes, Mom." She looked at Alec. "The remote is on the coffee table, if you two would like to watch TV."

As she moved to the kitchen, Eve heard the low drone of subdued voices behind her. She strained to hear, curious about Alec and the way he interacted with others. He was right. She didn't know anything about him beyond the combustible attraction her body felt for his. Maybe she should learn, if only in the hopes of discovering something that would turn her off enough to get over him.

As she opened the cupboard that held her plates and withdrew four, the voices in the living room grew in volume. Not because Alec and Mrs. Basso were moving closer or talking louder, but because Eve's hearing was sharpening. Every noise seemed suddenly amplified, as if her ears had an adjustable volume knob and someone had cranked it higher.

"I brought this for you, Mr. Cain," Mrs. Basso said.

Eve heard the paper bag exchange hands.

"Thank you." The surprise in Alec's voice made her smile.

"It was one of my late husband's favorite recipes. I included some of the spices that are sometimes harder to find."

Leaning around the support post, Eve craned her neck to get a look. They stood in the living room, the recessed lights bathing both of them in a white glow. Alec stood a foot taller than Mrs. Basso, giving the impression of a man speaking to a child. He was looking into the bag, and the perplexed frown on his face intrigued her.

"Add a cup of the Chianti to the sauce just before serving," Mrs. Basso said, "then enjoy the rest by the glass. You'll find the meal creates a mellow, luxurious mood."

"Mellow mood?"

Eve set the plates down quickly, fighting a building surge of humor.

Mrs. Basso cleared her throat. "Evangeline is so like me in some ways." Her face flamed with color. "We can appear tougher than we are. I think a quiet, romantic evening with good food will please her greatly."

Alec's head turned to find Eve and she faced forward swiftly, moving toward the silverware drawer in feigned ignorance of his conversation. She felt Alec's gaze on her back and bit her lip. Listening to Mrs. Basso give seduction pointers to Alec was priceless.

"Don't forget the forks," her mother chastised, pouring the curry from the pot into a serving dish. "Even when you plan on using only spoons, you should still set out forks."

"Hush, Mom," Eve said, waving her hand in an impatient gesture.

"Why are you whispering?"

"Uh . . ." Alec coughed.

"I worry about Evangeline." Mrs. Basso's voice strengthened. "A young, beautiful woman living alone. It's never been completely safe, but these days . . . These are rough times."

"You're right about that," Alec agreed grimly.

"She's such a lovely girl, inside and out. I would like to see her find someone special and this afternoon when you left . . . Well, she looked a bit lost. I think there's something there."

"Mrs. Basso—"

"I hope things work out between you, that's all. I won't embarrass you anymore. I feel like a meddling old woman as it is."

Eve caught the edge of the drawer and blinked back tears, deeply touched. It was then that she saw the large, clear glass bowl on the counter filled with water and a single, beautiful white water lily.

Her mother was an amateur horticulturist with an impressive green thumb. She often brought over plants and flowers from her garden. But she'd never brought over anything like this.

"The water lily is beautiful, Mom." Eve sniffled, arrested by its perfection.

"Isn't it? I am still reserving judgment on your Alec, but such thoughtfulness is a good sign—if he keeps it up. Men always try hard in the beginning, then they slack off. Anyway, you should put it on the table as a centerpiece."

"Alec brought that?" Eve glanced over her shoulder at the living room. He was seated on the couch with Mrs. Basso now.

"I guess so," her mother said, "unless you have another boyfriend somewhere."

"He's not my boyfriend." Would Reed have given her such a thing? She didn't know what to think about that.

Miyoko hummed doubtfully. "It was delivered when you were in the shower and Alec was changing his clothes. Nice delivery man. Refused a tip. Handsome, too. He reminded me of that blond actor from *A Beautiful Mind*."

Eve froze with forks in one hand and knives in the other. She felt like her heart should be racing, but it couldn't. Not anymore. "Paul Bettany?"

"Yes. That's the one. Very Scandinavian looking. Had a bit of an accent, too."

The water lily took on new meaning, changing from a lovely gift to a sinister warning. A whiff of something noxious wrinkled her nose and she realized what that meant. Eve's hands shook violently.

The Nix knew where she lived.

* * *

As soon as Alec heard the bathroom door lock behind Miyoko, he left the living room and went in search of Eve. He found her in her office seated before her computer.

Her work space was a large room, capable of comfortably holding two large desks—one for her computer and one drafting table for her renderings. It also held a contemporary futon in a soft camel color, a coffee table, and three bookcases.

"Your neighbor is . . . interesting," he said.

She laughed. "She thought you needed some dating pointers."

"I knew you were laughing at me." His hands settled on her shoulders. As he kneaded, his gaze came to rest on the monitor. She was Googling Nixes.

"What do you want to know?" he asked softly. "I can tell you more than Google can."

"Can I kill it with a bullet?"

A grim smile curved his mouth. Eve didn't think she was cut out to be a Mark, but he had no doubts. That didn't alter the fact that he was going to find a way to return her life to her.

"You can, if you blow his head off when he's in full mortal form," he said. "It won't work when he is in liquid form. Decapitation will kill everything except a hydra. You can also dehydrate Nixes by separating them from water. Unlike humans, a Nix will shrivel up within a couple of hours. But it's not as easy as it sounds. Any source of water can recharge them— tap water, puddles, tears, humid air. Unless you drop them off in the middle of a desert, the kill isn't guaranteed."

"That's it?"

"Fire is good. Flame-covered swords work, I've been told."

"And where exactly do I get one of those?" Eve blew out her breath and turned her chair around, forcing him to release her and back up.

"You'll be trained in how to request one."

"Eventually. Someday. If he doesn't kill me first."

His fingertips brushed along her jaw line. "You know I'd show you, if I knew how. I've never figured it out myself and since I've managed to survive this long without one, learning hasn't been a priority."

Her dark eyes were troubled. "What do you think of his gift?"

Alec crossed his arms. "I think he means to kill you."

The knowledge gutted him. He remembered eating at a sushi restaurant once where they'd served the fish still breathing. Slit down the belly, mouth gasping. He felt like that fish.

"Can he?" she asked quietly. "Is he allowed?"

"One of two things is happening here: either he's a rogue who hopes he can justify the kill after the fact, or he's sanctioned."

"Which is worse?"

"They're both fucking bad."

"I get that."

"Why did you have to leave the house, Eve?"

"This is my fault?" She stood. "You really want to blame me for this?"

Alec scrubbed a hand over his face. "No. Damn it, I don't blame you."

Her chin lifted. Despite her slender five-foot-four frame dressed in Betty Boop flannel pajama pants and matching tank, she looked formidable. She *was* formidable. Eve could knock him on his ass with a scowl.

"I left the house," she said, "because I needed a Bible for research. That's how I met the tengu. I hit the beach because I needed air after the tengu incident. That's how I met the Nix."

He blew out his breath. "Shit."

"Nothing is coincidence, you said."

"Right."

"So what is going on?"

"I wish I knew." The possibilities were many; none of them were good. "Did you find a Bible?"

"Yes."

"Are you scared?"

"Terrified."

"Good. You'll keep your guard up, then." He held his arms out to her. Eve hesitated, then stepped into his embrace.

The safest thing to do would be to get far away from her, to allow his scent to fade from her skin so that she couldn't be used against him. But there wasn't a soul he trusted to keep her as safe as he would. If she had to be out in the field, he had to be there with her. It was the only way he'd keep his sanity.

"What do we do?" she asked.

"If the Nix is rogue, killing him will end this. If he's sanctioned, we'll get one of two possible results—either the hunt was labeled personal, which would end with his death, or it was considered an affront to his whole unit and someone else will step in to finish what he couldn't."

"Yikes." She looked up at him. "How can I help?"

"You never leave my side. We'll watch your back. I'll make inquiries and see what turns up."

"We hunt him."

"*I* hunt him."

"I can't go into this blind."

"Angel—"

Her mouth took on a mulish cast. "I need to know what I'm up against, Alec, and I need to be more than a pain in your ass."

"You are *not* asking me to let you handle this as my partner."

"Of course not." She smiled and his breathing faltered. In that moment she was very much like the girl she'd been when they'd first met. "I'm just telling you that I *need* information, as well as your willingness to use me if you need me. Just promise me that you won't be stubborn enough to keep me in the dark."

Alec's instinctive response was to shelter Eve as much as possible. But he knew that would only alienate her and make her more stubborn, although it wouldn't make her foolish. Her quest for a Bible told him she still researched everything to a fault, a proclivity he'd noted the first time he made love to her. She had recited the pros and cons of several over-the-counter birth control methods before he managed to stop laughing and occupied her thoughts with something else instead.

"It's my job to lead, angel. *I* need to know that you'll follow, even if following means staying out of the way. And, for now, I don't want you leaving the condo without me."

She pondered that a moment. "What are we to each other?"

His brow arched, even as his hands slid down her back and cupped her buttocks.

"Behave," she admonished.

"You like me when I'm naughty," he purred, nuzzling his lips against her ear. He felt her shiver, even as she pushed against him. It was a bad idea to get more deeply involved with her when their parting was certain, but he couldn't resist.

When he let her go, she couldn't come back to him even if she wanted to. Yet if he kept her, if he tried to work off their penance in unison in the hope that one day he could be what she needed, he would lose her.

Evangeline Hollis had *family* written all over her. Husband, two and a half kids, a dog, and a white picket fence. Her sister was married with children. Her parents had passed their silver anniversary. The fact that she rarely dated wasn't so much a fear of commitment as it was a fear of wasting time with Mr. Wrong.

Alec couldn't give her the life she craved, and if he was honest, he would admit that he might never be capable of giving it to her. He was a killer, a murderer. Everyone had a talent, and ending lives was his. He'd never be the nine-to-five family man Eve wanted and deserved.

"I have enough on my plate at the moment," she said hoarsely. "I don't know when you're leaving, what I'm doing, where this mark is taking me, or how the hell I'm going to get my life back."

Alec smiled, the hunter in him relishing the chase.

She wriggled away from him. "I don't need any more complications. Now answer the question: what are you to me?"

"Every field-assigned Mark has a mentor. The training is thorough, but nothing can replace hands-on experience. Mentors guide new Marks in the transition from the classroom to the streets."

"Sounds organized. Training. Mentoring."

"It is. Very much so."

Eve nodded. "Okay. So now I know how to kill a Nix. How can I expect him to try and kill me? The normal ways? Does he have special gifts I should be concerned about?"

"They can kill with a kiss. Their lips seal to yours and they flood your lungs with water, drowning you. They can leech moisture from you, dehydrating you to death. But that takes time. You'd have to be immobilized. And they kill the old-fashioned ways, too."

"So my best option is the commonsense one—keep my distance."

"Definitely. With any luck, your body will acclimate quickly to the mark and you'll soon be able to smell him coming."

"I caught a whiff of him earlier." Her nose wrinkled. "A bit of residual odor on the outside of the vase."

Alec scrubbed a hand over his face. "Usually Marks start out smelling everything, then they learn to control their senses enough to focus on the little things. You're working in reverse. How the hell can you smell something so minor so quickly?"

Eve yawned. "Like I know. That's one too many questions for me today. I'm hitting the sack. I'm beat."

"Want some company?"

The corner of her mouth tilted up and his blood heated. "Not tonight, I have a mother in the house."

"Good point. Tomorrow we'll head out and find your little stone friend."

"Yipee," she said dryly. "Can't wait."

She walked away with a saucy wave.

CHAPTER 10

This is a bit out of the way for you, isn't it?" Alec asked, as Eve pulled into the parking lot of St. Mary's church.

"I drive when I need to think." Her gaze drifted over the roof of the building before she turned her attention to finding a spot.

"Busy congregation," he noted.

It seemed odd to Eve to have Alec in the car with her. For years, she'd pictured him on his motorcycle. He seemed at home astride it, a part of it, a virile man and his steel horse. But when he'd offered to drive she'd swiftly declined. She needed a clear head to absorb the surfeit of information he was imparting to her. There was no way she'd be able to think with his hips between her thighs and her arms wrapped around him.

"I guess so," she replied in response to his observation.

Eve put her car in park, pulled the key from the ignition, and undid her seat belt. Unsure of how their "hunt" would progress, she'd dressed in well-worn jeans, Vans, and a button-up, short-sleeved top. "Ready?"

He looked at her with a soft gleam in his eye. "Why didn't you just ask me what you wanted to know?"

"You were asleep."

Alec snorted. "That's a cop-out."

"What's the matter with wanting to read it with my own eyes?"

"It's hearsay. A lot of it is more fable than literal truth."

"And you're going to give me an unbiased play-by-play?"

In answer, he smiled and opened the passenger door. She remained seated as he alighted, her gaze riveted to his ass and long legs. He, too, wore jeans. His feet were encased in steel-toed Doc Martens and his torso was covered in a dark blue T-shirt. She was astonished by how normal he looked, when he was anything but.

She got out of the car before he could get the door for her. "Now what?"

"We case the church." Alec slipped on his sunglasses. "Then we spread out slowly on foot until we find where he lives."

"I thought churches were sacred."

"Stick with me, kid," he drawled. "You'll learn something new every day."

"Nothing I want to know," she muttered, slamming the door shut and pocketing her keys.

They weaved through the rows of cars with Alec in the lead. "Where did you see him?"

"Up there." She pointed at the arch. "There were other people around, but no one else seemed to notice him."

"They're not marked."

"Lucky them."

The wry glance he tossed over his shoulder brought a smile to her face.

"Ms. Hollis."

The husky, rumbling voice of Father Riesgo was unmistakable. She paused midstride and turned around, her smile widening at the sight of the approaching priest. She sensed Alec taking up a position behind her.

"Father," she greeted, finding him no less incongruent in the collar today than she had the day before.

She introduced the two men and was startled when Alec reached out his hand and spoke in a foreign language. Father Riesgo replied in the same tongue, his returning handshake firm and his green eyes sparkling.

Riesgo looked at Eve. "This must be the man who prompted you to study the church."

"Uh . . ."

"I am," Alec said, grinning wickedly.

"Excellent. Your relationship must be growing more serious." The priest glanced at Eve. "We have some wonderful couples' meetings you might enjoy."

Alec tossed an arm across her shoulders. "Eve is a bit stubborn."

"The more stubborn they are," Riesgo said easily, "the more devoted they can become. Are you here for morning mass?"

Eve shook her head. "I'm here for a different kind of research. I'm an interior designer. I was told there was a Gothic-style building around this area. Do you know of it?"

"You came to church for that?" He arched a brow. "Why not drive around and look for it?"

She glanced at Alec. His dark gaze was wickedly amused behind his shades. Eve scowled when she realized that he had no intention of helping her.

"It was his idea," she blamed, jerking a thumb toward him.

He responded by wrapping his arms around her. "It got you to church two days in a row, didn't it? I told you miracles happen."

Eve elbowed him in the gut, an act that only hurt her arm and made him laugh.

Father Riesgo smiled. "Mass begins in an hour. Hopefully you'll both be able to attend."

Waving lamely, she managed to urge Alec away.

"See?" he asked, as they left the parking lot. "No one believes you're a lost cause."

She kept walking.

"Are you giving me the silent treatment, angel?"

"I'm looking for my *friend*."

He hummed a doubtful sound and reached for her hand, linking their fingers.

As they rounded a corner and left the quieter side street for the main thoroughfare, the noise picked up appreciably, exacerbating the feeling that she was leaving safety behind and entering an unknown, dangerous new world. Cars traversed Beach Boulevard at the customary Southern California pace, a unique speed somewhere between distracted leisure and impatience. The vehicles that could have their tops down did. The rest had their windows down, allowing a steady stream of music to pour into the air in an eclectic mix of country and rap, alternative and pop.

The sky was powder blue, cloud free, and sunny. Just the right blend of warm sunlight and cool breeze . . .

A breeze that blew a noxious odor straight into Eve's face.

The stench made her nose wrinkle in protest. She couldn't describe the scent even to herself, having no point of reference for something that smelled so horrendous.

Instantly, Alec changed. His grip tightened and his casual stride, shortened to match hers, altered to a predatory deliberateness. Eve noted the change in him and felt the corresponding change in her body. Everything closed in. Narrowed. The background noises faded away, her vision sharpened, her muscles thickened. Adrenaline flowed hot and heavy through her veins. The sudden pulse of power was brutal. And arousing. Not entirely in the sexual sense.

"I smell them," she murmured, shivering. She felt as if she could run like the wind and tear a phone book apart with her bare hands.

Euphoria. That's what it was. And it was caused by aggression. How the hell did the two blend?

"Yeah." He glanced around, then gestured to a business suit–clad gentleman climbing into a Range Rover a few feet away. "There's one."

"Where's his detail?"

"Hidden beneath his clothes or hair. He's a lesser demon, hence the reason he stays in mortal guise for a full-time job."

Eve tugged on his hand, her mouth dry. He glanced at her in a distracted manner, then did a double take.

"I feel weird," she managed.

Alec gave a rumbling purr. "You look awesome. The mark is hot on you, angel."

It felt hot, too, in a wholly primitive way.

She breathed deeply, picking up a barrage of odors—exhaust fumes, heated asphalt, someone's fresh coffee, a rotting soul . . .

"German shepherd," she blurted, startled by the surety she felt in identifying the dog she smelled.

"Good job. The guy across the street with the Starbucks cup. What flavor?"

She sniffed, sifting through perfumes and fabric softeners. "None. It's black."

"Excellent." Alec jerked his chin down the street. "Can you read the headline of the newspaper in that stand?"

"No. It's lying down, smart ass." She narrowed her gaze. "But I can see that brick building about a mile away with a tiny gargoyle on the corner of the fourth floor."

He smiled. His expectation was tangible, thrumming across the space between them.

"You enjoy this," she accused, trying to ignore how infectious his excitement was.

"I'm good at it," he corrected. "Don't you enjoy being good at something, regardless of what that something happens to be?"

Eve released his hand, caught his elbow, and tugged him across the street. Two things astonished her by the time they reached the other side—one, that she'd been strong enough to veer him off course, and two, that they crossed the street before the pedestrian crossing countdown timer had ticked off more than two seconds.

No one could walk that fast. It wasn't humanly possible.

She paused, her brain trying to catch up with her body. "Whoa."

"Your Change is coming along," Alec said with his hand on her back and his gaze trained down the road. "But you'll have to learn how to keep a lid on your skills in public. We can move too fast to be seen, but it's still risky. If we aren't careful, it won't be long before we have widespread panic. Infernals feed off negativity, and they don't need any more fuel."

"It wasn't intentional."

"I know. Just sayin'."

Straightening, Eve blew out her breath. "Okay, I'm ready."

They continued at a more leisurely pace, but there was nothing else casual about them. The closer they drew to the building, the edgier she became and the more focused Alec appeared to be. Sounds and smells washed over her like lapping waves, sometimes intensely, at other times muted. The effect was disorienting and by the time they reached their destination, Eve wanted to lie down.

"It's still under construction," she said, noting that some of the upper windows still had the manufacturer's stickers on them.

"And I don't smell anything. This can't be the building."

"Alec, gargoyles aren't exactly a dime a dozen around here and the ones on this building are identical to the one I saw."

"If there was a tengu here the whole place would reek. Just like you can smell fish blocks away from a wharf."

She crossed her arms. "Okay, fine."

"Fine." He reached for the door, rattling it. "It's locked."

Eve peered through the window. The basic setup for a welcome/security desk and an occupant directory were in place but unfinished. There was a sign of some sort lying facedown inside the window. She suspected it was the property management company's contact information.

She cocked her head. "Hear that?"

"What?"

"Sounds like an air compressor." She stepped back to the very edge of the sidewalk. Leaning against a parking meter, she looked up.

"We'll need to get on the roof."

"Right, but how do we get up there?" Eve looked at him. "With a bionic leap or something?"

Alec glanced over his shoulder with a wry curve to his mouth. "No."

"Good." A sigh of relief escaped her. "I'm afraid of heights."

"We're climbing up the outside."

"*Four stories?*" She hugged the meter. "That's fifty-three feet above the ground. Are you insane?"

"No, I'm kidding." He winked and held out his hand. "Let's head around back and see if we can get in that way."

Growling under her breath, Eve walked past him and searched for a walkthrough that would lead them to the alley at the rear of the building. She found one just beyond the athletic shoe store, a few doors down.

After they made it to the other side, they discovered a chain-link fence protecting a makeshift construction site at the soon-to-be entrance of a subterranean parking garage. A dozen men in tool belts and hard hats littered the area. The sign on the fence said they worked for D&L Construction.

"Looks like they have a guard at the gate," she pointed out, referencing the man with a clipboard who was checking off who entered and left.

"Is that usual for a construction site?"

"Sometimes. Depends on how hazardous the site is and the expense of the decor. You want to limit your liability against injury and prevent theft of certain decorative items." She took stock of the building again. "With this type of retro design, it makes sense that the interior would follow suit with some costly period details."

"Excuse me," Alec called out, as they approached the sentry, a rent-a-cop with a massive physique. He looked as if he might eat steroids like breath mints. "What type of building is this going to be?"

"Office space. Really nice."

"Any chance we can take a look around? I'm looking to relocate my offices."

The guard shook his head and reached into his pocket. "Sorry. You have to make an appointment with the property management company." Gray brows drew together in a frown. "I ran out of the gal's business cards. The building is attracting a lot of attention so I'm giving out a dozen or more a day. I'm betting the space will be full long before it opens."

"When is the planned opening?" Alec asked.

"I'm not sure anymore. The contractor is behind schedule. Plumbing and electrical are still in the works." The guard shrugged. "Hang on a minute, and I'll grab some more cards."

The man was about to turn away when a large group of construction workers rounded the corner in a rowdy bunch. The fast-food cups in their hands suggested they were returning from break.

"Sorry," he said with a grimace. "I have to check these guys in first. We're having trouble with the time clock, so I have to keep track of their shifts as backup." His voice lowered. "They get pissy if their hours aren't right, and since the foreman just left for lunch, there's no one around to keep them in line."

Alec smiled. "I have an appointment in an hour and I'll have to change clothes between now and then. Do you mind if I just go grab a card myself? I'll bring you back a stack."

Eve tried not to look too surprised. What was the rush?

The guard's eyes glazed over. He gestured lamely toward a nearby mobile trailer. "They're in a holder on the foreman's desk."

"Thanks." Alec caught her arm and dragged her through the gate.

"How the hell did you get him to let you in so easily?"

"The mark makes us . . . persuasive."

She thought of how she'd felt compelled to be with Reed and her breath caught. "The Jedi mind trick is cool, but what's the point in this case? We need to come back with the Realtor."

"Not everything is a dead end. Always look for a detour."

"A business card is a detour?" She waited while Alec ascended the metal ramp and knocked on the trailer door. No one answered.

"The foreman just left for lunch, remember?" He smiled and turned the knob. "An unoccupied office filled with paperwork is a detour. Come on."

With a last, quick glance around, Eve grabbed the railing and vaulted up the ramp. She was quick, but Alec was quicker. By the time she shut the door, he was already sifting through the papers littering a large desk.

The long rectangular office space was devoid of any dividers. On the right-hand side was a small grouping of lockers and a beat-up sofa. On the left sat the desk and several metal file cabinets that were six drawers high. The walls were decorated with various blueprints of the building, and the linoleum floor was bare and badly scuffed.

"What the hell are you doing?" she demanded.

"These gargoyles look like your tengu, right?" He glanced up at her. With his sunglasses hanging on the back of his neck, he looked too relaxed to be a snoop. "Most likely they were made in the same location. Who manufactured them?"

She glanced nervously at the door. "I guess I'm the lookout?"

"No way, angel. You need to come over here and tell me where to look. All this construction/architectural stuff is familiar to you, but it's Greek to me."

Eve snorted. "Whatever. I bet you're fluent in Greek, too."

"You betcha. Now bring your hot little ass over here and help me out." He perused every inch of the room in a slow sweeping glance. "From what the guard said, it sounds as if this project has been plagued with problems—setbacks, unruly employees, malfunctioning equipment."

"It's not unusual. Some jobs are just more difficult than others."

"True. And some locations are just plagued with tengu."

"I thought you didn't believe me."

He looked at her. "Do you want to prove me wrong or not?"

"You're humoring me."

"Do you care?"

She sighed. "Who's going to be the lookout?"

Rounding the desk, she bumped him out of the way with her hip and settled into the dusty, duct-taped chair. She shook the computer mouse to wake up the system, then began to dig around the files.

"We don't have the time to waste," he said grimly. "We both need to be working. Just listen carefully. We'll hear them coming."

"Uh . . ." She frowned at the screen, her brain focused on finding what they needed as quickly as possible. "Listen?"

"Yeah." Alec moved to the filing cabinet. A moment later he asked in an amused voice, "Angel? Are you listening?"

"Huh?"

"That's what I thought. You don't multitask well."

"What?" She glanced at him. "Hush. I can't concentrate when you're talking."

He laughed.

Eve worked silently, assisted by her newly efficient body. Before being marked she would have been sweating, her heart racing, her fingers shaking. Now the only effect of their illegal activities was a powerful sense of excitement.

"I have the manufacturer's name here," she said, glancing aside at Alec. "Gehenna Masonry."

He pushed the drawer shut. "Then let's go."

There was something in his voice that disturbed her.

"What's wrong?" She closed the windows she'd opened on the computer and put it back to sleep, then she pushed back from the desk.

"That masonry. Ever heard of them?"

"Sure." Eve searched for the property management's business cards in one of three holders on the desk. They weren't there. Opening a drawer she found the box the cards came in, but it was empty aside from a "time to order more" reminder. "They're out of the biz cards."

"We got what we need." He opened the door. "I don't think the name of the masonry is a coincidence."

"Oh?" She stepped outside and breathed a sigh of relief when no one seemed to pay them any mind.

"In the Bible, Gehenna was a location near Jerusalem where forbidden religious activities were practiced. It was condemned, and became a place of punishment for sinners."

"Oh." Pausing at the end of the ramp, she looked up at the two gargoyles barely visible from her vantage point. She concentrated hard, willing her enhanced sight to kick in. Like an adjusting magnifying glass, the stone creatures came into view. They crouched, frozen, their faces carved with broad grins. And they were identical to the one that peed on her.

She sniffed the air.

Alec caught her arm and laughingly pulled her toward the gate. "You look silly."

"I'm trying to use my superpowers."

"We're done here."

They reached the gate and Eve explained to the guard that they were out of business cards. Then she and Alec started walking back toward the church.

"Be careful what you wish for," she said softly.

He looked at her. "What?"

"I'd been thinking about some kind of change in my life. Maybe a new employer, a shorter haircut, or a redesign of my condo."

"You're an adventurous woman." He shoved his hands in his pockets. "The way we got together proves that."

"I've never really thought of myself that way."

"Do you want a family?"

There was something in his tone, a kind of tense anticipation.

Her lips pursed. "This is the twenty-first century, Alec. A woman can have a successful career *and* a family."

"Don't get defensive, I'm just asking."

"I have to go into the office tomorrow," she said instead, "and hope Mr. Weisenberg hasn't fired me."

They paused at a streetlight and waited to cross.

"You want to go back to work?" Alec's brows rose above his shades. "Knowing all that you know, you're just going to go about your business? What if your boss is a Nix? Or your coworker is a succubus? You're just going to ignore that?"

"That's not funny."

"It's not meant to be." He leaned his shoulder into the lamppost and watched her. "They can smell you. They'll know what you are."

"What am I supposed to do? I have to work. I have bills to pay." Eve shoved her hands into her pockets. "Until I get called to class, I can't do anything else, right? There's no one I can talk to about getting out of this mark thing until then?"

"You can help me check out Gehenna Masonry."

"Why? You don't need me."

Alec straightened. "It's not about that. It's about right and wrong, and something is *wrong* here."

He caught her elbow and led her across the street. A group of tourists passed them, heading in the opposite direction. The women in the group stared at Alec, their heads turning to follow him with appreciative eyes.

"If I'm right about the tengu being in that building, will identifying him bring him up in the queue?" she queried. "Is taking a leak on a Mark worthy of getting your number called?"

"His number isn't up."

"Reed said there's a queue. No vigilantism."

"That's true. Now, if the tengu had tried to kill you, all bets would be off. Self-defense trumps the queue."

"So what are you doing?" she pressed.

"I'm investigating." He shrugged in a sinuous ripple of powerful muscles. "That's all."

Eve kept her eyes forward, but her thoughts were turned inward. There was a part of her that found the thought of hands-on, pounding-the-pavement research very appealing. The thrill of discovery and the sudden flash of understanding was a rush she craved. It was one of the aspects of her job that she most enjoyed—the pursuit of solutions to problems.

"You're quiet," he said, as they rounded the corner and the church came into view.

"Based on the name," she said, "what are your thoughts?"

"It's possible that when the masonry delivered the gargoyles to the construction site, they had the tengu on the truck. The one that came after you. Maybe he took a potty break while they were unloading. He might've caught wind of you, thought he'd play a bit without risk of repercussions, then rode off into the sunset."

"That's why there's no smell around here?"

"It makes the most sense. And if my theory is correct, we need to find out its final destination. Buildings with tengu have higher suicide rates than those that don't. Higher rates of business failures. Extortion. Evictions. Embezzlement. Adultery. Visit any dead mall in this country and you'll find evidence of tengu infestation. This particular tengu is bolder than most, so it's going to be more troublesome than most."

"Well, your theory also leads to speculation about how widespread this distribution might be," she added. "If you're right about the masonry be-ing involved, it might not be a one-time thing."

"Exactly." He smiled with approval.

Eve hit the remote for her car alarm when they were several feet away, noting that many of the parking spaces were now filled. From the church, faint sounds of voices raised in song could be heard. Sprinklers sprayed the nearby lawn, casting rainbows in the mist.

One of the corner sprinkler heads was broken, creating a stream of water that snaked across the asphalt. It caught Eve's attention only be-cause of the smoothness of the pavement, a rarity in California.

She had traveled extensively over the course of her life—family road trips when she was younger and job site visits when she was older. No-where else in the United States had she ever seen such bleached and cracked roads as there were in California. Repairs were made with topical appli-cations of tar, creating a haphazard web of black over gray that was often more prominent than the painted safety lines. But not here at St. Mary's. It was another sign of the health of the church's congregation.

More than that, however, the asphalt made Eve think of her life. Over the years it, too, had lost its color. As cracks had appeared, she'd slapped a Band-Aid on them and kept on driving. Her dissatisfaction almost felt like a midlife crisis, and at twenty-eight years old it was far too soon for that.

"I'll help you," Eve blurted, meeting Alec's gaze over the roof of her car. "But only to the extent that it doesn't interfere with my work."

"Deal." The curve of his lips drew her eyes to his mouth.

Shaking her head at her preoccupation with sex, Eve pulled on the handle and stepped out of the way of the swinging car door. Her gaze dropped to the driver's seat to facilitate sliding into it and the stench of a sewer made her recoil violently. Looking for the pile of shit she must have stepped in, she found herself staring into eyes of malevolent, crystalline blue. A face. In the puddle at her feet. She screeched, kicking instinctively, causing the visage of the Nix to explode in a shower of water droplets.

As her leg came back down, the spray regrouped in a rush, forming a rope of water that wrapped around her ankle. It yanked hard. Eve fell, the ground rushing up to meet her, the Nix's face leering with such glee-ful anticipation it struck terror in her soul.

CHAPTER 11

As Eve's knees buckled, she reached blindly for the car door, crying out as her forearms slammed into the thin metal lip that rimmed the top. She caught the edge with her fingertips, her body nearly dangling as water snaked around her calves and pulled at her.

Then Alec was there, catching her around the waist and chanting in a language she didn't recognize. What she did understand, however, was how furious he was. His large frame vibrated with it and his voice hummed with unmistakable menace. She kicked furiously at the puddle, her shins hitting the bottom of the door in her frenzy. The displaced water began to converge, evaporating with unnatural swiftness until it was no longer there.

"Shh," Alec murmured with his lips to her ear. "He's gone. It's okay. Calm down."

"Calm down?"

"I can't believe he came after you while I was here," he bit out. "He knew he didn't have the time to hurt you with me nearby. He's just terrorizing you."

She hiccuped, which brought to her attention the fact that she was crying. *"Just?* Damn it, that's enough!"

"No. It's too much." He set her down and urged her toward the passenger side. "I'm driving. You're shaken up."

"I'm pissed." And she was. She was scared, yes, but she was mad as hell, too. Her forearms and shins hurt, and aggression flowed across the surface of her skin like a hot breeze.

"We need to add the Nix to our to-do list."

"You're goddamn right we— Ow! Crap!" She hissed as her mark sizzled.

"Watch it."

Alec opened the door for her, then rounded the trunk and slid behind the wheel. He moved the seat back to accommodate his longer legs, then turned the engine over and slid the transmission into reverse. "You okay?"

"No. I'm not okay."

He squeezed her knee, then tossed his arm onto her headrest. He glanced out the rear window as the car backed out of the space.

The drive to her condo was made in silence. Eve wiped her tears, examined her already healing arms, and inhaled resolve deep into her lungs. When Alec pulled into her assigned spot next to his Harley, he sat for a moment with both hands on the wheel. He stared straight ahead at the cement block wall that framed the parking garage. Eve got out.

As she passed through the archway that led to the lobby, she paused at the mailboxes and waited for Alec to catch up. He dropped her keys into her outstretched palm and she opened her box. Mail poured out and littered the marble floor. Eve cursed and pried out the rest with effort. Some of the envelopes were torn, junk mail was crushed, and there were three receipts to pick up packages that wouldn't fit in the box.

Alec whistled, his brows arching. He handed her the mail he had retrieved from the floor. "Popular gal."

"It's been over a week since I checked my box," she reminded, stepping over to the nearby trash receptacle and beginning a cursory sift through the mass. She tossed the sales flyers, coupons, and catalogs. There was a letter from her sister and she set it on top, her fingertips lingering on the paper a heartbeat longer than necessary. She saved a Del Taco flyer with a sudden appreciation of her present hunger, then she paused, unblinking.

"What?" Alec looked over her shoulder. He stilled, too. Reaching around her, he plucked the postcard from her nerveless fingers and flipped it over. "It's stamped, not bulk mail."

"Yeah." A chill swept through her, like the old saying about a ghost walking over her grave. "The date of the cancel says it was mailed the day before I was marked."

Eve took the postcard back and read the text on the reverse. It was an invitation to view the Gothic-style building infested by the tengu. Olivet Place it was called. Only the date preprinted on the card was still a few months away and the collage of photos on the front included blank sections with notes like "insert lobby photo here." It was a mock-up and should not have been mailed.

"Someone wanted me to go to that building," she said, frowning.

"Looks like."

"Why?"

"That's the question." Alec mantled her with his body and rested his chin on her shoulder. "This isn't good."

"Ya think?" She exhaled in a rush, her gaze riveted to the suddenly threatening piece of paper in her hands. "What are the chances that I would be lured to a demonic building at the same time I was marked?"

"Slim to none, I'd say." His voice was grim, his touch possessive.

"Is there any possibility that the bad guys knew ahead of time? The two events have to be connected, right? Seems like too much of a coincidence."

"There is no such thing as coincidence."

She didn't say it, but she was glad Alec was with her. Yes, he'd gotten her into this mess to begin with, but at least he was around to help her deal with the aftermath. "So what do we do?"

"*Ms. Hollis?*"

Eve jumped at the sound of her name. Alec turned fluidly, pushing her behind him as he faced the man who addressed her. The visitor was dressed flawlessly in a three-piece suit of dark gray, his tall and slender frame motionless with his hands clasped behind his back. His hair and eyes were as gray as his garments, and his thin lips were curved in the vaguest glimpse of a smile that did not touch the rest of his face. Behind him waited a black limousine.

"Yes?" She stepped around Alec despite his protesting murmur.

"Mr. Gadara would like to meet with you now," the man said in a voice without inflection.

"*Now?*"

"Yes."

"How did you get in here?" The parking garage had a gate that required a remote or a resident code to enter.

One gray brow arched. "Gadara Enterprises is the trustee of this property for your homeowners' association."

Eve glanced at Alec, whose jaw and frame were tense. "I'll need a few moments to change," she said.

"I am afraid there is no time for that," the man in gray replied, pivoting to gesture at the open rear door of the limo. "Mr. Gadara has a flight at four."

"I'm wearing wet jeans," she pointed out. She had no makeup on, her hair was in a messy ponytail, and she probably had a shiny forehead and nose. Beyond that, however, Gadara had stood her up for their last interview, so she wasn't feeling too accommodating. "I also need my portfolio."

"Mr. Gadara is familiar with your work."

"He can't expect me like this."

Gray Man said nothing, simply waited patiently.

"Okay, fine," she conceded.

"I'm coming with you." Alec's gaze never left their guest.

"That is not advised," Gray Man interjected.

Eve's gaze narrowed. "He comes if I say he comes."

"Mr. Gadara will not appreciate the request, Ms. Hollis," Gray Man drawled.

"Well, I don't appreciate the last-minute notice to go see him," she retorted.

"As you wish." Gray Man moved to reenter the limo. "I will advise him of your sentiments."

Eve made a split-second decision. She could keep protesting the crap being shoveled her way, or she could do something about it. She looked at Alec. "I have a jacket in my trunk; could you get it for me, please?"

Alec looked startled, then none too pleased with the request. "You're not going alone."

"That's fine. I knew you wouldn't like being left behind."

She glanced at Gray Man, who had paused. He didn't seem to catch her hint, but Alec's pursed lips told her he hadn't missed it. "You could toss all the mail in there, too," she suggested with a wide innocent smile. She secured her mailbox and handed him the keys.

Alec headed toward her car, glaring over his shoulder. While he was occupied with finding the right button on the remote to open the trunk, Eve slipped into the backseat of the limo. "Let's go."

Without hesitation, Gray Man climbed in and they set off. Alec shouted something after them and Eve winced inwardly. She knew he was pissed at her, but she thought it best to dance to Gadara's tune for a bit and see what "shook out," as Alec said. She'd been marked in Gadara's building, after he stood her up. Since Alec insisted that there were no coincidences, Eve thought it was necessary to go back to the beginning. If the only way to do that was to go alone, so be it. She wasn't helpless; not with her new super skills. Clueless about being marked, maybe, but not helpless. And Alec would be only a step or two behind her.

Fear didn't enter into the equation. Or maybe she was scared to death and her brain was too scrambled by shock to notice. Without the accompanying physical reactions it was impossible to tell. She was grateful for that, since the lack of emotion kept her mind clear.

Reaching up, Eve removed the elastic restraining her hair and ran her fingers through the mass. Luckily, she had inherited her mother's thick locks, which seldom tangled too greatly.

"How did you know I wasn't at work?" she asked, taking a lame stab at conversation.

Gray Man's face split with his grimace-smile that made him look more constipated than pleasant. He said nothing.

"Is Mr. Gadara going on vacation?" she prodded. "Or is he leaving for a business trip?"

Again, nothing.

Eve refastened her hair and looked out the window at the passing scenery. Despite the uncomfortable silence, the trip to Gadara Tower passed swiftly. That was no doubt due to the traffic lights on Beach Boulevard, which stayed green for them 100 percent of the time. She had barely gathered her thoughts when the limousine drew to a halt outside the revolving front doors. Foot traffic was steady as usual.

As Eve followed Gray Man out of the car, she lamented her lack of heels and suit. She would have felt armored then. In jeans and a T-shirt—and reeking like a demon—she felt worse than naked.

They crossed the packed foyer on their way to the glass tube elevators. Unlike the last time she was here, she found the sickly sweet fragrance of the atrium flowers almost nauseating. She concentrated hard on turning off her Spider-Man sense of smell but it didn't work. And then something else drew her attention.

The door to the stairwell where she had been marked.

Memories hit her in a rapid-fire series of heated images. She could smell Reed's scent in her nostrils and feel his rough touch on her skin. The recollections were both disturbing and a turn-on.

She growled low in her throat. Her libido was now officially a royal pain in the ass.

"This way, Ms. Hollis," Gray Man said, gesturing to an elevator that was separated from the others.

Looking away from the past and ahead to the future, Eve began to notice the number of stares directed her way. They were prolific. She tugged surreptitiously at the hem of her shirt and lifted her chin. When the elevator doors closed behind her, she breathed a sigh of relief.

Gray Man inserted a key into a lock in the panel and the car shot to the top without pause. She looked down at the atrium below, watching normal-size people shrink into teeny ants. So industrious. So inconsequential. Is that what she looked like to God? Is that why he didn't care that he had set her life spinning like a top?

The elevator dinged, and the doors opened. Eve turned and found herself looking directly into a massive, well-appointed office. An intricately carved mahogany desk was angled in the far corner, facing the bank of windows on the opposite side. Two brown leather chairs faced the desk, a fire crackled in the fireplace, and a portrait of the Last Supper decorated the space above the mantel.

"Ms. Hollis. So glad you could come on such short notice."

Her head turned to find Gadara. He faced away from her, his attention on a file he read directly from a filing cabinet built into the wall. He returned the file to its place, then closed it. The drawer front settled into a clever wooden facade that looked like a wooden chest of drawers.

"Mr. Gadara."

"Please, call me Raguel." He faced her and smiled.

She had seen photos of him, but they didn't do him justice. Dressed casually in a guayabera and linen slacks, Gadara was no less imposing than he would have been in a suit and tie. He was African American, his skin espresso dark, his salt-and-pepper hair cropped short, his cheekbones dotted with sunspots. His eyes were dark and ancient.

He assessed her from head to toe, then gave a nod that seemed approving. "I apologize for missing our last appointment."

Her mouth curved slightly. He couldn't sound less apologetic if he tried.

Gadara's eyes narrowed when she did not reply. "Do you still want the job?"

"The position as described would be a dream come true. I'm sure you know that."

He gestured toward one of the chairs set before his desk. When she was seated, he rounded the corner and settled opposite her. His pose was deceptively relaxed, as if this was a social visit. He had one ankle crossed over the opposite knee and his forearms rested lightly on the armrests. But his gaze was as sharp as a hawk's and when he picked up a remote control from his desktop, she grew wary.

"I am not certain breaking into my construction site today was advisable then," he drawled, pushing a button that lowered a screen over the windows, blocking out the light and providing the canvas for a projection.

As images of her accessing the computer at the tengu site flashed in guilty testimony, Eve froze.

Gadara smiled. "I could have you arrested."

She pulled herself together. "If you wanted to do that, you would have done so already."

"True."

"So what do you want?"

His voice came with a sharp edge. "I want you to do your job the way you are supposed to."

Eve's erratic emotions kicked in with gusto. Her mouth spit out words before her brain fully caught on. "I don't work for you—*yet*—Mr. Gadara."

"You have been working for me for eight days now, a circumstance I am beginning to regret."

"Eight days?" She stood, unable to contain her sudden restlessness. She wasn't anxious so much as antagonized, and she was quickly learning that her new disposition didn't take well to antagonism.

"You are a loose cannon, Ms. Hollis, and that is the last thing I need in my firm."

"Your *firm*?"

Eve remembered her conversation with Reed at the beach. *Think of it as a bail bond agency. An archangel becomes responsible for bringing them in—like a bail bondsman.*

Was Gadara the archangel? She suddenly felt dizzy.

The phone on Gadara's desk beeped a subdued tone. He picked up the receiver. "Yes?" Satisfaction lit his dark eyes. "Send him in."

Glancing at the door, Eve fully expected Alec to enter, yet she was still oddly surprised when he did. Over six feet of aggravated, windblown male.

"Raguel," he barked, tossing a dark glare at Eve. "I don't appreciate you sending for my Mark without me."

"I wanted to see if she would defy you, Cain, and if you would be able to stop her if she did. Regrettably, you both failed to follow orders."

The screen retracted into the ceiling and the dimmed lights brightened. But not before Alec caught a glimpse of the matinee.

"You better find a tactic beyond intimidation," Alec warned. "That might work on other novices, but not this one."

She glanced back and forth between the two, feeling like she was myopic and unable to see the picture everyone else was looking at. However, one thing was painfully clear—Alec and Gadara knew each other quite well. Which couldn't be good.

"What's going on?" she queried.

"You violated one of the most basic tenets of initiation," Gadara said to Alec. "Taking a Mark out in the field prior to training—"

"We weren't in the field."

Gadara stood, thrusting both hands down on the table. The sudden break in his nonchalance was frightening. "Bullshit. She stinks like demon. Whether the assignment was sanctioned or not is moot."

"I can't leave her alone; Infernals are all over her. She's too vulnerable."

"You should have asked her handler for help."

"I would have, if I'd known who it is."

"I thought that was obvious. Abel will manage her."

"Are you shitting me? After the way he marked her?"

"Perhaps you would like to watch the tape?" Gadara asked silkily. "The marking was not as one-sided as you might choose to believe."

"There's a tape?" Eve croaked, knowing she'd be blushing to the roots of her hair if her physical reactions worked the way they used to.

Alec growled, his fists clenching. "I'll take you down, Raguel. I'm not one of your pawns."

"No." Gadara smiled. "But *she* is."

Alec tensed.

Eve stepped up. "I want that tape."

"He's got your life in his hands," Alec bit out, "and you want a sex tape?"

"Yeah." She scowled at Gadara. "If you don't want me around, let me go. I won't complain."

"He's not going to do that." Alec's tone was too subdued.

"How do you know?"

"Because you and I are a package deal, and having God's personal enforcer on his team is a coup he wouldn't give up for anything."

"Damn it!" she groused. "You are more trouble than you're worth, you know that?"

"I come with benefits, if you get around to using them. Besides, the best he can do is transfer you to another firm. Only God can free you completely."

Eve pinned Gadara with a sharp glare. "I hate being in the dark. Explain the firm to me."

Gadara gestured toward her vacated seat. "Sit down, Ms. Hollis, and I will explain—" he looked at Alec "—since your mentor has yet to."

"Save your breath," Alec said dryly. "You can't put a wedge between us." He tugged the second chair closer to hers and sank into it. He caught her hand and held it.

Gadara stared at the display of affection and settled back in his seat as if they had all the time in the world. "Just as Hell has various kings—"

"—Heaven has kingpins," Alec finished.

"I resent that term," Gadara complained.

"If the shoe fits . . ."

"It does not."

"Uh-huh . . ."

Eve squeezed Alec's hand in warning. "Keep going."

Gadara's brow arched at her tone. "The mark system is vast. It needs to be organized and self-sufficient. In order to accomplish that, capitalist ventures were launched that generated the income required to support a large number of Marks and their various activities within existing mortal society. Some ventures were more successful than others. In the end, seven of us rose to prominence. We are loosely divided by the seven continents, but we coordinate often, and those with larger areas share their burdens with those with smaller areas. For example, the African and Antarctica firms work in tandem." He smiled, his teeth brilliantly white against the darkness of his skin. "I am responsible for the North American Marks. All twenty thousand of them."

"Oh my God— Ouch!" She winced as her mark burned.

"Watch it," the two men said in unison.

"So every one of those people in the atrium are Marks?" she muttered, setting her hand over her arm. "That's why it reeks like the floor was washed in perfume?"

"Some of the people out there are mortals we do business with."

"What about you?"

"I am an archangel, Ms. Hollis."

She considered that a moment, then thought it best to question Alec about Gadara and not Gadara himself. "So I was assigned to your firm because I'm from North America?"

"No." Gadara's voice had a soothing, hypnotic quality. The more he spoke, the dreamier she felt. "Usually Marks are transplanted to make the transition easier. It is less traumatic to start a new life when you are not hampered by the old."

"Why wasn't that done with me?"

"Because of him." The archangel motioned toward Alec with an elegant flick of his wrist. "He tried to get you released. When his request was denied, he asked that you be kept close to your family. I suspect he extorted someone somewhere to get what he wanted."

Eve's gaze turned to Alec, who looked straight ahead with his jaw visibly clenched. Her eyes stung.

"Quite a sacrifice," Gadara purred. "Banished all these years and forced to roam. He could have uprooted you to his homeland. I am certain he misses it."

"Shut up," Alec rumbled. "You don't know what you're talking about."

Her grip tightened on his hand in silent gratitude. "What happens now?"

"You work for me. Your resignation at The Weisenberg Group was effective yesterday after a week's notice. Occasionally, your secular talents will be put to good use, but for the most part, your job is to train to the best of your ability and listen to your mentor, your handler, and me."

"I listen to my gut," she said. She wasn't a believer and thought she should put that out there right away.

"I will not tolerate insubordination," he retorted.

"Fine." Eve shrugged. "Just so we're clear."

Gadara's mouth curved in blatant challenge. The predatory expression didn't suit him. He was far too refined, his voice too cultured, and his words too precise. "What were you looking for this afternoon?"

"A tengu."

Gadara's eyes widened. Alec explained. By the time he finished, Gadara was visibly upset.

"I thought you cared more about your novice," the archangel chastised. "It was not your place to risk her so foolishly."

"What risk?" Alec snorted. "She's already been pissed on and threatened twice. There was more risk in doing nothing at all. And I told you, I can't leave her alone. The Nix knows where she lives."

"You are her mentor. If you wish to allow your feud with your brother to jeopardize your novice, far be it from me to intercede." Gadara's eyes took on an icy glint. "Proceed with your investigation, then. See it to its conclusion, including eradicating the threat."

Eve frowned.

Alec exhaled harshly. "You want to assign her before she's trained? No way."

"It is your choice, Cain. Allow your brother to do his job or you will have to do it for him."

"This isn't your call. Abel is the only one who can assign her to a mission."

Gadara laughed, a deep rolling sound. It was oddly pleasant, considering it wasn't meant to be. "He is a company man, something you would do well to emulate."

"You're both violating protocol." Alec's tone was almost a snarl. "I expect that of you, but Abel? He's never broken a rule in his life. You accuse me of putting her in danger, while Abel is ready to hang her out to dry?"

"It is perfectly acceptable to continue a deviation once it has been set in motion, if proceeding is the only reasonable course."

"Eve and I didn't deviate."

"That is debatable, is it not? I doubt either of us wants to take this upstairs, where we could both face penalties. Better to deal with this on our own, agreed?"

Pushing to his feet, Alec towered over the desk. Although Gadara seemed unaffected, Eve noted the deepening grooves around his mouth and eyes.

Gadara feared Alec. She tucked that information away for future use.

"How is sending an untrained Mark on a hunt the 'reasonable course'?" Alec asked with intemperate frustration.

"If the Infernals think she is hiding or that we are protecting her, they will go after her with a vengeance. With you as her mentor, she needs to be tougher than the average Mark. We cannot afford for her to look weak or frightened. We need to start as we mean to go on."

"No."

Eve stood. "I can handle it."

Alec's dark head swiveled toward her. "Angel—"

"I've got this." She looked at Gadara. It wasn't just the Infernals that needed to know she was tough.

"Good girl," Gadara murmured approvingly.

"Don't talk down to me," she warned. "Anything else I should know? Or can I go? It's been a long week."

Gadara reached into a drawer and withdrew a set of keys. He tossed them to her. "Those will give you access to this building and to your office. All of your belongings from your old employer were moved here. You will be paid by direct deposit and an expense account has been created for you."

"What are my hours?"

"They are 24/7. The office is a front; you will need it as part of your cover, but the field is where you will do the majority of your work. Your household expenses—mortgage, automobile, utilities, and so on—will be managed by the firm. You have also been tasked with the renovation of one of my casinos in Las Vegas. But we have several months before we get to that."

Eve was so stunned it took her a moment to reply. "And here I thought only the devil traded dreams for souls."

"Who do you think taught him everything he knows?" He lifted the lid of a wooden box on his desktop and withdrew a cigar. "All that you will need has been placed in your condominium."

"You had someone in my house?" Her foot tapped rapidly on the carpet. "I don't suppose your affiliation with my homeowners' association is a coincidence?"

"There is no such thing as coincidence, Ms. Hollis."

Alec caught her elbow. "We're done here, then."

"Not so fast," she muttered. "I want that tape."

"And I want world peace," Gadara replied. "I would also like to smoke this cigar, but my body is a temple. We do not always get what we want."

"We'll see about that." Eve smiled grimly and headed toward the elevator.

"Cain."

A shiver moved through her at the sound of Alec's name spoken in that cultured voice. The infamous Cain. Everyone knew his story. But having met both brothers, she knew there was far more to the tale than the few brief paragraphs mentioned in the canonized bible.

Alec paused. "Yes?"

"I have been authorized to credit you for every vanquishing, in consideration of your added responsibility as Ms. Hollis's mentor. Double the indulgences should cut your service in half, if you play your cards right."

The terrible stillness that gripped Alec alarmed Eve. She set her hand lightly on his hip. He caught and held it tightly.

"This isn't a game," he bit out.

"A turn of phrase," Gadara said. "Nothing more."

"Alec?" Eve murmured when he continued to stare, unmoving.

He shook his head as if in disgust, then continued to the elevator, pulling her with him.

When the doors closed behind them, Eve linked her fingers with his. She opened her mouth to speak, then her gaze lifted to the camera in the corner. She held her tongue until they exited the building.

The moment they breathed smog instead of Mark emanations, Eve blurted, "Double the indulgences." She fought an inconvenient urge to laugh hysterically. "He's bribing you."

"It's not going to work."

"It has to be tempting."

"Angel." His tone was as sharp as the look he gave her. "It's not going to work. Period."

"You called him a kingpin. Like the mafia?"

"You heard him and saw how he works. They're all like that. We always get a choice, but that doesn't mean the options are equal or favorable."

"So the picture he presented of seven head honchos working harmoniously together was crap?"

"I'd say they work together about as well as Democrats and Republicans." He unfastened the passenger helmet from the back of his bike, then freed her hair of its ponytail. "And they're just as politically minded."

"Lovely."

After settling the helmet on her head, Alec adjusted the strap beneath her chin. He kissed the tip of her nose. "Those in favor get bigger perks."

"Whatever he has against you is personal." She wasn't asking a question. "Because of me, you've played right into his hands."

Alec mounted the bike. Eve hopped on behind him and wrapped her arms around his waist. "The only person who's got their hands on me is you," he said over the rumbling of the engine.

"You'll have to come up with a better explanation than that," she shouted.

"I know." He rolled the hog back, his powerful thighs flexing against hers. "But not here."

They roared out of the parking lot.

CHAPTER 12

As Reed stepped onto the roof of Gadara Tower, he slipped his shades over his eyes and took in the majestic view. A helicopter waited on the nearby heliport, its blades still and shining in the late afternoon sun. A sliver of ocean was visible from this vantage point and the reflection of sunlight on nearby building windows made the sunny day even brighter. A breeze ruffled his hair, caressed his nape, and filled his nostrils with air untainted by the stench of Infernals.

"Abel."

His head turned to find Raguel exiting the stairwell to the rooftop. The man was dressed for the tropics with a straw hat on his head and leather sandals on his feet. An unlit cigar hung between his lips and his stride was elegantly unhurried.

"Raguel." Reed extended his hand and it was clasped in a firm, warm hold.

The archangel pulled the cigar free and said, "You were right. Cain had yet to explain to Ms. Hollis."

Pushing his hands into his trouser pockets, Reed smiled. Eve had been brought up to speed, which meant life was about to get a lot more interesting. "Excellent. When does the next training rotation start?"

"*When* she begins training depends on your brother. He has begun an investigation into a tengu infestation at one of my developing properties. It is a concern to me, so I have asked him to see the investigation through."

"What does that have to do with Eve?"

"Since he refuses to rely on you for Ms. Hollis's care while he proceeds, we will have to wait for them to finish."

"*Them?* You expect Eve to help him in the field?"

"Cain refused to have it any other way."

"That isn't Cain's decision to make."

"No. It was mine."

Reed paused midstep. Raguel continued a few steps before he realized he was alone. He turned around.

"You *assigned* Eve?" Reed was startled more by the roiling emotions he felt than by the blatant deviation from protocol. "Without consulting me?"

Eve was a member of Raguel's firm, yes, but assigning her to a mission was a prerogative that fell squarely and solely within Reed's purview. He liked rules. Perhaps even relished them. It was easier to exceed expectations when one knew what those expectations were. And with Eve, his position as her handler was his sole stanchion in a dynamic of two. He was wedging his way in as the third wheel and he wasn't going to give up his grip without a fight.

Raguel shrugged. "A bit presumptuous, perhaps, but I knew you would agree."

"I don't."

"Oh?" Raguel's brows rose. "What better way to teach your brother to work within the system?"

"What about Eve?"

"What about her?"

"Don't be dense," Reed bit out. "With Cain's scent all over her, she needs to be at the top of her game, not dangling from the bottom rung."

Rocking back on his heels, Raguel grinned. "You say that with such venom, as if the thought of your brother with Ms. Hollis is offensive to you."

"Ridiculous," Reed scoffed. "This has nothing to do with Cain and everything to do with my responsibility as Eve's handler. I don't like to lose Marks."

"This has everything to do with Cain and nothing to do with Ms. Hollis," Raguel countered, gesturing to the helicopter pilot with an impatient wave of his hand. "She is a means to an end. Her purpose is to act as a stick to prod your brother into line."

Reed's fists clenched within his pockets. "Did that come from above? Or from you?"

"It came from common sense." The helicopter's engine whined into motion, its blades whistling through the air in a rapidly increasing tempo. "Cain is a hazard if he does not learn to toe the line."

"He's incorrigible. You think you can succeed where Jehovah hasn't? Your head's getting too big."

"Not at all." Raguel smiled. "You are simply underestimating Ms. Hollis and her effect on your brother."

"You're thinking of her as a woman, not as a Mark."

"So are you."

Reed ignored the jibe. "I'm pulling her off the mission. She needs to be properly trained."

"You do that, and I will transfer Ms. Hollis to another firm and handler."

"Bullshit. You wouldn't pass Cain over for something so insignificant."

"Are you willing to gamble on that?" Raguel yelled, his voice carrying on the wind created by the revolving blades. "He might be less trouble screwing up another firm."

"Screwing up? He has a 100 percent success rate."

"Not for much longer if he disregards you as handler and manages Ms. Hollis by himself. One of them will be killed. As high profile as he is, the loss of him or his Mark under my watch would ruin centuries of prestige. I will not allow it."

Reed's jaw tightened. "You can't expect me to follow the rules if you don't."

"The three of you will be the death of either me or yourselves." Raguel stepped closer until only an inch or two separated them. "Whatever interest you have in Ms. Hollis, I suggest you keep it strictly professional. You have been given an unassailable position of power over your brother through Ms. Hollis. Keeping them together should be your priority. Now, I have to get to the airport to catch my flight. If you still have reservations when I return, we can discuss it further at that time."

"She might be dead by then."

"If that is God's will." Clutching his hat to his head, Raguel ran the distance to the chopper and climbed in.

God's will. Reed spit the bile out of his mouth. God's hand was far from this, separated from the mechanics by layers of seraphim, hashmallim, and angels. For some time now, Reed had begun to wonder if there was a lesson to be learned in the distance between Jehovah and the world. Perhaps it was to remind them that they couldn't hack it on their own. He tried to tell himself that the purpose was edifying—the harder they worked, the more they would appreciate the fruit of their labors. But truly, machinations like this always tested his faith.

"Damn you, Cain."

Once again his brother was disrupting the order of things, and Reed was expected to bend and adjust to make it work.

As the helicopter lifted into the air, Reed's mind sifted through the moves available to him with the same fury with which the wind whipped through his hair. He wanted another round with Eve, but making that move could push Cain completely out of the picture and without Cain, Reed would lose his chance to achieve his ambitions.

He couldn't let that happen. This was his best opportunity to further his long-held position that he was ready for advancement to archangel.

Reed knew, without any doubt, that he could manage a firm and manage it well. The world's population had grown exponentially. The existing seven firms were overtaxed, understaffed, and the archangels heading them were overappreciated because of it. They lusted for God's approval and infighting was rampant. Expansion was needed and Reed was determined to step into play when it happened.

Fucking Eve was hot as hell, but the pleasure was fleeting. If he kept his dick away from her, he could enjoy the extended satisfaction of governing something that Cain thought belonged solely to him.

He shouldn't be conflicted at all. There was no contest between the two options—Eve or the realization of all his goals.

"Eve," he growled, running his hands through his hair.

She was as helpless and vulnerable as a field mouse and Infernals were circling her like ravenous hawks. Hell, *he* was circling her.

Beware of the apples.

He should have foreseen how this would turn out when she gave him that scorching look in the lobby that first day.

Shit.

Reed spun on his heel and left the roof.

Alec pulled to a stop at a red light and balanced his bike with one leg on the ground. Because of Raguel's thirst for God's approval, Alec had known it would be risky to keep Eve close to home, but he never thought Raguel would risk her deliberately. If he'd even suspected that as a possibility, he would have requested a different firm. Antarctica, perhaps. Or Australia.

His knuckles whitened on the handlebars. He was being leashed by the one thing that he gave a damn about, which left him cornered, trapped between a disapproving God, an antagonistic brother, and an overly ambitious archangel who would do anything to achieve his aims. And Eve. Sassy, sexy Eve was the glue holding it all together.

Raguel assumed Alec wanted to shed the mark and return to a normal life. That was his biggest miscalculation. He thought the lure of double indulgences and the freedom they implied would be irresistible. He didn't understand that Alec had one skill, one talent—killing. Alec could no more turn his back on that and live a "normal" life, than he could stop loving Evangeline Hollis. But his ambition to head his own firm was a secret no one knew. He kept it close to his heart, hidden until the day he could present it as more than a pipe dream.

Eve.

Despite the volatility of his thoughts, nothing could fully distract him from the feel of her soft, warm body wrapped around his back. She was so delicate and fragile. He would have to train her himself for now, a solution that was less than perfect. He'd worked alone for so long. He had no idea where to begin, what to focus on, or . . . anything. He was completely clueless.

Eve tapped him on the thigh and shouted to be heard over the rumbling of the engine. "Go home. I want to check on my mom."

Home. With Eve. His mouth quirked with morbid humor. The part of him that wasn't homicidal was deeply enamored with that dream.

He nodded. When the traffic light changed, he altered his direction and headed for Eve's place. This time, he didn't need to wait for a resident to follow into the parking garage. Eve typed in the code and he rolled into the spot adjacent to the one that held her car. His and hers. The act of taking the place reserved for the significant other in her life affected him in an unexpected way—he grew hard. Dismounting from the bike became a difficult task, but he managed.

The knowledge that their time together was temporary . . . the threats against her . . . the fear that he might not be enough to save her . . . the pheromones her mark exuded . . . His body responded with a primitive desire to claim what was his. When she pulled the helmet off her head and shook out her hair, it was like waving a cape before a raging bull. He struggled against the sudden ferocious need to pin her to the wall and ride her to the finish. He backed away, putting distance between them.

She glanced at him and stilled. He watched the heat he felt spread to her, igniting her dark eyes with a sexual hunger that might match his. This wasn't the timid, inexperienced girl he had loved ten years ago. That girl had quivered when he touched her and cried when he kissed her. The woman who eyed him now made *him* quiver.

Eve locked the strap of her helmet to the backrest loop on his bike and muttered, "Catch me."

That was the only warning he got before she launched herself at him. As slight as she was, the mark gave her force and velocity. He stumbled back at the impact, his keys and helmet crashing to the cement floor. Her legs circled his hips, her arms wrapped around his neck. Her mouth met his without finesse, her soft lips slanting across his with a desperation that stole both his breath and his wits.

She tightened her thighs, levering up, forcing his neck back so that she hovered over him. Her position of dominance rocked him so hard there was no way they were going to make it upstairs before he got inside her. The scent of her lust was heady, sweeping through his senses and across his skin. There was no other fragrance in the world like it, the sensual fragrance of cherries, sweet and ripe. The mark intensified the smell, made it more luxurious, like whipped cream on top.

He gripped her ass with one hand and fisted the other into the thick silk of her hair. As Eve writhed over him, he tore his mouth away, gasping. In response, her fingers tangled in his locks and commanded his attention. His gaze was snared by hers. She was as hot for it as he was, but the determined glint in her eyes told him she wasn't yet completely lost to lust.

Alec set his mind to making her that way. He released her hair and cupped her breast, kneading the full weight, groaning in pleasure as her nipple hardened between the clasp of his fingertips.

Eve leaned closer, their harsh breaths mingling, her tresses shielding their faces in an ebony curtain. "Someone's watching us, right?" she whispered. "And listening?"

"What?" He urged her lower, notching the heated juncture between her thighs against his aching cock. He stroked her along his length. She took over, gyrating fluidly against him, making him shudder.

"My condo," she persisted, her eyes feverishly bright. "The common areas. Cameras. Microphones. There is no privacy anywhere, am I right? Gadara is watching and listening."

Reality pierced through the haze of his desire. "Probably." He remembered that Raguel was trustee of the community and growled, "Most likely. Yes."

"We can't talk freely."

"Who wants to talk?"

The clearing of a throat behind them jerked them both to an awareness of how public their ardor was. Their heads turned in unison to find Mrs. Basso standing by the mailboxes. She was facing away from them, awkwardly struggling with the lock to her box, but it was obvious she'd seen more than any of them wanted her to see.

"Put me down," Eve hissed.

Alec set her on her feet. "If the kiss didn't shock Mrs. Basso, my raging hard-on might do it."

Eve smacked him. "Behave."

"*You* attacked *me,* angel."

She winked. "Made you smile."

He stared at her a moment, lost in a déjà vu moment from a decade before. He laughed softly.

"I'm losing my touch," he drawled, adjusting himself in an unsuccessful bid for comfort. "You were thinking about Gadara while making out with me."

"I heard the camera move."

Alec paused at that. He wasn't too surprised that he hadn't heard anything. Disgruntled, yes, but not surprised. For the first time in his life, he'd been given something he wanted and he was enjoying her to the fullest. It was Eve's precise hearing that made the statement arresting. "You heard the camera move," he repeated.

Her smile was wicked. "I guess we didn't quite reach the brain cell frying point."

"Next time," he promised, bending down to collect his helmet and keys. "You're a smart cookie, angel. Turns me on."

"What if I didn't have a fondness for James Bond and Jason Bourne? I'd be giving Pamela Anderson a run for the money in the sex tape department."

He took the hit. It stung, but it was true. "I've never mentored before. I'm learning as I go."

"Great."

"I'm a quick study." He glanced toward the lobby. Mrs. Basso was gone.

"You better be." Sighing, she moved to the trunk of her car and opened it, retrieving her mail from earlier. "Or else we're a sorry-assed pair."

Alec grinned. There'd be no hysterics or drama from Eve. Bless her.

"Let's go. We have a lot of work to do." She headed toward the elevator with a determined stride. "And I have to think of something to say to my neighbor. How embarrassing is that?"

"Maybe she'll act like nothing happened." He followed, studying the way she moved and cataloging the self-defense techniques she might excel at. She had long, lithe legs and a hint of defined biceps. He thought kick-boxing might be good for a start.

"Ugh. I hate when people do that," she complained. "I'd rather just get it out in the open and clear the air."

Hard-charging, he thought fondly. That was his angel.

A soft mechanical whirring followed them, the sound of surveillance cameras keeping them doggedly in sight.

"Mom?" Eve called out as she pushed the door open.

"She's not here," her mother called back.

Relief filled her. She smiled at Alec, who just shook his head. As he set his helmet and keys on the console by the door, there was a sparkle of amusement in his eyes, but nothing could hide the set of his shoulders. They seemed weighted by the world.

Miyoko appeared from the hallway. Her feet were encased in Hello Kitty house slippers, her hair was in pigtails, and her arms were filled with freshly washed laundry. She looked like a teenager. "Are you hungry?"

Eve's stomach growled its assent. "Lately, I'm always hungry."

"Maybe you're pregnant."

"Mom!" Her protest was weak, her startled gaze moving to Alec. She'd missed taking her birth control pills for a week while she acclimated to the mark, and they'd burned up the sheets for hours . . .

Alec's jaw clenched. He gave a curt shake of his head. But how could he be sure?

It wasn't a question she could ask now.

"Unless you're a nun or sterile," her mother said, "it's possible."

Eve went to the kitchen. Decades of work as a registered nurse had made Miyoko brutally blunt when it came to discussing health matters. Setting her mail on the counter, Eve grabbed a soda from the fridge and wished a shot of rum would be worth the effort of pouring. Then she thought of babies and the effect of alcohol on them. She returned the soda to the fridge and grabbed a single-serving orange juice instead.

"Don't leave those letters there," her mother said, dropping the laundry on the couch before joining Eve in the kitchen.

"It's my house, Mom," Eve retorted, twisting the cap open and drinking deeply.

"Who cleans it?"

"Who asked you to? I keep my house clean, and I'm an adult. Don't act like I can't survive without you."

Miyoko's face turned into a mask. "I know you don't need me. You never have."

Alec walked into the kitchen. "How about I make some sandwiches?" he offered.

"I made *onigiri,*" her mother said tightly.

"Wonderful." Alec set his hand on the curve of Eve's waist. His voice was low and even in an attempt to soothe ruffled feathers. "I love *onigiri.*"

So did Eve, which is probably why her mother had made the little rice "balls" to begin with. Steamed rice flavored with various sprinkled seasonings called *furikake* were shaped into triangular patties. Eve had grown up on them, and they'd always been a relished treat.

Closing her eyes, Eve exhaled slowly. She hated feeling defensive around her mother. After all these years, she should be able to brush off the occasional pointing out of her shortcomings, but her mother had always been able to trigger volatile responses in her. One moment condescending and critical, the next cheerful and praising. Eve knew their chafing was due partly to culture clash. Her mother had come to the States in her mid-twenties and she returned to Japan for annual visits. While she was a naturalized American citizen now, Miyoko was still a Japanese woman at her core.

"I'm sorry, Mom," Eve said, setting her drink down and leaning heavily into the counter. Not for the first time, she made a small wish for a smoother relationship with her own children when she had them. "I'm having a really bad day. I appreciate everything you do."

Her mother stood there for the length of several heartbeats, her small frame tense with indignation and hurt. "Does your crabby mood have something to do with your new job?"

"How did you know about that?" Eve was superstitious—she didn't like to share anything good that wasn't a sure thing.

"I'm your mother. I know things."

Eve groaned inwardly.

"Someone stopped by while we were gone?" Alec asked, reaching into the container on the counter and pulling out a rice cake liberally sprinkled with beefsteak *furikake.* He handed it to Eve, then picked out another wrapped in seasoned *nori*—seaweed—for himself.

"Yes. Two young men. They left a briefcase and a box for you."

Straightening, Eve asked, "Where is it?"

"I put it in your office."

"Did they say anything?"

"They were very nice." Miyoko managed a smile. "I made some coffee, and they talked a little about Mr. Gadara's accomplishments. It sounds like a wonderful opportunity for you."

Eve shivered at the thought of Gadara's men around her mother, charming and impressing her. Winning her over. Snakes in the grass.

"So it that why you're grumpy?" her mother repeated. "Changing jobs is one of the most stressful events a person can go through. You need to take more vitamin B."

"That's part of it." All of it. She glanced at Alec, who eyed her orange juice with odd intensity.

"You didn't tell me you were thinking about quitting." Miyoko's tone was peeved.

"I didn't want to jinx it. Working for Gadara Enterprises is a monster leap, and I wasn't sure I would make it. Besides, I only had an interview."

"And it turned into an offer?" Her mother wiped the spotless counter with a dishtowel. "You shouldn't be so surprised. You're beautiful and smart. Anyone would be lucky to have you."

Eve's irritation fled completely. "Thank you."

Miyoko shrugged. "It's the truth. Is he Jewish? Or Middle Eastern?"

"Gadara? He's African American. Why?"

"His name. It's in the Bible."

"It is?" She glanced at Alec, who was reaching for another *onigiri*.

"Gadara is the place where Christ turned demons into swine," he explained before taking a bite.

"Did he pick that himself?"

"Who picks their own name?" Miyoko shook her head. "Aside from celebrities. Anyway, I'm going to finish the laundry and go home."

"Is Dad coming back today?"

"Tomorrow, but there are things I have to do."

Eve sighed, feeling terrible for having hurt her mother's feelings. "I wish you would stay."

"You have a guest. You don't need me."

"I don't have to need you to want you around, Mom."

"Not today." Miyoko rounded the island the opposite way and returned to the living room. She sat on the couch and folded laundry.

Alec rubbed between Eve's shoulder blades. "You okay?"

"No. My life sucks."

"I can help you forget about it for a while," he purred softly.

She pivoted and faced him head on. Her mouth opened, then shut again. The kitchen wasn't the place to talk about sex and the inevitable ramifications of it. Her hand fisted in his shirt and she tugged him to her office.

"I'm sterile," he said curtly before she could speak.

She gaped. Alec was the most virile man she'd ever come across. "W-what?"

"I watched you exchange the soda for orange juice. You're not pregnant."

Hurt straightened her spine. He said the words with such finality, his dark gaze cold and remote, his lips thinned.

"God forbid, right?" Her mouth curved in a mocking smile. "You wouldn't want the complication, I'm sure."

"Don't tell me what I want," he snapped. "There is nothing Heaven or Hell can dish out that is as painful as the loss of a child. Still, I might go through it again for you. But there's no chance, Eve."

"Why?"

"I almost lost my mind when the last of my children died. I said things to God that I regret. I couldn't understand why I had to be punished in that way, too. Why I had to live interminably while my children lived mortal lives."

Her throat clenched in sympathy. "Alec . . ."

"God *did* forbid it, angel." His arms crossed. "The mark sterilizes everyone now. Female Marks don't menstruate and the males shoot blanks."

Time froze for a moment, then rushed at Eve in a deluge. Years of dreams and hopes washed over her in a flood of tears that escaped in a hot stream down her face. "Will I get it back?"

"I don't know. Eve—" His entire frame vibrated. If she breathed deep enough, she could smell the turbulence in him. Alec was a man who felt as if every move he made was the wrong one. Another mistake in a lifetime of mistakes. He was passionate, impulsive, and headstrong.

But could she blame him for what was happening to her? He couldn't have foreseen how the decisions he made for himself would impact others. Bad shit happened to people. Rapes, beatings, muggings, abuse . . . and countless other horrifying things. Miscarriages, accidents, starvation. But being a victim was a choice one made, and Eve refused to be a victim.

"Angel?" Alec stepped closer, a move that was jerky instead of his usual graceful prowl.

"Give me a minute." She turned away to wipe her tears and was arrested by the tall, exceptionally dressed figure lounging in the doorway.

"Rough day, babe?" Reed murmured, his gaze examining her closely.

"It keeps getting better." She swiped impatiently at her cheeks.

"How can I help?"

"Get the fuck out," Alec snarled. "You've done enough damage."

"You only wish you could toss me out," Reed retorted.

Eve's circumstances were what they were. Everything happened for a reason. She didn't need to be religious to believe that. And it would take more energy to bitch than it would to do something about it. Instead of feeling crushed, her determination was strengthened. One thing at a time.

Figure out the tengu.

Deal with the Nix.

Lose the mark.

It was all doable.

"I'm going to take a shower," she said, wanting out of her jeans, which were stiffened by the dried water from the Nix. "Then I'm going to do some online sleuthing in regards to Gehenna Masonry. You boys can either kill each other, or help my mom fold laundry."

They stared.

"Or cook dinner, if you know how. I'm starved." She waved over her shoulder on the way out the door.

CHAPTER 13

Eve stared at her computer monitor with focused intensity. She had allowed herself a good, hard cry in the shower—a shower that now had an aluminum cross dangling from the showerhead. She, a lifelong agnostic, now had a cross hanging in her shower and the Mark of Cain on her arm.

Laughter at her situation had come first, then the tears that wouldn't stop. She let it all out, her frustration and anger, her sadness and worry. She was pretty sure she cried more tears than she ever had in her entire life. And then she told herself that was all the self-pity she was going to wallow in. It took too much out of her.

But the aftermath wasn't pretty. She felt wrung out like a dish towel. Both Reed and Alec watched her with guilt and wariness. She'd finally retreated to her office to save them all the discomfort.

Reed had folded laundry with her mom, while Alec made a thick hearty stew for dinner. Miyoko insisted on cutting vegetables and offering spice suggestions, then she left for home with obvious reluctance. Stubborn to the last. Eve fully expected a phone call tomorrow, asking why Reed— her supervisor—would come over for dinner and fold her clothes. She hoped she had a good excuse by then.

Presently, she was using Google in her search for information about Gehenna Masonry. She had been distracted for a time by a brief search of Meggido Industries. It existed. And Alec was listed as the CEO and founder. The name "Meggido" also came up as a location better known as Armageddon. Alec had called himself a headhunter specializing in disaster avoidance. She had to laugh at his twisted sense of humor.

"What's so funny?" Reed asked.

Eve glanced up and discovered him lounging in the doorway as he'd been when he first arrived. It was an insolent pose with his hands in his pockets and his pale blue dress shirt open at the throat. The room was dark, which allowed backlighting from the hallway to turn his silhouette into a dangerously compelling form.

She shrugged in feigned nonchalance. No matter what he did or said, she couldn't dispel the memories of their encounter. "Nothing. What's up?"

"What's up with you?"

"I'm researching the mason who created the tengu." Eve's gaze returned to the monitor.

"How's it coming?"

"Fine. It's hard to know if you've found what you're looking for when you don't know what it is." She watched him enter the room with that delicious stride that was just short of a swagger. The brothers moved so differently, yet they affected her equally. "Where's Alec?"

"Checking the balcony for any water leaks."

"Because of the Nix?"

"Yes."

"Can he get in that way?"

"He can get in anywhere there's a water source." Reed stood beside her, staring down. He watched her with that indecipherable look she was becoming familiar with but didn't understand. She got the "I want to jump your bones" part of it, but the rest—the confusion, regret, and sympathy—she didn't understand those.

Eve turned in her chair and leaned back to look up at him. She kept her exterior cool and unaffected, even though he presented an intimidating sight. With the planes of his face lit only by the glow from the monitor, he looked more devil than angel. "Gehenna is a relatively local company," she said. "They're based in Upland, California."

"That's what? Forty-five minutes from here?"

"Depending on traffic."

He nodded.

"Their web domain name is only a few years old," she continued. "They're obviously a new company, but they became solvent quickly from the looks of it."

The light came on and Alec walked into the room.

"We need to go there." He directed a narrowed glare at his brother. "Take a look around. See what they've got going on."

"Go yourself," Reed argued. "I'll stay with her. No need to endanger her unnecessarily."

"Bullshit." Alec approached the desk. "You should've considered that before you assigned her to this. You can't have it both ways."

"*I* assigned her?" The incredulity in Reed's voice was undeniable.

Eve's gaze darted to him, trying to visually verify the surprise she heard in his voice. She caught him quickly adopting a frozen mien that gave nothing away. But the brief glimpse of astonishment was enough to spark the suspicion that Reed wasn't as in charge of things as he should be.

"Didn't you?" she queried.

"He won't tell you the truth," Alec scoffed.

Reed's arms crossed. "Don't speak for me."

"You're a one-hit loser, bro. Better get that into your head. You're never going to be alone with her again."

Eve stood. "Enough. I find the 'hit' reference offensive."

Alec muttered, "Sorry, angel."

"I make my own choices," she said. "And right now, I'd really like to go back to that building with the gargoyles and take a closer look at them."

"Why?"

"Because we can't go out to Upland tonight; it's already too late. And I feel restless, as if I should be doing something. I don't like that feeling." She looked at both men. "It can't hurt."

"It's not going to be open."

"Is that normally a deterrent to you?" she challenged.

"It'll be guarded," Reed interjected. "But you should have a Gadara Enterprises badge. As one of his employees, any guards should let you in with no problem."

He glanced at Alec with eyes lit with triumph. "You've got a lot to learn, *bro*."

Turning to the black lacquered box that had been left for her earlier, Eve lifted the hinged lid with its inlaid ivory cross and rummaged inside.

"They left a box for you, too, Alec," she said, gesturing to a cardboard packing box waiting on the sofa. "It's in there."

"Fuck that," he snapped. "Raguel only wishes he could file me into his ranks."

Eve's box was the size of a large shoe box and it was filled with a haphazard collection of items ranging from some type of pepper spray to lip balm. She dug out a leather wallet-looking thing and flipped it open. Inside was a picture ID featuring the photo taken of her when she went in for the initial interview. She shivered thinking about how everyone had known she was minutes away from being marked, yet no one said anything or interceded in any way. If it had been the other way around, she would have told the recruit to run like hell and don't stop.

"That's it," Reed acknowledged, looking over her shoulder.

Eve's fingertips traced over the embossed Gadara logo. Reflective watermarks caught the light and prevented easy duplication. The symbols were a combination of familiar images—such as a cross—and others that looked like hieroglyphs. "I thought all of Gadara's employees were Marks. Can't they smell what I am? What's the point of this badge?"

"The employees who work in Gadara Tower are Marks," Reed explained. "They act as an early warning system to keep Raguel safe. It would be impossible for an Infernal to infiltrate the building undetected. But subsidiary companies and satellite buildings have some mortal employees."

"Keep him safe? I thought he was an archangel. Who would mess with him?"

"An Infernal looking for a major promotion."

"Couldn't an archangel kick their ass?"

"If they saw the hit coming. The seven firm leaders live temporal lives, aside from seven weeks a year when they are free to use their powers while training Marks."

"They lose their powers?"

"They have a choice," Alec corrected. "They can use their gifts, but every time they do, there's a consequence. It's up to them to decide whether the transgression is worth it."

She snorted. "Another example of God trying to drive someone crazy."

"How else would they sympathize with mortals, angel? The archangels need empathy and understanding in order to maintain their motivation. They refused to bow to man as God ordered. What better way to see the error of their ways than to walk a mile in mortal shoes?"

"Empathy and understanding?" Eve smiled without humor. "Frankly, I would be tempted to be frustrated and resentful. Why should I have to lose the privilege of using my powers to protect people that don't give a crap about me? Unless the archangels are truly angelic—which Gadara certainly didn't seem to be—the whole power-versus-punishment deal is just stirring the pot."

"'Angelic' and 'devilish' are mortal constructs," Reed pointed out.

"I caught that earlier. Gadara said demons pull their tricks from the same bag as angels. They're brethren, right? Fruit of the same tree, borne of the same father? It stands to reason that they'd be prone to the same vices, including getting pissed off that they're denied something through no fault of their own."

Reed scowled. "Why are we talking about this?"

Eve dropped the badge on her desk and stood. "Because it needs to be talked about. When do the archangels regain full use of their powers?"

"After Armageddon." Alec's arms crossed and his stance widened. It was a battle pose, one of readiness.

"So might it be possible that they'd like to hurry that along a bit?" she suggested.

"You're thinking like a mortal," Reed bit out.

"News flash: I *am* a mortal. This mark on my arm isn't going to change that. Tell me you haven't thought about the firm leaders playing outside the rules."

Reed's brows arched. "I haven't."

She rounded on Alec. "I know *you* have. You don't like to wear blinders."

"What are you implying?" Reed snapped.

"Gadara says you're a company man, Reed. You toe the line." Eve shrugged. "You want things to be a certain way and that's the only way you allow yourself to perceive them."

He took a step closer. "Don't try to analyze me! If you want to shrink someone's head, why don't you try the homicidal maniac you're fucking?"

"I touched a nerve," she drawled.

"You're talking smack. Want me to turn it around and see how you like it?"

"Step off," Alec warned. "Keep pushing her, and I'll push you back."

"Shut up." Reed's fists clenched. "If she wants to make wild conspiracy theories, she'll have to manage the aftermath on her own."

Eve studied the violence of Reed's response with a calculating eye. Alec was taking her questions with only minor tension, but Reed was strung tight as a bow. She looked at Alec. "So outside of the Gadara Tower, some of the employees are mortal."

He nodded.

"And if I flash this badge, they let me in, but they'll also record that we came by, right? And the company credit card, listening devices, video cameras . . . it's all cyberstalking in lieu of the divinely powered kind, right?"

"Sure. What are you thinking?"

"Nothing." Eve stepped around her desk. She'd said enough for the benefit of whoever might be listening through the bugs in her house. The rest she would keep to herself until she felt that she could speak freely. "Let me get ready and we'll go."

Reed moved to follow. Alec stepped in his path. "Leave her alone," he warned.

"I'm doing my job." Reed's voice was dangerously soft.

"Relax, Alec," she admonished.

A low, predatory rumble filled the air. She exited the room with a shake of her head. Those two were going to have to figure out on their own how to work together.

Eve was shutting her bedroom door when it was halted midswing and pushed back in. Reed entered, his gaze sweeping around the room and coming to rest on the bed.

"Feng shui," he murmured. "There's at least a little bit of believer in you."

"What does feng shui have to do with anything?" She watched him close the door, secretly impressed with his observational skills.

"You're trying to tap into energies you can't see or prove. Whether you think they come from God or not isn't as important as the fact that you acknowledge forces outside of yourself."

"You're giving me a headache."

He laughed, the velvet-rough sound flowing over her skin. "You can't have headaches anymore."

"That's what you think." She went to her closet and pushed the hanging wooden door along its track. It had taken her a long time to find two matching bleached pine panels of suitable size, but the effort was worth it. When she lay in bed, she studied the grain of the wood as she drifted to sleep.

"Listen." His tone was so grave that it drew her gaze to him again. "When Marks go on the hunt, they change."

"Change?"

"Their senses hone. You'll experience a kind of tunnel vision. You see it in felines when they crouch low and prepare to pounce. They're so absorbed in what they're doing, they don't register anything else."

"I think I caught a bit of that before."

"You might have. All mentors are specially trained to widen their focus to encompass their charges. Much like using bright headlights versus the regular ones."

Eve pulled out her most worn pair of jeans. "And Alec hasn't had this training."

"Right. He's really good at what he does, but I'm afraid he's going to leave you unprotected. You have to be extra vigilant. Somehow, you're going to have to remind yourself to take in everything."

"Are you telling me this to make your brother look bad, or are you serious?"

"I only wish I could make up stuff this good." He leaned back against the door. "You're going to have to trust me, babe. It's my job to keep you alive and working off your penance."

"I wouldn't say that assigning me to kill things prior to being trained is a good way to keep me breathing," she said wryly.

The tightening of his jaw was nearly imperceptible, but Eve was looking for it. Gadara was yanking them all around. She knew what leverage he had on Alec—her. But what was Reed getting out of this? Perhaps Gadara was holding something over him, too? It was in her best interests to find out.

Reed's glance moved back to her beautifully made bed and a smile curved his mouth. "You're not sleeping with Cain."

"How would you know?"

"His scent is fainter in here than in the rest of the condo."

"My mom just washed and made the bed."

"Uh-huh . . ." He looked at her with dark, slumberous eyes. Reed was like a firecracker, hot and explosive. The part of Eve that craved quiet evenings at home was shocked by how attractive she found that quality.

She turned away, determined to get ready for the task ahead and stop thinking about sex. "Don't get cocky and think his absence has anything to do with you."

"It has to do with something. You've been thinking about him for ten years, but now that he's here, you're keeping him at arm's distance?"

She thought of the make-out session in the parking garage and smiled. "My personal life is none of your business."

"Keep telling yourself that. Eventually you might believe it. But it still won't be true."

"Whatever. Got anything else for me?"

"Oh yeah, I got something for you, babe. Come and get it."

"Eww." Eve tossed an arch glance over her shoulder. "You just crossed the line from arrogant to crass."

His gaze dropped. "Sorry."

She sighed. He was faultlessly elegant on the outside, but on the inside . . . The man had some rough edges. Oddly enough, she didn't want to smooth them away. But she did want to understand them. "Where did that little bit of tastelessness come from?"

Straightening, Reed reached for the doorknob. "Hell if I know," he muttered, stepping out to the hallway.

The door closed behind him with a quiet click of the latch.

"It's cold," Eve muttered, pulling her sweater coat tighter around her.

Alec tossed an arm around her shoulders and bit back the obvious question. It was easily sixty-eight degrees outside, a temperature many individuals would say was balmy. The brisk stride with which they approached their destination would have kept most people warm. Eve's chill came from somewhere inside her, created by either her changing body or her somber mood—a mood Abel had also carried with him when he'd left the house.

Braced for some type of goading, boastful comment from his brother, Alec had been astonished when Abel simply exited Eve's bedroom and shifted away without a word. There one second, gone the next. Shifting was a blessing for all angels, except for Alec. He was the only *mal'akh* to have the gift stripped from him, another example of how he was denied even the basics. He'd been given very few breaks in his life, and now the one thing he cared for was at risk.

Intimacy. He hadn't been prepared for it to happen between Eve and Abel. Sex was sex. It was nothing compared to the nonphysical intimacy Alec sensed developing between them. Jealousy ate at him. He and Abel had used women to irritate each other in the past, but never had they cared equally about one. It was a threat Alec didn't know how to manage. After a lifetime of the same old, same old, he was now confronted with too many unknowns.

"It looks different at night," Eve said softly.

He looked at their destination. Strategically lit with exterior illumination, it appeared stately and established, as if it had existed for decades rather than mere months.

As they neared the front entrance, Alec inhaled deeply. No stench, no infestation. He slowed his pace and gazed up at the gargoyles. From the alley, two were visible and they were both in their positions.

"What's the matter?" Eve asked, reaching into her pocket for her badge.

"It doesn't smell, angel."

Her brow arched. "Not that again."

"I wanted to believe you."

She smiled. "I appreciate that."

Flashing her credentials at the guard, Eve led the way with that kittenish sway to her hips that had once lured him to sin. Who was he kidding? It still lured him to sin.

"Angel." He whistled after her. "Are you feeling frisky?"

She stopped at the bank of elevators and winked. They were met by a second guard in uniform who told them the elevators weren't operational yet. They'd have to take the stairs.

"Race you to the top," Eve challenged, before gripping the handrail and sprinting up.

He could catch her. His legs were longer. But it was far more fun to bring up the rear. They burst onto the roof in a rush of limbs and laughter . . . but the sight that greeted them quickly turned merriment into startled silence.

"Holy shit." Alec slid briefly along the metal roof before gaining purchase.

Eve, still new to her strength, almost skid directly into the bonfire that was the source of his astonishment. Instead, she fell on her ass. "Ouch!"

Feeling as if he were suffering the effects of a hallucinogenic drug, Alec gaped at the tengu who danced around the hellfire with gleeful chortles. None of his mark senses registered the beast in front of him. Aside from the frail mortal vision he'd been born with, there was no other way to detect the demon. Yet it wasn't that his senses had failed him. He saw the pit of hellfire. As a demonic conjuring that cast no illumination and no shadow, it was impossible to see with Unmarked vision.

But if his mark senses were functioning properly, he would also be able to smell the tengu and see his details. With that information, Alec would know which king of Hell he belonged to and how best to eradicate him. As it was, Alec was up shit creek without a paddle. And Eve was along for the ride.

Pivoting, he searched for the other gargoyles but found his view blocked by massive air-conditioning units. Were there more tengu to manage?

"Pretty Mark, Pretty Mark," the tengu sang, his beady eyes on Eve where she still sprawled. He didn't seem to notice Alec at all. "Pretty Mark came to see Joey."

"You piss on me again," she warned, pushing to her feet, "and I'll kick your ass."

"Joey's ass is stone, Pretty Mark. Pretty Mark break foot kicking Joey's ass." The tengu laughed, still hopping in a frenzied jig to some tune only he could hear.

"My foot's bigger," Alec rumbled.

The tengu looked at him and a smile split his face. "Cain, Cain, good to see you again."

"You know him?" Eve asked, stepping closer.

"Hell if I know. Without any details, I can't tell."

"What do we do?"

"Capture him."

She snorted. "How are we supposed to do that?"

"Pretty Mark want to dance?" Joey cried, then he lunged at her.

Alec leaped between them, grunting against the vicious impact of hard, heavy stone to his gut. He hit the deck on his back and rolled with the writhing tengu. A brick safety ledge surrounded the roof's perimeter and they crashed into it with a jolting thud.

The creature was hot to the touch, charged by the evil of the hellfire. As Alec grappled with the wriggling demon, his bare palms sizzled. The stench of burning flesh filled the air and he briefly considered tossing the damn tengu over the edge to shatter into pieces on the ground below. But he needed him intact so they could study him.

What the hell was it?

Aided by weight and his small size, the tengu crawled up Alec's torso. As he rose with both hands fisted together as a mallet and prepared to swing, Eve lashed out with a swift kick. Her boot caught the tengu in the face and sent him flying. Screaming, it crashed into the bonfire.

"We've got to put the flames out." Alec leaped to his feet. "It will keep recharging him, and we'll wear out before he does."

The tengu vaulted from the flames as a red-hot missile, and Eve ducked. He overshot and crashed into a van-sized air conditioner. A pipe feeding into the unit broke, spilling water across the roof.

"Will that work?" she asked.

"Only if it's holy."

"How the fuck are we supposed to get holy water up here?" She kicked droplets at the fire. The tengu disengaged from the massive dent he'd made in the AC unit and came running for Eve, screeching unintelligible words.

"Give me a second to work on that." Alec tackled the crazed demon before he reached her.

Eve stared in horrified fascination. The two combatants were so disparate in size, yet seemed almost evenly matched. Alec definitely had his hands full. She glanced around for anything that could be used as a makeshift weapon.

"*Adjutorium nostrun in nomine*—" Alec shouted. "—*Domini.*"

"What?" She raced around the air conditioner and was thrust backward with stunning strength. With the wind knocked from her, Eve could only gape up at the creature who sat on her. It was another tengu.

"I kill you," the tengu said, in a lilting feminine voice so at odds with her frightening visage.

Alec continued to yell at his opponent in what Eve guessed was Latin. She yanked her head to the side as the tengu swung at her. The sound of the metal roof rending near her ear was deafening and painful, but the pain dissipated as quickly as it came. Using the tengu's forward momentum, Eve tossed the heavy creature over her head and rolled to her belly. She scrambled to her feet, barely managing to gain her footing before the tengu was after her again.

"Alec!" she yelled, kicking the demon and sending her skidding through the growing lake of water. Eve was sick of being wet. Totally sick of it.

The tengu slid into the fire and popped up a moment later, laughing. Alec threw his tengu into the other one, causing a collision that cracked off the leg of one and the arm of the other. The two collected their missing appendages and leaped into the fire.

Standing over the gushing water, Alec made the sign of the cross. "*Commixtio salis et aquæ pariter fiat in nomine Patris, et Filii et Spiritus Sancti.*"

His voice rose in volume, the words rolling off his tongue in a richly nuanced incantation. Eve turned to the broken air conditioner, hoping her superstrength was fully operational. She grabbed the end of the broken water pipe and yanked hard, ripping a piece free. Wielding the section like a bat, she pivoted. "Joey" barreled toward her and she dispatched him with a home run hit that sent him flying over the lip of the roof. The pipe was ruined by the impact. She dropped it with a curse and searched for a replacement.

"Eve!" Alec barked as a tremendous crashing noise was heard from the street below. "We need one of them."

She winced. "Sorry. Don't know my own strength."

The one-legged tengu shrieked and hopped after Eve in retaliation, wielding her broken-off leg like a club. Alec lashed out with a fist, but haste threw off his aim. He struck the beast's rear lower flank, sending her into a tailspin. Her velocity increased, then she struck Eve, knocking Eve to her back.

The tengu landed on her thighs. Stone arms rose to brain Eve with the leg. Eve screamed and recoiled, shielding her head with her forearms. Braced for the beating, she squeezed her eyes shut.

Then a hideous stench roiled over her, turning her stomach and making her choke.

A roar filled the air, like the sound of a mighty waterfall. The ground slithered beneath her back, dragging her several feet. Her eyes flew open and she watched the scene unfold as if in slow motion.

The water surged into a tidal wave. An all-too-recognizable face emerged within the center of the liquid wall. The tengu shrieked and dropped the leg.

"She's mine!" the Nix roared.

In a churning, foaming mass, the Nix swept the tengu over the edge of the roof.

And took Eve with it.

CHAPTER 14

"Alec!"

Eve tumbled inside the wave like a wiped-out surfer. Her back hit the edge of the brick safety surround and she flipped over the top, arms and legs flailing. Her fingers grappled for purchase, one digit breaking in the effort. Then she was falling, weighted down by the tengu that clung to one leg and the Nix that was wrapped around her entire body in a swirling vortex of water.

As the lip of the roof escaped her vision, an arm reached over and clasped her wrist in a viselike hold. She glanced up, watching how her momentum and gravity pulled Alec inexorably until he dangled from the waist. She screamed. Not from the fear of falling, although she was deathly afraid of heights, but for Alec, who appeared ready to tumble over the edge with her.

"You're going to die," she yelled at Alec, kicking madly at the screeching tengu. "Let me go!"

"No way." He clutched at her with both hands. *"Deus, invictæ virtutis auctor, et insuperabilis imperii rex, ac semper magnificus triumphator—"*

As Alec continued to speak, Eve flopped from side to side. Her shoulders creaked with the tremendous weight of the beings hanging on to her. Her arms felt on the verge of ripping from their sockets. She was fairly certain that would have happened already if she weren't superhuman.

She looked down, aiming at the tengu's eyes with the heel of her boot and kicking at her with all her might. Alec slid farther over the ledge, his hips the only anchor keeping them from free-falling four stories to the ground.

"Per Dominum nostrum!" Alec roared.

The water exploded outward with teeth-rattling violence, knocking the tengu free and slamming Eve into the brick facade. Alec yanked her up and over the top with such force that they both landed in an ignoble sprawl of tangled limbs. From below, the reverberation of the crashing tengu caused a car alarm to wail.

"What the fuck happened?" she gasped, pushing her soaked hair out of her face.

Alec lay beneath her, laughing. "I asked for a blessing of the water. God made it holy and it kicked the Nix out."

"How can you laugh?" She smacked his shoulder. "This job sucks. And we're empty-handed."

"We're alive. And you were right." He cupped the back of her neck and gave her a quick, hard kiss. She cried out at the unintentional jarring of her broken finger. He set her beside him, then sat up. Catching her hand, he looked it over. "Angel . . ."

She couldn't look. Regardless of whether or not she was capable of physically vomiting, the thought of seeing her distorted finger made her sick.

"Come here," he murmured. Bending forward, Alec took her mouth, first gently and sweetly, then deeper. So startled was she by the action and the first tendrils of desire that she failed to register his changed grip until he yanked her finger into place.

Eve screamed just as the door to the stairwell burst open and the two security guards rushed out to the roof. Slipping in the water, they skid several feet before falling on their asses.

"My life just keeps getting better," she groused.

As Eve traversed the distance from the elevator in her condominium complex to her front door, she left a trail of droplets in her wake. From behind her, the sloshing of water in Alec's boots was clearly audible. It had taken a direct phone call to Gadara to get them off the hook with security. That had taken longer than she would have liked. She couldn't even think about the fact that he'd lagged on getting to the phone because he was schmoozing in Las Vegas while she waited sopping and sore: it pissed her off too much.

She was cold. She couldn't shiver and her teeth didn't rattle, but she was a Popsicle nevertheless. Her attire didn't help matters. When wet, her sweater coat had weighed a ton. She'd been forced to take it, and her shirt, off. Unfortunately, the only garment she'd had in the car was a black leather trench coat. Paired with her black lace bra and low-rise jeans, she looked like a prostitute, which wasn't conducive to improving her mood. Alec had tried to cheer her up, but finally realized that silence was wiser.

Eve looked at her once-broken finger. It was fully healed now, with no bruising or swelling to bear witness to the injury. If only her psyche could be set right so easily. There were some things a person shouldn't have to experience. Tidal waves on roofs, attacks by ghoulish creatures, and being suspended fifty-three feet above the ground were some of them.

"Got your keys?" Alec asked.

"Yep."

As they passed Mrs. Basso's door, it opened. She took in their appearances with one wide, sweeping glance. "You look like drowned rats."

"I feel like one," Eve muttered, though she managed a tight smile.

"What the hell were you doing if you don't mind my asking?"

"Uh . . . surfing?"

"With those clothes on?"

"It was spontaneous."

Mrs. Basso looked at Alec, who shrugged. She shook her head. "Young people these days. I get worn out just thinking about your courtship rituals. Whatever happened to drugstore chocolate shakes and drive-in movies?"

Eve laughed softly. Mrs. Basso reminded her that life was normal for some people. She wanted to feel that way again, if only for a short time. "I'm worn out, too, so you're not alone. I'll see you tomorrow."

"Mr. Cain," Mrs. Basso said. "Could I talk to you a moment?"

Alec's brows rose, but he nodded. "Sure. Let me get out of these clothes."

"Of course."

"Want to come over in about five minutes?"

Mrs. Basso glanced at Eve, who got the impression that she shouldn't be around when Mrs. Basso talked to Alec.

"I'm going to take a long, hot bath," Eve said, moving to her condo. It was ironic that she would want to sit in water after days of being soaked with it, but she couldn't imagine a faster way to warm up.

Once she was inside the sanctity and comfort of her home, she began to strip her way down the hall. She opened the louvered doors that hid the laundry alcove and shoved her wet clothes into the washing machine. A low whistle turned her head. Alec stood at the end of the hallway where it emptied into the living room. If the heat of his gaze had been less than tangible, she might have been embarrassed at her blatant display of nakedness. She was certain Mrs. Basso's likening of her appearance to a drowned rat was apt.

His voice came low and husky. "Your place has a great view."

"You got a thing for wet rodents?"

"I've got a thing for you. Hot, wet, and naked."

"Charmer." Her voice was come-hither husky. "No way you can start and finish anything in less than five minutes."

A slow, lazy smile curved his mouth. "I can make your bathwater safe."

She sighed. "That's not as sexy as what I was thinking."

"Hold that thought." He approached with the sultry stride she'd always drooled over. Catching her elbow, he led her through her bedroom to the bathroom, which was separated from the sleeping area by her closets. There, her sunken whirlpool tub waited to froth her worries away.

If only it could be so easy.

Alec plugged the drain, turned the taps, and blessed the water. Eve found herself swaying to the lulling cadence of his words.

"You better hop in," he drawled when the tub was full and he was done, "before you fall asleep standing up."

"Shouldn't the mark cure exhaustion?"

"Sleep reminds us that we're not invincible."

"Whatever."

He kissed the tip of her nose and cupped her bare breast. "You need to move out to the boonies," he whispered, the pad of his thumb brushing over her taut nipple. "No meddling neighbors."

"I'll get right on that. But she's not a meddler. She just worries."

Smiling, he left her and she sank into the steaming water with a sigh of relief. The sight of the cross hanging off the adjacent showerhead made her grumpy so she closed her eyes. A few moments later she heard a knock at the front door, a sound that would have been impossible to detect before having her super hearing.

The vague whisper of subdued voices reached her ears. She concentrated hard, trying to home in on the individual syllables. The Change was like putting a stethoscope to her ears.

"Mr. Basso saw it on TV one night a year or so ago," Mrs. Basso was saying, "and he started a monthly subscription. Now that he's gone, I have no use for them."

"I don't understand," Alec murmured.

"Take the box." Eve heard something rattle as it exchanged hands. "You're a fit young man, but swimming with your clothes on at night . . . and that business in the carport . . ."

Mrs. Basso cleared her throat. "Oh, this is terrible. I should learn to leave well enough alone."

Again the rattle came, like beans in a jar, and Eve frowned.

"Male enhancement?" Alec croaked.

Eve sat up so fast, water sloshed over the rim of the tub.

"The walls are thin," Mrs. Basso muttered. "A couple nights ago . . . No man can keep that pace indefinitely."

The silence from Alec was deafening. Eve bit her lip. He was speechless, and she was going to burst.

"You can't be any more embarrassed than I am," Mrs. Basso said. "Hear me out and I promise never to interfere again. Women with drive make the best wives, my late husband used to say. I know it can be exhausting, though, and intimidating. Just don't give her up without a fight. Don't give up, period. You'll never find another girl like Evangeline."

"I know." Despite how low Alec's voice was, Eve heard it clear as day. Her throat tightened and her eyes stung.

She grabbed her terry-cloth-covered inflatable headrest and leaned back with her eyes closed. Fact was, life wasn't bad when you had good friends, which brought her best friend, Janice, to mind.

Eve hoped her trip to Europe was fulfilling its purpose. They had both spent a year bitching about feeling stagnant. First, they'd blamed it on a lack of good men. Then, they'd realized that was just a tried-and-true excuse for the real problem—themselves. Janice had decided a complete change of scene would give her a new perspective and, as a bartender, she could easily take her livelihood with her. Eve had said her job prevented her from going, but that wasn't entirely true. She just hadn't known how to break the news to her parents, and the idea of backpacking seemed so far out of line with her desire to put down roots.

"Hey." Alec's voice penetrated her thoughts at the same moment she registered the shutting off of the spa jets.

She blinked sleepily up at him. "Hmm?"

"You have to get out, angel." He reached for her. "You've been in here so long, your skin is pruning. Considering you're a Mark, that's saying something."

"What?"

"You fell asleep." He plucked her out of the deep tub as if she was a child, heedless of how her wet body soaked his boxers. He was naked otherwise, and mouthwatering. She knew she had to be half dead with exhaustion, because her super libido could only manage a slight twitch of interest.

"Figures," she muttered.

He set her down on the rug and scrubbed her down with a towel.

"You're good at this babysitting stuff," she said. "Do this often?"

The question was only partly teasing. She did wonder if he'd cared for another woman with such tenderness before.

"Only for tasty Asian babes." He tossed the towel in the hamper.

She stepped back and eyed him. Long muscular legs, taut abdomen, beautifully delineated biceps, and a thick, weighty bulge in his drawers. She licked her lips. "Where's that male-enhancement stuff?"

His arms crossed. "Excuse me?"

"Think it'll work on me?"

Alec smiled. "You don't have the necessary parts."

"Oh yeah? Why don't you ask your parts if they think my parts are necessary or not? They might disagree."

"You're barely standing."

"I can lie down."

He tossed her over his shoulder. She almost protested, then pushed his boxers down instead and admired his flexing buttocks. He swatted her ass. "Behave."

"You like me naughty," she said, tossing his earlier words back at him.

"I like you awake, too."

Eve sighed. "Technicalities."

Alec tossed her on the bed and she bounced lightly. Catching the edge of the blankets, he covered her and kissed the tip of her nose. "Good night, angel."

"Where are you going?" She yawned.

"To bed."

"I've got one of those."

He tugged up his boxers. "You won't get any sleep if I join you and you need the rest. We have a conference call with Raguel tomorrow."

She snorted and curled into her pillow. "I'm taking tomorrow off."

"No such thing."

"Watch me."

As he closed the door, she heard him chuckling.

"Smells awesome."

As he fried bacon, Alec smiled at the sound of Eve's voice. He glanced back her, finding her dressed in her red kimono robe and wearing a towel on her head. "There's coffee in the pot."

"Will I get a buzz off it?"

"Nope."

"Good thing I like the taste of it, then."

She padded barefoot to the coffeemaker, poured herself a cup, and moved over to one of the stools on the opposite side of the island. He'd set the newspaper there and she immediately spread it out and began reading.

"After breakfast," he said, "we need to call Raguel."

"I told you, I'm taking the day off."

"Don't be stubborn." He set down the fork he was using to flip the bacon. "This is bigger than you and me now, angel."

"Because we couldn't smell them?"

"Or see their details. If there's a new faction somewhere operating completely outside the rest of the system, every firm needs to know."

Her lips pursed. "You can handle the talk with Gadara without me."

"Talk to me."

Eve looked up from the paper. She looked faultless, refreshed, and alert, but the lack of shadows under her eyes didn't hide the fact that she was weary. "I need a break, Alec. Just for a few hours, at least."

She let the paper rest on the counter. "I need some time to be normal. For my own sanity. Think about the last two weeks of my life, okay?"

"I understand."

"Do you?" Her slender fingers drummed atop the newsprint-covered granite. "Then handle Gadara by yourself. There's nothing I can add to what you're going to tell him."

"Fine." He turned back to the bacon and tried to hide his volatile response to her withdrawal. All morning long, he'd been whistling with contentment. The concern over the tengu and the possible rippling effect their existence would have over every facet of the mark system gave him a feeling of anticipation. Surely a new firm would be needed, and he had the only known hands-on experience with this new threat.

But Eve was unhappy and possibly scared. She had a right to feel both of those emotions. And he was an asshole for thinking only of himself.

"You're angry," she said.

"Not with you."

Silence followed. He continued browning the bacon and set to work on frying eggs. In another pan, he made pancakes. Behind him, he heard the rustle of flipping newspaper pages. It was a quiet domestic scene, but the intimacy he craved was lacking and sorely missed.

"There's a story in the paper about a series of animal mutilations," she murmured. "There's speculation that they're ritualistic."

"Then they probably are."

"I figured. And the fact that the latest animal—a Great Dane—was found in the back of a Gehenna Masonry pickup truck can't be coincidence, because there's no so such thing as coincidence, right?"

Alec turned off the gas burners and moved to the island. He read the story over her shoulder. The *Orange County Register* was covering the latest ultimate fight at the Upland Sports Arena. Lower down the page was the mention of a recent spate of dog mutilations and killings in the area. Two animal carcasses had been found in the arena parking lot just a week before—one of them had been found in the back of a Gehenna truck left in the lot overnight due to some construction the company was doing.

"I smell a rat," he said.

"I smell breakfast," she retorted, "and I'm hungry."

He pressed his lips to the crown of her head. "Yes, Your Highness."

Returning to the stove, Alec finished up the cooking, filled two plates, and brought them back to the island.

Eve looked at her overflowing plate. "You're going to make me fat."

He smiled. "Don't eat what you don't want."

"I want all of it."

"I'll help you work it off."

"How generous of you."

"I'm here to serve."

And that was the true crux of the matter, he realized as he stabbed at the yolk of one over-medium egg. He couldn't serve God's needs, his needs, and Eve's needs at the same time. Something had to give.

He found himself wishing that she would learn to like the mark, so he could have it all. Then he thought of the night before and remembered the terror he had felt as he watched her being swept over the side of the roof. If he'd been capable of having a heart attack, he would have had one.

"I think I'm going to take Mrs. Basso to the movies today," Eve pronounced before munching on a piece of crunchy bacon, "while you're talking to Gadara. The theater is away from water and far from the tengu building. I need a price on my head before anyone else can take a crack at me, right? So it should be nice and uneventful."

He swallowed hard. The thought of her going out alone scared the shit out of him. "I wish you wouldn't."

"I know." She set her elbows on the counter and rested her chin on her hands. "If you think it's really unsafe, I won't leave. I'm not an idiot. But if you're just worried, please let me go. I would really like to spend a couple of hours watching other people live average lives. I need the fantasy, if only for a little while."

Alec looked out the window. It was a crystal-clear day. No rain, no mist. If she went straight to the movies and came right back, she should be fine. "Don't use the john."

"Okay. Now let's talk about why I can't go to the bathroom. That Nix is stalking me. I can't figure out what his deal is. I swear I didn't do anything to him. He flicked his snake's tongue at me and I freaked. I said something offhand by complete mistake and it wounded him. He had to see that I was clueless and no threat to him. Why is he acting like I ran over his dog?"

"I don't know." Alec tapped the tines of his fork against his plate. "This is completely outside the norm. I'm going to talk to Raguel about it and see what he says. We can't sit here waiting for the Nix to strike again. We have to find and vanquish him."

"Sounds good to me." Eve pushed back from the island. She pulled the towel off her head and draped it over the back of her stool. "I'm going to run next door and see if Mrs. Basso is up for a movie. She wanted to see the new Hugh Jackman flick, and there's a matinee in an hour."

Alec nodded and continued to eat his now tasteless food, his thoughts occupied by the Nix. He listened to the multiple locks disengage, then the door opening. Perhaps talking to Raguel alone was the best way to go. Separating himself from Eve might help to alter the image of them as an indivisible team. Their paths would eventually diverge; they had to for her sake. Then he would need to continue on his present course alone. That would be difficult if it was perceived that he was useful only in regards to his association with her.

Of course, part of him wondered how useful he could possibly be without her.

As Eve exited to the hallway, she left her front door open. Her gaze returned to Alec against her will, her stride faltering just past the threshold. The sight of him in her kitchen—completely at ease and half dressed in only a T-shirt and boxers—was as bizarre as being attacked by the tengu. The incongruity of his presence in her life after a ten-year absence brought home a possibility she hadn't considered before—perhaps his return and the marking weren't the detours in her life. Perhaps the last ten years were.

It was a crazy thought, but how else could she explain why she wasn't a shell-shocked wreck at this point? Or why this new skin she wore felt so much more comfortable than the one she'd been born with?

And her sexual advances toward Alec . . . she could say that was an expected aftereffect of a near-death experience or blame her super libido. But she'd be lying to herself, and as screwed up as the rest of her life was, she needed her head on straight more than ever.

Eve stopped before Mrs. Basso's door and knocked. As she waited, she tightened the belt on her robe. She looked up and down the hallway, admiring the sunshine coming in through the window on the other side of her door. She spread her arms out and stretched, briefly wondering if she should have dressed before stepping out of her house. Luckily it was a workday and most of the residents weren't home.

She rang the doorbell, knowing that a knock was sometimes difficult to hear from the rear bedrooms. Her mark began to tingle, then burn, as it did when she took the Lord's name in vain. Frowning, she rubbed at it. Why the hell would the damn thing start bothering her now?

"Mrs. Basso?" she called out, just in case her neighbor wasn't answering in avoidance of solicitors. Salespeople weren't supposed to come into the building. Anyone caught putting up solicitations was quickly booted out, but often the easiest way to get rid of them was simply to ignore them.

Her mark throbbed something fierce. Aggravated energy pumped hard and fast through her veins, spreading outward from her arm until it inundated her body with restless anticipation. Eve's nostrils flared, scents intensifying with startling immediacy. Her eyesight sharpened, magnifying minute details such as the scrapes left by keys around the dead-bolt lock.

Before she fully comprehended what she was doing, Eve crashed into Mrs. Basso's door shoulder first. The door locks shattered through the jamb, spraying splinters through the air and filling the hallway with an echoing boom.

"Mrs. Basso!" Eve searched the living room with a sweeping glance.

The mark continued to pulse, pushing a steady stream of adrenaline through her body. Her super senses were functioning in high gear. The doors and windows were closed, but she heard the crashing of waves against the shore and the screams of seagulls as if they were directly in front of her.

"Eve."

Alec. She pivoted. Met his gaze. He stood on the threshold, barefoot but sporting hastily donned jeans.

"The mark," she explained. "It's freaking me out."

He entered. "Mrs. Basso?" he called out, his voice strong and steady.

"Maybe she's at the restaurant?"

The sheer lack of emotion on his face said more than words could.

Mrs. Basso's floor plan was the mirror image of Eve's, but the decor made the homes entirely dissimilar. While Eve's pad had a modern, minimalist style, the Basso residence was traditional Italian elegance. Faux painted walls and heavy leather furniture invited guests to linger in warmth and comfort. Yet Eve was chilled by the silence, broken only by the ticking of the beautiful clock on the living room wall.

She stared at its oversized numbers and wrought-iron scrollwork, marveling at the steadiness of her breathing and the rhythmic beating of her heart. Mentally she was panicking, but physically she could be visiting for espresso and tiramisu for all the stress her body felt. There was a brutal primitiveness to the combination of physical calm, coursing adrenaline, and super sensitivity. It was entirely inelegant . . . and seductive.

"*Eve.*"

Eve froze at the sound of her name, spoken softer than a whisper but heard louder than a gunshot.

"Mrs. Basso?" She moved down the hall, first tentatively, then faster.

"*Eve.*"

"Mrs. Basso!"

Bursting into the master bedroom at a run, Eve gasped in relief to find Mrs. Basso standing by the bed. Dressed in white slacks and a pale pink shirt, she looked lovely and ready for the day. Turning with a smile, Mrs. Basso eyed her from head to toe. "Cute pajamas."

Eve gave a breathy laugh, feeling silly for her overreaction. Her mark enhancements were obviously still whacky. "You scared me when you didn't answer."

"It's been an . . . *odd* morning."

Wincing, Eve recalled her abrupt entry. "About your door . . ."

"Is that what the ruckus was?" Mrs. Basso smiled. "You have so much energy."

Eve frowned. "I wanted to see if you'd like to catch that movie you mentioned."

"I would love to, but I'm afraid I can't."

Alec's hand touched Eve's back. She looked at him. His lips were thin and tight.

Mrs. Basso smiled at Alec. "Take good care of her, Cain."

"I will."

"I can take a rain check," Eve offered. "I won't go without you."

"You might think about keeping him, Evie," Mrs. Basso said, gesturing to Alec with a gentle jerk of her chin. "Especially if he masters that recipe I gave him."

Mrs. Basso turned back to the bed, affording Eve a view of the nightstand. A clear glass bowl waited there. It was half filled with water and showcased a lovely white water lily.

Eve's wide eyes shot back to her neighbor, who was leaning over the mattress. She was tucking in the frail figure lying peacefully amid the pillows—a figure easily seen through the gradually increasing translucence of Mrs. Basso.

Two of them. One ghostly, one . . . dead.

A sob escaped Eve, shattering the quiet. She covered her mouth.

The silver hair that fanned out on the pillow was wet, as was Mrs. Basso's skin, yet she appeared to be sleeping.

She looked so peaceful, so serene.

So lifeless.

CHAPTER 15

Eve accepted the sweater Alec handed to her and shrugged into it. She was frozen to the bone, her blood icy with grief, fury, and fear. They stood just outside her front door, staying out of the way of the paramedics and police detectives who swarmed around the Basso apartment.

"Now, let's run through this again," the detective said in a tone of voice that told her he didn't believe a word she said. Detective Jones, he'd said his name was. He was a nondescript man in a cheap suit dyed a shade of shit brown Eve was certain had been discontinued in the seventies. His partner was Detective Ingram. He had better taste in clothes, but was taller, fatter, and boasted a handlebar mustache.

For some reason, the two men offended Eve. They were so drab and worn, their voices monotonous and their eyes flat. Beaten down by the dregs of society and completely unaware of what they were really dealing with every day.

"What condition was the Basso door in when you found it?" Jones asked.

"It was locked," she said, wondering why she had to go over this so many times. She'd already told the story to two other detectives.

"Who broke in?"

"I did."

"Through two dead bolts?" Ingram was clearly disbelieving.

"Yes."

"Can you demonstrate how," Jones asked, "using your door?"

Eve exhaled harshly and turned around. She closed her door, then grabbed the knob with one hand and bumped the portal with her shoulder. "I used a little more force, of course."

"Of course." He wrote something in his notepad.

"You don't have to believe me," she said. "Just look at the security tapes."

"We will." His smile was tight. "Did you move the body?"

"I didn't move anything."

"The medical examiner says the body is wet," Ingram informed, "but the bed isn't. Someone moved the deceased to the bed. Then they tucked her in."

"I wouldn't know."

"Did Mrs. Basso have any family nearby? Or close friends?"

"Not that I'm aware of."

"Any children?"

She shook her head.

"The act of moving her and arranging her so nicely suggests that the person felt close to her. Do you know anyone who might fit that bill?"

Eve's lower lip quivered and tears welled. "No."

Thoughts of what the last minutes of Mrs. Basso's life must have been like made her sick. Eve swiped at the tears that coursed down her cheeks.

Alec altered his stance, moving from beside her to slightly in front of her. It was a protective pose and she was grateful for it. His hand reached back for her and she clasped it. "Ms. Hollis has been through enough today," he said. "I'm going to have to ask you to leave her alone for now."

Both detectives narrowed their eyes, then nodded in near unison. Ingram reached into his pocket and withdrew a business card, which he held out to Eve. "If you think of anything that might help, please give us a call in addition to the other detectives you spoke with earlier."

Eve frowned as she read the information imprinted on the card. "Anaheim Police Department? A bit out of your jurisdiction, aren't you?"

Then something more disturbing caught her eye. *"Homicide?"*

Alec's fingers tightened on hers. "You think this is a murder?"

"That's all we need for now," Jones said. "Thank you for your cooperation."

"Why do you think this is a murder, Detective?" Alec repeated, this time with an oddly resonant tone to his voice.

Persuasive. Eve watched the two detectives in silent fascination, wondering if the Jedi mind trick would work on them.

Ingram and Jones stood silently for a long moment, then Jones said, "Water lilies."

Eve's mark tingled and she released Alec's hand to rub at it. He glanced at her, then asked, "What's significant about water lilies?"

"It's an unusual flower to keep inside the house," the detective said.

"Explain."

"The lily is a calling card."

"How many have you found?" Alec prodded.

"A dozen in the last six months."

Eve leaned heavily into the door. "All in Anaheim?"

"Until today."

The Nix was a serial killer. In Anaheim. Where her parents lived.

"Detectives!" A young woman in a blue windbreaker jacket leaned out of the Basso apartment. "The M.E. is asking for you."

"Excuse us," Ingram said.

"God be with you," Alec murmured.

Jones smiled grimly. "Thanks."

Eve was inside her apartment in a flash, racing toward the console where she kept her purse and keys. She heard the door shut.

"What are you doing?" Alec asked.

"My parents live in Anaheim."

"So?" He stood with arms akimbo before the door, blocking the exit. "You go there now, you might lead him right to your family."

"It's not hard to find them, Alec. We have the same last name. Shit, he could have followed my mom home when she left here."

"Let the mark system do what it's supposed to."

"Which is what exactly? Fuck up everyone's lives?"

Alec came to her and pulled her close. Unfamiliar with relying on a man for emotional support, she resisted at first; then she sank into his strength, too weary to resist. He was so warm and hard. There was no external softness to him, no hint of weakness. Solid as a rock. But he wasn't truly. Nothing was solid when it was impermanent.

"Let's go to Gadara Tower," he suggested. "There we can access the resources needed to keep your family safe."

"I need to be with them. They can't fight him off."

"He's after *you*, angel. We can make them safer without you around. Grab what you need and let's go. If I don't ease your mind and you still want to be with them, I'll go with you."

Eve dug into her purse and withdrew her cell phone. She speed dialed her parents' number. It rang four times and with every ring, she grew more agitated. Then, finally, it picked up.

"Hi, you've reached Darrel and Miyoko Hollis . . ."

The answering machine. A terrible fear gripped her.

Then the line connected. "Hello?"

"Dad?" Eve collapsed into Alec. "Are you all right?"

"I was in the garden with your mother. What's up?"

It took her a moment to reply. "Nothing. Just wanted to hear your voice."

"You don't sound good. What's the matter?" Her dad was using the low concerned tone that always made her want to spill her guts. She'd learned to hold her tongue over the years. He was a great listener but a poor doer. It was Miyoko who argued with teachers and principals on her children's behalf. She was also the one who never let her kids live down mistakes, rehashing them whenever she deemed the time was right.

"My neighbor died this morning." Eve was croaking like a frog, but she couldn't help it—her throat was tight as a fist. Alec's hands stroked up and down her back, which just made it worse.

"Oh, I'm sorry, honey," her dad said. "I know how much you liked her."

"I did. Very much."

"Hang on. Your mother wants the phone." Her dad couldn't hide his relief. Dealing with emotions wasn't his forte.

Eve gave a shaky sigh.

"What happened?" Miyoko demanded in the clipped tone of a seasoned nurse. When a crisis hit, she always became no-nonsense and precise.

"Mrs. Basso died this morning."

"Heart attack?"

"I don't think so," Eve said.

"What did the paramedics say?"

"They haven't said anything to me."

"Hmph. Go ask."

"I can't."

"Why not?"

Eve grimaced. "Because I can't, Mom. And does it really matter *how* she died? She's gone, and I'm devastated."

The doorbell rang. Alec pressed his lips to her forehead, then moved to answer the summons.

"I have to go," Eve said. "I'll call you back in a bit."

"Okay. Call back soon."

She snapped her phone shut and shoved it back into its dedicated pocket in her Coach bag. She wasn't a designer junkie by any means, but she had to have purses that didn't fall apart. Period.

"Sorry to trouble you again," Detective Ingram said.

Alec kept him out in the hall.

Eve rubbed at the space between her brows. She didn't have an actual headache, but she definitely felt stressed. Making sure her parents were safe was vital, and she wanted it done *now*.

"I'm sorry, but I am in a hurry, Detective," she said impatiently.

"I just need to know if you touched anything next door." He had one hand at his waist while the other stroked the end of his handlebar mustache. "The forensic team will do their job, of course, but it's always nice to know what you're going to find."

"The phone in the living room," she said. "To call 911."

He nodded, his gaze moving past her to sweep across her living room. "Nice place. My partner says you're an interior designer."

"Yes." She adjusted her purse strap on her shoulder. "If you will excuse me."

Ingram stilled, his gaze narrowing on something beyond her shoulder. Eve turned to see what had caught his eye.

The bowl that had once held the water lily rested empty on the coffee table. Alec had moved it there after she'd ground up the flower in the disposer. Eve cringed inwardly.

"Can I help you with something?" Alec asked, stepping into the detective's line of sight.

Ingram attempted to peer around Alec's tall frame. "Where did you get that bowl on your table?"

"I bought it," she replied tightly.

"Do you have the cups?"

"What?"

He looked at her. His eyes weren't dull anymore—they were sharp as knives. "The cups that go with that punch bowl."

"I don't know what you're talking about."

"That is a three-gallon punch bowl from Crate and Barrel. It comes as a set with ten matching cups and a plastic ladle. If you bought the bowl, you must have the cups, too."

"I didn't get it at Crate and Barrel."

"Where did you get it?"

"I don't know. Salvation Army, maybe?" Eve shrugged. "It was a long time ago. Listen, I really have to get going."

"Ah, that explains the missing cups." Ingram tugged on his mustache. "Do you want to know why I know so much about punch bowls, Ms. Hollis?"

"Not really. I—"

"I've seen a few of those particular bowls lately," he continued. "Too many of them. Saw one this morning, actually. Right next door. Did your bowl come with a flower in it?"

"No." Her mark burned something fierce and her jaw clenched. Like a damned electric dog collar, the mark was acting like a behavior modifier. "Are we done now?"

Ingram's attention turned to Alec. "What about you, Mr. Cain? Do you have to run out, too? I might have a few questions for you."

"I can't add any more to what Ms. Hollis has already told you," Alec said. "And yes, I'm going with her."

Eve admired Alec's poise. He looked calm and relaxed, while she felt strung-out and edgy.

"Mind if I take that bowl?" the detective asked.

"Actually," Alec answered before she could. "We need that."

She looked at him with raised brows. She didn't want it in her house. Part of her also hoped the Nix had left something identifiable behind, like fingerprints.

"You promised to bring a punch bowl to the employee party," he said.

The sudden tension weighed heavily. It had never occurred to her that the mark system might need the item. Now the detective was even more suspicious. She could smell it on him.

She winced apologetically. "He's right, Detective. I'm sorry about that. You can have it when we're done with it."

"If it doesn't break or go missing first." Ingram's hands went to his hips in what she suspected was a customary pose for him. It spread the lapels of his suit wide and accentuated his portly midsection. "I'm trying to catch a serial killer, Ms. Hollis, and you know more than you're telling me. If this guy has contacted you, I need to know. If he's threatened you, I can help."

Eve held her pose for the length of a heartbeat, then all the rigidity left her. This man wasn't the enemy. He was a good guy, fighting the good fight. "If I had anything helpful, I would share it. I swear."

The mark didn't burn, because she was telling the truth. Nothing she could say would help the police. But it didn't make the situation any more comfortable.

Detective Ingram pointed a frustrated finger at her. "Don't travel far without letting me know where you're going."

She suspected she could argue the legality of that order, but didn't see the point. She wasn't going anywhere while that Nix was out there. "Okay."

Ingram left. Alec retrieved the punch bowl and they exited her home, locking the door securely behind them. She grimaced as she turned the key in the multiple locks. Once she'd thought such barriers would be a deterrent that would keep her safe.

No one was safe.

As they moved down the hall, a gurney rolled out of the Basso home. Eve halted in her tracks, devastated by the sight. Two paramedics stood at either side. She recognized one immediately, even without seeing the name *Woodbridge* embroidered on his shirt. He paused.

"Hey," Woodbridge said. "I thought I remembered seeing this address recently. How are you?"

Eve's chin lifted. "She was my friend."

"I'm sorry." Concern filled his blue eyes.

"Thank you. I appreciate that."

Alec took up a position beside her, his hand coming to rest at the small of her back. It was a proprietary gesture and it added to her stress. Her life was complicated enough as it was.

She watched as Mrs. Basso was taken away and the full force of her loss hit her. She thought of all the movies and meals they'd never share. No more unexpected visits that cheered her day. No one else to shop for when she went to the store.

Eve suddenly felt very much alone.

"We should go," Alec murmured, squeezing her hip gently.

Nodding, she skirted the people milling around the hall and waited for the elevator to return. She stepped inside and released the breath she hadn't known she was holding. As the doors closed, shutting out the view of the chaos on the floor, Eve absorbed the fact that her world had irrevocably changed.

Whether she shed the mark or not, her life as she knew it was over.

* * *

Stepping into a firm was always a heady rush for Alec, no matter which one he visited or where it was located. His entire body hummed with energy and his heart rate lurched into an elevated rhythm, as if the other Marks shared their energy with him. He breathed deeply, inhaling the scent of hundreds of Marks confined in one space.

Beside him, Eve made a choked noise. Her nose wrinkled, making him wonder what sensory input she received. She appeared to find the smell disturbing rather than pleasant. Then he pushed the thought aside. Of course everything would be disturbing to her. It was all new and unwelcome, and she'd received a terrible shock today. One thing at a time. Making sure her parents were safe was first on his agenda. He knew Eve wouldn't be able to function properly until that was ensured.

"This way," he said, directing her toward a set of elevators tucked away from general public use. Unlike the private elevators that went directly to Raguel's office, these cars only went down to the bowels of the building. There, nestled deep into the earth, existed a small complex complete with morgue and various specialized departments.

Eve didn't appear to notice where they were going. As the elevator descended, her gaze remained on the floor, unfocused. Alec adjusted his grip on the punch bowl and reached out to her, stroking her bare arm. She was so far away mentally she didn't register his attempt to connect. He withdrew and leaned against the metal handrail. He had no idea how to get inside her beyond the physical and it left him feeling . . . impotent, which in turn was driving him insane.

A heavy, impenetrable silence filled the car, despite the instrumental Barry Manilow elevator music that whispered around them. He listened to her breathing, then sharpened his hearing to listen to her heart beating. It was so impossibly steady, like a machine. He used to listen to his own heartbeat, and he'd curse the mark that stole its ability to race or skip. Was a person's humanity contingent upon that organ? And if so, was the removal of its frailties the catalyst that led to the removal of a Mark's soul?

In the past, it was only when he was in a firm that he felt truly vital. He had come to crave the feeling of renewal. Until he'd met Eve, he hadn't known of any other way to feel so alive. It scared him that the last time he had entered this building—in his pursuit of Eve—he hadn't felt anything at all until he found her.

The elevator slowed, then stopped with a ding. The doors opened and Manilow's "Mandy" was drowned out by pandemonium.

A screaming banshee's wail rent the air, as well as any nearby eardrums. Two writhing bodies, locked in combat, rolled past the elevator. One was covered in coarse animal hair, the other boasted flowing inky tresses. A werewolf and a lili. Around them, a crowd made up mostly of Infernals had gathered to feed off the negative energy.

In the corner on the left, a receptionist's desk was staffed by another wolf, this one in human form. She stood, dressed in a white blouse and black skirt, watching the melee with a wide smile. To the right, chairs lined the walls, filled with both Marks and Infernals waiting for processing. The untrained eye might see the crowd and think it was Halloween. The mixture of oddly dressed and naked Infernals wouldn't make sense on any other day of the year. Straight ahead was the hallway that led to the various offices. That's where Alec was headed, if everyone would get out of the way.

Alec stepped out of the elevator and held the door for Eve. She stared at the ruckus with wide eyes. Her fingers pinched her nostrils closed and she yelled, "What is this place?"

"Hell on Earth."

He didn't raise his voice, but the din around them quieted as if he'd shouted.

"Cain," the receptionist breathed, blinking momentarily before dropping into her seat. The standing crowd also sank into their chairs. The couple on the floor gaped at him; the wolf with his terrible maw and the lili with her perfect pouting lips. Locked together in a mock embrace, they seemed to forget that they had been tearing each other apart mere seconds ago.

"Are you done?" Alec asked them with a raised brow.

"It stinks down 'ere," Eve mumbled through her plugged nose.

"He insulted me," the lili said, disentangling herself and pushing to her feet.

"She has a nice rack," the werewolf rumbled, straightening.

Alec looked at the lili. "You couldn't take that as a compliment?"

"I could die today," she muttered. "I want to go out with some respect."

"We could all die today," Eve drawled, dropping her hand. The wolf shifted into his naked human form and she whistled.

Alec gritted his teeth. "It's not polite to stare."

"I have a better chance of dying than most," the lili retorted, glaring at Eve. She turned her demonic green gaze to Alec. "You suck. I thought older brothers were supposed to be protective."

"If I'm older than you," he countered, "I'm not your brother."

Eve's mouth fell open.

"You could act on the principle of it," the lili argued.

"She's a lili," he explained to Eve, grabbing her elbow with his free hand and tugging her away from the blatantly interested wolf. "One hundred of them die daily. They never know when their number is going to be up."

"*Brother?*"

"She wishes," he scoffed. "My dad hasn't talked to Lilith in ages. And that lili is too impetuous to be older than me."

"I'm confused. Who's Lilith?"

Alec looked at the receptionist just as she was lifting the phone receiver from its cradle. "Cain's here," she said to whoever had answered. She beamed at Alec, then winked. Wrapped around that flirtatious eye was the detail that labeled her a werewolf, formerly under the rule of Mammon, the demon god of avarice.

"Lilith was my dad's first wife." Alec hefted the punch bowl and directed Eve down the hall. The sound of their booted footfalls on the polished concrete echoed ahead of them. Behind them, furious whispers followed.

Eve's sloe eyes widened. "First wife? I thought Adam had Eve, and that was it."

He shook his head. "Don't worry about it."

"No, seriously. Why didn't I know that? No one's ever told me that."

"Angel." Alec opened a glass inset door that said Forensic Wiccanology in gold sticker lettering. "One thing at a time."

Inside the room, the overhead lights were out. Pendant lamps hung over various island stations, spotlighting specific work areas.

"Cain!" The coarseness of the voice was reminiscent of Larry King and it originated from the distant right corner. "It's been far too long since you came to see me."

Alec's head turned to find the robe-clad crone who approached with a shuffling stride. As she moved from the shadows into the light, she changed from a hunchback into a lovely, willowy redhead. Her robe altered from an all-encompassing shroud to a tightly fit and strategically cut gown.

"Hello, Hank," Alec greeted. He held out the punch bowl. "I need you to find the Nix who touched this."

Hank's full lips curved in a winsome smile. "I'll do my best." She looked at Eve, her head tilting. She shifted form again, taking on the appearance of a firmly muscled, carrot-topped male. The gown changed into a black dress shirt and matching slacks. "Nice to meet you."

Eve blinked rapidly. "Hi."

Alec touched her elbow. "Evangeline, meet Hank. Hank, this is Eve."

"Hi, Eve." Hank licked his lips.

Eve waved lamely.

"We'll check in later," Alec said, pulling Eve toward the door.

"Bring her with you when you come back." As Hank moved away, his form returned to that of a stooped crone.

Once they were in the hall, Eve took a deep breath and wondered if the stench of Infernals was affecting her brain. She looked at Alec. "I feel like one of my teenage acid trips has come back to haunt me."

"Not possible."

"What is Hank?"

"An occultist. A demon who specializes in the magical arts and tapping into the power that threads through all of nature."

"No, I meant is it male or female?"

Alec shrugged. "I'm not sure."

"Great. What is this place?" She tried breathing through her mouth to avoid smelling anything, but it was pointless. The odor was steeped into the walls. "Unless my nose is completely wrong, I'd say most of these beings are demonic."

"Your nose isn't wrong." He pointed down the hall. "It's an amalgamation of things. Various Infernal entities are kept here because they're useful in some way."

"Kept?" Eve took in her surroundings with an examining eye. The lower level of Gadara Tower reminded her of a fifties film noir with its muted lighting, inlaid glass doors, and smoky air.

"Some are held against their will," Alec clarified, "others come by choice, because they want protection. There's no such thing as honor among the damned. If you piss off the wrong guy, they'll hunt you down."

"You don't have to tell *me* that," she muttered, noting the occasional alcoves that boasted widows featuring a nighttime view of a metropolis. It was amazingly believable, but it was still daylight up above. "Is that real?"

"No. Most Infernals go nuts if they feel confined in any way. They prefer night to day, so that's what Raguel went with." Alec paused before a new door labeled Orange County Power and Water Management. Eve frowned, knowing that there was no such entity. He knocked and they waited. "The illusion of being topside keeps them functioning properly."

The door swung open, revealing a young, lanky man standing behind a desk situated directly before the door. He wore gray overalls with his last name—Wilson—embroidered on the breast and military-grade "birth control" glasses; nicknamed for their ability to make anyone look like shit. Beyond him, a partition blocked the view of the rest of the interior. Filing cabinets flanked his left and a large potted palm tree flanked his right. The air escaping the room smelled like cotton candy, which told Eve the man was a Mark and not an Infernal.

"Cain," Wilson said, smiling. "What can I do for you?"

Eve snorted softly. Alec entered a room and everyone started kowtowing. With every day that passed, the image she'd long held of an evil, reviled Cain wore away.

She was bringing up the rear when a group of three Marks rounded the corner—two females and one male. The girls were sporting an odd sort of look consisting of jungle boots, black parachute pants, and strategically ripped tanks in bright colors. The man wore jeans and a baby blue polo shirt. In unison, their gazes raked her from head to toe.

"She's not all that," one gal said to the other with a wrinkle of her nose.

"Cain gets all the pussy," the male said. "I hear Asian chicks are hot in bed."

"Excuse me?" Eve said.

"There's no excuse for sleeping your way to the top," hissed the second girl as they passed.

Eve turned to watch them go, feeling an odd mixture of anger and nausea. "There's no excuse for those clothes you're wearing either," she called after them. "News flash: the eighties ended a couple decades ago."

"Angel?" Alec's voice drew her gaze. He held a clipboard in his hands. "What are you doing?"

"Lagging." She left the hallway and the door clicked shut behind her.

"Come on." Alec held the paperwork out to her. "Fill out your parents' information. And yours."

She looked at the form, noting that it asked for name, address, and phone number for up to three individuals. "Okay."

He smiled. His expression was warm and pleased, telling her how much he appreciated her obedience. That surprised her, considering how easily he accepted the same from everyone else. He seemed more comfortable in command than Gadara did. Gadara manipulated to get what he wanted; Alec simply expected that his orders would be followed.

Alec looked at Wilson. "We have a Nix problem."

"We'll take care of it."

Eve looked up at him. "How?"

"As with any possible infestation," Wilson said, "we prevent the pest from gaining access in the first place. In the case of Nixes, we insert a deterrent into the main water pipe to the residence."

"After you do that, can I take down the crosses I have hanging in my showers?"

"You could." Wilson smiled. "It would only be a benefit to you, though, to keep them up."

She looked at Alec. "Since I'm living in a Gadara-managed building, why didn't I have something like that in place to begin with? It would have saved Mrs. Basso's life."

"We don't work like that." He pushed his hands into his jeans pockets. "Imagine if Infernals set up a barrier in the town of Baker, California. It would effectively prevent Marks from traveling between Nevada and California. We have to work case by case, Infernal by Infernal. Otherwise, we'd end up battling for territory, which would put mortals in the crossfire. We—Marks and Infernals both—need mortals to survive. Since we have a mutual need, we make certain concessions."

Her pen tapped against the clipboard.

He rocked back on his heels. "When, in the last two days, did we have a chance to come in here? Besides, you were safe with me. I never thought he'd hit your neighbor."

The phone rang on Wilson's desk and he answered it. Eve returned her attention to filling out the paperwork.

"They're right here," Wilson said into the receiver. "Yes, of course. I'll tell them." He hung up. "Raguel will be calling in ten minutes. He wants you to take the call in his office."

Alec nodded. Eve passed over the clipboard.

Wilson's gaze was sympathetic behind his glasses. "I'll send someone out immediately."

"Send two people simultaneously," she suggested, "so there's no one to follow from my house to my parents and vice versa." She set the pen on his desk. "Will whatever you're doing keep my parents safe?"

"The Nix doesn't know where they live," Alec reminded. "If he did, he would have gone after them instead of Mrs. Basso. Can he find another way in? Yes. If he finds them and he has the time, he can work it out. But this will slow him down. Hopefully long enough for Hank to find him."

She nodded. As far as feeling better went, it wasn't much, but what else did she have?

"One thing at a time," Alec repeated in a murmur. "We're dealing with the Nix. Now, we'll go upstairs and deal with Raguel. We'll get it all done. Trust me."

Her mouth curved ruefully. "You're good at this, you know. It's a shame you're stuck with someone clueless like me. You should be managing bigger fish."

Alec's face closed, although his pleasant mien did not change. It was more of a feeling she had of a sudden withdrawal, as if she'd struck a deep chord.

The sensation set her mind spinning. By the time they returned to the elevator, she'd thought of something she hadn't before: if nothing was a coincidence, how was it that she lived in a building for which Gadara was the trustee?

Had he been lying in wait for her? If so, what was the event or purpose that set her marking in motion?

And what would it take to be free of it?

CHAPTER 16

Hello, Cain. Ms. Hollis."

As the elevator emptied Eve and Alec into the antechamber of Gadara's office, the archangel's secretary greeted them with a wide smile. He was an elderly man, one who appeared a wee bit past the retirement age. He smelled like a Mark, though, which made Eve wonder what he could have done to get into trouble so late in life. "Can I get you both something to drink?" he offered. "Coffee, perhaps? Or a soda?"

Eve declined. Alec simply shook his head.

The secretary led them into Gadara's office and gestured for them to occupy the two chairs before Gadara's desk. He used a keypad to lower the projection screen and dim the lights. Eve was once again taken aback by the size of the room. It was cavernous and richly appointed. As an interior designer, she was well aware that a person's preference in room size and shape said a great deal about him. Gadara obviously felt a need to astonish and impress. How much of that was directed toward the mortals he did business with? And how much of it was for the benefit of the Marks under his command?

"A penny for your thoughts," Alec said, once the secretary had left.

"I'm not sure they're worth that." Her tone was as dry as her palms. After all she had been through the last several days, she should be a nervous wreck.

"Are you okay?"

Eve looked at him, noting that even in poor lighting Alec was drop-dead gorgeous. The planes of his face were strong and bold, but softened slightly by his overly long hair. She could get used to seeing his face every day. If she let herself. "I don't think everything has sunk in yet. Ask me again, once we've had a chance to settle down."

A soft beeping noise filled the air, then the screen flickered to life. Gadara's face appeared. His dark skin and eyes held a wealth of majesty and a touch of divine refinement that was enchanting. Eve was once again arrested by the sheer force of his charisma, evident even across the digital signal that broadcast him. Behind him was a window, and beyond that was a view she recognized immediately—the Las Vegas strip. He was dressed in a suit and tie today, and the more formal look suited him. It complemented his air of power and affluence.

"We've got a problem," Alec began.

"Yes, you do," Gadara drawled. "Where is Abel?"

Eve's brows rose.

"He doesn't know anything."

"Exactly." The archangel leaned back in his chair and ran a rough hand through his coarse gray hair. "He is her handler, Cain. He needs to be kept in the loop."

"If that's his job," Alec retorted, "he shouldn't need help doing it."

"The two of you are going to get her killed."

"If you don't manage to do that first."

"I'm not going to die," Eve interjected quietly.

The sound of clapping turned her head. Reed exited the elevator in an expertly tailored three-piece suit of graphite gray. The sheer perfection of his appearance—the faultless cut of his garments, the perfect combing of his inky hair, the sensual curve of his welcoming smile—took her breath away. "That's my girl," he drawled. "Don't let them push you around."

Alec pushed to his feet. "Eve was right. The tengu had no details and no scent."

Silence gripped the room so completely Eve could have heard a pin drop.

"What do you mean, 'Eve was right'?" Gadara bit out.

"When the tengu first attacked me a few days ago," she explained, "I noted that he didn't have any details. Alec and Reed both said my super senses hadn't fully developed and that's why I couldn't see them."

"'Super senses'?" Gadara laughed.

"But obviously, they were wrong," she continued. "Alec didn't see anything last night either. You can't tell me he hasn't come into his gifts yet."

Reed moved to the desk and leaned against it. "It's never happened before. All of these centuries, millions of Infernals . . . It's never been possible for an Infernal to hide its details. There has to be an explanation."

"Such as?" Eve asked.

"Perhaps his details are a similar color to the stone from which he's made."

"Okay. Why didn't he stink?" she countered.

Gadara made an odd noise, drawing all eyes to him. "Tell me everything that happened, Cain."

Alec went over the events of the night before, finishing with the death of Mrs. Basso.

Reed moved from the desk to Eve and set his hand on her shoulder. "Were you close to her?" he asked quietly.

"Yes. I loved her."

"I'm sorry for your loss."

"The police came," Alec said. "They say the Nix has been killing for some time. If that's true, why hasn't he been vanquished?"

"The order did not come down, until today," Gadara replied.

"That's sick," Eve said.

"It is the way we work, Ms. Hollis." Gadara's gaze was hard. "We are not vigilantes."

"He's killed at least a dozen people! We're not talking about vigilantism. We're talking about justice and protecting the innocent."

"Do not lecture me," Gadara said coldly. "You want to shed the mark and go back to your careless life. You do not give a damn about protecting the innocent."

A slap in the face could not have affected Eve more. "Don't make me feel guilty for wanting my life back."

"It is one thing to be ignorant; it is quite another to deliberately bury your head in the sand."

Reed moved to a spot a foot or so in front of her. "Don't attack her for our own shortcomings."

"We need to decide what to do about this," Alec interjected, his stance widening and his arms crossing. The pose made him imposing, depicting him as immovable, stalwart.

"What do you suggest?" the archangel asked.

"Both of the tengu on the roof lacked details and smelled normal. The first question I have is whether or not Gehenna Masonry has something to do with it. Did they create both? If so, we know the source."

"I pray we're lucky enough to have this restricted to tengu," Reed said.

Eve looked around at the grim faces of the three men. "Explain the possible ramifications of this to me."

"We do not have enough Marks." Gadara's voice was weary. "We supplement with mortal labor, like the guards you met at the building last night. We also do business with mortals. If Infernals hid in that guise, there is no limit to the places they could go and the information they could obtain."

"Infernals would have a tremendous advantage," Alec said. "They'd smell us coming a mile away, but they could be completely under the radar. If they've created a mask of some sort, we need to eradicate it."

Eve stood. "So we have to find out how they did it. We have to go to Upland, where Gehenna Masonry is."

All three men looked at her.

"Not with the Nix after you," Alec argued.

"And the tengu," Reed added.

"Yes." Gadara smiled like a proud parent. "You should go. The tengu seem to like you, Ms. Hollis, and the Nix has been assigned to a Mark, as of this morning. Right, Abel?"

"Right," Reed said tightly.

"Bullshit." Alec's voice was a low growl. "This is too important to use as a novice training assignment. Eve is in over her head. You need to send someone more experienced."

"Ah, but there is no one more experienced than you," the archangel pointed out.

"Then I'll go alone."

"I have to concur," Reed said.

"With who?" Alec snapped.

"You."

Eve might have laughed at Alec's blatant surprise, if the circumstances had been less somber.

"See, Ms. Hollis?" Gadara drawled. "Miracles do happen."

She looked at Alec. "I can't go home; I can't face it now. And I can't go to my parents' house. If you leave for Upland, what will I do?"

"You can wait for Hank's results."

A dry laugh escaped her. "I'm not going back down there. The Infernals creep me out and some of the Marks are hostile. After I'm trained and can hold my own, no problem. Until then, no thanks."

Alec frowned. "Hostile? What are you talking about?"

Reed drew abreast of her. "There is some jealousy in the ranks."

"She *must* go," Gadara said. "Once a mentor is paired with a Mark, they stay together until the Mark is self-sufficient."

"Don't start playing by the rules now," Alec snapped.

"And do not presume to dictate to me, Cain. If you separate from Ms. Hollis, I will make that separation permanent and pair her with a mentor who will keep her close at hand."

Eve's hands settled on her hips. "No one's buying your 'following the rules' line, you know. Why don't you just tell us the truth?"

Gadara's face split with a smile. "I want you to get your feet wet."

"Whatever," she scoffed. "I've gotten wet plenty of times in the last week."

Alec cleared his throat. Reed grinned.

"You know what I mean," she mumbled.

"Okay," Gadara conceded with laughter in his deep voice. "Whether you believe me or not, I would like you to get your hands dirty. I want you to see firsthand what we do and why we do it, and I trust that Cain will keep you safe under his watch."

I want you to get your hands dirty. Eve considered that statement carefully. Since Gadara didn't strike her as being overly altruistic when his own needs were involved, his statement made her contemplate whether or not her acceptance of the mark was important in some way. And if that was the case, what could her rejection of it mean?

"That settles it, then," she stated, determined to play the hand dealt to her until the end of the game. If Gadara insisted she go, she had to know the real reason why. And frankly, she *wanted* to go. There was a thrumming anticipation in her blood that was becoming all too familiar, a darkness like black velvet—soft, warm, and sensuous. She'd started the morning wanting a few hours of normalcy. Now she wanted to beat the shit out of something not human. Something that would give her a good fight, but wouldn't leave any guilt behind.

"It's not settled with me," Alec retorted.

Reed exhaled audibly. "Just be careful, Eve."

"What?" Fists clenching, Alec glared at his brother. "You're going to agree with this? You pansy-assed motherfucker!"

"Screw you," Reed bit out. "It's what she wants."

"I don't give a shit. She doesn't know better. She hasn't been trained and she's pissed off."

"Um, excuse me." Eve waved. "I'm right here. Don't talk about me like I'm not."

"Sorry." Coming up to her, Alec pulled her into a bear hug.

Eve rested her hand against his abdomen and tilted her head back to look up at him. "We didn't do so bad last night. We're both still kicking."

"You were almost splattered across the street like roadkill." His tone was exasperated . . . and resigned. "How much worse could it have been?"

"This is not open to debate," Gadara said. "Her handler and I are agreed."

Alec's head turned. He shot a killer glance at the screen. "You had better pray that nothing happens to her."

"I pray every day, Cain. Can you say the same?"

Eve tugged Alec toward the door before the situation grew any more explosive.

"This isn't a game, Eve," he warned darkly as the elevator doors shut out the view of a somber-faced Reed. With his hands propped on the handrail, Alec leaned back and glowered.

"It is to Gadara." Her mouth curved grimly. "But damned if I'll play the part of the pawn without making some moves of my own."

Reed watched Eve disappear behind the closing elevator doors, then he faced Raguel. "This is too serious for just one team to handle."

"I am inclined to believe it is their synergy that is causing the problem, not a mask." Raguel adjusted his tie. "I have a meeting with Steve Wynn in a half hour. I wish I looked as good in my suit as you do in yours."

"Are you kidding me? You're going to completely disregard what Cain and Eve told you?"

Raguel relaxed into his chair with a sigh. "You heard his story. He was as focused on Ms. Hollis as he was on the hunt."

"So? He was doing his job."

"Was he? Or is his heart ruling his head? There is a tremendous difference between happenstance and calculation. Cain hasn't been trained."

Reed felt a chill move through him. He knew deliberate obtuseness when he saw it. "You're gambling with something so potentially damaging that I'm at a loss for words. I don't understand why you're not erring on the side of caution."

"You want my job?" Raguel's voice was dangerously soft. "Be my guest. Manage the situation as you see fit."

"With what resources?"

Pristine white teeth flashed within the frame of coffee-dark skin. "With the ones you have at your disposal. I must function within my station. So, too, must you."

"Your station is greater than mine."

"Exactly," the archangel hissed. "Do not forget that."

The screen went black, leaving Reed in turmoil. He had twenty-one charges in total, including Eve. At any given moment, at least one of them was locked in combat that would lead to death—either the Mark's or his or her prey. From the heavens, orders streamed down into Reed's consciousness like water, forcing him to shift through the various threads. He assigned Marks to various hunts based on their experience, location, and a multitude of other factors, not the least of which was the needs of the firm to which he was assigned.

To his knowledge, no handler had ever thinned his charges by setting them on a task of his own design while relying on the others to pick up the slack. Doing so would weaken all of them. Some Marks were better able to handle specific Infernals than others. Assigning a less-talented Mark to the hunt because his more experienced team member was occupied by an unsanctioned task was so dangerous Reed couldn't believe he was even thinking of it.

But what options did he have?

He could use an Infernal, either one presently working within the firm or one scheduled for vanquishing. He could offer a bargain—cooperation or death. Infernals were survivors; they would do whatever was necessary to keep their lives. But it was not his place to decide which Infernals were worthy of saving and which were destined to burn in Hell. As with his previous option—using Marks—Reed had no idea what the ramifications would be for reaching so far beyond his assigned duties, but he knew they would be dire. He needed someone farther up the food chain than he was. Someone to take the heat, if necessary.

He needed an archangel to assist him.

It wasn't completely improbable. As long as he offered a perceived benefit, he could solicit help. Cain made devil's bargains all the time.

Reed avoided the elevator and moved to the reception area instead. He paused before the desk of the elderly Mark who answered Raguel's phones. "Do we have any visiting firms in the area or one scheduled to arrive shortly?"

The firms always kept each other appraised of visits. Putting two archangels into close proximity required greater security, plus they felt it was their due to be shown deference by whoever was visiting.

"The European firm sent seven Marks yesterday," the secretary replied. "Sarakiel is scheduled to visit next week."

Reed nodded grimly. "Thank you."

Of course it would have to be Sara. God forbid his task should be easy for him.

As he prepared to shift from his present location to her office, Reed steeled himself for the task ahead. She'd want his blood.

It was true. Hell hath no fury like a woman scorned.

It was a thirty-minute drive to Upland from Anaheim on a good day. To say the freeway traffic in Southern California was horrendous would be an understatement. Stop-and-go speeds added hours to most trips, and accidents often turned highways into parking lots.

Today wasn't too bad because it was still early afternoon, not yet the time when most residents began their commutes home. Alec stared out the passenger window, the fingers of his left hand brushing back and forth over the denim that covered his knee. He was quiet, contemplative.

He and Eve had left Gadara Tower through the subterranean parking complex using a Jeep Liberty that belonged to Gadara Enterprises. He hoped that move would throw anyone following Eve's car off the trail, which still sat in the street-level parking lot. With suspicious cops and an overzealous Nix, they couldn't be too careful.

Eve drove to a strip mall and parked. Exiting through the rear door of a nail salon, they walked up the road to a Hertz rental car agency and picked up new wheels. Alec paid with cash rather than a traceable credit card. Now they were settled in a Ford Focus whose satellite transponder wasn't monitored by Raguel—at least not at present. The archangel would catch on eventually and when he did he would tap into Hertz's tracking system. For now, however, they were off the radar.

Not a word passed between them during the exchange; there was nothing to say. Eve didn't trust Raguel and Alec couldn't defend him. The entire situation was fucked six ways to Sunday.

"He who is a hired hand," he murmured, "and not a shepherd, who is not the owner of the sheep, sees the wolf coming, and leaves the sheep and flees, and the wolf snatches them and scatters them."

"What?" Eve asked.

Alec glanced at her. "John 10:12."

"You're calling Gadara the hired hand? You think he's tossed us to the wolves, too?"

"I don't know what to think, angel." He leaned his head back against the headrest. "I'm having a hard time understanding how he can be so cavalier about something so important."

"He doesn't believe us," she said flatly. "It's either that, or he believes it and wants the shit to hit the fan. Any idea what reasoning he would have to allow that to happen?"

"No."

Alec had never liked the archangels. Similar to children, they curried the favor of their father. They competed with their siblings in the hopes of outshining them. Marks and their mentors and handlers were simply a means to that end. That was why Alec had come to appreciate his autonomy; it kept him far beyond their machinations.

"And that whole 'get your hands dirty' excuse is crap," Eve said crossly. "I'm not buying it."

"I'm not either."

"So what's the point?" She looked at him. "What could he possibly gain beyond pissing you off?"

"Are you asking me, or just talking out loud?"

"Of course I'm asking you." Her eyes went back to the road. They were traveling a respectable seventy-five miles per hour on Route 60. The windows were up so they didn't have to shout, but the air conditioner was on. The chilled air ruffled through Eve's hair, blowing loose tendrils from her ponytail across her cheek. She swiped at them impatiently. "You know what's going on better than I do."

"Not really," he said dryly. "That's the problem. I've never had a handler or worked within a firm. My orders come directly from Jehovah. I have no idea how to function within a framework. You and I are completely in the dark with this."

"Okay, then. How would you handle this if you were on your own?"

Alec didn't hesitate to answer, because he'd been thinking of his options ever since the night before. "I would set up camp in Upland. Infernals can smell me coming, so I would stake out the masonry and break in during off hours. Then I'd dig around."

"Let's go back to the smell thing." Her fingers flexed on the steering wheel. "If I was omnipotent and I created a legion of warriors to fight on my behalf, I wouldn't advertise them with a unique scent. I'd want to keep them hidden."

"Deer smell the wolves coming. This hunt isn't any different from what you see in the animal kingdom."

"It's like he's giving them a chance to get away with whatever they're doing."

"The Lord has a strong sense of fair play."

"Or a sick sense of humor."

"Angel—"

"So let's follow your plan," she said quickly. "We'll grab a hotel room, then stake out the masonry."

His eyes closed. He reached out blindly to set his hand on her thigh. "We don't have a choice. I'm sorry."

Her hand settled over his much larger one. Eve was slender and delicate, far too precious to risk so pointlessly. "One step at a time."

"You sound good," he murmured. "Focused."

"I know what we saw, or more aptly what we *didn't* see." Her voice flowed over his skin like sun-warmed honey. "I've never had aspirations of saving the world, but obviously I am not going to turn my back and pretend nothing is happening."

Alec opened one eye and turned his head. "Don't let what Raguel said get to you."

"That's easier said than done." The corners of her mouth took on a downward curve. "He's right. It's one thing to be ignorant by accident; it is completely different to be ignorant by choice. I wanted to go to the damn movies, Alec, when all Hell has broken loose—literally. What is the matter with me?"

"I understand why you wanted some time alone today. I can't tell you how many times I've wished I could be normal for even an hour. That doesn't make you a coward and it doesn't make you wrong."

"Doesn't make me right either."

Eve looked at him. The sadness in her eyes combined with the determined set of her jaw hit his gut like a blow. He was struck with the knowledge that more than one woman had died today. The young girl he had known and loved was gone, never to return. She had been ripped from her safe, orderly life and thrust into a world where demons hunted her and dear friends paid the price.

Scrubbing a hand over his face, Alec tried to hide his disquiet from Eve. As he mourned the loss of his first love, fury and frustration ate at him. In only a matter of days it had become too late to save her.

Yet it wasn't too late to save the woman sitting beside him now, the woman holding his hand and suggesting she stand with him as he tackled an assignment unlike any he had ever faced before.

"This isn't your fault, Alec."

A dry laugh rasped from his throat. "Are you trying to comfort me? After what you've been through?"

"This hasn't been easy on you either. You've given up a lot for me."

He stood to gain a lot more. But she didn't know that.

Beauty is in the eye of the beholder. One man's goddess was another man's nightmare. Sara Kiel, however, was beautiful to all who saw her. Tall, willowy, yet fully curved, Sara was physically perfect in a way that plastic surgeons would sell their souls to replicate. There had been a time when the mere sight of her could make Reed's blood heat dangerously. Now, he watched her with an indifferent eye, admiring her with only a vague interest.

"I find it nearly impossible to believe that Raguel has not acted on this information," she said, pacing gracefully. She reminded him of a tigress—golden, lithe, predatory. "Perhaps he knows something that you do not."

"Or perhaps he wants to keep the information as contained as possible," Reed countered.

Sipping from a glass of icy water, he lounged on the golden velvet chaise in Sara's Parisian office with one arm slung over the back. The head of the European firm of Marks was often assumed by theologians to be a male. They couldn't be more wrong. Sarakiel was a woman in every sense of the word.

Today she wore a pinstriped pantsuit and tie, an ensemble that might have made some women look masculine. On Sara, it only emphasized her divinely enhanced femininity. Her pale blonde hair was pulled into a classic chignon and her face was devoid of the makeup that funded her firm. Sara Kiel Cosmetics was a worldwide phenomenon, with sales inspired by the unequaled face of its owner.

There had been a time when Reed thought they were exceptionally suited to one another, but that was long ago. He had become jaded enough to admit that an outward sense of style and a mutual fondness for rough sex was not enough of a foundation for any sort of lasting relationship.

"Raguel knows," Reed continued, "that Cain is too much of a loner to approach anyone else for help and Evangeline is too green to do anything on her own."

"Ah, the notorious Evangeline," Sara cooed. "I plan to visit Raguel soon. I am dying of curiosity about Cain's woman. In fact, I sent a team to California yesterday to prepare for my arrival."

Notorious. Reed's jaw tightened. "She's just like any other woman."

"Is she? She is the only thing besides blood that you have shared with your brother." Sara's smile turned brittle. "Tell me, *mon chéri*, what is it like fucking a woman who bears your mother's name?"

"Who says I fucked her?"

"There is no way you could resist. And certainly she would not be able to refuse you."

He shrugged.

Sara returned to the topic at hand. "I am certain Raguel expected you to keep the news quiet, because doing so places your brother in jeopardy."

"Who knows what he thinks?" Reed dismissed.

"I am more concerned with what you are thinking. I admit to being surprised that you are here. Moreso than I am that he is not."

"This goes far beyond the North American firm. The development of an Infernal mask places everyone in jeopardy."

"So what do you want me to do?" Her fingers stroked sensuously along the length of her tie.

Behind Sara, Reed could see the Eiffel Tower glittering with lights in the darkness. Odd that the backdrop would be so similar to the one he'd seen behind Raguel just a short time past. Two archangels, two continents, same view. They had more in common than that; they were both ambitious and frighteningly competitive.

"I want you to lend me the team of Marks you sent to California," he said.

Sara laughed. "You do not ask for much, do you?"

"Nothing you can't afford."

"The question is: can you afford it?" The glint in her eye confirmed his earlier suspicions about what she'd want from him.

"You ask that as if it were a hardship," he drawled. He deliberately focused on not betraying his growing tension. "Don't forget how much you stand to gain beyond the immediate. To have your team outwit Raguel's would be quite a coup for you."

"I know how this benefits me, but what does it do for you?" Her blue eyes narrowed. "In addition to incurring Raguel's wrath, you are also foregoing the possibility of humiliation for your brother."

Reed stared through his drinking glass to the cubes of ice within. He rattled them absently before casting Sara a sidelong glance. "Forego Cain's humiliation? Darling, you wound me. What could be more perfect than being the instrument of his deliverance and the tool by which he is rescued?"

He didn't say that Jehovah might find his initiative pleasing, especially considering the possible consequences of failing to act. Pleasing God would only increase his chances of gaining a firm of his own.

But Sara was aware of some omission, as evidenced by the doubtful humming noise she made.

Setting his glass on the gilded coffee table, Reed stood. It was time to move in for the kill.

She held up one hand. "Did I not say that you would come back to me . . . on your knees?"

A smile curved his mouth. "But it's so much more fun for both of us when you are on yours."

Her lips parted and she backed up a step.

Reed moved toward her with deliberate leisure, his fingers on the buttons of his waistcoat. If he didn't see to his own undressing, Sara would tear his garments from him. She took such pleasure in ripping into his outer shell, as if that would somehow expose the man he was within.

He could see the anticipation race over her skin and knew her nipples would be tight and hard, her sex hot and slick. Two weeks had passed since he'd indulged in Eve. Two weeks of celibacy that should have left him hungry for the hard screwing Sara relished. He hadn't gone this long without a woman in centuries.

Shrugging out of his coat and waistcoat, Reed tossed them over the back of one of the chairs facing Sara's desk. He tugged off his tie and belt, adding them to the pile. With every article of clothing he shed, Sara's excitement grew. He could smell her lust, see it in the brightness of her eyes and the nervous licking of her lips. She reached into his pocket, withdrew his cell phone, and turned it off. Then she tossed it over to the chaise.

Reed reached for his fly. Her gaze dropped. He thought of stairwells and cameras and thickly lashed slanted eyes. His cock finally cooperated with his intentions, hardening from the heated memory.

"Before we get distracted," he murmured, "I want you to tell your team in California to get ready for a mission."

"I need them," she retorted. "I'll send another."

His hands dropped to his sides. "They may not get there in time. That isn't a chance I'm willing to take."

Sara's jaw tightened when she realized he'd leave if he didn't get what he wanted. "You drive a hard bargain, *mon chéri*."

"Isn't that why you like me so much?"

CHAPTER 17

Eve pulled into the parking lot of a Motel 6 just off the highway in Upland. There was a convenience store adjacent and a grocer's up the street. Turning off the ignition, she glanced at Alec before opening the door. He hadn't said a word over the last few minutes, retreating into himself and hoarding his thoughts. She knew this was as difficult for him as it was for her. If she'd ever consider praying to a higher power for anything, it would be for the ability to help him instead of hinder him.

She pushed the door open and exited. Resting her forearm on the roof of the car, she looked around. Upland was inland from Orange County, which made the temperature hotter and the air drier. She missed the ocean breeze already, but Eve suspected that was part of a general homesickness for anything familiar. She was separated from her family and her best friend, she'd lost her job, and Mrs. Basso was gone. A hotel stay in a strange town only added to her feeling of being a fish out of water.

Water.

Thinking of the Nix, Eve pushed away from the car and shut the door. Alec appeared on the opposite side. Tall, dark, handsome, and brooding. He slipped shades over his eyes, hiding his thoughts from her visual probe. There was a huge gulf between them at the moment. Like the tide against the shore, they crashed together and drew apart.

"After we get a room," she said, "I need to hit the convenience store for a soda and a prepaid cell phone."

He smiled. "You'd make a good spy, I think."

"I have a fondness for action flicks."

Alec came around the trunk and offered his hand. She accepted, but the closeness was only superficial. Emotionally, he was miles away, which was why she took a room with two double beds.

"You two got any pets?" the desk clerk asked. He was a young man in his midtwenties, Eve guessed. Overweight by about sixty pounds and a mouth breather.

She shook her head. "Just us. Please don't put us in a room that has had pets before. I'm allergic to cats."

"No problem." He leaned over the counter and lowered his voice. "Someone in the area has been stealing pets and hacking them up. It's in all the local papers. Just wanted to warn you."

"Hacking them up?" she repeated, remembering the article she'd read earlier that morning.

"Nasty stuff. Disemboweling, removing the eyeballs . . . that sort of thing." His tone was more gossipmonger thrilled than it was disgusted or disturbed. "I read once that most serial killers start out mutilating animals, then they progress to people."

"So this area isn't safe?"

"It is for humans." He shrugged, straightening. "Not so much for pets."

While she signed the paperwork, Alec paid the balance in cash. He stared at her from behind his shades, but didn't say a word until they went outside.

"Something you want to say to me?" he asked as they skirted the front office and crossed over to the 7-Eleven parking lot.

"About what?"

"About the two beds?"

"No pressure."

"Hmm."

An electronic beeping announced their entrance into the convenience store. Out front, three cars were filling their gas tanks at the pumps. Inside, an elderly woman with big white hair manned the counter and two teens stood by the coolers against the rear wall, looking at the soda.

Eve grabbed a hand basket by the door and moved to the prepaid phones hanging on an endcap.

Alec gestured to the soda fountain. "Want something to drink?"

"Diet Dr Pepper, if they have it. Otherwise, I'll get it in a bottle."

"Okay."

Alec walked away and she rounded the aisle, grabbing beef jerky, nuts, and Chex Mix. She had a vision of lying across her motel bed with junk food, soda, and a movie on the television. The mere idea of a few hours of decompression was heaven on earth. They wouldn't head out to the masonry until night, so she had time to vegetate and make sense of life as she now knew it. With that in mind, she grabbed chocolate, too—Twix, Kit Kats, and Reese's Peanut Butter Cups.

Eve was making her way around the next aisle when the Infernal stench hit her. She sought out the source of the putrid smell and settled on the teenagers by the rear cooler. One wore a hooded sweatshirt with the hood up. The other wore a Hurley T-shirt and unkempt hair. On his nape, a tattoo of a diamond animated. It rotated, displaying the glimmer of its various facets.

She gaped, unmoving. As if he felt the weight of her stare, the hooded boy turned his head toward her. Eve's gaze dropped, her obscenely steady hands absently pulling unknown items from the shelf into her basket. She continued down the aisle, witless with fear.

Look harmless and busy, she told herself.

"Angel."

Jumping a good foot into the air, Eve spun to face Alec, who approached with a rapid stride. He caught her elbow and drew her farther down the aisle, away from the Infernals.

They were everywhere. How could she have forgotten that for even a moment? The weight of the knowledge was crushing.

As they feigned a preoccupation with shopping, Eve and Alec furtively watched the two young men withdraw energy drinks from the cooler and head up to the register. The clerk greeted them cheerfully and rang up their purchases. Her eyes were rimmed with gobs of mascara à la Tammy Faye Bakker and her lips were rimmed with the wrinkles of a lifetime cigarette smoker, but her smile was genuinely warm and her manner sweet.

The woman had no idea what she was dealing with.

"You okay?" Alec murmured as the young men left the store.

Eve nodded and released her pent-up breath. "They just took me off guard."

He rubbed her lower back.

"You know," she said, "I appreciate being able to smell them. I think I'd always be terrified if I was second-guessing everyone I met."

Alec nodded grimly.

"I guess my nose still isn't working right, though," Eve noted. "You smelled them from across the store. I had to get within a yard of them."

"I didn't smell them."

"Then how did you know?"

He glanced at her. "One of those boys just got his number called."

It took a heartbeat's length of time before she understood. "You?"

"Yeah. Me." He urged her to the register. "Our stay in Upland just got a lot more complicated."

Reed's fingers were sliding between Sara's thighs when he felt the first wave of Eve's terror. Like ripples on water, the distance between them made the feeling faint, but it was unmistakable nevertheless.

Squeezing his eyes shut, he rested his forehead against the window where he'd pinned Sara. There were other sensations to process beyond Eve and the woman in his arms—there were the other twenty Marks under his watch, orders from the seraphim, and the occasional check-in from Raguel's switchboard.

"Tease," Sara whispered, her lips to his ear.

Distracted, he moved by instinct, parting her and stroking through her slickness. She moaned. He knew just how to touch her, how to pleasure her, how to give her exactly what she wanted.

Her teeth nipped his ear and he reacted accordingly. The hand he had pressed against the window for leverage moved to her throat. Reed fought the urge to hurry the business along. He had to keep her busy long enough to make their agreement worth Sara's while. Otherwise, she could withdraw her Marks from his command before they had a chance to be put into play.

Sara's manicured fingertips dug into his waist and her lungs labored, pushing against his chest in an elevated rhythm. Sex was one of the few times when a celestially enhanced body responded without restraint. Orgasm-induced endorphins were the drug of choice for many, including Reed.

As Eve's distress peaked, goose bumps swept across Reed's skin. Sweat dotted his upper lip and pooled in the small of his back. The urge to go to her was so strong he quivered with it. He told himself it was because she was untrained and therefore dangerously vulnerable. It was an occupational reaction, nothing more.

"I love it when you shake for me," Sara purred, her nails raking the length of his back.

Reed kept his eyes closed, imagining that the silky tissues that clutched at his thrusting fingers belonged to another woman.

I-I don't normally . . . do things like . . . this.

Eve's trembling voice whispered through his mind. She didn't know it—and he wasn't certain he would ever tell her—but their coupling in the stairwell had been raw in more than just the fierceness of the sex. He had compelled her away from the crowd, but once they were alone he'd done nothing to keep her there. He hadn't been able to, because he was too focused on her—the smell of her, the feel of her, the depth of her hunger. It had been as intimate an encounter as he'd ever experienced.

Sara liked rough sex, period. The person administering the roughness was moot. It was the thrill and the acts that she relished, not her partner. Eve, on the other hand, had been completely taken aback by her enjoyment of his handling. It had been *him* she responded to. No other man could have reached her the same way.

"Hurry," Sara hissed, her sex sucking voraciously at his pumping fingers. She released his waist and pushed impatiently at her wide-legged slacks. They fell to the floor in an expensive pool around her Manolos.

He stepped back long enough to shed his own pants. He briefly noted her black garter belt and silk stockings, then he gave a hard tug to her thong and dropped the ruined undergarment to the floor. She couldn't shrug out of her jacket fast enough. Before she could loosen her tie, he'd shoved her back into the window, pinning her to the cool glass.

Her smile lit up the room.

There was a brief moment when Reed thought about bending her over the desk and fucking her from behind. But this way had memories he was relying on to perform over the next several hours.

With his hands behind her thighs, he lifted her. Then he paused, his gaze locked with hers. "You know what to do."

Sara reached between them and positioned him at her entrance. He stepped forward and dropped her simultaneously, impaling her in one hard thrust. Her cry pierced the air and charged his nerve endings. With his erection clasped in slick, liquid heat, his body took over from his brain. Finally.

Using his arms and thighs, Reed moved her up and down over him, stroking deep and fast. The erotic slapping of their bodies filled the room and spurred his lust. He focused on the feel of her clenching and releasing around his aching cock, the sensation hardening him further, making him throb with the sudden rush of blood to the swollen head of his dick.

She moaned as he filled her, stretched her, the grip of her body becoming fistlike in its intensity. Physically, it was damn good. He worked her up and down his cock with greater fervency, charging forward in his drive to culmination. His balls drew up, his spine tightened, his lungs heaved with his exertions. Sara's orgasm rippled along his length, bathing him in the creamy, fiery wash of release. Her moans only added to his pleasure. For all her angelic beauty, Sara sounded like a porn star during sex. It roused the animal in him, turning him on to a near fevered pitch.

Which was still nowhere near as hot as he'd been in the stairwell.

Emotionally, he and Sara were on different continents. Sara's eyes were closed, her head thrown back, her thoughts her own. Reed's mind was with Eve, his sexual energy focused on her, his soul directed toward soothing the fear he felt in her.

His rhythm faltered when he sensed her reaching back, a chaste touch, like a handhold in the darkness. Her spirit brushed across his as ephemerally as smoke, yet it rocked him to the core. With a roar, he climaxed. Sara shivered into another orgasm with a high-pitched squeal.

Eve brought him to his knees before the glass, with Sara scratching at his back and hours of servicing her left ahead of him. In the aftermath, he gasped for breath and longed for a shower. Left unguarded by the force of his release, he wasn't prepared for the sudden piercing agony that broke his connection to Evangeline.

One of his Marks was dying.

Reed groaned in agony and pushed Sara away. His back arched, thrusting his chest forward and his arms out. Pain and sorrow radiated from him with white-hot heat. His skin glowed with the effort to contain the herald of his charge—an instinctive cry for help from Mark to handler that was occasionally so powerful it was sometimes sensed by mortals. A sixth sense, some called it. The feeling of something being "wrong" or "off," but they didn't know what.

"Takeo," he gasped, calling out the name of his charge. Takeo had waited too long to call for help; Reed could feel the power of the mark draining from him. It was an aching feeling of loss that was amplified through Reed and sent outward to the firm. The death of a Mark was news that was carried through the soul and not through secular lines of communication. As the force of the herald left him, Reed collapsed forward, gulping in air.

"I have to go," he panted.

"You cannot save your Mark." Sara's lovely face was flushed, her lips red and swollen even though he hadn't kissed her. "And if you leave before we are done, you will not save *her* either."

"Her?" Reed reached for his slacks.

"Evangeline." Her smile didn't reach her eyes. "You think a woman does not know when the man she is fucking is thinking about someone else?"

"Sara . . ." he warned, his fists clenching.

"It is too late to save Takeo and you know it. You just want to alleviate your guilt by consoling him in his final moments." She stabbed a perfectly painted red nail into his pectoral. "I want you to live with that guilt. I want you to remember how you failed your Mark because you were whoring for your brother's lover."

He slapped her, open-handed across the face. "You don't know what you're talking about."

She laughed and rubbed at the red mark left by his palm. Then she spread her legs, revealing the glistening pink folds of her sex. "Get to work, before I decide you are not worth the inconvenience you have caused me."

"How did you get called?" Eve asked, as Alec led her quickly across the parking lot back to the motel.

"The mark tingles," he said, "then burns. Toss me the car keys."

She did as he asked. "Like when you lie?"

He shot her an arch glance. "I don't lie."

"I did. And the mark burned."

Alec gave a wry laugh.

"It also burned when I entered Mrs. Basso's condo," she said. "It gave me the energy to break through the locks."

The line of his mouth thinned. "I know. The burning of your mark is just like getting an FTA—a failure to appear notice for a bail bond skip."

He unlocked her car door, then rounded the vehicle to the driver's side and climbed in.

"You didn't mention the door-breaking thing to Gadara," Eve said, just realizing that omission.

She accepted the bag of merchandise he set in her lap, moving it to the floorboards between her feet. Straightening, Eve was arrested by a sudden rush of warmth moving through her chilled veins. The sensation felt almost as if a warm blanket had been tossed around her shoulders. A blanket that smelled distinctly like Reed.

"I wanted to see if Abel would say anything." Alec turned the key in the ignition and backed out of the parking spot. "He's the one who triggered your mark. That's his job as your handler."

Eve watched him maneuver into traffic, still processing the rapid disbursement of her fear. One moment she was scared out of her mind, the next she felt cocooned and protected.

As if he was guided by radar, Alec quickly found the two boys strolling down a side street and fell into a safe surveillance distance behind them.

"What does that mean?" she queried. "Did he know about Mrs. Basso?"

"Handlers aren't necessarily aware of the particulars of the crime. They usually only know what class of demon the target is and which Mark in their stable is both local *and* qualified."

"Well, you can't get any more local than right next door."

"Or any less qualified that an untrained novice." He exhaled harshly. "Abel's job is to assign the most capable bounty hunter to each individual hunt, even if that means the Mark has to travel like we did today."

Eve's hands fisted in her lap. "Once a Mark is assigned, can another one step in?"

"Another Mark won't get the call, no."

Reed saved him for me.

Warmth blossomed in her chest, which scared her. She was grateful to be given a chance to kill. What did that make her? Besides homicidal?

"Raguel knew nothing about Abel assigning the Nix to you," Alec continued grimly, "which means Abel is acting on his own."

"Do handlers work for multiple firm leaders?"

Alec shook his head. "They work for one firm, that's it. But they are somewhat autonomous. They're *mal'aks*—angels—so they have full use of their gifts. They can route assignments to whomever they wish."

"Perhaps Reed doesn't trust Gadara either."

"Or maybe Raguel deserves the benefit of the doubt and my brother has something crafty up his sleeve," he snapped. "But I guess you don't want to think about that."

"Hey." Eve twisted in her seat, adjusting her seat belt for comfort. "Don't get pissy."

"Raguel is an archangel, Eve. His love for God is absolute."

"I don't buy it, I'm sorry. I haven't seen a drop of compassion in that guy. A lot of self-interest and bullshit, but love and compassion? Not at all."

"And you've seen love and compassion in Abel?" he scoffed. "When exactly was this? When he was banging you into servitude in the stairwell? Or when he blew off your training to assign you to a demon bent on killing you?"

Alec pulled the car over to the curb just before a cul-de-sac. The street sign named it Falcon Circle. The boys had turned the corner just a minute earlier. Eve hopped out before the vehicle stopped rolling. She continued on foot, anger and frustration riding her hard. On the left side of the road, the streets were open-ended. On the right side—the side she was traversing—all the streets were dead ends that butted up against a short field with a copse of trees beyond it.

The engine shut off and the driver's-side door slammed shut behind her, but Eve kept going. When she reached the corner, she paused and watched the two young men enter a home at the very end of the street. It was a two-story house with a deeply arched roof. The paint was a popular eighties-era scheme of light brown with chocolate trim. In the yard was a tricycle that had seen better days, and a lawn with bare patches and weed-infested flower beds. A covered car sat on one side of the driveway, while the adjacent side was stained with the remnants of an oil leak.

The day was bright and sunny, but a massive overgrown tree shaded the house and kept it in darkness. The residence was depressing, especially amid the other homes that showed signs of owner pride and attention. Alec's prey lived in the neighborhood eyesore, and the air of decay and neglect gave Eve the chills.

"Now what?" she asked when he drew abreast of her.

"Now I wait until the time is right. I know where to find him."

"Can you tell me how we're expected to get anything done? You're getting called . . . I'm getting called . . . we're both getting called together. How much shit is God going to throw at us?"

"He doesn't know what's happening, angel."

She snorted. "The all-seeing, all-knowing creator of everything is clueless?"

"He listens, He doesn't watch."

Eve opened her mouth to argue that point when she remembered that God hadn't known Alec had killed his brother. He'd had to ask to find out. "Maybe you should tell him to give us a break, then."

"Usually, a mentor's sole job is to teach. As Raguel said, once a mentor/Mark team is created, they are inseparable until the Mark is capable of functioning alone." Alec gestured impatiently back at the car. "In my case, God wasn't willing to lose me as an individual unit. I told Him I would do both jobs at the same time. It was the only way to be with you."

Eve's pique drained away in a rush. "Alec—"

"That doesn't explain why Abel is giving you hazardous assignments before you're ready or why Raguel doesn't know about it."

"You don't trust your brother at all."

"No, I don't. I have yet to see him give a shit about anything besides himself."

"That isn't how the popular story goes, you know."

The look he shot her was derisive. He opened the passenger door and waited for her to get in. "I know."

"So tell me what happened. What have you two been fighting about all these years?" She had to wait for him to settle into the seat beside her. Though it only took a minute or so, it seemed like forever.

As he pushed the key into the ignition, Alec kept his gaze straight ahead. "What do all men fight about?"

"Territory, goods, women."

"Right."

"Well, which is it?"

He put the transmission into gear and turned the car around, heading back the way they'd come. "All of the above."

Raguel returned to the penthouse suite of the Mondego Hotel in Las Vegas, Nevada, which he owned. It had been a long day and since it was only six o'clock in the evening, it was nowhere near over. The red tape involved in renovating a resort was daunting and exhausting. There were months of meetings and mountains of permits to file. Soon he would need Ms. Hollis's input to continue. It would give them plenty of time to work together and forge a bond, a bond that would assist him in managing Cain.

Raguel briefly noted the panoramic views afforded by the walls of windows around him, before turning his attention to the desk in the corner.

"Report," he ordered the secretary who waited there. Kathy Bowes wore dark slacks and a white turtleneck sweater, and looked every bit as young as she'd been when marked at the tender age of fourteen. She was kept close to home to keep her alive. There was more than one way to kill a demon, and some Marks were best suited to safer tasks than a physical hunt.

The secretary stood and read from a pad of paper in her hands. "Three Marks lost today. Two Marks acquired. Possible sighting of a new breed of Infernal. Uriel called and would like you to call him back—"

Raguel scowled. "Three Marks? Who were the handlers?"

"Mariel lost a mentor/Mark team to the Infernal she didn't recognize—"

"Is that the possible new breed sighting?"

"Yes."

He loosened his tie. "I want her full report."

"The recording is on your desk."

"Who else?"

"Abel lost one."

Raguel paused, disquieted. "Who did Abel lose?"

"Takeo, a former Yamaguchi-gumi yakuza member. He was very good. Forty-seven kills."

Relief flooded the archangel, and reminded him that he was taking a dangerous gamble. The loss of Evangeline Hollis would create an enemy in Cain that would jeopardize centuries of work. But the possible rewards were worth the risk.

Raguel knew that Ms. Hollis needed to find self-confidence in her abilities *in spite* of Cain rather than *because* of him. Past observations of her had revealed that she was ambitious and determined. Cain's mentoring of her had been a curve Raguel wasn't expecting, but he believed it was still possible for her to achieve an identity separate from her mentor.

The seven archangels were tasked with the training of new Mark recruits. They rotated the duties for the sake of fairness. For seven weeks a year, each archangel was given free rein to use his or her powers in the training process. Raguel had deliberately delayed Ms. Hollis's training so that it would fall into his rotation. He would give her a level of attention he'd never bestowed on any other Mark. A bond would form organically. He fully intended for her to align with him so completely that she related to him more than with her mentor and her handler.

Cain responded to stress with aggression; he always had. By keeping him edgy and off-guard, Raguel would promote tension between him and Ms. Hollis. Abel's obvious infatuation with his brother's lover would assist with that. She couldn't have both of them, and being torn between the two would prevent a deep attachment from forming with either one.

"Is Abel's report on my desk, too?" Raguel asked.

"He hasn't filed one yet. Just the herald has come in."

The archangel frowned. Abel was unfailingly prompt with all his reports, which were voice recordings made on the scene that were later transcribed onto celestial scrolls for future reference. While some handlers required time to absorb the loss of a Mark, Abel found solace in the act of witnessing the Mark's sacrifice for divine consideration. Some Marks were forgiven their trespasses, regardless of the number of indulgences earned.

Raguel moved to his office. He briefly skimmed the various items that had been left on his desk for perusal and approval. He flipped through several mock-ups of advertisements for his numerous ventures, pausing briefly on two options for invitations to the grand opening of Olivet Place. It was fortunate that the tengu had been vanquished prior to the ribbon cutting. Then he picked up the disk labeled Mariel.

Something niggled at him.

"Ms. Bowes!" he yelled.

"Yes?"

"Confirm Cain and Ms. Hollis's whereabouts."

"Of course, sir. I'll see to it immediately."

Eve never thought she would be happy to hang out in a Motel 6. Her personal preferences were much more upscale. But right now, she was looking forward to the tiny room off Highway 10 as if it were the penthouse suite in the Mondego.

She climbed out of the passenger side of the Focus and stretched. An aftereffect of the mark's release of adrenaline was the lingering sense of physical restlessness. Emotionally, however, she just wanted five minutes to enjoy some chocolate.

Pulling the motel key from his pocket, Alec unlocked their ground-floor room and ushered her inside. The space was small, about the size of Eve's guest bathroom. The two double beds barely fit inside, with the bed farthest from the door pushed up right against the bathroom wall and the nearest bed having scarcely enough room to fit in the window air-conditioning unit. The decor was motel classic—busy-printed coverlets that hid stains, nondescript wallpaper, and a three-paneled painting of the beach above the two headboards. A small fridge sat by the dresser and the sink waited beyond that, conveniently—though unattractively—built outside the shower and toilet area.

Alec set the keys and their purchases next to the television and pushed his shades onto his forehead. He leaned back against the dresser and crossed his arms.

Eve sank onto the edge of the bed nearest the door. "Can you pass me a Kit Kat?"

He reached for the bag. Digging inside, he laughed. "What the hell did you buy?"

She thought back to her time in the store. "I'm not sure. For a while there, I freaked out."

Alec straightened and dumped the contents onto the other bed. Eve stood and surveyed the pile.

"Antibacterial dish soap?" He arched a brow at her. "Floral air freshener. Unscented baby wipes. Two packages of lime-flavored gelatin. Beef jerky. Facial tissue enhanced with lotion."

She picked out the chocolate and the cell phone, arranged the pillows on her bed, and sprawled against the headboard. A moment later she was munching on what she considered to be manna from someone's god. She plugged the AC adapter for the phone into the outlet in the base of the nightstand lamp. Then she dialed her parents' house.

It rang three times before, "Hello?"

Eve breathed a sigh of relief at the sound of her mother's voice. "Hey, Mom."

"Where are you calling from?" Miyoko asked. "The caller ID says 'unknown caller.'"

"Long story. How are you?"

"I'm okay. Your dad isn't. He's mad."

Darrel Hollis's version of mad was a long-suffering look. He never raised his voice, never got physical. Eve suspected his blood pressure was on par with her new Mark stats. "Oh? About what?"

"The city turned off our water and started digging up the yard. They have to fix a leak. I told your dad it was time to resod anyway."

Eve smiled, relieved that the mark system had moved so promptly. "Tell him to look on the bright side," she suggested. "This might save you money on your utilities bill."

"Your dad says I'll spend the savings on the new yard, so he's not getting ahead."

Her mother's love of horticulture and feng shui had led to a desire for a curving stone walkway flanked by lush flower beds. Her dad, on the other hand, thought their straight cement pathway was just fine.

"He'll get over it," her mother dismissed. "Want to come over for dinner?"

"I can't tonight."

"You have a hot date?"

Eve laughed softly. "Not even close. I have to work."

"That's good. A woman should always be self-sufficient—" Eve's father said something in the background. "Your dad says congratulations on the new job."

"Tell him thanks for me. You're not going anywhere today, are you?"

"No. Why?"

"No reason. I've got to go now, Mom. Did this phone number show up on your caller ID?"

"Yes, the number is here. Just no name."

"Okay. Call me if you need me."

"Evie-san . . ." Her mother's voice took on a concerned tone. "Are you okay?"

"Yeah, I'm fine. There's just a lot going on right now."

"Take your vitamins," Miyoko admonished, "or you'll get sick. Stress weakens your immune system."

"I will. Talk to you later." Eve snapped the phone shut and stared at it for a long moment.

"Are they all right?" Alec asked.

She nodded and bit into a Twix bar.

"I want to stake out the masonry," he said. "Are you up for that?"

She was up for anything that gave her something to do besides contemplate how screwed up her life was. "Why did we come back here, then?"

"Bathroom break."

"Gotcha." Eve chewed with gusto.

Alec's arms crossed, causing his T-shirt to strain around his biceps in a way that melted the chocolate in her hand. As she licked her fingertips, he watched her with a guarded expression. "Are we fighting?"

Eve shrugged. "I'm just waiting for you to finish your explanation about your brother."

"I don't want to talk about him."

"Okay, then."

He exhaled in a rush. "I don't want to talk about him *with you*."

"I got it."

She turned her head to look out the window. The sounds of the nearby highway blended with the sound of blood rushing through her veins. She inhaled and smelled the familiar scent of Alec the instant before he climbed over her and caged her to the bed.

"Hey," he murmured, tossing his sunglasses onto the nightstand tucked between the two beds.

"Hmm?" She stared up at him, admiring the fall of dark hair over his brow. Every part of her tingled with awareness. Determined not to act as devastated by his nearness as she felt, Eve stuck the other Twix in her mouth.

Alec lowered his head and bit off the protruding end of the candy bar. A low sound of pleasure rumbled up from his chest. She watched him turn the act of chewing into foreplay, the steady clenching of his jaw a surprisingly erotic sight.

They swallowed in unison. Their lips parted in tandem. Then his tongue was stroking across hers. She shivered beneath him. Sexual tension and chocolate, could anything be more divine? Alec's hand moved to her waist and anchored her, his hips sinking between her thighs as she opened them.

Her arms wrapped around his shoulders, pulling him closer. His body mantled hers; his warmth and strength became hers.

"I'm sorry," he whispered.

Eve didn't know what he was apologizing for. His curtness earlier? Or maybe everything?

She pushed her fingers into his thick, silky hair. It felt so good to be held. A tear slipped down from the corner of her eye, then another. Tears that had been lying in wait since she'd found Mrs. Basso that morning.

Alec rolled to his back, taking her with him. He draped her over his body, whispering soothing words of comfort. In her mind, another soul touched her. She didn't know Reed at all, but that didn't matter. She found solace in the evanescent feel of him.

Together the two brothers gave her the brief respite she needed.

CHAPTER 18

Reed flinched away from the nails that scraped down his back. He stood with his forehead resting against a granite shower stall, one arm hanging at his side, the other pressed against the wall above his head. Steam swirled around him and scorching hot water sluiced down his spine.

"Leave me in peace," he growled, his lower lip throbbing from the sting of Sara's bite.

"The team is ready to go," she said. "They're waiting in Ontario, California."

She was docile now, appeased and somewhat contrite. It didn't matter. He hated her in that moment, hated how she made him feel about himself, hated that she'd seen motives he hadn't wanted to acknowledge. But most of all, he hated that Eve was in pain and he'd had to feel it while buried deep inside another woman.

He shouldn't give a shit about Eve. What did he know about her?

Sadly, the excuse had no validity. Cain didn't know any more about Eve than Reed did, but Cain loved her.

Reed shut off the water and accepted the towel Sara offered him. She wore a short white silk robe and her silver-blonde hair hung loose around her shoulders. She couldn't look more angelic. "You are truly worried about her," she said.

"You should focus less on her and more on the reason why there's cause for concern."

"I *am* focused," she retorted. "That is why I am accompanying you."

"Like hell." He scrubbed his head with the towel.

"You forget your place."

Dropping the towel on the floor, Reed brushed past her and moved into her office. He retrieved his clothes and dressed with deliberation. There was no point in arguing. He was in full control of his gifts. The archangels, however, paid a price for using their powers. Reed could be in California in a blink of an eye. Sara had a long flight ahead of her.

"I want you to fly with me," she said.

He glanced at her and smiled.

Her gaze hardened. "We were good together."

"Occasionally."

"Then why are you so distant?"

"You manipulate me, Sara." He crossed over to the wet bar and used the mirror there to adjust his tie. "I'm just an object to you."

"You used me, too."

"You're right, I did." He had once been foolish enough to hope that she might help him achieve his own firm. They could work together, he'd thought, and thereby be twice as strong. Then he realized that not only would she never allow her "boy toy" to achieve similar stature, she also didn't want to add to her competition. Perhaps more so than her six counterparts, Sara saw the other archangels as impediments in her relationship with God. "We both got something out of it."

"Then, why her and not me?"

His gaze met hers in the mirror's reflection. "You don't love me," he scoffed.

"I am not talking about *my* feelings. I am talking about yours."

A bark of laughter escaped him. He returned to her. "I don't love her."

She studied him with narrowed eyes. "But you want her."

"And you've hit on Cain in the past." His hands gripped her forearms through the silk, his thumbs stroking rhythmically. "Do I hold that against you?"

Her hands went to his waist and he released her, backing up. He pulled on his coat and waistcoat, then slipped on his shoes. "Let's not make this more complicated than it has to be."

"It could be wonderfully simple," Sara said. "We could work together."

Reed paused in the act of buttoning his vest. Why would she offer help now when she wouldn't before? "Doing what?"

"Getting Cain away from Raguel." Her arms crossed. "It would leave the field open for you."

Cain. Of course. Reed's jaw clenched. Raguel would no longer have such a heavy advantage over Sara without him.

"I'll think about it," he said, then he shifted to Takeo.

Eve splashed water on her face, then leaned into the counter. Her eyes stayed fixed on her own reflection. It was safer than looking through the open bathroom door at Alec in the shower. They'd received a discount on the room because they didn't need a bathtub. She hadn't considered that they might get a glass-enclosed shower stall.

"Angel?"

Her fingers dug into the counter. "Yeah?"

"Can you hand me a washcloth?"

She looked at the towel rack on the wall next her. Pulling a rolled washcloth free, she took a deep breath and entered the bathroom. Alec stood with arms akimbo and feet planted slightly apart. He faced her head-on, his mouth curved in a wicked smile. Surrounded by steam and dripping with water, he was the embodiment of her hottest sexual fantasies. Ripples of lust flowed over her skin, building with every passing second.

"You're rotten," she scolded, tossing the washcloth over the glass.

He caught it with a wink. "Care to join me?"

"I showered this morning." She set one hand on a cocked hip. "Besides, we've yet to have sex that didn't last several hours. We don't have that kind of time."

"A quickie?"

"I'm marked, too, if you've forgotten." Eve pulled open the glass door. She touched him reverently, brushing her fingertips over one dark nipple. His sharp inhalation made her smile. "I could probably ride you for *days* and call it a quickie."

Alec caught her hand and kissed her knuckles. "I'll take a rain check."

Revved up with nowhere to go, Eve returned to the bedroom. She busied herself with cleaning up the second bed, returning their convenience store purchases to the bag. That took about half a minute. Then she sank onto the mattress and gazed about the room.

"A stakeout." She reached for the nightstand drawer. As was to be expected, a Bible waited there. Eve pulled it out with a resigned sigh. Part of her had always believed it was fiction, or at least highly fictionalized. More like fables than absolute truths. But it was hard to deny the whole of it, when part of it was naked in the shower.

Eve reached to close the drawer. She paused at the sight of the postcards inside. They were generic cards for the motel, worn from frequent handling and boasting a photo taken many years back, if the cars in the picture were any indication. But it wasn't the image that arrested her, it was the card itself.

Alec came out of the bathroom whistling. He wore one towel low around his hips and used another to scrub at his hair.

"Hey." She caught his gaze. "We never figured out what was up with that invitation I received for the tengu building."

His arms lowered.

"You didn't tell Gadara about it either," she noted.

"I'm not used to sharing every little detail with someone."

"Are you sure it's not because you don't fully trust him?"

"I'm sure."

Her nose wrinkled. "Okay, so I'm playing devil's advocate here—"

"Sammael doesn't need any help." Alec tossed one towel on the bed, then pushed the one around his waist to the floor.

Eve glanced at the window, wondering if the sheers covering the glass really offered any privacy, or if some lucky gal was getting an eyeful. During the day they were opaque, but it was the other side of dusk now and their lights were on.

"What if Gadara orchestrated the tengu thing?" she suggested.

"Why?" He tugged on a pair of boxer briefs. She took in the view with a smile. David Beckham would be out of an endorsement deal with Armani if the advertising team saw Alec in his skivvies.

"As an excuse to keep me out of training?"

"Why would he deliberately orchestrate things to keep you untrained? There's no benefit to anyone."

"You have a better idea?"

"Maybe a masked Infernal did it."

"Why?" she tossed back at him. "Kind of stupid to draw attention to themselves, don't you think?"

"Unless they wanted you out of the picture before you Changed. Dead men tell no tales."

"Are you telling me that people in Heaven don't spill their guts?"

"You're agnostic, angel. Are you sure that's where you would go?"

Eve blinked at him. "Yikes."

He held both hands up in a defensive gesture. "Just sayin'. An Infernal would think similarly."

"The card was mailed the day before I was marked. That's cutting it close, don't you think? Why use the postal service? Wouldn't it have been safer to slip it under my door or something?"

Alec stepped into his jeans. "Good point."

"Okay, let's run with your idea. I'm harmless, so they weren't after me per se; they wanted to get to you. How did they know I was going to be marked? How did they know God had agreed to allow you to mentor me? No matter what—whether it was a masked Infernal or Gadara—it would have to be an inside job."

"Or a mystery." He straightened. The hair on his chest and abs was still damp. Eve fought the urge to lick him like a Popsicle. "Don't forget: Marks are trying to save their souls."

Eve smiled. "I didn't say a Mark did it. But you're thinking it's a possibility."

"Did I say that?"

"I'm learning to read between the lines with you. Maybe the situation is something like the Infernals working for Gadara? Satan has to have something to offer, right? And Marks are made up of sinners, not the pillars of society."

"I'm following, but where is this leading?" Alec pulled his shirt over his head.

"We're just speculating."

"I'm not a speculative thinker. Give me facts and proof."

"I'm a creative thinker. I like to explore all the possibilities."

"Okay, then." His arms crossed. "How about the possibility that God sent you to that church for a reason? And maybe that reason was to discover that Infernals were masking themselves. After all, you went there before the invitation ever had a chance to be put into play."

Her nose wrinkled. "What kind of facts are involved in that theory?"

"The spiritual kind."

Alec sat on the bed and reached for his socks. He shifted, pulling the wet towel out from under his ass and tossing it into the corner under the sink.

"Don't you know you're not supposed to put wet towels on the bed?" she asked wryly. Her gaze lowered. "Or the floor?"

"It's a guy thing."

"I don't think so. It's an Alec thing."

His dark eyes sparkled with laughter. "You've never had a boyfriend leave his towels lying around?"

"No."

"Bullshit."

She laughed. "I'm serious."

"You have obviously never lived with a man."

"With parents like mine? Are you kidding?" Eve shook her head. "My dad is the quiet type, but he has old-fashioned values. And my mom is a fan of Dr. Laura. Shacking up before marriage is a big no-no in my family."

Smiling, he stood and held out a hand to help her up. She accepted, then turned to put the Bible in the bag with their purchases. She was taking it with her to pass the time and the last thing she needed was for a motel employee to think she was stealing it.

Alec closed the blackout curtains and went to the door. "Ready?"

"As I'll ever be."

"What do you mean they are *gone*?" Raguel barked, glaring across his desk at Ms. Bowes.

"I'm s-sorry." She shifted her weight from one foot to the other. "I said that incorrectly, sir. They ditched the Jeep at a strip mall. A nearby rental car agency recognized their photos, so we know they aren't on foot."

"Of course they are not on foot! They went to Upland. They just wanted privacy while getting there." Which infuriated Raguel to no end. They could not be allowed to become a self-contained unit. "Abel knows where they are."

"He hasn't checked in since the herald."

Raguel sent an order through the celestial lines of communication that existed between the archangels and the *mal'akhs* beneath them. He was met with silence. "Get him on his cell phone."

"I've tried. It goes directly to voicemail."

Raguel stood and stepped out from behind his desk. The secretary backed up warily.

He told himself the three—Cain, Abel, and Eve—couldn't be working together. There was too much enmity between the two brothers. But what would explain how they all fell off the radar at the same time? What could they be thinking . . . planning? He couldn't afford to lose control of their trinity. He needed them to achieve his aims.

For the space of several heartbeats, Raguel considered using his gifts to find them. But in the end, he resisted the prod of impatience. He had enough transgressions to pay for and there were other ways to gather the information he needed. Although Abel was presently ignoring him—an aberrance of behavior that increased Raguel's alarm—the other handlers would not.

"I will send Mariel after Abel," he said, running a hand over his short, coarse hair. He had sprinkled it with gray about five years past, to simulate mortal aging.

"Yes, sir."

Ms. Bowes left the room in a rush, and Raguel moved to the window. He took in the view of the Las Vegas Strip below. Sin City. A hotbed of iniquity. And he was trapped here in this world, living a life that wasn't his, working to save the souls of man because God held them in such esteem. They were so small and weak, yet He adored them and considered them His greatest creation. Because of them, He waged a hidden war against the Fallen One, a conflict so deep beneath mortal consciousness that no ripples marred the glassy surface. The Lord would never bring the matter to a head. Devotion was more powerful when it came from faith and not from absolute proof.

So Raguel helped the situation along on his own. Step by step. Carefully planning and maneuvering. The sooner the arrival of Armageddon, the better. He was certain the Lord would appreciate the tapestry, once it was fully threaded. It was, after all, an incredibly clever scheme.

Cain and Abel had set the chain of events in motion by fighting to the death over a woman. It was only fitting that they should bring about the end of days in the same fashion.

The moon was hidden by the canopy of tree leaves above him, but Reed's enhanced sight had no trouble seeing in the darkness. He moved through the Kentucky forest like a wraith, swift and silent.

His veins still throbbed from the force of Takeo's herald, sent hours ago. Takeo meant "warrior" in Japanese, a fitting moniker. He had been a perfect Mark; his training as a yakuza assassin had stood him in good stead. Reed missed him already and knew he would miss him for years to come. None of the other Marks on his team had been as skilled in killing tommy-knockers—malevolent faeries with a fondness for mines. Which was why Reed was so shocked by his death. The assignment he had given Takeo should have been a simple one: vanquish a troublesome tommy-knocker.

A twig snapped to his right and Reed paused. The forest was deathly quiet aside from that one noise, a sure sign that nature had been seriously disturbed.

"Abel," a familiar female voice greeted.

"Mariel. What are you doing here?"

The *mal'akh* appeared from behind a nearby tree. Although the night robbed the color from everything, he knew her hair was red and her eyes green. She wore a floral dress, jean jacket, and cowboy boots, as well as an oppressive air of melancholy.

"Raguel sent me after you, most likely as punishment for losing two Marks today."

"I'm sorry."

"As am I." She pivoted and gestured to the right. "This way."

Reed followed her to the edge of a clearing. She paused there and he drew abreast of her. A chill swept down his spine that had nothing to do with the temperature.

The clearing was not a natural feature. Decades-old trees had been felled and pressed into the ground, deep enough to create a flat surface. The night breeze blew, whistling eerily through the limbs and boughs, fluttering through tissue that clung to stems and errant grass. Tissue bearing the colorful markings of *irezumi*—"hand-poked" Japanese tattoos.

"Dear God," he breathed, recoiling. "Is that skin?"

Blinking, Reed engaged the nictitating membranes that enhanced his night vision. The silver and black of the moonlit vista changed into living color.

Blood red. Everywhere. On every leaf and blade, on every inch of bark, all the way to the sky. As if Takeo had exploded from the inside out, splattering his body from the earth to the heavens.

"What happened h-here?" He cleared his throat. "What did this?"

As if in answer, an owl cooed its sorrow. A wolf howled in torment and was quickly joined by several of its pack. As the forest denizens sobbed their tales of the night's events, a cacophony of grief rose to the heavens. It hammered at Reed from all sides and nearly brought him to his knees.

Mariel's hand reached for his. She squeezed gently. "I don't know."

The din ceased as quickly as it had begun. A weighted sense of expectation replaced the mourning. They wanted to know who would save them from the fate they'd witnessed that night. They listened avidly, unmoving and barely breathing.

"One of my charges and her mentor were killed this way today," she said. "I felt the herald and I went to them immediately. *Immediately.* But it was already past the time when I could have done anything to help them.

The mentor was already dead. It was as if they waited too long to call me—"

"Or the Infernal struck too harshly and quickly."

She pivoted to face him. "The same happened to you."

He nodded. Exhaling a shaky breath he surveyed the scene again. There was nothing but gore left of Takeo. "Did you see what did this?"

"Barely." Her green eyes were wide, haunted, and shining with tears. "It was a monstrous beast; easily several feet in height. Flesh, not fur. Massive shoulders and thighs. It crawled inside my Mark . . . disappeared in her. She c-could not c-contain it."

"Mariel—"

"The slaying happened so fast. I barely saw it, didn't even smell it. I was so numb . . ." She gave a shaky exhalation. "I stared Sammael in the eyes once and I wasn't as scared."

No scent.

Reed closed his eyes and reached out to his charges, one by one. They touched him briefly, consecutively, assuring him of their safety. All save one.

Eve, he called.

Like the fluttering of a moth's wings, he felt her. Barely there, too green and untrained, too distant from her own soul to know how to reach out with it. What he felt most keenly was the silence where Takeo used to be. It was deafening.

"I need to make my report," he said softly.

Mariel nodded. "I'll wait for you."

"I have a favor to ask of you instead." Reed leaned closer and lowered his voice. "I need you to go to California . . ."

"Can I get out and stretch?" Eve asked.

Alec looked away from the masonry. He saw the dashboard clock and winced. Almost midnight. As usually happened during a hunt, he'd lost track of time.

Despite the lateness of the hour, the masonry yard was far from quiet. Trucks moved in and out. The perimeter was surrounded by a stonework fence topped with wrought iron. Through the bars, Alec watched bags of what appeared to be cement off-loaded, while various stonework pieces— fountains, statues, and benches—were loaded onto flatbeds and driven away.

Aside from the odd time, there didn't appear to be anything suspicious on the surface. But then again, when it came to Infernals, it was what you didn't see that was the most dangerous. There was also the added difficulty of searching through a facility that was never asleep.

"You must be bored out of your mind," he murmured.

Eve's smile was sheepish. "I'm sorry. I feel like I should be doing something or helping you in some way."

"Just having you here is enough." He reached out to her, catching her hand and lifting it to his lips.

Her fingers tightened on his. "I brought reading material, but I didn't think about the fact that there wouldn't be any light."

"I can help with that."

"Oh?" Her smile widened.

Alec caressed her cheek with his fingertips. "Close your eyes."

She followed his instructions. She waited with an air of expectation that reminded him of their first night together. He'd blindfolded her for a time, teasing her with feather-light touches and whisper-soft kisses until she quivered all over.

As he had back then, Alec drew out the moment, making her wait until she trembled in her seat, allowing the tension to build until it nearly steamed the windows.

"Alec?" she queried breathlessly.

Unable to resist, Alec closed the space between their two seats and pressed his lips to hers. A soft gasp of surprise escaped her and he took the invitation to deepen the contact. Tilting his head, he fitted his mouth to hers. Their breaths became one, mingling.

Eve surged into him with a soft sound of need, her fingers pushing into his hair and holding him close. She gave as good as she got, her lips slanting across his, her tongue stroking deep and rhythmically until his cock ached with the need to pull her over his lap and slip inside her. The mark on his arm began to burn.

Trouble was coming.

He tore his mouth away. "Do your eyelids feel heavy?"

"You have no idea," she husked.

"Roll your eyes behind your lids."

"They're rolled back in my head." She nibbled along his jawline. "My toes are curled, too."

A laugh escaped him. "Open your eyes slowly."

He pulled back enough to watch her. She blinked, then her head turned back and forth. "Holy strawberries, Batman." Her tone was awed. "I can see in the dark."

"Part of the Change you went through adjusted the nictitating membrane in your eyes. Rather than being useless, they now enable you to hunt with greater precision."

"This is really freaking cool," she said, surveying the world around her.

In the periphery of Alec's vision, a light went out.

"Perfect timing, too," she murmured.

His head turned to Gehenna Masonry and found that the exterior lights had been turned off. He glanced at the clock. Midnight.

"Hey." Eve's voice had lowered. "See that guy padlocking the front gate? Isn't that your assignment? That kid we followed from the 7-Eleven?"

Alec didn't have to confirm the identification visually. The throbbing of his mark and the subsequent pumping of adrenaline through his system told him everything he needed to know. "Yes, that's him."

The young man finished his task, then set off walking down the street with his hands shoved into the pockets of his jacket—a jacket that bore the Gehenna Masonry logo of a gargoyle on the back.

"He works there," Eve noted.

"Yep."

"There is no such thing as coincidence."

"Right."

"So now what? Do you want to go after him?"

"Not yet."

"Why not?"

He stroked the backs of her fingers. "Because he's a wolf. Killing wolves is a messy business. It has to be done in a way that doesn't incite the wrath of his pack. Survival of the fittest is something they understand and respect. A silver-coated bullet to the back of the head isn't."

"You don't have a gun. You're playing it safe because of me."

Alec didn't deny the accusation, because it was true. Eve was going through a trial by fire and he saw no benefit in making it worse. She didn't need any more death today. What she needed was a victory, however small.

"One thing at a time," he said instead. "Let's deal with the masonry first. Once we're certain the yard is cleared, we can hop the fence and take a look around."

"Breaking and entering?"

"Uh-huh."

"Great." Her tone was dry and resigned.

Alec reached over and patted her thigh. "This is just a reconnaissance mission, angel. We get in, look around, and get out. No problem."

"Things haven't worked out that well for me so far."

"The only constant is change," he said, tossing her a reassuring smile. "The tide will turn eventually."

A frown marred the space between her brows and her head cocked to the side as if she was considering something. "The tide, huh?"

She bent over and dug into the bag between her feet. "I wish I'd picked up bottled water instead of some of this other crap I snagged."

"You must be hungry, too."

"Ravenous." Eve straightened with a bag of beef jerky in one hand and something else that she stuck in the pocket of her pants.

"After this, I'll take you to Denny's."

She winked at him. "You big spender, you."

Alec laughed and exited the car. The masonry was dark and quiet.

Rounding the front end of the Focus, he opened the passenger door for Eve and stole a kiss the moment she straightened.

"What was that for?" she asked, eyes bright in the moonlight.

"For being so good about all of this." He didn't explain that he felt the weight of guilt heavily. If he hadn't intervened and requested to mentor her, she might have been assigned a nonfield position. In fact, she most likely would have been, considering she wasn't prone to violent acts. It was his determination to protect her that had put her in danger to begin with.

"Hold that thought." Her nose wrinkled. "I might royally screw things up in a minute."

He shut the door and caught her elbow. "Come on. Let's prove you wrong."

They walked up the road some distance, then crossed the street to the side the masonry was on. The area was industrial and therefore quiet as a cemetery at night. They passed a tow yard guarded by two Dobermans. The canines whimpered softly from a seated position, but made no other noise.

"Some guard dogs," Eve scoffed.

We're very good.

She stumbled. Alec helped her regain her footing. Wide-eyed, she stared at the animals.

"Yes," Alec confirmed. "You heard right."

"They talked."

I *talked*. The bigger dog's head tilted. *My mate is offended by your insult.*

Eve blinked, apparently too stunned to say anything. Then she found her voice, "I'm sorry. I didn't know."

You should train her, Cain.

"I'm trying," Alec replied. "Have you seen anything suspicious going on at the masonry up the road?"

No. They don't come down this way, and we can't see past the auto body shop from here.

"Okay. Thanks."

Alec urged Eve to keep walking.

"Be careful," she said to the dogs, thinking of the motel clerk's gossip.

You, too.

She faced forward, looking more than a little bit stunned. "Okay . . . I'm Dr. Doolittle."

"You're more animal than human now," he explained.

They reached the far edge of the masonry property. Looking through the bars, Alec studied the building and the surrounding displays and empty driveways. "I'll hop over first."

"Go for it."

"See you on the flip side," he said. Then he climbed over.

* * *

Eve tried not to be creeped out by the masonry yard, but it was difficult. She had warned Alec that she was a big chicken, but he didn't seem to believe her. Or perhaps he forgot she told him that. Either way, he was progressing through the outside displays with ease and she was jumping out of her skin at every turn.

So many of the marble statues were classical reproductions with their eyes turned heavenward and torment on their alabaster features. Gargoyles with leering maws played hide-and-seek among benches and bubbling fountains. The sound of water chilled her blood and exacerbated her feeling of dread. She was a Pisces and she was now afraid of water. Her hand went into her jeans pocket.

Her eyes never left Alec. Using hand signals, he directed her movements, telling her when to proceed and when to halt, when to crouch and when to stand still. There were cameras stationed at each fence corner and on the corners of the buildings, too. Alec knew just how to avoid them, and Eve found his expertise both impressive and reassuring.

They reached a door to the main building, which housed a showroom. He paused a moment, looking at the security system keypad. Then he signaled for her to keep going. They moved to a larger building in the back, one whose walls were made up of cement blocks. She wanted to ask why they'd skipped the other, but didn't dare make a sound.

Constrained to the shadows, Alec took several long minutes to maneuver the distance from the main showroom building to the workspace in the rear. When they finally reached their destination, Eve noted that there was no security pad on the back building and the doorknob had no slot for a key. Alec opened the door and sniffed the air inside, then he pulled her in.

"Why did we come here?" she asked.

"Gut feeling."

"Is that like a cramp? I've got one of those. I think it's fear."

He squeezed her hand.

Eve took in the gigantic room in a sweeping glance. Even with her super sight, the ceiling vaulted so high above them that it was nestled in shadow. Dominating the space was a massive kiln with rollered tracks leading into and out of it. It was presently cold. A pallet truck waited like a silent sentinel. Alec headed toward it. He moved fluidly, skirting around protruding pipes and hoses from the kiln. Eve attempted to follow suit and hit the floor in a face plant instead.

"You okay?" Alec asked dryly, standing over her with hand extended.

"Bruised my ego, that's all."

She accepted his help to gain her footing, then dusted herself off while looking for whatever had tripped her up. "Who the hell leaves bags of cement on the floor?" she groused.

Alec's head tilted to line up his sight with the lettering on the bag exterior. "The manufacturer's label says it's crushed limestone."

"Whatever. Shouldn't this be somewhere besides underfoot?"

Crouching, Alec scooped up some of the contents that had escaped from the hole she'd created with her boot tip. She sank back down and he held his hand out to her. The limestone hit her nose wrong. It was sickly sweet, but with underlying musky notes.

"It stinks," she said.

"It's bone meal."

"Smells weird."

"That's because it's part canine and part Mark."

Eve froze. *"What?"*

Alec punched through the thick brown paper exterior of a second bag lying nearby and she gagged from the resulting odor. He looked at her.

"Sorry," she muttered. Her body may not be able to vomit anymore, but that didn't stop her mind from sending the signal to wretch.

His hand came out covered in dark powder. "Blood meal."

"My mom uses that stuff for gardening. I didn't know they had any other uses."

"I don't think they do." He lifted his fingers closer to his nose. "Again, part animal and part Mark."

"How are they getting the blood and bone of Marks?"

"You don't want to know."

She swallowed hard. "Is that how they're masking the Infernals?"

"That's my guess."

"Why is this just lying around? Shouldn't they be guarding this stuff? It's just dumped here like—"

"Like they bailed in a hurry?" He stood and surveyed their surroundings. "If we scared them off, they know we're here."

Frantic scratching broke the silence. Eve leaped a good foot into the air. "Jesus! Oww—" Her hand covered the burning mark on her arm.

They both looked down the length of the massive space. In the far right corner two protruding walls met to create a separate room. From behind the door, the scraping grew more frenzied.

"The animal mutilations," Eve whispered.

"Right."

"We have to get them out of there."

"Yes." Alec dusted off his hands.

They hurried to the door. Grabbing the levered handle, Alec pulled, but the portal didn't budge. Whining could now be heard clearly from inside.

Eve set her hands over his and tugged with him. The door gave way with explosive violence, sending them to their backs on the floor. Nothing ran out in eagerness for freedom.

Alec leaped to his feet, then pulled her to hers, pushing her behind him.

"I've suddenly got a bad feeling about why there's no lock on the door," Eve muttered.

"You should."

Before she fully registered the source of the voice behind her, Eve was lifted and tossed like a rag doll against the kiln. She fell to the floor in an agonized pile. The lights inside the small room blazed to life, revealing a space crawling with tengu.

"Fuck!" Alec said, just before they yanked him inside and slammed the door shut.

Eve gained her hands and knees, lurching forward to help him. She was grabbed by the scruff of her neck and hauled upward. She blinked, finding herself staring into the face of the young wolf.

He didn't smell. He bore no designs. That was all Eve could register before he drew his fist back and knocked her out.

CHAPTER 19

Alec was on the wrong side of an ass kicking.

Backed into a corner, he was barely managing to keep the horde of tengu from overtaking him. There were at least two dozen of them, built of stone and giggling maniacally. Some swung from the shelves, others danced on the fringes, still others hopped from foot to foot and punched with their fists like miniboxers.

With sharp kicks, Alec kept most of them at bay, but the sheer number of them and their crushing weight were beginning to take their toll. It didn't help that he was scared shitless about Eve. He'd heard the force with which she struck the kiln. Even with her ability to heal rapidly, a full-body blow like that was devastating. She was untrained and completely on her own.

A tengu swinging from the ceiling kicked at the space between Alec's shoulders.

"Oomph!" He fell to his knees, groaning.

The tengu laughed and danced with greater frenzy.

"Cain! Cain!" they sang.

Alec glared and pushed to his feet, grabbing the closest tengu and bashing it into one of its brethren. They both shattered. The others recoiled to the walls with a collective gasp.

"Who's next?" he growled.

They hesitated, wavering. Tengu were more mischievous than malicious. They weren't combatants by nature and an implied threat to their lives was enough to send them scurrying for safety. Alec took the opportunity presented to him and lunged toward the door. As if he'd shattered the fear that held them still, they leaped toward him as a single mass, a ton of writhing stone bearing down on him.

They're going to crush me.

Steeling himself for the inevitable, Alec was startled by the sudden burst of power that flowed into him. It originated in his diaphragm, then exploded outward like a supernova, burning through his veins.

He recognized the cause immediately: there was a group of Marks in the area.

Alec hit the door with his shoulder and broke it completely from its hinges. Riding atop the slab, he skidded along the cement floor like a body boarder skimming across water. The tengu raced out of the room after him . . .

Then the lights came on.

Alec kept sliding parallel to the lengthy kiln. The marauding tengu paused. The momentum of those bringing up the rear was halted abruptly by those in the front who'd frozen in their tracks. They crashed into each other like a freeway pileup.

A cowboy-booted foot halted Alec's ride with jarring force. He looked up.

"Mariel."

The pretty redhead smiled. "Hello, Cain. Having fun?"

He sat up. Mariel held out a hand to help him to his feet. Behind her stood a team of several black-clad Marks, male and female. They were fully armed with 9 mm pistols strapped to their thighs—the personal guards of an archangel. They took a unified step forward. The tengu tripped over themselves scrambling back into their little room.

"Eve?" he asked, looking around the space.

"She's not with you?"

"No. She was attacked." Dear God. "I was delayed in there." Alec jerked his chin toward the corner where a few of the Marks were restoring the door to its space and securing it by moving the pallet truck in front of it. He breathed deeply, hoping against hope that some trace scent of the Infernal had been left behind for him to follow. But there was nothing.

As the rhythmic beeping of the truck warned any bystanders that it was moving in reverse, Mariel's head turned to watch. "We went to disable the alarms and cameras," she said, "but someone was there before us."

"There's also no way to see which direction they might have taken Eve." He glanced around. "Why are you here and not Abel?"

"Raguel detained him."

"Raguel sent his own guards, but not her handler?"

"They're not Raguel's," she said softly. "They're Sara's."

Alec stilled. His brother had gone behind Raguel's back . . . *for Eve.* Abel never did anything that didn't directly benefit himself in some way and he never broke the rules. Perhaps he expected Eve to be appreciative, or maybe he just wanted to show that Alec wasn't capable of his new and unfamiliar position.

Mariel reached out to him, her hand resting lightly on his biceps. "I saw an Infernal tonight, Cain. One with no scent and no details. Your brother wanted a team available to support you."

Fists clenching, Alec spoke words that cost him dearly. "We need Abel here. He's the only one who can tell us where Eve is."

A consoling smile touched Mariel's lips. "You two will have to work together for once."

He growled low in his throat. "I'm going to take half the team. Can you collect some of the contents of these bags and anything else you find, and get them back to the firm? The sooner we get to working on the mask, the better."

"Of course."

"And fire up that kiln. Burn whatever you can't take with you. Don't leave anything behind." He gestured toward the guards standing nearby.

"Come with me," he ordered, striding past them toward the door. "There's someone who might know where she is."

Reed glanced at his Rolex with clenched jaw. In Las Vegas time, midnight was when the party was just getting started. For him, however, he was achingly conscious of how late it was and how long it had taken to get from point A to point B. Almost twelve hours had passed since he left Gadara Tower. It seemed like twelve years.

Leaning against the railing of the Fontana Bar at the Bellagio, he watched the water show with barely restrained annoyance. How could Raguel go about his business with such insouciance after listening to both Cain's and Mariel's recountal of the day's events? And how could he insist that Reed report in person, knowing he was needed elsewhere?

"Where have you been?"

Reed turned and studied Raguel as he stepped out to the patio dressed in a classically simple tuxedo with a two-carat diamond stud in his right ear. Around him was an entourage of Marks—protection against Infernals. Once, the archangels had made every effort to keep as low a profile as possible. Now it seemed that with every new persona, they strove to outshine each other. They claimed it was necessary in order to create sufficient funding to manage their firms, but whether that was true or not only they would know.

Pride was one of the seven deadly sins. Had they forgotten that?

"Didn't you listen to Mariel's report?" Reed asked.

The archangel's arms crossed. "Of course."

Reed tossed the jump drive that held the final words spoken on Takeo's behalf. He prayed his advocacy would be enough to spare the Mark's soul. "The same thing happened to my Mark."

"Do you agree with Mariel that the Infernal is of a new class of demon?"

"I don't know. I didn't see it or any trace of it; nothing remained that would assist in an identification. With the extent of the destruction, the clearing should have reeked for yards away, but whatever it was, it left neither a scent behind nor anything of Takeo beyond his skin and tissue."

Raguel stared at him.

"Have you nothing to say?" Reed asked tightly.

"Your brother and Ms. Hollis dropped off the radar this afternoon."

"She doesn't trust you." And Reed was beginning to feel similarly. He might have commented on the weather for all the concern Raguel was displaying.

"She needs to."

"Then give her reason to." Reed straightened. "I don't understand what you're doing—or more aptly, *not* doing. How is a novice supposed to?"

There was a long silence, then, "Is she safe?"

"So far."

"Are you going to her now?"

"If you don't mind."

"Tell Cain to report in. I want to know where in Upland they are."

Reed smiled. "You could send a team with me, you know. I wouldn't mind. I'm sure they wouldn't mind either."

"You worry about your job, Abel. I will worry about mine."

With a mocking bow, Reed skirted the archangel and his guards, and crossed through the busy bar. The location of their assignation didn't escape a deeper perusal. Raguel said he had a meeting there that he couldn't be late for. However, Reed suspected there was more to the choice. Perhaps it was a definitive statement of Raguel's disregard for the unfolding events of the day.

But if that was the case, why was the archangel so certain of his safety? Had arrogance truly made him ignorant? Or did Raguel know more than he was willing to admit?

Eve woke to an icy deluge. Choking, she struggled to curl away from her torment and found herself strapped to a spindle-backed chair with her wrists bound in her lap.

Blinking, she glared at the young wolf who held a newly empty bucket in his hands. The air stunk of blood, urine, and shit.

"What is it with Infernals and water?" she snapped.

He simply stared at her, his face devoid of expression. He looked to be around sixteen years old. His hazel eyes were cold and barren, soulless. His hair was a mop of dark curls, his chin was weak, and his lips were full and pouty. The boy had the sullen look down to a science. His jeans were baggy and ripped in several places, and his Gehenna Masonry windbreaker was filthy.

"You shouldn't have taken her," admonished a voice from a speakerphone on the wall.

The tone was androgynous, or perhaps it only sounded that way because of the white noise in the background. Was the owner the other boy she'd seen in the convenience store?

Infernal or not, there was no way two teenage kids pulled off an endeavor as enormous as this one by themselves. An adult owned the masonry and secured the permits, vehicles, and contracts. And an adult certainly knew about this hellhole.

Eve shuddered as she studied her surroundings. The space was decorated in horror movie chic. A lone naked lightbulb hung from the ceiling, casting a distinct foot-wide circle. The cement floor was stained with reddish-brown splatters she thought might be blood. There was a noticeable pattern to it, a distinct line where unmarred floor gave way to gory floor. On the very edge of the circle of light was a horizontal bar of silver metal—the edge of a gurney, like the ones she'd seen in the medical examiner's room on *CSI*. It had been pushed aside to make room for her.

Beyond the gurney, the shadows whimpered and writhed. Because of the intensity of the wattage above her, Eve's nictitating membranes weren't useful at all, leaving her blind but for the young wolf standing in front of her.

"I tried to draw them away, but they didn't follow," the boy said petulantly. "By the time I came back to see where they'd gone to, they were digging around the kiln room. What else was I supposed to do with her?"

He tossed the bucket aside. It crashed into something metallic and Eve jumped. A dog's frightened bark rent the air. A kennel, maybe? The resultant din of scratching and shifting suggested there were several creatures restrained in the darkness.

"How did they find us?" the voice asked.

"How the hell would I know?" the wolf muttered. "If not for Jaime, I wouldn't have even known we were being watched."

"What did Jaime do?"

"He didn't do anything, besides knock his girlfriend up. He had a delivery in Corona, which only took him an hour and a half, so he came back hoping to make another run. He noticed them sitting in a car on a side street before he left and again when he came back. He thought it might be Yesinia's dad looking to take a bat to him. He mentioned it to me, and I checked it out."

"Mortals do have their uses."

"Occasionally."

"Where's Cain?"

A maniacal light lit the boy's eyes. "Cain is dead."

Eve winced, her gut churning. An ache grew in her chest and spread. Laughter came from the speaker. Again, the sound held both masculine and feminine notes. Like a prepubescent boy whose voice had not yet fully changed.

"You think you killed Cain?" the person asked. "*You?* Better demons have tried and they have all failed."

"The tengu grabbed him."

There was a pause. "How many of them?"

"Twenty or more. However many there were in storage."

"Well, perhaps they've at least injured him. I'll check on him when I get there."

Eve realized then the poor sound quality was not entirely inherent to the speaker in the phone. It was the sound of traffic. Whoever was talking was on the way. Her heart dropped into her stomach.

"So what do you want me to do with her?" the boy asked, his feet shuffling on the gruesome floor.

"She might be more valuable to us alive than dead. If Cain survives—which he has proven is inevitable—he might forfeit a great deal for her return."

Fury started to burn its way through Eve's fear. She was sick of being mauled. No amount of chocolate could improve her mood enough to avoid the nuclear meltdown she felt was coming. And there was one basic undeniable truth—there was no way in hell she'd allow anyone to use her against Alec.

Her head turned slowly, her eyes narrowing in an attempt to see a way out. Where was she? The house on Falcon Circle? If not, she was screwed, because she would have no idea where she was, or which direction to run for help.

Eve glanced down at her watch. Through the water droplets on the face, she saw it was just after one in the morning. The kid couldn't have moved her too far from the masonry. Not enough time had passed.

If this were a real slasher movie, this room might be a basement of horrors. But this was California, where earthquakes made basements a rarity. She was either on the ground floor or above it. For some reason, that made her feel better. As long as she was above the ground, she might have a chance of escaping to the street outside or being seen from a window. If she screamed loud enough, she might be heard.

The door is to your left.

The sound of the female voice took Eve aback. She glanced around furtively. One of the animals was talking to her and she didn't sound good. Her voice was weary. Resigned.

It opens inward. If you make it to the hallway, run to the right and don't stop.

Eve had no idea how to reply without her voice, how to say she would come back for them if she lived through the night. She refused to leave them behind and let them suffer whatever fate awaited them on that gurney.

We're counting on it.

Mentally girding herself, Eve wiggled in her seat, trying to see if her legs were bound in any way. They weren't.

"You can bleed her until I get there," the person on the speakerphone said. "Just don't drain too much."

The wolf's slow smile sent Eve's anger into overdrive. A rough growl escaped her. She lunged forward, aiming her shoulder at the boy's stomach like she'd seen football players do when tackling. The maneuver worked. They both tumbled to the ground and crashed into a malodorous kennel. The animals began to bark, hiss, and screech.

Shouting came through the speakerphone. "What's going on? *Tim?* Answer me! What the fuck is happening?"

Struggling to her knees, Eve then lurched to her feet. One with the darkness now, her night vision kicked in, allowing her to see the proliferation of bloodstained tools hanging on racks suspended from the ceiling. There were also at least a dozen kennels holding animals so ravaged, Eve couldn't tell what species some of them were.

"Bitch!" the boy cried, swinging for her legs with both arms.

Eve stumbled, then turned and kicked at where he lay on the floor. "Asshole!"

Reaching the door, she fumbled for the knob. Grasping hands scratched her ankles and shins but couldn't get purchase. Yanking the portal open, Eve leaped around it and fled to the hallway.

Behind her, the wolf cursed and gave chase.

Alec bypassed the patio area of the masonry at a run, heading toward the main gate that led to the street. His footfalls combined with the Marks' behind him in a rhythmic pounding that built his anxiety. He was a yard away from the gate when a familiar figure appeared on the other side. The man grasped the wrought-iron bars, revealing the diamond-shaped detail on the back of his right hand—a detail that was identical to the one on the kid from the convenience store.

"Bad timing, Charles," Alec bit out.

"What are you doing here, Cain?"

The Alpha of the Northern California pack was in the wrong place at the wrong time. Alec wasn't in the mood to play. "Leaving. Get out of my way."

"I'm looking for someone; a young male from my pack." One hand dug into his pocket and withdrew a newspaper image of the Upland Sports Arena. In the periphery, the boy stood beside a Gehenna Masonry truck.

Alec smiled. "Good luck with that."

The Alpha's eyes glowed golden in the moonlight. He was tall and sinewy, handsome in a way that lured too many mortal women astray. He was dark and intense. Magnetic, some said. And wily enough to avoid Jehovah's wrath. At least so far. "It can't be a coincidence that you're here."

"You're the one outside of your territory."

Charles settled more firmly on his feet, showing his determination to block the exit as long as necessary. Since the padlock was on the exterior of the gate, Alec wouldn't be able to access it without reaching through the bars, a move that would put him at an unacceptable disadvantage.

"Point me in the right direction," Charles said, "and I'll step aside."

"There's no help for your rogue wolf. Go home."

"I can't let you kill him."

"That's not your decision to make."

"He's young, and he's my son." Charles's knuckles whitened. "His mother was a witch. Her parents believe I'm denying him his magical birthright. They've turned him against me."

"I don't give a shit."

"Because he's a half-breed," the Alpha continued, "he can't control his wolf, so he's rejected it and fled."

Alec's arms crossed. "You're breaking my heart."

"Let me handle this within the pack."

"It's too late for that." The evening breeze blew through the bars, ruffling through Alec's hair and filling his nostrils with the stench of Infernal. "Among other things, a Mark has been taken."

"Whatever Timothy has done, it's been at the will of his grandparents. Let me give them to you in return for my son."

"I want my Mark," Alec bit out, agonizingly conscious of how much time had passed since Eve had been taken.

"I understand. I want to help you."

"Then get out of the way."

The Alpha's grip loosened. "Do we have a deal?"

Alec inhaled sharply. "Sure."

Eve was right. The mark did burn with a lie.

CHAPTER 20

It was a hallway, and at the end there was a faint, almost imperceptible glow.

Eve raced toward it, suddenly aware of just how much swinging arms helped a person to run. With her wrists bound in front of her, she felt off-balance and front-heavy.

The screeching cries of the animals ceased abruptly with the closing of the door Eve had fled through, telling her the horror room was sound-proofed in some way. The thudding footfalls of her pursuer, however, were loud and clear. And gaining on her.

Flanking either side of the hallway were other doors, only a few, but they were all closed. There was no wayward moonlight to give her bearings. There was no artificial illumination and no windows to tell her where she was. Only the glow at the end of the tunnel that hinted at a window.

The hallway emptied into another. She turned the corner and found herself dodging sofas and end tables. Moonlight flooded the space through picture windows. She was on the ground floor. If she'd been a religious person, she might have sent up a prayer of thanks. As it was, she thought it was about time she'd been given a freakin' break.

She saw the double-door exit that led to the outside.

Almost there . . .

"Stupid slut!" the boy grunted, skidding into the wall as he rounded the corner behind her.

Eve sensed a tackle coming and leaped the last yard to the door. The mark burned with a rush of power, giving her the strength required to shatter the lock and leap out into the night.

Her foot hit the ground wrong and she stumbled . . .

. . . directly into the chest of an immovable masculine form.

Fishtailing around the corner of Falcon Circle, Alec stood on the brakes and squealed to a halt before the brown house at the end of the street. It

was the only unlit home on the cul-de-sac; a dark hole in a suburban tapestry of welcoming lights. Behind him, a dark blue Suburban filled with
Sara's guards and a black Porsche driven by Charles followed suit. Bringing up the rear was a van of wolves. The multitude of vehicles clogged the
driveway and spilled out to the middle of the street.

Alec hit the pavement running, the driver's-side door of the Focus left
hanging open.

This sort of melee was not the way things were done. Sting operations,
raids, ambushes . . . Aside from being strongly discouraged because of
their inevitable attention-grabbing value, they weren't in Alec's repertoire.
He preferred the quiet, clean kill.

The soles of his boots skidded around the corner of the garage. He
charged toward the front double-doors.

One side burst open in a rush and a running figure tumbled out, crashing into Alec. If his heart could have stopped, it would have.

"What the fuck is going on?"

The voice wasn't Eve's.

Eve didn't need to look up to know that the man holding her was Reed.
His scent was unmistakable and relief filled her.

But she was still pissed.

Leaning into him, she kicked back with one leg, nailing the pursuing
kid directly in the chest. The force of the blow traveled through Eve and
was absorbed by Reed. The young wolf caught air and was thrust backward at least a yard. He slammed into the stationary side of the door, col-
liding with an audible crack of his head against the thick glass. Knocked
unconscious, he slid down and came to rest, sprawled and harmless.

"Nice," Reed said. He assessed her physical condition. "You're wet
again."

"Was I ever dry?" She held out her bound wrists. Her hands were
shaking terribly, but there was nothing she could do about that. "Take
this off!"

"Where's Cain?" His fingers deftly unraveled the nylon rope that restrained her.

"Fending off tengu." At least she hoped he was still fending them off.
The knot in her stomach tightened.

Reed freed her. "Let's go save his ass, then."

Eve kicked at the wolf's sneakered foot. "We need to keep an eye on
him. He's your brother's target."

"I'll restrain him." He doubled up the rope in his hands and snapped it.

"There are also dogs in there . . . animals," she said, pointing at the
showroom. "They're hurt bad. And someone else is coming. They're on
the way here. I don't know how many. Only one guy was talking, but who
knows if there were more with him. Or her. The voice was weird."

"We'll need Cain," he said grimly. He was so calm, so self-possessed. And wearing a ridiculously expensive suit that smelled of a woman.

Eve pushed the thought aside. "Right. Tie up the boy. I'll get Cain."

A wry smile curved his lips. "By yourself?"

"There are only two of us. What else can we do?"

"I asked for reinforcements." He pulled out his cell phone. "Let me see where they are."

"Okay, then. We have a plan."

"We do?"

"Sure. I have a way with tengu. They'd rather pick on me than Cain and that should give him a break." She caught Reed by the lapels and shook him. At least, she tried to. He didn't budge. "Don't get hurt. You hear me?"

Reed winked. "I'll be sure to protect your favorite parts."

"Jeez," she muttered. "You're terrible."

"Hey." He caught her arm before she turned away. His voice was low and grave. "Be careful."

"Will do." Eve took off running toward the back of the lot, skirting all the statuary and fountains that littered the patio area of the showroom.

They weren't nearly as frightening as before.

Alec stared down at the kid he had by the shirt. It was the other boy from the convenience store. Another wolf, although Alec wasn't certain which pack claimed him because his details were hidden beneath his clothing.

"Where's Evangeline?"

"Who?" the kid asked. "Dude, you're tripping. What the hell are you doing tearing down the street like the *Dukes of Hazzard*? You scared the crap out of me."

"Where's your friend Timothy? The kid you were with earlier?"

The young wolf scowled. "How the fuck should I know? He hasn't come back from work yet."

The Alpha's voice rumbled through the darkness. "Do you know who you're talking to, Sean?"

The boy's eyes widened with fear. Not because of Alec, but because of his Alpha. He began to struggle violently. "Let me go!"

Alec looked at Charles.

"He ran away with Timothy," the Alpha explained, his gaze never leaving the writhing teenager. "Where is he, Sean?"

There was an undertone to the Alpha's voice that drained all the fight out of the kid. He sagged in Alec's grip and said, "I think he's still at work. He called a little bit ago and asked for Malachai to meet him there."

"Malachai?" Alec asked.

"His grandfather," Charles explained.

Still at work. Alec released the kid and exhaled harshly. Was Eve still at the masonry? Had she been right under his nose?

All this time . . . wasted.

"Back up!" he yelled, skirting Charles and the other wolves to return to the Focus. "Back the cars up!"

A female Mark attempted to run by him. He caught her arm. "Get a hold of the team we left with Mariel," he said. "Tell them to search the premises."

"Yes, Cain." As she ran to the Suburban, she pulled out her cell phone.

Alec slid into the driver's seat and put the car in reverse. Once again he'd screwed things up. He should have killed the boy when he had the chance.

He wouldn't make the same mistake twice.

Eve wrenched open the door to the rear building. Heat assailed her, as well as an exceptionally noxious odor.

She ran in. The kiln was on, and there was a dark-clad man feeding bags into it. Eve briefly debated whether he was a friend or foe, but the barest whiff of sweetness revealed him to be a Mark. She wanted to know why he was there, but that could wait. A quick glance down the length of the room confirmed that the tengu were secured.

"Where is he?" she asked.

"Looking for you," the Mark said. He assessed her from head to toe. "Are you okay?"

"Not really, no." Eve tried to look collected, but the sudden release of terror and tension left her limp like a deflated balloon.

"You didn't get yourself hurt, did you?"

Something about his tone bugged her. "It's not like I planned to get snatched, you know."

"Well, we all know you didn't plan to *not* get snatched either. You have no business being on a mission like this at your stage. Look how much trouble you've caused."

"Excuse me?" Her hands went to her hips. "Who said I wanted this gig?"

The Mark made some kind of grunting noise that she found offensive.

She shook her head. "I'm going back to check on the wolf-boy in the showroom. He had better social skills."

"Hang on," he muttered. "I'll go with you. Just let me wash this crap off my hands."

Eve opened her mouth to protest.

"Don't argue." He rolled his eyes. "You need someone to watch out for you before you get yourself killed."

"I've kept myself alive so far, haven't I?"

"By the will of God," the Mark argued. He moved over to a plastic utility tub sink in the corner.

As he busied himself there, Eve glanced around impatiently. The tengu were eerily quiet and she couldn't help but wonder what condition Alec had left them in.

Her foot tapped with frustration. She really wanted to say "to hell with you," but the fact was, this guy was trained and she wasn't. He was also sporting attire that suggested his position was an important one, or at least one that was distinguishable from the basic Mark in some way. Surliness aside, he could help her and she wasn't in a position to reject assistance of any kind.

His cell phone went off, playing a "Low Rider" ring tone.

"Can you hur—" she snapped, facing him. "Holy shit!"

Water poured from the tap like a twisting rope, wrapping around the Mark's body and face. He struggled, but any sounds he would have made were muffled. He was blue from his exertions and lack of oxygen.

"Hey!" she shouted. "Back off. It's me you want."

The Mark was dropped to the floor, unconscious. Maybe dead. She couldn't tell.

Leaving Eve alone with the Nix.

Reed straightened from a crouch with the bound teenage boy tossed over his shoulder. Opening the showroom door, he carried his burden inside. He tossed the kid on a waiting room sofa and took stock of his surroundings.

Gehenna Masonry had the sort of upscale style that Reed gravitated toward. They'd spared no expense in their presentation. The couches were leather, an espresso machine waited by the receptionist's desk, and samples of materials, colors, and tiles were mounted on mahogany displays.

A clever disguise, he thought. Not what he would have expected.

His gaze returned to the unconscious teenager. There was no greater proof of the masking Cain had suspected than the body in front of him. Reed had no idea what kind of Infernal it was. If not for the present circumstances, he wouldn't even know the boy *was* an Infernal. That was almost as frightening as the look on Eve's face when she'd burst out of the showroom. He'd felt her fear as if it was tangible, but seeing it had been too much.

Yet she continued bravely, worrying over both Cain and himself. She'd only been marked a couple of weeks, but she was more concerned about the oldest members of the mark system than she was about her novice self.

Where the hell was Sara's team? After what he'd paid for them, they should be here.

Reed reached into his pocket, withdrew his cell phone, and turned it on. The phone played a little tune as it powered up, followed shortly by the beeping that said he had text messages and voicemails waiting. The subdued sounds were loud in the stillness. He glanced around warily, then moved toward the receptionist's station. It was time to shed some light on the situation.

He was reaching for the switch on the wall when the stench of rotting soul wafted by his nostrils. Reed shifted from behind the desk to the waiting area. He sniffed the air around the kid and frowned. Werewolf.

"It wears off," he murmured, a smile forming. If they destroyed all knowledge of the masking agent, things could go back to the way they'd been before.

Reed turned the lights on in the showroom, then took off down the hallway in search of the employee and purchasing records. Anyone or anything connected to the masonry would have to be secured. He dialed Mariel.

"Abel," she greeted. "Where are you?"

"At the masonry, where are you?"

"Cain found some suspicious materials and he wanted me to get them to the Gadara lab immediately."

"Cain is with you?" Reed spun around and headed back into the waiting area. Eve was on a goose chase. Or worse, walking into danger.

He paused at the end of the hallway. The couch was bare but for a gnawed length of rope.

The wolf was gone.

Reed was so horrified by the thought of Eve in danger that he failed to sense any hazard to himself until a sharp-ended metal rod pierced clean through his right shoulder from back to front.

Bellowing in pain, he dropped the phone. He gripped the protruding end of the pipe and yanked it free. It was four feet in length, hollow, and about an inch in diameter. Pivoting, Reed wielded it against his attacker. The blow struck the assailant in the face and he crumpled.

It was an elderly man, if the silver threading the dark hair at his temples was any indication. A mage. Sprawled at Reed's feet in his mortal guise—khaki slacks, loafers, and polo shirt. Harmless by all appearances.

Reed healed his wound and freed his wings. They unfurled through his garments to extend their full span. His features and voice contorted, taking on the face of his fury. The air stirred around him, swirling in response to the surge of his power.

The mage recoiled as he realized his mistake. A wand lay on the floor next to him, but he was too stunned to reach for it. He'd thought he wounded a fragile Mark, perhaps even Cain, not a *mal'akh* with full gifts.

Stupid. He should have smelled the difference.

"Vengeance is mine!" Reed roared, thrusting the pipe through the mage's heart with such strength it cracked the floor beneath him.

Blood bubbled on the mage's lips, but he smiled. "And mine." He exploded in a burst of white hot embers, leaving only a body-shaped pile of ashes around the protruding spear.

Reed scowled. Then he smelled the smoke. His gaze lifted to the hall-way. Shadows danced on the walls, betraying licks of flame.

"Eve."

Retracting his wings, he turned toward the front door. As he neared the exit, it wrenched open and Cain raced in.

"Where is she?" his brother demanded.

Three of Sara's guards came in after him. Followed by a group of wolves. One was clearly an Alpha—Charles Grimshaw, one of the more powerful pack leaders.

"Where are the tengu?" Reed queried. "Wherever they are, is where she is."

Alec gestured toward the blood on Reed's shirt and vest. "What hap-pened to you?"

"*That* happened." Reed pointed to the ashes on the floor. "A mage."

Smoke began to pour from the back rooms, rolling down the hallway like a churning wave.

"Malachai," Grimshaw said. "Where is my son?"

"Down there." Reed pointed toward the rear of the building.

The wolves ran headlong into the fire.

Reed looked at Cain. There was a flash of comprehension in his brother's eyes.

Together, they raced after Eve.

Eve backed warily away from the Nix, who took on a human shape but remained clear as water. She'd seen something like it in a movie once. *The Abyss,* she thought it was. A bark of laughter escaped her. She was losing her mind. Here she was, about to die, and she was thinking about motion pictures.

"It's warmer in Las Vegas," the Nix purred.

She would have expected that his words would come out garbled be-cause of the water, but he sounded normal. At least as normal as Germanic-accented English could sound.

"Why would I care about the weather in Vegas?" she retorted, reaching into her pocket.

"Have you seen the water show at the Bellagio? It's magnificent. You always come away with something new. Tonight, I found out where you were."

"Lucky you."

"Not so lucky for you."

Eve shook her head. "Why me?"

"I do what I'm told," he said, his lower half beginning to swirl like a vortex.

"What?"

The door opened. Eve gasped in relief and turned her head to find Reed. What she found was the wolf.

Her heart went to her throat. *Reed. Are you okay?*

"Sorry to interrupt." The kid grinned. "I'll leave you two alone."

"You little shit!" She lunged toward him.

But he skipped out, slamming the door. A second later a heavy thud against it suggested he'd blocked the exit in some way.

The Nix laughed and sidled closer. He was toying with her. She knew he could nab her in less than a heartbeat, but he wanted her to squirm. He wanted to frighten her half to death before he killed her.

Eve backtracked toward the kiln. Her plan was lame and probably doomed, but it was all she had. As she moved closer to the kiln it became warmer. The Nix advanced, smiling.

She pulled the small pouch from her pocket, praying the plasticized lining was intact. Otherwise, she was screwed.

"What is that?" he asked, his lower half spinning with such agitation that he looked like a genie.

"A present for you."

"Oh?"

Tearing the package open, she was relieved to find green powder inside. It hadn't gotten wet. "Do you like limes?"

"What?"

Eve leaped to the side of the kiln opening and the Nix surged toward her. She tossed the powder at him and the water took on a verdant cast. The eddy slowed and he tilted precariously. She quickly ripped open another and chucked that at him, too. The Nix tottered toward her.

"W-what have you d-done?" he gurgled.

Focusing on her super strength, Eve caught him as he tipped. She tossed him onto the rollers, then shoved his inert, semigelatinous form straight into the kiln.

He screamed and she stared, horrified. The floor began to shudder, then the walls. Dust sifted down from the exposed metal rafters. The pallet truck bounced along the violently vibrating floor and the door to the tengu room dislodged.

Eve grabbed the downed Mark and dragged him to the exit. She tried to open it, but it wouldn't budge. Pounding against the door, she shouted for help, trying to be heard over the horrible whining that emanated from the kiln. The tengu raced toward her in a rambunctious aggregation.

"Help!" she yelled, beating at the door. "Help!"

Suddenly the door gave way and she fell . . .

. . . straight into Alec's arms. He squeezed the air from her.

"Time to go," he muttered, tugging her out. He reached back in for the Mark, tossing him over his shoulder in a fireman's carry.

Reed stepped out of the shadows. He held the young wolf by the scruff of his neck. He tossed him into the kiln room and shut the door. Then he picked up a length of wood and propped it against the portal, trapping him inside.

The sound of sirens turned Eve's head and she saw the showroom engulfed in flames.

"The animals!" she cried, setting off at a run.

Hard arms caught her about the waist and held her back. She fought against Reed's hold, but he was too strong.

"Eve," he said, his voice to her ear. "It's the Lord's will."

But it was too senseless for her to accept. If God had loved them, he would never have allowed them to suffer as they had. He would have allowed them some tiny bit of comfort before death. Instead he'd used her to give them hope, then cruelly shattered it.

"We've got to go," Alec said, running toward a group of people dressed like the guy he had slung over his back.

"Where are the wolves?" he asked when they reached them.

"Still inside," a female Mark replied. She stuck two fingers in her mouth and whistled.

Another Mark came running from a shedlike building. As he drew to a halt before them, he reported, "It would take days to sort through all the materials in there."

A tremendous whining noise came from the kiln building, the sound of metal stretching and tearing. Alec shook his head. "We don't even have minutes." He looked at Eve. "What did you do to it?"

"I put the Nix in there."

"Dear God," the female Mark breathed.

"Shit," Alec muttered. "That thing is going to blow. Run!"

Eve sprinted behind him to the car in a daze. They managed to drive a block's distance before the kiln exploded.

The fireball was seen from miles away.

CHAPTER 21

Gadara paced behind his desk in the penthouse office of Gadara Tower. Dressed in jeans and a white denim button-down shirt, he looked both handsome and leisurely. However, he definitely *wasn't* the latter.

"You are a menace, Ms. Hollis," he said grimly. "There is no other word for you."

From her seat in front of the archangel's desk, Eve glanced first at Alec, who sat on her left, and then Reed, who sat on her right. Two days had passed since the incident in Upland. Yesterday had been recovery time to make up for the twenty-four hours without sleep the day before. Today was the day of reckoning.

"You told us to take care of the tengu," she reminded. "We did."

"By destroying a brand-new air-conditioning unit and crushing a custom Lexus," the archangel retorted. "You failed to mention that when you related the events a few days ago."

"Think how much the tengu would have cost you over the long haul," Alec suggested. "We saved you money."

"And what is the benefit of the disaster in Upland?" Gadara queried crossly.

"You told me to get my hands dirty," Eve said.

He paused, glaring. "You blew up an entire city block!"

"I didn't, the Nix did."

"How did you manage that, by the way?" Reed asked in a conversational tone. As usual, he was dressed to the nines and looked very divine.

"Jell-O."

"Really? Clever."

"Totally an accident. I didn't think it would work."

Alec reached over and picked up her hand. The complete opposite of his brother, he was wearing leather pants and a T-shirt. "But it did. It was brilliant."

He didn't say it wasn't a coincidence that she had picked up instant gelatin in the convenience store, but she knew he was thinking it.

"Excuse me." Gadara's palms hit the desk and he leaned forward. "Are we done patting ourselves on the back?"

"Ya know," Eve drawled. "If I didn't know better, I would think you *wanted* us to fail."

"Ridiculous," he scoffed. "I benefit only when you succeed, but at this rate, you will drive the firm into bankruptcy."

"I have a plan," she said. "I'll just stay home quietly until it's time to start training."

It took a moment for his glower to fade into a reluctant smile. "You start training next week."

"Oh?" Reed straightened from his lounging position. "Whose rotation is it?"

"Mine"

Eve didn't miss the sudden tension in the men on either side of her.

"Better me than Sara, yes?" Gadara asked, staring at Reed.

Reed made a choked noise. Alec shook his head.

"Rotation?" Eve asked.

"The archangels share training duties in a rotation," Alec explained.

"Oh." She looked at Gadara.

"I am the best," he said modestly.

She laughed. "Of course you are."

"Anything from Hank regarding the stuff Mariel brought back from the masonry?" Alec asked.

"Like Ms. Hollis's gelatin idea," the archangel said, sinking into his seat, "Hank says it is very clever. But there is something missing, and considering the creators are mages, Hank is certain there was an incantation of some sort involved."

"I wonder how many people knew the recipe," Reed said.

"Not many, would be my guess."

"Mine, too," Alec agreed. "The rarer it is, the more value it had to Malachai and his wife."

"Hank believes it would have been a couple's spell," Gadara continued, "something a man and woman would cast together in order to affect the largest number. By your accounts, several types of Infernals were successfully able to use it."

"Unless there were several kinds of masks," Eve offered.

All three men looked at her.

She shrugged. "Just sayin'."

"I killed Malachai," Reed said. "The rest of the materials were destroyed in the explosion."

"The house on Falcon Circle was raided," Gadara finished, "and anything of interest was removed. I have a team investigating the various leads we found there."

"The Alpha might be able to help us find the woman," Reed suggested.

"I doubt it." Alec's face was grim. "We killed his son. He's not going to be feeling too charitable."

"If the grandparents hadn't led the boy astray, he probably wouldn't have attracted notice. The fault lies with them."

"Try telling that to a grief-stricken parent," Eve said. "They don't always have their head on straight."

"Right." Alec squeezed her hand.

"Anything else?" she asked Gadara.

He reached into the wooden cigar box on his desk and withdrew one. She wondered what he did with them, since he didn't smoke. Just gnaw on them until they got soggy? The thought grossed her out, so she pushed it aside.

The archangel studied her. "In a hurry to go?"

"Yes, actually."

"Stay on the radar," he admonished. "It is there to protect you."

"No worries. I have a date with my couch and the first season of *Dexter* on DVD."

"Odd viewing choice."

Eve stood and all three men pushed to their feet. "Considering my life? Are you kidding? It's like watching *Leave It to Beaver*."

She moved toward the elevator. Alec followed after her.

"Abel." Gadara's voice arrested everyone. "I'd like you to stay and go over your report regarding the death of your Mark."

Reed nodded and hung back.

Turning inside the car to face him, Eve's gaze met his just before the doors closed.

His wink good-bye followed her all the way home.

Yellow police tape and a crime scene sticker sealed Mrs. Basso's door. Eve couldn't help but stare at it as they passed. Alec tossed an arm around her shoulders and tugged her closer, offering support.

"This is terrible in so many ways," she said.

"I'm sorry, angel."

"I loved her." She struggled to push her key into the lock of her door. It was hard to see through tears.

Alec took her keys from her and worked his way through the dead bolts. He pushed open the door and gestured her in.

"I liked her," Eve continued, setting her Coach bag atop the console table where she kept her gun. The screen door to the patio was open and a crisp sea breeze wafted through her sheer curtains, billowing through them like a ship's sails. "Really liked her. Some people you only like a little, some you only like on certain occasions, and some you only like when you're drunk. But I liked her all ways and all the time."

He pulled her into a tight embrace.

Her hands fisted in his shirt. "I'm going to miss her. And I'll probably hate whoever moves in next door."

"Don't say that," he murmured. "Give them a chance."

She rubbed her face into the cotton of his T-shirt, drying her tears. "What am I going to do with you?"

"Can I offer a suggestion?"

Leaning back, Eve met his gaze. "I mean about our living arrangements."

His mouth curved in a smile that curled her toes. "Of course I'll move in with you, angel. I was just waiting for you to ask."

"My dad would kill me."

"This coming from the gal who survived a tengu, a Nix, and a wolf in a week?"

"They have nothing on my dad's silent treatment, let me tell you." She pulled away. "I mean he's silent most of the time, but when he is peeved about something, he becomes *really* silent. Oppressively silent. I hate it. Makes me squirm."

"Guess I better go with plan B, then."

She frowned. "What's plan B?"

"Moving in next door when the police are done with it."

"What?"

"It's perfect."

"It's creepy."

"She was a sweet old lady, angel. She's with God now; she's not hanging around worrying about us."

The doorbell rang.

They both stilled. Alec arched a brow in silent query. She shook her head. Knocking came next, an annoying impatient rapping.

"*Ms. Hollis?*"

Eve groaned in recognition of the voice.

"*It's Detectives Ingram and Jones from the Anaheim Police Department. We'd like to speak with you.*"

Blowing out her breath, she went to the door and opened it. "Hello, Detectives."

"Can we come in?"

"Certainly." She stepped out of the way, her heels rapping on the hardwood floor. She'd dressed for business to see Gardara—skirt, blouse, and chignon. Now, she was doubly glad to be formidably attired.

The two policemen entered and she was once again struck by what an odd pairing they were. One short and thin, the other tall and portly. But there was a synergy between them that told her they had been working together a long time.

"Would either of you like some coffee?" she asked.

"Sure," Jones said, unsmiling.

Eve led the group into the kitchen and began preparing the coffeemaker. "So what brings you to my door?"

"We found a local florist who remembers selling water lilies on two separate occasions to this man," Ingram said.

She looked over her shoulder. The detective held up a sketch artist's rendering. Mostly she found the ones she saw on television to be useless for identification purposes, but this one was good. It looked eerily like the Nix. She took the carafe over to the sink.

"Have you seen this man, Ms. Hollis?" Jones asked.

"No." The mark burned.

"What about you, Mr. Cain? Have you seen him?"

"I haven't, no." Alec moved to the cupboard that held the mugs.

"I don't believe you," Ingram said bluntly.

Eve sighed and filled up the water reservoir of the coffeemaker. "I'm sorry about that."

"So are we." Jones propped one foot on the rail that ran along the bottom of the island. "You see, either both you and Mrs. Basso received flowers—which is what we think happened—or another woman in Huntington Beach has been targeted. The rest of the lilies were purchased at various locations in Anaheim. We don't want to waste our time on you, if there's another victim out there."

Holding her tongue was killing Eve. She could hear the frustration in the detectives' voices and it broke her heart. She hated to send them on a wild goose chase, but what else could she do? Telling the truth wasn't an option.

Alec pulled the bag of coffee beans out of the freezer. "Did you look at the security tapes?"

As Eve took the bag from him and poured the beans into the grinder, her hands were steady but she was shaking inside.

"We did," Jones admitted. "This man visited Mrs. Basso."

"But not Ms. Hollis," Alec finished.

Eve realized he'd planned ahead and doctored the video. She was both grateful and admiring.

The din of the grinder blocked out all conversation for a few moments, then she filled the filter and turned on the coffeemaker. She wiped her hands on a dishtowel and faced the two detectives.

"I really wish I could help you," she said softly.

Ingram smiled grimly and toyed with his handlebar mustache. "We think you can, Ms. Hollis. You'll be seeing us around until we're sure either way."

"I'll have to stock up on coffee, then."

Alec moved the mugs from the counter to the island. "Now that the pleasantries are out of the way . . . Cream and sugar, anyone?"

* * *

Eve was curled up on her living room sofa watching *Wildest Police Videos* when the knock came on her front door.

She debated ignoring it. Today was the first day in three weeks of training where she didn't feel like she had been hit by a truck. She didn't want any unwanted visitors ruining it. Even with her ability to heal rapidly, Mark combat training was hard work and it was six days a week. She'd come to seriously appreciate the classroom-only days. And Sunday. Now known affectionately as "vegetation day."

The knocking came again, louder.

With a small grunt, Eve pushed to her feet. Out of habit, she paused at the console table by the door and withdrew her gun. Then she peered through the peephole. Alec stood there, smiling.

"Angel," he called out in that rumbling purr that caressed like warm velvet. "It's just your friendly neighbor."

Pulling the door open, she waved at him with her gun hand. He was wearing shades, a tank top, knee-length Dickies shorts, and pure sex appeal. No one wore it better.

He pushed his sunglasses up and smiled. "Pretty soon you'll be more deadly than that weapon."

"I still like the way it feels." She hefted it reverently. "Weighty, solid."

With one hand on the jamb, Alec leaned in. She watched, riveted. He stopped with his lips a hairsbreadth away from hers.

"I've got something weighty and solid," he murmured, his breath gusting across her lips. "Wanna take it for a ride?"

"That's so crude," she whispered back. "I think it turned me on."

He kissed her. "I was talking about my bike."

Her mouth made a moue.

"I want to take you out," he said. "Let's have some fun and relax a little."

"We can have fun here."

"And we will." His dark eyes burned with promise. "Later."

"What's wrong with now?"

Alec laughed. "Much as I love having sex with you—and you know I do—we've never been on a date."

Eve frowned. "A date?"

"You. Me. Outside. In the sun. Doing things together in public that won't get us arrested."

"What things?"

He shouldered his way in and plucked the gun from her hand. "I was thinking we could take a ride down the coast to San Diego. It's a beautiful day."

She watched him return her weapon to its padded case and zip it up. Then he tucked it back into the drawer.

A date. Something warm and fuzzy expanded in her chest. "Let me change."

"Don't. You look hot."

Eve looked down at her outfit of shorts and tank top. Totally, ridiculously unsafe for motorcycle riding. But then again, there were some perks to being marked. Alec had hyper reflexes and she was built like a tank. Kinda. Sorta.

"If you turn off the television," she said, "I'll go get my boots."

Alec caught her arm. "Wear those." He pointed to the flirty flip-flops tucked beneath the console.

"Not very practical on a bike," she pointed out.

"Let's be impractical. It's Sunday. You're supposed to take the day off."

She opened her mouth to protest.

"Have I ever told you," he purred, "how sexy those little flowers you have painted on your big toes are?"

Eve slipped on the shoes. "What's in San Diego?"

"Seahawks versus Chargers."

"That's such a guy date," Eve teased, smiling.

He grabbed her keys and shades. Then he pulled her out to the hallway and locked the door. "We'll take care of the girl parts later."

AUTHOR'S NOTE

There are some projects in an author's career that are inspired. The Marked series is definitely that for me. Eve came to me like Athena of Greek mythology, springing from my head fully armed and prepared for battle. Her story was then expanded upon by random synchronicities. I won't attempt an explanation for how often random events offered prompts and clues at the exact moment I needed them, but I'm grateful.

Residents of Huntington Beach and Anaheim will note that I took creative license with locations. The fictional Henry's Ice Cream shop is located where Lorenzo's Pizza used to be on the corner of Cerritos and Euclid. Both the Circle K and Lorenzo's are gone now, leaving a hole in my life that only Lorenzo's pastrami sandwiches could fill.

St. Mary's Church as described in the Marked series is nothing like the actual St. Mary's by the Sea, which is located in a different part of the city and is much smaller and older. My St. Mary's more closely resembles Saint Vincent de Paul in some aspects of appearance and location, but it's fictional in every way.

I've taken other liberties with my beloved hometown area. Locals will spot them; non-locals won't care. I hope you enjoyed the story in either case!

EVE OF DESTRUCTION

To all our soldiers serving in the United States military: Thank you. You are respected and deeply appreciated.

For those of you on foreign soil: Come home safe. We love and miss you.

My time in the military was deeply enriched by the soldiers who crossed my path. From Foxtrot Company, 229th Military Intelligence Battalion: Oglesby, Frye, Antonian, Doughty, Anderson, Edmonds, Calderon, McCain, Slovanick, and Pat.

Christine: You will always be the sister of my heart.

I love you, guys. Never Quit.

ACKNOWLEDGMENTS

My deep gratitude goes to:

My editor, Heather Osborn, for giving me the time I needed and for all the cheerleading she does behind the scenes to support this series.

Nikki Duncan (www.nikkiduncan.com) for the McCroskey name and enthusiasm over *Eve of Darkness*.

Jordan Summers, Karin Tabke, Sasha White, and Shayla Black for always being there for me. *You rock, ladies!*

Melissa Frain at Tor for loving the first book enough to clamor for this one.

Seth Lerner for breaking one of his cardinal rules. I'm honored.

Denise McClain and Carol Culver for assisting me with the French dialogue.

Giselle Hirtenfeld/Goldfeder, whose first name I gave to a nightmare in this book. The real Giselle is actually a dream to work with.

Susan Grimshaw of Borders Group, Inc., whose last name I appropriated for an alpha werewolf. Far from being villainous (like my Alpha turns after the loss of his child), Sue is one of my heroes. *Thank you, Sue, for all the support you have given to me and my books over the years.*

My father, Daniel Day, for his help with the Italian dialogue. *Thanks, Dad!*

Therefore whosoever slayeth Cain, vengeance shall be taken on him sevenfold. And the Lord set a mark upon Cain, lest any finding him should kill him.

—GENESIS 4:15

ANNO DOMINI 2008
Class R4AD08

Student/Origin:
Callaghan, Kenneth: Scotland
Dubois, Claire: France
Edwards, Robert: England
Garza, Antonio: Italy
Hogan, Laurel: New Zealand
Hollis, Evangeline: United States
Molenaar, Jan: Holland
Richens, Chad: England
Seiler, Iselda: Germany

Number of Graduates:
classified

Number of Casualties:
classified

Status:
pending internal review

CHAPTER 1

Evangeline Hollis woke to the scents of Hell—fire and brimstone, smoke and ashes.

Her nostrils flared in protest. She lay on her back, unmoving, willing her brain to catch up with her circumstances. Licking her lips, she tasted death, the bitterness coating both her tongue and mouth in a thick, immovable wash. Her muscles shifted in an attempt to stretch and a groan escaped her.

What the hell? The last thing she remembered was . . .

. . . being burnt to a crisp by a dragon.

Panic assailed her with the memory, quickly followed by her mind lurching into full awareness. Eve jackknifed up from her sprawled position, sucking in air with such force it was audible. She blinked, but only inky darkness filled her vision. Her hand reached up to her arm and her fingertips found the raised brand there. The Mark of Cain—a triquetra surrounded by a circlet of three serpents, each one eating the tail of the snake before it. The eye of God filled the center.

The mark burned whenever she took the Lord's name in vain—which was often—and whenever she lied, which was less often but useful on occasion. When dealing with Satan's minions, playing dirty leveled the playing field.

Where the fuck am I? In her upright position, the smoky stench in the air was magnified. Her nose wrinkled.

Maybe I'm in Hell? As a longtime agnostic, she still struggled with facing the reality of God. Heaven, Hell, souls . . . They were concepts that couldn't be explained with reason.

Besides, if there was a merciful God and a Heaven, she'd be there. She had only been cursed with the Mark of Cain for six weeks and she hadn't yet been properly trained in how to kill Infernals, but during that short time she had eradicated a tengu infestation, killed a Nix, and managed to vanquish a dragon. She'd also helped put a lid on a major new threat to the good guys—a concoction of some sort that allowed Infernals to temporarily hide in the guise of mere mortals. *And* she'd managed to get Cain and Abel to work together for the first time since they were kids.

If all that wasn't enough to save her soul, she would take her chances with the Devil. Maybe he'd have a better sense of fair play.

As Eve's mind struggled to catch up with her present, the sound of singing penetrated the fog of her thoughts. She couldn't understand a word, but it was familiar all the same. The language was Japanese; the voice, her mother's.

The idea of sharing Hell with her mother was oddly both comforting and chilling.

Eve's hands clenched tentatively, testing the soft surface beneath her, attempting to discern where she was. She felt satin, like the sheets on her bed. A cool breeze touched her brow and Eve's vision exploded into living color. She jerked violently in surprise.

She *was* in her bedroom, sitting atop her king-size bed. As if her senses had been muted, the steady crashing of waves against the Huntington Beach shoreline increased in volume. The soothing rhythm drifted down the hall from her living room balcony and brought welcome relief.

Home. As her tension dissipated, Eve's shoulders relaxed. Then, a brief glimmer in the periphery of her vision made her turn her head.

Lifting her arms to shield her eyes from the blinding light, she barely made out the silhouette of a winged man standing in the corner between her bleached pine closet doors and her dresser. Eve blinked back an unusually thick wash of tears. She risked another glance at the angel and found that, once again, her mark enhancements knew what to do even when she didn't. Her arms lowered. She could see him now without damage to her vision.

The angel was tall, with brawny arms and legs displayed by a knee-length, sleeveless robelike garment. The gown was white and belted with a tan braid. The black combat boots with wicked spikes running up and down the outside were a surprise, as was the impossible perfection of his features. His jaw was square and bold, his hair dark and restrained in a queue at his nape. His irises shimmered like blue flame, and he had an air about him that warned her to keep on his good side.

His gaze lowered to her chest. Hers followed. She was nude.

"Yikes!" Grabbing the top sheet, Eve yanked it up to her neck.

Miyoko Hollis appeared in the doorway, buried in an armful of laundry.

"Hey, you're awake," her mother called out, her voice flavored with a Japanese accent.

"I guess so." Eve was so happy to see her mom, her eyes burned. "It's good to see you."

"Eh, you say that now." Striding toward the bed with the brisk stride of a retired nurse, Miyoko was a compact whirlwind of energy, a tornado that often left Eve feeling exhausted. "You didn't move a muscle for a while. I nearly thought you were dead."

Eve *had* been dead, that was the problem. "What day is it?"

"Tuesday."

Another noxious breeze assaulted her nostrils and Eve waved a hand in front of her face. Her gaze found the source on her dresser—an incense stick.

"Whatever fragrance that is," Eve muttered, inwardly reeling that she had lost two days of her life, "it stinks."

Miyoko moved to the end of the bed and dumped the still-warm pile of clothes onto the comforter. She wore Hello Kitty pajamas—pink flannel pants and a T-shirt that had a giant Hello Kitty face on the front. With her black hair in pigtails and her unlined face, she looked more like Eve's sibling than a parent. She also acted as if she owned the place, which she didn't. Darrel and Miyoko Hollis lived in Anaheim—home of Disneyland, California Adventure, and Eve's childhood. Still, whenever her mother visited, Eve found herself fighting for her place as alpha female in her own house.

Eve watched her mother walk right past the angel without batting an eye. Standing with crossed arms, widespread legs, and folded wings, he was impossible to ignore . . .

Unless you couldn't see him.

"Aromatherapy aids healing," Miyoko pronounced.

"Not when it smells like shit. And why are you doing my laundry again? I wish you could come over and just relax."

"It's not shit. It's jasmine-chamomile. And I am doing your laundry because it was piled up. Can't relax in a messy house."

"My house is never messy." Her mom did laundry every time she came over, despite the fact that at twenty-eight years of age Eve was perfectly capable of doing her own. No matter how spotless her condo might be, her mother cleaned it—rearranging everything to her liking in the process.

"Was, too," her mother argued. "You had an overflowing basket by the washing machine and a sink full of dirty dishes."

Eve pointed at the boxer briefs, men's shirts, and towels in the pile. "Those aren't my clothes. The dishes aren't mine either."

She wondered what her mother would do if she learned that she was washing Cain and Abel's clothes. The brothers went by the names Alec Cain and Reed Abel now, but they were still the siblings of biblical legend.

"Alec has been using all the towels and leaving his clothes on the bathroom floor." Miyoko's tone was starkly chastising. No man was good enough for Eve. They all had some flaw in her mother's eyes, no matter how small. "And both he and your boss get new glasses every time they have a drink."

"Alec lives next door. Why doesn't he go mess up his place?"

"You're asking me?" Her mother snorted. "I still don't know why Reed spends so much time at your house. It's not natural. Or why your boyfriend is CEO of a corporation like Meggido Industries, but I've never seen him in a suit."

The thought of Alec in a suit made Eve smile. "When you run the place and you're good at it, you can wear whatever you want."

Eve stretched gingerly, wincing at the lingering tenderness in her spine. Then, she hollered, "Alec!"

"Don't yell."

"It's my house, Mom."

"Men don't like to be yelled at."

"Mom . . ." She heaved out a frustrated breath. "What do you care, anyway? He leaves towels on the bathroom floor."

It was a pet peeve of Eve's, too, but she didn't think it made a man unsuitable for marriage.

"It's inconsiderate," Miyoko groused. "And unhygienic."

Eve glanced at the angel, embarrassed to have him witness their squabbling. His burning gaze met hers, then his nose wrinkled.

"Mom!" Eve's tone was more urgent. "Put that incense out, *please*. I'm serious. It stinks."

Miyoko grunted, but moved to tamp out the incense stick. "You're difficult."

"And you're stubborn, but I love you anyway."

"You're awake," Alec interjected, walking through the open bedroom door. He stared at her with fathomless eyes, his gaze darting over her in search of any cause for concern. "You scared me, angel," he said gruffly.

Angel. It was a pet name only he ever used. Every time she heard it, her toes curled. Alec's voice was velvet smooth and capable of turning a reading of Hawking's *A Brief History of Time* into an orgasmic experience.

Dressed in long shorts and white tank, he looked hotter than most men did in a tuxedo. His black hair was a little too long and his stride boasted a bit of a swagger, but no matter what he wore or how casually he moved, he looked like someone you didn't want to piss off. It was the hunter in him, the predator. Alec killed for a living and he excelled at it.

He was the reason she'd been marked. He was also her mentor.

His brother Reed entered the room behind him. Their features were similar enough to betray them as siblings, but they were otherwise as different as night and day. Reed favored Armani suits and sharp haircuts. Today he wore graphite gray slacks and a black dress shirt open at the throat and rolled up at the wrists. He was her superior.

Every Mark had a handler, a *mal'akh*—an angel—directly responsible for assigning them to targets. Reed had once likened the mark system to the judicial system. The archangels were the bail bondsmen, Reed was her dispatcher, and she was a bounty hunter. She wasn't a very good one . . . yet. But she was learning and trying.

In the meantime, Reed was responsible for her assignments and for peripherally ensuring her safety. As her mentor, Alec's sole responsibility—under usual circumstances—was keeping her alive. But God had been unwilling to lose the talents of his most established and powerful enforcer. Alec cut a deal to be with her, and the result was that Reed often had more liability where she was concerned. Considering the festering animosity between the two brothers, the setup was fucked all around.

"Welcome back to the land of the living, Ms. Hollis," Reed greeted. He smiled his cocky smile, but his dark eyes held an uncertainty Eve found endearing. He had no idea what to make of his feelings for her. Since she was in a relationship with his brother, she couldn't help him with that. She tried not to think about her feelings for him. It was just too complicated. Her life was already a disaster of biblical proportions.

Both men spotted the angel in the corner, who stood unmoving. They bowed slightly in deference.

Because Miyoko was too busy glaring at Eve, she failed to catch the gesture. Eve used her job as an interior designer as an excuse for Reed's frequent visits. As far as her family knew, she worked from home most days and if Reed wanted to see what she was up to, stopping by was the best way to do it. But Miyoko didn't believe the lie. She assumed all male interior designers were gay and Reed was most definitely *not*. Eve had no idea what her mother thought was really going on, but she knew the obvious animosity between the two men was fodder for suspicions.

Alec's smile warmed her from the inside. "How are you feeling?"

"Thirsty."

"I'll get you some ice water," Reed offered.

She smiled. "Thank you."

Alec bent and pressed his lips to her forehead. "Are you hungry?"

"A banana would be nice." She caught his wrist before he could draw away. "I had a dream. A nightmare. I was killed by a dragon."

"Your subconscious is trying to tell you something," her mother interrupted. "But you couldn't have dreamt you died. I heard if you die in your dreams, you die in real life."

"I think that's a myth."

"There is no way to know," Miyoko argued as she folded laundry. "If it happened to you, you would be dead and couldn't tell us."

Alec sat on the edge of the bed, watching Eve with an alert gaze. He knew she couldn't say what she meant while her mother was in the room.

"It's over now," he soothed. "You're safe."

"It was so real . . . I don't understand how I'm sitting here now."

"We'll talk later, after you've had a chance to eat." He squeezed her hand. His expression held the softness he showed only to her. "Let me get you that banana."

He left, and her mom returned to the side of the bed. Leaning over, Miyoko whispered loudly, "He fights with your boss. About *everything.* You would think they were married. Too much testosterone in those two. Not enough brains."

The angel made a choked noise.

"Mom . . ." Eve glanced at the corner. He looked pained. It was an expression her father wore often.

Miyoko straightened and gathered up the now-folded clothes. "A *thoughtful* man would carry sunscreen to the beach. He wouldn't let you get burned."

Sunburned at the beach. Eve snorted at the excuse. If only she'd been bedridden for something so simple. "I can count on one hand the number of guys I've seen carry sunscreen."

"A good man would," her mother insisted.

"Like Dad?"

"Sure."

"I've never seen Dad with sunscreen."

"That's not the point."

"I thought it was."

Eve loved her father, she really did. Darrel Hollis was a good ol' boy from Alabama with an even-keeled temper and a gentle smile. He was also oblivious. Retired now, he rose at dawn, watched television or read, then went back to bed after dinner. The most unexpected thing he had ever done was marry a foreign exchange student (and Eve suspected her mother hadn't given him much choice in the matter).

"Stop dating pretty boys," Miyoko admonished, "and find someone stable."

Eve shot a beseeching glance at the angel in the corner. He sighed and stepped closer. His voice had a soothing resonance no mortal could create.

"You want to replant the flowers in the pots by your front door," he whispered in Miyoko's ear. "You will go to the nursery, then home, where you will spend the rest of the afternoon indulging in your passion for gardening. Evangeline is fine and no longer needs you."

Her mother paused, her head tilting as she absorbed the thoughts she assumed were her own. The gift of persuasion. Eve hadn't mastered that one yet.

"You should get a spa pedicure, too," Eve added. "You deserve it."

Miyoko shook her head. "I don't need—"

"Get a pedicure," the angel ordered.

"I think I'll get a pedicure," Miyoko said.

"With flowers painted on your big toes," Eve went on.

The angel shot her a quelling glance.

Eve winced. "If you want," she amended quickly.

Alec returned with the banana. Standing by her bed, he peeled it, arresting her with the sight of his flexing biceps.

"I'm going home," her mom said suddenly. "The laundry is done, the dishes washed. You're fine. You don't need me."

"Thank you for everything." Eve intended to stand and hug her mother, but remembered that she was naked between her satin sheets.

Miyoko waved her off and headed toward the door. "Let me change first and get my stuff together, then I'll say good-bye."

Reed's voice rumbled down the hallway and swept over Eve's skin like the warm caress of the sun. "Let me help you with that, Mrs. Hollis."

Eve looked at Alec, who resumed his seat on the edge of her bed. Then, she glanced at the angel. "Hi."

"Hello, Evangeline." He stepped forward, his heavy boots making no sound on the hardwood floor. He had an inordinate number of feathers and appeared to have three pairs of wings. He was beyond impressive; he was the most perfectly gorgeous creature she had ever seen.

"Who are you?" she asked before taking a bite of the fruit. The first chunk was swallowed almost whole, followed immediately by another. Her stomach growled, reiterating that the mark burned a ton of calories and she was expected to keep up by eating frequently.

"Sabrael."

Chewing, she glanced at Alec again.

"He is a seraph," he explained.

Her eyes widened and she chewed faster, embarrassed to be naked in such company. The seraphim were the highest ranking angels, far above the seven archangels who managed the day-to-day operations of the mark system here on Earth. Alec was a *mal'akh*—the lowest rank of angel—as was his brother. Eve was a lowly Mark, onc of thousands of poor suckers drafted into godly service for perceived sins. They worked for absolution by hunting and killing Infernals who'd crossed the line one too many times. A bounty was earned for every successful vanquishing, an indulgence that went toward the saving of Mark souls.

"Can I get dressed?" she asked, wiping her mouth with the tips of her fingers.

Alec stood and took the empty peel from her. "Sabrael won't leave until he speaks with you. Celestials have a different view of nudity than mortals do. Tell me what you need and I'll get it."

Eve directed him to a beach cover-up that hung in her closet. It was made of pale blue terry cloth and sported a hood, short sleeves, and a pouch in the front. Alec dropped it over her head, and she shoved her various body parts through the appropriate openings.

"Okay, Sabrael," she began, brushing her hair back from her face. "Why are you here?"

"The better question would be: Why are *you* here, Evangeline? You should be dead."

She bit back a groan. Another riddle. It seemed all the angels spoke in them, except for Alec and Reed. Those two spoke so bluntly she'd be perpetually blushing if not for the mark, which prevented her body from wasting energy. "I thought I was."

"You were. But Cain claims you have knowledge we need."

Eve looked at Alec. "You brought me back from the dead to grill me for information?"

Sabrael's arms crossed in front of his massive chest. "You were going someplace where we would not have been able to ask you. It was the only way."

Her gaze moved heavenward. "You're not winning any brownie points with me," she called out.

"It is not your place to demand Jehovah prove himself to you," Sabrael said in a terrible voice.

"You said we missed something in Upland," Alec prompted, his fingers lacing with hers.

She thought back to her last assignment—vanquishing an Infernal in one of the men's bathrooms at Qualcomm Stadium. Alec had taken her out on their first "date"—a Chargers versus Seahawks football game. Reed had come along and said it was time to parlay her classroom instruction into the field.

"A wolf," she murmured.

"What?"

"I assigned her to a werewolf," Reed said from the doorway. He approached the opposite side of the bed and passed a chilled bottle of water across the expanse to Eve. "A kid. Easy pickings."

"Only it wasn't a wolf," Alec retorted. "And it sure as shit wasn't easy."

"But there was one there," Eve explained. "One of the kids we spotted in the convenience store in Upland."

Upland. She'd never think of the town the same way again. They had been sent there on an investigation. Just as Marks bore the Mark of Cain on their arms, Infernals bore "details" that betrayed what species they were, and what their rank in Hell's hierarchy was. Sort of like military insignia. They also reeked of rotting souls, which made them easy to detect. When Eve stumbled across an Infernal who bore no details and no stench, she and Alec had been tasked with discovering how that was possible. They'd found that a masking agent had been created, a concoction that could potentially tip the balance between good and evil enough to set off Armageddon.

The operation had been run out of a masonry in Upland. The place was gone now, blown to smithereens when Eve shoved a water demon into a fired-up kiln. But it appeared the original problem still remained to be dealt with. The dragon had been odor-free, a condition made possible only by the mask.

"He said the Alpha sent him," she went on. "They wanted me dead as retaliation for the death of his son."

Alec's face took on a hardened cast that chilled her blood. "Charles."

"The bigger issue," she said quickly, "was that the dragon he brought with him didn't stink or have any details."

"There has to be more of the masking agent somewhere," Reed said. "A stockpile or a new batch."

"Perhaps the mask is permanent?" Sabrael suggested.

"No, it wears off. I saw it happen."

The seraph's gaze moved to Alec. "You did not smell the Infernal either?"

"I told you, I didn't pay attention." Alec continued to focus his attention on Eve. The muscle in his arm twitched just below the mark, as if it pained him, and she knew immediately what he was doing—he was lying. The mark burned when sins were committed.

Turning his head to look at Sabrael, Alec said, "I haven't been trained as a mentor. I don't know how to focus on both the target and Eve at once. I only know how to hone in on her."

To bring her back from the brink of Hell, he'd lied to someone in power. A seraph. Or maybe God himself. Alec would pay for that . . . somehow, some way. And now he was lying again. For her.

Her grip on his hand tightened until she was white knuckled, but he didn't complain.

Miyoko bustled back into the room, her gaze narrowing at the sight of the two men on either side of Eve's bed. "Okay, I'm ready to go."

Alec stood so Eve could get out of bed, but he held her back when it became clear that she was too dizzy to complete the effort. She held out her arms for a hug instead.

"When did you get your scar removed?" her mother asked as she bent over.

Her fingers brushed over the Mark of Cain. All of Eve's childhood scars had been removed with the mark. Her body was a temple now. It ran like a well-oiled machine—precise and without deviations such as sweating, a racing heartbeat, or labored breathing. Except when sex was involved. Then everything worked in full mortal fashion. It made orgasms as addicting as a drug, since it was the only time a Mark could get "high."

Eve frowned when her mother didn't say anything about the mark on her deltoid. Her younger sister Sophia's first tattoo had been lamented with the statement, "You used to be such a beautiful baby."

"I get a tattoo," Eve said dryly, "and you're worried about a mole?"

"You got a tattoo?" her mother screeched. "Where?"

Eve blinked and looked down at her arm. She glanced at Alec who shook his head.

Her mother couldn't see it.

Sadness settled over Eve, weighing her down. The barrier between her and her old life wasn't just metaphorical.

"Just kidding," Eve husked, her throat tight.

"That was terrible," her mother complained, pushing her gently in recrimination. "I almost cried."

They hugged, and her mother straightened. "I made some *onigiri*. It's in a container by the coffeemaker."

"Thank you, Mom."

Reed moved to the door. "I'll help you carry your things down, Mrs. Hollis."

Miyoko beamed. Eve's condo was on the upper floor and the carport was subterranean.

"Kiss ass," Alec muttered, as they left.

Eve smacked him. "She needs help."

"I was going to help her, if he hadn't jumped all over her."

Sabrael cleared his throat. "You will hunt the Alpha wolf, Cain."

There was a long moment of stunned silence, then, "Eve is in training."

"And she will remain that way," the seraph assured. "The classroom is the safest place for her to be, but you must go."

Alec shook his head. "No way. You can't separate a mentor/Mark pair."

"Charles Grimshaw is connected to the Infernal mask. His son was at the masonry where the concoction was being manufactured and the masked dragon that killed Evangeline was sent at his behest. Time is of the essence. He must be put down before he causes more damage. Your agreement was that you would still perform individual hunts as well as your mentored ones."

Alec ran both hands through his dark hair. "Once it becomes known that she's still alive, they will hunt her. She'll need me nearby to protect her."

"Raguel has full use of his gifts at the moment. I doubt even you can offer better protection than an archangel in full regalia. Also, don't forget that you are earning double indulgences for every vanquishing. Killing an Infernal of Grimshaw's prominence will advance you by years."

Alec's jaw tightened. "And I'm just supposed to say, 'Sorry, angel. I'm off to save my own ass, so you're on your own'?"

Eve winced.

"I'll be okay," she reassured, her thumb brushing soothingly over his palm. "Shouldn't be any trouble at all. You and Reed can go about your business without worrying. We all know Gadara won't allow anything bad to happen to me, since he needs me to bully you two."

"That doesn't mean," Reed drawled as he returned, "that we're not going to worry. You always manage to find trouble."

She almost argued that Gadara liked to shove her face first into trouble just to irritate Alec, but that wouldn't make them feel better.

"I especially don't like that this week is field training," Alec said, glancing at Reed. "It's one thing to be in Gadara Tower. It's another to be out in the open."

"Fort McCroskey is a military base," Sabrael said.

"A *closed* base."

"It still has a military presence, and Raguel will travel with his entourage of guards."

Eve frowned at all three men. "What are you talking about?"

Reed explained. "Raguel is taking your class up to Northern California. There's a former Army base there that he likes to use for field exercises."

Eve groaned inwardly. A week-long trip with a class of newbie Marks who resented her for having the infamous Cain as a mentor and the equally revered Abel as a handler. She figured the coming week would be as much fun as a Brazilian wax.

"Doesn't the Alpha live in Northern California?" she asked.

Alec nodded. "A couple hours north of the base. Fort McCroskey is near Monterey, the Grimshaw pack is nearer to Oakland."

"A couple of hours' drive is quite convenient," Sabrael pointed out. "You could have been sent on assignment to the other side of the world."

"You can't make me like this," Alec bit out. "But I'll take Eve up to Monterey, then continue on."

Reed grinned. "I'll keep a close eye on her while Cain is busy."

"You have an Infernal to classify," Sabrael reminded him. "You both must trust that Raguel will see to Evangeline's safety."

Eve sighed. "Anyone want to switch places?"

"Sorry, babe," Reed said. "Mark training isn't a place to play hooky."

"She's not your babe," Alec snapped.

Reed held both hands up in a gesture of surrender that was belied by the mischievous twinkle in his eyes.

Their feud wasn't helped by her past intimacy with Reed. That happened before Alec had reentered her life, so he didn't hold it against her. But to say that he didn't trust his brother to be within a mile of her would be an understatement.

Alec looked at Eve, his features softening. "You'd rather hunt real demons than pretend to?"

"Maybe I was resurrected with a different personality," she suggested. "Like *Invasion of the Body Snatchers*."

"Or maybe you're pissed off at getting killed, and want a little payback."

Her mouth tilted at the corners. How well he knew her.

"But if you are a pod person," he continued, "you have great taste in bodies."

A tingle moved through her. His wink told her he knew it.

"Four more weeks, angel. Then we'll tear 'em up."

Four more weeks of class, one of which was a camp-out. Eve sighed. She was definitely back among the living.

Hell would have more direct means of torture.

CHAPTER 2

I'm sorry about Takeo."

Reed glanced at the Mark who entered Gadara Tower beside him. "Thank you, Kobe."

Kobe Denner scrubbed a hand over his face and cursed in his native Zulu. "He saved my life once. I still owed him one. He was a good Mark."

"My best." Avenging the Mark's death was at the top of Reed's to-do list. But first he had to classify the Infernal who did the deed, then he needed to learn how best to vanquish it.

"I heard some unknown demon-type did it."

"Yes, that's true."

"Must have been a badass to take out Takeo."

"I've never seen anything like it." The graveness of the situation was evident in Reed's somber tone.

"Shit." Kobe's dark eyes were sad. His features were kept youthful by the mark, but nothing could hide the weight of experience that burdened his five-foot ten-inch frame. Killing demons took a terrible toll on the soul. "It's already bad out there."

"We'll find and kill it. We always do." Reed was grateful to sound more confident than he felt.

Kobe paused beside one of the many planters that decorated the lobby atrium. "Do you think Takeo got in?"

Reed inhaled deeply, contemplating the best answer to the question. It was a common one among Marks. They were working for absolution and all wanted to know if they would be granted access to Heaven if they lost their lives before collecting enough indulgences.

"He deserved to," Reed answered.

It was the best answer to give that wasn't a violation of the Decalogue, but it clearly wasn't the answer Kobe wanted to hear.

Still, the Mark accepted it with a grim nod. "If you need me for anything, let me know."

"I will." Reed shook the Mark's hand, then they separated. Kobe headed toward the tucked-away bank of elevators that led to the subterranean floors, an area that was restricted to Marks and Infernal allies and prisoners. Reed crossed the bustling lobby to reach the private elevator that would take him directly to Raguel Gadara's office.

At least one hundred business-minded pedestrians congested the vast space. Fifty floors above them, a massive skylight illuminated the atrium and served as an architectural invitation to God's blessings. The steady hum of numerous conversations and the industrious whirring of the glass tube elevators testified to both the effectiveness of the design and Raguel's widely lauded business acumen. On the surface, all was well at the headquarters of the North American firm. Mortals conducted business here in blissful ignorance of Gadara's true purpose—the oversight and control of thousands of Marks.

The seven archangels were responsible for funding their firms in a secular fashion. Raguel had a knack for real estate, which had created a multibillion-dollar empire and a notoriety that rivaled Donald Trump and Steve Wynn. Gadara Enterprises owned properties the world over, from resorts in Las Vegas and Atlantic City to office buildings in Milan and New York. As a handler assigned to Raguel's firm, Reed had traversed the various halls so often he could do it with his eyes closed. But ever since he had marked Eve here, he could no longer do so comfortably.

Without volition, his gaze moved to the stairwell door that concealed the landing where he'd taken Eve. Memories hit his brain in a rapid-fire series of graphic images. The recollections were so vivid, he could feel her lush curves beneath his hands and smell her perfume. His dick hardened and he adjusted himself for comfort.

"Damn you," he growled, as much to Cain and Eve as to himself. He needed her to advance his ambitions, but he didn't need to admire her. Or covet her.

Entering the elevator, Reed stabbed at the lone button on the panel. There was a long pause as the camera in the corner focused on his features, then the security guard on the receiving end of the feed set the lift in motion. It shot up the thirty flights to the penthouse in a matter of seconds, but Reed could have shifted across the distance in the blink of an eye. Teleportation was a blessing given to all *mal'akhs*—except for Cain, who'd had the gift stripped from him. Reed chose to take the slower secular route today in order to gain the time needed to get himself under control. By the time the doors opened, he felt ready to deal with Raguel.

He exited into the massive, well-appointed office as if he owned it. An intricately carved mahogany desk was angled in the far corner, facing the bank of windows on the opposite side. Two brown leather chairs faced the desk and an eternal fire crackled in the fireplace. Above the mantel, a portrait of the *Last Supper* as imagined by Da Vinci brought God into the space, as did the crucifix adorning the wall behind Gadara's chair.

The archangel himself stood at the windows with his back to Reed. His hands were shoved in his pockets, and his bearing was regal and relaxed. The contrast between his cream-colored garments and his coffee-dark skin enhanced both beautifully.

"How is Ms. Hollis?" he asked, without turning his head.

Adjusting his slacks, Reed settled into the chair before the archangel's desk. "Recovering and putting on a brave face."

"Cain is not capable of arranging Ms. Hollis's resurrection alone." Raguel pivoted away from the Orange County vista. "You must have helped him."

"Help Cain? *Me?*" Reed's mouth curved slightly. Whether he had or hadn't was for him alone to know. The ambitious archangel didn't need any more ammunition.

The mark system had been built to work cohesively and, at one time, it had. Now, however, the race to please God better and more often than their counterparts had led to dissension and subterfuge among the archangels.

"Not that I mind, of course," Raguel assured. "It would have been a tragedy to lose her."

"It's a miracle it hasn't happened sooner, considering the deviations from protocol that she's suffered through."

"She has to be put through her paces. She has to be better than her peers, tougher and quicker. Unafraid. Her work with Cain will always make her the target of Infernals like Charles Grimshaw."

Reed's fingers curled around the ends of the armrests. Raguel was using her to further his own ends . . . and to aggravate Cain. "She became a target because we had her waving in the wind."

It was a coup for the archangel to have Cain on his team, and that was possible only because Eve was assigned to the North American firm. If anything happened to take Eve from Raguel's power, Cain—and all the prestige he brought with him—would be lost, too. Which was why Raguel was dragging Reed into the whole mess. He hadn't counted on Eve throwing a wrench into his plans.

"What does not kill her will make her stronger."

Reed's gut twisted with the memory of her scorched and broken on the bathroom floor. "She's already been killed once. Guess it can't get any worse."

"Your sarcasm is ill placed."

"What do you expect, Raguel? You ask if she's okay when you're the reason she was dead in the first place."

The archangel exhaled audibly, a soft but chastising sound. He was in his element while class was in session, the only time an archangel was given free use of his celestial gifts. Power thrummed through the air around him and divine radiance burnished his appearance with a golden glow. If he chose to, he could extend gold-tipped wings to a thirty-foot span. But he only had four weeks left before his students would graduate and he would once again be trapped within his temporal guise.

The training of new Marks took seven weeks, and the archangels rotated the duties so they could each enjoy their God-given power. The rest of the year the Lord *suggested* they live mortal lives. He believed the archangels would be more sympathetic to His beloved mortals if they suffered the same inconveniences.

The archangels could choose to disregard the suggestion, of course. Jehovah was a strong proponent of free will. But there was a price to pay for every transgression. Considering the heat of the competition between the archangels, they were loath to incur even the smallest setback.

Raguel changed the subject. "We have to find the Infernal who killed your Mark."

"Yes, we do. Has there been word of further sightings?"

"One possible. In Australia."

Raguel moved toward his desk. Elegant in build with coarse black hair liberally sprinkled with gray by design, the archangel didn't age as mortals did, but he was forced to simulate the passing of years in order to allay suspicion. Eventually, this incarnation of Raguel would have to die and he would be reborn as someone else. Sometimes slipping into the role of a descendant was possible. At others, a full reinvention was the only viable way.

"Was another Mark lost?"

"Yes."

A chill swept through Reed. He would never forget the manner of Takeo's death. There had been nothing left of the Mark but skin clinging to forest branches and fluttering in the night air. "You can't mistake this Infernal's signature for any other's. If it's the same demon, it will be obvious. Was there a witness?"

"Yes, the handler was present at the time."

Mariel, another handler under Raguel's purview, had heretofore been the only celestial to glimpse the demon. Only briefly, but long enough to bring a haunting terror to her eyes when she spoke of it.

It crawled inside my Mark, she'd said. *Disappeared in her. She c-could not c-contain it.*

What remained was an explosion of tissue and skin in quantities not sufficient to make up a body. Where did the bones and blood go?

Reed exhaled harshly.

Raguel leaned one hip against the front of his desk. "Perhaps you and Mariel should go to Australia and question Uriel's handler yourselves."

"I want the Infernal, not reports of it."

"It will not take you long. A few hours, at most."

"If you insist, I'll go. Otherwise, I don't see the point." But Reed's outer capitulation came with inner doubts. Aside from having lost a Mark to the beast, he had nothing to offer in the way of assistance. Hands-on investigative work was the duty of Marks. His job was simply to know the strengths and weaknesses of those under his watch and to assign them to hunts where they had the best probability of success.

"You do not seem pleased," Raguel noted. "I thought you would be."

"Why? Because I want retribution for Takeo's death? It won't bring my best Mark back. I can only pray that my testimony was sufficient and he is with God now."

"Something else is troubling you, then. What is it?"

"This whole thing troubles me. Violence is escalating. Now there's a mask Infernals can hide behind and a new class of demon that's tipping the balance."

"We do not know that there is more than the one."

"It's killed three Marks in three weeks," Reed bit out. "One is enough. How long do you think it'll be before Sammael deems the trial run a success and makes more of them?"

The Fallen One was always eager to exploit any advantage.

"Jehovah never gives us more than we can handle. The Infernals are not the only ones who are improving."

Reed pushed to his feet. "That knowledge isn't helping me at the moment."

Raguel opened the humidor on his desk and withdrew a cigar, placing it between his lips uncut and unlit. He didn't smoke, but he enjoyed the act of holding a cigar in his mouth for reasons Reed had never grasped.

"Are you having a crisis of faith?" the archangel asked, his words spoken around the cigar.

"If this Infernal continues to murder Marks at a rate of one a week, we'll need to step up recruitment, training, mentoring—just to maintain our numbers. And if it keeps taking out our best and brightest, we'll soon be left with only novices."

"You paint the direst of pictures, Abel, as if this demon will charge through our ranks unchecked."

"It's my job to anticipate and prevent."

"Which is why I think you should accompany Mariel."

"I'm going." Reed stood. "I'll call her and we'll head out."

There was more behind Raguel's request than preventive measures. The archangel wanted his firm to be the one responsible for the identification and vanquishing of this new demon. He didn't want Uriel to take that honor, or any of the other archangels.

"I will be assembling the class and taking them to Fort McCroskey this evening. Report your findings to me there."

"Fine. Keep an eye on Eve."

Raguel withdrew the cigar from his smiling mouth. "Of course. She is my star pupil."

"Is that because she's already good? Or because you want her to be?"

"She is passably proficient." Raguel shrugged. "She could be brilliant, if her heart was in it. As it is, only determination drives her, and that is not enough to achieve the heights she might be capable of."

"How many new Marks have their heart in it? They're all drafted into service." Reed ran a hand through his short hair, reminded again that Eve was not at all the sort of mortal who usually became a Mark. She was/ had been agnostic and she hadn't committed a crime of sufficient severity. Her only offense was being a temptation to Cain; the shining, delicious apple in his garden of demons and death.

"Ms. Hollis is different," Raguel said, his resonant voice rolling gently through the air. "Marks always come to us with varying degrees of faith within them. She has none at all, and she is hindered without it. Other Marks find strength in their desperation to save their souls; she lacks that edge and that deficiency might be the death of her."

If Raguel didn't see to that first. "Are the other Marks still hostile toward her? She might be 'dumbing down' to avoid further antagonism."

"I have never witnessed any hostilities."

Reed's mouth curved wryly. "That doesn't mean they're not there."

Because Eve was paired with Cain, a legend in the field for both his 100 percent kill rate and his autonomy, she was tormented by those who were jealous of her "good fortune." They assumed Cain did the lion's share of the work and she stood around looking pretty. They didn't bother to learn how wrong they were.

Cain had also pulled strings to keep Eve close to her family. Marks, as a rule, were transplanted to foreign firms. They were mostly loners, those who had either distanced themselves from family and friends or didn't have any for a variety of reasons. Their lack of strong emotional ties facilitated their acclimation to the life of a Mark. It also created a divide between them and Eve that was undeniable.

But Raguel blindly—or conveniently—ignored how the other Marks treated her.

"Just keep her alive while I'm gone," Reed said. "That's not asking too much."

"Keep *yourself* alive, Abel," Raguel returned. "We have a great deal of work ahead of us."

As if Reed could forget that.

Armageddon. It was coming. Sooner, rather than later.

Alec pulled Eve's Chrysler 300 into her assigned spot in the subterranean garage of Gadara Tower. Turning off the engine, he glanced at her, noting her set jaw and taut posture. Her long, dark hair was pulled back in a ponytail and her slender body was dressed in a black cotton tank top and khaki shorts. He reached out to her, kneading her tense shoulder muscles. "Are you okay?"

She nodded.

"Liar," he murmured.

"Let's just say I would prefer to go camping with a different crew, if I had a choice."

His hand wrapped around her nape and pulled her closer. He nuzzled his nose against hers. "I'll miss you."

An impatient thumping on Eve's trunk shook the car and drew his attention to the rear window.

"No place for muckin' aboot!" a masculine voice shouted.

Alec pushed up his sunglasses, noting that the heckler was one of a group of three people walking by. He was tanned, blond, and looked to be in his early thirties.

"That's Ken," Eve said with laughter in her voice.

Ken's eyes darted between them, widening with horrified recognition. He quickly retreated, holding both hands up in a gesture of surrender. He had a duffel bag draped over one shoulder and teeth white enough to blind. "Sorry, Cain. I didnae ken it was you."

"Smooth move, arsehat," one of his companions muttered, shoving him.

"Ken, huh?" Alec grinned. "I was just thinking he looks like a Barbie doll."

"Don't let that pretty-boy exterior fool you. He's the best in the class."

Alec climbed out of the driver's seat and rounded the trunk. Opening the passenger door, he helped her out and asked, "What's his nickname?"

Eve had assigned names to all the Marks in her class. He thought he knew why. A nickname could serve two purposes: it could dehumanize a subject or it could personalize them. Alec suspected Eve's use of nicknames was due to both reasons.

"Just Ken," she said, "since he does look like a Ken doll."

Catching her elbow, Alec led her toward the elevators.

She shot him a wry glance. "You know, Gadara isn't going to like me riding up to Monterey with you instead of with the others."

"Gadara could use one of his planes to transport you all up there. Since he doesn't want to make life easy for you, we're not going out of our way to make life easy for him."

"You keep breaking rules for me."

He shrugged it off.

She looked at him in a way that made him want to take her back to bed. "The wolf in the bathroom told me you made a deal for my life. Then broke it."

"You believe everything an Infernal tells you?" He didn't want her gratitude. Not when he was the reason she was marked to begin with, and certainly not when he was hoping she would learn to like being a Mark.

"Thank you," she said softly, killing him.

They rode the elevator up to the atrium level.

Eve's nose wrinkled. "I don't think I'll ever get used to the smell of so many Marks in one enclosed space."

"You have to admit, it's more pleasant than the stench of rotting Infernal souls."

"Yeah, but it's too much. Makes it hard to breathe."

The lush vegetation in the atrium planters created a humidity that intensified the sweet smell created when a hundred-plus Marks gathered. The effect was pleasant to Alec, as was the surge of power he felt whenever he was surrounded by Marks. Stepping into a firm was always a heady rush, no matter which firm he visited or where it was located. His blood thrummed with energy and his heart rate lurched into an elevated rhythm, as if the other Marks shared their energy with him. But Eve's senses were still very sensitive. He wondered how long that would last. Since he'd never mentored before and had yet to be trained for the task, he had no benchmark to compare her to.

They crossed the marble lobby to a recessed hallway where a private set of elevators would take them to the bowels of the building.

"What do you know about this fort we're going to?" Eve asked. "Anything?"

"Fort McCroskey was closed in 1991. There are some services still available—a commissary and some family housing for the students of a nearby military school—but otherwise it's a ghost town."

"Why are we going there?"

"There's enough infrastructure left to facilitate training. The Army still uses it for that reason on occasion and since our purpose is the same—the defeat of an enemy through force—it serves our needs just as well."

"Fun."

Alec linked his fingers with Eve's. The next week would be rough for her. "I'll be back before you even have a chance to miss me."

The cast of her features changed from disgruntlement to worry. "I'm an idiot. Bitching about learning how to defend myself while you're on assignment."

"I'll be fine. You just take care of yourself."

Eve eyed him carefully. "But it's not going to be easy, right? He has subordinate wolves to protect him; you're alone."

"It's no fun when it's easy."

"I wish I felt that way." She leaned against the metal handrail that surrounded the elevator car and crossed her arms. It was her *you-are-not-going-to-bullshit-me* pose. "Have you done this before? Gone after an Alpha while he's home with his pack?"

"Piece of cake."

"Now who's lying?"

Alec grinned and took in the view from the top of her head down to the combat boots on her feet. Eve was the type of exotic beauty people looked more than twice at. Creamy skin, inky dark tresses, red lips. His own paradise, his refuge from the rigors of his life.

It had been lust at first sight ten years ago and nothing had changed since then, despite being apart the entire time. She was his apple, his temptation. He was her downfall. Talk about a shitty foundation for a relationship. They had baggage, hurt feelings, regrets. Eve was the kind of woman a man married. White picket fence, kids, and a dog. Alec was aiming for advancement to archangel and heading his own firm.

The elevator doors opened and they stepped into the training center. The entire floor was dedicated to creating the best fighting force of Marks possible. There were classrooms with desks as well as dojos, indoor firing ranges, weight rooms, and fencing studios. Alec sometimes stayed to watch the instructions, impressed with the level of efficiency. As the original Mark, he'd been forced to survive by the skin of his teeth. Some said he was born to kill, built for it, and he agreed.

Eve led the way to a glass-enclosed conference room. As they entered, the conversation died and all eyes turned toward them. There were a handful of people in the room, ranging in age from late teens to middle age, male and female. Some sat around the long table that dominated the center of the room, others sat atop it with their legs dangling over the sides. Ken was pouring himself a glass of water from the silver pitcher on a nearby console. They all looked at Eve, then glanced furtively at Alec, except for a nearby blonde who assessed him boldly from head to toe.

"How are you feeling, Hollis?" asked a dark-haired Hispanic man in jeans and a button-down flannel shirt.

"Good. Thanks for asking."

As Alec joined Eve in the far corner, he returned every stare. Eve hopped onto the widow ledge, her lithe legs dangling and her fingers curled around the lip. They were white knuckled, betraying her unease. The tension in the room was thick and it pissed him off.

He leaned back and crossed his arms, facing the room dead-on. Uncomfortable shuffling ensued, then a return to the previous discussion.

Ken cleared his throat. "I cannae wait to get started."

"You're two sammies short of a picnic," a petite redhead said derisively, flipping her hair over her shoulder.

"Well," Alec murmured for Eve's ears only. "The girls are easily pegged with their nicknames, I think. 'Goth Girl' especially. I'm assuming the redhead is 'Princess,' since she's covered in glitter."

Eve smiled. "I am so high school, aren't I?"

"It's not your fault they're easily identifiable. Besides, I liked you in high school," he purred, alluding to the ill-fated tryst that led them to where they were today. He couldn't regret it, and he took every opportunity to remind her of why she shouldn't regret it either.

Eve bumped her shoulder into his. "Can you guess which one is 'Mastermind'? That one's a bit harder."

Alec looked around. There were seven people in the room besides them-selves. Since he had already identified four of the Marks, he quickly ruled them out—Ken, the red-haired princess with her glitter mascara and lip gloss, the Goth girl with her pale blonde hair and pixie-perfect features, and the "Fashionista" whose height and rail-thin figure were the stuff of supermodel dreams. The remaining occupants were the guy who greeted Eve when they entered, a wan and slightly portly teenage boy in a nylon jogging suit, and a gray-haired gentleman in dress slacks and polo shirt.

"The old guy?" he guessed. "He kinda has that Magneto vibe."

"You're older than he is," Eve reminded. "And no, he's 'Gopher.' His name is Robert Edwards."

"Okay. Then it's the guy in the jeans."

"Nope."

Alec's eyes widened. "The kid? You're shitting me."

Laughing, she said, "No, I'm not. He's older than he looks. Early twen-ties. Name is Chad Richens. He and Edwards are both from England, so I'm guessing that's one of the reasons why they gravitated toward each other. The other is that Richens can come up with schemes, but he doesn't like to do the dirty work."

"Like what?"

"Like the time he had Edwards swap out everyone's bayonets with dull ones from the previous day. We all worked twice as hard as he did that session, because he and Edwards were the only ones to have freshly sharp-ened blades. It was Richens's idea, but Edwards was the one who actually made the switch. Claire freaked when Ken figured it out. I thought she was going to give herself an aneurism."

"The fashionista?"

"Yes, Claire Dubois, from France. Isn't she gorgeous? She says she wasn't before the mark. Apparently, she used to be a meth addict. She burned her apartment down and killed her boyfriend in the process, which is why she was marked. She's still very high-strung and fidgets a lot."

Alec studied the teenager. "How is Richens doing in the physical por-tion of the class?"

"Not good. Even with the help of the mark, he has trouble with the combat training, which is why I think he tries to get through the sneaky way. He's a video game junkie and strategy is his strength, not his fists. He also has a short fuse." Her voice lowered. "Edwards told me Richens's dad was abusive. I think he carries some of that around with him."

It didn't escape Alec's notice how well Eve had researched her class-mates in order to better understand them. It was a sign of a natural hunter. Killing wasn't merely a physical act. It was also cerebral. "There must be some potential in him, or he would have been assigned to a nonfield posi-tion."

"He killed someone. I don't know the details. He won't talk about it."

"Murderers usually end up with field work automatically."

"Stupid," she muttered. "I think his being here is a major screwup on someone's part."

"Watch it." Alec shot her a chastising glance. Eve's beliefs were her own and he respected her right to have them, but sometimes she voiced her opinions in a way that was too irreverent to be safe. "So, that leaves us with the dark-haired guy. He's 'Romeo,' I take it."

Eve nodded. "Antonio Garza, from Rome. But that's not why I call him Romeo. He's got a thing going with Laurel . . . and being discreet isn't his strong suit."

"Which one is Laurel? The princess?"

"That's the one. Laurel Hogan. Romeo wooed the Goth girl first, but she says he's too much of a gigolo for her tastes. He's better off with Laurel anyway. If you ask me, Izzie is missing a few tools in the shed."

Alec studied the petite blonde with a calculating eye. She was slender, pale, her blue eyes rimmed with thick kohl and her mouth painted a dark purple. He would describe her as "delicate," despite her spiked collar and cuffs. "Why do you say that?"

"Izzie's pulled a Bowie knife on damn near everyone in this room at some point or another. She doesn't like any of us."

"That's an odd name."

"It's short for Iselda. Iselda Seiler. 'Izzie' suits her more than 'Goth,' I think. Like the other girls, her nickname is more of a description than anything else."

Alec noted the guarded way Eve watched the other woman. Not that he blamed her. The blonde had been mad dogging him since he entered. "You don't like her."

"I don't mind her," she corrected. "But she sure seems to have a problem with me. More so than the rest of the class, and that's saying something."

"Is there anyone here you get along with?"

"Well . . ." Eve shrugged. "I don't *not* get along with anyone, but I haven't made any friends either. I just keep a low profile and stay out of the way."

Alec turned to face her. He asked her about her experiences in class every day, and every day she found a way to redirect him to another topic. Their present conversation was the most she had shared to date.

"How does Raguel feel about that?" he asked. "I bet he wants you front and center."

Her nose wrinkled. "Sure, so he can pick on me and point out all the ways I'm doing things wrong."

Alec's jaw clenched. When he was done with Charles, he would deal with Raguel. Eve had innate talent. It was a travesty that she didn't know it because the archangel withheld his praise.

As if Alec's thoughts served as the archangel's cue to appear, Raguel entered the room by floating through the glass door, displaying for one and all a small portion of his power. He was dressed casually in loose-fitting indigo linen pants and tunic, but the intensity that radiated from him belied the outward appearance of leisure.

A brief nod passed between Alec and the archangel, then Raguel looked around the conference room. His lyrical voice rolled though the room like smoke, "Good afternoon."

"Good afternoon, *moreh*," the class greeted in unison, using the Hebrew word for "teacher."

Raguel frowned. "Where is Molenaar?"

"He hasnae shown his face yet," Ken answered.

Alec glanced at Eve, trying to remember which classmate was absent. Her lips formed the words, *the Stoner.*

Nodding, Alec wondered at the composition of students in the class. Two former drug addicts, a teenager with poor motor skills, and an elderly gentleman most likely set in his ways. Marks came in all shapes, sizes, pasts, and temperaments. But only select Marks became hunters rather than behind-the-scenes personnel with occupations like personal assistant or travel coordinator.

It was Dubois and the absent stoner who most disturbed him. Addicts had the hardest time acclimating to the mark. In addition to the loss of their homes, family, and friends, they also lost their crutch. The mark was an instant cure, changing the body so that mind-altering substances were no longer effective. Some novice Marks went crazy facing reality. They hadn't been capable of functioning without drugs in their ordinary mortal lives. It was impossible for some to cope with sobriety in an extraordinary world filled with demons who wanted them dead.

"We will leave on the hour," Raguel said, "whether Molenaar is present or not."

Eve raised her hand. "What is the purpose of this field trip?"

Raguel widened his stance and crossed his arms. He raked the room with a sweeping glance. "All of you carry fear. You must face it and learn to see past it. You have been tasked with eliminating the vilest of Hell's denizens. The horror movies you enjoyed in the past are nothing compared to what you will face daily. I am taking you to a place where fear will be your closest companion. You will learn to function at your best when confronted with the worst."

Alec felt Eve shiver.

He reached for her hand and tugged it from the lip of the window ledge. His fingers linked with hers, a silent offer of comfort. To say he felt shitty for his part in her marking would be an understatement, but that wasn't the worst of it. He couldn't change what happened in the past. He could, however, change the future. But he wasn't working as hard on that as he should be.

Eve wanted him to help her shed the mark and he'd promised that he would. But her desire to be free competed with his need to keep her around long enough to learn the mark system from the ground up. It was the best way for him to position himself as the most obvious choice to head a new firm. The Infernal threat was growing and more Marks were needed. Alec wanted to step into position as soon as expansion was finalized. He couldn't do that as the outsider he'd always been. The wanderer, cursed to roam. Through Eve, he was finally established in one place, watching Marks from their inception. Once he completed mentor training, he would have hands-on experience with every aspect of the system. No one would be better suited to lead than him.

"You will learn to work together," Raguel went on. "You are not in competition with one another, although some of you act as if you are. You are a team; your goal is the same. The loss of one weakens all of you. By the time we are done, you'll have become accustomed to both surviving and helping your brethren survive as well."

"Sounds flash," the princess—Ms. Hogan—said.

"*Sì.*" Romeo winked at her.

Richens shifted uncomfortably. Izzie yawned.

Edwards, however, drummed his fingertips into the tabletop. "I've been to Fort McCroskey. The place is a dump. Overgrown with weeds and crawling with vermin."

"Eww." Laurel's nose wrinkled. "I've changed my mind."

"I will protect you, *bella,*" Romeo drawled.

"You will all protect each other," Raguel corrected.

Ken rubbed his hands together. "We can do this."

"Is there Wi-Fi?" Richens asked.

"Of course." Raguel smiled indulgently. "All the modern conveniences. I do not want to completely isolate you. The intent of this exercise is to simulate actual field situations."

"Simulate?" Eve's fingers tightened on Alec's. "Are the Infernals we're hunting simulated, too?"

"In a fashion. Your prey will be real Infernals. There's nothing on Earth capable of reproducing their scent, so we have to use actual demons."

A ripple of laughter moved through the room.

"But they work for me," Raguel went on.

"A pity that," Ken muttered. "I was hoping we'd finally get to kick some demon arse."

"All in good time, Mr. Callaghan. Gather around the table, please. Let us pray for success in our endeavors before we depart."

The students stood, forming a motley group that made Alec ponder the future of the mark system. Eve freed her hand from his grip and slid off the ledge.

His brows rose.

"I'm going to step outside," she whispered.

Izzie approached. "I'll join you."

"I would prefer you two remain," Raguel called out, having picked up their exchange with his celestial hearing. "Whether you join us in prayer or not is moot. We need to act together in everything."

Alec caught Eve around the waist and drew her back against him. He said a prayer for both of them. With the way their luck had been so far, he knew they needed all the help they could get.

CHAPTER 3

As her car approached the unguarded entrance of Fort McCroskey, Eve took in her surroundings. In the glow of the setting sun, the signage delineating the end of public land shimmered from a recent coat of fresh paint. The road beneath her tires darkened as she crossed the threshold, compliments of a new layer of asphalt. Ahead, lights attracted customers to the commissary, the parking lot of which boasted more than a few cars.

"It doesn't look abandoned to me," she said. "Maybe I have an over-active imagination, but I pictured this place looking a lot different. Cob-webs and tumbleweeds. That sort of thing."

Alec glanced at her from the passenger seat. "You haven't seen the best parts yet."

"Oh, great. Something to look forward to."

"Look forward to me coming back," he purred, giving her one of his looks. He was, quite simply, ferociously sexy. And he knew it, which made him even more dangerous.

She jerked her attention back to the road. "You're going to get us into an accident. It's hard to drive when your toes are curled."

Eve slowed to maintain the distance between the front of her car and the white van carrying the other Marks. The white Chevy Suburban be-hind her carried six of Gadara's personal guards, as well as a week's worth of provisions and all of their equipment.

Occasionally, some of her classmates looked back at her, but never with any show of friendliness. She probably should have ridden with the group to foster solidarity, but she didn't have the energy. She didn't know if com-ing back from the dead was supposed to feel like killer PMS or not, but she was seriously cranky and sluggish.

They drove down streets lined with homes whose architecture ranged from 1950s duplexes to 1980s single-family dwellings. The residences were all well lit, with cars in the carports and large manicured yards. She'd done some research on the place and learned that it had been established in 1917, became an official fort in 1940, and closed in 1994. Nowadays, it still served a variety of uses, both civilian and military. The homes they passed now were occupied by married soldiers attending the nearby Defense Language Institute and the Naval Postgraduate School.

Eve lowered the window and let the crisp, salt-tinged air into the vehicle. Although the base hugged the same Pacific Coast as her condominium, the northern climate was very different. The temperature was cooler, the sky more overcast, and the trees were pines instead of palms. She wished they were riding Alec's Harley instead, but the seven-hour ride would have been tough even for a mark-enhanced body.

"I bet the soldiers who were stationed here loved it," Alec said.

"It's a shame it's closed. I had a friend whose brother was stationed at Fort Leonard Wood, Missouri. He called it 'Fort Lost in the Woods, Misery.' I'm sure he would much rather be here."

"No doubt."

They followed the van around a bend in the road. Eve caught sight of a building with boarded-up windows and butterflies took flight in her stomach. She told herself it was a mental thing—her body wasn't supposed to react to stress—but that didn't help. She was nervous and scared. "So . . . Do you know anything about the training that goes on here?"

He reached over and squeezed her knee. "I checked around while they were loading up the Suburban. Raguel has only used McCroskey a couple times so it was difficult to find anyone who has been through the experience. The two Marks I spoke with said it was a pivotal assignment for them, one that changed their perception of everything."

"For the better?"

"So they say."

"Only two Marks?" She swallowed hard. "What happened to the rest of them?"

Alec shot her a wry look. "They're out in the field, doing their job. They're not dead."

Eve exhaled in a rush. "Good to know."

"I *will* get you out of this before it kills you," he vowed, looking grim and determined. "You're not going to end your days marked."

Her reaction to his promise was so mixed, Eve couldn't decide how she felt about it. Three weeks ago, her reply would have been, "You bet your ass." Now, she was ambivalent. She had never in her life quit something because she didn't like it. She made it to the end before saying she'd given it her all.

"You know," she began, "I've gone through this training with a 'one-day-at-a-time' attitude."

"That's not a bad attitude to have, angel. Sometimes, it's the only way to get by."

"Yes, but in this case, I think I need to see the bigger picture."

Alec pivoted in his seat. His movement was fluid despite his size. At six feet four inches and two hundred and twenty pounds of lean, mean muscle, Alec had a body that was coveted by both men and women. Even with the mark—which made him preternaturally powerful—he worked out regularly to maintain his prime physical condition. He took his work very seriously and she admired him for that, even as she chastised herself for being far less committed.

"And what would you do with the bigger picture?" he asked.

"Hell if I know." Her shoulders lifted lamely. "I just can't help feeling as if throwing myself headfirst into the whole marked business makes it easier for God to keep me here for a while."

His fingertips stroked down her forearm. "Jehovah doesn't recognize easy or hard. He does what he thinks is best."

"Well, *I* recognize easy and hard," she retorted. "And what used to be hard is becoming easier and sometimes it's not so bad. But then sometimes—like dying in a dirty men's restroom—it's really fucking awful."

"So try it out this week," he suggested. "Give it your all for seven days and see what happens."

Eve's fingers wrapped tighter around the steering wheel. "I don't want to like this, Alec. I don't want to become comfortable."

The van turned a corner, taking them into a less-populated area. The homes on this street were dark, the yards yellowed. The sun was setting, adding shadows to the mix. Suburbia faded into desolation and Eve shivered.

"What do you want, angel?"

"I want normal. I want marriage and kids. I want to grow old." Eve glanced aside at him. "And I want you. Most of the time."

When the van pulled into one of two parking spots in front of a darkened duplex, she stopped in the street and stared at the home. The Suburban passed her and took the remaining space.

Alec's head turned away from her. "I don't come with normal," he murmured.

"I know."

The van rear door slid open and Ken leaped out, stretching. Then he set his hands on either side of the frame and leaned in, appearing to listen to instructions passed along from someone inside. He glanced at Eve idling in the street and gestured for her to park at the curb.

She sighed. "Here goes."

After parking the car, Eve climbed out of the driver's seat and joined the others. The rest of the group poured out of the van. Gadara stood between the two vehicles and waved his arm in a sweeping motion. The exterior lights blazed to life.

"Brilliant," Laurel said, popping her chewing gum.

Shedding some light on the situation didn't ease Eve's discomfort. Instead, it brought the disrepair of their living quarters into stark relief. Paint peeled from the siding and trim, cracks marred the cement walkway, and the asphalt in the drive was crumbling. A cockroach ran between the two cars and Laurel screamed.

Izzie rolled her eyes and stomped on the bug with her Dr. Martens. "It is dead," she said in a tone made gruffer by her German accent. "You can quit screaming now, please."

"I am not staying in a place infested with bugs!" Laurel cried.

"I told you this place was cocked up," Edwards said. "I brought some insecticide."

"We do not kill God's creatures," Gadara admonished.

Claire snorted. "Are you certain they aren't Infernal creatures? I believe cockroaches and mosquitoes are demon spawn."

"They are moving out, Ms. Dubois. Give them a few minutes and they will find another home in the area to occupy."

Richens shoved his hands into the front pouch of his hooded sweatshirt. "We're truly holing up here?"

"Yes, we truly are. Gentlemen in the duplex on the left, ladies to the right."

"I hope none of you snore," Izzie muttered.

"Why can't we stay in the nicer neighborhood?" Laurel asked.

"For the ladies' benefit?" Romeo added.

"And scare the noobs with our mad ways?" Ken scoffed.

"Mr. Callaghan is correct." Gadara walked to the rear of the van and opened the back doors. "Our hours will be erratic, we will often be armed, and we are an eclectic group. We want to attract Infernals, not mortal curiosity."

"I wish I could stay," Alec said. "Sounds like fun."

Eve looked at him. He offered a reassuring smile and she made an effort to return it. Although she had never in a million years imagined the scenario she presently faced, there was no point bitching about it. It was what it was. She would just have to make the best of it.

"Yeah, right," Richens grumbled, picking up his backpack and hefting it over his shoulder. He hit the back of a guard who was unloading equipment from the Suburban. "Sorry, bloke. Unintentional."

Ken collected his duffel. "Yer a lot of feartie-cats. I'm chuffed o'er this holiday."

"Of course you are," Claire said. "You are insane. Hand me the burgundy bag, s'il vous plaît."

Returning to her car, Eve hit the trunk release on her remote and rounded the back to get her duffel bag. Alec beat her to it, whipping around her and catching the handle before she could.

His gaze met hers. "You know I always have my cell on me. Call me anytime, no matter what the hour."

The last thing Alec needed while moving in for a kill was to be distracted by a phone call. She shook her head. "Don't worry about me. You just take care of business and come back in one piece."

"You gonna miss me, angel?" he purred.

She smiled in answer. She felt the same way about Alec as she did about her training—she was afraid to commit herself too fully to either. Lose one, lose them both. He was a fixture in her life only as long as the mark was, and keeping the mark wasn't an option. Marks lived outside the normal order of man. They couldn't die of natural means and they couldn't create life. Eve wasn't prepared to accept that.

But those were concerns for another day. Right now, a man she cared for deeply was heading into danger.

"Of course I'll miss you," she said. "Be careful."

"Listen." He set his free hand atop her shoulder. His eyes were hot, his mouth firmly set. "You're a natural. I know Raguel hasn't bothered to tell you that, but you are. You have an innate talent."

"I got killed!"

"But not before you sent the dragon back to Hell," he reminded. "You know how few Marks can make that claim? I'm probably not supposed to tell you this. In mentor training, they'll most likely tell me to tell you to follow the rules. But I'm telling you to follow your gut, you hear me?"

Eve stared up at him, arrested by his intensity. "Follow my gut?"

"Yeah." Alec tapped a blunt fingertip against her temple. "And your head. You're a smart cookie, angel. Fuck the rules and go with your instincts."

She nodded. He kissed the tip of her nose. "And miss me. A lot."

A moment later, he was pulling away from the curb and she was left alone with her classmates. Eve trudged up the drive, steeling herself for a week of being emotionally isolated.

Ken was shutting the rear doors of the van when she joined the rest of the group at the end of the driveway.

"Divide by gender," Gadara said, "and begin preparing the homes for habitation."

"Where are you going?" Laurel asked, frowning.

Gadara's brows rose at her tone, but he replied calmly, "To the commissary."

"You need to be military to shop in the commissary," Edwards advised.

"I have clearance, Mr. Edwards."

"He's an archangel," Izzie muttered, "not an idiot."

"Sod off."

Eve smiled at the exchange, but her merriment faded when she caught Gadara's gaze.

"Ms. Hollis. Please ensure that things flow smoothly in the women's quarters. There are air mattresses over there." Gadara pointed at the pile of equipment in front of the garage.

Laurel scowled. "Why is she in charge?"

"She is the only one of you to have actual field experience."

"Yeah, and she got the shit kicked out of her."

The class didn't know that she had died, Eve realized with some surprise, which made her wonder if her resurrection was a big secret.

Gadara's dark eyes took on a warning gleam. "Humor me, please, Ms. Hogan."

Laurel shot an arch glance at Eve. Romeo set his arm around her waist and murmured in her ear.

Eve's chin lifted. Of course Gadara would stoke the animosity. From the beginning, he'd made her marking as difficult as possible. It was his way of keeping Alec under his thumb.

"Mr. Edwards." The archangel turned away. "Please oversee the arranging of the men's quarters, especially the kitchen. We will begin dinner preparations when I return."

"Are we hunting tonight?" Ken asked.

Gadara shook his head. "No. Tonight is about settling in and preparing for tomorrow."

"Then we better get started," Eve said before heading toward the ladies' side. The other women fell into step behind her.

The sun was dipping low on the horizon, streaking the sky with jeweled hues. The view was breathtaking, and Eve paused on the small cement porch step to take it in.

"Maybe it won't be so dodgy here after all," Laurel said.

"Maybe," Eve agreed, hoping that was true.

The comfortable stillness was shattered by the howl of a wolf in the distance. A chill coursed down Eve's spine.

"There are wolves at the beach?" Claire asked in a whisper.

"*Were*wolves," Izzie corrected grimly.

As the color of the sky took on the hue of blood, Eve's enjoyment in its beauty fled. The evening air took on an ominous, oppressive weight.

They were out there. Infernals. Waiting, as the Marks were, for orders to kill. They passed their time toying with mortals, leading them to the edge of Hell, then shoving them over.

Eve pushed open the unlocked door and gestured for the others to enter to safety before her. "Let's get inside."

"G'day, mates."

Reed smiled at the Aussie greeting. "It's past midnight."

"Sorry to keep you waiting," Les Goodman said, gesturing them into his small but well-kept house in Victoria Park. As the Australian handler who'd witnessed the most recent attack by their mystery Infernal, he was the reason Reed and Mariel were Down Under. He'd been tied up with the formalities that followed a Mark killing and had finally called Reed to come over about thirty minutes ago.

"I wanted to record my report while everything was still fresh in my mind," Les explained as they moved into a comfortable living room furnished with brown leather furniture and sturdy wooden pieces. "Not that I will ever forget, mind. I'll have nightmares about what happened to my Mark forever."

"Thank you for agreeing to see us, Mr. Goodman," Mariel said. "We wish we were here under happier circumstances. We're very sorry for your loss."

"Thank you. Call me Les, please."

Mariel wore a loose floral dress and coordinating blue sweater, which gave her a casual and approachable air. Her wild flame-red hair, however, was pure seduction, but Les didn't appear to be affected as most single men were.

"You know Abel, of course," she said.

Les extended his hand to Reed. "Yes, of course. Welcome, Abel. It's an honor to have you here."

Reed accepted Les's handshake, noting the strength and confidence conveyed by the *mal'akh*'s grip. Les was blond, his skin darkened and weathered by the sun, his appearance arrested to look as if he was somewhere in his midforties. Grief weighed heavily upon his broad shoulders and bracketed his mouth and eyes with deep grooves of strain. Such physical manifestations of emotion were rare in *mal'akhs* and were only caused by the loss of a beloved. Les's Mark had meant a great deal to him.

Affairs sometimes formed between Marks and their handlers, since they shared a connection that transcended the physical. A Mark could share fear and triumph and a handler could reassure and offer comfort across many miles. Also conducive to work-related romance were the isolated lives led by Marks and the lure of their Novium, which was brought on by the thrill of their first hunts. Even *mal'akhs* weren't immune to a Mark awakening to full power.

"We appreciate you taking the time to answer our questions," Reed murmured, thinking of Eve and his own growing connection to her. God help him when her Novium hit, which would happen soon after she finished training and began hunting in earnest.

He glanced at his Rolex. It was early evening in California. She would be in Monterey now. By the end of the week, she would be three weeks away from graduation.

Les's jaw tightened. "I'll do anything necessary to catch that demon. I've never seen anything like what happened to Kimberly. I pray I never see anything like it again."

"Did you see the Infernal?" Mariel asked in a soothing voice.

"Yes." A haunted look came to the handler's blue eyes. "It was built like a brick shithouse. Nearly six meters in height and two meters wide at the shoulders."

Reed looked at Mariel with both brows raised. She had described the demon far differently.

The high-pitched whistle of a teakettle came from the back of the house. Les motioned them to follow him.

"Come along." His booted steps thudded heavily across the hardwood floor. "We'll talk in the kitchen."

They settled around a scuffed linoleum-topped table. Les turned off the gas stove and poured boiling water into a waiting teapot. His domesticity contrasted starkly with his rugged appearance—worn flannel shirt, faded jeans, and large belt buckle.

"The Infernal I saw," Mariel began, "was a little over seven feet tall, nowhere near as large as the one you describe."

Les set the pot on the table, then returned to the counter to retrieve a paper bag. He shook the contents—scones—onto a plate.

"Well, here's the thing." He glanced over his shoulder at them. "It wasn't that big before it killed my Mark."

Reed's cell phone vibrated in his pocket. He withdrew it quickly. He normally kept the damn thing off, but with Eve in training he wanted to be accessible. Glancing at the caller ID, he cursed silently. *Sara.* He hit the button that sent the call to voicemail.

Sarakiel was both an archangel and his ex-lover. She helmed the European firm, her flawless angelic features fueling the sales of the multimillion-dollar Sara Kiel Cosmetics empire. She was also on his shit list, so he had been avoiding her calls for the last few weeks. That wasn't going to change right now.

"You're saying the Infernal grew in size?" Reed asked, returning his full attention to the conversation.

"Yes." Les set out three teacups, then pulled out a spindle-backed chair for himself.

"Did you witness the attack?" Mariel asked.

"Just barely. If I'd blinked, I would have missed it. The blooming thing was fast. Impossibly fast. It rushed at Kim in a blur. Ran on all fours— fists and feet to the ground. Almost like an ape, but graceful like a canine. Kim screamed and the Infernal leaped into her open mouth, just disappeared inside her. I couldn't believe it. By the time I figured out what happened, it was over."

"What did happen?" Reed asked the question, but he already knew the answer.

"She . . ." Les swallowed hard. "She *exploded.* But it was wrong. All wrong. What was left behind . . . there wasn't enough. There wasn't enough *of her.* No bone, no blood . . ."

"Just muscle and skin," Reed finished, declining Les's silent offer of tea.

"Yeah, that'd be right. So where does everything else go?" Les poured two servings of tea, his hands visibly shaking. After he set the pot down, he looked between Mariel and Reed. "I think the Infernal absorbed the rest. That's how it grew."

Mariel accepted the cup Les handed to her. "Were you responding to a herald?"

A herald was an instinctive cry for help from Mark to handler that was so powerful it was sometimes felt by mortals. A sixth sense, some called it. The sensation that something was "off," something they couldn't put their finger on.

Les shook his head. "I didn't wait for it. I'd sent her after some *Patupairehe* faeries that were causing trouble for tourists. They were her specialty, so when I felt her fear, I knew something was wrong."

Reed leaned back in his chair. "Raguel didn't say anything about the Infernal growing larger."

"He doesn't know." Les broke off a piece of a scone. "Uriel wanted to keep the news to himself until he could figure out what to do with it."

"This is not the time for the archangels to be territorial," Mariel protested.

"My thoughts exactly, which is why I'm telling you. There is something else." Pushing away from the table, Les twisted around in his seat and collected an item from the counter behind him. He set it down in front of Mariel.

She picked up the zippered sandwich bag and examined its contents. "It looks like there's blood on this rock."

"There is. Open her up."

Mariel did as directed. Instantly the honey-sweet smell of Mark blood filled the air. It was unusually robust and Reed found himself breathing through his mouth to diminish the potency of the scent.

"Your Mark's blood," she noted. "Why are you keeping it?"

Les's lips thinned. "That's the Infernal's blood. I put a hole in the thing when it came at me."

"If your scene is anything like the one I saw," Reed muttered, "that could be Mark tissue. There was nothing within three yards that wasn't completely covered with gore."

"I shifted some distance away before I discharged my pistol," Les said. "That blood didn't come from my Mark, because we were at least a kilometer's distance from where she was killed."

"How did the Infernal know where you were shifting to?"

"That's the question, isn't it, mate? My theory is that the Infernal absorbs not only the blood and bone of the Marks it kills, but also some of the connection to the handler. I'm guessing it's only temporary. Before I finished emptying my clip, it became impervious to the bullets. Could have been some kind of warding or could have been acquired vulnerability from my Mark that faded when the connection did. The Infernal certainly had no idea I was going to shoot it."

"Even temporary is too long." Reed's foot tapped against the floor. "How much information can it absorb? How long does it retain what it learns? We need to know if your theory is right."

Mariel carefully closed the bag. "Can we go to the scene? I'd like to take a look for myself. I'm the only one who's seen all the locations of attack. I would like to see if a usable pattern emerges."

"Of course." Les drank his tea in one swallow. "The area is remote. Stick close during the shift."

He disappeared.

Glancing at Mariel, Reed stood. "Let's go."

CHAPTER 4

Reaching around Izzie—who refused to move—Eve set a large bowl of salad on the makeshift dining table. They had combined three folding card tables into one larger table in the men's dining room. Seating was still cramped, but Gadara insisted they eat together. Eve understood that he was trying to foster a familial connection between the Marks, but after three weeks of sharing lunches at Gadara Tower, she couldn't see why it would work now when it hadn't before.

"I hate tomatoes," Laurel griped, looking into the bowl. "Couldn't you have kept them separate?"

"Feel free to help," Eve retorted.

Gadara entered the dining room from the adjacent kitchen. He carried a fresh-from-the-oven pan of lasagna—without the safety of gloves.

Glaring at Eve, Laurel tossed her strawberry-blonde hair over her shoulder with a practiced flick of her wrist. She was in her early twenties, her skin freckled in a becoming way, her eyes a pretty cornflower blue. She was a couple of inches taller than Eve, slightly more slender and less athletic, and gifted with the ability to complain about nearly everything. Eve had no idea how that proclivity had gone over in her homeland of New Zealand. Here in America, Laurel's charming accent softened the annoyance factor some. She was one of the classmates Eve wondered about. What could Laurel have done to end up marked? Her self-preoccupation was annoying, but otherwise she struck Eve as innocuous enough. And she seemed like the type who needed a lot of friends, not a loner.

Gadara looked at Eve with a questioning glance and she shook her head, silently telling him not to worry about it. She was having a hard time adjusting to the new image of the archangel she was forming. Before she'd been marked, she had held Gadara in high esteem for his secular talents. Donald Trump aspired to be Raguel Gadara when he grew up. As an interior designer, Eve had applied to Gadara Enterprises for a job, hoping to be a part of the redesign of his Mondego Hotel and Casino in Las Vegas.

Now, she was working with him—just not in a way she could ever have imagined.

Of course, their association wasn't happenstance. Alec swore nothing was a coincidence and everything followed a divine plan. If that was true, the loss of her virginity to Cain and her subsequent marking had both simply been a matter of time. Therefore, working for Gadara had also been inevitable.

To her, the whole thing was wack.

Richens appeared from the kitchen. He skirted Gadara and set a plate of store-bought garlic bread on the table. "I'm starved. Let's eat."

"Who will say grace?" Gadara looked at Eve.

Her brow arched.

"I will." Claire stood, towering over the table.

The Frenchwoman's brown hair was super short and looked as if she had cut it herself. Her skin was porcelain perfect, her lashes thick and dark behind cute black-framed glasses that were worn for aesthetic reasons only—the mark cured myopia and every other imperfection. She was so beautiful it was hard not to stare, yet she didn't pay much mind to her looks. She wore no makeup or hair products. However, she did have a weakness for clothes. For this short trip, she had brought a duffel almost as big as she was.

The moment the short prayer was finished, the group settled elbow-to-elbow at the makeshift table and began passing the food around. It wasn't gourmet cuisine, but it was still pretty good. For a while, everyone was too busy shoveling food to talk—sating the need to refuel often and in large quantities—then excited discussion about the week's upcoming events kicked into high gear.

Eve ate mechanically, feeling disconnected from the boisterous atmosphere by a fuzzy sensation she called a "brain cloud." She felt as if she was coming down with a nasty cold. She was exhausted and suspected she was running a mild fever. Since the mark prevented illness, she was more than a little concerned. As soon as she had a moment alone, she planned to call Alec about it. She didn't feel like discussing any weakness in front of the others.

"So what's on the agenda for tomorrow?" Ken asked, always ready to leap in headfirst.

"My training plans are a closely guarded secret, Mr. Callaghan," Gadara said, smiling. "Besides, in actual field conditions you will have to think on your feet."

"What should we do to prepare?" Eve asked.

"Dress in layers. It is chilly in the morning here and depending on how well you progress tomorrow, we may be out until evening."

"That is when the ghosts come out and play," Izzie said in a deliberately affected low and dramatic tone, followed by a *bwa-ha-ha* bark of laughter that sounded even funnier with a German accent. "Maybe they will visit us tonight."

"Don't make jokes," Claire muttered. "Real Infernals are bad enough."

"Who says I'm joking? I watched a television show on this place just last week. One of those ghost hunter series."

Richens nodded. "We have similar programs in the U.K."

"What are you talking about?" Claire asked.

"There are people," Edwards explained, "who go to allegedly haunted locations and try to find proof of supernatural activity. They record their activities for television."

"*Vraiment?*" Claire's brows rose. "With what type of equipment do they search?"

Ken laughed. "A camcorder and a torch. Mostly all you see is screaming in the dark."

"Yes," Izzie agreed. "That is what I saw. It was strange that they waited until the middle of the night to 'investigate.' They deliberately turned the lights off, too. What is the reasoning behind doing that? If there are Infernals in the place, they don't give a shit if the lights are on or not."

"Torches?" Eve asked.

"Flashlights," Gadara explained.

Claire frowned. "What is the purpose?"

"Entertainment," Richens muttered.

"For whom? The persons screaming in the dark? Or the television viewers?"

"I don't get it either," Eve said, figuring she could contribute at least that much to the discussion.

Everyone looked at her, then resumed speaking.

"So are there truly Infernals in this place?" Claire asked. "Or just overactive imaginations?"

"There are Infernals everywhere," Gadara reminded. "But what fuels these shows are rumor and conjecture. However, if there are Infernals nearby when the shows are filming, they sometimes play along for their own amusement."

Eve pushed back from the table and stood, taking her plate with her. "I need to make a call before it gets too late."

"To Cain?" Laurel's smile was brittle.

"Who I call is none of your business."

"You are fortunate to have someone to answer you," Romeo murmured, rubbing his fingertips up and down Laurel's spine.

Eve knew her situation was rare. She couldn't decide if that was a blessing or not. Did her lingering connection to her family mean she didn't have many indulgences to earn to gain her freedom? Or was her connection to Cain so valuable that her family ties were worth overlooking?

Setting her plate on the counter by the sink, Eve exited out the kitchen door and sat on the cement stoop. Above her, the sky was a gorgeous mid-night blue. An inordinate number of stars twinkled between rapidly moving clouds. In her hometown, pollution created a charcoal gray night that hid much of the universe's celestial beauty, but Eve would gladly trade being there for here.

She punched in Alec's number. As the phone rang, Eve brushed her hair back from her damp forehead. She became dizzy if she moved too quickly, and her breathing was coming fast and shallow. The mark only allowed such reactions when arousal or a hunt was involved. Stress and illness weren't factors.

So what the fuck is wrong with me?

Her physical acclimation to the mark had been screwy from the get-go, fading in and out like someone twisting the volume knob on a radio.

"You've reached Alec Cain. Leave a message or call Meggido Industries at 800-555-7777."

The sound of Alec's voice made Eve's throat tight. "Come back in one piece," she told his voicemail. "And call me when you can."

Feeling in need of some fussing, she speed-dialed her parents and waited impatiently for one of them to pick up. They would check the caller ID first, since they never answered calls from numbers they didn't recognize—

"Hey, darlin'."

Eve smiled at the sound of her father's familiar drawl. "Hey, Dad. What are you doing?"

"Watching television and telling myself to go to bed. How about you?"

"I'm up in Monterey."

"Oh, that's right." The smile was evident in his voice. "Your mother told me you had some work up there."

"Yes. Work."

"Well, take some time to see the aquarium."

"I'll try."

There was silence for the space of a few heartbeats, but Eve was used to it. Her father was the master of silence—companionable, awkward, and disapproving. She could handle screaming shrews and bellowing assholes, but Darrel Hollis's wordless disapproval could make her feel smaller than an ant.

Usually she'd try to fill the void with inanities, but tonight she was just glad to have an open line to someone who loved her.

Her father cleared his throat. "Your mom isn't here right now. She went to her tanka group."

"That's okay. I'm fine with just talking to you."

"Is something on your mind? Are you having trouble with Alec?"

"No. We're good."

"You both should come over for dinner when you get back into town."

"Sure. We'd like that."

Another stretch of silence, then, "Are you having work trouble?"

Not that she could share. "Nothing's wrong, Dad. I just called to say hi. I miss you."

"I miss you, too. Looking forward to having dinner with you." He yawned. "I'm going to call it a night, honey. Don't work too hard."

Eve sighed, wishing they were capable of doing more than making small talk. "Say hi to Mom for me."

"Of course. And find a way to the see the aquarium. You can't go to Monterey without seeing the aquarium."

"I'll do my best."

"Night, Evie."

She snapped the phone shut just as the kitchen door opened behind her. As she pushed to her feet, a hand settled on her shoulder and urged her to stay down.

Eve looked up. "What's up, Richens?"

"Stick around," he said, joining her on the small step. "I could use the company; this place gives me the screamin' abdabs."

"Is that like the creeps?"

"Yeah."

It was the first real overture any of the Marks had made to her, so she stayed.

She slid over a little to give him more room. "Me, too."

"Is that why you called home?"

"Kinda." She was keeping her health to herself.

"Your old man isn't very chatty, eh."

"Didn't anyone tell you that eavesdropping is rude?"

"No. So what's your sin?"

Glancing at him with arched brow, Eve was struck again by his youth. He'd been a pudgy teenager when she met him just three weeks ago. He would retain that youthful appearance until he lost the mark, but the baby fat was gone. The mark made the body too efficient to carry around extra weight. His acne had cleared up, too, and the scars from them. What remained from the transformation was a young man of average height and build with somber features and wily gray eyes.

"Is that like 'what's your sign?'" she queried.

Richens shook his head. "I wouldn't piss off Cain by hitting on his girl. Besides, you're a bit long in the tooth for me."

"Ouch."

He shrugged. "So, what did you do to end up here?"

"Cain."

"That's it?" He scowled. "You're here for shagging?"

"So I'm told."

He muttered something under his breath.

"Sorry to disappoint," she said.

"It's okay," he said magnanimously. "It can still work out."

"What can still work out?"

"My plan. I killed people. Two of them. That's why I'm here."

Eve blinked. "You?"

She'd pegged him as the type of kid who drank too much soda, ate too much junk food, and played too many intricate, complicated video games. Murder, however, did not become him.

"Don't act so bloody startled." He shoved his hands in his sweatshirt pouch. "The owner of the store where I worked was an arseface. I was doing his job, too, but not getting paid for it."

"You should have quit, not killed him."

"I didn't kill *him*."

"Oh. Sorry."

"It was supposed to be a simple robbery. I knew how much money came in and when it went out to the bank. I'd helped to select the security system for the place, so I knew all the codes. The scheme was aces. I was to work the counter and play the victim, and my girl's cousin was to pull off the heist."

After her initial surprise, Eve didn't find the tale too unbelievable. Richens was so detached, so cerebral. He would have viewed the whole thing as a game. "Something went wrong, I take it."

"I was swizzed," he bit out. "That's what went wrong. The bloke wasn't her cousin at all, she was banging the git. They thought they'd hie off with *my* share of the spoils? Not bloody likely."

Eve didn't know what to say to that, so she said nothing at all.

"Then the blighter shot a kid dead," Richens continued, his voice rising along with his temper. "Wasn't no more than ten years old, I'd guess. Buying some chocolate. That's when I pulled the gun out from under the counter and shot *them* both dead."

"Why are you telling me this?"

"Because I think teaming up is the way to get ahead." He looked at her. "Like that television show *Survivor*, I think working together in small groups is the way to win."

"But we're not trying to eliminate each other in order to win a prize."

Richens's gaze narrowed. "So? We can still help each other. You're the brawn, I'm the brains. Better to be at an advantage than at a disadvantage, wouldn't you say?"

"Why me? What about Edwards?"

"Edwards is in with us. He has his reservations, of course, because he doesn't want to irk Cain, but he'll come around. It's easier to work with girls. Less chest thumping. He'll see that."

Eve laughed. "You could have approached Izzie. She's brawnier than me."

"She's also 'round the twist," he scoffed.

"Aren't we all?"

He stood. "If you're not interested, just say so."

She noted his short fuse for future reference.

"I'm all for working together," Eve murmured. "I could use some friends around here."

His smile was nothing less than charming. It transformed his features and brightened his eyes. He held out a hand to her and helped her to her feet. "We've got a deal, then."

"Sure." The coming week was going to be interesting.

Richens opened the kitchen door, which swung inward, and stepped inside, completely foregoing the "ladies first" rule. Eve shook her head and was about to enter behind him when the low growl of a canine rumbled through the evening air. Chills raced down her spine.

Pivoting on the narrow stoop, she blinked and engaged the nictitating lenses that allowed her to see in the dark. She searched the nearby area, the heat of her already fevered skin rising.

But she saw nothing. No gleam of moonlight in malevolent eyes, no betraying movement. She sniffed the air and smelled the sea.

Still, she knew something was out there.

The bushes dividing their yard from the neighbor's rustled. Eve leaped to the yellowed grass and landed in a crouch. A tiny puff rushed out at her and she caught it, lifting it by the scruff and drawing her fist back to strike.

Hold it, sweetie! the toy poodle cried, flailing its tiny legs.

Eve paused midswing, her marked senses retreating as quickly as they'd come, taking the overwhelming urge to kill with it. The mark created power and aggression in highly intense quantities. The sensations were base and animalistic, not at all the elegant sort of violence she might have expected the Almighty to use in the destruction of his enemies. The surge was brutal . . . and addicting.

Don't punch the messenger.

"Jesus—ouch!" Eve winced as her mark flared in protest. Since she wasn't a pet owner, days could go by without any animals speaking to her. She often forgot that the mark had given her new senses, such as the ability to converse with all of God's creatures. "What are you doing running at me like that?"

I'm in a hurry. Put me down. This isn't dignified.

Eve set the little creature down and watched as the obvious stray shook herself off. Despite the filth that darkened the poodle's cream-colored fur to a café au lait color, the dog was adorable. "Why are you growling at me?"

Not at you, doll face. The teeny poodle pranced daintily and looked at Eve with somber, puppy-soft eyes. *At those around you. You feel it, too. You're smack dab in the middle—*

An explosion rent the air. Eve jerked in surprise, then found herself splattered with gore and fur.

"What the hell?" she screamed, leaping to her feet.

Izzie stood in the doorway with a gun. A second later, the light from the kitchen was blocked by the number of people crowded behind her.

Eve looked at the carcass on the ground and the mark's potency rushed through her. "You idiot! What did you do that for?"

"It was attacking you," Izzie said, shrugging.

"It was the size of my shoe!"

Gadara materialized on the stoop and held his hand out for the gun. Izzie passed it over.

The archangel looked at Eve. "Are you okay, Ms. Hollis?"

"No." She looked down at the blood on her clothes. "I'm really fucking far from okay."

"What happened?"

"A stray wanted some dinner scraps." She glared at Izzie. "And ending up getting blown to smithereens instead. What the hell caliber pistol is that?"

Gadara turned his attention to the gun, then to Izzie. "This is yours?"

"Yes."

"You were told to come unarmed. I will provide everything you need."

Izzie's purple stained lips thinned stubbornly. "I told you, I saw that ghost program on television. I could not come to this place without protection."

"You have no faith," he said, eyeing her with a narrowed gaze. "You have no belief in me. I am here to help you rebuild you life and attain the skills to live it to the fullest."

"And there are millions of demons prepared to end it," she argued.

The archangel hovered above the stoop, his silence as condemning as shouted rebukes. Even Eve shuffled nervously and she had done nothing wrong.

"What happened?" Ken yelled from the back of the kitchen.

"Seiler shot something."

"What? Let me by."

"It was only a dog," Izzie muttered, looking mulish.

"A dog?" Ken scoffed.

"Everyone back in the house," Gadara ordered, his voice resonating with celestial command.

The persuasion was so forceful, it was nearly tangible, and Eve took an involuntary step forward. She forced herself to stop by supreme effort of will.

"Why were you packing heat right now anyway?" she asked Izzie. "And where did you hide it?"

Izzie turned on her boot heel and shouldered her way back into the house.

Eve quickly moved to follow her. She didn't feel sick anymore, at least not physically. Sick at heart, yes. And so furious with Izzie she wanted to strangle her.

Gadara caught her arm as she rushed by. "Leave her."

"Her problem is with me."

"And now it is with me." His dark eyes burned into hers, taking on a golden sheen. "You suffer from lack of faith, too, Ms. Hollis. It is why you often find yourself in situations such as these."

She opened her mouth to protest, then snapped it shut again. They both knew what was really going on. Reiterating wasn't necessary. "I want to know what answers she gives you."

He smiled indulgently, his teeth white against his brown skin. "You assume I mean to question her."

The cryptic reply was so like him. So like all the angels actually.

Gadara gestured toward the driveway. "Take Dubois and two guards with you back to the other side of the duplex. You can clean up and prepare for bed."

"I don't feel . . . right," she said, surprising herself. She wasn't quite sure why she was telling Gadara that when she didn't trust him.

He studied her. "In what way?"

"I'm hot."

His brows rose.

"Hot flashes. Intermittent fevers. That sort of thing."

"That is impossible."

"Tell that to my body."

"You are under stress, Ms. Hollis, and experiencing dramatic and rapid change. It is not surprising that your mind would expect your body to have physical responses to such extreme pressures . . . even to the point of phantom maladies."

"Which is just a convoluted way of saying it's all in my head." She dismissed him with a frustrated wave of her hand. The *persuasive* undertone in his voice wasn't lost on her, but it wasn't effective either. "My on-the-fritz brain and I will just run along now."

He dismissed her as easily, turning his back to her and levitating over the remains of the stray. As he spoke a foreign language in a low tone, his arm made a wide gesture over the gore, turning it into ash, which sank into the earth.

Eve was depressed by the waste and tantalized by the tiny bit of information the poodle had managed to impart before dying.

. . . those around you. You feel it, too. You're smack dab in the middle—

Smack dab in the middle of what? And what did the people around her have to do with it?

CHAPTER 5

Alec made it as far as Santa Cruz before he pulled off Highway 1 and secured a motel room. He didn't want to travel any farther in Eve's car. The Alpha had obviously sent his dogs to track her, hence the attack at Qualcomm Stadium. Alec would need to switch to a rental to avoid being recognized before he drove into Brentwood—the Black Diamond Pack's den.

As he pushed his key card into the door lock, Alec thought about Eve at Fort McCroskey. Frustrated by circumstances he had long ago lost control over, he pushed the door open with undue force. She wouldn't be the same person by the end of the week. The experiences that came from being marked changed people in both drastic and subtle ways. He loved who Eve was and that wasn't going to change, but he also missed the eighteen-year-old girl who'd given her innocence to him. That was one of the penalties for his sin, the same penalty his parents had paid when they gave in to temptation—you can take what you shouldn't, but in the end you still won't get what you wanted.

I'm coming for you, Charles, he thought, looking around the motel room with distaste. *If you had left well enough alone, I wouldn't have to be here.*

Unfortunately, the Alpha's death would set off a chain of events that could ripple outward, affecting other packs and creating room for new—possibly more dangerous—Alphas.

"Better the demon you know," Alec muttered.

When Charles was gone, his Beta would step up. Pack members would scatter, reinforcing other packs or creating new ones. Charles, for all his many faults, was familiar and—previously—fairly cooperative. His demise would most likely give birth to greater threats, since the inheritance of power was often accompanied by an initial display of force, not goodwill toward the enemy.

Alec stepped deeper into the room. The door shut behind him. For years he'd lived on the road like this. A new town every few days. A different motel room. Another forgettable girl to screw when the need to do so distracted from the hunt. There had been no one to worry about him and no one for him to look forward to going home to. He'd spent thousands of nights lying in the dark, watching the glare of vehicle headlights drifting across unfamiliar ceilings. Nowadays, he had a sweet condo on Pacific Coast Highway, right next to his dream girl, and he resented having to settle for less.

Eve was in his life full time now, and he spent many of his nights in her bed. Sometimes she sent him home, but he knew she wanted him to stay. She hoped it would make it easier to say good-bye to him if she practiced doing it now. But Jehovah's intent was to make choices difficult, and nothing she could do would change that.

Restless, Alec hit the streets on foot. He needed an Infernal. Or more accurately, he needed an Infernal's blood. He had to find a cocky, stupid one who would throw caution to the wind and want to brawl. There was at least one in every town. He just had to find it. Sometimes the search took hours; other times he was lucky and stumbled across one fairly quickly. Tonight he didn't care how long it took. He wasn't heading into Brentwood until the morning and he knew worry over Eve would keep him awake most of the night.

He strolled over to the downtown area of Santa Cruz and the bustle of Pacific Avenue, whistling all the way. Boutiques and sidewalk cafés commingled with music and bookstores and countless restaurants. Pedestrians were attired in a wide spectrum of styles ranging from business suits to torn fishnets paired with Dr. Martens.

Perfect. Alec smiled. Infernals loved crowds. More mortals to play with.

His first stop was at a coffee/smoothie shop where he ordered a cherry-laden concoction because it reminded him of Eve. The girl at the counter was mortal, pretty, and a flirt. A month ago, he would have arranged to meet her after work. No promises, no entanglements, and he'd sleep hard in reward. Not any longer. Tonight he'd exhaust himself with a different kind of exertion. His biceps flexed at the thought.

There was no steady pump of adrenaline, as would accompany a sanctioned hunt, but it would come later. Marks weren't vigilantes; they couldn't attack Infernals at will. The loophole was that if a Mark was endangered, he had free rein to defend himself to the death. There was always a back door, if you knew where to look.

As Alec moved leisurely through the milling shoppers, he stayed watchful. There were Infernals all around him, the scent of their rotting souls competing with the smells of food, hot beverages, and human perfumes. He was in search of any demon who could be goaded into a fight, one whose blood would create his signature fragrance—*eau de Infernal*—a scent that would disguise his and give him the cover he needed to penetrate a den full of wolves.

He knew the moment he'd found what he was looking for.

She stepped out of an Irish-themed pub several feet ahead of him. As suited her Norwegian heritage, the Mare was fair skinned and blonde. Her demonic blood made her willowy and stunning, an irresistible lure to most men. Someone, however, had turned her down, if her scowl was any indication. She was irritated, agitated, and tense. Everything about her screamed "end of my rope," which hinted that the right amount of goading might provoke her to overlook both the rules and his identity.

Mares were shape shifters who thrived on nocturnal torment. Chest pains, horror-filled dreams, tightness of breathing . . . The blonde bombshell in front of him fed off the distress she created in her sleeping prey. Her class of demon was the reason the term "nightmares" had come into wide use, and they were easily riled when denied a particular target. Correction: they were easily riled, period. Any sort of dispute created the negative environment they craved.

As he approached, he grinned. "Crash and burn?"

She bristled visibly. "Go away, Cain."

"What turned him off? Did you push too hard?" He studied the dark circles under her eyes, bags carefully hidden beneath expertly applied makeup. His focus altered from confrontation to curiosity. "You've waited too long to feed."

She attempted to pass him.

He sidestepped into her path. "A gorgeous Mare like you should have dinner crawling all over her. Why leave empty-handed?"

"I'll scream," she warned.

"Do it," he goaded softly, his smile fading. "Let's see what happens."

Fear added an acrid tinge to her scent. The cheekbones he'd admired from afar were prominent due as much to gauntness as to breeding. With proximity, she appeared to be famished. That went against a Mare's very nature. They tormented sleepers for both sustenance and pleasure. Even if she didn't need the former, she wouldn't deny herself the latter.

Her crimson sheath dress left her arms bare. Circling her forearm just above her elbow was a moving band of twisting vines and veined leaves—her detail, proclaiming her a servant of Baal, the demon king of gluttony. Another reason she should be well fed.

"What do you want?" she asked crossly.

"I wanted to brawl. Now I want to know why you haven't eaten." Alec gestured at the throng around them. "There's no lack of food."

"Why do you care? Go pick a fight with someone else."

He stepped out of the way. "Fine with me. You don't look capable of giving me the stress relief I'm looking for."

The Mare remained unmoving for the length of several heartbeats, clearly suspicious of his easy capitulation.

"Go," he ordered. "You're boring me."

She departed with swiftness, her stilettos clicking impatiently down the sidewalk. Men watched her walk, looking for any sign that an advance would be welcomed. But her posture rejected any overtures and the aggressive set of her frail shoulders caused other pedestrians to clear the way.

She reached the corner of Locus Street and glanced back. By then, Alec had moved to the short wrought-iron fence that surrounded the patio tables of the pub. He sat on the railing and lifted his smoothie cup in toast.

As soon as the stoplight changed, the Mare bolted across the street.

Alec took off, too. He raced across Pacific Avenue with preternatural speed, dodging the moving cars with such dexterity the drivers never saw him. From the opposite sidewalk, he shadowed the Mare, using the crowd for cover. Music poured out of a busy coffee shop and a group of slightly tipsy women tried to detain him, but Alec kept pace. He watched the Mare withdraw a cell phone from her purse. She paused at infrequent intervals, looked backward, sensing his pursuit but unable to confirm it visually.

Fucking complications.

Nothing came easy for him. All he'd needed was a pint or two of Infernal blood. Now he was chasing a desperate Mare and facing the possibility of being outnumbered. If she had anyone in her corner, she'd be calling for reinforcements.

As if he didn't have enough on his plate with Charles.

Walk away.

His mark wasn't burning. She wasn't a target. She'd refused to take the bait. He couldn't hunt her.

Alec growled and the couple in front of him leaped to the side, clinging to each other.

He could no more back off now than he could resist Eve. When his attention was caught, it was firmly snared. Until he knew why a Mare was killing herself—starving while surrounded by an all-you-can-eat buffet—he couldn't let it go. Someone or something was exerting enough pressure on her to make eating unpalatable. Her survival instincts had goaded her to hit the clubs in search of a meal, but fear had prevented her from taking a victim home.

It didn't make sense for a higher ranking Infernal to order a minion to commit suicide, so why had her superior done that to her? Infernals wanted to rule the world. The greater their numbers, the better. If they wanted something dead, they killed it and made sure the deed was done. They didn't leave it to chance, such as waiting for starvation to take its final toll.

The Mare reached the end of the downtown section of Pacific and rounded the corner, heading into a somewhat quieter area of town. The foot traffic began to subside and the businesses changed from high-end and trendy establishments to smaller, less affluent merchants. As the energy of the surrounding venue changed, a new atmosphere descended, swirling around Alec like an evening mist—damp and chilling. He hadn't sensed it on the other side of town, but here it was prevalent.

Something wicked this way dwells.

Alec shot an accusing glance heavenward. It wasn't a coincidence that he had exited the highway at this particular destination.

He watched the Mare turn into the delivery bay of a hotel. Unlike the serviceable but amenity-less lodging he was staying in, this was a full-service establishment with a dozen stories worth of rooms. He noted the gargoyles rimming the roof of the building and a grim smile curved his mouth. Ever since he and Eve had investigated a group of tengu demons masquerading as grotesques, he knew to be on his guard. As long as Infernals had a way to mask their scent and details, everything was suspect.

Increasing his gait to a lope, Alec reached the mouth of the alleyway. Beneath the smell of motor oil and rotting garbage in Dumpsters was the stench of Infernals. More than one. Rolling his shoulders, Alec limbered up for the battle ahead. The demons were desperate and frightened; he could smell their disquiet. That made them more dangerous. When you had nothing to lose, there was no reason to hold back for safety's sake. He knew that from centuries of personal experience.

Alec walked into danger without preamble or stealth. There was no point. They smelled him coming.

There were a half dozen of them, four men and two women, one of whom was the Mare. They were a ragtag bunch, their clothes and hairstyles as varied as the downtown crowds. They faced him as a unit, arranged in a half-moon formation. And they all looked emaciated.

Their weakened states evened the odds considerably, but deepened the mystery.

"Are you hunting Giselle?" the other girl asked.

It was a reasonable question. If the Mare was an assigned target, nothing could save her. But if his pursuit was due to any other reason, they might be able to bargain her out of trouble.

"No." Alec stepped forward. "I just didn't want to miss the party."

"Leave her in peace," one of the men rumbled. He held a fat cigar between lips hidden by an unkempt beard. A kapre. He was a long way from his native home in the Philippines. The protective stance he adopted in front of the second girl—whose Baphomet amulet betrayed her as a witch—offered a possible reason why. Kapres followed their loves for the entirety of their lives.

"Make me," Alec said.

"We're no threat to you." But the kapre's voice lacked conviction and his eyes shifted nervously.

None of the Infernals would look Alec in the eye.

A frisson of warning skated down his spine. His Mark senses burst into full acuity in a brutal rush of power. Giselle's gaze darted to a spot just over his left shoulder.

Confirmation of the impending ambush came with the whistle of a blade. Alec dropped to a crouch. As the katana sliced through the space where his neck had been a split second before, the kiss of a breeze told him how close he'd been to decapitation.

Twisting at the waist, Alec lunged at his attacker. His shoulder rammed into the Infernal's diaphragm. They hit the ground with jarring force, Alec on top, the winded demon pinned beneath him.

In the blink of an eye, Alec noted the demon's mask and head-to-toe black attire. He registered his assailant's small stature, then the pillow of breasts against his chest.

A female.

For Alec, fatal battles were as familiar as sex and just as fluid. He was a creature of instinct and homicidal precision. He didn't plan or panic, he didn't flinch or hesitate. When his life was in danger, he didn't think twice. And he loved the hunt. Every minute of it. Predation created a high that couldn't be replicated. Only another hunter would understand the allure. The hunger. The dark need that was both savage and seductive.

Alec drew back his fist and swung. Two rapid blows to her covered face. The crush of bone echoed in the semienclosed loading bay, as did the clattering of her sword to the ground.

The Infernal grappled to regain her weapon. Her fingernails pierced through her gloves, shredding the skin on the back of his hands. She tried to knee him in the balls, but he shifted, absorbing the blow with his thigh. She lost necessary purchase with the miss, he took the advantage.

He wrestled the hilt free, then bit out, "It's been fun."

Aiming at the tender spot between throat and arm, Alec thrust the length of the two-foot blade diagonally into the demon's body, bisecting her chest cavity from left shoulder to right hip. His aim was perfect, nicking the heart. Instantly she exploded into a pile of sulfuric dust, and Alec dropped to the ground, prone. He rolled to his back, then jumped to his feet, brandishing his new weapon with affected insouciance. The fact that none of the other Infernals had tried to join the fray while he was distracted was puzzling. Demons played dirty, always.

The witch standing beside Giselle crumpled to the ground, her multiplicity spell broken by the death of her warrior half. A moment later, she burst into ash, unable to survive without the part of herself Alec had killed.

The kapre bellowed in agony. It turned and leaped to the brick wall that enclosed the end of the bay. Punching through the facade with fingers and toes, he crawled halfway up the building. Then he threw himself from the sixth floor and hit the oil-stained cement in an explosion of ash.

"What the fuck?" Alec was stunned.

In centuries of hunting, he'd witnessed only a handful of suicides. Infernals would rather go down fighting. It was the best way to ensure Sammael didn't hold their demise against them . . . too much.

But he quickly shook off his astonishment in favor of saving his own ass and getting what he needed from the remaining demons—blood and information.

"So . . ." The word was drawled, the mark regulating his breathing and heartbeat so that they remained as steady as a ticking clock. He brushed at the ash on his shirt and jeans with the back of his free hand. "Did you draw straws? Or should I just pick one of you to vanquish next?"

Someone was going to answer his questions and someone was going to give him some blood. The only question was: which one?

The male on the far right volunteered. With a roar that drowned out the sounds of the city around them, he leaped forward and bared his fangs. A vampyre.

"I just had a smoothie," Alec said. "I should be extra sweet . . . if you can manage to get a bite."

The demon withdrew a stake from the small of his back. Alec beckoned him closer with a wriggle of two fingers and a cocky smile.

"*Servo vestri ex ruina!*" the Infernal snarled.

Alec raised his sword. "*Dei gratia.*"

The vamp thrust his weapon deep into his own chest and exploded into dust.

Another Infernal pounced from the depths of the ashy haze that filled the air. The third male. This one tilted his leonine head back and howled at the moon. A werewolf.

"It's my lucky night," Alec muttered. "I got a mixed bag of nuts."

The wolf was short and stocky. His barrel chest and thick forearms and thighs warned Alec that this particular tussle was going to take some effort.

Or it would have, if the wolf hadn't put a gun to his temple and blown his brains out.

"Holy fucking shit."

If Alec hadn't seen it with his own eyes, he wouldn't have believed it. As the report of the shot reverberated around him, he wondered if his smoothie had been spiked. In his reality, mass suicides among Infernals were unheard of.

When the ash from the third Infernal took too long to clear, he widened his stance and adjusted his grip on his blade, prepared for a charge. But nothing rushed at him from the depths of the churning cloud. It only grew bigger, more opaque, as if being continuously fed.

Were the others checking out, too?

Alec's gut knotted. The order of his existence—so damn repetitive he had begun to think he was living his life on a loop—had been thrown completely out of whack since Eve had been marked.

As the floating debris in the compact delivery area finally began to dissipate, his suspicions were confirmed. There was nothing left of the Infernals. No one remained to explain what the hell was going on.

Disturbed and disgusted by the waste, Alec tossed the katana into one of the Dumpsters and exited back out to the street. Every step he took away from the scene was heavy with reluctance. Leaving empty-handed went against his very nature, but what choice did he have? Without an Infernal to pursue, he had no leads to follow.

Raguel, he called out.

Yes? The archangel's voice was as resonant in thought as it was in reality.

You need to send a team of Marks to Santa Cruz. In explanation, Alec relived his recent memories through his connection to Raguel.

There was a moment's stillness, then, *Call me.*

What? Why?

A jolt caused Alec to stumble mid-stride, followed by the silence of a severed communication.

Raguel?

He reached into his rear pocket for his cell phone, cursing when he realized it was still in his backpack in the trunk of Eve's car. He had tossed it there before they left Gadara Tower, figuring that the only person he was interested in talking to would be sitting right next to him. Now he'd have to wait until he reached his room to call Raguel, a delay that was too lengthy. What game was the archangel playing? Raguel needed to send a team of Marks out here immediately. Someone had to figure out what the hell was going on, and it couldn't be Alec because he had places to go and a wolf to kill.

Two blocks away from his hotel, Alec knew he was being tracked. He veered off the sidewalk and entered a convenience store. Skirting his way past the public restrooms, he ducked into the employees-only area. Within moments, he was exiting out the rear service door and rounding the building to catch his shadow unaware.

But it was he who was caught by surprise.

She hid in an unlit corner of the lot, her shoulders hunched forward and her Nordic appearance hidden under the glamour of a dark-haired Latina beauty. The red dress, however, was unmistakable.

Alec slipped along the low cement block wall that bordered the edge of the parking lot and came up on her from behind. The Mare was functioning so far below normal she didn't scent him until he was a few feet way.

"Cain." She faced him. Her face was tear-streaked and her mouth bracketed with lines of strain.

"Giselle." His arms crossed. "You change your mind about that brawl?"

"It was the only way," she whispered. "They have to believe I'm dead or they'll find me. They'll kill me."

"Who?"

Her blue eyes, so hard and wary earlier, were soft and pleading now. "Take me with you when you leave Santa Cruz. Then I'll tell you everything."

* * *

Eve was tired of staring at the water stains on the ceiling. It was driving her nuts to lay unmoving in her bed when she felt so restless and sticky with heat. On the opposite side of the room, Claire's steady, rhythmic breathing illustrated the other Mark's continuing slumber.

Lucky, she thought grudgingly.

Sighing, she tried closing her eyes to see if that would put her to sleep. She had spent the last two hours ruminating over the same questions in a frustrating loop.

Why hadn't Alec called her back?

What did Richens really want?

What had the dog intended to tell her?

What the hell was wrong with Izzie?

Something was rotten; that was all Eve knew for certain. And speculation over what it could be was keeping her awake.

The dog smelled something I'm not picking up. And no one else was catching it either. How was that possible? She could understand her classmates being behind the curve, since they were all still growing accustomed to their new "gifts." But what about Gadara? And his guards?

Eve slid her legs over the side of the bed and pushed her feet into a waiting pair of flip-flops. Her flannel pajama bottoms and matching top had seemed like a good idea that morning. Now that she was suffering from a low-grade fever, she inwardly cursed her choice. She'd never be able to fall asleep when she was too hot for comfort.

As she picked her way to the bedroom door, the hardwood floors creaked and groaned despite her best efforts at a stealthy exit. Claire mumbled in her sleep and rolled to her side, facing away from the disturbance that Eve was creating.

When she gained the hallway and closed the door behind her, Eve exhaled her pent-up breath with relief. Izzie and Laurel were in the master bedroom, which shared a wall with the room she occupied but was farther away from the common areas. Lack of window coverings allowed plenty of moonlight to illuminate the empty living room, delaying any need for her nictitating lenses.

Pausing in the center of the main living space, Eve shook off the feeling of a ghost walking over her grave. The men's half of the duplex was on the other side of the master bedroom walls and the three other females were only feet away. Yet her body was tense and her stomach was knotted. Every creepy, awful horror flick she'd ever seen was brought to life by the musty smell and unfamiliar noises of the house and surrounding exterior. The illusory perception of some homicidal maniac standing behind her made her want to shiver . . . if only the mark would let her.

"Damned sadistic imagination."

Eve. The rumble of Reed's voice hit her as the sensation of a hot summer breeze—a warmth drenched in the darkly erotic scent of his skin—engulfed her.

She reached back to him, grasping for the thin thread of awareness that flowed between handlers and their Marks. She'd heard that some Marks were able to share whole thoughts with their handlers, but she didn't have that ability. For her, it was only distant echoes of emotion. She secretly wondered if that was her fault, if she was afraid to let him in because of Alec.

Or maybe . . . due to more personal misgivings.

Feeling too exposed, Eve retreated both mentally and physically, stepping out of the shaft of moonlight and into the shadows. As she withdrew, she felt Reed lunge for her. She froze, startled by his vehemence. His concern and apprehension were so strong she felt them as if they were her own. Something was wrong wherever he was, something that had him checking on her and assuring himself of her safety.

Eve rolled her shoulders back. Alec and Reed had their own burdens to bear. They had more experience, but their jobs weren't any easier than hers. She was a big girl and she needed to take care of herself.

I'm okay, she told him. *Don't worry—*

A group of dark forms moved through the moonlight, arresting her in midthought. Their shadows raced across the patch of light she'd just vacated.

Frightened, Eve's gaze shot to the window and out to the view beyond. The street was eerie in its lifelessness. The streetlights were dim, the houses across the way were dark, the road was empty of cars.

"Just a flock of birds," she whispered, wishing she was one of those people who weren't afraid of anything. "You need sleep, that's all."

A large hunchback shape lumbered across the lawn toward the men's side of the duplex, moving in the opposite direction of the shadowy figures.

"Christ," she breathed, then winced as the mark on her arm burned in chastisement. Her mark enhancements woke with a start, stealing her breath. Her fever returned with a vengeance, but instead of wiping her out with exhaustion, she was possessed by a wild, edgy energy. She'd ridden on a roller coaster once that had made her feel much the same. The car had shot from the station like a bullet, building speed with every second, hurtling her toward a towering precipice framed with a ring of fire.

Eve sprinted to the front door and opened the locks. She looked outside, engaging her nictitating membranes to see. The two guards who had been stationed at the front and kitchen doors were already in motion, running stealthily around either end of the hedge fence that bisected their property from the neighboring one.

But they were still heading in the opposite direction of the hunchbacked form.

Her gaze lifted beyond their retreating backs. There *were* other unwanted visitors out there. She could see what looked to be half a dozen tall and lean forms moving rapidly in a disjointed pack. Their presence prevented her from calling out to the guards or even whistling.

She glanced down the hallway at the other bedrooms and considered waking the girls. But Infernals had hearing as good as hers and trying to keep quiet would eat time she didn't have. If that lumbering thing was after Gadara, she couldn't allow it to get any closer.

Threats are to be neutralized, not minimized, the archangel had taught. *Do not prevaricate. They learn with every confrontation and you do not want to give them the chance to ambush you in the future.*

"Go," she muttered to herself grimly. "You can scream for help *after* you stop it."

Locking the door behind her, Eve took off around the front of the house. Blood lust spurred her stride and her muscles flexed in anticipation. Her senses were so acute she could hear the faint sounds of a television show coming from an occupied house a couple of blocks away.

Usually archangels were ensconced in buildings filled with Marks who acted as an early warning system. It was impossible for a stinky Infernal to sneak past all of them and get to an archangel. At least it *had* been impossible before the creation of the Infernal mask. Now, all bets were off.

Gadara had only four guards to protect him and a class of newbie Marks who couldn't even smell whatever the poodle had detected.

Kicking off her sandals, Eve ran barefoot across the coarse dead grass that covered the shared lawn. Ahead of her, the bulky creature rounded the front of the duplex and disappeared down the cement pathway that led to the entrance of the men's side. A light was on in the living room, but a sheet had been draped over the window, blocking the view of the interior. As Eve ran past, she heard Gadara speaking. The resonance of his voice betrayed his power, creating a potent lure to an ambitious Infernal.

You can do this. She deliberately ignored the size of the Infernal she hunted. The demon was easily six and a half feet, with massive shoulders and a protruding back. Eve had no idea what class of Infernal fit that description or what its specialty might be. It could have razor-sharp teeth and claws, or it could spit fire like the dragon that killed her on Sunday. Or perhaps it had some other, deadlier talent.

Don't think about it. She swiped strands of her hair off her hot and sticky forehead.

The demon stood on the unlit porch. The far side of the stoop was enclosed by a thin wooden partition that blocked the moonlight. It loomed as a large void before her, drenched in shadow, the finer details of its form indiscernible even with her enhanced sight. There was only the massive back and disproportionately thin legs. Nothing else was defined. The scent of it was unusual, more bitter and acrid than rotting. It was an anomaly, which frightened her, but the power of the mark goaded her to leap first and ask questions later.

Eve lunged, tackling the beast and shoving him through the partition. The shattering of the wood was like a thunderclap in the still of the night.

They crashed to the ground on the other side of the step, tangled with splintered rubble and each other.

"Help!" Eve yelled, grappling with the unwieldy beast. It was softer than she expected and oddly unresisting.

"Help!" the Infernal screamed.

She froze.

The porch light came on, and men tumbled out of the duplex.

CHAPTER 6

Help!"

Eve blinked rapidly, startled to recognize the thickly accented voice. She gaped down at her capture. *"Molenaar?"*

Like an overturned turtle, the Mark wobbled precariously atop the military-style rucksack on his back. "You're insane, Hollis!" he screeched. "A maniac!"

"Ms. Hollis." Gadara caught her beneath the arms and hefted her up as if she weighed nothing. "What are you doing?"

Eve watched Romeo help Molenaar to his feet. A large shawl was tangled around the man's neck, but it had previously been wrapped around his head, shoulders, and backpack, giving him the hunchback appearance. "You stink," she accused.

"So you thought I am a demon?" Jan's blue eyes looked ready to pop out of his head. "I was forced to hitchhike to here after I was left behind. The driver I traveled with did not care about his odor."

The girls came charging around the corner of the house—Izzie in pigtails, Claire sans glasses, and Laurel sporting a green beauty mask caked to her face.

"What is happening?" Claire demanded, eyeing the gathering with arms akimbo. "When did you arrive, Molenaar?"

"I wish I had not come now!" He glared at Eve.

"You shouldn't be sneaking around in the middle of the night," she argued.

Gadara turned his head to look at her, his gold hoop earring catching the light and glinting. "Were you defending us from a perceived threat?"

"It's dark. With that thing on his head and back, I couldn't tell what he was. And where the hell are your guards?"

"Right here." A dark shape appeared from around the corner, his stride surefooted and confident. Eve recognized the voice as belonging to Diego Montevista, Gadara's chief of security and one badass Mark. "Chasing down some delinquent teenagers. But there should be two guards here."

"On point, sir," Mira Sydney replied from her position on the stoop. As large and forbidding as Montevista was, Sydney was the polar opposite. Fair to his dark, petite to his bulk. But she was his lieutenant, and it was clear they had developed a strong affinity. "When you went after the trespassers, we closed ranks and moved inside."

Gadara stepped closer to Eve. He pressed his wrist to her forehead and his gaze narrowed. She looked back at him with a challenging tilt to her chin. She felt as if she was burning up and knew he had to feel it, too.

"Well done," he said. Nothing more.

"Excuse me?" Molenaar protested. "She almost killed me!"

"You should not have been tardy this morning, Mr. Molenaar," Gadara dismissed. "Then this misunderstanding would not have happened."

Laurel spun on her heel and stomped away. "This is ridiculous," she tossed over her shoulder, "and I'm tired. Good night."

"I will walk with you, *bella*," Romeo offered, jogging after her.

Richens snorted in disgust. "That's devotion if he can still shag her with that shit on her face."

"Mr. Richens." Gadara's voice was disapproving, as was his frown. "You will keep such vulgar thoughts to yourself. Please show Mr. Molenaar into the house and help him settle in."

"I'm hungry," Molenaar said, shrugging off his rucksack.

"You're always hungry," Ken scoffed.

Claire yawned. "I am returning to my bed." Her gaze settled on Eve. "Please do not wake me when you come in."

Eve's return smile was forced.

A cell phone with a Handel's *Messiah* ringtone rang inside the men's quarters. Her brows rose.

Gadara smiled. "That would be mine, of course."

"Of course." Archangels with cell phones, such was her life. Ready to crawl under a rock, Eve offered a brief wave, then moved around him. "I'm calling it a night."

"You should wait a moment, Ms. Hollis," he suggested. "Cain will insist on speaking with you."

"How do you know—" Eve stopped. Of course he would know, he was an archangel.

"Because I ceased communicating with him when we heard the disturbance out here." His dark eyes were bright with amusement. "And I told him to call."

"Oh. Right." As if Alec took orders well.

"Come in where it is warm."

"I'm not cold. I told you that." And the fact that he wouldn't acknowledge her condition made it even more suspect.

Still, Eve followed Gadara to the men's side of the duplex. Edwards was pouring himself a glass of milk in the kitchen. Richens was leaning against the counter and speaking in rapid, heavily accented British English that was unintelligible to her. He acknowledged her with a jerk of his chin, then looked back at Edwards, who was examining her with an assessing glance.

She fought the urge to flip them the bird.

"Everything is as it should be," Gadara said into the phone. "Yes, there was a disturbance . . . Fine. In fact, she is extraordinary. I am quite impressed . . . Yes, I told her you would. Just a moment."

The archangel held the phone out to her. Accepting it, Eve moved to the far corner of the living room where a massive spider web occupied much of the space.

"Hi," she said in a subdued tone that made her feel better but wouldn't prevent mark-enhanced eavesdropping.

"Hey." The sound of Alec's gruff, purring voice filled her with relief. "You're not answering your phone."

"I had to turn it off so it didn't disturb my roommate."

He growled. "Put it on vibrate and keep it on you."

"I tried that, but then I left the damn thing under my pillow when I couldn't sleep."

"What's going on, angel? Are you hurt?"

"I'm fine."

"Raguel cut me off, and you weren't answering. Scared the shit out of me."

"It was a stupid misunderstanding."

"Couldn't have been that stupid. You impressed Raguel."

"What can I say?" She shrugged. "He's easily amused."

"Does he have you training already? It's after two in the morning."

"I told you, I couldn't sleep."

"You miss me." There was a smile in his voice.

"That, and it's too hot to nod off."

"Hot? In Monterey at night?"

Eve rubbed at the space between her brows. "I think I'm coming down with something. I'm pretty sure I have a fever."

There was a long pause. "You can't get sick."

"You have to believe me, I'm not giving you a choice. Gadara won't listen to me and—"

"*I'm going to take a shower.*"

She stiffened at the sound of a woman's voice in the background on the other end of the phone. It was throaty and seductive, as if the speaker had just woken up . . . or just had a screaming orgasm. "Who is that?"

Alec groaned. "A mess."

"Sounds like a woman."

"She's a Mare."

Eve's foot tapped against the hardwood, her earlier feelings rushing to the fore. "She doesn't sound like a horse to me. I bet she doesn't look like one either. Where are you?"

He laughed, the low rumble as enticing when she was mad as when she was completely besotted. "She's a Mare, as in *night*mare. And I'm in my room. It's the middle of the night, where else would I be?"

"You have a naked woman in your room in the middle of the night."

Edwards gave a low whistle. Eve turned around and flipped him the bird.

"She's not naked yet," Alec said calmly.

"Well, I don't want to hold you up so I'll let you go."

There was a pregnant pause, then, "Tell me you're kidding."

"Sounds as if the joke's on me."

"Give me a fucking break."

Eve pinched the bridge of her nose. "Ignore me. I'm not feeling well."

"She's an Infernal."

"I'm not rational."

"She's not you."

"Got it."

"Nothing to worry about. Understand? And anyway, you don't strike me as the jealous type."

"I'm not jealous of you, I'm jealous of her. She's naked with you. Call me back when I'm shacked up in a motel with a naked guy and see how you feel about it."

"I'm not shacked up, and she's not naked within eyesight. But . . . point taken."

A reluctant smile curved her mouth. "Why do you have an Infernal taking a shower in your room?"

"Bad luck?" He exhaled his frustration. "Something is really screwed up around here. She offered information if I'd get her out of the area."

"Like Hank?"

The Exceptional Projects Department—located in the subterranean floors of Gadara Tower—housed Infernals who worked for the good guys. Some did so by force, others were defectors from Hell. They all used their various talents to further the Mark cause.

"Yes. Like Hank and the others."

"How will creating nightmares be helpful?"

"Mares see into dreams. Sometimes that helps in learning what Infernals have planned."

"Subconscious eavesdropping?"

"Exactly. They can also make subliminal suggestions."

"What about the Alpha?"

"Giselle will have to tag along." Alec's tone was blunt and uncompromising. "I'm not interrupting my hunt, it's keeping me away from you."

Eve forced herself to ignore his use of the Mare's first name. She knew it was nothing. *Knew* it. But her agitated emotions were seeking any outlet. "Can you trust her?"

"You worried about me, angel?" he asked softly.

"You know it."

"I'll make you a deal: I keep myself in one piece and you do the same."

"You're on." She yawned against her will.

"Go to bed," he ordered. "I need to finish talking to Raguel, then I'm crashing, too. I want an early start."

"Listen," she looked over her shoulder at the rest of the room's occupants, then lowered her voice, "a dog tried to talk to me earlier."

"Oh?" The rise in his interest was palpable. "About what?"

"That's the thing, I don't know. She said something was fishy around me, then Izzie shot her."

"*Shot* her?"

"Yeah, for no other reason than she felt like it, as far as I can tell."

"The dog is *dead*?"

Eve winced. "Yes."

"How do these things happen around you? I've only been gone a few hours!"

"Hey," she said defensively, "I didn't do anything."

Molenaar yelled from the kitchen, "You attacked me, *krankzinnige vrouw*!"

"Why is he calling you a crazy woman?" Alec asked. "And why did you attack him?"

"Ignore him." She crossed the living room and exited the house for privacy. Due to lack of heating, the house wasn't much warmer than the outside, but the addition of a breeze helped cool her overheated skin.

"Shit."

"Not my fault. Besides, you're supposed to take my side. You're my mentor."

"Okay." He exhaled with deliberation. "Let's take it from the top. The feverish feeling is probably just your body's adjustment to the changes it's going through. You remember how it was when you went through the first part of it."

Oh yeah, she would never forget. She had felt as if she was on fire from the inside out and the need for sex had nearly driven her insane. Who would have thought God would tie two such disparate concepts as killing and loving into the same event? Then again, Eve had always thought the Almighty had a sick sense of humor.

"Probably?" she persisted, picking up on his slight hesitation. "What else could it be?"

"Well . . . there is the Novium."

"The Novium?"

"It hits Marks right before their mentoring ends and they've achieved some autonomy."

"So it can't be that."

"Right. It's way too soon. So you're adjusting, that's all."

She kicked at the ground. "Sucks."

"I bet. As for you jumping your classmate . . . He apparently didn't like what you did, so it's not sexual. Since that's the only thing I would give a shit about—aside from you hurting yourself—we'll just chalk that up to you being you."

"I hope you're not expecting a warm welcome when you get back," she muttered.

"Hot and sweaty, actually. Can't wait." A seductive purr rumbled across the cellular waves.

Eve's mood changed from hot and irritable to hot and bothered. "Better be nice to me, then."

"I'll be very nice to you, angel. You've never had any complaints. Now about the dog incident . . . I admit, that bothers me. What is Raguel doing about it?"

"Nothing that I can see. He told me to let him handle it."

"There must be a reason why he's not pressing the issue."

"Apathy?"

"I know you don't trust him, so trust me. He's got it covered."

Eve's free hand went to her hip. "You aren't here, Alec. He didn't even blink when Izzie killed that poor dog."

"As an archangel, he's closer to God. I'm guessing the connection is similar to trying to watch television and carry on a conversation at the same time. He's distracted, not careless."

"So you say."

"When I'm called to stand before Jehovah, I lose all sense of everything—time, feelings, reality. It's very . . . serene. I can't imagine how the archangels make it through their days with that connection open all the time."

"Regardless, I'm watching my own back." She looked around, making sure she was still alone. "I can't help but think that it's a little too convenient that Izzie acted when she did."

"I know you can't stay out of trouble, but can you please keep yourself safe?"

"Ha. So says the man with a naked demon in his shower."

The door opened behind her. Eve faced it. Montevista gestured her back with a jerk of his chin.

"I'm being summoned," she said, as she moved toward the house.

"Phone on you at all times. Got it?"

"Hey, I tried to call you earlier and you didn't answer."

"Won't happen again." Alec's voice softened and filled with warmth. "I am here for you, angel, even though I'm not there."

"I know."

"Try and get some sleep. It'll help you with the side effects of the transition."

"Will do." She passed Montevista, who held the door open for her, and entered the house. "Stay safe."

"Back at ya."

Gadara leaned elegantly against the old kitchen countertop, his appearance flawless despite the late hour. She held out the phone to him.

He traversed the distance between them in the blink of an eye. His fingers wrapped around hers, cooling her temperature with a single touch.

"Thank you," he murmured, his dark eyes filled with an age's worth of knowledge. "Your concern on my behalf pleases me greatly."

Although it was contrary to her desire to get her old life back, Eve appreciated the archangel's praise. "You're welcome."

They shared a brief smile. Gadara took the phone and resumed his conversation with Alec. Eve stepped into the kitchen for a bottle of water before she headed back to the girls' side of the duplex.

"Stick close tomorrow," Richens said, watching her from his position by the sink.

"Okay." The whole covert association thing was weird to Eve, but she'd play along at least until she figured out what was going on.

Edwards grunted. "And try not to be all over the place."

"I hope I'm not the only one of us who would have acted first and asked questions later," she shot back. "With that backpack and shawl over his head, Molenaar didn't look human. And he was heading toward Gadara."

"I am touched," Gadara called out.

"Stop eavesdropping." She glared at him, peeved to find him grinning. It made him look boyish and almost . . . cute. And Gadara wasn't cute. He was ambitious and blessed with celestial gifts she could only wonder at. He was also on a power trip where Alec was concerned, and she bore the brunt of his machinations. Eve didn't want to like him. She certainly didn't want to like his adorable grin.

"I think your superpowers are messed up," Edwards muttered.

Eve grabbed a water bottle from the stash on the counter and headed out. "See you guys in a few hours."

Leaving the house with Sydney in tow, Eve headed back to the girls' side. They rounded the corner and found Izzie waiting in the driveway at the front of the duplex. Without her usual cosmetics, the blonde looked startlingly young and delicate. Her skin was as pale as cream, her features finely wrought. She was as short of stature as Eve, but much less curvy. It looked good on her, as did her rainbow-striped knee-highs and black baby-doll pajamas. Izzie had the appearance of a pixie with a Goth edge.

Eve eyed her warily. Her inner warning bells went off whenever Izzie was near.

"Hello." Izzie straightened from her leaning position against the front of the Suburban.

"What are you doing out here, Seiler?" Sydney asked.

"Waiting for Hollis."

Both of Eve's brows rose. Two overtures in one day? After three weeks of cold shoulders? "Did you need something?"

"Can we talk?"

"I'm listening."

They continued forward. Sydney deliberately fell behind.

"He asked me, too, you should know," Izzie said.

"Who asked you what?"

"Richens."

Eve's steps faltered, then she realized she wasn't all that surprised. "Really."

"He did not tell you?" Izzie sighed dramatically. "He said I was the only female in our class worthy of asking."

Ignoring the dig, Eve asked, "Do you know what he's thinking?"

Izzie shook her head. "I do not care. There is something wrong with him."

There was something wrong with all of them as far as Eve was concerned. And the fate of the world rested, in part, in their hands. How scary was that? "Why are you telling me this?"

"I thought you would wish to know."

"You haven't told me much of anything yet."

The blonde sighed. "Also, I thought perhaps we should join forces, too."

"*We?* As in you and me?"

"Yes." The word was said with exasperation, as if Eve was slow to catch on. "Richens has a purpose for why he wants his own group. If we could understand, it would be of use to us."

"'We' as in *me*, right," Eve murmured wryly, "since you turned him down?"

Izzie smiled, but it didn't reach her blue eyes. "Right."

"If you want to know what he's up to, why didn't you play along and find out?"

"Patience is difficult for me." Izzie glanced aside with a slight smile, her short pigtails swaying in the damp evening air.

Eve wished she'd been a fan of the reality show *Survivor*. She might have picked up some tips about how to backstab, a skill she suspected her classmates had long ago mastered. "How old are you, Izzie?"

"Thirty. Why does that matter?"

Eve would have guessed that she was younger. She shrugged. "Just curious."

"You don't wish to know why I was marked?"

"Sure. Are you going to tell me?"

"No." Izzie climbed the short steps to the front door and opened it. Her loosely laced Dr. Martens thudded onto the hardwood of the living room. Sydney brought up the rear, locking them inside the house while another guard kept watch outside. Four guards, two for each duplex.

The moon had drifted farther along in the sky, shining less light into the space and creating more shadows. Eve was suddenly exhausted and a giant yawn escaped her.

"Tell me why you are here," Izzie said, kicking off her boots.

Eve headed down the hall to her room. "Not tonight, I have a headache."

"We can help one another."

Eve paused at her door. "How exactly are you going to help me?"

The blonde shrugged. "I will think of a way."

"Don't hurt yourself." Stepping into her room, Eve shut the door and crawled into bed. She was asleep almost as soon as her head hit the pillow.

Festive tropical music poured from hidden speakers while a warm ocean draft gusted through the open French doors of Greater Adventures Yachts, the manufacturer of the multimillion-dollar boats that funded the Australian firm.

Reed feigned the appearance of examining the photos of various ships on the wall, but in truth, he didn't see any of them. Instead, he saw the horror of the night before—the blood splattered over acacias and broken melaleuca trees, the wide circular depression in the wild grasses, the skin of Les's Mark torn from the missing body. Caught on various twigs, the flesh flapped in the evening breeze as a macabre banner, taunting them with their helplessness.

What the hell were they dealing with?

"Are you all right?" Mariel asked from her position beside him.

"Not really, no."

"If it's any consolation, you're good at what you do because you let the shit get to you."

He managed a slight smile. "Flattery will get you everywhere with me."

"Abel!"

Reed turned at the sound of the familiar, jovial voice. Uriel approached with his ever-ready wide grin and bright blue eyes. Sans shirt, the archangel sported only tropical shorts and flip-flops. His skin was tanned mahogany and the ends of his longish hair were bleached by the sun.

Bowing, Reed showed his respect and appreciation for the courtesy Uriel paid him by allowing him to investigate on Australian turf. As he straightened, the archangel clapped him on the shoulder.

"It is good to see you again," Uriel said.

"And you as well."

Uriel accepted Mariel's extended hand and kissed her knuckles. "Let us go up to my office."

They left the large waiting area and ascended a short flight of steps up to an expansive loft. A glass-topped, white wicker desk faced another set of open French doors. The stunning view of the beach beyond was a bit like the vista Eve's condo enjoyed. However, the water in Huntington Beach was a dark bluish-gray. The water here was bluer. Beautiful. Reed found himself wishing Eve were here to see it.

Dropping into the chair behind the desk, Uriel said, "It is unfortunate that you are not here under more pleasant circumstances."

Mariel took a seat.

Reed remained standing. He noted a small rack on a nearby console that held several bottles of wine. He crossed over to it and carefully lifted one, reading the brilliantly colored label. "Caesarea Winery?"

"A new venture," the archangel explained.

"I hope it does well for you."

"It always pays to be cautious and plan for contingencies, which is why I invited you to come out here."

"We appreciate the invitation," Mariel murmured.

"Where's Les?" Reed asked. "I would like him to be present, if you don't mind."

"On the beach. He will be up in a moment." Uriel's features were grave. "He is taking the loss of his Mark very hard. I told him to hit the waves for a bit and clear his head. Everyone needs to be focused on the puzzle at hand."

"It's a terrible puzzle." Mariel's voice was soft and filled with sadness. "Something truly heinous."

As if on cue, Les entered through the balcony doors, dripping wet and sprinkled with sand. No one missed the catch in Mariel's breathing, least of all the handsome Aussie, who gifted her with a slight smile. "Hello."

Uriel launched into the discussion without hesitation, looking between Reed and Mariel. "What did you determine last night? Is this situation similar to what you both experienced with your Marks?"

"Yes." Reed returned the wine bottle to the rack. "The same."

"So you believe it is the same Infernal?"

"Or the same *classification*," Mariel said. "We don't know if this is one demon or several."

Uriel looked at Les, who nodded his agreement. "It's a possibility to consider."

"Three attacks in three weeks." Reed thought back to the order he'd received to vanquish a tommy knocker causing trouble in a busy Kentucky mine. The faeries were Takeo's specialty; the Mark had vanquished many of them. "For a new class of Infernal, there seems to be no learning curve. This demon has jumped straight into killing on a mass scale. And it's not attacking defenseless mortals or novice Marks; it's taking out our best and brightest."

"I sent Kimberly after *Patupairehe*," Les said grimly, "but we never saw any. So I'm wondering what happened to the original assignment."

"Perhaps this Infernal is killing other demons, as well as Marks?" Uriel suggested.

Reed crossed his arms. "Or the seraphim are vulnerable in some way. Either erroneous information is leaching into the system or our lines of communication aren't sacred. An Infernal could be intercepting the assignments as they're sent down to us."

"How would that be possible?" Mariel breathed, clearly horrified by the thought.

Uriel leaned forward with his forearms on the desk. "Marks graduate from their mentors every day. Killing one established Mark a month barely puts a dent in our numbers. It hurts, yes. But it is not fatal."

"I'm not sure the goal is a thinning of our ranks." Reed's cell phone vibrated. He looked at the caller ID, sent Sara to voicemail *again,* and passed the conversation over to the Aussie handler. "Les has a theory."

Les ran a hand through his dripping wet hair and laid it out. "I think the demon might be absorbing the Marks it kills. Parts of the physical body, and also some of the Mark's thoughts and connection to their handler."

The archangel paused. His gaze moved over all three of the *mal'akhs* before him. "What evidence do you have for such a claim?"

"The Infernal knew where I was shifting almost before I did."

"That is hardly proof," Uriel scoffed. "I would call it dumb luck, unless it happens more than once."

"It *will* strike again." Mariel's tone was resigned. "But learning from our failures doesn't sit well with me."

Uriel arched a brow at Reed. "Suggestions?"

"To find it, we need to know how it hunts. I've been considering the similarities between the three kills, trying to find a pattern we can use."

"All three Marks were in remote areas," Mariel said. "Places the Infernal couldn't have simply 'stumbled' upon them."

"All three were hunting an Infernal they specialized in," Les added. "They were in their element."

"All three were under the direction of established, prominent handlers." Uriel's mouth was a somber line. "Handlers with years of experience and information."

Reed believed Les was onto something with his theory, which led him to a horrifying realization . . .

"Eve . . ." he breathed, his gut clenching.

She wasn't safe. She had been paramount in his thoughts at the moment the Infernal had absorbed Takeo . . . and possibly Takeo's connection to Reed. If Sammael knew about her, he would exploit her to the fullest extent. Cain had been a focus of his since the dawn of time and he would seize any opportunity to minimize Cain's effectiveness or turn Cain against God.

The archangel stared at Reed, comprehension dawning in his eyes. "Would he not have gone after her directly? Why come here first?"

"Maybe Kimberly and I had something he thought he could use?" Les suggested.

"Or maybe there's more than one," Mariel repeated. "The Infernal who killed my Mark was much smaller than the one you saw."

"We need to coordinate with the other firms," Uriel said.

"We can start by establishing teams to covertly accompany experienced Marks on remote hunts for Infernals they specialize in." Reed's gaze touched upon Mariel and Les, then came to rest on Uriel. "We can also set a trap to prove or disprove Les's theory."

"How?"

"We can feed the Marks false information and see what happens."

Uriel nodded. "And what if the only way to access that information is through death?"

"It's a chance we have to take. We need to know."

"I agree." The archangel's smile didn't reach his eyes. "You have no qualms. You should have my job."

That was Reed's plan. Not to take Uriel's place, but to join him in the rank of archangel. The creation of a new firm was long overdue. Reed fully intended to step into position as firm leader when the time came. Handling Eve was going to help him do that. By supervising her—and therefore Cain—he would prove that he could handle any task. From the training of new Marks, to the managing of the most powerful Mark of them all.

"I wouldn't go that far," he demurred. "I hate to lose Marks, whether they're mine or not. But casualties are inevitable in war."

Mariel's verdant eyes were sharp and assessing. "You have someone in mind?"

"Not yet. I'll work on that. In the meantime, Eve is in training now. In light of the possible danger, I will shadow her until Cain returns."

"Understandable," Uriel said. "I will arrange a conference call with the other firm leaders."

Mariel pushed gracefully to her feet, her long red hair swaying around her shoulders. She offered a shy smile to Les, who managed to return the gesture despite the grief that shrouded him.

Reed and Mariel left Australia in the blink of an eye. They shifted to Gadara Tower, landing in the subterranean Exceptional Projects Department.

Touching his arm, Mariel said, "Sara is going to be livid when Uriel calls."

"That's her problem."

"And subsequently, yours and Ms. Hollis's."

Reed's jaw clenched. Ambitious, masochistic, and shrewd, Sara had wanted to head any investigation into the rogue Infernal creature so that she could take the credit for its eventual vanquishing.

"There's nothing to be done about that," he dismissed. "The Infernal has never hunted on her territory. She's in no position to lead an investigation."

"She'll expect that your relationship will give her an advantage."

"We don't have a relationship." They'd never had one. He had been a stud to service her and she had been diverting. Once he realized she would rather sabotage his efforts to advance to archangel than help him, he'd ended the affair. However, although she didn't love him, she didn't want anyone else to have him either.

Mariel studied him carefully. "Has Sara seen you with Ms. Hollis?"

"No."

"You better pray she never does."

His mouth curved. "You've never seen me with her either."

"I've seen you without her, that's plenty."

Reed caught her elbow and led her down the long hall, away from the traffic and Infernal stench that distinguished the lobby area. Eve said the E.P.D. reminded her of noir films. He could see the resemblance in the muted lighting, inlaid glass doors, and smoky air.

"What are you going to do now?" he asked.

"Pay attention to all the orders that come down and protect my Marks. I'll skip a call before I send one of my crew to get slaughtered."

"Uriel isn't one to delay."

"Thank God. And you? Are you leaving to join her now?"

Reed kept his face impassive. "After I grab a few things."

"Be careful." Her tone told him she wasn't fooled by his nonchalance.

He pressed a kiss to her temple. "You, too."

"My worries aren't even half of yours," she muttered. "You're on shaky ground, my friend. I don't want to see you fall."

Walking toward the elevators, Reed thought of Eve and suspected it was already too late. God help him.

"God help us all."

CHAPTER 7

M onterey was a chilly, foggy town in the morning. The gray sky and thick, misty ground cover added to the somber mood of the training area. Lined up shoulder-to-shoulder with the other Marks, Eve gazed warily at the view beyond Gadara, who stood before them. Peeling paint, broken windows, and haphazardly leaning structures formed a dystopian city occupied by rotting mannequins and junkyard cars.

"Welcome to Anytown," the archangel said in his luxuriant timbre. "Where anything can happen."

He was smiling and looking far too anticipatory for Eve's taste. His attire of khaki green sweat suit emblazoned with GADARA ENTERPRISES was overly casual in her estimation. She had never seen him so laid back, and the skeptical side of her brain wondered if he expected to be camped out here for a while.

For her part, she'd dressed in comfortable jeans, T-shirt, and sweater jacket. On her feet she wore what she now considered to be necessary footwear—combat boots. All of her pretty heels and sandals were stored away. She missed them, but she valued her life more than her fashion sense.

"As Ms. Hollis so heroically demonstrated last night," Gadara continued, "vanquishing a target is only half the battle. First, you must confirm that you have acquired the correct Infernal before proceeding. That is the focus of today's training exercise."

"Was that the plan before last night?" Ken asked.

"Why do you ask?"

"I wantae ken if our training was goosed because Hollis and Molenaar were scrapping like a bunch of haddies."

"She attacked me!" Molenaar cried.

"This particular assignment was scheduled for later in the week," Gadara conceded. "But this is a simple rearrangement, not a replacement. You will not be deprived of anything, Mr. Callaghan. I promise you that."

Ken leaned forward and looked down the row at Eve. His expression clearly said he wasn't pleased. She smiled and waved. He wore all black today—black jeans, black turtleneck, and black ski cap. On someone else the outfit might have been too stark and slightly intimidating. Ken, however, looked like he'd stepped out of the pages of *GQ* magazine.

"This exercise is designed to simulate actual field conditions." Gadara began to walk down the line, inspecting each Mark. "In this scenario, you are hunting a rogue faery."

"What is the alleged crime?" Edwards asked.

"You are not concerned with *why* you are hunting, Mr. Edwards. That is something you will rarely know."

"Got it. Sorry."

Gadara held up a black armband, which he produced out of thin air. "For training purposes, you will wear these directly over your marks. It holds a thin metal pad that will heat up when in proximity to a similar band worn on your target."

"The smell of the Infernal will not be enough?" Romeo asked.

Laughter swelled through the group.

"If there was only one, yes. But when will you be in an urban situation such as we are staging today and have only one Infernal in the area, Mr. Garza? Today's exercise would not be a very realistic simulation with only one demon present."

"So there's more than one," Eve murmured.

"Of course. In addition to your target, there are other Infernals within the designated training area. Some are working in collusion with the demon you hunt and they will try to distract you. The others are simply bystanders. Later on in the week, we will also be training alongside an Army platoon, which will add mortals to the mix and force you to work without arousing suspicions. But in the beginning, you will be focused on hunting your designated target among a group of Infernals."

"Well," Ken said, grinning. "If our bands burn, we'll know what tae do."

"It is not quite that easy, Mr. Callaghan. You will see how fear alters your judgment and goads you to act rashly. That is the reason we train Marks so extensively. You must learn to ignore your terror and work through it."

"What does the winner get?" Richens asked.

"You will succeed or fail as a team, which leads me to the rules of engagement. Number one: take pains to avoid wounding your fellow Marks. Anxiety fosters careless mistakes."

"Yeah, Hollis." Laurel blew a bubble with her chewing gum, then popped it. "Watch out."

Eve looked at her and rubbed the space between her brows with her middle finger.

"Are you flipping me off?"

"Ladies, please." Gadara shook his head. "You may save each other's lives one day."

"How much time do we have to catch the Infernal?" Romeo asked.

"This is not a timed assignment. We will remain at the training site until the Infernal is captured." Gadara moved over to the nearby tent and picnic table. He set his hands on one of several large coolers resting on the tabletop. "There are sandwiches and drinks here, if you need them."

"We should begin now," Claire said. "I have no wish to be out here after dark."

"It's morning," Izzie drawled. "There are eight of us. We will not be out here long."

"Will we be given weapons?" Ken asked.

"To a certain extent." The archangel swept his hand in a wide swath before him. A tarp covered with various knives and pistols appeared on the ground at his feet. Eve bit back a smile. The twinkle in his eyes told her he was thoroughly enjoying the free use of his celestial gifts.

Ken frowned. "I dinnae ken."

"Injuries inflicted with these items are survivable. The bullets are rubber and the knife blades are short to ensure shallow wounds. So whether or not they will be of any use to you remains to be seen."

"What's the point, then?" Richens muttered. "A bloody mug's game. That's what this is."

"Rule of engagement number two: this is *not* a hunt to kill. The Infernals work for me, so refrain from overzealousness. Some of you will strike first and ask questions later. It will take time to learn how to suppress your instincts long enough to use mental reasoning."

"I thought learning to trust our instincts was the point," Edwards said.

"When you are frightened and something lunges out at you, what is the usual instinctive response?"

"Fight back," Izzie said.

"Or run," Claire offered.

"Correct. But you are marked, Ms. Dubois, and you will not flee. The mark will have filled your veins with adrenaline and you will thirst for blood. And if it was a mortal who happened to be in the wrong place at the wrong time? Someone who is as frightened as you and fighting for his life, mistakenly believing you are the enemy? Instincts are blunt instruments; reasoning minds are sharp."

Silence weighed heavily over the group.

"Any further questions?"

Eve spoke up. "What would you consider a successful mission?"

The archangel smiled. "Since the goal of this exercise is discovering that answer for yourselves, telling you would defeat the purpose. I can tell you what I would consider to be failures: the injury of one of you, failure to cooperate among yourselves, or the injury of one of my Infernals. There are more, but those are the outcomes I would find most disturbing."

Ken rubbed his hands together. "I'm ready to go."

"Excellent. Chose your weapons. One per person, please."

Eve watched the others pick over the selection. Izzie and Romeo both selected knives. Edwards picked a revolver. Molenaar went for a 9mm, as did Laurel after rejecting all of Romeo's varied suggestions. Claire liked the Glock. Ken went with brass knuckles. Eventually, only Richens and Eve remained. The others moved with Gadara over to the tent area to be outfitted with their armbands.

"I hate this," Richens muttered. "Why did I have to get a field assignment? Why didn't they put me to work doing something I'm good at?"

"You're asking the wrong person." Eve studied what was left to choose from—a couple of knives, a revolver, a 9mm, a telescoping baton, mace, and a taser.

"Take a gun," she suggested. "A knife requires proximity."

"Right, then. You take a knife. If the Infernal gets through you, I'll shoot it."

Eve glanced aside at him. "Are you kidding?"

"Hey." His boyish features took on a sullen cast. "I'll be analyzing the scene for clues. If you watch my back, we'll get done a lot faster. Brain and brawn, remember?"

"That might work if you knew anything about faeries. Since you don't, you're no better off than me. Is Edwards watching your back, too?"

"Edwards is a pain in the arse."

"Not interested in being a bodyguard, eh?"

"He's still griping about you. He thinks Cain is going to blow his top and kill us if something happens to you."

Her brows rose. "What would you guys have to do with anything bad happening to me?"

"My point exactly! If anything, Cain should appreciate that you had colleagues."

"I'm sure Edwards would have preferred it if Izzie had said yes," she trawled, "instead of me."

"Screw Edwards." He scowled. "I'd never work with Seiler."

"She says differently."

"She's loony." Meeting her gaze directly, Richens reiterated. "I didn't ask her for a damn thing. I didn't like her before and I like her even less now, the bloody liar."

"How would she know what you were up to?"

Although she asked the question, Eve found herself believing him. He seemed sincere. Izzie . . . well, she had seemed sincerely insincere, which was honest in its own way.

"Maybe she was in the kitchen when you and I were talking. I don't fucking know." He ran a rough hand through his short hair. His hooded sweatshirt was black and had KILLER RABBIT! screened across the front along with an image of a predatory hare attacking a medieval knight.

Eve's mouth curved.

"What the hell is so funny?" Richens snapped, his compact frame vibrating with anger.

Her smile faded. She'd forgotten about his quick temper. "Your shirt."

Dropping to a crouch, Eve selected the 9mm. She checked the magazine, then straightened and walked away.

"Hollis! Wait."

But she didn't. She joined the others just as Romeo volunteered to outfit the class with the armbands. They had come to McCroskey with a skeleton crew and every Mark was expected to pitch in when he or she could.

Romeo's gaze met hers, so dark she could see why Laurel would want to drown in him. "Come here."

Eve shoved her gun into her waistband at the small of her back, then shrugged out of her sweater and presented her arm. He attached the band directly over the Mark of Cain and double-checked it for a tight fit. It was slender, maybe a quarter of an inch wide, just enough to cover the eye in the center. The intricate triquetra and circled serpents remained visible.

"How does that feel?" he asked, his voice velvet smooth and seductive.

"Fine." She looked at him, noting his heavy-lidded stare. Izzie had called him a gigolo and Eve could see how she had come to that pronouncement. With his slumberous eyes, fit physique, and accented voice, he fit the "Italian Stallion" image to perfection. Eve could believe a woman would pay for his sexual favors.

"Flex," he ordered.

Complying, she fisted her hand and tautened her biceps. The band tightened, but didn't become prohibitively uncomfortable. "Still fine."

"*Buono,* go wait with the others."

Eve grabbed her sweater off the picnic table bench. "Need any help with yours?"

He tugged up his T-shirt sleeve, displaying his band. "No, *bella.*" A faint smile curved his mouth. "Thank you for asking."

"No problem."

Laurel walked up and set her hand possessively on Romeo's waist. "Hi, babe."

"*Cara mia,*" he greeted.

If looks could kill, Eve thought as she walked away. Laurel was the jealous type, apparently. Having experienced the green-eyed monster herself the night before, Eve understood. But Laurel and Romeo were such an odd couple. There appeared to be little true affection between them. Theirs was a liaison created by circumstances, which was fine if that worked for them. Eve wasn't going to dwell on it. She had her own difficulties to deal with.

She rejoined the group. They waited at the start of the street that led

into the training area. Once again, she looked over the visible area. A
female mannequin wearing a sun-bleached and tattered coat stood on a
nearby corner, her wig askew and flapping in the salt-tinged breeze. She
was pushing a carriage that was missing a wheel. The smell of mold and
decay permeated the air and emphasized the sense that time forgot this
place. The tableau made Eve's stomach churn.

"Can you think of how the insides must be?" Izzie asked, drawing
abreast of her.

"We'll find out in a minute."

"I can't wait." The blonde palmed her blade with obvious familiarity.
Her pretty face was fully made up with darkly rimmed eyes, pale powder,
and purple lips. The palette was oddly beautiful on a woman so fair. She
still managed to look dainty, despite the spiked collar around her neck. "I
visited California once before, for Knott's Berry Farm's Halloween Haunt.
I went three nights. It was great."

"Good for you."

"You do not look excited."

"Not my cup of tea." Which was a total understatement. She kept pic-
turing *The Texas Chainsaw Massacre* in her head. It didn't give her the
warm fuzzies.

Izzie's voice lowered. "You have killed an Infernal before. What was it
like?"

"You just . . . do it."

Eve thought about the water demon she vanquished. He had been trying to kill her. His umpteenth attempt, which made him officially a nuisance. She had been terrified, but something inside her reared up and
fought back. She was still astonished that she succeeded. She was also surprised that she wasn't haunted by her actions. Fact was, she would do it
again.

Izzie snorted. "That is all you can say? Only 'do it'?"

"Yep."

The sudden apprehension Eve felt wasn't due entirely to the creepiness
of the fake town. A lot of it had to do with the eagerness of the others in
her class and her lack of the same. Ken was pacing in his impatience to
start. Claire had a camera with her, as if this was a sightseeing event and
not training for murder.

"Those things take dodgy photos," Laurel said, walking up with Romeo and Richens.

Claire shrugged. "I won't jeopardize my good camera."

"What do you need one for?" Eve asked. When Marks and Infernals
were in their element, they didn't show up on film. They functioned on a
different plane altogether. Eve assumed that was why her mother couldn't
see the Mark of Cain on her arm.

"Posterity."

"You should take one now," Eve suggested, trying to find the same enthusiasm the others exhibited. Maybe posing for a group picture would foster solidarity among them. It certainly couldn't hurt. "Of all of us."

Claire gestured to Sydney, who stood nearby in full black urban commando garb. "Will you take the picture for us?"

Everyone lined up into two rows—men kneeling in the front, women standing in the back. Claire asked Gadara to stand to one side. The result was an assemblage reminiscent of an elementary school class photo.

Yanking up her poplin sleeve, Claire said, "Show your armbands, *s'il vous plaît*."

The group posed with funny faces and proudly presented biceps wrapped with the armbands. The mood was festive.

Which made Eve wonder why she felt as if something was about to go horribly wrong.

"You've reached Evangeline Hollis. Leave a message, and I'll return your call as soon as I can."

Alec terminated the connection with a quick tap to his headset, then he applied more pressure to the accelerator. The black convertible Mustang's 300-horsepower engine rumbled with pleasure, hurtling the sleek sports car along Highway 17.

"You're going the wrong way," Giselle said.

He tossed her a dry glance.

As they passed a freeway sign, she pointed at it. "You're going north."

"I know where I'm going."

"Gadara headquarters is in Anaheim. To the south."

"Do you have a point?"

Giselle frowned behind her new five-dollar sunglasses. They'd purchased more appropriate clothes for her at a truck stop—shorts, a tank top emblazoned with *California,* flip-flops, and a kerchief to wrap around her head.

They were cruising with the top down. Hot wheels, beautiful day, wrong girl. Alec would say two out of three wasn't bad, but he missed Eve too much.

And his girl wasn't answering her cell phone.

He knew she was in training, but after their conversation the night before, he needed to talk to her and make sure she was feeling better. He also needed to ease the sense that something was off, and only the sound of her voice could do that.

"You promised to take me to safety," Giselle argued.

"No. You asked me to take you with me. I've done that."

She pivoted in the seat. "We can't go north!"

"Why not?" Alec kept his hands relaxed on the steering wheel, but inside he was still and watchful.

"Because it's too dangerous."

"You'll have to give me more than that."

"Where are you going?"

"I'm hunting." He glanced aside at her. "Don't be coy."

"I'm not coy, damn you. I'm scared."

He knew that much was true; he smelled the fear on her. "Tell me why."

"Tell me you're not going after Charles Grimshaw."

Alec smiled. "I'm not telling you shit. The sharing between us only works one way."

"That's not fair!"

With a quick glance at the rearview mirror to check for traffic, he eased diagonally across the second lane and pulled to a stop on the shoulder. "If you don't like the rules, get out."

Her features altered into the enraged mask of her Infernal soul. "You're a dick."

"You're right."

"You need me."

"You wish."

She crossed her arms. "You have no idea what you're up against."

Cars and trucks roared by, shaking the Mustang on its wheels and stirring exhaust in the slightly chill air.

"Make me care," he challenged. "Tell me why I should."

"Do you want to die?"

"Not gonna happen. I've known Charles for years."

"No one knows the Alpha, not really."

"Don't talk in riddles."

Her too-slender fingers fidgeted with the hem of her shorts.

"Okay." He backtracked. "What does Charles have to do with you?"

Mares and wolves weren't known to associate. They were too different; one a physical aggressor, the other a mental marauder.

Giselle chewed her lower lip, her eyes darting over their surroundings, running in the only way she could—mentally. Alec was more than alert now. There was no doubt she wanted to reveal only the amount necessary to stem his questions.

"I don't have time for this," he snapped.

"If I tell you everything here," she whined, "what leverage do I have to get you to take me back to Anaheim?"

"You have no leverage. I need your blood, that's it. Obviously, I don't need you alive to get it."

"I'm running from Charles," Giselle blurted. "I need to get *away* from his territory, not drive *into* it."

"Does he have anything to do with what happened last night?"

"Start driving south and I'll tell you."

Alec's mouth curved. "Nothing you can say will get me to turn around. I have business to attend to and until it's done, everything else takes a backseat."

She looked prepared to argue, then her gaze met his and she knew it was pointless. "If you won't listen to me, will you listen to Neil?"

"Who is Neil?"

"The vamp who staked himself."

He recalled the events of the night before. *Servo vestri ex ruina.*

"Save myself from ruin?" he scoffed. "I'm getting a tan; Neil's dead. He should have taken his own advice."

"Save yourself from *destruction,* you idiot. And trust me, if Destruction gets a hold of you, you'll be dead, too."

Alec tossed his arm over the back of her headrest and pushed his shades up with the other hand. He stared at her with cold eyes. "Want to rephrase that?"

She pouted. "Sorry."

"Start from the top."

Giselle groaned and collapsed back into her seat. "Can we talk about this in Anaheim?"

Knowing they would attract the California Highway Patrol if he stayed on the shoulder too long, Alec faced forward and eased the car back into traffic. He pulled off the freeway at the next exit and into the parking lot of a gas station/convenience store. From the sudden gleam in Giselle's eyes, he knew she thought their stop was a good sign, which just showed how different the reasoning was between Infernals and Marks. Alec knew who ran the show in his world. He had been given an order by God. Ignoring it was not an option. Demons, on the other hand, were all egomaniacs. None of them wanted to admit that Sammael ruled the roost in Hell. They all preferred to delude themselves with the thought that Sammael's commands were optional and they followed them because it was fun.

"Okay." He slid the manual transmission into first gear, pulled up the emergency brake, and turned off the engine. "What is Destruction?"

Giselle's mouth took on a mulish cast. Her arms crossed.

Alec opened the driver's side door and unfolded from the seat. Rounding the trunk, he reached into the passenger side and plucked her out. She hadn't worn a seat belt—against California law—and he hadn't cared enough about her well-being to enforce it.

He returned to his side of the car and slid behind the wheel. "See ya."

"You are not leaving me here!" she protested, her lips white. "You need my blood."

"I also need my concentration, and being pissed off at you affects that." He reached for the ignition.

"Destruction is Sammael's pet."

Pausing, Alec glanced over at where she stood. "His *pet*?"

"A hellhound, but unlike anything you've ever seen before. It's a hybrid of demon and Cerberus, nephilim and Mark."

His jaw tightened.

Giselle's shoulders slumped and she looked even more gaunt, which he hadn't thought possible. "Sammael has been working on a new breed for centuries. None of them were viable; they all died."

"Except for Destruction."

"Right." She pulled the door open and dropped wearily into the seat.

"Was it the Mark blood that made the difference?"

"Yeah. Mark blood regenerates; it held all the parts together."

Holy shit. They were using Marks to create new demons. "What does Charles have to do with this?"

"Charles was the key. He's the Hound Whisperer. Sammael was able to keep the mutt alive, but he couldn't train it."

"Use a canine to train a canine."

Charles was one of the most powerful Alphas in the world. He ruled his pack with an iron fist. He was also wily enough to stay under the radar, which enabled him to expand his territory with only minor interference from Marks. He might have continued to grow in power, if he hadn't sought revenge for the death of his son by killing Eve in the Qualcomm Stadium bathroom. And now this.

"What does this have to do with you?" he asked.

"Once Sammael saw how successful Charles was in training the beast and how destructive it was, he wanted more of them. The hound is powerful and ravenous." Giselle's eyes turned fever-bright and she began to pant, her body thrumming with excitement. "If there were enough of them, they would wipe you all out. Every single Mark and angel. Every archangel. Even God. They're unstoppable."

Alec growled low, disgusted by her joy. "Answer the fucking question. What does this have to do with you?"

The glazed look of pleasure faded from her expression. "Every Infernal from the Oregon border down to Seaside, California, was tasked with feeding the growing pups. They take decades to mature, and they eat. And eat. And eat." She growled. "Why do you think I look like this? You try getting a plate of food and only eating ten percent."

"They're feeding *from* you?" he asked, incredulous.

"Like I said, ten percent is our share. That's why Neil and the others checked out. Sammael gave strict orders—no leaks of the Lebensborn-2 program. If we're too weak to fight off a Mark attack, we are to take ourselves out of commission before we're captured. I thought Charles would back me up when I argued against that, but I was wrong. He's hot and a great fuck, but I'm not going back to Hell for anyone or anything. Especially not for a guy who thinks I am just a disposable piece of ass."

Lebensborn. Alec's fists clenched. Sammael considered the Holocaust his greatest masterpiece, his trial run for Armageddon. That he would revisit the horror, even in name only, made Alec fit to kill. "I've never met an Infernal willing to commit suicide."

"You've never met an Infernal with Destruction on his tail," Giselle retorted. "Charles warned us that if we returned to Hell as a traitor to the program, Sammael would make us pay. When the choices are to get ripped to shreds by a hellhound then tortured by the Prince or to kill yourself and wait in the earthbound queue, suicide is the lesser of the two crappy options."

"You didn't follow through."

"Thanks to you." She smiled. "What are the chances that you would come along? Cain of infamy, the only Mark powerful enough to give me a shot at staying on Earth. It has to be fate."

Alec's gaze lifted heavenward. He never knew at moments such as this whether he was following a divine plan or just monumentally cursed to always step into shit. Perhaps this was all part of an elaborate punishment for his machinations to resurrect Eve. If so, he would consider the price worth it.

"Are the puppies still with Charles?" he asked.

She nodded. "That's why we want to drive in the other direction. They're housed in a kennel dead center of a gated, wolf-only community. You're good, but you aren't *that* good."

Alec turned the ignition. "Was that a dare?"

Giselle paled. "No! I didn't mean it that way."

He backed out of the parking spot and headed toward the northbound on-ramp. Brentwood was an hour away. "I've never been one to turn away from a challenge."

Raguel. The archangel needed to be brought up to speed. Then, Alec would grill Giselle to formulate a plan of attack. And when he found a private moment, he would touch base with Eve and make sure she was okay. As long as she was doing fine, he could manage the rest.

"This isn't a challenge, you idiot!" Giselle screeched. "This is a kamikaze mission. We. Are. Going. To. *Die.*"

Alec grinned, then opened the throttle.

CHAPTER 8

Eve hated horror movies. She didn't believe she had ever watched an entire one. Usually she had her face buried in her hands or she left the room. Her best friend, Janice, refused to sit next to her during slasher flicks and boyfriends quickly learned that it was safest to stick to blow-'em-up action films. She loved to watch stuff explode, but creepy music and waiting for mass murderers to pop out of closets was too much suspense for her.

Too bad Richens hadn't figured that out yet.

The Mark lagged behind her, as if she would be of any help at all during a surprise attack. He also exacerbated the problem by stage-whispering all manner of provoking statements, like: "Did you see that?," "What was that noise?," and "Do you smell anything?"

Thankfully, Edwards held his tongue, bringing up the rear with a silent stride. They were searching through the ground floor of a three-story building that was dressed as an office unit. It was the tallest building in Anytown and perhaps the most inhabited by vermin. Roaches climbed gray walls and rats dashed across the retro-patterned linoleum. A worn mannequin with a broken face staffed the receptionist desk, its dead eyes staring blankly. Eve shuddered and tried not to look at it. Her overactive imagination made her feel as if she was being watched with malicious intent.

Morning light spilled in through the windows, many of which were broken. Shards of glass shimmered on the dusty floor and crunched beneath their booted feet. Outside, the cries of seagulls filled the air with a mournful cacophony.

"This would have worked better at night," Edwards said gruffly. "We're open targets in the daylight."

"Gadara says fifty percent of hunts are conducted during the day." Richens snorted. "I'll be asleep then."

"You can't sleep through a call." Eve's tone was wry. "The mark burns like hell."

"I can sleep through anything."

No point arguing. He'd figure it out soon enough.

"Ow!" he screeched, lurching into her.

She stumbled. Her armband heated to burning, defeating any need to ask him what his problem was. From the outside, Ken whooped a joyful war cry. A smile curved her mouth, and Eve pivoted to face her companions. "Too bad you're not asleep."

Richens glared.

Edwards hissed, "How can you joke at a time like this?" He spun around wildly, his posture hunched and his revolver up.

Eve sniffed the air. "The Infernal isn't near enough to smell. Yet."

"It's around here somewhere."

Richens looked at Eve with wide eyes. "Now what? Is this how it happens in the field?"

She nodded. "Your handler will also communicate with you, either in person or with some kind of telepathy."

"Crap." Edwards's jaw tautened. "I don't want someone poking around in my head."

"You'll appreciate it when the time comes." Eve thought of Reed and how she sometimes leaned heavily on his support. He calmed her in times of stress, though he was often miles away. It was a bond of some sort. A connection. And it was screwing with her equanimity. She was a one-man woman. At least she always had been.

A hot, spice-scented breeze wafted over her. It was stronger than usual, more forceful. *Reed*. Either he was close in proximity or their tie was strengthening. Both possibilities gave her a tingle of apprehension. He was responding to her, letting her know that he knew she was thinking of him. How much of her emotions did he feel? How deep into her thoughts could he go?

Richens set his hand on Edwards's wrist, pushing it—and the gun— down. "Put that away before you hurt someone." He glanced at Eve. "So what now?"

"We hunt." A flutter tickled her tummy at the words. The feeling was a mental trick, like sympathy pains. She wasn't brave or kick-ass. Tracking and killing evil beings from Hell scared the shit out of her.

"Lead the way," Edwards said, sketching a mocking bow and gesturing her forward with a wide sweep of his gun hand.

"No way."

"What the hell are you here for, then?"

Her shoulders went back. "I led the way in here. It's someone else's turn now."

"Don't be a baby, Hollis," Richens said.

"Screw you," she retorted. "Be a man."

"We're scared," he whined, reminding her that he was barely past his teens.

"So am I. If you wanted a fearless leader, you should have tagged along with Ken and his brass knuckles." She was glad they hadn't. It was doubtful that anyone else would have teamed up with her, and the thought of searching through the creepy fake town alone made her nauseous.

Edwards stilled. "*You're* scared?"

Eve growled. "Of course I'm scared! Why wouldn't I be? Four weeks ago the most stressful thing I faced was fitting a client's wish list into her budget. Now I'm lucky to survive the day, between the Infernals that Cain pissed off in the past and the ones I'm annoying right now."

Sighing, Edwards's features softened. He patted her awkwardly on the shoulder. "I'll take the lead."

"Someone do it," Richens snapped. "Before one of the others bags our faery."

"It's not a race," Eve reminded, wondering how a petulant narcissist had come to be selected as a Mark.

"The hell it isn't. We're talking about our *souls* here, Hollis. I'm playing to win. Besides, if this was a group effort, wouldn't we all be together instead of wandering around separately?"

Edwards shrugged. "He has a point. Okay. So we'll search this building, then move on if we don't find anything."

Starting out tentatively, they began with the bottom floor and worked their way up. As they opened the stairwell door to the uppermost landing, the scent of Infernal drifted into their nostrils. Edwards held up one hand, slowing them to a halt. He made eye contact with both of them and placed a finger to his lips in a gesture for silence.

Richens rolled his eyes and mouthed, *We're not bloody idiots.* Then, he pushed Edwards over the threshold and into the hallway.

Edwards made a strangled noise and brandished his revolver with terror-goaded carelessness.

Eve marveled at their dynamic, whatever it was. Richens was a kid. Edwards was middle-aged. Why he deferred to the younger man was a point that inspired much speculation.

Richens peered around the jamb, his head swiveling to get a 180-degree view. Eve put her foot to his ass and kicked him into the hallway.

What's good for the goose . . .

"Mind out!" he shouted, stumbling into Edwards, whose weapon discharged into an overhead fluorescent light fixture with a thunderous boom. Plastic and glass rained down on the two. They cursed in unison, lifting their arms to shield their heads. The report echoed through the once-quiet floor, killing any hope of a stealthy entry.

"Oops." Eve vacated the stairwell behind them, unable to watch Edwards's obvious fear and not join him. "Sorry about that."

"Are you *insane*?" Richens barked, pointing his gun at her.

"No, but I'm beginning to think you are." He didn't appear to be frightened at all. More like curious, watchful. Like a spider.

"*What is going on out here?*"

They all turned their heads to find the source of the clipped female voice. They found her down the hall, standing in the doorway of an office. She looked to be in her midfifties, her silver hair restrained in a chignon and her mouth a grim line. She wore a business suit in gray—a knee-length skirt and matching jacket. She reeked of rotting soul.

Her gaze dropped to the three guns pointed in her direction. "I am ringing the authorities." She pivoted on her heel and slammed the door.

"Maybe we should shoot her," Richens suggested.

"She's not the one," Edwards said. "My armband isn't hurting."

"Yeah, but she might call the faery and warn her we're coming."

"True."

Eve waited for her armband to signal a proximity warning. After a long moment, she shrugged off the possibility, opened the stairwell door, and left. Hurried footsteps followed . . . *and* approached.

"Where are you going, Hollis?" Edwards called out, tripping down the stairs after her.

She slowed on the second-floor landing and raised her hand in a gesture for silence.

Edwards drew abreast of her, his gun hand trembling.

Richens paused two steps above them. "We left a witness behind."

Eve glared at him. "We're not vigilantes. She's not the target and that means we don't take her out."

Clutching the handrail with white-knuckled force, she shot a quick glance down the center of the spiraling staircase. A flash of platinum caught her eye. She straightened quickly.

Izzie.

"Everyone heard the gun go off," she said. "They'll all come running to this one location."

Richens smiled, catching on. "The faery will see that we're all distracted."

"It would be the perfect time to move," Edwards finished.

"Right." Eve turned back. "Let's go."

In unison, they raced up the stairs. They burst onto the rooftop and ran to the edge, their booted feet crunching atop the gravel. Without discussion, they spread out, taking in the view of the city beneath them. As they'd anticipated, Marks had rushed toward the building from all directions. Izzie was already on the premises. Claire was still a few blocks away. Romeo and Laurel appeared a few moments later, both looking suspiciously disheveled.

"Freaks," Edwards grumbled, voicing Eve's thoughts. She couldn't imagine that there would be any clean, nonspooky places in Anytown to indulge in some nooky.

"Where's Callaghan?" Richens asked.

"Maybe he's already in the building," Eve suggested, keeping a few feet between the lip of the roof and the toe of her boots. None of them raised their voices despite the distance between them. With their mark-enhanced hearing, volume wasn't necessary. "I would expect him to be first."

"He certainly wouldn't be last. That's Molenaar's place."

"I see him." Edwards's voice was low, filled with curiosity. "But he's not coming this way."

Eve and Richens joined him. They watched the blond Mark slip furtively along a shadowed wall a couple of streets down, then turn a corner and disappear from sight.

"He's tracking," Eve murmured.

"We have to follow him without alerting the others," Richens said.

Her brows rose. The rest of the class was crawling all over the building now. "And just exactly how are we supposed to do that?"

He gestured over his shoulder. "There's a fire escape over there."

Eve froze. "Very funny. How old is that thing? How many years has it gone without maintenance?"

"How many hours do you want to spend in this shit heap?" he countered. "We could be celebrating by noon, if we bag the faery now."

"No way." She retreated even farther from the edge.

"Why are you so—?" He gaped as comprehension dawned. "You're afraid of heights? Crap. Is there anything you're *not* afraid of?"

"You. I can take you. Don't push me."

Edwards laughed.

Richens scowled. "Come on, Hollis. Get over it."

"It's not a contest. Let's get the others and do this right." Foreboding weighed heavily in her gut, a sort of sixth sense she'd had her whole life. Right now it was ringing the alarm loud and clear.

"No way. They're idiots. We were the ones smart enough to have a workable plan."

She backed up. "I'm not risking my life for your ego."

"Risk it for your soul, then."

Eve snorted. Frankly, she wasn't hanging off a rusty fire escape for that.

When she didn't budge, Richens made an impatient gesture and set off toward the fire escape. Edwards hesitated a moment, then followed. Eve didn't waver. She left the roof and took the stairs. Gripping the railing, she hurtled down the three flights, passing Claire with a brief wave. Izzie was nowhere to be seen.

Eve hit the sidewalk at a run, but despite her speed, Richens and Edwards were at least a block ahead of her. Just as her brain kicked its way past her competitive drive and asked, *Why are you so into this?*, the mark kicked in, too, pumping the heat of the chase through her veins and urging her into a swifter gait. There was no labored breathing, no throbbing pulse. The lack of physical stress allowed feelings of euphoria and omnipotence to take precedence, inspiring false courage and confidence.

"I'm just watching out for them," she muttered to herself, skidding around a corner in time to see a glass door swinging from recent use. "Good Samaritan and all that."

The building was long and squat, its exterior a shiny silver metallic reminiscent of a 1950s Airstream trailer. Above the entrance, a crooked and faded sign read FLO'S FIVE AND DINER.

Eve went in with gun drawn, hissing as her armband burned her skin. Cracked and torn red vinyl booths lined the wall beneath the many grimy windows. Plastic food on plates decorated tabletops and the counter. Two mannequins in pink and white uniform dresses stood at the coffeemaker and the register, respectively. Lifting to her tiptoes, Eve peered through the opening to the kitchen but saw nothing at all.

Had they run out the back?

She continued cautiously, one step at a time. Her next step hit the ground wrong and she lost her footing, skidding atop something on the ground. Grabbing for the back of a barstool, she nearly fell as it swiveled under her grip. She glanced down, saw that she'd slipped on an armband, and guessed that Richens had lost his short temper over the annoyance.

A shout followed by a crash rent the air.

A dark shape flew past the food service window. Eve dropped to a crouch. A hand touched her biceps and she caught it, yanking hard. Claire tumbled into her lap. The Frenchwoman shrieked at the same moment pots banged wildly against each other. Clamping a hand over Claire's mouth, Eve strained to hear.

"Let him go, lovey," Richens cooed.

"Make me, darlin'," purred a sweet feminine voice.

Claire tensed.

With a narrowed look of warning, Eve pushed Claire up to a kneeling position. *Go around back,* she mouthed. The Frenchwoman nodded and crab-walked awkwardly to the front door. Eve waited until she was gone, breathing in the smell of mold and dust, her emotions fluctuating from excitement to dismay.

Part of her was enjoying the hunt.

You're losing your mind, she told herself, crawling the length of the counter to its end. Peeking around the corner, she saw the aluminum swinging door to the kitchen. The quilted surface and round glass window were covered in grime. Through the two-inch gap at the bottom, Eve searched for shadows that would betray movement on the other side, but all she saw was darkness. She moved closer.

We could be celebrating by noon, Richens had said.

Who was the faery holding hostage? Ken? Edwards?

There should be three Marks in there. Where was the third man?

"Come any closer," the faery said, "and he gets it."

"He 'gets it'?" Richens laughed. "What rubbish."

"Shut your mouth, Richens!" Ken gasped. "This knife is jaggy."

Eve paused a moment, surprised to learn that it was Ken who was captive. She was further astonished when she pushed the swinging door open a couple of inches and took in the enfolding situation courtesy of her nictitating lenses.

Richens stood with his back to her. Two yards in front of him, Ken was kneeling. Behind Ken, a portly and kindly faced woman with gray hair hovered gracefully, supported by impossibly tiny wings.

It was one of Sleeping Beauty's faery godmothers; cherry red cheeks, pastel dress, and pointed hat included.

Unsure of whether to laugh or freak out, Eve surveyed the rest of the kitchen. It was staged as if the owners had walked outside for a short break. Pots and pans sat on the stove, knives and cutting boards littered the island. She looked for Edwards and found him prone on the floor, unconscious. Her feelings of unease increased. The sight of an unmoving body on the filthy ground was just too realistic for her tastes.

How far would this simulation go? What was the best way to bring it to an end?

Ken's eyes were wide, his neck arched away from the blade pressed against his skin. "What do you want?" he bit out.

"You're coming with me, toots." The faery smiled and the result was so sweet-looking and innocuous, Eve had a hard time reconciling it with the reality of the knife in her chubby little hand. "We are going to slip out the back and make our getaway."

"You're not going anywhere." Richens's voice held a chilling amusement. "I'll shoot him before I let you walk out of here."

A dark cloud moved over the faery's features, briefly revealing the horror of her demonic soul. An Infernal could never be tamed or trusted. But they could be understood. They were similar to infants—self-centered, impatient, ravenous for attention and stimuli.

The faery made a *tsk*ing noise. "You should have crossed over to the dark side, sugar. You would have made a great Infernal."

Eve took aim and shot Richens in the ass.

He screamed like a girl. The gun fell from his hand and hit the floor, firing a bullet into a cast-iron skillet hanging on a pot rack above the stove. The bullet ricocheted, squealing through the air and waking Edwards, who bolted upright. His upthrust head smacked the underside of a cutting board whose edge protruded beyond the lip of the island. The knives atop the board leaped into the air. They spun and twisted, then fell to the counter in a deadly riot. They skidded across the surface as a single writhing mass, hitting a small metal canister and sending it toppling over the side. It struck Edwards on the crown of his head, dumping its contents over him before rolling to the floor with a resounding *gong*. The resulting cloud of flour billowed outward, expanding in unison with Edwards's choked curses.

Ken tossed the startled faery from his back, sending her careening into a tailspin. She crashed into the overhanging rack, her "Oh, shit!" muffled by the stockpot that fell from its perch and dropped over her head. She toppled to the floor with a substantial thud, landing still as death.

Richens was still screaming. Ken lunged to his feet and hit him with a perfect right hook. The Mark crumpled to the floor beside the faery, knocked out.

"Arsemonger," Ken muttered.

His gaze met Eve's. She looked at Edwards, who resembled Casper the Friendly Ghost or an uncooked corn dog, depending on the turn of his head. His eyes were two blinking black holes in an otherwise white face, his mouth a round "O" as he stared at the two prone bodies on the ground.

Eve's brain caught up to the series of events.

The screaming hadn't stopped. It had just moved outside.

"Claire," she breathed.

She jumped over the unconscious bodies and sprinted out the service door. For a split second, her nictitating lenses hindered her sight, then she retracted them with a deliberate blink.

Claire stood in the center of the narrow alley, her beautiful features frozen into a mask of terror. Her mouth was wide and a hideous wailing poured out. Her eyes were locked on a spot beyond Eve's shoulder, and madness stirred in the cerulean depths. Eve turned her head, her gaze following the Frenchwoman's line of sight.

She choked, then stumbled, the world spinning. Ken's tall form emerged from the unlit kitchen, his head turning to align with theirs.

"Holy mother of God," he gasped.

Pinned to the exterior wall of the diner was Molenaar's body. Arms splayed and hands affixed to the metal facade with iron nails through the palms. Urine soaked his pants and puddled on the crumbling asphalt. His sightless eyes gazed heavenward, his mouth lax and lips spattered with crimson. A circlet of rusted barbed wire hugged his head, completing the sick re-creation of the Crucifixion.

Where was the blood . . . ?

"*Sa tête est—*" Claire doubled over, but no vomit came up, her body too perfect to succumb to her emotions.

It was then that Eve realized Molenaar's head had been severed from his body. It was held in place above his neck by nails staked through his ears.

Terror chilled her fevered skin.

Eve screamed, her fists clenching even as her knees weakened.

A flock of seagulls joined them, screeching to the sky and the God who allowed such things to happen to those who served him.

CHAPTER 9

Reed pulled off Highway 1, the fabled Pacific Coast Highway, at the Fremont Boulevard exit. A moment later his rented Porsche was purring across Fort McCroskey.

He could have been with Eve already if he'd shifted directly to her, but he knew Raguel too well. The archangel would have his students holed up together with no chance of privacy. That was fine for training. It wasn't fine for dealing with the turmoil Reed sensed in Eve.

Through their handler/Mark connection, he felt her alienation from the rest of her class and sensed that she was dealing with it by shutting herself off emotionally. She was running on autopilot and that was dangerous for a Mark. He suspected he'd need to get her away from the strain of her classmates before she would relax enough to talk about what was troubling her. Hence the need for wheels.

The fact that the car was also a babe magnet was a bonus. Eve had been attracted to Cain and his Harley. It wasn't a stretch to hope that she might find the 911 Turbo Cabriolet a turn-on, too. With a top speed just shy of two hundred miles an hour, Reed hoped to open the throttle on both the engine and Eve's stress.

Using his connection to Eve as an inner tracking device, Reed maneuvered across the base. Raguel would want a report on the trip to Australia, then the archangel would try to make Reed leave, which wasn't going to happen. He wasn't going anywhere while there was any hazard to Eve's well-being.

Although he would never admit it, he was still reeling from losing her last week. Seeing Cain broken had only added to the surreal quality of his torment. All his life, he had wanted to see his older brother humbled by something. *Anything.* Yet he'd discovered that losing Eve to accomplish that aim was too high a price to pay.

He had handled countless female Marks over the centuries, sharing a connection with them as deep as the one he shared with Eve, yet she was the only one with whom he'd ever felt so conflicted.

She blamed his fascination on the animosity between him and Cain. She said he was only interested in her because she represented an opportunity to hurt his brother. But they both knew that wasn't true. Reed wished it was. Everything would be so much easier that way.

Rounding a bend in the road, he slowed as he came upon the duplex with the unmarked white van in the driveway. The license frame read GADARA ENTERPRISES. Reed pulled into the vacant spot beside it. He didn't need to knock on the door to know that no one was home. He felt the yawning vacancy before he turned off the engine.

Reed exited the car and set off on foot, walking in Eve's wake. As he passed the house, he noted the shattered partition by the entrance of the far side of the duplex. The mess looked fresh and gave him pause.

The first wave of terror hit Reed with enough force to hinder his stride. The second rolled over him like thunder, building in tension until it exploded with such force that he began to run. The leather soles of his Gucci moccasins gained little purchase. He shifted in midsprint and materialized beside Eve.

She was screaming. A quick glance at the building she faced told him why. Reed snatched her close, snapped open his wings, and surged into the air. Airborne, he held her tightly, containing her struggles.

"Shh." His arms wrapped completely around her slim body. "I'm here."

"Reed." She clutched at him, her face buried in his neck, her tears sliding across his skin.

He alighted onto the neighboring rooftop and retracted his wings, but didn't release her. Her fear, grief, and horror pulsed through him in rhythmic beats that left him unable to erect the barriers he used with his other Marks.

And the feel of her . . . the smell of her . . . It had been weeks since he'd touched her.

He had been *forbidden* to touch her.

"D-did you s-see?" She pulled back to stare up at him with tear-filled eyes.

"Yes." He didn't tell her that she would inevitably see much worse.

"I can't do this."

And in that moment, Reed didn't want her to, which screwed up everything—his ambitions, goals, and dreams. They all hinged on keeping her around. And he wanted her again, damn it. His entire body was hard for her.

Along with every-fucking-thing else, he was obsessed. How the hell was he supposed to get over that, if even a dead Mark and her terror couldn't diminish it?

"Help me get out," she begged.

His forehead dropped to rest against hers, which was hot and damp. Shit. Deep shit.

Her fingertips dug into the muscles framing his spine. "Say something, damn you!"

Inhaling sharply, he slipped into the tried and true lines he always used to calm skittish Marks. "I know this is tough for you. But think of the good works you will do, the people you will save—"

"Like him?" Eve gestured viciously at the alleyway below. "Isn't that what he was told, too? What about his good works? What about the people he was supposed to save? Are they just as fucked as he is now?"

"Eve . . ."

She shoved him away. "Tough for me? That's all you've got to say? Some propaganda bullshit? There is a dead man down there. Without . . . his . . . head!"

"Give me a break, Eve," he snapped, angrier with himself than with her. "I'm trying to help."

"Try harder."

Her lithe form vibrated with her inner turmoil. She was covered in jeans, shirt, and sweater jacket. Her hair was in a simple ponytail that accentuated the exotic tilt of her eyes. Her face was devoid of makeup, allowing the porcelain perfection of her Asian skin to take the stage.

Reed struggled with his attraction to her, a magnetism that started in his gut and worked its way out. Having been surrounded by brunettes for centuries, his first exposure to blondes had spurred a fascination with fair-haired beauties like Sara. Yet here he was, fighting an itch that wouldn't quit over a woman who looked nothing like his "type."

"What kind of training is this?" Eve rubbed her eyes with her fists. "No one said anyone was going to *die*!"

"Accidents happen, rarely. Overzealous and frightened Marks are unpredictable. But never like this. Never murder."

The sky darkened as clouds rolled in so fast they appeared to be on fast-forward. The breeze turned chilly, whipping the long strands of Eve's hair across her face. Reed watched her frame stiffen and her fists clench. He shifted to the edge of the roof and looked down at the scene unfolding beneath them.

Raguel hovered several feet above the ground, his arms and wings spread wide. His head was back, his eyes glowing gold and trained heavenward. His mouth was open in a silent scream. It was a riveting sight, both eerie and beautiful.

As Eve drew abreast of Reed, her hand pushed into his. She leaned over cautiously, her balance maintained by her death grip on him.

"What is he doing?" she asked, her voice ripped away by the furious wind.

"Lamenting. Sharing his grief with the Lord."

"I have something to share with the Lord," she muttered. "A piece of my mind."

Thunder cracked, booming through the dark gray sky.

"Watch it," Reed admonished, squeezing her hand in warning.

"Did the faery do this?"

"Faery?"

Eve pulled wind-whipped strands of hair out of her mouth. "The Infernal we were hunting in this exercise."

"You always blame us first."

Reed turned to face the speaker. So did Eve.

A dour-faced woman with gray hair that matched her gray suit stood just outside the stairwell door. Her laser-bright eyes told him she was an Infernal a second before the scent of her decaying soul did. She was staring at his hand holding Eve's, which seemed to remind Eve of the connection. She tugged her hand free.

Eve shouted to be heard above the storm. "Don't get pissy. It's a valid question."

"Pox on you." The Infernal approached with a pigeon-toed stride that did much to mitigate the intimidating force of her glower. Her details weren't visible, but her accent and haggard appearance suggested that she was a Welsh gwyllion—a demon known for its ability to inspire trust and confidence while leading mortals directly into danger. "We're out here in this dump, playing your idiotic war games, training assassins how to kill our kind. Yet every time something goes wrong, we are the first to be blamed."

A bark of laughter escaped Reed. He couldn't help it. A self-righteous Infernal? Now he'd seen everything.

Eve stared at the gwyllion for a long moment, then she started forward, her steps deliberate and unwavering. "That's total crap. You're not here out of the goodness of your rotten soul. You're here because you can't be wherever you would really like to be and you want to save your damned hide."

The demon halted and crossed her arms. "That doesn't mean you should accuse us first!"

Pointing toward the alley, Eve asked, "Doesn't that look like Infernal handiwork to you?"

The dourness faded into a broad smile. "It's brilliant, that much is true. So precisely rendered and creative."

"I have a loaded gun." Eve aimed it at the demon. "Perhaps you might reconsider your admiration?"

The gwyllion's merriment faded instantly. "Quite right. Terrible. Only a sicko could have done something so heinous."

"Who?"

"Wasn't me."

"Make a guess."

Reed held his tongue, watching Eve work, noting the stubborn set of her chin and determined glint in her eyes. She didn't know her own strengths, at least not when they applied to her marking. The selfish part of him smiled, thinking that maybe she could manage to accept the calling without becoming jaded and hardened. Maybe she would learn to take pride in her accomplishments and find something worthy in what she was doing, some positive amid all the negative. Maybe she would become a believer and find her faith.

Miracles were known to happen in his line of work.

The wind died down and the clouds separated. In the wake of the abrupt storm, silence reigned. The air was heavy with uncustomary humidity. It was oppressive, reflective of the confusion, horror, and sorrow that permeated their immediate vicinity.

"There are three of us working this training session," the gwyllion said. "Griselda, Bernard, and me."

"And you are?"

"I'm Aeronwen."

"That's . . . lovely," Eve said grudgingly.

Reed grinned. "It's derived from the name of the Celtic goddess of carnage and slaughter."

"Why do these things keep surprising me?"

"I like it." Aeronwen beamed.

"Of course. Griselda is the faery?"

"No, Bernard is the faery. Did you like the godmother glamour? He's so fun like that."

"A laugh a minute. What's Griselda?"

Raguel appeared at the edge of the roof, levitating over the lip and landing beside Eve. He pointed to the shacklike protrusion that shielded the stairs from the elements. Eve's sharp inhalation told Reed that she saw the dragon peering around the corner.

"Great," she muttered. "My favorite type of demon."

"Hello, Raguel," Reed greeted.

"Did she herald you?" the archangel asked.

"No."

"Then why are you here?"

Reed arched a brow in an expression that asked, *Do you really want to talk about that here and now?*

Raguel nodded. "You frightened the others with your abduction of Ms. Hollis."

A shrug was Reed's reply. The other Marks were Raguel's concern.

The archangel's gaze passed over the two Infernals, then settled on Eve. Deep grooves framed his lips and eyes. He could hide them, if he wished, but he chose not to. "What are you doing, Ms. Hollis?"

Eve felt her mouth curve, although she found nothing at all humorous about the mess that was her life.

"Freaking out. Losing my mind. Take your pick." Outwardly she probably looked composed, maybe even serene. But the knuckles of her gun hand were beginning to hurt from the force of her grip and the set of her shoulders was causing a crick in her neck. She was still screaming, even if no one could hear it.

"You should be with the others."

"No, I should be in Orange County. Designing the interior of someone's dream house. Looking out my windows and considering hitting the beach. Reminding myself to get my car washed and speed-dialing Mrs. Basso to see if she needs anything from the store." Her foot tapped rhythmically into the gravel. "But I can't do that, because she's dead. And the poodle is dead. And now Molenaar is dead. I'm sick of people dying around me, Gadara."

"Let me deal with this."

"What are you going to do? Make us pack up our toys and go home?" She made a sweeping gesture with both arms, causing the two Infernals to duck below the arc of the gun. "This is a perfect training exercise. We have something to hunt down and slaughter. You couldn't have planned it better if you tried."

Gadara stared hard at her. It took everything Eve had to hold his golden gaze. He was a handsome and elegant man, but when enhanced by the full force of his divine gifts, he was blindingly beautiful. His dark skin like silk, his features finely wrought by a deft and loving hand. "This is far beyond your limited training, Ms. Hollis."

"So we learn as we go."

"It is against protocol. You know that."

"I also know that it's 'perfectly acceptable to continue a deviation once it has been set in motion.'" She shrugged out of her sweater jacket, switching her gun from hand to hand until the garment fell away from her overheated body. "Isn't that what you said when you assigned me to hunt tengu and travel to Upland before I was trained?"

"If proceeding is the only reasonable course," he added. "Remaining here is far from reasonable."

"I agree with him, Eve," Reed said, his voice smooth and dark. Comforting, even when contradicting her.

Eve tried not to look at him, knowing it would just make her even hotter, but she lost the battle. He stood with his hands thrust into the pockets of his tailored black slacks, his pale yellow dress shirt sans tie and open at the throat. The wind ruffled his dark hair, draping the locks across his brow. Like his brother, he watched her with a predator's stare, hungry and determined.

He held her gaze. If he'd touched her, it couldn't have felt more real. In some ways, the brothers were very much alike. In others, they couldn't be more different. One warmed her with a slow, steady burn. The other ignited a scorching fire.

With Alec the world stilled, external concerns faded away. She enjoyed him as she would a fine wine, with delicate sips and limitless time. With Reed her response was like a runaway train, increasing in velocity until she was breathless and reckless.

Eve looked away, rolling her shoulders to ease the knotting there.

"We are vacating the base," Gadara said.

"What if that was the goal of the attack?"

"Why?"

"I don't know, but it's a possibility."

"A far-reaching one," Reed interjected. "And regardless, it's too dangerous for you to be here."

Gadara continued to watch her intensely. "I have already ordered an investigative team up here. They are far more qualified and are therefore at less risk."

Eve knew she couldn't argue with that. She also knew that doing nothing at all wasn't an option. "Will you let us participate in the investigation from the safety of the tower? Studying evidence or whatever else can be done?"

A hint of a smile touched the archangel's mouth, but she was too upset about Molenaar to chafe over playing into Gadara's hands. So what if she was determined to participate? That didn't mean she was married to the idea of being a Mark.

"I am certain something can be arranged," Gadara said magnanimously.

Reed gestured for Eve to head toward the stairs. "I'll take the class back to the house."

Gadara nodded. "You can record your report and transfer it to my desk."

"I'll be sticking around awhile."

"That will not be necessary."

"You haven't heard my report."

Eve frowned. "You're worried about something else?"

He caught her elbow as she came closer and started to escort her off the roof. "I'll tell you later."

There was no way to avoid inhaling the unique scent of his skin. It was musky, exotic, seductive. It flowed through her senses, creating tingles where she didn't need them and aches where she didn't want them. The heat of his touch burned through her shirt to her flesh. Sweat dotted her upper lip. Her body remembered the feel of his. Craved to feel it again.

Reed glanced at her. She kept her own line of vision firmly on the ground. He opened the rooftop door, and she was about to step inside when something long, gray, and quick darted past her booted foot.

Eve yelped. The rat stilled halfway down the stairs. It turned its head, staring at her with teeny beaded eyes.

Are you screaming 'cuz of me? it asked.

A mental shudder rolled through her. The sight of the rodent's long, ribbed tail was revolting. She swallowed back her disgust and asked, "Did you see anything when you were up there?"

Rearing up on its rear legs, the rat made a noise suspiciously like a laugh. *I scared ya. Gotta love newbies.*

She aimed her gun. Reed chuckled and lounged into the stairwell railing.

Take it easy, doll, the rat said hastily. *Where's your sense of humor?*

"What's your name?"

A loud screeching was his reply.

Eve cut him off with a wave of her hand. "Okay, let's call you Templeton."

What kind of name is that?

"A rat's name."

"*Charlotte's Web,*" Reed murmured.

Startled that he would know such trivia, Eve looked at him with a widening smile. "I'm impressed."

Who is Charlotte? Templeton barked.

"Never mind," Eve dismissed. "Did you see anything on the roof?"

Nope. Nada.

"You're lying."

Prove it.

"Come on," she cajoled, firmly squelching the voice in her mind that shouted, *You're talking to a rat!* "You had to see something."

It's not true.

"What's not true?" She glanced at Reed, who shrugged and grinned boyishly, the combination briefly distracting her. She cursed her raging libido, which seemed to be fueled by her low-grade fever.

What they say about rats. Templeton's whiskers twitched in a manner that seemed . . . affronted. *It's pigs who squeal, the miserable bastards. They'll do anything for food.*

"I like pigs. They're useful. They make bacon and ham. What have you got to offer?"

Entertainment?

She waved the gun carelessly. "I have to be honest, it's not looking so good for you right now, Templeton. You're giving me the willies, not information."

You'd shoot an innocent rat? Man, that's low.

"Gimme something, then."

Did you see the lip around the roof? It's at least three feet high. I couldn't see shit.

Eve considered that. "What did you hear?"

Struggling. Gurgling. Hammering.

She swallowed hard. "That's not helpful."

Templeton dropped back down on all fours. *Told ya. Can I go now?*

Her gaze shot to Reed. He raised both brows and straightened. The air around him stirred, causing his scent to waft to her. She changed her line of questioning. "Did you *smell* anything?"

Nope. Nada.

"I don't believe you."

Templeton looked at Reed. *Tough crowd, Abel. You sure she's worth the effort?*

Reed looked at Eve, his dark eyes soft. "She's worth it."

Eve forcibly ignored the physical response she had to his tone and words. "You're a rat, Templeton—"

You're brilliant.

"—which means you have a great sense of smell. You can tell me what kind of Infernal did . . . *that*."

Templeton shook his head. *I didn't smell anything but Mark.*

Her head tilted to the side. "I could maybe see that if there was blood everywhere, but there isn't any."

Right, doll. So you tell me . . . No blood to stink up the air and a killer exerting himself strenuously, but all I could smell was Mark. How is that possible?

"What are you—" Reed's hand came to rest at the small of her back. She swallowed hard. "Are you saying there wasn't an Infernal down there when Molenaar was killed?"

Seems that way.

The chill in her gut spread. "Then who did it?"

Templeton's whiskers twitched. *That's the question, isn't it?*

"Who was the last person tae see Molenaar?" Ken asked, his gaze raking over the other Marks.

They were waiting in the men's side of the duplex for Gadara to return from Anytown and the tension was thick as fog. Eve stood on the open threshold between the dining and living rooms. Reed leaned a shoulder into the wall beside her, a causal pose she knew was only a facade. She was unusually antsy, with a simmering need to *move*. The itch to leap into offensive action crawled over her skin like a thousand tiny ants.

The smell of mold and decay in the house was more pronounced now, almost oppressively so. The weak rays of sunlight shining through the windows showcased every flaw the moonlight had concealed: the stained and warped hardwood floors, the crumbling walls, the scuffed baseboards. The air was choked with the proliferation of dust that swirled around them like tendrils of smoke. Eve found herself becoming more agitated by the moment.

Inside her mind, Reed murmured words she couldn't understand in a soothing tone. Their connection was too weak to convey more than impressions, but she got the gist. He wanted her to take it down a notch. She was hot and irritable, and she wanted to cry but her eyes were dry as bone.

"Well?" Ken demanded, looking oddly fierce in his ski cap, like a bank-robbing felon. "The last time I saw him was when we entered Anytown. I went tae the left. I saw Hollis, Edwards, and Richens go intae the office building. Who went tae the right with Molenaar?"

Claire raised her hand. She stood with feet wide and arm wrapped around her waist in a defensive posture that belied the aggressive tilt of her chin. "I did, in the beginning. We separated when I entered a video rental store. He continued without me."

"What time was that?"

"Half past eight?" She muttered something in French. "Maybe eight. What does it matter?"

"What about you?" Ken directed his question to Romeo.

"I was with Laurel."

Ken stared a moment at the pretty Kiwi, who looked chagrined and might have blushed if she wasn't a Mark. "You two make me sick," he bit out.

Laurel blinked, then recovered. "Fuck you, Callaghan."

"Isnae that what he was doing?" Ken jerked his chin toward Romeo. "While Molenaar was losing his head, you two were houghmagandying on a training mission!"

"You didn't save him either," Laurel snapped. "What were *you* doing?"

"Where was Seiler?" Edwards interjected.

"She was following us," Eve said.

"I was not!" Izzie protested.

"You came onto the scene awfully quick," Eve drawled, deliberately goading.

"I am fast. That's all. I do not care about what you are doing. You have problems if you think I would."

"Since you and Richens keep contradicting each other, it's clear that one of you is a liar. Which one of you is it?"

"I am confused," Romeo said, frowning.

Izzie palmed her blade and spoke with dangerous softness. "Do not call me a liar."

Eve crossed her arms. "We don't have time for these games you and Richens are playing. Until one of you admits that you told me a lie, I'm not going to believe either of you."

"Sod off, Hollis," Richens bit out. "My arse still hurts, you know. I told you to pick the knife!"

"I shot you on purpose," she said wryly.

Reed's hand touched her elbow. She caught his frown and shrugged it off.

Ken stepped closer. "What are you talking about, Hollis? What lies?"

"They know what I'm talking about. Let's go back to what happened to Molenaar. Did anyone else notice the lack of Infernal stench around Molenaar's body?"

A stillness came over the group, then a cluster of protests. Eve cut them all off with a wave of her hand. "I understand you were all freaked out. I am, too, but we need to stop thinking about how we feel about this and do something about it instead."

"I didnae smell anything but Mark blood," Ken said.

The others quickly concurred.

"Right." Eve's gaze raked over everyone, searching. "So what does that mean?"

"We weren't paying attention?" Edwards suggested gruffly.

"Or maybe the only thing to smell was Mark. Maybe there was never an Infernal there."

"You accuse one of us?" Romeo cried, dark eyes wide. *"Sei matta! Come puoi dire una cosa del genere?"*

"I have no idea what he said," Laurel snapped. "But I agree!"

Reed's grip on her arm tightened. "Come with me." He dragged her toward the door.

"She is lying," Izzie said with a smile in her voice. "I think it was the faery."

Pausing, Reed faced them. "Leave this matter to Raguel and his team."

"If there's a traitor among us," Richens said, "we have a lot to worry about."

Reed snapped his fingers at the two guards standing watch just outside the front door. "No one leaves."

Without waiting for their acquiescence, he yanked Eve down the steps and away.

CHAPTER 10

Eve stumbled after Reed as they rounded the driveway corner and stepped out of sight. He tugged her around the hedges that separated the duplex driveway from the drive next door and faced her, scowling. "What are you doing?"

"Talking."

"Bullshit. You're instigating infighting on purpose."

"I have a really good reason," she said. "Maybe they'll wake up and smell the stench."

"You aren't in any position to train others."

"This is just a game to them. Richens acts as if we're playing for points and not lives. Ken chose brass knuckles for his weapon. Brass-fucking-knuckles, against Infernals? And Romeo and Laurel were *screwing* for christsakes—*ow!*" She glared at the sky and rubbed her mark through her armband. "That doesn't count!"

Reed's mouth thinned into a disapproving line. "You should be working together, not fighting among yourselves. You know none of them did it."

"Says who?" she challenged, spoiling for a fight. "We can't rule anyone out. We need to be looking very closely at everything and everyone around us. We can't afford any blind spots."

"Marks don't do shit like this, Eve! They're not capable of it."

"And demons don't exist. Sometimes what we think is an absolute truth is completely false." Eve stabbed a finger viciously toward the house. "They have to step outside of the cocoon they're living in and face facts. You can't trust anyone, and if you turn your back, don't be surprised to find a knife in it."

He growled. "Not the conspiracy theory again."

"Gadara has wiretaps in my condo and cameras on every floor of my building. You think he doesn't have Anytown scoped out?" Eve ripped off the Velcro-secured armband. "We're all wearing these. They're supposed to simulate a call, but I would be willing to bet they have GPS locaters in them and maybe bugs, too."

"Will you listen to yourself? You're nuts, and you're driving me nuts, too. Gadara wouldn't let a Mark *die,* Eve."

"Why? Because he's an archangel?"

"Because losing a Mark during training looks bad," he bit out, his powerful frame taut with frustration. "Really, really bad. It will take Raguel centuries to regain the standing he lost today."

Eve's hands went to her hips. "Then why didn't he stop it from happening?"

A muscle in Reed's jaw ticced. He knelt down to get the armband. "You're leaping to conclusions based on assumptions. Look—" he straightened and snapped the metal plate of the band in half, "—there's nothing in here. It's solid. Raguel's running on full power now; he doesn't need secular electronics. These are for your benefit. The pressure on your arm keeps you focused and the metal gives Raguel a concentrated area to heat."

"Are you telling me there's no way Gadara could have known about the attack and prevented it?"

"He's an archangel. Not God."

"I don't see how—"

"Do you think he's evil?" Reed demanded, shoving the destroyed band into his pocket. "Is that what this boils down to? You think he watched your classmate getting butchered on a live feed and ate popcorn?"

She rubbed at the bead of sweat that ran down her nape. Said in that manner, it did sound implausible. "No."

"Everything happens for a reason." His voice softened. "You have to believe that."

"I *don't* believe, Reed. I'm agnostic."

"You're a pain in the ass." He caught her face in his hands and tilted it up. With his thumbs brushing over her cheekbones, he examined her. "Shit. You're burning up. Why didn't you say anything?"

"I did say something," she groused, "to both Gadara and Alec. One says it's all in my head, the other says it's just my body adjusting to the mark."

He snarled something in a foreign language. Eve meant to ask what it was but was distracted by the feel of his touch, which cooled her. The scent of his skin filled her nostrils, altering the tension that gripped her from anger to something far more dangerous.

She caught his wrists and tried to pull his hands away. "Uh . . . Maybe you shouldn't touch me right now."

"No wonder you're so combative," he said roughly. "The Novium is on you."

"You sure that's what it is?" Her voice was a whisper, her throat clogged by the images that filled her mind of *him* on her.

"Oh, yeah. No doubt." He released her abruptly. His gaze was sharp . . .

and frighteningly fervent. "You're crawling out of your skin. Marks don't reach this stage until much later, but you're primed like a veteran."

Her hand lifted to her face, coming to rest over the spot where he had touched her. The skin tingled and was cooler. "Why?"

"You were made for this work, babe. It's just that simple."

"No, I wasn't. You said it yourself; I wouldn't be here if Alec had kept his dick in his pants."

"I said that to fuck with you and get you pissed off at Cain."

"This isn't me," Eve argued. She couldn't face days on end of this job. She would lose her sanity. "Remember? I'm the one who screams at the idiots in horror movies who grab a weapon and pursue the maniacal killer instead of running for help."

The negating shake of his head infuriated her as much as if he had covered his ears with his hands.

"I didn't commit a sin worthy of being marked," she insisted. "This is all just a monumental fuck-up to punish your brother."

"You know how many mortal women have fucked Cain?" Reed's smile was tinged with malice. "And of those, how many of them have ended up where you are now?"

Her chin lifted. "He loves me. I can be used to hurt him. That's the difference."

"You want to toss around theories and conjecture?" He advanced. "Let's take it further. What if Cain is in this mess because of you, instead of the reverse? I've been watching you, babe. You're a natural. What if you two met because you have the inherent skill to rival him and no one else could mentor you as well as he can?"

"That's r-ridiculous."

"No, that's a possibility." His quiet conviction sent a chill down her spine. "You've survived demons no untrained Mark should have."

Eve took a step forward. Reed's suggestion pounded through her skull like a migraine. Her skin and muscles ached as if she had the flu. Even the roots of her hair tingled with a prickling that maddened her. *Don't kill the messenger,* or so the saying went. But she wanted to. Unease slid sinuously around her insides, hissing like a serpent. "I love how you all conveniently forget that I was *dead* just a few days ago!"

A visible shudder moved through him.

That telltale sign devastated her. With everything around her unfamiliar and hostile, what she longed for most was something familiar. Someone who cared for her.

Her arm lifted toward him. "Reed—"

He turned away, his shoulders set against her. "I can feel the heat of the Novium moving through you. It's making me . . . edgy and agitated."

"I'm sorry."

"I need to stay away from you while you're like this, Eve."

She realized then that her bloodlust was translating into a different kind of lust, which created an entirely new problem on top of all the others. She could fight her fascination for Reed, but not his returning fascination for her. "Does that mean you're leaving?"

"I can't," he said gruffly. "Not yet."

Eve would have asked why, but she had a more pressing question. "What *is* the Novium, exactly?"

Reed looked over his shoulder at her. "A change, similar to the change you went through when you were marked. Over time, a mentor and Mark pair become connected. Emotionally and mentally. They learn to think and move as one unit. When the time comes for the Mark to work alone, that bond has to be severed. Cauterized. Some Marks call it 'the Heat' instead, due to the fever that accompanies the process."

"Bond," she repeated, "like you and I share? But I can't feel Alec's thoughts and feelings like I do yours."

"There hasn't been time. Neither of you has been trained. You haven't hunted together. The connection has yet to grow."

"And now it won't?"

He shook his head.

"And what about my connection to you? Will that go away, too?"

"No. It's a rite of passage—similar to leaving a father's household for a husband's. The handler/Mark link grows during the Heat, as does the Mark's connection to his firm leader."

"Gadara."

"In your case, yes."

"Boy, that sure works out for him, doesn't it?" She watched the confusion drift over his handsome features, his train of thought following hers.

"It doesn't work that way. It's not vulnerable to manipulation."

Eve rounded him so that they faced each other again. The transition was akin to stepping out of a cool house into sweltering desert heat. Her temperature shot up to an alarming degree, making her dizzy. "Tell me how it works."

His gaze was as hot as she was. But when he spoke, his voice was calm and sure. "A Mark is trained. Then exposed to missions. They witness deaths and battle various Infernals. They absorb information from their mentors. Somehow, that combination eventually sets off the Novium."

"Okay. Let's see." She started counting down on her fingers. "I've been exposed to missions. I've witnessed deaths and battled various Infernals. And I have a romantic relationship with my mentor. Good enough?"

"You're forgetting time."

"Maybe it's not so much time as it is a buildup," she speculated. "I've had everything thrown at me at once, then I was killed and resurrected, which has to mess with a person, right?"

"Right, which exonerates Raguel."

"Not necessarily, since he's the one who sent me on the missions to begin with. Plus, he's been suspiciously stubborn about acknowledging my present condition."

"There's so much more to this than that, such as how you met Cain and how you were killed. Raguel didn't have a hand in any of that."

"I'm not saying he orchestrated this thing from the very beginning, but once he realized how it had been set up, he could have manipulated things from there. If I'm more connected to him than I am to Alec, it benefits him exclusively."

Growling, Reed ran both hands through his thick hair. "What do these paranoid delusions have to do with your classmate dying?"

Eve studied him, noting the fine sheen of perspiration that glistened on the skin of his throat. She would guess it was no more than fifty-eight degrees in Monterey today, but they were sweating as if it were double that temperature. If she concentrated hard, she could feel the morass of thoughts and emotions roiling within him.

"Answer me, Eve!"

She shook her head, trying to dissipate the ethereal connection to him that was making it hard for her to think. Instead she lost her balance and fell into him. Jolted by the collision with something so hard and solid, she gasped and clutched at him. The sudden surge of cooling relief she felt was so astonishing and so welcome that she sobbed her gratitude.

"Babe . . ." His arms tightened around her and his lips pressed to her sticky forehead.

She stammered over her dry tongue, "How l-long does this l-last?"

"The Novium usually begins during a hunt," he murmured, "and ends with the kill. A few days, usually."

"Days!" Her nails dug into his skin through his shirt. "It hasn't even been one yet and I'm sick of it."

"This is supposed to happen in the field, where it actually helps a Mark by imparting confidence and fearlessness. Without the culmination of a kill, I don't know how long it will last, and since you're restrained, all that energy and bloodlust has nowhere to go."

It was going somewhere all right. To intimate places on her body. The familiar and longed-for sensation of his embrace only exacerbated her condition. "Touching you helps," she whispered.

"It's killing me."

Her hands moved of their own volition, unclenching and resting flat against him.

Reed stiffened. "Don't do this, Eve. I'm not a saint."

"I'm not doing anything." She was barely moving, arrested by the volatility between them.

"You're thinking about things you shouldn't be. You're a one-man woman."

"There's just one of you."

He moved too fast to register. His fist captured her ponytail, arching her back. She found herself wrapped with him, mantled by his powerfully aroused body. There was no denying that he was hard for her, not when she could feel nearly every inch of him against her.

Armani and steel. Elegance and brutal passion.

Desire burst across her mark-regulated senses, exploding across her nerve endings and leaving her shaken. She groaned into his hovering mouth, her nipples hardening and thrusting into his chest.

"You're playing with the wrong brother." His lips moved against hers, his words so softly spoken they were menacing.

"I'm not playing with you," she whispered, repeating the words he had once said to her.

Reed's tongue followed the line of her cheekbone, then dipped into her ear. "Then, what are you doing?"

Eve swallowed hard. "I g-guess I'm . . . coveting."

He cupped her buttock with one hand and ground his erection against her. The lewd gesture was so patently Reed, it made her weak in the knees. "You can't covet what belongs to you."

Reed was deeply pained by the admission, she could feel it. That only made his feelings more precious to her.

How was it possible for her to love Alec, yet want Reed so strongly? However her affection had grown, it needed to stop. Alec had killed Reed—*again*—for touching her the last time. She couldn't put any of them through that twice. It wasn't fair. It hurt people she cared about. It made her not like herself. She wasn't a cheater; she respected herself and her partners too much.

"Remember what I told you in the beginning?" His voice was low and gruff, the words breathed into her mouth. "You're a predator now. Predators like to fuck. That's all this is."

"Don't lie. Not about this."

His tumult was palpable and added to hers. She felt safe with Alec; she felt far from it with Reed. The fact that fear pushed her forward instead of urging retreat scared her. *What if he's right about me? What if killing things is what I'm meant to do?*

No, she refused to believe that being a Mark was her destiny. She *couldn't* believe it, because if she did, it meant that all of her childhood dreams and hopes had to die. There would be no fairytale wedding, no possibility of a family. Everything and everyone she loved, the very aspects of her life that made her who she was, would grow old and leave her life. Who would she be then? Someone she didn't know. Someone she might not like.

"Don't count on me to put on the brakes, Eve. I'm selfish. I won't say no to a prime piece of ass."

She couldn't stop the smile that curved her lips. "Isn't that what you're doing now?"

His mouth took on a mulish cast. "I don't want you like this. I've seen the show, I know how it ends."

"It was a good show." Really good. Reed was rough, edgy, wild in a way she never expected to like, let alone crave. The fact was, the mark . . . Novium . . . *whatever* . . . didn't make her want him. It only lowered her inhibitions enough to free her existing attraction.

He nipped her lower lip, then licked across the spot to soothe the sting. "Come to me again when you're not strung out with the Heat. You'll get a different answer."

"Reed—"

"Enough." Tilting his head, his mouth slanted across hers, taking her breath until she grew faint.

His fist in her hair tightened, arching her further backward, forcing her to mold into him. Her scalp ached with the pressure, the pain intensifying until she whimpered in protest and writhed. The prodding of the gun into her lower back was the final injury that pushed her over the edge.

She stomped on his foot and wrenched free, stumbling a few feet away. "You're hurting me!" she accused.

Reed wiped his mouth with the back of his hand, then adjusted the prominent bulge in his slacks with impatient movements. "Look what you've done to me. Look what you *keep* doing to me, you fucking cock tease."

Eve blinked, shocked by the vehemence of his attack. And the justification behind it. "I'm sorry. I—"

He cut her off with a glare. "Cain's the one getting laid. That means he's the go-to guy for your crap, not me. I want to fuck you, not carry your baggage."

"Jesus," she breathed, wincing at the resulting burn from the mark. A bucket of ice water couldn't have doused her lust faster. "You know I feel like—"

"—you haven't had sex in three weeks? Join the club, Eve. Don't expect sympathy from me."

A hand touched her elbow. She jerked in surprise, her head swiveling to see who joined them. Gadara's gaze moved over her, pausing on the labored lift and fall of her chest and her clenched fists.

"Ms. Hollis," he murmured.

The tension rushed out of her like water down a drain, fleeing her body at the exact spot where the archangel touched her. Eve was suddenly chagrined and emotionally exhausted. Still aching and slick between her thighs, she nevertheless was now capable of coherent, rational thought.

"Walk it off, Abel." Gadara's order resonated with divine command.

Reed spun on his heel and left them, the leather soles of his shoes thudding angrily upon the cement drive and sidewalk. It took everything Eve had not to chase after him. The set of his shoulders told her so much about his mood. She'd backed him into a corner, then wounded him. Her frustration turned inward.

"You should be inside with the others," the archangel said. His irises were an iridescent gold rimmed with obsidian black. He was so beautiful it hurt to look at him. "Our plane will arrive within the next two hours. We will need everything packed by then."

"I don't want to leave."

His brows arched.

"I need to be here," she continued. "I can't go. You might not want to admit it, but the Novium is on me."

Gadara stood silently, eerily composed in the face of the day's events.

"There has to be something I can do here that we can both live with," she persisted.

"It is too dangerous. I prefer your original suggestion to assist from the sidelines."

"I don't think that's going to be possible. Not in the shape I'm in."

"We can resume training next week. A hunt conducted under controlled conditions should suffice—"

"*Next week?* I can't stay like this for—"

The rhythmic thumping of an approaching bass beat halted Eve's tirade midsyllable. Her head turned toward the sound, her eyes catching sight of the pea-green van that turned the corner. It was followed by a white sedan, which in turn was followed by a red pickup truck. The procession slowed, then pulled into the driveway of the duplex directly across the street.

"Is that your investigative team?" she asked, her gaze riveted on the exiting occupants of the vehicles. They seemed far too rambunctious to be long-standing Marks. They tumbled out with whoops and excited chatter.

He stepped forward, taking an almost protective position in front of her. "No."

"Then, who are they?"

"Good question."

"They're fresh faced," she noted. "Maybe a college study group? Biology or chemistry, if all that equipment they're unloading is any indication."

"No one is supposed to be here while we are."

Glancing aside at Gadara, Eve registered his alertness. His sweat suit wasn't capable of softening him completely, not with his ramrod-straight posture and elegant bearing.

"Did you tell whoever's in charge that we're clearing out today?"

"Yes." He returned her gaze. "But the military rarely moves quickly when civilian requests are involved. We began talks for this year's training two years ago. I fail to see how they could have granted permission to a new group in so short a time."

Eve started across the street. Every step was a relief. She needed to walk it off, too.

"Ms. Hollis." The archangel's tone was admonishing. "What are you doing?"

"Saying hi to our new neighbors." She looked down the road toward Anytown, which was within walking distance. Far too close for mortal comfort.

As she approached the new arrivals, Eve caught the attention of one of the girls—a somber-looking brunette with black-framed glasses and orange camisole. The girl elbowed the lanky man next to her, gesturing toward Eve with a jerk of her chin. He turned with a frown that dissolved into a smile when he saw Eve. He had unruly brown hair, a peach-fuzzy goatee, and slumberous hazel eyes that were emphasized by the olive-colored T-shirt he wore.

"Hey," he drawled, sauntering down the drive to the sidewalk.

"Hello." She extended her hand. "Evangeline Hollis."

"Roger Norville." He lifted her hand to his lips and kissed the back. "What's a babe like you doing in a place like this?"

She was taken aback by the line, thinking it was too cocky for such a laid-back guy. "I'm teaching a class on interior design."

The answer rolled off her tongue as if it was her idea, but she knew it wasn't. She didn't have to look behind her to know Gadara was watching and listening through her . . . and compelling safe replies into her brain. Mind rape, but it had its uses.

"In this dump?" Roger's brows rose. "No amount of decorating is going to fix these homes."

"Interior *design*," she corrected. "How spaces are laid out."

"Oh, gotcha. Sorry."

"No problem. How about you?"

He released her hand and shoved his hands into the pockets of his brown corduroy jeans. "We're going to be filming the next episode of our show here."

Eve frowned. "Show?"

"*Ghoul School.*" Roger stilled when she just stared blankly. "On Bonzai. The cable channel."

"Sorry." She shrugged. "I'm not familiar with it."

He beamed, his vaguely smarmy countenance changing to one more genuine. "That's good news."

"It is?"

Roger laughed. "Forgive the corny pickup line. I thought you recognized us."

She smiled, but was bemused.

"Chicks like geeks and television personalities," he clarified, "but not sleaze."

Eve laughed softly. "Whatever works."

He gestured toward the brunette. "Linda, come meet Evangeline. She's teaching an interior design class across the street."

Linda walked over, her lips curved shyly. She was so short, the top of her head barely reached Roger's shoulder. Her attire was deceptively casual at first glance, but closer inspection revealed a penchant for pricey designer pieces and her bob hairstyle was cut with expensive precision. "You must be part of the group we're supposed to steer clear of."

Roger nodded. "Right. Evangeline, this is my girl, Linda."

"Please, call me Eve," she corrected. She felt Gadara in her mind, sifting through her thoughts and leaving new ones behind. To her knowledge, he had never been able to do that before. Considering how new the Novium was for her, he seemed able to leap right in and make use of it without any trouble.

"So, what's *Ghoul School*?" she asked, the thought coming from Gadara. "If you don't mind my asking?"

"We're a paranormal investigative club based out of Tristan College in St. George, Utah. For a while, we were putting our investigation videos up on YouTube, but someone from the Bonzai network found us and gave us a weekly slot."

"Paranormal investigations?" She glanced back at Gadara. "Like *Ghostbusters*?"

"The opposite, really," Linda said. "We don't go into an investigation hoping to find something. We go in hoping to disprove it. We're skeptics."

"You're hoping to disprove something here?"

"At the request of the commandant," Roger said. "She granted permission for another show—*Paranormal Territory*—to investigate a few months ago and they suggested that areas of the base are haunted. She appreciates our more scientific approach. Basically, she wants a second opinion."

"That's fascinating." In a wholly alarming way, considering Molenaar's tragedy just hours ago.

Roger draped an arm around Linda's shoulders. "Are you a skeptic, Eve?"

She shook her head.

Linda grinned. "We've found a believer."

"I wouldn't call myself that," Eve said dryly. "But there are unusual events and situations—"

"Beings?"

"—that are unexplainable."

"Want to come with us?"

Roger shot a startled look at his girlfriend.

Linda's returning glance was mischievous. "Don't look so surprised. Eve's interior design expertise could prove useful. Plus the contrast between her belief in the supernatural and our skepticism would make for great television. She'll reinforce *Paranormal Territory*'s position on the hauntings; we'll debunk it. Gently, of course."

"Ms. Hollis." Gadara's voice poured over the three of them like warm water. It affected Roger and Linda immediately, bringing an enthralled look to their faces.

Eve made the introductions and rehashed the information the archangel had already heard through eavesdropping.

"My brother is a big fan of yours, Mr. Gadara," Roger said, shaking the archangel's hand. "He's a house flipper who wants to be like you when he grows up."

Gadara's smile was a thing of beauty. "Real estate can be wonderfully lucrative."

"That's what he says. Of course, he needs to learn how to budget first. So far he's managed to barely break even."

"Tell him to detach himself from the project. It is business. No more, no less. He should not approach the assignment with his own desires and needs in mind." The archangel looked at Eve, but she already understood that he was talking to her as much as to them.

"I'm impressed that you would take time out of your schedule for a class," Roger said. "The waiting list for that course must be years long. Maybe I could get my brother on it? I forgot his birthday last month."

"It is a private class, given to select employees."

"Lucky employees." Linda smiled. "So . . . would you be interested in roughly thirty minutes of fame? It's an hour-long show, but commercials and setup eat up time. We would love to have you along. We've never had a celebrity guest before."

"I am hardly a celebrity," Gadara protested, but Eve sensed he enjoyed the thought.

"You're very nearly a household name," Roger countered. "As well known as Donald Trump."

"Your presence would boost our ratings," Linda cajoled. "Plus, it's fun."

Gadara smiled boyishly. "Where are you investigating?"

"Anytown."

If Eve hadn't been looking for his surprise, she might have missed it.

Archangels are brilliant actors.

Startled by the new voice, Eve's gaze darted to find the source. A deep bark brought her attention to the Great Dane leaping from the passenger seat of the red pickup. A pretty redhead exited from the driver's side and called out, "Don't bark at the neighbors, Freddy."

Freddy rolled his eyes, then dipped his large head in a bow to Gadara.

"You have a dog," Eve said.

"Yeah." Roger snapped his fingers, and Freddy padded over. "Animals have keener senses. When the viewers see that Freddy is bored, they know nothing paranormal is at work."

Obviously, I'm a brilliant actor, too.

Eve winked at him.

Gadara cleared his throat and looked suitably regretful. "We are utilizing Anytown at the moment."

"No worries," Roger assured. "The commandant warned us. We film at night, so we won't get in your way."

Curious to see how he would maneuver his way through this new curve, Eve watched the archangel closely.

"Hang on." Linda pulled away from Roger and ran back to the van. She dug into a duffel bag resting on the threshold of the open sliding rear door, then returned with a DVD case that she extended to Gadara. "Here's the episode of *Paranormal Territory* that was filmed here at McCroskey. Take a look at it. We won't start filming until midnight. Hopefully that will give you plenty of time to consider it."

Gadara accepted the video, then made their excuses. Eve waved to Freddy before falling into step beside the archangel.

"We can't leave them here alone," she said.

"Clean-up is progressing as we speak, and I will speak with the lieutenant colonel again."

"Going to put the persuasive whammy on her?"

"I will simply suggest that she delay them until we are completely cleared out."

"Shouldn't we catch whoever killed Molenaar before we say we're done here? We can clean up and go, but that doesn't mean the killer won't be left behind."

"You no longer believe the culprit is one of your classmates, Ms. Hollis? Or me?"

She also had concerns about the Infernals working for him, but she'd keep that to herself for now. "I never said it was any of you."

"Not directly, but the implication—the suspicion—is there."

"Okay. That mind-pillaging thing is just plain creepy. If I have something to say to you, I'll say it. Please don't dig around in my brain."

"It is concern for you that motivates me."

"Really? And that's why you decided to ignore the Novium that's tearing me up?"

Stopping by the Porsche, the archangel faced her with narrowed eyes. "Tell me how you think I can best help you."

Eve's fingers touched the trunk, seeking a connection with the vehicle in lieu of Reed. The car was sleek, expensive, and dangerously fast. Just like the man who drove it. "They invited us to go with them. I think we should. We could protect them."

The archangel shook his head and handed her the DVD. "Let me speak with the colonel before we consider that. In the interim, go inside with the others and help them pack. Make sure that we are prepared to go."

She took the video. "The girls' side is done and ready to load."

"Excellent. Now concentrate on the provisions and equipment."

With two guards still in Anytown and two always on point with Gadara, that left only the Marks to do the grunt work. "All right, I'll play along," she said, disgruntled. "For now."

"And stay away from Abel," he added. "He needs to cool down some, as do you."

Eve shot him a wry glance. "So you finally admit I'm running a fever?"

His mouth thinned, briefly reminding her of her dad's style of silent chastising.

She shrugged it off and headed toward the house.

Reed stood in the shade of an oak tree and watched as Eve ran her fingers over his car as if it were a lover. Her mind followed suit, returning to musings of him and her confusion over her attraction. She loved his brother but she wanted him, too. In ways she had never wanted anyone else.

His jaw clenched so tightly it ached.

I covet you.

The words should have been his, not hers. And if she settled into her fate as a Mark, he would have numerous years with her. A blessing, if he was able to head a new firm and snag her for his team. Or a curse, if she remained in love with Cain even after their mentoring relationship was over.

I want to fuck you, not carry your baggage.

The truth mixed with a lie. He wanted everything, which pissed him off to no end. If his brain hadn't been scrambled by her Heat, he would have pulled her into an abandoned home and pinned her to a crumbling wall. He would have pounded himself into her until neither of them could breathe, think, or walk. He would have spilled every drop of his lust into her writhing body, thereby deepening the ethereal connection between them. He also would have irrefutably checkmated Cain by severing their connection before it had a chance to fully form. Eve might have hated him afterward and hated herself for giving in to the desire she didn't understand, but he would've had her in every way that mattered.

But his brain had fried when she laid her feelings on the line. Without a driver behind the wheel, his gut had taken over and fucked it all up.

I want to fuck you, not carry your baggage.

He was such a dick. He'd felt how deeply the words cut her and had relished her pain because it mirrored his.

He could have had her body, but taking her while under duress wasn't enough. He wanted her sober, cognizant, and fully willing. No remorse, no regrets.

"*Hello.*"

Pulled from his thoughts by the greeting, Reed dragged his gaze away from Eve to find the pretty blonde with the dark fashion sense approaching. Her wrists and throat were hugged by spikes and leather, her palms were covered in fingerless gloves, and her legs were wrapped in black-and-white-striped knee-high socks.

He used to seek out women like her—light-haired women with harder-than-usual edges. He'd considered them his type.

His head tilted slightly in silent acknowledgment.

The blonde's gaze followed his previous line of sight and came to rest on Eve, who stood talking with Raguel.

"If it's any consolation," she said, "she's not accessible to your brother either. He has been ringing her cell phone all morning."

"It's not," he said gruffly. Another lie. If there had to be a gulf between him and Eve, he wanted the same distance between her and Cain.

Then why did you let her go?

"Perhaps I can help you."

He turned, leaning his shoulder into the tree. "In what way, Miss . . . ?"

"Call me Izzie." Her stained lips curved in a come-hither smile. "In any way."

Reed knew the invitation had as much to do with Eve as it did with him. Rivalry, perhaps. Or jealousy. Catty girl crap. He wanted to shut her down just for that, just to choose Eve's side. He didn't. Eve wasn't celibate, why should he be?

His gaze dropped to the blonde's lips. "You have a pretty mouth, Izzie."

She nodded, comprehending what he wanted. She turned around and led the way. He followed. Once he dealt with his raging hard-on, he might manage to hold himself together until Eve was safe and he could once again put distance between them. They couldn't keep butting heads. He'd gambled a great deal in order to help Cain resurrect her. He couldn't afford to wreck all of his plans by alienating her beyond repair.

Sparing one last look over his shoulder at the driveway, Reed found that both Raguel and Eve were gone. The Marks would be clearing out soon. Eve would be squired away to safety. Class would end, the blonde would be assigned to a mentor, and he would never see her again. No harm, no foul, no complications.

That didn't stop him from feeling like shit.

CHAPTER 11

D on't leave me like this! What if the maid comes in?"
Alec smiled down at Giselle, who wrestled futilely against the handcuffs that secured her to the pipe beneath the hotel room sink. "I'll put the Do Not Disturb sign up."

"Cain! I'll scream, I swear. They'll call the cops."

He bent down and tugged the handkerchief off her head.

"No!" she protested. "I was just kidding. I didn't—*Mmphfff* . . . !"

He secured the gag with a tug and stood, stepping clear of her kicking legs. "Don't wear yourself out. When I get back I'll need some blood from you, so you should save your strength."

The metal links of the cuffs were muffled by the pipe insulation used to protect the legs of wheelchair-bound guests. Still, Alec shut the bathroom door and turned on the television as added camouflage. Then, he grabbed his black leather messenger bag and crossed into the adjoining room. He shut both connecting doors, then moved to the desk set against the opposite wall. He withdrew the various components of his satellite videophone, but paused to hit redial on his cell phone before assembling them.

The line rang three times. He was about to hang up when Eve's voice, breathy and filled with relief, answered. "Alec!"

"Angel." Concern straightened his spine and canceled his plans to chastise her for not answering his other calls. "Is everything all right?"

"No—"

"Are you okay?"

"Yes, but—"

"Are you hurt?"

"No, but Molenaar—the Stoner—is dead."

"*What?* How?"

He listened to her explanation with a growing sense of urgency. "I want you out of there," he said when she finished. "Right now."

"That's Gadara's plan. We're packing up as we speak."

He knew her well enough to pick up the stubbornness underlying her tone. "Don't fight him on this, angel, although I can't imagine why you would. Sounds like just the sort of thing you would want to avoid."

"No shit. Where's my scaredy-cat sense of self-preservation when I need it?" She sighed. "I've been told I'm going through the Novium. It's making me bitchy."

Alec stilled. It was impossible. It was years too soon.

"I would take that with a grain of salt," he said gruffly. "Raguel doesn't have enough experience with the Heat to make that diagnosis."

"Well, your brother agrees with him."

"Abel is there?" His concern for her safety turned into something baser, an emotion that was darker and more selfish.

"Yes. He has something going on with Gadara. I don't know what it is."

Alec was more concerned with his brother having something going on with Eve. She shouldn't be so susceptible to the Heat so quickly. By design, the Novium helped train Marks to overcome their lingering fears so they could achieve successful independence. Eve hadn't been marked long enough to be affected, plus they hadn't attained the sort of bond he'd seen in other mentor/Mark pairings. If she went through the Novium now, not only would he lack a vital part of the experience he hoped would help him advance to firm leader, but he would also miss the opportunity to bind Eve more tightly to him.

With a growl, Alec moved to the bed and sat. It was time for another argument with God about the return of his *mal'akh* powers. Eve, bless her, was somewhat of a disaster magnet. "Are any of the other students showing signs?"

"I have no idea." Her tone was weary. "They're argumentative, and Romeo and the princess are still screwing like rabbits, but other than that . . . ? I don't know what to look for."

"They're not important. Just take care of yourself." If it was only Eve, he would have to seriously consider if her acclimation was being manipulated. And if so, who was responsible.

"Take care of myself how? I feel like shit, Alec. As if I have the flu. Isn't the mark bad enough? Why does my process have to be so out of whack with the norm?"

"Angel . . ." Fuck, he should be with her now. She shouldn't be alone. And she damn well shouldn't be anywhere near Abel, whose connection with her would strengthen while his waned. "I'm guessing the Stoner's death triggered your Heat early. Maybe you're being affected so strongly because you've already been on a hunt."

"That's what I told Reed. This sucks. I'm not a dog; I shouldn't feel like a bitch in heat."

"It's not like that."

"You're not the one going through it, Alec," she argued. "Trade places with me, then tell me how it feels."

Inhaling sharply, he forced himself to remain seated and not break speed limits back to Monterey. Not for the first time, he damned the fact that he was as untrained in his role as she was in hers.

"I hate being clueless," he growled, shoving a rough hand through his hair. "This whole situation is fucked all to hell. Everyone's got their thumb in the pie and we're stuck cleaning up the mess."

"No one's finger is in my pie," she said dryly. "And sadly, I'm disappointed about that. The Novium is making me horny. How insane is that?"

Alec stilled, considering. He'd come across all types of mentor/Mark pairs over the years. Romantically linked teams were rare, but they did happen. One Mark had sworn that the best sex of her life had come during the Novium. She'd wondered whether it was melancholy over the end of her mentor relationship that had made the sex so hot or whether it was due to the Heat itself. Either way, the Mark had said her emotional attachment had strengthened during that time despite the imminent end to the training bond.

And Abel was there with Eve . . . Damn it.

"I wish you were here," she said in a small voice. "I don't know what to do with myself. I feel like a stranger in my own skin."

There was something he could do for her from this distance, one way to ensure that she didn't fall into Abel's greedy hands like a ripe, juicy apple. "I don't have to be with you to help you."

"Talking helps. But honestly, that's the last thing I want to do with you right now."

"All action. My kind of girl." Alec piled the pillows against the headboard and made himself comfortable. He pictured Eve in the grip of lust— her eyes glassy with need, her lips red and parted on gasping breaths as he pumped hard, fast, and deep into her.

With his voice low and thick, he asked, "Are you alone?"

Her hesitation told him that she registered the change in his mood. "No. I'm with the others, helping them pack up the equipment."

"Can you find someplace where you will be within a safe distance but far enough away to prevent anyone from overhearing you?"

Eve's breath caught, then was exhaled in rush. "I think so."

"Then get there. Quick."

Raguel unfolded from the back of his bulletproof Suburban and slipped on a pair of sunglasses. Before him stood the headquarters where the garrison commander, Colonel Rachel Wells, oversaw the nuts and bolts of what was left of Fort McCroskey and the adjunct installations.

He had called ahead and she was expecting him, but the tone of her voice had warned him of trouble ahead. Debunking the ghosts was important to her for a reason he had yet to discern. But her motivation was moot. He would *persuade* her to postpone the filming of the ghost-hunter show long enough for his team to purify the area. A few days, at most, were all he needed.

Montevista exited the front passenger seat. With practiced movements, the guard straightened the fit of his navy blazer, effectively concealing the bulge of his shoulder holster and gun. From behind dark sunglasses, the Mark scanned their surroundings with a sweeping glance. "I can't stand feeling vulnerable."

"You have the strength of an army in you."

"Flattery won't save you if we're attacked by whatever butchered Molenaar today. You and the students should be on the move as we speak, sir."

Raguel brushed a careless hand down his dress shirt. The time for leisure was over and his change of attire reflected that. "Charles Grimshaw will circle us for a while before he strikes again. He just wanted us to know he was here, hunting."

Montevista looked at him. Although the Mark's shades were dark enough to be impermeable to mortal eyes, Raguel's enhanced vision saw through them as if they weren't there. The Mark was clearly taken aback. "Grimshaw did this? How do you know?"

"Molenaar was hunted by an animal. He was targeted because he was the weakest and slowest member of our group. And the manner in which he was killed was a message, one guaranteed to reveal the sender."

"What is the message?" Sydney asked. She was a petite blonde, less than five feet tall. Delicately feminine, she downplayed her fragility with a severe chignon, starkly cut pantsuit, and button-down dress shirt. Like Montevista, she wore dark shades and her right ear was wrapped with an earpiece that kept her connected to the rest of his security detail.

"He intends to cut off God from the people—hence the decapitation of a crucified man—through those who are lacking and vulnerable."

Montevista's hazel eyes narrowed consideringly. This was why Raguel trusted him with his life. The Mark examined everything. "How is that Grimshaw's signature?"

Raguel moved to the walkway that led to the headquarters entrance. On the lawn to the left, a bronze statue celebrated a person or event rather than the hand of God who guided all. He looked away, noting instead the number of cars in the parking lot and the proliferation of uniform-clad soldiers scurrying like ants around the various buildings.

"Charles once told me that Infernals are not an accident. He claimed they were created by design and our time here on Earth is merely a test. Survival of the fittest, he said. One day, only the strongest and wiliest will remain. That is who God seeks, he claims. Not the most faithful, but the most ruthless."

"What do you think, sir?" Sydney asked.

"I think Charles lost his originality with age. His actions are not motivated by survival of the fittest; they are spurred by his own misplaced
grief and self-recrimination. Nearly everyone blames God when they lose
a loved one. I expected better of him."

Montevista's face took on a stony cast. "The loss of a child is something you could never understand unless it happened to you."

Raguel was well aware that Montevista—a former police officer—had
approached the acquitted murderer of his six-year-old daughter and fired
six rounds from his service revolver straight into the man's heart. One for
each year of her life. It was why Montevista was marked.

"The Lord gave," Raguel murmured, "and the Lord hath taken away."

"Job 1:20–21," Sydney offered.

"It's a brutal test even the most pious fail." Montevista's voice was
tight. "A demon like Grimshaw didn't stand a chance."

"Perhaps that was the point." Raguel reached into his pocket for his
beeping cell phone. He withdrew it and read the text message from Uriel.
Satellite conference @ 18:00 EST.

He checked the time and exhaled harshly. It was just past noon. He
still needed to speak with Abel, who would explain what happened in Australia. Going blind into a meeting with the other archangels was not an
option. There were very few things he disliked more than discovering that
he knew less than his siblings.

Once he learned all he could from Abel, Raguel would send him away.
The *mal'akh*'s appearance so swiftly on the heels of Molenaar's murder
had created a volatile situation Evangeline was not prepared for. Later, she
would serve God's purpose. For now, Raguel wanted nothing to interfere
with his own work with her. He fully intended for her to align with him
so completely that she related to him more than she did with Cain and
Abel. He could manage them through her. Together, he and the two
brothers could form a triumvirate that would ensure his position in the
celestial hierarchy. And bringing the warring siblings together would prove
unequivocally that he could accomplish any task. Ascension to the rank
of *hashmal* wouldn't be far behind.

Raguel's fingers wrapped around the cool metal handle of the door.
The entrance to the headquarters was set into the side of the building,
shielded by an overhang that kept the doorway in shadow. Free of the sun's
glare, the glass was as clear as still water. Even without his enhanced sight,
he could see directly through to the twin doors on the opposite side of the
long foyer.

The lights were out. Nothing moved. He listened closely and heard only
silence.

Montevista rushed in front of him, preventing him from opening the
door. Sydney pressed her back to his, shielding him from a possible rear
attack.

"Take him back to the truck," Montevista ordered.

"Not yet." Glancing over the Mark's shoulder, Raguel noted the flashing red light on the wall. "Someone set off the fire alarm."

"I don't smell smoke."

"Neither do I." If it were present, he could smell it from a mile away. Literally. "A drill, perhaps."

"I don't like it," Sydney said. "Something's off. I can feel it."

"Sir, if you'll wait in the car with Sydney," Montevista suggested, "I'll investigate and find the colonel."

"Not this time," Raguel demurred. "Under the circumstances, I prefer that we remain together."

Something weighty and cool was pressed into his palm. Raguel glanced at Sydney, who gave a nod. Then, his gaze dropped to the gun in his hand. His lip curled in distaste. Such a blunt and brutal weapon, lacking all elegance and refinery. That he was forced to carry, and possibly use, such an instrument was insulting. Against an Infernal, he could unleash the full force of his God-given power. But against a mortal—a Satanist or possessed soul—he had to restrain himself to inflicting wounds that wouldn't destroy the body or betray what he was.

The restrictions on his gifts chafed deeper every day. To his knowledge, the other archangels were happy with their lot. Uriel loved the ocean. Raphael loved the Serengeti. Sara had earthy appetites. He, however, would leave mortal life behind in an instant to return to the heavens. There was little here that appealed to him. He found it all so primitive. Despite centuries of technological advances, human nature had yet to mature beyond its infantile stages.

Raguel handed the gun back. "I changed my mind. Wait here."

"I don't—!"

He shifted before Montevista could finish the sentence. He winked in and out of every room in the building. Signs that the occupants had vacated in a hurry were prevalent—open e-mail in-boxes on monitors and cold drinks sitting amid puddles of condensation.

Yet it was calm outside. Whatever alarm had been triggered here hadn't alerted anyone beyond these walls. A drill would explain that, but it didn't explain the chill that moved through Raguel. Something was wrong; he simply had to discover what it was.

Pausing his search inside the colonel's office, Raguel glanced out the wall of widows that overlooked the field below. His brows lifted at the sight of the formation on the grass a few hundred yards beyond the building. A hundred or more soldiers stood at parade rest in neat, precise rows.

"What are you doing?" he wondered aloud.

Footsteps thundered up the stairs, the pounding beat echoing through the hallway and reception area.

Sydney and Montevista.

"In here." Raguel's voice came at conversational volume, knowing their enhanced hearing would pick it up. With the casement windows ajar to invite in the breeze, he was hesitant to disturb the ranks below.

The two guards rushed in behind him. Sydney dipped into the adjacent garrison Command Sergeant Major's office, searching for hazards. Montevista took up a position at Raguel's right shoulder.

"Everything okay, sir?"

"So it would appear."

He scanned the visible area, spotting the baseball game taking place on the opposite side of a thick barrier of Monterey pines. Off-duty soldiers at play. What had started out as a gloomy morning had turned into a sunny day.

"Uh . . . Sir," Sydney said from the CSM's office. "There's a disturbance at the tree line. I can't make out what it is from here."

Montevista leaned forward as if doing so would improve his vision. Old habits died hard. "Where? What are you looking at?"

Raguel's gaze honed in on the swaying of a twenty-foot pine. He pointed. "There."

Enhancing his vision, he looked through the trunks and watched some . . . *thing* struggling. A huge creature, pale enough to glimmer like a pearl even in the shade of the towering trees around it. A creature capable of shaking a mature pine down to its roots.

"What in hell can move a tree that size?" Montevista asked.

Mariel's voice echoed through Raguel's mind, *It was a monstrous beast; easily several feet in height. Flesh, not fur. Massive shoulders and thighs.*

"I believe we have found our mysterious Infernal."

"Or it found us first," Montevista said grimly. "If that's the thing Mariel and Abel are after, what is it doing here and how do we kill it?"

This creature was much bigger than what she had described, but size was moot. The thing in the trees was evil, a being so afflicted in the soul that it tainted the air around it. Its thrashing and writhing sent waves of horror outward in shockwaves. The branches recoiled, their creaking a cry for help that reverberated inside him. Below, the formation shivered in unison. They felt the *wrongness* but were incapable of discerning the source.

Raguel breathed deeply, inhaling the fresh air entering through the window. The faintest hint of sweetness teased his nostrils.

Mark blood.

With a roar only enhanced ears could hear, he shifted through the glass and plummeted along the outside of the building, leaving his cell phone spinning like a top on the office floor behind him. As the ground rushed up to meet him, his wings snapped outward like a flag in a Santa Ana wind. He caught the current and soared over the formation, his upward surge sending a torrent of air across the soldiers. Their hats scattered, twisting and tumbling.

A unified cry of dismay followed him. Blinded by their mortality, they couldn't see his celestial form, but they felt him. Not just in the wind, but in the inner sense that connected them to the heavens. A sense dulled by time and misuse, but still inherent nevertheless.

The beast returned Raguel's war cry with one of its own, a fulsome growl that caused every animal within a goodly distance to sound out in fear, giving voice to the hidden reality of the battle about to ensue.

Accelerating to a speed faster than mortal time, Raguel noted how the world around him slowed. The wayward hats hovered in midair, arrested. Birds hung in midflight. The only thing moving at his pace was the Infernal. The creature broke free of its confinement and leaped out onto the field, felling two trees and leaving a depression in the ground.

It was a flesh-colored mass the size of a bus. The beast barreled toward the unsuspecting formation with a speed that was stunning considering its bulk. It ran on all fours, fists punching into the earth with unrestrained ferocity. The shoulders and thighs were disproportionately gigantic, a grotesque contrast to the smaller head and tiny waist. But the crowning atrocity was its mouth, a yawning cavern lined with rows of yellowed teeth.

It crawled inside my Mark, Mariel had reported. *She screamed and it lunged into her mouth. It disappeared inside her. It should have been impossible. The creature was many times her size . . .*

The falling trees were at the midway point in their rush to the ground. Tucking his arms close to his sides, Raguel beat his wings, increasing his velocity.

He was one of the holy angels. *He who inflicts punishment on the world and the luminaries.*

But he had no problem kicking the ass of *anything* vile. Sammael had been gunning for him since he was cast from Heaven. Raguel supposed it was time to give his fallen brother what he'd long wanted.

"Out of the belly of Hell I cried," Raguel said grimly, zeroing in, praying for strength and the blessing of God. "And You heard my voice."

So much time had passed since his last battle. Time wasted. Time misused. He'd grown arrogant. Sloppy. And an innocent, untrained Mark had paid the price. Jan Molenaar's soul would now wait in *Sheol*—purgatory—its owner denied the chance to redeem it. Raguel prayed his next act would redeem them both.

The Infernal reared up on its hind legs, attaining a breathtaking twenty-plus feet in height. It screamed with open-throated hatred at the heavens, beating at its chest in an awesome display of power.

Retracting his wings at the last second, Raguel dived into the gaping maw.

*   *   *

Eve was striding down the hallway before her brain fully registered Alec's intent.

Get there. Quick.

Her aching body was galvanized by the purring rumble of his voice, a seductive timbre that even cellular reception couldn't diminish. She hurried through the kitchen and opened the rear door. Richens sat on a folded-up jacket on the lowest step, his head turning to see who joined him.

"Hollis." His eyes and expression were eerily blank. "I need to talk to you."

"Lose Mastermind," Alec ordered.

For some silly reason, it meant a lot to her that he remembered her nicknames. "Getting there," she muttered.

Eve shook her head at Richens in silent negation. *Later,* she mouthed. She jumped off the step and onto the dead grass.

"You just showed up and now you're leaving again?" he groused. "We have to pack."

She didn't bother pointing out that he wasn't doing anything to help. "I forgot something next door."

"That's what Garza and Hogan said . . . before they headed in the opposite direction."

Eve waved him off, unsurprised. Garza was going to get calluses on his dick if he didn't slow down soon.

"You still moving?" Alec asked.

"Yes. By the way, this Novium business is damned inconvenient. I really needed to talk to Izzie. She should have reached Molenaar around the same time as me. But she didn't show up until ten or fifteen minutes later. Where the hell was she?"

"The Novium is never convenient, angel. And you can't do anything about your classmate now anyway. Raguel has you packing and you can't work alone."

"So I'm just stuck being miserable?"

"Your brain is seeking the sensation of a kill, so we'll trick it—temporarily—into thinking you've done that."

"How?"

"Phone sex, angel."

She stumbled over a protruding patch of dead weeds. "Killing demons is orgasmic?"

"How did you feel after you killed the Nix?"

Euphoric. Slightly drunk. "O-kay . . . That's really kinda sick, Alec."

"Hey, they're the bad guys, remember? The scourge of the Earth. Evil incarnate. It's okay to feel good about vanquishing them."

Rounding the backside of the duplex, Eve bypassed the kitchen door and went to the main entrance of the girls' side. It was unlocked and she hurried in. A pile of duffel bags and backpacks rested on the threshold to the dining room, including hers. "Can you go upstairs and ask God for a little help here?"

"You know better than that."

"Can't you try?"

She should be a basket case right now. Traumatized for life and frightened into paralysis. Instead, the memory of Molenaar's death filled her with an aggressive, wild energy. The need to move, to act, to rip something apart was difficult to fight. But a good hard screw would do just as well. That bothered her more than she could say.

"Angel—"

"Why is sex so much a part of being a Mark?" She swiped at a drop of sweat that trickled down her temple. "Sex brought us together in the first place. Then, it was involved when Abel put the mark on me, and again when I went through the physical changes with you. Seems to me that being marked and being a nymphomaniac go hand in hand."

"It's balance, Eve. You're a killer now. You'll wake up in the morning for the sole purpose of murdering something and you will usually go to bed having accomplished that task. Sex connects you to someone. It forces you to give and take intimacy. It keeps you human."

"Balance would be sex one day and hunting the next." She leaned against the living room wall. "Mixing the two is just . . . kinky."

"Sex isn't the reason we hooked up."

She quivered at his rumbling tone. "Liar," she breathed. "It's all we had time for."

"Liar," he rejoined gruffly. "It took us half a second to see where we were headed. Time had nothing to do with it and the sex was a bonus."

Eve would never forget the sight of him on his Harley outside the ice cream store where she worked after school. He'd had her at the first glance. "You made my mouth water," she confessed. "Still do."

"Right now, I could tell you to cool off with a shower and an ice pack. I could tell you to pick a fight with that blonde who has issues with you and knock out some of the stress that way. I could suggest that you slip away and get yourself off without me. But I'm not going to let you do any of those things, Eve, because I need to be your go-to guy." He paused, then, "And I need Abel to *not* be that guy."

Sagging into the wall, Eve knew she couldn't feel any worse. Reed had run like hell, but she couldn't say that without explaining what he'd been running from. And it didn't matter anyway. Alec was a damn good guy and she was lucky to have him in her corner. He wouldn't be there forever, but right now was better than nothing.

"Eve?"

"Gimme a minute. You slayed me."

He laughed softly. "I'm glad you don't need wine and roses."

She wiped at her wet cheeks with her free hand. "You make this all bearable, you know."

"Just bearable? I'll have to work harder."

More than bearable. He made her feel safe and sane. He didn't put her off or undermine her. He treated her with respect when everyone else was manipulating her into cramped corners.

"I miss you like crazy," he murmured. "You're in my head even when I'm sleeping."

"Did you have a wet dream?"

"Damn near. You were lying beside me, naked and hot as hell. I got hard just watching you sleep."

Eve understood that. Admiring him while he was sleeping was a favorite pastime of hers. Sleep softened him in a way nothing else could.

"I pulled you under me and slid into you before you were fully awake. You made those sexy little noises you always make when I'm deep in you. I could almost feel you fisting around me. And the way you can't stop coming . . . Drives me fucking crazy that I can get to you that way."

The images that flooded her mind concentrated the heat of the Novium and dropped it low in her belly. Alec's voice, roughly seductive like velvet, always left her weak in the knees. He was inexhaustible, and his need to get her off until she couldn't take any more had pretty much ruined her for other men.

"I wish you were here with me now," he purred. "I'd strip you bare and lick you from head to toe."

She gave a shaky exhale. "You have an oral fixation."

"Which you love." The smile in his voice sparked an inner quivering.

Alec never did anything in half-measure. Unlike Reed, who rode a woman hard and put her away wet, Alec took his time during sex. He used his mouth first, then his hands. From head to toe, front to back, every curve and crevice. Whispering praise both lewd and tender. Taking hours.

"Are you thinking about my mouth on you?" he murmured. "Are you hot and wet?"

"Are you alone?" Eve locked the front door. The big picture window was covered by a white sheet that let milky light in, but made viewing impossible. It was as private as she was going to get without venturing off to someplace farther away. "Do you have an audience?"

"I'm all yours. Why are you whispering? Aren't you alone yet?"

"Yes, but we're having phone sex, Alec. And I'm inexperienced. It would be embarrassing if someone overheard me. Where's the horse?"

He laughed. "Giselle is handcuffed to the bathroom pipes in the adjoining room."

"Handcuffed? Sounds kinky."

"Stop it. Tell me you miss me."

She sighed. "A lot. Are you naked?"

"Not completely. Just enough to get the job done. I've got work to do, too, but you come first."

"We'll come at the same time," she breathed. "Are you touching your-self?"

"Yes. Are you?"

"Not yet."

"What are you waiting for?"

Her eyes closed against the building ache in her chest. "You."

She'd been waiting for him for ten years. Staying away hadn't spared her punishment, so when she'd been marked he'd come back for the duration. But now that she had him, she sometimes turned him away and sent him home just to prove to herself that she could still live without him. Because one day, soon, she would have to.

"I'm here, angel," he purred. "Hard and ready. I'm in heat, too. Thinking about you always gets me that way."

It was her complete trust in him that gave her the courage to say, "I wish you were in my hands."

"Fuck, yeah. Me, too."

"I want to hold you. I love how soft the skin of your cock is. How thick the veins are. They make you look so brutal, when you're really so tender."

"Trace them with your tongue."

"What?"

"The veins. Use your tongue."

Eve's mouth watered. Alec wasn't the only one to have an oral fixation. What really got to her was how much he loved it. He was so unabashed in his enjoyment, his hands fisting in the sheets or her hair, his voice hoarse as he cursed at her for stripping him down to base animalistic need.

"I love that sensitive spot just beneath the head," she whispered. "I like to flutter my tongue across it just to hear you fall apart."

Alec groaned. "Touch yourself while you're sucking me."

Eve's fingers went to the top button of her jeans and flicked it open. "It gives me a thrill to know you're so hot for me."

"I'm beyond hot. I'm about to go up in flames."

She imagined herself kneeling over him, holding his fly apart so nothing impeded her working mouth. The fantasy was so real she could hear the slick suction noises. Her hand pushed into her jeans, forcing the zipper pull to slide down.

Suck harder.

Eve lost her balance, sinking into an off-kilter crouch.

It wasn't Alec's voice she heard in her mind; it was Reed's.

CHAPTER 12

Eve's eyes stung with welling tears.

Why Reed's voice? Why *now,* when she was deep into an intimate moment with another man? A man she'd loved for as long as she could remember.

The gun at her lower back shifted dangerously, freed from its position by the loosening of her fly. She grabbed for it, then set it down on the dusty floor beside the luggage, her fingers clenching spasmodically around the grip.

"Damn, that feels good," Alec gasped. "You suck cock as if you were starved for it."

Her mind was inundated with sensation—the rhythmic drawing of a hungry mouth, a tongue flickering, a fist pumping the thick root. It felt as if she was inside his brain, enjoying their fantasy through his senses. Sweat dotted her brow and upper lip. Heat rippled along her skin in a prickling wave, the Novium burning through her in double time, yet she felt closer to him than ever before.

An orgasm hovered just out of reach. Through no physical manipulation at all, she was about to climax from the feel of Alec's pleasure. She cried softly, nearly dizzy from the surfeit of sensual perception. "Please . . ."

"Yes, angel." His voice was sandpaper rough. "Come for me. Let me hear you."

A pained female whimper yanked Eve back from the edge, cruelly halting her hurtle toward climax.

Her eyes flew open. *She* hadn't made that sound . . . could never make that sound with Alec. He was too gentle. Despite the ferocity of his ardor, he always treated her as if she was breakable.

Eve slid from her crouch to a seated position on the floor. A brazen wet sucking noise rent the quiet of the house, followed by a serrated masculine groan.

Unmistakable sounds with an unmistakable cause.

She wasn't alone. And, worse, she wasn't unaffected. The knowledge that a sexual act was taking place somewhere nearby ratcheted up the tension to painful intensity.

Alec growled in her ear, knowing her well enough to pick up on her sudden preoccupation. "Don't stop! Fuck, I'm about to blow."

"Do it," she urged, struggling to her feet. He could come and keep going. It was a gift.

"Not without you. Are your fingers inside you?"

"Yes," she lied. With deliberate steps, she managed to walk carefully to the hallway without her heavy boots giving her away.

She didn't recognize herself. She wasn't a voyeur. In her previous life, she would be hightailing it out of there, not salivating for a lewd peek. Especially of Romeo and Laurel. Part of her brain was revolted by the thought; the rest of her brain was so inundated with Alec's approaching orgasm it couldn't string a sentence together.

"I can't hold off much longer," Alec bit out. "Are you close?"

"Yes." But her answer referred to her proximity, not her orgasmic state. The fellating noises were spilling into the hall from the farthest open bedroom doorway. Another couple of steps and she would be able to look inside.

Eve hugged the opposite wall. The panting and groaning grew in volume, as did the erotic sound of hard suckling.

The couple came into view and she stumbled. Her free hand covered her mouth, stemming the low moan of torment that rose up unbidden. Her chest constricted.

Reed.

He occupied the center of the master bedroom, standing with head back and eyes closed. Izzie kneeled before him like a supplicant, the bobbing of her pigtailed head betraying the enthusiasm with which she sucked his cock. His fingers were shoved into her restrained hair with white-knuckled force, pulling the blonde tresses in a way that caused her pained whimpers. He moved her as he wanted, his hips thrusting at a breathtaking pace. His neck was corded by straining muscles and his handsome face twisted with a carnal grimace of pleasure and fierce concentration.

Eve was bombarded by a dark and cold desire, as if the walls between them had stemmed a tide that the open doorway now freed. His struggle to climax rushed at her like an oncoming tsunami, carrying her back, beating her against the wall.

Ravaged by jealousy and the aggressiveness of the Heat, Eve watched with horrified eyes, understanding that the sensations she had thought were Alec's were actually Reed's. They traveled to her through their growing emotional link, hitting her in real time with Izzie's movements.

But it wasn't Izzie he pictured behind his closed eyelids.

"Angel?" Alec's voice was strangled. "You're fucking killing me. If you were here, I'd have my mouth between your legs, tonguing your clit until you went off for me."

Alec's intrusion triggered an emotional flood—remorse and longing, sorrow and love. It was so potent, it was tangible. The hairs on her nape prickled.

His breath caught. "I can *feel* you."

Reed gasped and straightened. His gaze found her, his lips moving without sound. *I can feel you.*

And she felt them. Both of them, pushing into her, inundating her with their desire and raw needs, seeping into every pore, every memory, every hidden thought. She was bared in a way only a true . . . *possession* could make possible.

Two men. Inside her at the same time.

They swirled around her like billowing smoke, battling within her, shoving at each other like children over a favored toy and inadvertently discovering her tragic fascination with both of them in the process. Triumph and pain, joy and misery, envy and passion, love and hate—the way they responded to the revelation was destroying all three of them.

The roots of her hair grew damp with sweat. Her skin burned as it had when the dragon killed her, a blistering pain she hadn't survived the first time. Alec and Reed were overpowering her, too focused on their endless rivalry to realize how their centuries of memories and bickering were drowning her.

Sucking in air, Eve pushed her hand into her open fly and cupped her sex. The subsequent flare of pleasure and relief was like a beam of light in the darkness. The two men recoiled from each other and she took the advantage, pushed them backward, slipping into them the way they had come into her.

They each wrapped around her, their mental embraces as heated and passionate as their physical ones. But she was divided and untrained, torn by guilt and confusion. She lacked the sheer strength and knowledge required to see into their souls the way they'd seen into hers. Still, Eve tried to probe their minds even as her fingers delved between her thighs. She moaned as she pushed two fingers inside, feeling how hot and swollen she was, how desperate and greedy. Both men growled in unison, feeling her pleasure as she felt theirs.

It seemed as if there was no separation between them. She felt Alec's strong fingers wrapped around his cock, pumping with unrestrained ferocity. She felt Izzie's lips and tongue around Reed, felt the rhythmic suction and drenching heat.

But mentally, she was the deliverer of both forms of pleasure. The two men saw her in their minds' eyes, a revelation that caused tears to blind her.

Eve . . .

Which one spoke, she couldn't discern. The voice was too guttural, too coarse from the knife's edge of orgasm. Suddenly, the hand between her legs wasn't hers. It was theirs. Both of them. Together. Spreading her, stroking her, filling her.

Her resulting climax devastated her, bringing a cry to her lips that was lost in the conjoined roar of their orgasms. In that moment, at the height of pleasure, there was no distinction between them. They were one, a triumvirate of souls. She melted, crying both inside and out, her skin so hot her sweat steamed off it.

It wasn't until the first brutal surge had passed that she realized their transient embraces weren't meant to cherish but to restrain. As she struggled to explore them while the singular connection existed, they bound her tightly. Too tightly. Preventing her from looking deeper. Their history was behind her, an open book. But their futures—their hopes, dreams, and motivations—were beyond, and they wouldn't allow her to see them.

What are you hiding? her two halves asked, their voices an eerie chorus that sent a shiver down her spine.

She lost her grip on her phone. Her marked reflexes kicked in, enabling her to withdraw her hand from her jeans and fumble for the cell within the blink of an eye. As she struggled to make the catch, she took several stumbling steps down the hall before slipping into the guest bedroom where she'd spent the night. Eve held herself flush against the wall, reeling from an encounter she could only liken to a mental ménage à trois.

Gulping in air, she was arrested by the vortex of emotions that swirled through all three of them. Alec was sick with jealousy, Reed was tormented by guilt, and she . . . she felt an all-pervasive confusion.

What the hell had just happened to them?

Inside Eve, something shifted and solidified. Time passed without her registering it. It wasn't until she heard Izzie's quick, light footsteps pass the open doorway followed by Reed's heavier, more arrogant stride that she realized they had finished and were leaving. In her hand, her cell phone vibrated, urging her to answer. *Seven missed calls,* the display read, and she hadn't felt a one. She turned the phone off, shoved it into her pocket, and refastened her jeans.

The comfort of her waistband reminded her—she'd left her gun on the living room floor.

Galvanized, Eve darted out of the bedroom. She was halted by a collision with a steely chest.

"Let go, Reed."

Part of her took comfort in his need to see her. Another part resisted the lying in wait. Perhaps that was all she was to him and Alec, a prize to be won.

He held fast. "It's too late for that now."

Eve opened her mouth to protest, but was silenced by a piercing female scream.

"Shit," she breathed.

"Stay here," Reed ordered, shifting out of the room.

Running to the living room, Eve dug through the backpacks looking for her gun, missing the feeling of safety the weapon imparted.

A shout. This one male, but not Reed's.

She'd have to find the damned gun later. Rushing out the door, she'd just hit the rear lawn when Reed shifted in front of her.

"I told you to stay put," he bit out, his features hard.

"I should be with the others."

"Damn it." He sidestepped into her path when she tried to pass him. She shoved at his chest with both hands. "Get out of the way."

Reed hesitated, then cursed in a foreign language. He caught her elbow and she increased her pace to a jog to keep up with his long-legged stride. She could feel their physical connection through his senses—the feel of her flesh in his hand, the scent of her perfume, the growing irritation for the yawning emotional chasm between them.

She also sensed Alec. Through her, he felt her interaction with Reed and she felt the way that affected him. The pain and frustration. The fury and bloodlust. She would have expected his emotions to feed into the Novium, but she was cool and calm. Focused on her external problems.

They rounded the corner of the house and the other side of the duplex came into view. Izzie, Ken, and Edwards stood facing the back door, their shoulders set in a way that set Eve's teeth on edge. Sobbing rent the quiet afternoon and drew her attention to Claire who sat crumpled on the ground. The wind blew gently, bringing the scent of sweet Mark blood with it.

As Eve altered her trajectory to skirt the small crowd, her viewing angle changed. The recessed kitchen doorway came into view . . .

. . . as did the disemboweled body that hung upside down from the rafters there. Richens.

"God!" She barely felt the pain of the recriminating mark. Spinning away, she wanted to gag.

"I tried," Reed bit out. "You're too damn stubborn, Eve. You need to—"

Her helpless gaze silenced him midrant. "I-I can't k-keep doing t-this."

Reed caught her to him. His scent was stronger now, more virile. Comforting. Alec reached out to her, too, but she pushed him away. He would worry about her, when he needed to be focused on his own safety.

She didn't understand the connection nor know how long it would last. It didn't matter. She needed it now and it was there.

"*Mon esprit, c'est perdu, perdu . . .*" Claire sobbed. "*Je ne peut plus rien faire. J'ai perdu toute raison.*"

Eve didn't need to understand French to comprehend that Claire was losing it. The cracking voice and wrenching sobs were heartbreaking. Leaving Reed, Eve crouched beside the fallen Frenchwoman, reaching out a hand out to touch her shoulder.

Claire surged into her arms, rambling incoherent words. "Did you see? *Did you see?* Who could do such a thing to another person?"

"Not who." Reed stood over them, his gaze on the doorway. "*What.*"

Izzie moved closer. Her lipstick had worn off, leaving her looking younger and oddly innocent. "How could this happen? Where was everyone?"

Edwards spoke, his lips white. "Callaghan and I were loading the Suburban in the driveway while Dubois packed up the food in the kitchen. We didn't hear or see anything."

"Where is the rest of your class?" Reed asked, surveying their immediate surroundings.

"I've no idea. Seiler and Hollis took off—"

"They were with me."

A length of silence followed Reed's pronouncement, during which Eve looked at Izzie and caught the narrowing of the blonde's eyes on her. Then, Edwards cleared his throat and said, "Garza and Hogan are shagging somewhere. It's all those two know how to do."

"Where is Gadara?" Ken barked. "We should not be here alone."

Reed pulled his cell phone out of his pocket and turned it on.

"Can't you do that popping in and out thing you do?" Eve asked.

"I'm not leaving you here," he retorted grimly.

Claire looked up, her eyes wild. "We are all going to *die* out here."

"Shut up," Edwards snapped. "The last thing we need is melodrama."

"We're not going to die," Eve soothed, patting her back.

Reed walked a short distance away, his focus on his phone, which beeped a missed call or text message warning.

A growling noise brought Eve's attention back to Ken. He looked ready to blow a gasket. "What good are guards when they cannae stop us from getting killed?"

"We need to forget packing and clearing," Eve said. "I don't think getting out of Dodge is going to solve this problem."

"Aye, we should hunt."

"Bloody hell," Edwards muttered. "You're both daft."

"You are crazy!" Claire's spine straightened. "We should get in the cars and leave this place. Don't look back. Go to Gadara Tower and leave such things to those who know what they are doing!"

Edwards nodded. "I second that. Run like hell. That's the ticket."

"What about the kids across the street?" Eve asked.

"What about them?" Claire shot back. "They are mortal. The Army invited them, they can protect them. Nothing is going to save *us* other than common sense. God helps those who help themselves."

Ken moved between the corpse and Claire, who was growing more distraught by the minute. "Killing the miserable bajin would do the same."

"Who was the last person to see Richens alive?" Izzie asked.

"I *just* saw him," Eve answered, "about twenty minutes ago." Now she would never know what he'd had to say. That made her indescribably sad.

She had scarcely done more than glance at what remained of Richens's body, but she couldn't forget the sight of him. Strung up by the ankles and wrists like an upside-down starfish. Gutted. His entrails ripped from the now-gaping body cavity and wrapped around his head. Stuffed into his mouth. Blood overflowed from his nostrils and soaked his hair, but it didn't drip. Below him, there was no puddle. Where had the blood gone?

How could this have happened right under their noses? Why hadn't Richens screamed? Did he know his attacker? How else could such an elaborate staging take place on their very doorstep without a sound made?

So many questions and all the immediate answers were terrifying.

"What was he doing?" Edwards asked.

"Sitting on the steps."

"He was lazy," Izzie muttered. "He was always looking for someone else to do his work for him."

Eve shook her head. "You shouldn't speak ill of the dead."

Looking toward Reed, she caught him scowling at his phone. Obviously, he didn't like whatever messages he'd had waiting for him.

Ken's head went back and he growled at the sky. "I didnae hear a thing. Nothing. How is that possible?"

The distant sound of the doorbell caused the group to freeze in place.

"Who's that?" Edwards hissed, looking as if he wanted to bolt.

Eve pushed to her feet. "I'll go look."

Ken came forward. "Allow me."

"*Eve?*" Linda's voice floated around to the side yard where they stood. "Is everything all right?"

"Shit." She looked at Ken. "I'll stall her. Get him down from there!"

She was running around the corner before she'd finished speaking, nearly crashing into Linda, who was leaning against the side of the house and peering through the sheet-draped window.

"Whoa!" Linda stumbled.

Eve caught her by the forearms and yanked her back upright.

"Where did you come from?" Linda gasped. "One second you weren't there, the next minute you were bowling me over."

"Sorry."

Freddy sat on his haunches beside Linda, his gaze trained at the walkway Eve had just traversed. He whined softly.

"He was barking like mad a little while ago," Linda said, "and looked ready to eat through the front door, which is really out of character for him. Then, we heard the screaming."

"Horrendous wallpaper," Eve improvised. "Some of the fashionistas didn't take it well."

You bullshit good, Freddy said. He looked up at her. *Whatever it was, it came around our pad first and circled the outside.*

If her heart could have stopped, it would have.

I think my barking scared it off. I'm sorry I couldn't help your friend. I tried to get out.

Eve rubbed behind Freddy's ears. She would have to question him in depth later. The fact that he'd caught the scent of danger opened another can of worms. A Mark's senses were animalistic in their acuity. Why hadn't the Marks sensed the killer coming?

"Wallpaper?" Linda's dark eyes sparkled behind her black-framed Bulgari glasses. "And here I thought it might be the DVD we lent you."

Eve smiled. "I should share that with the class. It might cheer them up after lime green and orange paisley."

"I like orange." Linda gestured at her tank top. "Can I check out the horror?"

"No!" Eve winced inwardly when Linda's eyes widened. "They hated it so much, they tossed it in the fire."

"Really? That's too bad. And having a fireplace in class? I'm taking the wrong major, I think. Unless Mr. Gadara has a spot for a psychologist."

"How does a psychologist get into ghost hunting?"

Eve's acute hearing picked up the sounds of movement from behind her—rope being cut, grunts of exertion, Claire's muffled gasp followed by more sobbing. The knowledge of what was happening kept Eve on edge. She pushed Alec and Reed to the far corner of her mind, shutting off the view of Richens that filled Reed's vision.

"Unfortunately, parapsychology isn't yet a widely accepted course of study, so I settled for the closest thing."

"*Para*psychology? Wouldn't that make you a believer?" Eve gestured toward the girls' side of the duplex. "Come inside."

Unfortunately, that side lacked the food and refreshments that would have helped break the ice.

Linda fell into step next to her. With a quick side glance, Eve reconfirmed what she'd noted before. Linda's hair was beautifully, perfectly cut. Her camisole was silk and her leather sandals were Manolos—identical to a pair Eve had at home. The girl was wealthy, but attending a small college in Utah. Eve doubted the production company paid enough to keep her in style, especially considering the lack of a professional camera crew. Had she been born into money? If so, what fueled the desire to hang out in dumps like this with other students far below her social class?

The questions weren't goaded by curiosity. Eve had to learn what Linda's hot buttons were and which ones would get the college kids to pack up and go home.

"I love what you've done with the place," Linda said when they entered the house.

Eve wrinkled her nose. She didn't know whether it was a trick of the mind or not that she still smelled Reed in the empty space. She looked again for her gun, knowing that its presence would be difficult to explain, but it wasn't visible from a cursory inspection.

"I can imagine how cute these homes were once upon a time," she said. "The bones are here—the hardwood floors, the picture windows, even the sea-foam-colored tiles in the bathroom are worth keeping. But neglect has done a number on them, I'm afraid."

"And the bugs." Linda shuddered. "These homes should be condemned."

"I'm really surprised they put you up here instead of in the guest quarters."

"Billeting for guests is on one of the annexes; they don't have anything here at McCroskey. And they don't take pets."

"Gotcha." Heading toward the kitchen, Eve crossed her fingers and hoped there wasn't anything lying around that would incriminate them or arouse suspicions. She was relieved to find only an ice chest in the spot where a refrigerator should be.

"Are you leaving?" Linda asked.

Eve turned and found the brunette looking down at the pile of backpacks and duffels. "Gadara would like to," she admitted, "but I'm still hoping to talk him out of it. I think we still have a lot to learn here."

"Well, I hope you stay, and I hope you'll come with us tonight."

"Problem is," Eve said with regret, "if we stay longer, I don't think you'll be able to film in Anytown."

"We'll just have to work something out," Linda said determinedly. "We have to leave tomorrow for the Winchester Mystery House. We've been granted permission to film some night footage there, but only tomorrow night. Who knows when we'll be back out this way? And honestly, I know having Mr. Gadara on the show would boost ratings. Television is all about ratings, you know. We're not getting rich off *Ghoul School*, but it does fund things we would otherwise have to forgo."

Moving to the sink, Eve washed her hands using the foaming hand wash she'd put there the previous evening. She ripped a paper towel off the roll by the sink, then faced the cooler. She approached it cautiously, unable to stop imaginings of decapitated body parts inside.

"You look like you're expecting something to pop out of there," Linda teased.

Freddy padded over. *I'm ready. No worries.*

Eve winked at him. "This cooler wasn't here earlier. Who knows if the cheese is moving or the bologna has gone bad."

I'll take them.

"Is bologna ever good?" Linda queried with an exaggerated shudder.

I think it's delicious.

"I like it fried." Eve pushed the lid open the rest of the way and peered inside. A variety of beverages, both canned and bottled, were nestled in a soup of melted and semimelted ice. So was a small bag of Styrofoam bowls. Leftovers from the long road trip the day before. "There's soda and water. Are you thirsty?"

"Water would be great."

Ditto.

Grabbing three bottles and the bag of bowls, Eve knocked the lid back down with her elbow and handed a water to Linda. Then, she filled a bowl and set it down on the floor for Freddy.

"So, when will you know if you're staying?" Linda asked.

"We're waiting for Gadara to get back from a meeting with the post commander."

There was a pause as they all drank, then Linda said, "Honestly, this place gives me the creeps."

"You hide it well."

Isn't she a gem? The others freak out, but not Linda. She's always got it together.

"I'm left-brained," Linda explained. "My imagination is dull and boring, so I don't think about zombies chasing me or mass murderers leaping out of dark corners. I don't believe locations can be haunted by those who once occupied them. People once lived here, and now they don't. It's just that simple. That's why the vibe from this place really bothers me."

"You say that," Eve smiled to soften the sting of her words, "but if you didn't believe at all, why would you dedicate so much time to researching the validity of other people's claims?"

"I don't believe, but people close to me do."

"So you want to prove them wrong?"

"I want to help."

"I'm intrigued." And hopeful that there was an exploitable hot button in the story somewhere.

Linda set her half-full bottle on the counter. "Do you have any siblings?"

"A sister."

"Are you close?"

Eve nodded. "She's younger, but she married before me and has two beautiful children. She lives out of state, so I don't see her as much as I'd like to, but we talk often and she sends lots of pictures."

"That's wonderful."

"And you?"

"Only child. But I had a best friend who was like a sister to me. We were inseparable until after high school. I was all set to go to college; Tiffany joined the Army."

"Brave girl."

"Practical. Her parents died when she was young and joining the military was the only way she was going to get college money." Linda sighed. "When word came back that she was killed in action, I was devastated. My grades suffered. I dropped out of school. My boyfriend and I broke up. Everything fell apart."

"I'm sorry."

Linda accepted the condolences with a grim nod. "Have you lost someone close to you, Eve?"

"I recently lost my neighbor, who was also a dear friend."

"Then, perhaps you can understand how difficult it was to learn that Tiffany wasn't dead at all."

Eve frowned. "You lost me."

"It was all a great big cover-up, including a letter from the Department of Defense and a military-provided funeral service." Her voice hardened. "I should have known something was wrong when they couldn't produce a body."

"Why would the government fake her death?"

Freddy moved from his spot by the cooler to sit at Linda's feet. She stroked the top of his head with a distracted rhythm. "I don't know for sure why they did it, but my guess is that she was exposed to some whacky chemicals out in the desert. Something that really messed with her head and they didn't want us to find out about it because of the scandal that would ensue."

"But you figured it out?" Eve suddenly had an inkling of what she must sound like to Reed when she went off about Gadara being shady.

Linda nodded. "My parents took me to Europe in the Spring, hoping the change of location would help my grief. We weren't there a week before I spotted Tiffany at a bakery in Münster, Germany. I called out her name, but when she caught sight of me, she ran. I've never seen anyone move that fast until you. Today."

Eve shifted her gaze away to avoid revealing her dawning unease.

"Fact was, Tiff *wanted* us to believe she was dead. Whether she was protecting her grandmother and me, or the government, or all of us . . . I have no clue. It took me a week to track her down after that incident in the bakery. I looked for her everywhere, haunting the neighborhood until I finally spotted her again. She didn't run that time. She knew I wouldn't let it go. I'm too stubborn."

"What was her explanation?"

"She swore she had been chosen by God to save mortals, like Joan-of-fucking-Arc or something. She said there were demons among us, hunting us, and it was her mission to kill them."

Eve reached out to the counter to steady herself. "Yikes."

"That's an understatement," Linda muttered. "She was completely delusional, pointing at normal people and saying they were evil, that she could smell their souls rotting. She saw marks and tattoos on her skin that weren't there. She said I couldn't see them because I'm not one of the chosen."

"Lucky you," Eve said sincerely.

Someone has to fight the good fight.

Eve wrinkled her nose at Freddy.

Just sayin'.

"Tiff could tell I didn't buy a word she was saying. I begged her to come home with me. I told her how much her grandmother missed her. How much *I* missed her. I promised to help her get back on her feet. But she wouldn't budge. She said it was better if she was dead to us, because the demons would hurt us if they thought they could get to her that way. She said the only thing I could do was believe. 'When you believe,' she said, 'then I'll come to you for help.'"

"Wow."

"No kidding." Linda straightened. "I never saw her again after that. We stayed in Germany another two weeks, but she didn't contact me at the hotel, even though I gave her the information. I came back to the States and hired a private investigator to find her, but he never did. Sometimes I wonder if I dreamed up the whole conversation in some sort of grief-induced delirium. Then I remember that I have no imagination. I couldn't make that stuff up. So I've been trying ever since to believe her, or at least give the impression that I believe her. I have a blog detailing our investigations, hoping she'll find it and realize I am trying. I figure the show is another way to reach Tiff, too."

"You're a good friend."

Eve couldn't help but consider her own obligation to Mrs. Basso. Her friend and neighbor had died because of Eve's connection to her. What had she done since then to justify that sacrifice? Nada, aside from making a sorry, half-assed attempt at going through the motions. She was shamed to realize how little she'd done to honor the memory of such a wonderful woman.

Shrugging, Linda said wearily, "I wouldn't go that far. Tiffany always did more for me than I did for her and that hasn't changed. Because of her I began researching paranormal investigations, which is how I met Roger. I think he's the love of my life. And we receive letters every week telling us how much *Ghoul School* helped someone in one way or another. It's very rewarding."

Eve wondered where Tiffany was now. Was she still alive? Was she still marked? "What's her last name?"

"Tiff's? Pollack. Tiffany Pollack." Linda polished off her water and screwed the top back on. "I need to take a nap or I'll be worthless tonight. Thank you for the water."

"Any time." Eve smiled. "Or at least as long as we're here."

Linda hooked her thumbs through the belt loops of her shorts and smiled. With the empty water bottle tucked between the palm of one hand and her hip, she looked like a Wild West sheriff with gun at the ready. "I will be seriously disappointed if you don't join us tonight, you know."

"I'm still working on Gadara," Eve said, "but you can count on me tagging along if you end up going."

Her mind was set; she wasn't leaving McCroskey without Linda, Roger, Freddy, and the rest of the *GS* gang. Not unless she knew—without a doubt—that it would be safe to leave them behind.

"Oh, we're going," Linda insisted. "This is the first time a military installation has requested our services. We wouldn't miss it." Linda did a little victory hop. Then she hugged Eve. "You won't be sorry, and I will be eternally grateful. Whether Mr. Gadara comes or not."

"I can't say I'll be good for anything more than screaming inconveniently," Eve warned. "Anytown gives me the chills in the daylight."

And that was before Molenaar had been killed there.

"I'll protect you from the bogeyman," Linda promised with a wink. "Don't worry."

"Keep her safe for me, Freddy," Eve said, giving the Great Dane a quick rub behind the ears.

He woofed in reply. *Watch your back, too.*

Eve gave him the thumbs-up. Then she followed them into the living room to resume the search for her gun.

CHAPTER 13

Alec was exiting the bathroom when his cell phone rang. He sprinted the short distance to the bed where he'd tossed it. Glancing at the caller ID, he winced.

"Shit." He ran a hand through hair he'd just finished dousing in the sink, an ineffectual attempt to cool off his raging temper. He was ready to kill. Starting with Abel.

The last person he wanted to deal with was . . .

"Sarakiel," he bit out before the phone reached his ear.

"Sorry, *mon chéri*," Sara purred. Forbidden to use her archangel gifts at God's *suggestion*, she relied heavily on the power of her feminine wiles to make up the lack. "I can hear your disappointment, and I do sympathize. Your brother has not been answering his phone, so I, too, have been waiting to speak with someone."

He really didn't give a shit about Sara's issues with his brother, but that wasn't something he could say to an archangel arbitrarily. It wasn't her fault that he was infuriated by the distance between him and Eve, and the closeness he sensed between her and Abel. He was confused by the singular connection between all three of them. How common were such meldings? How long did they last? What were the ramifications?

"How can I help you, Sara?" She wouldn't be calling him unless she wanted something.

Sara laughed softly. "Do you know why there is an emergency conference call in a few hours?"

His brows rose. Considering the events of the last two days, he didn't know where to start, and he damn well wasn't going to take a stab in the dark. He liked to keep his cards hidden. "Who initiated the call?"

"Uriel. Who else would have something worthy of bothering all of us?"

"It must have something to do with that new class of Infernal." He didn't bother to answer her question.

Moving to the table in the corner, Alec began connecting the various cords that would power up his satellite videophone. He needed to talk with

Raguel about the hellhounds before the archangel spoke with the others and since the archangel was playing his power games and refusing to answer his summons, Alec was forced to reach him the secular way. He also wanted to touch base with Uriel. Uriel would explain what happened to him, Eve, and Abel this afternoon without withholding vital information, as Raguel and Sara were likely to do.

"Yes." She didn't sound pleased. "That is what I suspect, but I was hoping for confirmation."

"Well," he drawled, "I imagine that's why you are having a meeting."

"Do not toy with me, Cain."

"Of course not, Sara. I would never do that." The mark on his arm burned in reprimand for the lie. "Listen, I have my own shit pile to shovel through at the moment, but I can tell you that Raguel assigned Abel and Mariel to investigate the most recent sighting in Australia. That guarantees they're the two most knowledgeable *Malakhim*. If you want to stay one step ahead, you might want to stick close to one of them."

"That might be possible, if your brother ever bothered to answer his phone. Where is he?"

Alec had known Sara would disregard contacting Mariel. The archangel had never gotten along well with other women, even easygoing ones.

"He's with Eve," he replied, knowing what the answer would do to Sara. Hell hath no fury like a woman scorned. While Alec couldn't agree with that statement absolutely, he did concede that the two had their comparative qualities and he wasn't above using jealousy to get his brother out of the way. "Considering the danger involved, he's keeping a close eye on her."

"I bet he is." Sara's voice was tight. "I never took you for a trusting soul."

"I trust Eve." And that hadn't changed. She was certain that she was in love with him, regardless of her infatuation with Abel. While that didn't alleviate the feeling that he'd been sucker punched in the gut by a rakshasa demon, Abel had fucked himself six ways to Sunday by messing around with the blonde. As usual, his brother had no idea how to put someone else's feelings before his own.

"Where are they?"

"Fort McCroskey."

Sara made a disgusted noise. "A dreadful place."

"Lucky you're in France." But not for long, he'd bet.

"Actually, I am on a plane."

His smile turned into a grin. "Where are you headed?"

"California."

Beautiful. "When do you arrive?"

"I have only been in the air thirty minutes." Her frustration at her inability to use her gifts was evident in her disgruntled tone.

She wasn't as far along as Alec would like, but it was better than nothing. Sara would keep Abel on his toes and away from Eve. She would also have a contingent of guards with her. Security was never tighter then when two archangels were in close proximity. Eve would be in the safest spot in the world.

"They were planning on pulling out of McCroskey," he advised. "They should be back in Anaheim by the time you arrive."

"Thank the Lord for small favors. I will check in with you in a few hours. Find out where they will be when I land. And keep your phone on."

"If it won't get me killed." Alec snapped the phone shut.

It behooved him to help her, but he only took orders from God. Presently, his latest order was to kill the Alpha, and that took precedence over everything else—including his need to deal with his relationship with Eve.

If he had his way, he'd be on Grimshaw land by nightfall. He definitely wouldn't have his phone powered on then, although he would have it with him. Charles was the reason Alec wasn't with Eve, so sending the Alpha to Hell had to happen as soon as possible. He certainly wasn't waiting for a call from Sara to get things started.

Pulling out a chair, Alec sat and used his cell to call Raguel, inwardly cursing the unnecessary inconvenience. The phone rang longer than usual, then, "Montevista."

He paused a moment at the unexpected voice. "Where's Gadara?"

"Cain." The relief with which his name was spoken increased his unease.

"Who is this?"

"I'm Diego Montevista, the head of Gadara's security team."

Alec leaned into the seat and asked quietly, "Where is Gadara?"

"I t-think—" Montevista cleared his throat. "I think Gadara is dead."

"Say that again."

"There was a creature here, a beast. It s-swallowed Gadara."

"Impossible!" Alec bolted upright, knocking the chair to the floor. "He is an *archangel*."

"Yes, I know, Cain. I've lived at his side for years. It doesn't change the fact that he was eaten alive by a . . . a *thing* the size of a tank. I saw it with my own eyes, and I'm not the only one who bore witness." The conviction in the Mark's voice was undeniable.

"What happened to the Infernal?"

"The earth opened up and sucked it down. One moment the beast was there, the next the ground split and it sank into the fissure. There were mortals everywhere. An entire company of soldiers stood a few hundred yards away, but all they saw was the felling of two trees."

Alec stared at the blank video screen, his chest lifting and falling in its same measured rhythm even as his world spun haphazardly.

An archangel. Dead. He couldn't imagine it. Not like this. Without fanfare or storms from the heavens. Without a shockwave that reverberated through the world.

It was too quiet. Too still. All wrong.

"How long has he been gone?" Alec asked.

"Less than thirty minutes." Montevista exhaled harshly. "It gets worse."

"How the fuck can it get worse?"

"I just got off the phone with Abel. There was another fatality in the class."

Alec gripped the edge of the table, images of Raguel's students sifting quickly through his mind. He reached out to Eve, felt her touch him in reply. Cool and collected. Controlled. She had pushed him aside earlier. He'd thought it was because she was mad at him; now he suspected she just hadn't wanted him to cloud her mind with his worry.

"Chad Richens," he murmured, seeing the scene through her mind's eye.

"How did you know that?" Montevista asked. "Did they call you first?"

"No. You need to get back to the other students."

"I'm on my way now." In the background, a car door slammed shut and an automobile engine rumbled to life. "Gadara suspected Charles Grimshaw of this morning's attack, but I'm not sure this second killing fits the Alpha's MO. Gadara said he would circle us for a while before striking again—"

"Charles thinks he has the upper hand; he's not going to play it safe anymore." And it would only worsen when he learned about Raguel. "Why was Richens alone after what happened this morning?"

"He wasn't. All of the other students were nearby."

Yet no one heard a thing, and Eve had been *right* there. Alec considered his options. He could get back to Monterey in a couple of hours . . .

But first he had to understand what he was walking into. Charles wanted *him*. A trap wasn't inconceivable.

Montevista growled. "I know how bad this sounds, but my team isn't inept. We're being ambushed. Stalked. It's against the rules to—"

"Fuck the rules." Charles had obviously tossed them into the fire. They would, too. "How did you get Raguel's phone?"

"He left it behind."

"Was his confrontation with the Infernal *planned*?"

"Totally. He was gunning for it."

Alec's thoughts raced. "Did you check the phone for messages?"

"No."

"Do it."

Standing, Alec walked through the adjoining door and headed to the bathroom. Giselle lay on the pile of towels he'd spread out on the floor—still cuffed, gagged, and now deeply asleep. As he watched, she made soft chuffing noises of pleasure. His gaze lifted to the far wall. He'd bet there was a poor soul in the next room, taking a nap and having a doozy of a nightmare. Feeding the Mare.

"Power up," he muttered to her. "You're going to need it."

"What did you say?" Montevista asked.

Alec shut the door quietly. "Nothing. Find anything?"

"A text message from Uriel about a conference call at three o'clock. That's only a couple hours from now."

"Right. I'll be there. Make sure Abel is there, too. Don't let any of the Marks out of your sight, especially Evangeline Hollis. Don't expect her to cooperate either," he said dryly. "Sometimes she does, sometimes she doesn't."

"She's a woman," Montevista said, as if that explained everything. Which it did.

"She's *my* woman."

"Understood."

Alec rubbed the back of his neck and looked out the window at the Mustang parked just outside the door. Hop in, hit the gas. So easy. He wished.

"Cain?"

"Yeah?"

"I don't know what to do." The Spanish inflection in Montevista's voice was more pronounced, deepened by sadness and confusion. "Who should I notify? Who do I take orders from? You?"

"Yes, me. I'll take care of the peripherals."

Whether Raguel was truly gone was debatable. Alec had known the archangel the whole of his life and he had yet to see Raguel do anything completely self-sacrificing. A kamikaze attack wasn't in keeping with what Alec knew. But there was no benefit to what-ifs at this point. The fact was simple: a once-in-an-immortal-lifetime opportunity had arisen. He could step up to the plate and take over the firm for the present, proving he was capable of the position.

But . . . the odds of him securing the necessary blessings without manipulation were slim, and thanks to Eve's penchant for landing in trouble, he was running out of favors and secrets to exploit.

"What do you want me to do?" Montevista asked.

"Your job is to keep those students safe until you can be extracted. What's holding things up in that department?"

"Hank is flying up here, along with a crew to investigate the earlier slaying. Once they bring Gadara's private plane, we can fly out. I tried to arrange an immediate departure, but the Monterey airport is tiny and none of the airlines had the space to accommodate the whole class on such short notice. Breaking up into smaller groups was just too risky."

"And venturing out in public while you're waiting would endanger mortals. If an attack is coming, you want to be somewhere you can fight back."

"Exactly."

And yet no great battle had been fought for Raguel's life, despite the proximity of a literal—albeit mortal—army. "Why was Raguel near a company of soldiers?"

"The base commander gave permission for a television show to film at Anytown—the place where Jan Molenaar was killed this morning. Gadara hoped to convince the colonel to reschedule."

"Get Abel to follow up with that." A television show. Somehow he'd missed that.

"You say that as if he'll listen to me. I'm only a Mark."

"—who's following my orders. He'll do it. And tell him to answer his phone when I call. I'll get with him in a few minutes, and he sure as shit better pick up."

He checked the clock on the nightstand. Two hours before the conference call.

The mark on his arm burned with vicious intensity, reiterating Sabrael's order to put down the wolf.

Alec scowled heavenward. As if he could forget. He was hoping that killing the Alpha would kill the problem.

But first he had to get over his aversion to blitzkrieg attacks. He was a sniper by nature, choosing to wait for the perfect moment. One strike, one kill. He didn't have that luxury now. The longer Charles was alive, the bolder and more dangerous he would become.

"I'll talk to you at the time of the conference," Alec said. "But if you need me beforehand, you have my number."

"I wish you were here. Protecting an archangel against possible threats is a hell of a lot different from protecting a multitude of untrained Marks from actual danger."

"I promise to get there as soon as I can."

Alec snapped the phone shut. Then he set to work on keeping that promise. Turning with the intent to wake up Giselle, he nearly ran into the giant occupying the doorway between the two adjoining rooms.

"Sabrael," he greeted, only slightly surprised. He blinked, engaging the wash of celestial tears that protected his eyes from the blinding brilliance of the being before him. Sabrael stood in his customary pose—arms crossed and legs spread wide to better anchor him to the ground.

The seraph's piercing blue eyes examined him. "You will proceed with your assignment, Cain."

"You know about Raguel?"

"Of course." Something dark passed over Sabrael's features.

"I'm going to manage the firm in his absence." Alec never asked for what he wanted, since the answer was always no.

"You are far from qualified."

"Prove it," Alec challenged with a jerk of his chin. "Tell me who's lived with the mark longer than I have."

"Foot soldiers do not advance to generals overnight, regardless of how well they have performed on the battlefield."

"I would hardly call the passage of centuries an overnight occurrence."

Sabrael's head tilted to one side. His unrestrained ebony hair slid over a massive shoulder and the top of a wing like liquid silk. "Perhaps Abel would be the better choice," he murmured. "He is in the thick of things, as they say."

Alec laughed through the clenching of his gut. "Abel won't want the responsibility. He doesn't even keep his cell phone on."

"But he follows the rules."

"Is that what you need right now? With one archangel out of commission, a rogue Alpha with an ax to grind, a rash of slaughtered Marks, and an unknown breed of Infernal on the loose? You want someone who does only what's required and follows the rules?"

There was a length of silence before Sabrael spoke. "I never knew you had such lofty ambitions."

"There is a lot you don't know about me."

"True. Such as, how badly do you want this?"

Inside Alec, frustration and fury raged. He'd played this game before; it kept his hands dirty. "What do you want, Sabrael?"

"I have yet to decide."

"Makes it hard for me to decide, then. Of course, Abel won't give you a damn thing."

A frightening shadow briefly transformed the seraph's features. His bluff had been called and he didn't like it. "I will speak to Jehovah on your behalf. As an *interim* solution."

Alec snorted.

Sabrael's slow smile chilled Alec's blood. "But you will owe me, Cain of Infamy."

"You'll have to take a number."

"Number one."

Pointing a finger at him, Alec said, "Get me the go-ahead first. Then, we'll see where we're at."

"What are you doing?"

Reed watched as Eve bolted up from her crouch. Raguel was gone, two Marks were dead, and she was alone; a state that had led to two Mark deaths already today. To make matters worse, he could feel Cain like a phantom limb. Altogether, his patience was short and his temper shorter.

She spun around, her long ponytail arcing through the air. "Jeez! You scared me."

"What are you doing here by yourself?" he barked. "You should have come back as soon as the girl left."

"I lost my gun."

He wanted to shake her. "I don't give a shit. What's your aversion to a flame-covered sword? You know you can summon one at any time."

The line of her mouth turned sullen. "I'm not so great with swords."

"You killed a dragon with one," he reminded. "Forget the gun for now and rejoin the others. You're less likely to be attacked in a group."

"What if one of the group is the killer?"

Pausing, he stared at her for a long moment. Then he exhaled harshly. "Enough, Eve."

"Richens didn't make a sound. Perhaps his attacker wasn't perceived to be enough of a threat to elicit a scream or a fight."

"Or the Infernal was a witch, warlock, wizard, mage, or faery who bound his vocal cords."

"Like the faery who participated in the exercise today? The faery who was within several feet of Molenaar when we found him?"

"Your conspiracy theory is mucking things up in your brain. Did the faery stink or not?"

"To high heaven," she groused.

"The Infernals who work for firms have a compelling reason to stay in the archangels' good graces—they can't go home. You know that. You said it yourself."

"It seems foolish to rule them out, though."

He chastised her with a shake of his head. "In the history of Marks, we've never had a rogue Mark in training. After a few years, yes. But not fresh. They're too new to the realities of Celestials and Infernals to decide to go one way or the other. They just float with the tide for a while until they catch their bearings."

"Okay," she conceded. "Hang with me; brainstorming helps me think. So, let's run with the bad guy Infernal theory for a bit. They must be wearing that masking stuff to hide their scent, or Templeton would have smelled them."

"Or the rat was lying."

Eve ignored him and went on. "There was no residual smell around either of the bodies. With that level of brutality, the killer would have to be worked up. Blood pumping, soul rotting . . . maybe they cut themselves. I saw a forensic show on television where they said most knife wielders injure themselves. In any case, the scene should have stunk at least a little if it was really an unmasked Infernal who did it."

Reed felt himself smiling, despite the events of the day.

"You're laughing at me," she accused.

"No. I'm congratulating myself. You're going to be a great Mark, babe. If you don't get killed first." He gestured toward the front door. "Speaking of which, we should be tossing these ideas around with the others. Just don't get them all riled up this time."

"Alec says sometimes you have to shake things up," she grumbled, "to see what falls out."

"Everyone has been shaken up enough." And it was about to get worse. Somehow, he had to tell them about Raguel without inciting total pandemonium. The Frenchwoman in particular seemed fragile.

She nodded. "You're right. We have work to do, too. Garza and Hogan are missing, so we should—"

"Romeo and the princess are back. Looking rumpled and slightly worse for wear."

"Maybe there's something in the water. Seems to be going around."

"Could be. Toss a little aphrodisiac in the food, get everyone so horny they're too busy getting off to fight back, and *wham*! Take 'em out. Brilliant Infernal strategy."

Eve snorted. "You're a riot."

"It was your idea. And where did you come up with those nicknames?"

"Don't you know?" She stared at him. "You were in my head."

And what an experience that had been. He had no idea how other women's brains worked, but he knew he liked the way Eve's did. It was convoluted and slightly twisted—as he'd come to accept as the norm for females—but regardless, it functioned with what he considered to be the perfect mix of creativity and common sense. She also had the hots for him. Not just the horny kind of hots, but the deeply rooted type of fascination that could lead to something that scared the shit out of him.

"I was interested in other things at the time."

"Hope you enjoyed the view," she said testily. "I got nothing out of you, besides a swift kick in the ass."

He hadn't had a choice. He couldn't allow her to see his ambition to ascend to archangel. And her role in that. "Sure you did. You're so attuned to me now, you have no defenses. I walked right up to you and no alarms went off."

"It's called distraction." But her frown belied her words.

"You wish that's all it was."

She blew a stray strand of hair out of her face and looked adorable while doing it. "Why can I still feel you and Alec in my head?"

He was still reeling from the experience. He had a picture of Cain in his mind, one built by a lifetime of association. Yet Cain, as seen through Eve's eyes, was not the same. "Hell if I know. I've never heard of anything like it."

"Well, someone has to know what happened and how long it will last."

"Yes. And I intend to find out. In the meantime, let's rejoin the others. We have a lot to discuss."

Eve scrubbed both hands over her face. "I feel naked without a gun."

The statement would have sounded melodramatic coming from most people, but Eve had spent a few hours of every week for the last few years practicing her aim at a Huntington Beach shooting range. As a single woman, living alone, she'd felt as if she needed the added protection. Reed was more inclined to think her senses had picked up on the Infernal undercurrents, even if her brain hadn't yet been trained to catch on. She was made for this work.

He gestured toward the door. "We'll ask the others if they've seen it."

"Ugh." Eve's nose wrinkled. "I'd prefer to think it was around here somewhere."

Reed crossed his arms. "Why?"

"I set it down earlier. You know . . . *before.*" Her gaze moved to the hallway, which was clearly visible from where they stood. "I don't want to think about one of them seeing . . . hearing . . . I would rather believe I didn't embarrass myself."

"You would rather pretend it didn't happen," he corrected. "I won't let you."

Eve glared. "If you want to remember your tryst with a tart, go ahead. But don't presume to make that decision for me."

"A tryst," Reed repeated wryly, indulging in an inner smile. "With a tart. My . . . You *are* jealous."

"Fuck you."

Irritated by his own feelings of guilt, he taunted her by reaching for his belt buckle.

"Whip it out," she challenged. "See what happens."

Pausing, Reed assessed her warily. He couldn't get a read on her thoughts. "What do you intend to do to it?"

"Did Izzie get the third degree, too?"

"No." His hands went to his hips. "I told her what I wanted. Her opinion didn't matter."

"Yes, that seems to be the only way you like it."

Reed's jaw clenched. She was referring to their lone encounter in the stairwell. He hadn't been able to get in her fast enough. Everything in his way—her clothes and conscience—was disregarded in the intensity of his need.

"It's the way you like it, too," he bit out.

"A one-shot deal." Her mouth thinned to a fine line. "Lucky for you, you found greener grass elsewhere."

It didn't escape his attention that she was starting to sound like Alec. "The grass wasn't greener. It just didn't have a guard dog."

"Don't blame this on Alec. He didn't deserve to be hurt the way he was today."

"He's a big boy, Eve."

She ran a hand over the top of her head and growled softly. "It's one thing to know that what you're doing can hurt someone. It's another thing altogether to feel their pain as if it was your own. Alec really cares about me and I repay him by having a stupid crush on *you.*"

Reed struggled to stem cruel words. Damn it, that stung. He could tell her that what happened today wouldn't have been possible if they didn't have feelings for each other, but she knew that already. It was simply eas-ier for her to pretend otherwise. Too bad for her, he was sick of pretending.

"The hurt you felt was your own," he shot back.

"And you love that, don't you?" Her lovely face took on a hardened cast, shutting him out. "It didn't matter to you who you stuck your dick in, but you're gloating that it mattered to me."

"Think how much worse you'd feel if I'd stuck it in you. I did us both a favor." And he was an asshole for doing it. He'd lied to himself about hiding the encounter from her. Her discovery had been inevitable, and some part of him had wanted to get to her that way. To show her how it felt to him, knowing that Cain could have her any time.

She laughed, the sound absent of any joy or humor. "You went to Izzie for *me*? What a great line. Pass all responsibility for your actions to my shoulders."

He grabbed her arm and yanked her closer. "You would have spread your legs in a heartbeat if I'd bothered," he snarled, "and we both know it. But like I said, I've seen that show. I'm waiting for the episode where you come to me."

As short as she was, Eve still stood up to him. Her chin lifted, her shoulders went back. "You don't need me, Reed. You *want* me, sometimes—apparently only when Alec is around to be irritated by it—but that's as far as it goes. I won't give up what I have for that."

Reed pushed her away. "Then you should be really damn happy I played the gentleman today. Lord knows I didn't do it for me."

Reaching into his pocket, he withdrew his cell phone and turned it back on, keeping his gaze on the illuminating face rather than meeting Eve's wounded and furious gaze. Due to Sara's frequent calls, he had powered up his phone only long enough to call Raguel. He had no one to call now, but the act of playing with the damn thing gave both him and Eve the chance to cool down. They needed to work together on this, not bicker about what couldn't be changed.

His phone beeped as it woke to full operation, but there were no wait-ing messages. That bothered him more than a full voicemail box. Sara was more inclined to escalate her attempts than to give up.

Eve acted as if she were focused on dusting herself off. "Let's go."

"Listen." Reed looked at her. "I don't know how long these residual connections between us will last."

"We can't get rid of them soon enough for me," she muttered.

"You're starting to use some of Cain's phrasing, and we've established that we can feel each other's emotions. That could be disastrous for all of us, if we don't get it under control."

"How so?"

"If Cain is gung-ho in his hunt for Charles, you could feel the same recklessness."

Her frown altered into raised brows. "And if I feel fear, he could feel it."

"Right. Which means we need to keep you even-tempered and focused while he's hunting Grimshaw." Not for his brother's sake, but for Eve's. If she was inadvertently responsible for crippling Cain in battle, she would never forgive herself.

"Then you should probably know," she began with a determined glint in her dark eyes, "that if Gadara can't get the base commander to delay those kids across the street, I'm going with them into Anytown tonight."

Reed froze. "You are *not* going back there."

"We can't leave them here alone!"

"Raguel is dead, Eve."

Eve stumbled back as if struck. He'd meant to break the news with more tact, but her pronouncement took him off guard.

"*Abel.*" A grim masculine voice broke the heavy silence.

Reed didn't move his gaze from Eve, but she glanced at the door, her eyes wide like a deer caught in headlights.

"Montevista," she breathed. "Where is Gadara?"

The guard replied unflinchingly, "In the belly of an Infernal."

Reed studied the Mark, taking in the man's stocky build and jaded eyes. There was a calm, steadfast air about him that inspired confidence. Reed could see why Raguel had relied on this Mark for his safety.

Eve's lower lip quivered. "What happened?"

Montevista explained, visibly weary as he spoke. He looked at Reed when he was done. "Cain wants you to turn your phone on so he can call you."

Reed glanced down at his cell, understanding now why he'd turned it back on to begin with. He was still connected to his brother in some way. He glanced at Eve, who seemed not to notice his dismay. She might be the conduit, but if so, she didn't feel the information passing through her.

"What type of Infernal was it?" Eve crouched and began digging through the duffel bags again.

"I have no idea."

She looked at Reed. "Was it your mystery demon?"

"The description is the same," he said.

"We need to go back to that copse of trees and see what's there that might help us go after Gadara."

Montevista exhaled harshly. "You don't believe he's dead?"

"She doesn't believe anything," Reed growled, still stinging.

Eve glared at him. "Gadara doesn't strike me as the type to commit suicide. Isn't suicide a sin?"

"Murder defies God's command," Montevista answered. "Suicide is self-murder."

"So it's doubtful Gadara would do it, right? He must have had a plan."

"We can hope, but how would he know how to deal with a class of Infernal we've never heard of before?"

"*We* haven't, but maybe *he* has. It's the first time he's seen it right? Maybe he recognized it."

"I doubt that," Reed said. "Mariel and I described the creature very clearly."

"I'm just tossing out ideas." Eve finally gave up looking for her gun and stood. "We also have to take into consideration the setup you walked into—fire alarm set and Infernal restrained outside. If they'd wanted the soldiers dead, they would have killed them before you guys got there."

Montevista looked at Reed. "Was she a cop?"

"Interior designer."

"She's pretty good at this for a novice."

"Enough to be dangerous," Reed agreed.

"Hey!" Eve pushed his shoulder, which didn't budge him at all. "I'm right here."

He shrugged. "You're here. Whether or not you're right remains to be seen."

"You agree that the culprit is probably Grimshaw?" Montevista asked.

"If Gadara and Alec think so," she said, shrugging, "I'll follow their lead."

"That's a first." Reed's jaw set. "But you're not going back to Anytown. That's not debatable."

"It makes sense that it would be the Alpha," she continued, ignoring him. "He's the only demon we know of who has openly declared war on us."

Montevista tensed. "He has?"

"He's already killed me once."

"*He has?*" Running a rough hand through his close-cropped hair, Montevista cursed in Spanish.

"And we're not having a repeat performance," Reed said grimly, "which is why you're not going to—"

His phone rang, interrupting his words. As he pulled it from his pocket, the muffled tune of his "Jessie's Girl" ringtone became crystal clear. The caller's name glowed on the screen.

Cain.

Growling, Reed lifted the phone to his ear. "What?"

"Fuck you, too," his brother retorted. "Has Montevista reached you yet?"

"Yes. And we're busy."

"Have you arranged to meet with the colonel?"

Reed's jaw clenched at the impatience in Cain's tone. It didn't help matters to see Eve and Montevista huddled together in conversation. "That's none of your damn business."

"It's absolutely my business, since I'm heading Raguel's firm in the interim."

"No fucking way." *Raguel's absence had created a firm vacancy.* Shit. He should have made that mental leap earlier. His focus was still on finding Raguel, not replacing him. Once again, Cain was ahead of him, knocking him out of the running before he even had a chance to play.

"Yes way, little brother." Cain's tone was so smug, Reed wished he was nearby so they could talk with their fists.

"Then shift over here and deal with the colonel yourself!" Reed hung up, his mind whirling.

Cain's *mal'akh* gifts had been curbed. He couldn't shift from one location to another in any celestial way. His wings were clipped and discolored a dark, inky black. Why would *he* be given the power to rule a firm when he couldn't be trusted with an angel's gifts?

It was so unreasonable, Reed couldn't believe it. Cain was a nomad, a wanderer, a sociopath. Aside from Eve, Reed couldn't recollect anyone whose feelings Cain had put before his own. How could he be charged with the safety of millions of people?

And why in hell did he sound so damn pleased about it?

CHAPTER 14

Alec briefly considered redialing his brother, then thought better of it. Abel would need to digest the state of affairs for a while. The dig about shifting was a knee-jerk reaction. All the archangels were stripped of their powers except for seven weeks of the year. They managed without them; so would Alec.

He dialed 4-1-1 instead and requested the phone number to the commandant's office. A few minutes and connections later, he was told that the colonel had left for the day and wouldn't be available until tomorrow.

"Shit." He needed a Plan B. After considering his options, he called Hank.

"Cain!" The coarseness of the answering voice was reminiscent of Larry King, yet Hank's true gender was a mystery. An occultist who specialized in the magical arts, Hank was a chameleon, changing form and gender to suit the client. The only things that never changed about Hank was the flame-red hair and head-to-toe black attire. Those were staples.

"To what do I owe the pleasure of your call?" Hank husked.

"Death and destruction."

"Sounds like my kind of party." Hank made a choked noise, then shouted, "Be careful loading that box! The contents are irreplaceable."

"Where are you now?"

"At the Monterey Municipal Airport in Northern California. Raguel called me up here. I had to bring my equipment, so I was forced to fly. Can't expect Marks to understand how important my gear is. If I left it to them, they'd break everything in transit. Even loading up the rental van seems to be too much for them."

Alec considered Hank his favorite Infernal. In the dozen centuries or so since Hank joined Raguel's team, the demon had proven to be extremely helpful. "Who's with you?"

"Two investigators from the Exceptional Projects Department and two guards."

Alec exhaled with relief, then explained the situation as it now stood.

"I know," Hank said. "I felt it the moment Raguel was gone."

"How?" After noting the complete lack of celestial reaction to Raguel's disappearance, Alec was more than startled to hear that an Infernal had sensed what no one else appeared to.

"We've been working together a long time. He bonded with me just as he has to all the Marks who work for him."

Alec reached a hand out to the wall, bracing himself against what he considered to be an earth-shaking revelation. "Do all Infernals working for archangels bond with their firm leaders?"

"Sure. Why not?"

Holy shit. Infernals bonding with archangels. Sharing information. Seeing how each other's minds worked.

Shaking off his astonishment, Alec went back to the original point of his call. "When you get to McCroskey I need you to report all of your findings to me in real time. Don't wait for an official report."

There was a short pause, then, "Have you stepped into Raguel's wings?"

"In a manner of speaking."

"You give orders like an archangel, my friend. But you do not sound like one."

Archangels had a unique resonance to their voices that inspired both awe and capitulation.

"Roll with me on this," Alec said.

"As you wish. I look forward to seeing your lovely girl again."

"Keep her out of trouble for me, will you?"

"And away from Abel?" Hank purred. Working for the good guys didn't mitigate the innate desire Infernals had for chaos and conflict.

"That, too. Call me when you know something."

"Will do."

Alec hung up and headed into the adjoining room's bathroom. He stood over Giselle and called out, "Wakey wakey."

The Mare didn't budge.

Alec turned on the faucet. He filled his cupped palms with the flowing water, then dumped the whole of it on Giselle. As she sputtered and lurched into a seated position, he backed up swiftly. Her attempt to swipe at her eyes was arrested by the handcuffs, resulting in a yanked arm and a string of muffled bitching.

He crouched beside her and pulled the gag down to hang around her neck. "Sweet dreams?" he asked, smiling.

She glared at him through wet, spiky lashes. "What did you do that for? I wasn't finished."

"Yeah, you were."

"You suck, Cain," she grumbled. "Totally suck. Get me out of these cuffs."

"I need you to draw a layout of Charles's compound. You gonna give me a hard time?"

The petulant curving of her lips changed to a bright smile. "Does this mean I don't have to go with you? I'll draw you the best map ever. Then I'll just wait here for you to finish and we can drive—"

"I need some blood, too."

"—down to Anaheim and—" Giselle's blue eyes widened. "My *blood*? After you chained me to a bathroom sink? You've got to be—"

"Okay." Alec pushed to his feet with a dramatic sigh. "Have it your way."

"Where are you going?"

"To get my knife. If you don't squirm, it might not scar too badly."

"Wait!" she called after him, the handcuffs rattling against the pipes. "Let's talk about this some more. You didn't give me a chance to think. You can't wake a girl up in the middle of a meal and expect her to be fully coherent."

He stood just outside the door with his back to the wall, smiling.

"Cain! Damn you," she complained. "Didn't your mother teach you any manners? This is not the way you're supposed to treat guests!"

Backtracking, he kneeled at the sink and pulled the cuff keys out of his pocket. "When you're an uninvited guest, all bets are off."

He released her and stood.

Giselle rubbed her wrist, then she held out her hand to him for assistance gaining her feet. Her blonde hair was a mess from both the handkerchief and bed head, but the look was a good one on her. "This floor is hard and cold."

"If you hadn't wiggled so much, you might have been somewhat comfortable."

"You shouldn't cuff people to pipes!"

"Don't make me gag you again."

"You are really not a very nice person."

"Says the demon who gives people nightmares," he retorted.

"I have to eat!"

Alec preceded her out of the bathroom. He went to the nightstand and withdrew the hotel letterhead from the drawer. Setting it on the tabletop along with the provided pen, he said, "Draw. Now."

"Go. To. Hell." But she plopped onto the edge of the bed and caught up the pad. Her hand began to push the pen across the paper. "It's a gated community. I don't see how you're going to get past the guards. You stink."

Alec opened the backpack he'd set on the other bed and pulled out a bottle of body wash. The contents had already been laced with an anticoagulant. He just needed some Infernal blood to add to the mix.

"You're going to fix that." He faced her.

Giselle's eyes dropped to the syringe in his hand. Her mouth fell open. "Uh . . ." She swallowed hard. "I'm afraid of needles."

"It will only pinch a minute."

She shook her head violently and stood. The pad dropped to the floor. "You don't understand. The sight of blood makes me vomit."

Alec's brows rose. It figured that he would end up with the one demon who had a gore complex. "You don't want to find out what happens if you puke on me."

"Then don't stick me with that! What kind of sick torture is this?"

"You know damn well what I'm doing." He gestured to the bed with a jerk of his chin. "Sit down."

"Can't we have sex instead?" she suggested, setting her hand on her hip and trying to look seductive. "You'll smell just as nice, and it's less painful."

"For you maybe. Now sit."

Giselle opened her mouth, but the look on his face must have warned her off. She dropped back onto the bed and held out her slender arm, turning her face away.

Alec kneeled and said, "I'm good at this. It'll be over before you know it."

She kept her head turned. "People only say that about things that last forever."

"Count to twenty." He secured the tourniquet. As always, he took a moment to absorb the similarities between them—the beating hearts, the pumping blood, the fragile shell of their skin.

"*Ett, två,*" she began, shivering as he tapped the inner fold of her elbow with his fingertips, "*tre, fyra—*"

Alec slid the needle into a plumped vein.

Giselle screeched and jumped to her feet. Her knee struck him in the chin, sending him toppling backward into the neighboring bed.

He started to laugh, then pain lanced his brain like a white hot poker. Clutching his head, he yowled in agony.

She screamed, too, then smacked him on the shoulder. "You scared the shit out of me! What are you doing yelling like that?"

Falling onto his side, Alec curled into the fetal position.

"Oh, please," she muttered. "Drop the drama. I barely touched you."

Acid pumped through his veins, eating its way through his system from the inside out. Tears burned his eyes and his throat clogged.

"Are you serious?" Giselle prodded him with her foot. "Cain. Are you bullshitting me or not?"

Alec's back arched and his frame tautened like a bow. He writhed in torment, his bones altering with such alacrity he felt as if he were being ripped apart.

"You're not kidding," she breathed, standing over him. "I really did a number on you."

If he lived, he was going to kill her.

"This could save my ass!" Giselle clapped her hands. "I can tell Sammael that I didn't return to Hell because I had a shot at knocking you out of commission! This is perfect. I'll be a hero. Charles is going to be sick with envy. A Mare taking out Cain of Infamy. Who'd have thought?"

He grabbed her ankle and squeezed. Hard.

"Ow!" She yanked her leg free. "You're hurting me in your death throes."

Heat pooled in his belly, scorching and heavy. It began to radiate outward, lengthening his limbs and extending his fingers and toes. Pulled like a victim on a medieval rack, Alec was ready to pray for death when he felt Eve moving through him. As solid as the pain and just as intense. Phantom arms embraced him, calm and cooling. He struggled into her, grasping at the ethereal feel of her as a drowning man would a lifesaver, dragging her into the anguish with him.

Alec. Her voice. Filled with worry and growing alarm.

Eve began to panic as she sank deeper into his pain, but he couldn't release her. His instinct to survive was too powerful.

His body began to convulse and Giselle screeched. She leaped over him and rushed to the door.

"Stay."

It was his vocal chords that created the sound, but the voice wasn't his. What he heard was deeper, darker. *Resonant.*

Giselle froze with her hand on the knob.

Insanity lapped at Alec like waves of dark, cool water. He sank beneath the surface with Eve in his arms, his body a prison of torment.

Cain!

Alec jerked at the sound of Abel's roar—a reverberating bellow of fury in the still darkness of his mind. Eve resumed her struggles with renewed vigor, reaching upward with flailing arms and gaining purchase. She was ripped from his embrace and pulled away, too far to reach her despite Alec's clawing attempts.

Like a firefly in the darkness, she flitted away. He followed her upward through the suffering of his body, then through the more painful ache created by the knowledge that she was connected deeply enough to his brother to be stolen away.

Then his misery was gone as quickly as it had come.

Peace enveloped him, soothed him, relaxed every muscle and tendon, loosened the fist of heartbreak that tightened his chest.

His eyes flew open. The ceiling was lowering to him.

No, he was rising toward it. Levitating.

The roaring of blood in his ears faded to the background and pitiful sobbing filled the gap. He straightened from his prone position, his feet aimed toward the earth, his head pointed toward the heavens.

Shrugging off the lingering tension with a roll of his shoulders, Alec's wings burst free. His feathers were black as night—as they had always been—but now tipped with gold.

"My life sucks," Giselle cried, drawing his attention. She sat crumpled by the door, her lovely face wet with tears.

Alec smiled, reveling in the power that flowed through him like an electrical current. His feet touched down on the carpeted floor and he stood a moment, soaking up the flood of knowledge that poured into his consciousness. What was most pleasant, however, was the tranquillity he felt. His emotions no longer ruled him. In fact, he scarcely felt them at all.

"Sammael will never take me back now." Giselle sniffled and scrubbed at her running nose. "I've turned Cain of Infamy into an archangel."

Eve jolted as the doorway between her mind and Alec's slammed shut with violent finality. Drained and devastated, her knees gave way, but she was caught by strong arms and held tightly. The scent of Reed's skin drifted across her nostrils and brought her back to herself.

Her back was to his front, his lips at her ear. She blinked and recognized the interior of the girls' side of the duplex.

"What the fuck was that?" Montevista's gaze darted between both of them. "One minute we're having a conversation and the next, you two are off in some kind of zombie trance!"

Gasping, Eve's hand lifted to her shirt. She'd half expected to find it dripping wet, but it was bone dry. The sensation of floating on an inky sea had seemed so real . . . And mind-breakingly terrifying.

"Something *awful* just happened to Alec." She broke free of Reed's hold and faced him. "We have to find him."

Reed's face was set into an unreadable, yet ominous mask. His dark eyes were cold, his lips hard. "He almost killed you."

Hearing the words said aloud was a shock to Eve's system. Although their connection had felt that way, she couldn't believe that had been his conscious intent. "He would never hurt me."

"He's not the same person anymore, Eve."

She frowned, fighting off the lingering fuzziness in her brain. "What do you mean?"

Reed's jaw tensed, then, "He has been promoted to archangel."

"Huh?" Dread sank like a heavy stone in her gut. "How is that possible?"

"Raguel is gone. Alec was tapped to step into his shoes."

"Alec?" Her arms wrapped around her middle. "How do you know . . . ?"

"He told me," he bit out. "He's never given a shit about anyone in his life, and now he is responsible for caring for thousands of Marks."

Eve had no idea how she was supposed to react. What did this mean? What would happen to her and Alec now? She pulled out her cell phone and speed-dialed Alec.

Sydney called out from her position on the stoop. "A van just pulled up."

Outside, an automobile horn honked twice.

"Reinforcements?" Eve asked, frowning when she reached Alec's voice-mail.

A cell phone went off, its ringtone a Paul Simon song that Eve couldn't quite place. Montevista dug into his pocket and withdrew a sleek silver smartphone.

"That's Raguel's," Reed noted.

"Yes, it is." The phone fell silent. However, the caller ID was apparently still visible on the face, because he said, "Hank's here."

Eve hurried toward the door. Just as her foot stepped over the threshold, she paused, causing Montevista to bump into her from behind. She tripped but caught herself on the partition that framed the back of the cement porch step—the twin to the one she'd tackled Molenaar through on the boys' side.

"Are you all right?" the guard asked, frowning. "Maybe you should take it easy."

"Where are the Infernals?"

He blinked. "Which ones?"

"The ones Gadara brought with him. The faery, the dragon, and the gwyllion. And whoever else there might be."

"It's just the three. The faery can work with any glamour."

"Where are they now?"

"They're staying in a house around the corner." He gestured in the direction of Anytown.

"Why aren't we using them?"

"We are. They're helping my team with the bodies."

The mention of "bodies" made Eve shiver inwardly. "What are they doing with them?"

"Field autopsies."

"You brought equipment for that?"

His look was wry. "That's why we're using the Infernals."

"Gotcha. Where is this happening?"

"In Anytown. Lots of space, no public access, and it's near the scene of the first attack, which was still being examined at last check-in."

Reed brushed past them and headed out to the driveway.

"Have you looked over the area yourself?" she asked.

"A cursory inspection, but my job is to stay with Gadara." A cloud passed over Montevista's blunt features. "My job *was* to stay with him."

Eve touch his biceps gently, imparting silent comfort. She still didn't know the whole story about what happened to Gadara, but she would be there when it was explained to Hank and could catch up then. With that in mind, she started moving again. Montevista fell into step beside her.

"What are you getting at?" he asked.

"I would imagine you're going to head over there soon."

He glanced at her. "There's no way Cain or Abel is going to allow you to go back there."

"Can you really tell me that it's safer here than there? Especially if you're there and not here?"

His mouth curved. "Not really, no."

"See? Don't worry about them. I'll get them on board," she assured. "If they let me check out the area now and we keep it under surveillance afterward, I'll have no problem making my regrets to the *Ghoul School* team."

"I can't wait to see this. Can you tell me why you're pushing this so hard? You know we're all doing the best we can to figure out what's going on."

"I just feel like I'm missing something, and I can't let it go until I know what it is."

He bumped her shoulder with his. "Good Marks always follow their guts."

They reached the driveway where Ken, Edwards, and Romeo were helping Hank—whose sole contribution to the effort appeared to be dire warnings—unload a variety of wooden crates from the back of a black van. Izzie, Lauren, and Claire sat in the shade of an oak tree on the edge of the driveway. Their attention was divided between something they watched on Claire's laptop and Hank's appearance, which altered from a buxom, beautiful, Jessica Rabbit–type redhead in a Morticia Addams dress and a tall, well-built, red-haired hunk—depending on the gender of the person he was speaking to. The transformations were fluid and instantaneous. A blink and they would be missed.

As Eve approached, Hank caught sight of her. Altering to the masculine form, the occultist moved toward her with a wide smile and leisurely stride. He was dressed in a black dress shirt and black slacks, the severity enhancing the red currant color of his hair.

He held his hands out to her, studying her with both pleasure and curiosity. "Lovely Eve, so good to see you again."

She placed her hands in his. She always got the impression that he enjoyed her as a scientist enjoyed experiments. "Hi, Hank."

The Infernal paused, head tilting to the side as he read her. "Cain has altered. Advanced. Blossomed. You don't like it."

"That's not true," she protested, deciding that she really hated how people were just popping in and out of her head. "I don't understand it. I'm hoping you'll explain it to me."

Ken cursed and Hank spun around, morphing into the red-hot female before he'd completed the rotation and shouting in a masculine growl, "Be careful with those! Please."

"What have you got in here?" Edwards gasped, limping under the weight of a smaller box. "An elephant?"

"Must I do everything myself?" Hank muttered. Holding a hand aloft, Hank snapped his fingers and the box was gone from Edwards's hands.

Without the weight to balance his contorted pose, the Englishman toppled over. "Bloody hell! If you could do that the whole time, why didn't you?"

Hank faced Eve again, as a man. "Novices are so tiresome."

"I'm a newbie."

"You are unique."

Uniquely plagued with bad luck. She visually searched the area. "Where did the box go?"

"Into the house." Linking their arms, Hank started toward the men's side of the duplex.

She glanced over her shoulder at Montevista. "Don't leave without me."

The guard gave her the thumbs-up.

As she and Hank passed the girls, Eve asked, "Do you know what they're doing?"

"Watching a video they found in the kitchen."

Eve frowned. "A video?"

"A television show about ghosts here at the base."

"Oh . . . right."

"I can't tell you much about Cain's advancement," Hank went on. "To my knowledge, no one has been promoted to archangel in the history of . . . well, in history. Period."

"Great."

"You worry that you've lost him."

She shook her head. "I worry that he's lost himself. I was with him—in him—when the change happened. I don't know how anyone can live through pain like that and still be the same person. I could feel his . . . *soul* separating from his body."

"He did not lose his soul, Evangeline. It has simply connected more fully with God. Sammael is known for his ability to lure the weak to worship, but he has yet to achieve the level of expertise that God enjoys."

"Are you saying that God is *luring* Alec away from me?"

Hank smiled. "He can make Cain happier without you. You bring turmoil. God will give him peace."

"Peace."

"It is easy to entice someone to have sex, yes? Sammael does it every minute. It's much more difficult to convince someone to forsake it, *forever,* yet God manages to do that regularly. With the strong, not the weak."

Eve tried to picture Alec—the most virile man she knew, along with Reed—forsaking sex. "Uh . . . I don't think that—"

"—Raguel is dead?" The sparkle in Hank's pale blue eyes told her that he knew what she'd intended to say.

"You're right, I don't."

They reached the porch, and Hank surveyed the damaged partition.

They had cleaned up the destruction as much as possible, but it was clear that things were not what they should be.

The front door was open to facilitate the moving of the boxes. Hank entered first, which made Eve wonder if Hank was really a woman or just clueless about etiquette. Moving directly to the largest crate, Hank circled it. "It isn't by chance that the number of archangels has been immutable," he murmured.

"No, I wouldn't think so."

He looked at her, smiling. "I love that you aren't naïve, you know. Makes you much more interesting."

"Thanks. You're pretty interesting yourself." She gestured at all the crates. "Can I help you with any of this?"

He pointed to three crowbars propped up against the wall by the door. "There has to be a balance. Just as the kings of Hell are still alive and well, so are the archangels. They both make a great show of protecting themselves, because they don't want to insult the other by making it too easy."

Eve grabbed a crowbar and picked the nearest crate, which was chest height. "Like nuclear weapons in the Cold War? The United States and the Soviet Union spied on each other, lied to each other, and were prepared to blow each other up, but in the end, no one wanted to tip the balance. The cost was too high."

"Exactly."

"But," she tugged on the crowbar, venting her frustrations with physical exertion, "Alec might remain an archangel, regardless of what happens to Gadara?"

Hank's arms crossed over the top of a crate. "Maybe. He could be demoted back to *mal'akh,* which would create more issues to deal with. It's easier to adjust to an improvement in one's circumstances than it is to taste success and slide backward into failure."

Pushing down on the bar with all her might, Eve pried the top open amid a cacophony of protesting nails. "Can you find out who or what killed the two Marks with this equipment?"

"I can certainly give it my best shot. I take it you don't want to talk about Cain anymore?"

"I want to talk *to* him." She managed a half-smile to soften any sting her words might cause. "Although I appreciate what you've shared so far."

She dug through the sawdust that filled the box and withdrew . . . a lampshade. A child's lampshade with a cartoon theme featuring stars and moons. Her brows raised and she looked at Hank.

Blushing, Hank explained, "Frame of mind is as important to success as tools."

"I'll go with that." Which brought home the fact that her frame of mind had been skewed all day. She needed to slow down, take some time alone, and rehash everything she knew about the events with a fine-tooth comb.

Her phone vibrated in her pocket. Hoping it was Alec, she was in such a rush to get it out that she nearly dropped it. But the name on the display was *Mom*. Eve briefly considered sending the call to voicemail, then thought better of it. She needed a hefty dose of reality right now. Her old reality, not her new one.

"I have to get this," she said to Hank. "I'm sorry."

"Don't be. I will still be here when you're done."

"Hi, Mom," she greeted, while moving down the hallway for privacy.

"Your dad just told me you called yesterday. Is everything good?"

Eve winced, but said, "So far. We're busy, but that's to be expected."

"Is Alec with you?"

"No, he's away on business." Not for the first time, she felt what it might be like to live a normal life with Alec. She grieved for that imaginary life when she allowed herself to think about it.

"And Reed?" Miyoko asked. "Is he there?"

"Yes."

"Strange. There is something wrong with Alec that he puts up with that."

Eve smoothed her brow with her fingertips. Her skin felt damp and hot, which worried her. "I would think there was something wrong with a man who interfered with his girlfriend's job."

"Jobs don't last forever," her mother said. "Marriages do."

Unwilling to touch that with a ten-foot pole, Eve looked into the first bedroom as she passed it. It had been completely cleared out. "Is there anything exciting happening with you?"

"Just my children giving me gray hair. Sophia got another tattoo. Two of them."

"Really?" Eve's sister had been fond of tattoos when she was a single girl, but she hadn't indulged in new ink since her marriage. "What did she get?"

"Cody and Annette's names wrapped around her ankle."

"I think that's sweet, and the kids might think their mom is really cool for doing something like that." She went on to the next room. The master bedroom had only a couple of sleeping bags and duffel bags left in it, bearing witness to the interruption of Ken and Edwards's efforts to pack up the vehicles. Richens's laptop case was set neatly atop his bag and a shaving kit that resembled a camera case was set on top of that.

Camera.

"Don't sound so happy about it," Miyoko complained. "I hope you never get one."

Eve thought back to the conversation they'd had a few days ago when she'd thought her mother noticed the Mark of Cain on her arm. Instead

she'd learned that the mark wasn't visible to mortal eyes. "I'm not planning on it, but never say never."

"Evie . . ." her mother said in her best warning tone.

"I have to go, Mom."

"What did you call for last night?"

"I was lonely." Eve pivoted and left the room. "Now I'm busy, so I have
to run."

"Eh. You call me later, then."

"I'll try. Love you." She hung up and noted the time on her cell phone.
It was almost two. Barely enough time to get what she wanted.

Rushing down the hallway, she waved at Hank as she passed him. She
nearly ran into Ken as he backed up the steps with a crate that was steered
by Montevista on the opposite end. She jumped off the porch and ran
around the back of the house to the girls' side where Claire and Sydney
were just returning.

"I need your camera," Eve said to the startled Frenchwoman.

Claire seemed confused for a moment, then her face cleared. *"Bien
sûr . . . of course."*

Eve waited outside while Claire retrieved the camera.

"You'll have to hurry with whatever photos you want to take," Sydney said. "Cain is adamant that we clear out of here immediately."

"Did he call?" Eve looked at the phone in her hand. No missed calls.

"He's in the driveway talking to Abel."

Eve looked down the walkway toward the drive, but the angle was bad
and she couldn't see anything more than the driver's side of the white van.

Claire stepped out onto the porch with the camera in hand. "There is
a lot of room left in the memory."

"That's fine. Thank you!"

Grabbing the camera, Eve took off at a run toward the driveway.

CHAPTER 15

Reed was debating whether punching his brother as an archangel would have different consequences than knocking him out as a *mal'akh* when Eve rounded the duplex corner at a flat out run. His fist stayed clenched, but his biceps relaxed. The look on her face was enough to stay him. She could tear into Cain much more effectively than he could.

Hank was in the house with the rest of the ill-fated class, using their labor to set up his equipment before they left for the airport. Reed wished the occultist was present for this impromptu visit from Cain, just to see if his reaction to his brother's new incarnation was unique or not. Montevista was the only Mark, aside from Eve, who was present, and he just looked relieved. He was a Mark after all, and they thought Cain was the best thing since sliced bread. The heavy artillery was here and all would be well.

"Alec!"

His brother turned and smiled at Eve's enthusiastic greeting. "Hello, angel."

Eve skidded to a halt a few feet away, her lovely face marred by an uncertain frown. He greeted her as one would a friend, not as a lover he had craved deeply over a decade's separation.

"How are you?" she asked, watching him approach with concerned eyes.

"I'll be better after you've been moved to safety."

Cain didn't sound like himself, his resonant words spoken at a slower tempo and slightly clipped. He also didn't look like himself, his eyes rimmed with gold, his caramel-colored skin luminescent. In his jeans and tank, Cain took the position of archangel to another level. Reed knew that level was now beyond Eve's reach.

"Are you okay?" she persisted. "How are you feeling?"

"I'm fine." As he brushed stray strands of hair from her face, Cain's smile was kind. "Are you packed?"

Reed leaned back against the front of the Suburban and crossed his arms, watching with avid interest. In the past, the two had been combustible together. Now, he'd call them lukewarm at best.

"Yes, I'm packed," Eve answered, "but I'm not ready to leave."

"Because of the crew across the street?"

She nodded.

"I've arranged for them to stay overnight on Alcatraz, but the offer is only open tonight. The last ferry leaves at ten to seven, so they'll need to leave quickly if they want to go."

"Wonderful," she replied, but her tone was flat. The look in her eyes was confused, wary. Her fingers clenched and released against her thigh. "Have they been told already?"

"I was hoping you would take care of that."

"Okay." She backed away, then stopped. "The Alpha . . . ?"

"Not yet. After this."

"Don't leave until I get back. Please."

Reed knew how much it cost her to say that—Eve was not the type of woman to cling to a man—but with the detachment his brother was displaying, it was a valid concern.

Montevista stood poised to follow her. Cain moved first, closing the small gap she had created between them. He gripped her by the biceps and stared down into her upturned face.

"The conference call is in less than an hour's time, and I still have to deal with Charles."

"What's wrong?" she whispered. "I can't feel you anymore."

His lips pressed to her forehead. "Things have . . . *changed,* angel. When everything here is resolved, we'll talk about it. There's a lot I don't know or understand. I'll have to find answers before I can give them to you. I need some time to do that. Can you give me that?"

Eve gave a jerky nod.

Reed was fairly certain she had just been kicked to the curb. From the wounded look on Eve's expressive face, she thought so, too.

Her shoulders went back and her chin lifted. "Be careful."

"Don't worry about me." Cain released her and stepped back. "Take care of you."

Recognizing a golden opportunity when he saw one, Reed straightened and said, "I'll go with her."

"I'll go," Montevista offered. "You're needed here."

"Quite the opposite actually." Reed smiled. "My entire reason for being here is Eve."

"Don't you have something to tell me about your trip to Australia?" Cain asked with narrowed eyes. That was the only sign that he was affected at all by Eve's departure and Reed's offer of accompaniment.

Reed watched Eve reach the other side of the street, then glanced around to ensure privacy. "We think the Infernal grows with every attack," he said in a low tone. "The one in Australia was considerably larger than the one Mariel first saw and the one that attacked Raguel was even larger than that."

"You don't think it could be more than one?"

"Maybe, but Les—the Australian handler—watched the creature increase in size after it destroyed his Mark."

"All right. Thank you." Cain looked away, dismissing Reed altogether.

Shock threw Reed for a loop for a half minute. He almost told Cain about the Infernal's suspected ability to absorb its target's thread of awareness and connection to the handler. But in the end, he wanted to join Eve more than he wanted to give his brother any advantage in the upcoming conference with the other archangels.

Heading across the street, Reed reached the front door of the *Ghoul School* duplex and knocked. One dog bark and a minute later, the door opened and revealed a pretty redhead in a pink and purple sundress.

"Hi." She grinned, checking him out.

"Hi. I'm looking for Eve."

"He's with me," Eve called out.

The redhead held out her hand. "I'm Michelle."

"Michelle." Reed lifted her hand to his lips. "Reed Abel."

She stepped back and waved him in. He entered a dormlike space filled with an inflatable sofa, a few folding lawn chairs, lots of cardboard boxes, and a couple of air mattresses. The air was redolent of insecticide and nacho tortilla chips.

Reed offered an all-encompassing wave and took note of the various occupants in the living room—a brunette in glasses shared the couch with a goateed guy in corduroy slacks. Another guy in jeans and white T-shirt was snoring from his spot on a nearby bed. A brown Great Dane paced the perimeter of the room, while Michelle pulled up a lawn chair and offered it to him. He declined the hospitality with a shake of his head and a grateful smile.

Eve made the introductions, then continued with her interrupted conversation. "So there you have it. We're really sorry about the inconvenience."

"Hey," Roger grinned, "We're not going to get upset about a shot at Alcatraz at night. We've been signing up for the lottery there for two years now, but never get in. And even if we did, there's no guarantee we'd be allowed to film there."

"I'm not sure," Linda said. "We were asked specifically to come out here to McCroskey. I hate to burn that bridge."

"I'm certain the invitation will be reextended," Reed reassured smoothly, celestial *persuasion* resonating through his tone. "Gadara simply wants to make some small restitution for imposing on you. He hadn't expected that we'd be using the area in the evening, too."

"That's very nice of him," Michelle said, her eyes dazed.

"What the heck can you all do at night, anyway?" Linda asked.

Reed's brows rose. The brunette seemed unaffected.

"Lighting," Eve improvised. "Exterior and interior."

"Linda doesn't like spontaneity," Roger explained, "but I'm excited. Alcatraz at night isn't an inconvenience."

Linda frowned. "We'll have to talk it over and let you know."

Reed looked at Eve. *Tough cookie,* he thought.

Her mouth curved. *I like her.* Aloud she said, "Well, let me know what you decide. But don't wait too long. It's a two-hour drive from here, without rush-hour traffic."

"I really want you to participate in an investigation."

Reed was taken aback by the fervor with which Linda made her pronouncement. He had assumed Eve was pushing herself to go along with them. He hadn't realized she was facing pressure from the "ghost hunters."

"I'll take a rain check." Eve smiled. "I promise."

A few minutes later, Reed was standing on the sidewalk next to Eve and they were both staring at the Mark duplex across the street. From the outside view, the place was still and quiet. Everyone was inside, all the vehicle doors were closed, all the equipment packed away.

"I'm going to Anytown," she said. "Coming with me?"

He looked down at her, noting her stubborn chin and challenging gaze. "I can stop you."

Her lips pursed. "Why?"

"Safety?"

"Right now, there are three of Gadara's Infernals, two guards, and two investigators working in Anytown. If you come, I'll have a guardian angel, too. A veritable army."

Reed seized the opportunity. "You'll owe me."

Eve paused, then crossed her arms. "Owe you what?"

He looked at her hands with their slender fingers. Certain she'd had a camera in hand when she set off toward the *Ghoul School* house, he asked, "Where's your camera?"

"I left it inside."

"Want to go back and get it?"

"Want to stop changing the subject? What will I owe you? It can't be sex."

"Why not? Maybe that's exactly what I'll want." Might as well lay it all out there. He didn't want her saying later that she had no idea what she was getting into.

She snorted. "You didn't want it from me a short while ago."

"And you didn't hesitate to get it on the phone with Cain," he countered. "We both found substitutions for what we really wanted."

"You can't even compare the two. They're not even in the same ballpark. I care about Alec. You—"

"And that makes you better than me?" he challenged, cutting her off. "I'm an asshole for blowing off steam with someone who doesn't give a shit about what I do, but you're on the high road for using a guy who cares about you?"

"I wasn't using him!"

"Bullshit." Reed scrubbed a hand over his face. "This is all jealous bullshit."

Snorting, she said, "Jealous? You flatter yourself."

But her mind filled with images of him with the blonde—some were memories and some were made up in her head. She was torturing herself by imagining him doing things he hadn't done. He couldn't appreciate her possessiveness because it was driving her crazy. Some women could live with sharing. Eve wasn't one of them. Remorse slithered inside him, then fury.

His arm shot out and caught her nape, yanking her closer. With his nose touching hers, he whispered, "Your jealousy has got nothing on mine. I feel it every time you come. *Every* time. Think about that for a minute."

Reed licked across her lips, then released her. "So maybe I'll want you to wash my car in a bikini," he bit out, "or cook me dinner. Maybe I'll want you to answer my phone for a week or wear a particular outfit. Or maybe I'll want to fuck you senseless. I'm not sure. But whatever it is, you have to do it willingly."

Her shoulders went back. "You're a pig."

He grinned wolfishly. "You love it. And Cain just kicked you to the curb so you have no obligation there."

"He did not!"

"Okay, if he didn't—nothing sexual. If he did, all bets are off." His confidence rattled her further, he could tell. But he knew a Dear John speech when he heard one and he had no problem using it to get back in her pants.

"You're asking for a hell of a lot for a quick look around an abandoned town," she complained.

He stepped one foot into the street as if to cross over. "Take it or leave it."

"If I leave it and go anyway?"

"Try it. I dare you."

A wicked light lit up her brown eyes. "Fine. But I want more."

"Babe," he drawled, "you could barely handle what I gave you last time."

"I need you to track down a European Mark for me."

"Who?"

"Never mind who. Will you do it?"

Reed held out his hand, "Deal."

Eve shook on it, then took off without him. "Come on, then."

He quickly fell into step beside her. "Do you know what you're looking for?"

"Not really." She glanced aside at him. "But I'll know it when I see it."

He reached out and caught her hand, linking their fingers together. "I want you to tell me what you think about the new Cain."

Her grip tightened. "I liked the old Cain better."

"That's it?"

"I've got bigger things on my mind at the moment, Reed."

He sifted through her thoughts, trying to see if there was more she wasn't telling him. There wasn't. So he pressed on, hoping to milk the situation for all it was worth. "You can only be truly in love with one thing, Eve. Cain is so focused on Jehovah he doesn't have room for you now, and look how much happier he seems to be."

Reed didn't tell her that he longed for advancement even more, thirsted for it like a vampire thirsted for blood. What a relief it would be to lose his fascination for her. How much easier his life would be if he weren't thinking about her all the damn time. But he thought about the ramifications as they related to Cain, not to himself. If Eve was in his head, she would misunderstand his thoughts on the matter.

"That's a lie," she said, her gaze trained straight ahead.

"Excuse me?" *She couldn't be that good at reading his mind* . . .

"The only-loving-one-thing part. And Alec doesn't look happy, he looks brainwashed. Lifeless."

He almost asked her if she'd ever loved two people at once, but he bit back the urge. Damned if he'd get hopeful over something that was temporary by necessity.

"How are you feeling physically?" he asked, noting that she was still sans the sweater jacket she'd discarded earlier. It was probably a balmy day for the locals, but for a Southern California gal it had to be chilly. The air moved briskly around them, smelling of salt and sea.

"I'm trying not to think about me either."

"How's that working out for you?"

"Not as great as I'd hoped." She looked at him with a rueful smile. "How about you?"

While Reed really wanted to address *her* issues, he was willing to go first . . . and pick her brain through their connection in the interim. "I'm worried about Raguel. It's easier on us to believe that he knew what he was doing when he went after that Infernal, but we're just guessing. If he's truly gone, we are in deep shit."

"You don't think your brother will be a good firm leader?"

"I . . . I doubt it. He's been a loner a long time and he's been disconnected from the mark system since its inception."

"You've been anticipating the creation of a new archangel for a while," she noted, rifling through his brain in his moment of weakness. "You wanted the job."

"No," he lied, training his thoughts to follow as if he were speaking the truth. "I think a new archangel should be familiar with all aspects of the system, like I am. You misread me."

"Hmm . . . but you do think there should more than the seven arch-angels? Did I get that part right?"

"The world has exploded from a population of two to a population of billions, yet the number of archangels hasn't increased."

"Makes sense. So even if Raguel comes back, Alec could stay the way he is."

"Yes."

"I would need a new mentor, then."

"Yes. You could also, possibly, be reassigned to a different firm."

Eve didn't say anything to that, but then she didn't have to. He felt her distress as if it were his own. He squeezed her hand.

They reached Anytown. Reed took in the view he had missed in his first visit to the training area. The mannequins in various states of disre-pair were especially effective in creating an atmosphere guaranteed to set trainees on edge.

"Once a coveted community," he intoned in mimicry of an announc-er's voice, "Anytown has suffered a steady decline in recent years and is now in dire need of revitalization."

"Totally." Her nose wrinkled. "This place creeps me out."

"That's the point. Every time I come here, it's deteriorated further, but it's been a mess as long as I've known of it."

She slowed, then stopped. Facing him, she asked, "McCroskey isn't considered an international tourist destination, is it?"

Reed laughed. "No. Unlike Alcatraz, which has tours almost daily, the McCroskey tour is an annual one."

"So, would you find it strange for a foreign national to have visited McCroskey?"

"Depends. But for the most part, yes. I would find that noteworthy."

Eve nodded and resumed walking, but at a slower, more contempla-tive pace. "Edwards said that he's been here before."

"Any details?"

"Not really, but he did say there were a lot of bugs here. He called the place a 'dump,' I believe. Said it was overgrown and crawling with vermin."

Reed's brows rose. "You can't tell that from the public areas."

"Right. When we first got here, I remember thinking that it wasn't what I expected. It was clean, well maintained. I told Alec I thought the troops probably missed this base." She glanced at him. "So how would a Brit know its state of disrepair?"

"A Google search would probably reveal that."

"But it doesn't explain why he's been here before."

"Right."

They turned a corner at the end of the main street and Reed saw the diner up ahead.

"Izzie's been to California before, too," Eve said. "And she showed up to training with a gun, against Raguel's orders."

"Izzie?"

She stared at him. An image of the blonde who'd sucked him off popped into his brain.

"Oh . . ." He winced. "That didn't look good."

"No, it didn't."

Reed quickly changed the subject. "Are you thinking Edwards is involved in some way?"

"Honestly, I really can't see how he would be involved. I've trained alongside him for three weeks and there's nothing even remotely Infernal-like about him."

"And remember, the masking agent wears off. At some point or another, an Infernal in your class would've reeked."

"Izzie, though . . . There's something going on with her. I just can't put my finger on it. She gives me the evil eye a lot."

Reed smiled wryly. "She's probably jealous. You're smokin' hot. Makes me hard just to smell you."

"Eww." Eve smacked him. "Don't be crude."

They paused at the end of the alley where Molenaar had been killed. The Mark was long gone. Since he'd been drained of blood before being pinned to the wall, there was very little left behind to proclaim that a soldier of God had died here. A couple of holes in the wall, that's it. Two men and two women occupied the narrow space. Two in black—Raguel's guards—and two in navy blue jumpsuits with the initials E.P.D. on the back—the investigators from the Exceptional Projects Department.

A female guard caught sight of him first. "Abel."

"Draw any conclusions?" he asked, leading Eve closer with a hand at her back.

The nearest investigator glanced up. He had a lanky frame, gray hair, and intelligent green eyes. "We're still collecting evidence, but the jaggedness of the wound edges suggests that the head was severed with a physically wielded blade."

"Because magic would have left a clean slice, like a laser, right?" Eve asked.

"Right. There are also contusions on the wrists and ankles. Our attacker was hands-on with this killing. But preliminary tests show no signs of Infernal blood. Usually in knife attacks, the assailants injure themselves. The hilt becomes slippery with blood and their grip slips."

Reed smiled, remembering Eve saying something similar earlier.

"How do you test for Infernal blood?" Eve queried.

"By spritzing the area with holy water. Even the smallest trace will sizzle and steam. It doesn't have the wow factor of luminol," he said dryly, "but it works the same."

"I have a question," she said. "When we first discovered the masking agent, we learned that it was Charles's in-laws—a mage and a witch—who had cast the spell that helped create the Infernal mask. Hank said it was the combination of mage and witch, male and female, that allowed the mask to work on all Infernals, regardless of classification or sex."

"Right."

She pointed at Reed. "He killed the mage, but we never found the witch. Could she have found a new partner, someone who could alter the spell sufficiently to make it longer lasting?"

The investigator scratched his head. "Doubtful. I think it's more likely that the intimate relationship between the original pairing made the spell potent to begin with. Unless she's fallen madly in love with another mage or wizard, any other combination would lack that edge."

"*I agree.*"

The voice came from behind Reed, forcing him to turn his head to see who was speaking. Hovering at eye level was a tiny blonde pixie in a minuscule green dress. Bernard. In a Tinker Bell glamour.

Reed scowled.

Eve leaned forward to look around him. "Hi, Bernard."

"Hey, toots. What a day, eh?"

"Has it only been a day?" she asked, weariness evident in her tone. "Seems like an eternity."

"Let's take a closer look," Reed said, dismissing the Infernal.

She shook her head. "No, thanks. I saw enough earlier. I'll just hang out here with Bernard."

"I thought the whole point of coming to Anytown was to check things out."

"I wanted to guesstimate the time it would take to get from the video store—where Claire last saw Molenaar—to here. When you're done, we'll walk the various routes and see if we can get an average timeline."

"We'd appreciate it," the investigator said. "When we were called out here, it was for one scene, not two. We're understaffed."

Reed looked at Eve. "Give me a second, then we'll go."

She winked at him, a playful gesture that rocked him back on his heels. She took hits, but kept on trucking. That trait made him admire her, and that admiration was leading them both into dangerous territory. Especially now that Cain had apparently stepped aside.

He'd traversed half the distance between Eve and the murder site when his cell phone vibrated. He pulled it out and looked at the caller ID.

Unavailable.

He turned the power off and shoved it back into his pocket.

Prolonged exposure to darkness destroyed minds. Prisoners who were sent to "the hole" in prisons usually emerged disoriented and senseless. Even *He Who Inflicts Punishment on the World and the Luminaries* felt claustrophobic dementia flirting with the edges of his mind, and he had only been in the belly of the beast for a few hours at most. But then a prison "hole" would be preferable to the gore he was presently stewing in.

If he was forced to fight now, Raguel would be at an undeniable disadvantage. He'd been cramped into the fetal position for hours, cocooned in his wings to protect his flesh from acid, lacking water and sitting in a waist-deep pool of Mark blood. The beast purred and cavorted gaily, inundating him with noise and nauseating jostling. Raguel definitely wasn't at the top of his game, and that would worsen the more time passed.

But Sammael would make him suffer for as long as possible. Not only for retaliation purposes, but because his freedom would come at a steep price.

By the time the vessel within which he waited finally cried out its agony and collapsed, Raguel was ready to claw his way out. Light pierced into the obsidian darkness with a sword's blade. It seeped in while the blood poured out, the exchange courtesy of the downward slice through the beast's torso.

Raguel was borne into the depths of Hell in a gush of crimson, his body emerging through the widening gap in the Infernal's gutted belly. He skidded along the hot stone floor, until the blood pool became too shallow to carry him further.

"Brother," Sammael greeted, his deep purring voice laced with malice and fury. "You owe me a dog."

Raguel rolled to his belly, then pushed up onto his hands and knees. His brother came at him in a blur of red wings and black velvet, kicking him in the gut and wringing a cry of pain past his lips. Raguel was returned to his back, gasping, but when the next attack came he was ready. He yanked his body to the side when Sammael's cloven foot stomped down toward his face. Raguel's wings burst free, spraying blood and launching him upward. He didn't achieve sufficient height to fly, but he did regain his footing.

Facing his brother with scarlet-stained feathers, Raguel struggled to stay upright without swaying. The air was sweltering, the stench of decaying souls cloying when mingled with the Mark blood seeping from the freshly killed Infernal.

They seemed to be alone in a vast receiving room. The appointments were impressive—the vaulted ceiling with a replica of Michelangelo's *Fall of Man,* the mosaic stone floor, the white marble walls, Corinthian columns, and the massive throne positioned beneath a chandelier that levitated and moved with Sammael. Statues of various historical figures—such as the Marquis de Sade, Hitler, and Stalin—decorated symmetrically placed alcoves that lined the walls. The room was the size of a football field, yet the Prince of Hell did not appear dwarfed by it. In contrast, Raguel felt small and helpless.

He studied Sammael carefully, looking for any sign of the brother he had once known. Possessed of awe-inspiring beauty, Sammael had hair dark as ink, golden skin, eyes a brilliant green, and a mouth designed to lure the faithful to sin. The Angel of Death. He had once been the most favored archangel, trusted with the meting of punishments and the overseer of two million *mal'akhs*. Raguel had once admired and envied Sammael. Like Cain and Abel, Sammael did everything wrong while Raguel did everything right, yet Sammael had been loved in a way the other archangels had not.

"A clever way to get what you wanted." Sammael gestured to the fallen hellhound with a graceful wave of his hand.

"Desperate is more apt."

"How did you know Havoc could only die by an Infernal's hand?"

"I did not know."

Sammael's smile was icy. "You took a chance hoping I would save you rather than let you die and spark the war. Patience is not one of my virtues. Perhaps I am ready for Armageddon."

"I had no choice. Your beast was set on killing hundreds of mortals." Raguel widened his stance for better balance and shook out his wings.

Sammael smiled . . . and circled him. "With your blood-soaked wings you resemble me now, brother. Perhaps you will consider staying. I would love to have you."

Raguel laughed without humor, sidestepping to maintain the gap between them. He kept his gaze on his opponent, but he was always completely aware of his surroundings. Demons never played fair; they didn't see the point. Winning was all, so an ambush was not only likely, but expected. A sudden apparition or a trapdoor. "Perhaps *you* will come home with *me*."

"Impossible. Father and I have fundamental differences in our views."

"Creation versus destruction," Raguel murmured.

"Coddling versus challenging."

"Generosity versus selfishness."

Sammael snorted. "Arrogance versus acceptance. We complete each other. Yin and yang."

"Up and down."

"It is not so bad here, is it?" A warm, seductive chuckle rumbled up from Sammael's chest. "You look so disappointed. Did you think I was pining for His good graces? Did you believe the mere chance of begging, groveling, and giving up all autonomy would have me crying in relief?"

"I am autonomous." Raguel coughed, choking from the heated air.

"Within the limits of a system I created here on Earth. Where would you be without me?"

It was a testament to Sammael's charisma and powers of persuasion that Raguel could almost believe that his brother was happy in this mire he'd created for himself. But Raguel couldn't shake the memories of the man Sammael had once been. A man like Cain—capable of dark acts, but for a just cause. "I am certain that I have yet to see the best of your hospitality."

"True. But we can rectify that," his brother purred, his eyes sparking with malevolence.

Raguel carefully extended claws from his fingertips, keeping his hands tucked behind his thighs. He couldn't kill his brother. Not because he was restrained by sentimental reasons, but because Sammael had powers that terrified him. Still, he would not go down without a fight. "Why set the trap you did today?"

Sammael *tsk*ed softly, twice as horrifying because his magnetism was enough to lure even the most frightened of souls like moths to a flame. Even a painful death was no deterrent. "Does that seem like my style to you, Raguel? Do you remember so little about me?"

"Nothing stays the same. Change is inevitable."

"Not for Father. He never learns. Never grows."

They were circling each other, each move perfectly gauged. Sammael could be fully human in appearance, but he chose to wear hooves for effect. Each clopping step he took was like a gunshot in the quiet. There was no doubt that he was the predator and Raguel was the prey.

"Why?" Raguel asked again, wondering why his brother seemed unconcerned about the death of his pet. Fact was, Havoc had been an unmitigated success, and if it was true that it was vulnerable only to an Infernal's hand, then its loss should be a lamentable one to him.

"It was a transgression, a show of cockiness by a lower-level demon flush with his first successes."

"Are you losing control of your domain?"

"Never." The word was spoken with such vehemence it reverberated through the room around them.

The door at the far end of the chamber opened and Azazel entered. The archdemon had been Sammael's lieutenant forever. He bowed before his ruler and waited to be acknowledged.

"You will see for yourself," Sammael said, his focus still on Raguel, "since you will not be leaving. I cannot kill you . . . *yet*, my brother, but I can keep you. And I shall."

"My liege," Azazel murmured. "Forgive the intrusion. I bring news of importance."

Sammael's growl echoed through the vast space. He turned his back to Raguel and stormed away, his form changing as he moved into that of a fully realized man in Tudor-era hose with waistcoat, doublet, jerkin, and gown. His hair was long, past his shoulder blades, and it moved as a separate entity. Lifting and shifting as if caressed by a breeze. But the air was sulfuric and stagnant here. Oppressive.

The Prince of Hell took his throne, lounging with long legs extended and arms draped over the thick, carved wooden armrests. He was majestic, and as graceful as a feline. "What is it?"

Azazel approached. Aside from similar height and build, he was as opposite from Sammael as opposite could be. His hair and eyes were white, his skin like ivory. Dressed in breeches and doublet of silver and blue, he looked as cool as the snow . . . in a place as hot as Hell. "Cain has been advanced to archangel and placed as head of the North American firm."

Raguel stumbled, the room suddenly spinning around him. He had been gone only hours . . .

His gaze shifted wildly, his brain struggling to catch up with the ramifications. He saw the dead beast on the floor; its massive body lying on its side, its opened gut still oozing gore. Its legs were sprawled, its male genitalia clearly visible.

He froze.

Why have reproductive organs? *Unless it had a mate . . . ?*

"See how easily you are replaced?" Sammael gloated with a triumphant smile lighting his darkly beautiful face. "Discarded and forgotten. Expendable. Where is the love and loyalty Father promised you all of your life?"

Raguel spread his wings for balance as the room began to spin. *Did no one find and recognize the clues he'd left behind? Did they think he was dead to them . . . lost forever?*

Why Cain, of all the Marks? Once again, Jehovah favored one who was far less than perfect. Raguel would not have chosen him as his successor.

"What are your orders?" Azazel asked.

"Orders?" Sammael made a careless gesture with a flick of his wrist. "I have none."

"None?" The archdemon glanced at Raguel.

"My brother's presence does not hold my tongue. This is cause for celebration, not alarm. Cain is removed from the field. Raguel has learned how little he means in the grand scheme of things." Sammael stroked his chin thoughtfully. "However, it does me little good to keep Raguel if it is believed that he is dead. The word of his capture can be spread, of course."

"And quickly," Azazel added.

"Yes. But I think it might be more effective to return him to a world in which he has lost importance. I will have to consider the matter further." Sammael's malice-laced smile was riveting. "You can always choose to stay of your own accord, brother. I welcome you with open arms."

"Never," Raguel spat.

Sammael snapped his fingers and Raguel found himself contained in a cage suspended over the fiery pits of Hell. Smoke, ash, and heat billowed upward and wrapped him in a cocoon of torment. But what was worse was the dead space inside him that he hadn't noticed while consumed by fear.

For all of his life, his mind and heart had been filled with a steady influx of orders from the seraphim, reports from handlers and mentors, and the occasional comment from Jehovah himself—new assignments for his

Marks, reports and receipts, commentary and encouragement. It had sounded like the faint buzzing of hundreds of flies, a steady hum that was the rhythm of his existence. The beat to which he marched, the tempo of his heart, the cadence of his life. The sudden awful silence within him was like a yawning black hole.

Discarded. Forgotten. Expendable.

Raguel sank to his knees and cried.

Azazel approached his prince, his face schooled to impassivity so as not to give away his surprise. He would not have expected his liege to act so boldly in regards to the archangel Raguel. Terror and temptation were expected. Torture and imprisonment were not.

He looked at the fallen hellhound and shook his head at the loss. "The boy is a loose cannon. He is a danger to us all."

Sammael smiled. "He thinks he is invincible and who can blame him? He was at ground zero in an explosion that took out an entire city block, yet he lives to cause more trouble."

"I request permission to kill him."

"Kill him? He walks among Marks as one of them. The glamour he wears is so perfect none suspect him. If he pulls this off, he will prove that we are being too cautious."

"He is an abomination," Azazel said. "I would celebrate that fact, if he were not also an idiot."

"When his time comes, you may have him." The prince stood. "In the meantime, we have many successes to relish. Our position has not been so favorable in a very long time."

Azazel shifted with unease. "Will you keep Raguel, then?"

"No. I will hold him only long enough to despair and doubt his faith. The rest he will do to himself, because of jealousy and resentment. It is more fun that way."

"Cain's advancement could be quite a coup for you," the lieutenant agreed. "You might consider telling him the truth."

Sammael laughed. "I am still waiting for his mother to do the honors."

"After all these centuries? I doubt she intends to."

"The time will come," Sammael said, his gaze dreamy and his thoughts on some future Azazel could not see. "When it does, all Hell will break loose. What a day that will be, my friend. What a day."

CHAPTER 16

Alec didn't shift directly into the Grimshaw compound. Instead, he paused at the convenience store across the street and studied the main entrance from a safe distance. He breathed with concentrated steadiness, willing his system to become accustomed to his long-repressed *mal'akh* power to shift from one location to another.

From the exterior, the Charleston Estates gated residential community looked like many others. A fountain occupied the center of a circular drive. A guard station stood at the entrance. A tall stucco wall surrounded the entire perimeter, providing privacy for the homeowners inside. Mature trees dotted the winding streets, providing shade and an exterior appearance of tranquility. While the developer's brochure listed some upscale amenities—tennis courts, a helipad, and a concierge house—there was nothing to proclaim it as the domain of the Black Diamond Pack. But every single resident was a wolf under Charles's command.

It was ingenious, actually. An ideal way to keep tabs on his subordinates . . . and to ensure that secrets stayed secret.

Like the Lebensborn-2 program.

Thanks to Giselle, he had a fairly thorough map of the community in his mind. The Mare was frightened by his transformation to archangel and equally wary of what would happen if he were to be captured with the motel room key on his person. She would not fare well if Charles found her in the possession of Cain the Archangel. It wasn't a risk she was willing to take, so he trusted that the map she drew him was as correct as she could make it.

The question now was whether he should go to the kennel first and kill the hellhound pups, or whether it would be wiser to take out Charles, then deal with the Alpha's mess. He glanced at his watch. It was quarter after two. Forty-five minutes until the conference call. This might have to be a reconnaissance mission. Get the lay of the land. Get out. Come back later.

But he'd much prefer to strike during the day when the wolves least expected it, when they were at their laziest and most vulnerable. Maybe he would blow off the conference call instead. The other archangels weren't expecting him. It might be better to allow them time to adjust to his new role.

The sooner he finished this task, the sooner he could return to Eve. That was still his motivation, although it was a conscious decision rather than an emotional compulsion.

He felt her. Tangibly. As if she stood beside him with her hand in his. But in reality it wasn't his hand she was holding, it was Abel's. He felt no personal response to that, a lack of reaction that made him feel like a stranger in his own skin. Worse yet, in lieu of his own feelings, he felt Abel's—a brutal, covetous, consuming lust for Eve that fed off Alec's connection to the hundreds of Infernals under Raguel's command. The ties to the demons were thready, but what he did absorb was cool, dark, and very seductive.

Alec could only conclude that just as the Novium found a loophole around the lack of physical response, his brain was finagling around the lack of emotional reaction. It was telling him that Abel's feelings for Eve were *his,* not his brother's.

In short, he was screwed.

Instead of the peaceful disassociation archangels enjoyed, he felt the frustration and lust that were Abel's. Mixed with the confusion and heartbreak Eve was experiencing, Alec was suffering like a teenager with a megadose of pubescent hormones.

It wasn't supposed to be this way; archangels were serene. But Eve's Novium was throwing a wrench into everything, along with the fraternal bond between him and Abel, her affection for both of them, their pressing desire for her, and the triumvirate of mentor/Mark/handler. The whole morass was completely unique, creating an environment that fostered an anomalous connection that had to be addressed as soon as possible. With the overwhelming influx of information pouring into him from both the seraphim and Raguel's Infernals, Alec didn't have the energy left over for . . . angst. He felt as he suspected schizophrenics might, with hundreds of voices in his head telling him what to do and when to do it, while his own mind was telling him that Eve was still important to him no matter how he felt. Or didn't feel, as the case may be.

Archangels weren't supposed to experience romantic love. With everything else they dealt with, they weren't equipped. They were kept detached by the hand of God, which is why they were discouraged from using their powers. The restriction was the most efficient way of cultivating the sympathy for mortals and Marks they would otherwise be incapable of feeling. But they had an advantage he lacked: they didn't know what they were missing. It was easy to turn down something when you'd never had it. Far more difficult to resist something you were addicted to. While he didn't feel the urge for a fix any longer, he still remembered what it felt like to be high and the sensations filtering in from Abel and Eve kept the memories potent.

"Eve."

He wanted to reach out to her, but was afraid to. The connection to the Infernals had . . . awakened something. Like a hidden coiled serpent unwinding from its den and making its presence known. Alec was forced to feel Eve's turmoil without the ability to comfort or explain.

Until he finished here.

Alec supposed he could assign a Mark to the task of killing Charles now that he was no longer a Mark himself, but he didn't. Charles had killed Eve because of him. He would, therefore, be the one to avenge her.

The kennel was where he decided to start. He could use the death of the pups as psychological warfare. Fear of Sammael's retaliation would knock Charles off his game and give Alec another advantage. With luck, that would add a layer of unrest to Charles's last day here on Earth and added torment when he returned to Hell.

Alec shifted to the far side of the building, which was built off of the red-tile-roofed community center in the very heart of the compound. Children played in the nearby Olympic-size pool. Adults basked on white plastic loungers in the sun. It was a demon's paradise and its existence was one of the reasons why Charles's wolves were so loyal to him. It was also a warning to Alec—everything breathing within a two-mile radius wanted him dead with a vengeance.

Reaching the rear double doors, which were made of reinforced steel, Alec attempted to shift inside and was prevented by a ward of some sort. He would have to get inside the old-fashioned way.

He tried the levered handle and found it unlocked. He was slightly surprised, despite how difficult it would be for anyone with a nefarious purpose to get this far without detection. A camera was trained at the doorway, but it wouldn't register him. Secular technology was good, but it wasn't capable of registering beings functioning on a different plane, such as archangels using their full powers. Which meant it was there to catch Marks and mortals. The question was—was it catching them going in, or running out?

A sense of foreboding tightened his jaw. He depressed the handle with his thumb and the lock gave way without a sound. He cracked the door to look inside and was immediately assailed by the sweet odor of Marks and the cacophony of multiple creatures protesting their confinement.

The building was soundproofed.

Peering through the narrow slit between the two doors, Alec took in a long hallway that made an uninterrupted line to the other side of the building. A stocky wolf in human form stood an arm's distance away with his back to him. Alec waited for the guard to scent him. When the wolf pivoted and attacked in half-form with claws and canines extended, Alec jerked the door open and lunged for the guard's throat. His fingers dug into the flesh, piercing through it. Fisting the trachea, Alec ripped it free. The wolf fell, unable to voice a sound and paralyzed, his life's blood spurting from his carotid in thick, powerful pulses.

In full wolf form, he would have turned instantaneously to ash. *For you were made from dust, and to dust you will return.* In half-form, the process took longer and was sometimes incomplete, leading to semiburned bodies that mortals attributed to spontaneous combustion.

Alec waited for the welcome and familiar rush of bloodlust to heat his veins and thicken his muscles. It didn't come. The absence was excruciating, like blue balls from fucking without the resulting orgasm. Loving Eve and killing Infernals were the only things in his existence that brought him pleasure and both had been taken from him. He understood now why the archangels were so ambitious. What else did they have to live for?

Dropping the remnants of the throat onto the man's chest, Alec stepped over him, finding a modicum of relief by siphoning his frustration through to the Infernals connected to him.

Cages lined either side of the hallway. The walls were windowless, whitewashed cement block, and the ground was polished concrete liberally scarred with claw marks. Small trenches were dug into the juncture of the exterior walls and the floor, with steadily flowing water running the length like a river.

Driven into a frenzy by the scent of blood, the beasts snarled and leaped into the bars without regard for their own safety. A quick count told him there were a dozen of the creatures, each one at least five feet tall. Fleshy and lacking fur, they had thickly muscled shoulders and thighs, and tiny midsections. They panted like dogs, but ran like apes, their hands fisted and punching into the concrete floor. The more excited they became, the sweeter they smelled. Like Marks.

Alec yanked open a glass door that protected a wall-mounted display of shotguns. He would rather not use his newly acquired archangel powers, if he could help it. The force required to kill an Infernal would send out a ripple that would be easily detected by the adult wolves sunning themselves just beyond the door.

Alerted by the ruckus, another wolf in human form emerged from a room at the end of the hall. She charged Alec, growling with a fury that incited further frenzy from the caged beasts. The bitch altered to canine form midstride and leaped. Alec shifted to a position behind her and fired, severing her spinal cord at the nape. Reduced to ash that exploded outward, the bitch's remains dusted the creatures in the nearest cells. They grew rabidlike in their mounting hysteria, slamming into the bars with such force they rattled the anchors and filled the air with clouds of debris.

Pumping another round into the chamber of the shotgun, Alec began searching the rooms of the building, looking for further threats. In the end, he didn't find anyone else, which wasn't a great surprise. Giselle had said the pups took decades to mature, plenty of time for security to grow lax. Since the Infernals hadn't been caught yet, there was no reason for them to believe they would be now.

What he did find of interest was a rolling metal cart protruding from the doorway the second wolf had appeared from. Its shelves were covered with a dozen five-gallon-size aluminum bowls filled with a putrid stew. Giselle had said she kept 10 percent of her meals; the rest went to feeding the pups. Which meant the contents of those bowls—and the puppies' stomachs—was an amalgamation of evil from an assortment of Infernals.

He looked again at the beasts that were creating a racket that was capable of shattering mortal eardrums. Those that were close enough to the dead wolf at the rear door were extending their long tongues to lap at the widening pool of blood. Those that were too far away continued to beat themselves against their cell bars.

Alec lifted the shotgun to his shoulder, pushed the muzzle between the bars of the nearest cage, and squeezed off a round. It was a dead-on hit to the temple. The bullet went clean through and embedded in the wall on the other side. The beast sat and growled, the picture of forced docility. It looked at Alec with a malevolent gaze. There was no visible wound.

"Shit." Adding a prayer to the mix, he shot the Infernal again, this time between the eyes. The beast became even more accommodating by sliding into a prone position. Same result—no injury and an embedded bullet in the cement block.

The guns were behavioral tools.

"How the hell do I kill you, if I can't even hurt you?"

One of the other hellhounds was lying on its belly, licking at the wolf blood that was creeping beneath the bars. Its tail was protruding from the cage into the hallway. Crouching, Alec used a trick Eve had taught him and summoned a flame-covered dagger. He pressed it against the appendage. It was like pressing against solid stone. There was no penetration, no scorching. The creature snarled and glared at him, but was otherwise unaffected.

"Fan-fucking-tastic," Alec muttered, sending the blade back with a flick of his wrist. It had been centuries since he'd run across an Infernal he didn't know precisely how to vanquish.

He was about to abandon the kennel and make Charles tell him how to kill the damned things when he noted that the tail he'd touched was damaged, its end chewed off and healed raggedly. Pivoting, Alec looked at all the hellhounds, noting that some had torn ears, while others had scars on their limbs.

So . . . they weren't completely impervious to injury.

They were caged separately. Fed separately. But clearly at one point they hadn't been. Were they vulnerable only to each other? Or were they just protected against Marks?

Alec moved to the dead wolf, whose corpse was beginning to smoke. One arm in particular was nearly severed, the elbow area having melted into a gory puddle. Gripping the wrist, he picked it up and carried it back to the distracted hellhound. He crouched and hammered the severed hand downward, claws first. They sank deep into the tail, causing the beast to leap away with a furious roar.

"Gotcha." Alec grinned. He couldn't kill the dozen with one clawed hand, but he had a better idea.

He returned to the office he'd searched earlier. Via the computer, he quickly acquainted himself with the kennel setup. Each cage floor was hydraulic, lowering to an underground dog run set up like a maze, with each pup segregated from its siblings by cleverly placed walls. A set of drawn schematics pinned to a corkboard above the desk showed that live bait was occasionally brought in for hunting and training. The kennel doors could be opened remotely for cleaning while the pups were below.

Alec smiled. "I love it when a plan comes together."

He left the office. Moving to the metal meal cart, he pulled it completely out of the doorway it protruded from and wheeled it down the hallway. The beasts went wild. He paused by the first cage and lifted a bowl.

"Requietum." His voice resonated with command.

All the Infernals immediately quieted and sat, waiting. There had been other commands listed in the office, but the rest of them were only useful if you wanted something hunted. The pups eyed him with obvious malice, obeying him only because they were instinctive creatures that wanted nothing so much as to eat.

Shifting with lightning speed, Alec entered the first cage. He dumped the contents atop the Infernal's head and shifted back out. Rinse and repeat, all the way down the line. The last two were the hardest, since the first few were screaming in protest by the time he reached the end.

Spattered with the noxious meal, he shifted back into the office and locked the door. With a quick downward wave of his hand, he removed all traces of puppy food from his clothes. Then, he hit the release for the cage locks. The subsequent collision of powerful bodies was like listening to eighteen-wheelers crashing on the highway at top speeds. Alec grinned and text-messaged Abel—*Not going to make the conference.* He cc'd Raguel's phone, too, since Abel was unreliable about using his.

Outside the office door, the screams were deafening.

"Ten minutes." Eve looked at Reed, who was rubbing the back of his neck. *"If*—and that's a big 'if'—Molenaar was walking at a slug's pace, and Claire is right about last seeing him at eight-thirty."

They stood outside the video rental store where Claire had last seen Molenaar alive. They'd occupied the same spot a half dozen times over the course of the last forty-five minutes and the conclusion was undeniable.

"That's not enough time," he said, "to cross the distance from the store

SYLVIA DAY

to the alley, pin him up, then mutilate his body . . . Not while using bare hands. Magic . . . maybe."

"So, how did the killer gain time?"

He shot her a bemused look. "Good question. She did say the time could be closer to eight."

Eve shook her head. "Not possible. We entered Anytown at eight."

Reminded of the ticking clock, she glanced down at her watch. "We have to head back. It's five minutes to three."

"Did you get what you needed here?" His fingers circled her wrist.

"Yes, I'm all set." She wondered if he noticed how often he reached for her, both mentally and physically. Luckily, their physical connection seemed to short-circuit the mental, which afforded her some privacy, but she wouldn't have bitched even if it hadn't been convenient. Right now, she needed to be touched.

To say she was smarting from Alec's personality transplant would be the understatement of all time. Eve had a few absolutes in her life—her parents would always be married, her sister would always be wild, Janice would always be her best friend, and Alec would always be madly in lust with her. The loss of one of those made her doubt the others, which in turn made her wonder if there was anything she could count on at all. Silly to pin so much on the affections of one man, but there it was.

"Are you sure?" Reed insisted. "No coming back?"

"I'm sure." They hadn't examined every crack and crevice of Anytown, but an exhaustive search wasn't necessary. She didn't have the same feelings of dread she'd had at the start of the exercise, a familiar cloud of foreboding that had hovered over her from the very beginning of training. All this time, she believed the sensation of being disliked and an outcast in her class had been externally generated. Now she understood that disquiet came from inside her.

"Unless the *Ghoul School* team decides they want to stay," she equivocated. "Then we'll have to revisit."

He nodded, apparently satisfied with that. "They think this place is going to be lit up like Times Square. I doubt they'll decide that's conducive to filming eerie-looking night vision footage."

"I don't know. Linda isn't doing this as a lark." She related what the young woman had told her earlier.

"This Tiffany person," he began when she finished. "She's the European Mark you want me to check up on?"

"Yes." She glanced up at him and felt her stomach clench. He was boyishly handsome when he smiled, but when he was somber, he was devastating.

"Why? They can't be reunited, babe. Not unless Linda gets marked."

"Don't say that," she admonished. "I don't expect that Linda will ever know what happened to her friend, but she'll be all right. She's got Roger to lean on when she needs to, and a calling that gives her purpose. It's

Tiffany I worry about. I think if she knew about Linda's blog and the show, maybe she'd find some comfort in knowing how much her friend still loves her."

"Marks are cut off from their old life for a reason."

"You promised."

Reed shook his head. "That was before I knew what you wanted the information for. Rules are rules."

"Hey, I don't know what you want from me. There's a lot of ground to cover between wild gorilla sex and washing a car."

His slow smile made her toes curl, not exactly a convenient thing when walking in combat boots. "True."

She didn't really believe sex would be the forfeit or she never would have agreed. Reed wanted her to come to him on her own. Since he wouldn't take her during the Novium, he certainly wouldn't take her for a bet.

"It's not as if Linda's actions are covert," she argued. "Her weblog, episodes of the show, their website, the website of the network . . . It's all public domain."

"So let the Mark find it—or not—on her own. If you're claiming inevitable discovery, allow her to discover it inevitably."

"If you renege on our deal, I'm free to do the same."

He growled, looking so disgruntled she couldn't help but find humor in it despite her worry over Alec.

"Hey." She bumped her shoulder into his. "Just say the deal is off and you're free."

"So you can sucker some other poor soul into trouble with you?"

"You're claiming selfless motivation?" She laughed. "That might have more impact if you weren't blackmailing me."

"You started it by dragging me here."

"You would have come, regardless," she countered. "I just got myself invited."

She was pretty sure she could have swayed Montevista, if she'd had to. At worst, she could have proceeded without him, which would have forced him to tag along for safety's sake. But she was much happier to have Reed with her. Despite his rough edges, she enjoyed his company, and while he was a risk to her in many ways, he was also protective. Sometimes.

They passed the boundaries of Anytown, then reached the street. Turning left, they headed toward the duplex.

"You just barrel through everything," he grumbled, "rules be damned."

"Break the deal." Her voice was low and taunting. "I double dog dare you."

Reed met her gaze with narrowed eyes. "Not on your life."

His look promised all sorts of wicked consequences and a fission of attraction moved through her.

Eve shrugged it off by necessity. "I don't understand what you and your brother are fighting about." Or why she had to be stuck in the middle.

"What does Cain have to do with anything?" he snapped.

Growing cautious at his harshness, she replied carefully, "You tell me."

He stopped and faced her, his back to their destination. Blocking her way. "Explain your convoluted female thought process to me."

"Can't you read my mind?"

"Not without screwing up my own."

"If I'm going to be the rope in your tug of war, shouldn't I know what the war is about?"

He gave her an aggravated look. "What does Cain have to do with finding this Tiffany person?"

"You obviously don't want to find her for me," she explained, "but you want our little agreement more. I have to think that has something to do with Cain. You don't seem like the type of guy who breaks the rules arbitrarily."

And a bet with her was arbitrary, no doubt.

Reed's lips thinned and a vision of her bent over his knee popped into her head. "When I do something with you because of Cain, I'll let you know."

"Spanking isn't my thing, caveman." She crossed her arms. "And I'm not talking about you and me. I'm talking about you and Cain."

"You can't say it's not your thing until you've been spanked properly." He caught her elbow and pulled her toward the duplex.

"We were having a discussion," she protested.

"No, you were prying."

"Alec said it had something to do with a woman."

Reed stared straight ahead. "On the periphery."

"And the fact that you are both interested in the same woman now doesn't signify?"

"Not anymore. Now there's just one of us interested." He glanced at her. "Note that Cain's defection didn't affect me at all. What does that tell you?"

"That you don't think he got over me that quickly either."

"He's an archangel, babe. Archangels don't feel love like you know it."

"Are they celibate?"

He laughed. "Hell, no. They can even feel fond of a lover, like an owner with a pet. But love . . . that is reserved for God."

Eve sighed. Until she spoke with Alec at length, in private, she wasn't jumping to any conclusions. "So get back to the origins of your fight with your brother."

"Get over it, Eve."

"Were you ever close?"

Shrugging, he said, "My mother says we were once, but I don't remember it."

"Your mother *says*?" Not past tense.

The wry smile he shot her was a knee-weakener. "She'll tell you all about it when you meet her. Like most moms, she loves to share embarrassing childhood stories."

Eve was too stunned to reply. Alec and Reed . . . with their mother. The singularity of meeting the Original Sinner had nothing on the thought of seeing the two potently virile men she knew with their mom.

As they neared the house, they spotted Linda and Roger outside with Freddy. Linda waved, then crossed the street.

"Hey," she said, smiling. "We all talked it over and we've decided we're going to stick around tonight. We tried reaching the commandant, but she's gone for the day. If we had gotten a hold of her and she agreed to let us come back, we would have headed up to Alcatraz. But since we couldn't reach her, we feel like it is best if we stay. All we have is our reputation. We need to protect it."

Reed's hand settled at Eve's lower back, intensifying the rush of his thoughts in her mind. He wasn't at all happy with the turn of events.

"Completely understandable," he said. "And admirable. But Eve's been called away and won't be available to join you tonight."

Setting her boot heel on his toes, she shifted her weight to that side. *You're an ass. You could have at least talked to me about it first.*

You've been there, done that, he countered, pushing her off his foot with a firm but gentle hand. *No more.*

Why not? If it's safe enough for them, it's safe enough for me.

Not as safe as Gadara Tower.

I won't argue that, but I can speak for myself.

"I haven't decided," she said to Linda, smiling, "whether I'll be leaving or not."

Reed's fingertips tickled her spine. "She's needed in Anaheim."

"Tonight?" Linda asked, frowning.

"No," Eve said.

"Yes," Reed interjected.

Eve shot him a warning glance. "We'll have to discuss it."

"Okay." Linda looked warily between them. "Let me know. We're going to head over there around midnight. You should be mostly done with whatever you're doing by then, right?"

"Sure," Eve said.

"Doubtful," Reed qualified.

Linda returned to Roger and Freddy, who were cavorting in the empty driveway. Freddy in particular was rambunctious in a way that was out of character with his behavior so far. Eve's gaze narrowed on him. He caught her looking and settled down.

Reed led Eve back to the house. They went to the men's side, where Hank had set up shop. The occultist was seated at a folding card table that was serving as a makeshift desk. In the guise of a man, Hank's gaze met Eve's.

"Your friends across the street left—"

"—something here for me?" she asked, cutting him off.

He eyed her for a moment, then nodded. "Yes."

She accepted the compact disc he held out to her. Their fingers touched and he read her, seeing more than she wanted him to. But also what she needed him to see.

"Interesting," he murmured. "Let me know what you find out."

She stared at his red hair, thinking of the last redhead she'd talked to. When Hank pulled away, she caught his wrist.

His brows rose. "Clever girl."

"Will you do it?"

Hank smiled. "Yes."

Reed moved over to the kitchen, where Montevista had set up a satellite video phone. Eve wondered why they didn't just use a webcam, but that question would have to wait until later.

Moving down the hall, she returned to the room where she'd seen Richens's laptop earlier. It was still there, as were all the rest of the men's bags. She closed the door and sat cross-legged on the floor. It only took a couple of minutes to power up the laptop, then she slid the CD into the drive and waited for the photos on it to load.

Her sister had once told her that she'd hacked a disposable digital camera and used it multiple times on vacation. Eve didn't ask Sophia how it was done, but she'd asked the *Ghoul School* kids if they knew. Michelle was familiar with the process, so Eve left Claire's camera with them.

The photos began to appear on screen, thumbnailed within some type of photo editing software. Eve skipped over the two of Gadara Tower, and also the ones taken of Monterey Bay and the entrance sign to McCroskey. She clicked directly on the last known photo of Molenaar and Richens, the one taken that morning before they began their excursion into Anytown. With bright eyes and big smiles, the group was arranged like an old elementary school class photo, with two rows of students—men at the top, women at the bottom. Raguel stood regally to the side, his elegance undiminished by his gray sweat suit. The students had all pulled up their sleeves, displaying their armbands for posterity.

Eve blew up the photo and examined each student carefully.

"Bingo," she whispered.

Her mother hadn't been able to see the mark on her arm, because it was undetectable by mortal eyes. Secular technology was also unable to register them. So when Eve's eyes discovered the edges of the mark peeking out around the silver plate of a student's armband she knew she'd found what she had secretly hoped she wouldn't—a fake Mark, hiding in plain sight. Only it wasn't whom she had suspected. It was worse.

Everything fell into place.

"Sneaky. But I caught you."

She heard footsteps thudding atop the hardwood floor of the hallway. Hitting the eject button on the disk drive, Eve closed the window for the photo software and folded the laptop shut. She scrambled to her feet just as the door opened and he walked in.

"Hollis. What are you doing in here?"

Eve tried to appear nonchalant. "Just checking my e-mail." But mental images of the corpses of Molenaar and Richens flashed incessantly and something must have shown on her face.

His friendly mien changed. His lip curled and he snarled like a wolf. Another Mark appeared behind him.

Eve feinted to the right, then bolted left, shouting for help. He lunged, tackling her to the floor.

Her skull hit the hardwood and the lights went out.

Reed stared at the text messages on the screen of Raguel's smartphone and felt his stomach knot.

KIEL, SARA—13:08—1K
ON MY WAY. WILL ARRIVE AT LAX EARLY TOMORROW A.M.
ASK ABEL TO TURN ON HIS PHONE.

He growled. There was so much shit piled on him right now, he could barely breathe through it. Cain was running through his brain on the periphery, using his experience to deal with the influx of information from the seraphim and handlers. It kept Reed edgy and infuriated. Why hadn't he been selected for advancement, when Cain obviously wasn't capable of functioning without his help? "Montevista, I think—"

A yelp from Eve at the rear of the house stiffened his spine to the point of pain. Midpivot, a deluge of information poured into his mind, a confusing disjointed morass that made him stumble.

He was in motion before his brain fully understood why, rounding the makeshift dining table and bolting toward the hallway. His shoulder bumped into Hank's, who was also responding, and his heel was clipped by a pursuing Montevista. They were nearing a bottleneck when Eve stepped out to the hallway from one of the bedrooms. Seeing the stampede, she winced and looked sheepish.

"Are you all right?" Reed barked, hating the fear that gripped him.

"I'm fine."

"What are you screaming for, then?"

"Uh . . ." She shifted nervously. "Big spider. Huge."

Montevista exhaled and leaned into the wall. "You scared the crap out of me, Hollis."

Hank's voice came low and somber. "Anything I should know?"

She frowned at him for the length of a heartbeat, then her face cleared. She smiled. "No. Nothing."

He nodded and walked away.

"You slayed a dragon," Reed said, curious enough to probe her thoughts but finding her as calm as if she were dozing, "but freak out over a *spider*?"

"I told you it was big," she said defensively.

He released his tension with a frustrated exhale and caught her elbow. "Come on, then. Show me where it is and I'll move it outside."

He reached for the doorknob.

"No!" She stayed him with a viselike grip on his wrist. "I'm over it. Forget it. Really."

Reed stared for a long moment. "You sure?"

She nodded. "Yes, I'm sure."

That worked for him. He had enough to worry about without adding spiders—big or not—to his list. Like preparing both himself and Eve for Sara . . . If it was possible to do anything more than brace themselves for the impact. "The conference call is about to start. You coming?"

"Wouldn't miss it," she said, smiling.

They headed back to the dining room.

CHAPTER 17

It seemed like hours before the kennel finally fell silent. Alec pushed up from the wheeled, black-leather office chair and shifted into the hallway. The destruction in the main area was plentiful. Blood and tissue covered every surface. Very few of the pups remained in recognizable form. Most were in pieces. Only two were capable of movement—a faint twitch of a tail and an ear. They'd be dead within minutes due to copious blood loss.

Alec tried to shift into the underground dog run, but was prevented by more warding. He could shift freely once he was inside, just as he was able to shift within the kennel. It was the gaining entry part that caused trouble.

Returning to the office, he activated the hydraulic lifts in the cages and shifted to the nearest one. He was lowered into the maze, his nostrils flaring at the scent of death and decay that permeated the space. He moved carefully through the vast underground complex, which was dimly lit and cooler than the kennel above. The walls here were metal, the ductwork-covered ceiling low, and the floor more polished concrete. He cursed when he found a liquid nitrogen tank where embryos were being stored.

"I don't want to know how Charles got the goods to make those," he muttered to himself.

He searched the lablike room and found a heating element. Five minutes later the various cans that held the embryo straws were sitting in a deep metal tray set atop the hot plate. Alec wasn't going to take the chance that they might be rescued. The last thing the world needed was a legion of rampaging, ravenous, indestructible-by-Marks hellhounds running around. He would rather burn the place down, but until he killed Charles, he didn't want to risk any smoke signals. In this case, literal ones.

Satisfied that he'd crippled the breeding operation, Alec took the subterranean tunnel that led to the garage of Charles's castlelike home. Because the structure was built atop a small rise in the center of the community, the Alpha was both cushioned from his enemies and able to view the extent of his domain.

From the exterior, the home was majestic and lovely. Gray brick covered the exterior, which was distinguished by two turret-shaped corner staircases that connected the three stories. A large, rolling green lawn and imitation gas lamps lining the driveway gave the home a storybook quality. A coat of arms featuring a black diamond decorated the space above the front double doors. There was nothing to tell mortals that a demon ruled from here, quietly biding his time until he could attempt to destroy the world.

Pausing a moment, Alec took time to appreciate his situation. While there were plenty of mortals filtering through the gated community—postal workers, gardeners, pool cleaners, baby-sitters, and the occasional police patrol—it wouldn't have been easy for him to get this far as a Mark. And getting to the pups? That would have been impossible. Yet Jehovah had given him this task—a task he'd needed an archangel's gifts to accomplish.

The Lord worked in mysterious ways . . .

Alec shifted into a lower-floor guest bathroom. The stench of rotting souls was overwhelming in the house, as was to be expected. Every pack member traversed the halls here on a regular basis and Charles—an unmated wolf—was known for his insatiable appetite for sex, which kept a large quantity of women in the house.

That was why Alec started in the master bedroom.

The private domain of the Black Diamond Pack Alpha suited a wolf. Wood paneled walls, tan carpet, and forest green drapes gave the impression of the great outdoors. As Alec expected, two women lounged there, naked and decorated with details that betrayed one as a witch and the other as a wolf. A console at the foot of the bed was raised, revealing a hidden television. They were too busy giggling over a talk show to notice him standing in the shadows of the unlit sitting room. Charles was absent.

Alec kept moving, shifting from room to room, growing more uneasy by the moment. Aside from servants, the home appeared to be empty. Where the hell was everyone? When an Alpha was in residence, his home was usually crammed.

Pausing in the office, Alec searched the desk but found nothing of note. Just rosters, dues spreadsheets, and mating and birth records—the tools of a healthy pack. So he returned to the bedroom, shifting to a seated position atop the console television with his legs dangling in front of the screen. He spread his ebony wings with their gold tips and waved at the naked ladies.

The women screamed.

He knocked out the spiky-haired blonde with a single burst of lightning from his fingertips to her chest. He leaped atop the brunette and covered her mouth with his hand. She stared up at him with wide, horror-filled hazel eyes. Every Infernal with the most basic of training knew who he was on sight.

"Howl," he warned darkly, "and I'll stab you through the heart with a flame-covered silver sword. Nod, if you understand."

She moved her head in the affirmative, her tousled curls tumbling around a pretty face.

"Where's Charles?" He removed his hand.

"He left."

"You should try telling me something useful," he murmured. "Like where he was headed."

"I don't know, Cain. I swear. He left in a hurry."

"Why?"

"Whatever the reason, it has to be important. When he's in full rut, nothing can drag him away."

"What was said to get his attention?"

"Devon, our Beta, said he had an important phone call. Something about Timothy."

"Who's Timothy?"

"His kid." She swallowed hard. "The one you killed."

Alec's gaze narrowed. "Did you overhear the call?"

She pointed to the sitting room. "He took it in there. I couldn't hear him, but he wrote something down. Then he dressed and grabbed a change of clothes. That's all I know. I promise."

An Infernal promise was worth about as much as used toilet paper, but the smell of the wolf's fear was potent. If there was anything that passed as truth with Infernals, it was that they'd do anything to save their own skin.

"How long ago?"

"Twenty minutes, maybe."

Touching her neck, he sent a surge of power through her that rendered her unconscious. He leaped from the bed and moved into the next room. There was a small writing desk with an old-fashioned corded phone. A blank pad of paper and a pencil waited for the next note or message, while a desk lamp sat unlit and oddly placed, as if it had been shoved aside hurriedly.

He picked up the pad and pencil. Rubbing the tip of the lead lightly over the page, he revealed the imprint of the prior messages.

Right at commissary
Right on Pvt. Mitchell
Left on Garrison Way
White van, black Suburban

Directions to the duplex where Eve was staying. Why? The consensus was that Charles was responsible for the terrorizing of Raguel's class. If that were true, why would he be jotting down Eve's location as if he didn't know it? And why would that information, which he should have already had, cause him to leave two willing women in bed?

Alec shifted back to the motel. He freed Giselle, whom he'd once again cuffed to the sink. "Come on."

She scrambled to her feet and ripped the gag from her mouth. "Is he dead?"

"Not yet. But the pups are."

"All of them?" Her tone was both awed and horrified.

"Yes."

"Oh, man . . ."

A surge of alarm struck him, a rolling wave of emotion from Eve that halted him midstride. He reached out to her, but the sensation was gone as quickly as it had come, leaving behind a quiet, peaceful stillness.

"Hurry up," he bit out, urged to haste by the mystery.

"Where are we going?"

"Monterey." He returned to the bedroom.

"Yay!" She clapped. "That's south. We're finally getting somewhere."

"Don't get too excited." He touched her and tried to shift to the other room, just to see if he had the skill to move them both. He made the trip. She didn't. He shifted back, cursing.

Giselle's eyes were lit with amusement. "Doesn't work on Infernals. Our cooties don't travel well with angels."

"I'll have to leave you here, then." He glanced at the clock. It was shortly after four. "The way things are going, we might all be dead soon. You should go do something you always wanted to do before you croak."

"Ha! Archangels can't die. And you're not getting rid of me. Cain of Infamy turned into Cain the Archangel, and I had to be in the vicinity when it happened. I'm half dead already. At least with you I have a chance of saving the other half."

Alec pulled the car keys out of his pocket and set them on the dresser. "Archangels aren't invincible."

"Might as well be," she scoffed. Then a stunned silence permeated the space between them. "Wait a minute . . . Something happened to one of them, didn't it? Which one?"

"You can head down to Anaheim. I'll let them know you're coming."

"That's why you're an archangel now, isn't it?"

He pulled out some cash and set it next to the keys. "Grab everything that's here and take it down with you. I don't want to have to come back here, if I can help it."

"Cain, damn it! Talk to me."

He moved into the adjoining room and took a last look around, praying that he wasn't forgetting something. With the enormity of information passing through him—from the handlers underneath him and the seraphim above him—he was barely keeping his own thoughts straight.

"Are you a *machine*?" she cried. "Don't you care at all about what this means? I'm not ready for the world to end yet."

"Can anyone ever be ready for it?" he retorted, aggravated by her outburst.

Giselle skirted him and got in his face. Hands on her slim hips, she demanded, "What about that woman you were talking to on the phone last night? I heard the tone of your voice. She's special to you. Do you care about what the end of the world means to *her*?"

Alec paused and exhaled harshly. Examining his feelings for Eve was like trying to see through fogged glass. He knew they were there, could see the shadows and shapes, but the details were lost to him. It was similar to being served his favorite dessert and discovering he had no appetite.

"Yes," he said, honestly. "I care about what happens to her." There was more than sex and love involved in his feelings for Eve—respect and admiration, affection and nostalgia. The best days of his life had been spent with her. Being an archangel didn't change everything.

She nodded. "Okay, then. Tell me what's going on, so I can help."

He related the bare minimum required to bring her up to speed, while simultaneously reaching out to Eve. She seemed to be . . . napping. She was presently a blank slate, hovering in the space between consciousness and REM sleep. He frowned, wondering if the panic he'd felt from her a moment ago had been part of a dream. Having never shared a connection like this with anyone before, he wasn't certain how they worked. He reached out to his brother and found him unconcerned about Eve beyond what Alec would expect.

Abel expelled him forcefully. *Stay out of my head, Cain, before I find you and kill you.*

Alec gave the mental equivalent of flipping him the bird.

"Wow." Giselle sank onto the bed. "I can't guarantee I'll be any help, but I will sure try."

His brows rose. "What happened to the Mare who thought we were on a suicide mission?"

"She hooked up with an archangel. Kinda changes the odds, you know."

"Pack your stuff. We leave in five."

The conference call was anticlimactic. Raguel had, of course, been absent. His replacement was a no-show. Sara had a poor connection. It was decided to postpone the bulk of the conversation until all seven firms could be represented.

Reed left the crowded interior of the duplex in favor of the driveway. He was trying to figure out a way to keep Eve out of Anytown short of tying her up, when a low female voice drew his attention.

"Hey."

He turned his head and watched the blonde—Izzie, the Goth girl—approach. She had her fingers shoved into the teeny pockets of her black skirt and her eyes were half lidded.

"Hey back," he replied.

"I hear Cain was around earlier."

"You didn't miss anything."

She shrugged. "I've met him before."

"I'm sorry."

A smile teased the corners of her pretty mouth. His gaze rested there, his thoughts returning to what that mouth had done to him earlier. The memory had as much impact as remembering to get his hair cut—convenient and good for the vanity, but not necessary. He wished he could say that about Eve.

"It was not so bad," she said. Her gaze locked with his. "In fact, it was very good."

Reed froze, absorbing the innuendo with growing unease. Her accent was Germanic. "You're from . . . ?"

"Germany."

"Sarakiel," he growled.

"I was marked by one of her team, yes."

"When?"

"A few weeks ago. I arrived in California the day class started."

"And which firm will you be attached to when class is over?"

Her smile widened. "This one."

He rubbed the back of his neck. In the normal order of things, Izzie would have had anywhere from one to seven weeks to settle into her new country and firm. She would have been assigned housing, given a vehicle and a bank account, shown around the city, and had a tour of Gadara Tower *before* starting training. In some cases, Marks were transplanted to their new firms, then found themselves back in their home countries for training if that's the way the schedule fell. But following that bit of protocol would not have placed Izzie in the same class with Eve.

Nothing was coincidence. Sara had known of Izzie's past and put it into play against Eve. Izzie's selection was the hand of God, but using her as an irritant . . . that was pure Sara.

"You are not happy about this," Izzie murmured.

"Why would I care?"

"Sara believed you would be pleased. But then, I do not think she knows how you feel about your brother's girlfriend."

He kept his face impassive, despite her dig.

"You called Eve's name," she continued, "when you came."

Screw beating around the bush; he didn't have time for it. "What do you want?"

"The same thing you do. Cain away from Hollis."

He laughed. "Did no one tell you that Cain has been promoted to arch-angel? He's incapable of giving a shit about either of you."

"I do not need him to care. I just need him to give me an orgasm." Her lashes batted coyly. "You and I can help each other."

Seeing the similarities between Izzie and Sara filled him with fury. With his wings spread wide, Reed lunged across the distance between them, his face contorted with the rage of angels. He caught her by the throat and lifted her feet from the ground. Her eyes were like saucers in her pale face; her stained lips parted in a bid for breath.

In a terrible voice he warned, "You forget your place. We are not equals."

"I d-did not m-mean—"

"Keep your distance from Eve. You will do nothing to her. *Nothing.*" His free hand lifted and cupped her face, his thumb pressing into her lips and smearing her purple lipstick along her cheekbone. "Or you will an-swer to me."

Her hands wrapped around his wrists. "P-perhaps *you* w-will answer t-to Sara . . ."

His grip around her neck tightened.

"Abel." Montevista's sharp tone snared his attention. "What are you doing?"

Reed tossed Izzie to the grass that bordered the driveway. She puddled, but he knew she wouldn't stay humbled for long. He faced the guard, schooling his features into a less frightening mien. "It seems Ms. . . . ?"

"Seiler," Montevista provided grimly.

"It seems Ms. Seiler has too much time on her hands. Perhaps you have something you can occupy her with?"

Montevista nodded. "Come with me, Seiler."

Izzie stood and straightened her skirt. Her slow smile with its ruined lipstick was macabre and served as a warning to Reed. Like Sara, she believed life was all about the game—the maneuvering, the planning, the winning. Cain was a prize to be won and Reed had played right into her hands by joining his brother as a notch on her belt.

Retracting his wings, he turned away. Shit. Sara being here would only add to the tension. Cain was out of commission, but the obstacles in Reed's path hadn't diminished; they'd just changed. And women were much sneakier than men.

He looked at the house across the street, returning his attention to the most pressing problem. The redhead—Michelle—had come outside with a camcorder. The Great Dane and the Scottish Mark—Callaghan, the Ken doll—stood nearby. She appeared to be filming the neighborhood, whether for the show or for fun, he didn't know. He was concerned, however, by Callaghan's presence. The class was supposed to be in the house, helping Hank with the processing of evidence. Observing the many duties of the

Exceptional Projects Department was part of training. Why wasn't Callaghan participating?

Reed shook off the thought. Eve's paranoia was filling him with suspicions, too. Fact was, Callaghan was a man and Michelle was pretty and possibly available. In the Mark's shoes, Reed would think that making out with a hot redhead was more fun than hanging out with Hank and his potions, too.

Sensing Reed's stare, Callaghan looked up and waved. He said something to Michelle, then walked over.

"Montevista asked me tae keep an eye on them," Callaghan explained when he reached Reed. "So they dinnae wander off."

"She's cute."

Callaghan grinned. "Aye, that she is. She wanted tae see Anytown now for some daytime filming, but I think I talked her out o' it."

"Where are the others?"

"In the house."

Reed made an aggravated sound. "This whole thing is fucked all around. We don't have the time or resources to baby-sit them."

The unmistakable sounds of gagging preceded the abrupt appearance of the French Mark—Claire, the fashionista—lurching from around the corner.

She paused at the sight of them, swallowing hard. "I never thought I would wish for the ability to vomit," she said.

"What's wrong?" Reed's gaze lifted to the side of the house she'd emerged from.

"The E.P.D. investigators are examining R-Richens's body." She bent over and clutched her knees, inhaling and exhaling carefully.

The urge to puke was all in her head, but as with the Novium, knowing the cause didn't make the phantom feeling seem any less real. Reed sympathized. He wasn't fond of cadavers either, especially grisly ones.

"I have to leave," she said. "I hate this place."

"We're trying," he murmured, also sympathizing with whichever handler ended up with her. She was going to need a lot of help acclimating to the mark.

"I hated him, too," she said.

"Who?"

"Richens. He was an asshole."

"Aye," Callaghan agreed.

"And now I feel terrible to have thought about him in that way," she muttered.

Reed smiled.

"How much longer do we have to stay?" she asked.

"As soon as they go," he gestured across the street with a jerk of his chin, "we can go."

"What do they want?"

"To prove or disprove that there is paranormal activity in Anytown."

"Where is a tengu when you need one?" she groused.

Reed paused, considering. A sense of déjà vu washed over him, as if he was meant to think of the idea that popped into his head. "Good idea."

"Excuse me?"

"Why wait for them to figure it out for themselves?" He looked at Callaghan. "Let's go with them now. We'll rig something to give them the proof they want, then there won't be any reason for them to stay."

"They dinnae want proof of it," Callaghan said. "They're here tae disprove."

"I watched the video they gave Hollis," Claire said. "Mostly it was nothing for the first half an hour or so. Then they went to the video store and there was a shadow that looked like a DVD case floating in midair."

"Perfect. So we give them a reasonable explanation for what the other crew saw and they're done here."

"Can I accompany you?" Claire asked. "I cannot go back in that house. Not now."

"Where's Hollis?"

"Helping Edwards. He is worse than me. He liked Richens."

"And Hogan and Garza?"

"Hogan is fine with the corpse. Better than the rest of us. Garza accompanied Hank back to Anytown. He had to carry the equipment."

"Let's keep Hollis out of this." Eve was safer surrounded by her class, the guards, and the E.P.D. investigators than she was anywhere else.

"Callaghan." Reed looked at the Scottsman. "Offer to accompany the ghost hunters to Anytown, then lead them around to the video store. Claire and I will go on ahead, and set things up."

"Will do." Callaghan set off across the street.

Reed turned his attention to Claire. "Are you ready to go?"

She nodded. "I'm ready."

"Good. Let's get—"

A wolf howled. A long, drawn out cry followed by excited yips.

The rapid whirring of an approaching helicopter's blades shouldn't have bothered Reed, not considering the number of military installations in the area. But the wolf—far from indigenous to the area—sounded almost . . . *joyful* at the sound. Welcoming. Its tone set off alarms. Reed listened to them.

"Callaghan."

The Mark turned back. "Aye?"

"Get the redhead in the house, and keep the rest of the kids in there."

The urgency of his tone brought a gleam to Callaghan's eyes. The Mark nodded grimly and stepped up his pace.

"I will go with him," Claire offered. "At least there are no dead bodies in their house."

"Yes, go. No one comes in or goes out until I say otherwise."

She took a step forward, then looked at him with blue eyes wide behind her trendy black-framed spectacles. "I'm scared," she whispered.

He reached out to her, touching her shoulder in a silent offer of comfort. "You can do whatever needs to be done. God would not have chosen you otherwise."

Seemingly reassured, she jogged after Callaghan.

Reed pivoted on his heel and strode toward the house.

CHAPTER 18

Eve woke to a dull throbbing at the back of her head and a phantom shiver coursing down her spine. The howl of a wolf had woken her. Had it been a dream, or reality?

She wiggled, trying to find a more comfortable position. Instead, she realized she was strapped to a wobbly metal chair with her wrists bound behind her. A gag was in her mouth, the knot of which was pressing hard to a sore spot at the back of her skull. She must have been nearly brained during the attack, otherwise the mark would have healed her by now.

Groaning, she willed her foggy mind to catch up with her circumstances. She sat in near darkness, light filtering in through two thin vertical cracks on either side of her. She extended one leg, trying to gauge the amount of space around her. It connected with hollow wood that swayed outward, briefly allowing more light to enter. She tried to rock backward, but discovered a wall behind her.

She was in a closet with sliding track doors. The kind of closet that was in the McCroskey duplexes.

Was she still in the home Raguel had arranged for? Or had she been moved to a vacant one? Where was everyone else?

Eve focused on her superhearing, but registered only her own breathing. Then it came again, unmistakable and chilling—a wolf howling in what sounded like victory.

A whirring in the periphery of her consciousness grew in volume and she recognized it as an approaching helicopter. There was no reason to put the two together, aside from her instinctive belief that they were connected.

Follow your gut, Alec had said.

Using her feet, Eve worked the closet door over in small but regular intervals. Her mind was working as well, reaching out to Reed and Alec, then recoiling as pain lanced through her skull. She moaned into the gag, wishing her hands were free so she could check the back of her head for the stake that had to be driven through it.

How the fuck was she going to get out of here? She tried again to connect to either of the brothers. Same result. Pain intense enough to make her fear unconsciousness.

She needed a knife. And a new brain, because the one she had was killing her.

Feeling completely hypocritical, Eve closed her eyes and asked—as nicely as she could under the circumstances—for a sword. Frankly, she would prefer that such things were provided without her begging or that she could get a gun instead, but she knew the drill. The Almighty preferred the biblical flame-covered sword for a dash of drama. Flashy intimidation was one of his fortes.

She hadn't told Reed earlier when he asked, but truth was, she was always surprised when her request for the weapon was granted. She believed that one day the Almighty would turn his nose up at her and say her lack of faith had tried his patience one too many times. The possibility didn't inspire confidence.

Thankfully, this time *wasn't* the time when God left her to the wolves. The sword materialized in her hand. Actually, it was more like an envelope opener. She almost dropped it, but retained it with a fumbling grasp and a muffled scream. Even as it burned through the rope around her wrists, it scorched and blistered her flesh. The smell reminded her of dying in a men's bathroom at Qualcomm Stadium and strengthened her resolve.

Damned if she'd let these fuckers kill her again.

The rope gave way and Eve dropped the knife. She pulled her sizzling hands into her lap and felt the blood rush into the extremities with sharp tingles. The damage repaired before her eyes, the ruined flesh dropping away like torn gloves, leaving unmarred skin behind. The pain faded away at a much slower rate, but Eve pushed it aside. She didn't have time to focus on herself. She had to know where the rest of the class was, and she had some Infernal killing to do.

Tugging the gag from her mouth, Eve sucked in a deep breath. She stood and bumped her head into the underside of a shelf. Cursing, she froze, wondering if anyone had heard her. Wondering if it mattered.

The dagger continued to burn on the floor. She could stop it by sending the blade away, but she didn't. There was more than one way to call for help, and she'd use the old-fashioned smoke signal just as well as preternatural means. As the varnish melted and exposed the vulnerable wood beneath, smoke began to tendril upward. Pushing aside one of the closet doors, Eve rushed out and found herself in the bedroom where she'd been knocked out. She also found the mauled and lifeless corpse of another classmate.

A scream was trapped in her tightening throat.

Behind her, the drywall caught fire and burst into flames.

*　*　*

Etheric projection was never easy. The concentration required to be in two places at once was always draining. Fortunately, the rush inherent in the hunt and subsequent kill energized. Without that, there was no way to have maintained the duplicity this long.

In less than an hour, they would all be dead.

What a coup! Just weeks ago, all had seemed lost. All *had* been lost—killed, destroyed, ruined. Then, exactly like a phoenix emerging from the ashes, the hopes and dreams of every Infernal had arisen from the remnants of the Upland masonry.

Since that night, they had achieved more than any demon ever dreamed was possible. They had lived with an archangel, spoken face-to-face with both Cain and Abel, mingled among the most traitorous of their own kind, and through it all they remained undetected.

The entire balance of power had shifted now. They could do anything, go anywhere. Soon, Abel would be in Hell. He'd killed Malachai at the masonry. He deserved to suffer the torments of the damned. He deserved to watch Evangeline Hollis die to see what it was like to lose someone he cared for.

But that was not to be . . . yet. Sammael planned to use her. One day, though, she would be expendable, too. And the next time she died, they would be certain it was irreversible. They would sever her pretty head and impale it on the gate to Sammael's palace for all to see. They would be heroes, revered and feared in every corner of Hell.

In less than an hour, they would have it all.

From the singular vantage attained by hovering over the ghost hunter group, it was easy to see that Callaghan was destined for greatness. He studied the nearly empty living room with narrowed eyes, his enhanced senses picking up the anomalous etheric body hovering over him and the others. He was the only one to notice; even the rambunctious dog seemed oblivious to the malevolence waiting to strike.

The redhead in the pink and purple dress studied photos of Anytown. "These dummies are creepy looking."

"Psychological warfare," the brunette in orange said from her seated position atop an ice chest. "They could easily replace those mannequins, if they wanted to. But then they'd lose the freak-out factor inherent in having them decayed and riddled with vermin."

"I love it when you talk dirty," the goateed man at her feet drawled. "Makes me hot."

"Roger." The brunette poked his thigh playfully with a pedicured toe. "I can only imagine how much worse the place looks at night, with shadows thrown into the mix. I can see why *Paranormal Territory* would get psyched out enough to think they saw something here. But I researched the area thoroughly. While it's a training ground for both military and local law enforcement, there have been no deaths or unfortunate accidents here."

"We should have gone to Alcatraz," Roger muttered.

"We were asked to come here," the brunette said, sounding exasperated. "It would have been fucked up to take off just because we got a better offer."

The sound of an approaching helicopter grew uncustomarily loud and snared the attention of everyone in the room. Callaghan, in particular, widened his stance as if preparing for battle.

"Why does that chopper sound like it's flying directly over us?" the redhead breathed, her arms wrapping around her middle.

"I am certain that is normal for a military base," Claire said, but the quaver in her voice ruined any chance of her words soothing.

They were completely clueless. It was all too much fun.

The brunette stood and moved to the front picture window. "It does sound awfully close. Almost like it's going to land."

They were too distracted to notice when the doors and windows were sealed, both with secular locks and a containment/warding spell. No one could come in, and no one could get out. There would be no escape.

Within the hour, they would all be dead . . .

The men's side of the duplex was abuzz with activity.

Richens's pale cadaver was splayed on a collapsible gurney. Two E.P.D. investigators bent over his remains, probing into the gaping wounds to collect evidence and reach some helpful conclusions.

There had been a lot to like about Richens—selfishness, arrogance, lack of remorse, the way his intestines had gushed out of his body like fat, slippery sausages. A shame he'd been marked. With his fondness for half-truths and manipulation, he would have made an amusing court jester.

"Hey." One of investigators looked up with a smile, which faded when she saw the bloodstains on his clothes. "What happened to you?"

Laurel turned to face him, her pretty glittered face changing from welcoming to concern. "Oh no! Are you hurt?"

With Havoc home with Sammael, there was no longer any need to save the Mark blood to feed the hellhound with. And with the Marks' deaths imminent, there was no more reason to hide who he was. He would greet the Alpha with his war paint on—the evidence of his kills dripping from his muzzle and claws.

He took in the room's occupants with a sweeping glance. Two investigators and two female Mark trainees—Seiler and Hogan. Three guards and Montevista were locked outside. Callaghan and Dubois were across the street. Hank—the only possible fly in the ointment—was occupied in Anytown, along with two more guards. They all expected the threat to come from without rather than from within.

He made a show of stumbling as if wounded and was caught by Laurel's soft, pale arms. She was sexy, susceptible to manipulation, and blessed with a ravenous, juicy cunt. Just the way he liked his women. She'd spread her legs every time he snapped his fingers and in doing so, had spread her Mark scent all over him.

"Let her go, Garza."

Hollis's voice momentarily took him aback, then a slow smile curved his mouth. What few weapons they'd brought with them were packed in the Suburban and Hollis's skill with a sword was mediocre, at best. He had every confidence he could take her.

Deliberately keeping his back to her because he knew nonchalance would rattle a newbie Mark, he said, "Make me, *bella*."

"Bugger off," Laurel snapped. "Find your own man."

"You cannot have all the men, Hollis," Seiler intruded.

Women. They were their own worst enemy.

"He's not a man," Hollis retorted.

Laurel tossed her hair over her shoulder. "Uh, I think I would know if he wasn't."

"You should sit this one out, Evangeline," he said, glancing over his shoulder. "The Alpha is here now. In just a few minutes, this will all be over."

"It'll be over *for you*," she corrected.

She stood at the mouth of the hallway, her dark eyes hard and wrathful, her fists clenched. But her frown gave her away. She knew he wasn't a Mark, but she didn't know who he was or remember their history together. She couldn't recognize him through the glamour.

"What the fuck are you talking about?" Laurel demanded. "Why do you have blood all over you, Antonio? And why are you squeezing me so tight? I can't breathe."

His smile widened into a grin. "The better to kill you, my dear," he whispered for her ears alone.

Gripping Laurel tightly to him, he set his hands on either side of her spine and extended his claws, ripping deep into her liver and kidneys. She would have screamed if he hadn't restricted her chest. She looked at him with horror-filled blue eyes, her lips lovely as they parted to expel her last breath. He inhaled it deep into his lungs like a lover's kiss.

His animal senses picked up the whistle of a blade, and he jerked to the side to narrowly avoid the flame-covered dagger aimed at his head. "You suck," he taunted Hollis.

A rapid volley of blazing knives shot toward him. He dropped Laurel's corpse and ducked.

Spewing a stream of German, Seiler tackled Hollis.

Regaining his footing, he took on his wolf form and lunged for the nearest investigator. His teeth perforated the jugular before they hit the hardwood. Sweet, syrupy blood gushed down his throat, and he growled with open-throated triumph.

Pounding came to the door and the guards yelled for entry. The cacophony created a unique and provocative requiem. It made him want to howl with joy, so he did.

Seiler and Hollis continued to fight like hissing cats. The second investigator withdrew a pistol from beneath her lab coat and aimed. The fired bullets pierced excruciatingly through fur and flesh, but the mask mitigated the silver that would otherwise slow him down. Finally, the gun clicked repeatedly with no report. Realizing the magazine was empty, the investigator screamed.

He vaulted forward and took her down for the kill.

In the "ghost hunter" house, the sound of panicked shouting in the neighborhood lured everyone to the window. The group stood shoulder-to-shoulder as a unit, exposing their backs as they watched the guards across the street scurry like ants.

"Why can't they get in?" the brunette asked. "Look at them. They're pounding on the doors and windows."

"I should be there," Callaghan said, tension gripping his powerful frame.

"Go," the redhead said. "They need you."

He shook his head. "I gave my word tae stay here."

"We're fine," the brunette insisted. "We'll just—Wow!"

"What the hell?" Roger's tone was awed. "There are at least a half dozen of them!"

Wolves. Big ones. Running from the direction of Anytown in a cohesive pack. A large wolf with a white diamond patch on the forehead led the group.

The Alpha was here. After three weeks, the time had finally come. She had hated him once. Detested him for raising her grandson as a wolf rather than the mage he was. Her only child had died giving birth to his son, and Charles repaid her memory by ignoring Timothy's magical birthright. She had done everything in her power to turn Timothy against his father, but now she looked to Charles as the deliverer of her vengeance.

"Ready to die?" she asked sweetly.

They turned and faced her. Callaghan scowled. "What?"

She smiled and killed the dog first, throwing a ball of pure, icy evil that the stupid creature chased and bit into. It screamed and rolled to its back, legs sticking upright and jerking quite dramatically.

"Jesus, Claire!" the brunette cried. "What the hell did you throw at—?"

Shedding the glamour of the Frenchwoman, Kenise revealed her true form. Then, she went after Callaghan.

She hit him with enough force to lift him from his feet and slam him through the nearest wall, embedding him in the drywall. He hung splayed like a starfish, his black turtleneck smoldering right between his pectorals. A direct hit.

That left her with the mortals, who stood frozen with shock. She smiled and rubbed her hands together.

She struck Roger next, knocking out the kids in order of threat level. The men first, then the girls. But when she turned to the brunette, the redhead lunged at her, toppling her to the floor.

Stunned by the unexpected attacked, Kenise began to laugh. A mortal taking on a witch? It was comical. Then, the redhead pushed up and smiled a cat-with-cream smile that chilled Kenise into silence.

The pink and purple dress changed, turning to black as if afflicted with a spreading ink stain. It swept over bare arms and legs, turning into long sleeves and floor-length skirts. The strawberry-blonde tresses lengthened, the hue deepening into a darker, richer shade of red. The pretty features morphed from fresh youth to stunning, bewitching beauty.

"Evangeline was right," it murmured, in a gravely male voice so at odds with the highly feminine appearance. "She swore the traitor would come after the college kids if they were given the opportunity."

Kenise gaped, her brain arrested in midthought by utter surprise.

The rapid clicking of canine paws turned her attention and her head. Her eyes widened at the sight of the Great Dane, who changed midstride, growing in height into a lumbering dragon. "Cain's woman is a smart cookie," it rumbled.

Roger pushed up from the ground, dusting himself off. He sighed over the gaping hole in his chest that went clear through to the other side, then altered into a faery of such blinding beauty Kenise was enamored with the sight of him. Tall and lean with pale blond hair, pointed ears, blue eyes, and a winsome smile, the prince was the most gorgeous creature she had ever seen. "I was certain the empty driveway and house would give us away," he said. "You're dumber than you look."

The gravity of her situation sank into her stunned brain along with the horror sinking into the very marrow of her bones. Three Infernals. There was no way for her to fight them all off. She would have to appeal to their dark side and pray to Sammael that they could be lured home.

A groan came from the wall and Callaghan slowly roused. "'At wis a helluva dunt tae my heid."

"How . . . ?" Kenise gasped, feeling her hopes die. She might have had a chance if only Infernals were present, but with a Mark around it was a long shot convincing them to return to the fold.

"We protected him with warding. Couldn't leave him hanging out to dry," the dragon explained in his guttural voice. "We like him."

"What should we do with this, Aeronwen?" the redhead asked, looking at the brunette while gesturing to Kenise.

"Let's train the Mark how to vanquish witches." The brunette's glamour fell from her like a shrugged-off cloak, revealing a gray-haired woman in a gray suit. A gwyllion. Incapable of creating her own glamour, which meant one of the others had created it for her while wearing his own.

Four powerful Infernals and a Mark. She had no chance. None.

The faery shifted into the guise of Pinocchio's Blue Fairy. "I agree. No need to let her go to waste."

"I don't smell you," Kenise managed through dry lips. "Any of you."

The redhead's smile lacked even a semblance of warmth or humor. "Did you think you were the only one who could create the mask? Once I had the materials, the rest was simple. Of course, I admire your pioneering spirit. The mask was very clever."

"You are a traitor to your own kind!"

"My kind?" The gwyllion stepped forward. "My kind is those who want to keep me alive."

"Sammael would take you back," Kenise said quickly. "You have insider knowledge he desires."

"You presume to speak for Sammael?" the faery asked quietly. "You *are* stupid."

The redhead stood, removing her not-inconsiderable weight, but when Kenise attempted to regain her feet, she was restrained. With just a single snap of the faery's fingers, her arms were splayed and palms staked into the hardwood in semblance of a crucifixion. Screaming, she fought the magic and broke free, only to be repositioned just as quickly as the first time. She continued to struggle until exhaustion set in.

Murder by numbers. There were too many of them. Infernals who had used her own creation against her. The plan had been perfect. Brilliant. They would have gotten away with it, if it hadn't been for that meddling Evangeline.

"We can do this all day," the faery drawled. "Or we can just get on with it and you can rejoin your dear Malachai in Hell."

Malachai. Her spouse, lover, partner-in-crime. His contribution to her spell had made the mask possible . . . and it had cost them his life by Abel's vengeful hands.

"Go help the others," the redhead said to the dragon. Her gaze moved to the gwyllion. "Bernard and I will commence training."

Callaghan came forward, shaking off the drywall debris. "I'll ask fer explanations later. Right now, I just want tae know how to kill this bajin."

Kenise closed her eyes and thought of Malachai.

CHAPTER 19

"What the fuck is the matter with you?" Eve shouted, yanking on Izzie's hair. Smoke was roiling down the hallway, churning through the air like a tidal wave, clogging her throat and burning her lungs. Somewhere in the house, a window shattered.

"What is—" Izzie gasped for breathable air, "the matter with *you*? Attacking Garza—"

Gaining her knees, Eve yanked the blonde up by her hair and pointed at the wolf presently devouring the investigator's throat. "Does that look like Garza to you?"

Izzie froze. Eve hauled back and socked her square in the jaw, knocking her out. She dropped the blonde back onto the floor and struggled to her feet, screeching when she was hauled upward and clasped back-to-front to a steely frame.

"Did you have to hit her?" Reed asked, his lips to her ear. He was scorching hot, as if he were giving off a great deal of energy.

"Yes, actually, I did."

His hand fisted between her breasts and ripped something from around her neck. Instantly, a surfeit of emotion poured into her—his and Alec's. As soon as they reconnected, Alec shut himself off like a spigot, but Reed's mind latched onto hers with something akin to desperation.

She looked down at his hand and in his palm saw the Sigil of Baphomet amulet—the official insignia of the Church of Satan, a symbol adopted by Sammael himself because he thought its design was clever. Reed dropped it, revealing a smoldering burn in his palm.

Her gaze returned to the wolf, who lifted his head and leered at her with his bloody, gaping maw. The pounding on the door stopped. A moment later the sounds of battle rang out in the yard—growling and barking, shouting and cursing. Screaming.

"Get Izzie out of here," Eve said, tensing for her own fight.

"I'm not leaving you in here with him."

"And I'm not leaving Izzie to the wolf, even if she is enough of a pain in the ass to deserve it."

"Shit." He released her. "Two seconds."

She felt him collecting Izzie behind her, followed by the soft breeze that accompanied his shifting away.

"Can you take me in mortal form?" she goaded the wolf. "Or do you need to be in animal form to win?"

The wolf shifted before her, taking on the shape of a ghost she recognized. At least he should have been a ghost, considering she'd killed him once already. Recognition hit her hard, followed by an immediate chill down her spine.

"You," she said.

"Me." He smiled.

Eve's heart dropped into her stomach. How was she supposed to kill something that wouldn't stay dead?

"You're going to break the steering wheel if you don't ease up." Giselle shouted to be heard over the roar of the Mustang's powerful engine and the surrounding freeway traffic.

Alec glanced at his white knuckles, startled to see a visible sign of tension he didn't feel. He forced his grip to relax. They flew past Gilroy, weaving through cars as recklessly as possible.

Forty-five minutes to Monterey. But then it should have been an hour and a half to Gilroy. He'd cut that travel time almost in half.

He was changing lanes between two cars when Eve hit his brain like a ton of bricks, blackening his vision and thrusting his head back against the headrest. Swerving, Alec lost control of the Mustang, the car fishtailing and skidding recklessly.

Giselle screamed. Car horns blared. Tires squealed.

Jerking the steering wheel, Alec fought to keep the sports car on the road. Vehicles flew by all around him. It was only by the grace of God that they reached the shoulder of the highway without hitting another car. Yanking on the emergency brake, he maneuvered the Mustang into an abrupt, violent halt just an inch shy of a guardrail.

"Jesus fucking Christ!" Giselle shouted, gasping. "What the hell was that?"

He unhooked his seat belt. "I have to go."

"*What?*" Her hand whipped over and caught his. "Go where?"

"To McCroskey." His gaze met hers. "He's there already. He flew."

She stilled. "Oh, shit."

Alec pushed open the door and climbed out. "Just keep driving south and follow the signs."

"To where?"

"Wherever. Anaheim. Mexico. Hell. You might end up there anyway within an hour or two."

Her jaw tightened and she crawled over to the driver's seat. "I'll meet you there. Don't get yourself killed."

He was already gone.

Eve stared at the teenage son of the Alpha and wondered how he could look the same, yet different. She'd guess he was sixteen. Seventeen at the most. His hair was still a mop of dark waves that fell to his shoulders. He still had a weak chin, and a pouty, sullen mouth. But his hazel eyes were colder, more barren than before. Soulless, and drowning in malice and bloodlust.

He was also buck naked, which gave her the willies. Pubescent boys had never been her thing. She'd kept her virginity until she was almost eighteen, then she gave it to Alec. A virile, potent *man* . . . several centuries her senior.

The pounding at the door resumed, Reed shouting words she couldn't understand. His near-panic, however, was palpable and gave her courage. The wolf was using his magical side to keep Reed out.

I'm coming, Reed thought grimly. *You stay alive until I do.*

No worries, she said with pure bravado. In truth, she was scared nearly witless. A wolf with magic. Just what she'd always wanted.

In response, Reed bolstered her the best way he could. The mark on her arm began to tingle and burn, pumping celestially enhanced adrenaline through her system. Her senses honed, her muscles thickened. Permission granted to kick some demon ass.

"He can't come back for you, you know," the wolf murmured, circling around Richens's corpse. "I've locked us in a warding/containment spell."

"Great. No one to interfere while I kill you."

"For years," he continued, "I couldn't control my wolf or my magic. Now, thanks to being cooked in Mark bone and blood meal, I can control both."

As understanding dawned, Eve exhaled in a rush. He'd been locked in with the kiln in Upland when it exploded—a kiln that had been stuffed with all the ingredients to make the Infernal mask, including Mark blood and bone meal, which were remarkable for their regenerative properties.

It's how they made the hellhounds, Alec said.

Hellhounds?

I'll explain as soon as I get in there.

Alec was outside with Reed. Her heroes. Unfortunately, it looked as if she would be stuck saving herself. Against a wolf with magic. Without a weapon she was proficient with.

She sidestepped in opposition to him, keeping him directly across from her. At least the gurney hid the lower half of his body from view, although it kept Richens's mutilated cadaver a bit too close for comfort. She tried not to look. "I really don't give a damn about your existential angst or your shitty childhood," she retorted. "All I care about is how to kill you so you stay dead."

Smoke tumbled across the ceiling, black and gray, like specters on the hunt. In the rear of the house, the fire ate through wood and drywall with gleeful cackling. To make things worse, she was facing a hybrid who had a lot more experience than she did, despite his youth.

"Aw, gimme a break," he teased, as if they were friends or people who liked each other. "I don't want to kill you. I want to turn you over as a gift. You're not a believer anyway. What does it matter which side you're on?"

Eve choked on smoke. "You're k-kidding."

"I'm going to get a car out of my dad for this." His dead eyes brightened at the thought. "A Porsche like the one in the driveway. The bitches will love it."

She'd love to run him over with it, the little bastard. She tossed a flaming dagger at his right side just for the hell of it, then followed it up with another to the left. When he ducked away from the first, the second nicked him on the shoulder. Then it smashed into a jar of something on a crate behind him that exploded into flames. The ignited liquid splattered on him and he cursed, tamping the fire out with swats of his hands.

Eve raised her arms in triumph, relishing the wild aggressive energy the mark was pumping through her veins. "Yes!"

"Stupid whore." His lips curled back from his teeth.

"Asshole," she countered.

He feinted to the left, then the right, trying to psych her out. She laughed instead. It was a shaky, rather unconvincing sound, but it was still a shock to hear, which was the point. Sometimes bullshit was all a Mark had to keep the tension even.

The wolf growled and shoved the table at her, prompting her to jump back. Richens's body tumbled to her feet.

Then she realized she had a weapon after all—his temper. She'd seen it before, the last time they met. When she provoked him, he'd become careless and violent. He'd run straight into her roundhouse kick and gotten his dumb ass knocked out.

The house is on fire, Alec said.

No shit? I thought it smelled like barbeque.

You're *going to be barbequed,* Reed snapped, *if you don't get the hell out of there.*

From the ruckus outside, she guessed they were brawling. Hopefully against the Infernals and not with each other.

Bummer, she thought, *I was hoping to hang out here awhile. It's so pleasant and—*

Eve! they shouted in unison.

"You should have dropped the glamour before you killed Laurel," she said to the wolf, "let her see what she's been fucking the last three weeks. Or were you afraid to?"

"I'm not afraid of anything! I've done what no other Infernal ever has."

The smoke began to thicken and lower from the ceiling, swirling around their heads and blistering their breathing passages.

"She said you sucked in bed," she went on. "No finesse. But the Antonio glamour was hot enough to make it bearable. Wonder what she would have thought if she'd seen that you're just a kid."

"I'm not a fucking kid!"

Eve opened her mouth to continue, but he threw a bluish glowing ball straight into her sternum. The impact lifted her feet from the floor and slammed her into a crate the size of a refrigerator. She crashed through plywood and into sawdust, the room spinning from the force of the blow.

"Is that all you've got?" she wheezed. "No wonder Laurel was bored."

He leaped across the overturned gurney and landed in a crouch. "You should have heard her begging for it," he snarled. "She couldn't get enough."

She squirmed free of the crate and fell to her knees, sucking scorching, ashy air into beleaguered lungs. The mark helped her to heal fast, but it didn't make her invincible. At least there was less smoke closer to the floor. "So you say . . . but that's not what she told me."

His fingers and toes lengthened into claws. The skin across his back rippled with fur, then returned to skin. "I'll show you," he growled, stalking forward. "I'll fuck you till you scream."

The ground fell away. Eve found herself levitating a foot above the hardwood floor, then slamming backward into it, splayed. Magic stayed her. She couldn't move more than her head, fingers, and toes. Fear coiled insidiously through her gut, despite the steady pumping of adrenaline and bloodlust through her veins.

The wolf came closer, half boy and half beast. He was leering, his eyes triumphant, his cock hard.

Eve laughed softly, knowing she was either going to succeed beautifully or fail miserably. "Do your worst," she taunted. "With a dick that small, I won't even feel it."

He pounced, altering into his wolf form midleap.

She waited, holding off until the last possible moment, shaking like a leaf and grateful she couldn't vomit.

As if in slow motion, he came at her, hovering over her. His mouth was wide, his teeth bared.

"Now," she whispered, crossing her fingers that she wouldn't be denied. A flame-covered silver sword appeared in her hand, facing upward and ready.

He speared himself cleanly, the blade sliding through fur and flesh like a hot knife through butter. A horrendous howl turned into a sick gurgling.

As the magical hold he'd had on her released, Eve rolled, taking the top. She lurched to her feet, yanking the blade free and swinging it downward with all her might. The instant the tip hit hardwood, both the severed head and body disintegrated into ash.

"Eve!"

"Angel."

She spun to face the two men who charged into the house. Freed from the necessity of watching the wolf, Eve took in the state of the house. Fire licked along the walls from the hallway, rushing toward the fresh air introduced through the front door. The blaze she'd started in the bedroom had spread to the kitchen. The whole house creaked in protest, shuddering at its impending collapse.

Alec reached her first, snatching her up and tossing her over his shoulder. The sword clattered to the floor.

"Time to go," he muttered.

The next instant she found herself by the Porsche, disoriented and barely breathing. Around her was chaos. Twin piles of ash dotted the lawn, as did the bodies of two Mark guards. Two wolves fought with those who remained standing. The dragon was acting as cover for the Marks, spewing fire according to the directions shouted from the gwyllion, who stood on the roof of the van.

"Is he d-dead?" she gasped, clinging to Alec as the sky swirled madly above her. "Is the wolf really dead this time?"

Reed's voice came clipped and furious, "I'd say so."

"Are you sure?" she persisted. "We burned him up before and the son of a bitch came back."

Alec pressed his lips to her forehead and released her. "Ash is ash, there's no coming back from that. Can you get Montevista out of here?"

Eve blinked. "What?"

He gestured to the passenger seat where the guard lay crumbled, his black shirt glistening wetly, his throat torn and gushing. If he were mortal, he'd be long dead. As a Mark, he was damn close to it. Defenseless and vulnerable.

Reed pressed keys into her palm. "Go."

A piercing howl rent the air. They turned their heads and saw a massive wolf on the front steps. It stared at them with bared teeth and glowing red eyes. The white diamond on its forehead told her who it was, but she asked anyway, "Is that Daddy?"

"Get the fuck out of here!" Alec yelled, his wings snapping free with such force that Eve was plastered to the hood. Reed joined the fray, the two brothers launching forward, intercepting the wolf, who charged at her full-bore while flanked on either side by two wolves.

Black and white wings, powerful masculine bodies, ferocious beasts . . . She was arrested by the sight. The eternal conflict between angel and demon. The battle cries and howls of pain. The smell of fire and ash, of blood and urine.

"Hollis . . ."

Montevista's weak voice snapped her back to reality. Eve slid off the hood. She leaped over the driver's-side door of the open convertible and hopped into the seat. She turned the key in the ignition and the powerful engine roared like a dream. She squealed out of the driveway in reverse, running over an attacking wolf in the process.

Gripping the stick shift, she slammed the transmission into gear and punched the gas. She adjusted the rearview mirror, trying to see the fracas behind her. Montevista yelled in terror. Eve's gaze shot forward and she screamed, too. She stood on the brake. The Porsche's rear end fishtailed wildly, the car skidding down the street passenger side first . . .

. . . straight for the house-size, flesh-colored beast thundering toward them.

The car juddered to a halt.

"Fuck me," she breathed, then coughed as her lungs burned. Was that the hellhound?

Turn around and run, Alec bit out. *Only Infernals can kill it.*

Wasn't that just really damned inconvenient?

She looked back at the blazing house and the two winged men who circled low over it, combating the wolves that poured out of a widening hole in the ground. Satan was sending reinforcements. They couldn't deal with the behemoth from Hell on top of that. No way.

One wolf broke free of the melee and raced toward her, foaming at the mouth and lathered at the throat. The Alpha.

Eve restarted the stalled car and spun around, hurtling toward the wolf with the same reckless intent he displayed. If it was just a game of chicken between a canine and a car, she'd know who would win. But against a werewolf . . . She gripped the steering wheel tighter and shifted gears in rapid succession.

A foot away from impact, the wolf leaped onto the hood, his massive claws piercing through the metal. He roared at her through the windshield, his red eyes wild and filled with evil. He lunged headfirst into the safety glass, shattering it.

Fucking A.

Downshifting, Eve yanked the steering wheel hard left and spun the car back around, skidding across the empty street and hitting a curb. The bump dislodged the wolf, who slid across the hood and almost fell off before gaining purchase at the very nose.

She gunned it, putting the Porsche through its paces as she accelerated toward the approaching mega-Infernal. Zero to sixty in less than four seconds.

"This might not work," she shouted at Montevista.

"Go down in a blaze of glory," he said back.

"Give me your gun."

Montevista pulled the weapon free of his thigh holster and racked it, then handed it over. She aimed and fired through the wolf, the Glock autoloading and discharging again and again and again. The sixth bullet widened the hole in the Alpha's shoulder and pierced through the other side, hitting the hellhound. Covered in werewolf blood, the bullet penetrated the beast's hide. Eve continued to fire, punching through the back of the wolf to injure the hound with nearly every shot.

The hound screamed in fury and lunged. Eve punched the gas. With the Alpha as a hood ornament, she hit the beast head on. The wolf's head sank muzzle-first into the hellhound's belly before he disintegrated into ash. The Infernal bellowed, then exploded, spraying Eve and Montevista with a deluge of gore.

Unable to see, she ran the Porsche over a curb and crashed into an oak tree. The air bags deployed and her head slammed forward into the pillow, then back into the headrest.

The world came to an abrupt stop.

Eve groaned and looked at Montevista. He was slumped over the dash, eyes open and sightless. Crying, she tried to open the driver's-side door, but was unable to.

Strong arms plucked her out. She fell into Reed's embrace with a sob of relief. "He's dead. Montevista's dead."

The arms that held her were shaking. "You're fucking nuts, you know that? Absolutely insane. What the hell were you thinking?"

Thinking? Her brain had stopped working when Alec beamed her out of the house. "I—"

A massive explosion shook the very ground they stood on. Looking around Reed's shoulder, she saw flames from the duplex shoot toward the heavens. Another enormous *boom!* had her ducking her face into his chest.

Then her feet left the ground and they were moving.

"What—?"

"Gasoline," he bit out, tossing her over his shoulder as Alec had done.

Eve smelled it then. Her head lifted to watch and found Alec fast on their heels. They were barely across the street before the Porsche went the way of the house, erupting into a billowing inferno.

Reed put her down and stared at the destruction with an arm around her shoulders. Alec drew abreast of them and took a position on the other side of her. The light of the twin blazes set him aglow, burnishing him in a way that made her look twice.

"You okay?" he asked.

She patted herself down, searching for any spots of soreness or grotesquely protruding bones. "I think so."

An unknown blonde in shorts and a tank top came running toward them. "Un-fucking-believable!" she shouted.

"Do we know that person?" Reed asked.

"You do now," Alec replied, sounding resigned. "Meet Giselle, the Mare."

"She just ran over Sammael's dog!" Giselle yelled, clutching her head.

A blazing chrome wheel rim rolled toward them and came to a shuddering stop at the curb.

"And destroyed another expensive car," Alec said.

"And blew up another building," Reed added.

"What does that matter at a time like this?" Eve snapped, fighting to stay upright. Everything around her was spinning like a top, and blood and tissue were dripping from her hair and clothes.

"If I think about how this place got this way," Reed muttered, "I might go stark raving mad."

The Porsche collapsed to the ground with a loud groan. The passenger door popped open and Montevista's charred body tumbled free.

Eve thought she might pass out. Then the body got up and walked toward her, and she really did.

CHAPTER 20

I am impressed with your performance, Evangeline."

Eve stared at the stunning blonde at the end of the conference table and felt uneasy. The way Sarakiel said her name was . . . creepy, as was the intensity with which the archangel watched her.

They sat in one of the conference rooms in Gadara Tower. In addition to her and Sara, both Reed and Alec were present, plus Montevista and Hank. On one of the walls, a bank of video screens aired feeds from the offices of the other archangels. Five impossibly beautiful faces stared at her, watching her with the same intensity as Sara. It took every bit of self-control Eve had to sit still and not wiggle nervously.

Two days ago it had seemed as if Armageddon was here. Today they were drinking tea from a Victorian-style tea service and recapping the events that constituted the worst training disaster in Mark history.

"What made you think of the photographs?" Sara asked her.

"I needed proof," she explained. "I suspected there was a traitor in the group after Reed and I established a timeline for Molenaar's murder. Since Claire is the one who provided the benchmark and she didn't have an alibi, I thought of her first. It wasn't until I saw the picture and realized Rome—*Garza* had a visible mark, too, that it hit me: he was the one who volunteered to put the armbands on everyone. Probably because he didn't want to risk either his grandmother or himself getting caught."

"You did not see this when you read her, Hank?" Michael asked, his voice as resonant as a harp. Eve kept her eyes downcast, unable to look at him without quaking. As gorgeous as he was with his dark hair and brilliant blue eyes, he was also terrifying. There was something . . . lethal about him. A darkness in his eyes that hinted at volatile, frightening depths. If someone told her that he was Satan, she'd believe it. As formidable as Raguel and Sara were, they seemed almost friendly in comparison.

"The last time I read her was before she saw the photos," Hank said. Presently in the guise of a man, he lounged with studied insouciance and offered the occasional supportive smile to Eve. "I knew she suspected someone and I followed her plan to assume the guise of the ghost hunters, but I was clueless as to the identity of the Infernals until after they attacked."

Eve waited for someone to ask why Alec and Reed didn't know, considering their insight into her mind, but no one did.

They don't know we're tied together, Alec said.

She looked at him. He sat at the opposite head of the table from Sara. While Sara was dressed faultlessly in a blood-red pantsuit, Alec was wearing his own classic attire of worn jeans and a fitted T-shirt. His hair needed a cut and deep grooves rimmed either side of his mouth, but neither detracted from his appearance. He was still hot as hell.

His dark eyes narrowed slightly. *We're keeping that information hidden from them—for now—but we're going to have to figure out how you hid information from us.*

She'd hidden her thoughts on purpose. They so firmly believed that the mark system was impenetrable by Infernals that they'd refused to listen to her. But . . . maybe she wasn't supposed to be able to hide her thoughts from them?

"It was Hank's penchant for red hair in all his guises that gave me the idea," Eve offered, earning a wink from Hank.

"How did the Infernals get into the class to begin with?" Uriel asked. He seemed to be the most laid back of the archangels, but that didn't make him less forbidding.

"As near as we can tell," Alec said, "they were watching Sara's firm. When the real Antonio Garza and Claire Dubois became marked, Timothy and Kenise took over their identities. Once they were in training, Timothy's sexual activities with Hogan kept him smelling like a Mark. Kenise wore glasses that had porous arm sleeves soaked in a concentrate of Mark blood proteins. Her beauty supplies were also laced with it. The masking agent was continuously administered through their watches, which had reservoirs on the underside."

"There is more to identity than mere appearance and smell," Sara said defensively.

"If we assume that Les Goodman's theory is true, they probably used the hellhounds. The hounds absorbed Garza and Dubois's memories, which they passed on to Timothy and Kenise. Because the two Marks had yet to be assigned to a handler, they didn't have the ability to send out a herald. There was no way for anyone to know they were dead."

"Refresh my memory," Raphael said. "Why do we wait until after training to assign Marks to handlers?"

"Because it's a pain in the ass otherwise," Reed said. Dressed in a three-piece Versace suit, he put everyone in the room in the pale—except for Sara, who eyed him with obvious hunger. Eve tried not to think about how that bothered her. "The trainees were sending out heralds during exercises, distracting the handlers unnecessarily and putting other Marks in danger."

"There could be more imposters," Eve mused.

Everyone looked at her.

Sara shook her head. "Once they graduate and establish a connection to a handler, they would be discovered."

"But how much damage can be done in the interim?" Gabriel asked. His unshakable demeanor reminded Eve of Raguel. Both archangels projected the appearance of having an inner core so solid it made them unflappable. The others seemed more capricious. "We should test every untrained Mark to be certain."

"Montevista." Remiel's voice flowed through the room. "How are you feeling?"

The guard straightened. "Better than ever, actually."

The archangel turned his gaze to Hank. "Can you explain what happened? Why is Montevista with us today?"

"The same thing that happened to Grimshaw's son," Hank replied. "In a nutshell: high heat combined with the masking agent. There are other factors involved—animal DNA, a spell or two—but that's the gist. The hellhounds were made viable by using a similar Mark blood/bone mixture as the Infernal mask, so when the hound's blood splattered over Montevista and the car exploded, it created a situation not unlike the kiln incident."

"Only Jehovah should have the power to preserve life," Michael said in a tone that made Eve want to hide under the table.

"Do we have any idea how many of the hellhounds are in existence?" Sara asked.

"One. A male. Eve killed the bitch. I took care of the pups. That leaves only the sire."

"Have we heard anything about Raguel?" Uriel asked.

"No," Reed answered. "Nothing."

"Perhaps he is dead."

"Jehovah would have told us if that was true," Alec countered.

Frankly, Eve thought it was pretty fucked that God didn't tell them how to get Raguel out, but that wasn't a discussion she was going to have in present company.

"I've got something." Eve reached for the cell phone Montevista obligingly pushed her way. She flipped through the menu until she came to the ringtones, then she played the default one. When it finished, she said, "When I first heard the tune, I recognized it as a Paul Simon song—my mom's a big fan—but I couldn't place the name. Now, I know it's 'Jonah.'"

The group stared at her.

"'They say Jonah was swallowed by a whale,'" she sang softly, "'but I say there's no truth to that tale . . .'"

More silence.

"Didn't Jonah survive in the belly of the whale and come out unscathed?" she prodded. "Can't be a coincidence, right? I'm always told there's no such thing."

Montevista nodded. "Blows me away that you caught that."

"Thank you, Ms. Hollis," Gabriel said. "We will take it from here."

Take it where? Would they go as far as Hell?

Raphael moved on. "How many of Raguel's trainees are left?"

"Three." Alec's fingertips drummed into the tabletop. "Hollis, Callaghan, and Seiler."

"They will have to join the next class." Raphael bent his dark head—only Sara and Uriel were fair-haired—to read something on his desk. "Which will be Michael's."

Eve swallowed hard.

"I can pick up where Raguel left off," Sara offered. "Since I am already here."

Shit.

The curse came from both Reed and Alec simultaneously, which took Eve aback. But the other archangels readily agreed.

"Thank you for your input," Sara said, looking at both Eve and Montevista. "You are both dismissed."

They stood and left the room. Eve didn't look back. She didn't have to. If Reed or Alec had anything to say, they'd do it in her head, not with their expressions.

"We live to fight another day," Montevista said, winking at her.

Eve reached out and gripped his hand. "I'm glad."

Oddly enough, she really was.

Cap and gown. Eve never thought she would wear them again. Yet here she was, walking across a stage with diploma in hand and a crowd of fully fledged Marks applauding madly. The day was clear, warm Southern California perfection. The setting sun's rays fell like a benediction through the skylight of Gadara Tower onto the crowd in the atrium below. It was late Sunday afternoon and the office was closed to the public.

Eve stepped down from the stage and a tall, dark figure intercepted her.

"Congratulations." Reed's voice was a purring, seductive rumble. He was always exquisitely dressed, but today he seemed especially so. His graphite gray suit was set off by a pristine white shirt and robin's egg blue tie. His hair was both the perfect length and perfectly styled. His scent was subtle but addictive, luring a woman to lean closer to get a deeper whiff of it. The outer civilized trappings were so deceptive. Beneath them was a primitive man with very rough edges. But she rather liked him that way.

She pulled the cap off her head. "Thank you."

"Have any plans tonight?"

In her heart of hearts, she had hoped Alec would get in touch with her, at least on this day. But she hadn't seen nor heard from him since they spoke at the meeting with the archangels more than a month ago. Considering that they lived next door to each other and their condos shared a wall, she could only conclude that he was avoiding her. Her parents assumed they'd broken up. Eve figured his failure to appear at her graduation was proof of that. "No. No plans."

"Care to go out to dinner?"

"I would love to."

Reed had stayed away, too, although mentally, he'd been there. Rumor had it that there was history between him and Sara, which kept him at bay. Those whispers had prompted Eve to keep her head down the last four weeks of class, which actually hadn't been difficult, considering how intensive training was. While it wasn't said implicitly, there was the sense that they were preparing for more than just regular Infernal hunting. Eve hoped they were gearing up to go after Gadara. She still believed he was alive somewhere, waiting for them to come and get him.

"Give me a minute," she said, "to get out of this robe."

Half expecting a crude offer of help, she was surprised when he simply nodded. "My car is out front. Meet you outside?"

"Okay . . ." She sensed that something was different about him today. He was more somber, perhaps. More serious.

Eve hurriedly dropped off her cap and gown in an anteroom. She retouched her lip gloss and adjusted the straps of her black satin dress. Pausing, she took in her appearance—the strappy heels she hadn't worn in so long they made her feet hurt, the dress that was a size too big now that she was exercising so much, the silver hoop earrings that would be a hazard in a fight. She'd given herself leeway today, figuring she had earned the right to dress up and be normal. Especially in the safety of Gadara Tower. Now she was grateful that she looked edible (if she did say so herself) because for once, she complemented Reed instead of looking like a charity case.

She found him in the circular drive, sans coat, leaning against the passenger door of a silver Lamborghini Gallardo Spyder. The top was down, his shades were on. Together *mal'akh* and machine made a lethal combination. Her breath caught at the sight of them.

He stared at her for a long, taut moment in which she was certain he undressed her mentally. She could almost feel it through the bond between them—the whisper of his fingertips against her skin as he pushed her straps aside, the press of his lips against her throat, the low groan of desire.

But it wouldn't be that way at all. That was Alec's style. Reed was rough and tumble.

"A guy can change," he murmured, opening the door for her.

Eve smiled as she slipped into the seat. "Who says I want you to?"

He took her to Savannah on the Beach on Pacific Coast Highway, not too far from where she lived. They sat by a window, but she didn't enjoy the view of the water. She was too busy studying him and trying to figure out what he was thinking. He seemed pensive, which didn't jibe with a celebratory dinner.

"So," she began, breaking the silence, "do you always take your graduating Marks out to dinner?"

Reed's lips pursed, then he shook his head. "They don't get assigned to a handler until a week or so after graduation."

"To what do I owe this honor, then?"

There was a drawn-out pause before he said gruffly, "Today was the day you finally decided that you're single."

Wow. Okay. "Is this a date?"

"Yeah . . . Am I doing it wrong?"

It took a moment for her to realize he was serious. An internal shiver moved through her. She shouldn't be surprised that an actual date wasn't part of his repertoire. He was the kind of man who picked up a woman just by giving her "the look." Hell, that's how he'd picked *her* up. Next thing she knew, she'd been in the stairwell of Gadara Tower getting the ride of her life.

She leaned back in her chair. "You're a little tense." She'd tell him to drink a little, but mind-altering substances had no effect on celestially enhanced beings. The body is a temple and all that.

"Loosen me up, then."

There he was, Reed's internal caveman. "Should I sing and dance?"

"I've heard you sing, so no thanks. But dancing? Depends. Will it be exotic?"

"Pig."

He reached over and caught her hand. "Show me how not to be, I'm willing to learn."

"Where is this leading?"

"A sanitarium, if you keep trying to blow yourself up. Beyond that . . ." He shrugged. "Hell if I know."

"I'm not ready," she said honestly.

His dark eyes were amused. "Neither am I. But I'll keep taking you out, you'll keep dressing like that, and we'll enjoy the ride. Wherever it goes."

Eve took a deep breath and jumped in. "Okay. Deal."

It was with great relief that Eve slipped off her heels in the elevator. The image of Reed standing by his car in the subterranean garage of her condominium complex was indelibly etched into her mind. She suspected it would follow her into her dreams. Alec had once looked at her with similar hunger. It was hard to get over wanting to be wanted like that.

The car reached the top floor and the doors opened with a soft *ding*.

Padding out to the hallway, she came to an abrupt halt. Alec sat on the floor in black jeans and leather motorcycle jacket. His back was to the wall between their two condos and his long legs were stretched out into the hall.

He stood when he saw her. "Hi."

She just stared.

"You look . . . amazing," he murmured.

"You look different." Darker, leaner, his hair a luxurious mane of black silk that tumbled around his broad shoulders. Still had the golden sheen of an archangel. And the distance between them yawned wider than ever before.

He nodded, waiting.

"Why are you out here?" she asked, gesturing at the length of the hallway.

"I'm waiting for you."

"You could do that in your condo."

"I wanted no distractions from thinking about you."

Convoluted reasoning, but then . . . when had she ever really understood him? The man was a mystery.

Eve didn't mean to sound resentful when she said, "I graduated today."

"I was there. Congratulations. I'm proud of you."

"I didn't see you."

"I saw you," his lips thinned, "leaving with Abel."

"I haven't heard from you in a month."

Alec came toward her. "I've been traveling. Researching what happened to us."

"You could have called. E-mailed. Written a letter."

"Yes." He reached her. His hand lifted to tuck her hair behind her ear. "At first, I thought it was best to stay away from you."

"You're not my mentor anymore?"

"Not while you were in training."

"And now?"

He exhaled harshly. "There's something . . . in me, angel. I didn't know it was there until I became an archangel."

She frowned. "Something *in* you?"

"I can't explain it, other than I want to keep it away from you."

Eve sighed. "What do you want me to say to that, Alec?"

"I want you to say that you'll let me try and fix this."

"Fix what?"

"You and me."

Stepping around him, she headed toward her condo.

"Eve?" He followed.

She unlocked the multiple dead bolts that had once given her a feeling of safety. Setting her shoes beneath the console table by the door and her purse on top of it, she looked at him standing in her doorway. "How do you feel about me?"

He didn't misunderstand. "Confused. Detached."

"You don't love me anymore?"

"I *want* to love you." His deep voice was low and fervent. "I remember what it felt like to love you."

Her head ached. "I think you need to figure out what you're doing with your life, before you try and do me."

Alec stepped inside and shut the door. "What means more? When someone wants you because they can't help it? Because of hormones or some chemical reaction in the brain? Or when they want you because they choose to want you? Because they make the conscious decision to want you?"

She groaned. "You're too fucking complicated."

"We'll start slow," he suggested, stepping closer and moving in for the kill.

"Like what?" she asked, suspicious.

His smile made her toes curl. "A ride on my bike along the coast. That slow enough for you?"

Eve's gaze narrowed. Far from innocent, a ride on his Harley would put him in her arms and between her legs. The gleam in his eyes told her he was thinking the same thing.

"Only if I'm doing the driving," she said.

He hesitated, well aware that she was talking about more than the bike.

"Otherwise, no deal," she pressed.

"Fine. Deal."

Her tummy fluttered. Where had she heard that before?

For a second she wondered how this would work. Even now, she could feel both men in her head bristling at each other with their backs up. Then she gave a mental shrug. They all knew what was going on. They were all adults. Mostly. And she was a one-man woman. They would both be at arm's distance for a while.

The moment she thought it, she felt how well *that* went over.

Smiling, she headed down the hallway to change.

AUTHOR'S NOTE

For some it will be clear that Fort McCroskey is based on the former Fort Ord, an Army base on Monterey Bay, California. I fictionalized it to free me creatively. The Defense Language Institute and Naval Postgraduate School, however, are very real. DLI not only trains some of the best and brightest military personnel in the world, it also holds some of the most vivid memories of my life. My father-in-law attended to learn Vietnamese for the Marines. Years later, I attended to learn Russian for the Army. And years after that, my sister attended to learn Arabic for the Air Force. How times change.

Many languages are taught at DLI, all in the continuing mission to keep the United States military the most formidable in the world.

God bless our troops.

EVE OF CHAOS

To all the readers who've followed Eve on her adventures so far. Thank you.

ACKNOWLEDGMENTS

Faren Bachelis, copy editor at Tor, for the attention paid to my books and for all the lovely notes of praise that sprinkled the margins, both of which I deeply appreciate.

Gary Tabke, for making the delicious One-Eyed Jacks that Eve loves in this book.

Everyone at Tor who went the extra mile for this series. You rock! I appreciate all of you.

Kate Duffy, who went above and beyond, as always. Thank you for the patience and support.

And to Patricia Briggs, for her generosity and kind words. There is nothing in the world like receiving compliments from an author whose work you would camp out on a bookseller's doorstep to get to.

*God will stretch out over Edom the measuring line of chaos
and the plumb line of desolation.*

—ISAIAH 34:11

CHAPTER 1

Evangeline Hollis watched with clenched jaw as a kappa demon served *yakisoba*—Japanese pan-fried noodles—to her mother with a broad smile. Eve guessed that the ratio of mortals to demons at the Orange County Buddhist Church's annual Obon Festival was about fifty-fifty.

After three months of living with the Mark of Cain and her new "job" as celestial bounty hunter, Eve was resigned to the reality of Infernals mingling undetected among mortals. However, she was still surprised by the number of transplanted Japanese demons who had come out to play at the festival. There seemed to be an inordinate amount of them present.

"You want some?" her mother asked, holding out the plate. Miyoko had lived a mostly quintessential American life in the United States for thirty years. She was a naturalized citizen, a converted Baptist, and her husband, Darrel Hollis, was a good ol' boy from Alabama. But she appreciated her roots and made an effort to share the Japanese culture with her two daughters.

Eve shook her head. "I want *yakidango*."

"Me, too. It's over there." Miyoko set off, leading the way.

The festival was contained within the gated parking lot of the temple. To the right was a large gymnasium. To the left, the temple and school complex. The area was small, but still managed to hold a variety of food and game booths. A *taiko* drum was elevated in a *yagura* tower overlooking a space that would later showcase Bon Odori dancers. Children competed to win prizes ranging from live goldfish to stuffed animals. Adults hovered over displays of trinkets and homemade desserts.

The Southern California weather was perfect, as usual. A balmy seventy-eight degrees with plenty of sunshine and very few clouds. Adjusting her sunglasses, Eve relished the kiss of the sun on her skin and breathed in the scents of her favorite foods.

Then a foul stench wafted by on the afternoon breeze, assaulting her nose and ruining her rare moment of peace.

The putrid smell of rotting soul; it was unmistakable. It was a cross between decaying flesh and fresh shit, and it amazed Eve that the Unmarked—mortals lacking the Mark of Cain—couldn't smell it. She turned her head, seeking out the source.

Her searching gaze halted on a lovely Asian woman standing across the aisle from her. A *yuki-onna*—a Japanese snow demon. Eve noted the Infernal's white kimono with its delicate *sukura* embroidery and the detail on her cheekbone that resembled a tribal tattoo. In truth, the design was the demon's rank and it was invisible to mortals. Like the Mark of Cain on Eve's arm, it was similar to mortal military insignia. All Infernals had them. The details betrayed both which species of damned being they were and what their rank in Hell's hierarchy was.

Contrary to what most theologians believed, the Mark of the Beast wasn't something to be feared as the start of the Apocalypse; it was a caste system that had been in place for centuries.

Eve's mark began to tingle, then burn. A call to arms.

Now? she asked with a mental query, exasperation clear in her dry tone. She was a Mark, one of thousands of "sinners" around the world who'd been drafted into service exterminating demons for God. She was expected to kill at the drop of a hat, but her mother was with her and they were at a house of worship.

Sorry, babe. Reed Abel sounded anything but. *You're in the wrong place at the right time. Her number's up, and you're closest.*

You've been singing that tune all week, she retorted. *I'm not buying it anymore.*

She'd been vanquishing a demon a day—sometimes two—for the last several days. A girl needed more than just Sundays off when her job was killing demons. *Why am I always closest?*

Because you're a disaster magnet?

And you're a riot.

Reed—aka Abel of biblical fame—was a *mal'akh,* an angel. He was a handler, a position that meant he was responsible for assigning hunts to a small group of Marks. It was a lot like skip tracing. The seven earthbound archangels acted as bail bondsmen. Reed was a dispatcher. Eve was a bounty hunter. It was a well-oiled system for most Marks, but to say she was a squeaky wheel would be an understatement.

Dinner tonight? he asked.

After that wisecrack, cocky bastard?

I'll cook.

She followed her mom, keeping an eye on her quarry. *If I'm still alive, sure.*

In the back of her mind, she heard and felt Alec Cain—Reed's brother—growl his disapproval. Alec was her mentor. Once known as Cain of Infamy, he was now Cain the Archangel. She and Alec had a history together, starting ten years ago when she'd given him her virginity. Nowadays, his position as archangel had stripped him of the ability to have an emotional attachment to anything other than God, but Alec held on to her anyway.

What means more? he had asked her. *When someone wants you because he can't help it? Because of hormones or some chemical reaction in the brain? Or when he wants you because he chooses to want you? Because he makes the conscious decision to want you?*

Eve didn't know, so she was drifting along with him, trying to figure it out.

She was certifiably insane for stepping in the middle of the oldest case of sibling rivalry in history, especially since the three of them shared a unique bond that allowed a free flow of thought between them. Eve often asked herself why she played with fire. The only answer she came up with was that she just couldn't help herself.

I'm calling dibs on breakfast tomorrow, Alec insisted gruffly.

One-Eyed Jacks? No one cooked them like Alec. Grilled pieces of bread with a hole in the middle to hold a fried egg. Buttery and crispy, and served with syrup. He also toasted the centers and sprinkled them with cinnamon-sugar to serve on the side. Delicious.

Whatever you want, angel.

It was a given that Reed wouldn't be around for breakfast, since dating two men at once meant that all three of them were sleeping alone at night.

The *yuki-onna* excused herself from her handsome companion and moved toward the gymnasium, taking the tiny steps dictated by the tight fit of her kimono and the *geta* wooden clogs on her feet. Eve was at an advantage with her attire. Her stretchy capris and ribbed cotton tank top didn't impede her range of movement at all. Her Army-issue "jungle boots" were breathable and functional. She was ready to rock. But that didn't mean she wanted to.

"I have to wash my hands," Eve said to her mother, knowing that as a retired registered nurse, Miyoko would appreciate the need for cleanliness.

"I have antibacterial gel in my purse."

Eve wrinkled her nose. "Yuck. That stuff makes my hands sticky."

"You're too fussy. How many dangos you want?"

"Three sticks." The rice cake dumplings were grilled on wooden skewers and coated with sweet syrup. They were a childhood favorite that Eve enjoyed too rarely, which aggravated her disgruntlement. If the demon ruined her appetite, there would be Hell to pay. Seriously.

Eve handed over a twenty-dollar bill, then set off in pursuit of her prey.

She overtook the demon and entered the gym where picnic tables had been arranged to provide seating for diners. Dozens of festival-goers filled the vast space with echoing revelry—laughing, conversing in both English and Japanese, and eating. Mortals mingled with Infernal beings in blissful ignorance, but Eve noted every one of Hell's denizens. In return, they knew what she was and they eyed her with wary hatred. The mark on her deltoid betrayed her, as did her scent. As rotten as they stunk to her, she smelled sickly sweet to them. Ridiculous really, since there was no such thing as a sweet Mark. They were all bitter.

Tucking herself against the wall, she watched through the tinted glass doors as the *yuki-onna* approached. From the forward vantage, Eve could see the demon's feet hovering just above the ground. Backing up slowly, Eve rounded the corner to stay out of sight. A glass case was mounted to the wall at her shoulder, displaying trophies and a lone katana within its lighted interior.

Eve glanced around quickly, noting the distraction of the rest of the gym's occupants. With superhuman speed, she pinched off the round metal lock with thumb and forefinger, and withdrew the sheathed blade. She held it tucked between her thigh and the wall, hoping it was more than a decoration. If not, she could always summon the classic flame-covered sword. But she'd rather not. Buildings had a nasty habit of catching fire around her, and she had greater proficiency with the sleeker, moderately curved "samurai sword" than she did with the heavier glaive.

Her prey entered the gym and turned in the opposite direction, heading toward the restrooms just as Eve had guessed she would. Closing the women's bathroom while food and drink were present in copious quantities was always a bad idea, but Eve didn't have a choice. Her mother was waiting, and she couldn't risk losing her target.

Her present dilemma was one of the many reasons why Marks weren't supposed to have family ties. The sinners who were chosen were usually loners easily transplanted to foreign soil. Relatives were a liability. Eve was the sole exception to the rule. Alec had fought to keep her close to home because he knew how much her parents meant to her. He was also motivated by guilt, since their indiscretion ten years ago was the reason she was marked today.

The wheels of justice didn't turn any faster in Heaven than they did on Earth.

When the bathroom door swung shut behind the demon, Eve followed. The mark throbbed hot and heavy within the skin covering her deltoid, pumping aggression and fury through her veins. Her muscles thickened and her stride altered. Her body's reaction was base and animalistic, the surge of bloodlust brutal and addicting. She had come to crave it like a drug. Too much time between kills, and she became short-tempered and twitchy.

Despite the rush, her heartbeat and hands remained steady. Her body was a temple now, and it ran like a machine. As she entered the bathroom, Eve was calm and focused. When had she become so at ease with her murderous secondary life? She would have to ponder that later, when she had some privacy and time to cry.

All of the stall doors were slightly ajar, except for the handicapped one at the far end of the room. The stench of decaying soul permeated the space. Affixed to the wall near the door was a tube that held a collapsible Wet Floor sign. She tugged it free and set it outside in the hallway, then closed the door and turned the lock. It wasn't quite as useful as an Out of Order cone, but it would have to do.

There was no way to stave off the sudden deluge of memories of another bathroom, one in which she had fought a dragon and paid with her life. She'd been resurrected to kill another day because of a deal Alec had made with someone, somewhere. She didn't know the details, but she knew the cost had to be steep. If she hadn't been in love with him already, his willingness to make that kind of sacrifice would have sealed the deal. She wasn't ready to die just yet, despite demon killing and a crazy love life.

One day she hoped to marry and have children, enjoy a successful career and family vacations. But she would have to shed the mark first—either by manipulating someone in power or by collecting enough indulgences to work off her penance.

Of course, there were loopholes in the indulgence system. She'd killed the teenage son of the Black Diamond Pack Alpha werewolf *twice*, but had only been given credit for the second kill. Bullshit like that really got under her skin. What was a girl supposed to do when even God didn't play fair?

A soft whimper arrested Eve midstride. The sound had a high, trembling note that sounded childlike. She rolled her shoulders back and waited. Hunting was less about the pounce than it was about positioning. She stood dead center in the most open space in the room. The exit was at her back. The Infernal had no way out but through her. Damned if she would move just to hurry things up a bit.

The mark continued to flood her with adrenaline and hostility. Her senses honed in on her prey, flooding her mind with information. Her stance widened.

"Come out, come out wherever you are . . ." she crooned.

The lock on the handicapped stall turned. The door pulled inward. A child's face appeared, wan and tear streaked. A pretty girl of Asian heritage in a light summer dress with a watermelon design around the hem. Maybe six or seven years old. Shaking with fear. A moment later, the lovely visage of the *yuki-onna* appeared above the girl's head.

Eve growled. "A hostage was a bad idea."

When she had kids of her own, she wasn't letting them out of her sight.

"I will walk out of here with the child," the Infernal said in her lilting, accented voice. She stepped out of the stall with her hand on the girl's shoulder. "Then I will release her."

The child's teeth began to chatter and her lips took on a blue tinge. Gooseflesh spread from the point where the demon clutched her.

"You're going to die," Eve said matter-of-factly. The *yuki-onna* had been targeted. Marks would hunt her until she was dead.

"So are you," the demon retorted. "Do you really want to waste your last moments killing me?"

There's a hostage, she told Reed, ignoring the standard demon intimidation and bargaining tactics. *A little girl. I need you to get her out of here.*

A warm breeze moved over her skin, tangible proof that her handler was always with her. He was forbidden to assist his charges in their hunts, but clearing mortals out of the way fell under his purview. *On your cue,* he murmured.

Eve had no idea where in the world he was, but as a *mal'akh,* he could shift—or teleport—in and out of a location faster than the blink of an eye.

"I was going to take you down fair and square," she told the demon, holding the sheathed katana aloft. "I should have known you would want to fight dirty."

"I have no weapon." A lie. Demons all had certain gifts, like the *yuki-onna*'s ability to create extreme weather. Marks had only their own wits and strength. They were celestially enhanced physically—able to heal and react quickly—but lacked any supernatural "powers."

"I'll give you mine," Eve offered grimly, "if you let the kid go." She ripped the katana free of its sheath and hurled the lacquered wood at the demon's head.

She reached out to Reed. *Now!*

The demon's arms rose to ward off the projectile. The child was snatched by Reed before the *yuki-onna* caught it.

The Infernal's cry of rage was accompanied by an icy gust that burst through the room like an explosion. Eve was thrust backward into a heated-air hand dryer with enough force to hammer it flush to the wall. She held onto the hilt of the katana by stubbornness alone. Her booted feet dropped to the floor with a dull thud, and she hit the ground running.

Arm raised and blade at the ready, Eve rushed forward with a battle cry that curdled her own blood. The child's fear lingered in the air, the acrid scent mingling with the stench of decaying Infernal soul. The combination sent her mark into overdrive. She leaped, slashing down on the diagonal, but the demon spun away in a flurry of snow. The temperature dropped drastically. The mirrors fogged around the edges, and her breath puffed visibly in the chilled air.

Eve pursued her, feinting and parrying against the sharp icicles the demon threw at her. They shattered like glass against her flashing katana, sprinkling the tile with slippery shards.

Crunching across the hazardous floor, she advanced with precision. The beautiful kimono fluttered with the Infernal's retreat, the thick silk shredded by Eve's calculated attacks. Once the sorriest swordswoman in her class, Eve had practiced exhaustively until she stopped embarrassing herself. She still wasn't much beyond passably proficient with the weapon, but she no longer felt hopelessly inept.

She began to hum a merry tune.

As she'd hoped, the demon floundered, caught off guard by the implied boredom. The *yuki-onna*'s next salvo lacked the speed of the previous ones. Eve caught it with her fist, hissing as the ice splintered its way across her palm. Blood flowed, its scent goading the demon into roaring in triumph, a sound audible only to those with enhanced hearing.

Eve lobbed the icicle back, followed immediately with the katana. The Infernal deflected the first projectile with an icy blast, but was left vulnerable to the second. The blade sliced along the demon's right triceps, drawing blood before impaling the wall behind her. A crimson stain began to spread through the pristine white of the kimono.

"Checkmate," Eve taunted. "Your blood for mine."

The Infernal retaliated with an icicle that pierced straight through Eve's right thigh. She cried out and dropped to one knee. Agonized, she sent up a silent request for a sword. She held her palm open to receive the gift . . .

. . . which didn't come.

Shock froze Eve. She'd gambled with the loss of the katana and rolled snake eyes. She always feared this day would come. Formerly agnostic, she didn't show the deference to the Almighty that others did. She wasn't disrespectful per se, but she might be too forthright in voicing her inability to understand the way God handled things.

She asked again, throwing in a "please" for good measure. The result was the same. Nada. Eve growled, furious that she would be denied the tool required to complete the task she was forced to perform.

The *yuki-onna* quickly deduced what had failed to happen. She giggled, a lovely melodic sound. "Perhaps he realizes that saving you is hopeless and not worth the effort."

"Fuck you."

"It is rare that Sammael sets a bounty so high or allows everyone in Hell a chance to claim it." The demon grinned. "But then, this is the first time someone has run over one of his pets."

"What bounty?" Eve hoped she hid the sudden fear she felt. "Is Satan upset that I ran over his *dog*? That's hysterical."

I'm not laughing, Alec snapped.

I know. Eve sighed. *My life sucks.*

She struggled to her feet, favoring her impaled leg. Reaching down, she yanked the ice dagger free and tossed it aside. Blood spurted from the gaping wound, then gushed. She ignored it for now. She had bigger problems.

"What is funny," the *yuki-onna* retorted, "is how you will be ripped apart by everyone in Hell."

"Everyone, huh?" Eve shrugged. "He'll have to do better than that, if he hopes to take me out."

That's my girl, Alec praised. *Never let 'em see you sweat.*

But she heard the unease in his voice. She also felt him poised to leap to her rescue.

I've got this, she said, staying him. She wasn't sure how, but she would figure it out on her own. Damned if some ice bitch in clogs would kick her ass.

"Sammael wants you," the demon taunted. Her disheveled hair and wide eyes only made her more beautiful. "And I will be rewarded for bringing you in."

Laughing through her growing panic, Eve made a third request—not quite a prayer—for a sword. Again, she was ignored.

She deflected the demon's next icicle with her forearm, then darted to the left to catch another. She threw it back. It was knocked off course by a burst of frosty air. All the while, she closed the distance between herself and the wall that held the katana.

"You can take hostages," Eve taunted, "but you can't take me."

Bravado. Sometimes it was all a Mark had.

"I am beginning to think otherwise," the demon retorted with a malicious gleam in her dark eyes.

Pounding came to the locked door, followed by a string of anxious-sounding Japanese. Not for the first time, Eve wished her mother had taught her the language. All she knew was that someone wanted to come in, and the demon she was fighting was no longer eager to get out. In fact, the *yuki-onna* seemed energized by the intrusion.

Eve took another step closer. Her boot slipped on an ice shard and she skidded, her balance compromised by her injured leg. She was inspired by the near fall, her mind seizing on a possible means to the end.

Dependent upon God's willingness to cooperate and give her a damn break, of course.

Kicking hard, she sent up a spray of water and ice. As the *yuki-onna* retaliated with a rapid volley of icicles, Eve shot forward, using the slush on the tile to drop to the floor in a careening, feet-first slide into home plate.

"I could really use that sword now," she yelled skyward, as the white tile rushed past her in a blur. *"Please!"*

Nothing.

Time slowed to a trickle . . .

The demon leaped gracefully and was held aloft by icy air currents. Levitating into a prone position, the Infernal let her facade of beauty fall away, revealing the true evil beneath—eyes of blood red, a gaping maw of blackened teeth, and grayish skin with a network of inky veins that spread into her hairline. Her arms splayed wide, spears of ice appeared in her hands like ski poles.

Alec and Reed roared in unison, their shouts reverberating in Eve's skull with such volume they drowned out everything else. In slow motion, she watched the demon hovering like a ghostly apparition, her white robes in tatters, her hair a sinuously writhing mane. Eve raised her arms to ward off the coming attack, then jerked in surprise as a heavy weight forced her forearm to drop to her chest . . .

. . . weighted by the miraculous appearance of a glaive in her hand.

Her grip tightened on the hilt and her back arched up. Hurling the blade forward like a javelin, she struck the *yuki-onna* straight in the chest. The glaive pierced deep with a sickening thud.

The demon exploded in a burst of ash.

Eve continued to slide until she slammed into the wall. At impact, the katana dislodged from its mooring, twisting to fall point down toward her head. She jerked to the side, rolling to avoid the blade. It pierced the floor where she'd been an instant before. Behind her, the glaive—no longer embedded in the demon's body—clattered to the tile.

"Holy shit," she breathed.

A pair of steel-toed boots appeared next to her head, then a hand extended into her line of sight. Looking up, her gaze met eyes of rich chocolate brown. Once, Alec had looked at her with a heat so scorching it burned her skin. She missed that look. Then again, she got hot enough for the both of them just checking him out.

At a few inches over six feet, Alec was as ripped as one would expect a skilled predator to be. He was God's most revered and trusted enforcer, and his body reflected that calling. His hair, as always, was slightly overlong, but she would fight off anyone who approached him with shears.

"Could God have waited any longer to bail me out of the mess he put me in?" she groused.

"Did you note the lack of fire?" His voice—dark and slightly raspy—was pure seduction, even when laced with the resonance unique to archangels. It didn't sound that way when he spoke to her telepathically, which was sadly appropriate. Who he was in reality was far different from who he was in her mind.

She blinked up at him. "*You* bailed me out? What the hell? Was he just going to let me die? *Again?*"

"Obviously not, since you're not dead. It was a lesson in faith."

"More like a lesson in 'I am God, see me fuck with you.'"

"Watch it," he admonished.

Eve accepted his proffered hand. As he pulled her upright, his powerful chest and tautly ridged abdomen flexed noticeably beneath his fitted white T-shirt. She couldn't help noticing stuff like that, even though she couldn't touch what she was looking at.

"What is it with demons and bathrooms?" she asked. "Grimshaw started a trend when he sent that dragon to kill me. I swear I've vanquished at least half a dozen Infernals in bathrooms since then."

The dragon had been a courtier in Asmodeus's court, but he'd killed her for Charles Grimshaw—former Alpha of the Northern California

Black Diamond Pack and father of the wolf she'd had to kill twice. Demon retaliation was a bitch.

Alec cursed at the sight of her thigh. Her toes were squishing in the blood soaking her sock and puddling along the sole. She would need a new pair of boots.

He bent to examine her wound more closely. "I would have gotten here sooner, but I had to scare off the crowd of Infernals in the hall first."

"Crowd?"

"I don't think the ice bitch was kidding about the bounty."

"What do you know that I don't? You wouldn't believe an Infernal without some sort of proof."

Alec had assumed control over the day-to-day operation of Gadara Enterprises—the secular front for the North American firm of Marks—since the archangel Raguel had been taken prisoner by Satan a couple of months back. That meant Alec was privy to almost every hellacious and celestial happening that occurred between the top of Alaska to the end of Mexico.

"The number of Infernals in Orange County has tripled in the last two weeks."

Which was when she'd graduated from training. As she was often reminded, nothing was a coincidence. "No wonder it's been so busy around here."

He gave her a resigned look. "It will get busier, if Sammael's set his sights on you."

"With a free-for-all bounty open to all classes of demons? Jeez, you'd think I kicked his puppy or something. Oh wait . . . I did." Eve put weight on her wounded leg and winced at the immediate throb of agony.

Alec tucked his shoulder under her arm to support her. "We need to bandage that leg, smart ass."

"You *like* my ass, and not because of its IQ."

"Love it." He gave her butt an affectionate squeeze. Alec might be restricted from feeling emotional love for her, but lust wasn't a problem. "But I love the rest of your hot body, too, and I'd like to keep it in one piece."

The mark enabled her to heal super fast. In an hour or two, only a pink scar would remain, and by nightfall, the injury would be nothing but a memory. But she could help move things along in the recovery department by closing the hole with some butterfly bandages. She'd have to hurry; her mom was still waiting for her.

I'll take care of Miyoko, he assured her.

"I'll take Eve back to her place to change," a deep voice intruded.

They turned their heads to find Reed by the door. The men's features were similar enough to betray them as siblings, but they were otherwise polar opposites. Reed favored Armani suits and faultless haircuts. Today he wore black slacks and a lavender dress shirt open at the throat and rolled at the wrists. It was a testament to how completely, robustly *male* he was that he could look so damn fine in such a soft color.

Alec's arm at her waist tightened. The two brothers were like oil and kerosene together. Dangerously flammable. They refused to tell her what started their lifelong feud, and they kept the memory so repressed in the darkest corners of their minds that she hadn't yet been able to find it. Whatever the sore spot was, the murderous rage it incited was easily goaded. They'd been killing each other for years—Cain more so than Abel—but were always resurrected by God to fight some more.

Which was just nasty in her opinion. Why God enabled the two brothers to keep fighting was beyond her comprehension.

"What are we going to do about this mess?" She offered a soothing smile to Alec before stepping away from him. A trail of blood marked her recent kamikaze slide across the floor. The rapidly melting ice was spreading the crimson stain along the grout lines, creating an oddly compelling map.

Stepping into the water, Alec snapped his fingers and the liquid and blood filled the nearest sink, transferred so quickly she hadn't caught the movement even with her enhanced senses. She would go home with Reed in similar fashion.

Thankfully, Marks had handlers to pick up after them. She was luckier than most in that she had Cain, too, although that created some friction with many of the other Marks who thought she had an advantage. They didn't take into consideration how many demons wanted to use her to get to the deadliest Mark of them all. She might as well wear a bull's-eye for cocky and rash Infernals to aim for.

Then again, it looked like Satan had taped the target on for her.

"Come on," Reed said, extending a hand to her. "Before your mother calls in the cavalry."

"Forget the cavalry." Alec winked at Eve. "Miyoko would charge in herself."

She was halted midlaugh by the stench of a sewer. Looking for the demon whose proximity had to be the cause, she found herself staring into an inexplicably lingering puddle at her feet . . . and familiar eyes of malevolent, crystalline blue. A face in the liquid. She stomped instinctively, destroying the visage of the water demon in an explosion of spraying droplets.

"What the hell?" Reed barked, catching her as her wounded thigh caused her to stumble.

In the literal blink of an eye, Eve found herself in the kitchen of her third-floor condo in Huntington Beach. "Did you see him?" she gasped, leaning heavily into his hard body.

Reed's arms tightened around her. "Yeah, I saw him."

He's gone. Alec's tone was grim. *I'm heading out to hold off your mom, but we need to address this when we're done here.*

The demon was a Nix—a Germanic shape-shifting water spirit. He'd targeted her almost from the moment she had been marked, then made a nuisance of himself until she killed him. Correction: She'd *thought* she killed him.

She *would* kill him. This particular Nix had taken the life of her neighbor Mrs. Basso. Sweet, forthright, widowed Mrs. Basso who had been a beloved friend. Eve's need for vengeance was what motivated her when the damned Infernal bounty hunting got tough.

Pulling away from Reed, she limped down the hallway to her master bedroom. The crash of the waves against the shore pulsed in through the living room balcony's open sliding glass door. In her premarked life, she'd been an interior designer. Her condo had been one of her first projects, and the space remained one of her favorites. Even the mistakes she'd made in the layout were fond ones. She wouldn't change a thing. She felt safe here, less like a demon killer and more like herself.

Eve absorbed the calm she found in her home with deep, even breaths.

Reed called after her, his tone both seductive and challenging. "Need help getting naked?"

She sighed inwardly. Outside these walls, the worst of Hell's denizens were converging en masse. She would need to be ready when she ventured out again.

As if her love life wasn't dangerous enough.

CHAPTER 2

Eve climbed onto one of the Shaker-style bar stools at her kitchen is-land. "You know, I wish the demons I killed would stay dead."

In truth, they usually exploded into ash like the *yuki-onna* had and were returned to Hell, where they were punished for blowing their chance to play with mortals. She was the only Mark to have vanquished the same demon more than once.

"Hey," Diego Montevista protested from his seat on the stool beside her. "I'm alive for the same reason they came back to haunt you."

She smiled. "That's right. And you're worth it."

Montevista—previously the archangel Raguel's chief of security and one badass Mark—bumped shoulders with her. "Damn straight."

Mira Sydney frowned from her position at the other end of the island. Like her partner, Montevista, she was dressed in head-to-toe black—parachute pants and cotton T-shirt, with thigh holsters for both a 9mm and a dagger. "I still don't understand how that worked."

Montevista was large and forbidding, but his lieutenant was tiny and sweet-natured. Fair to his dark, Caucasian to his Latino. But it was clear that decades of working together had created a strong affinity between them. Alec had assigned them to Eve's protection detail after the Obon festival. After all, Cain of Infamy didn't need the same protection that the other archangels did. Eve didn't mind. She'd bonded with both Montevista and Sydney during her training—infamous for being the worst Mark train-ing disaster in history. Out of a class of nine, only three survived. And Raguel Gadara had been taken; the first and only successful archangel ab-duction.

"The world's gone to shit since Eve hit the scene," Reed grumbled from the stove where he was stir-frying homemade Kung Pao chicken. He was clearly unhappy to have company during their date.

"Gee, thanks," Eve said.

His mouth curved in a devilish smile that contrasted sharply with the wings and halo he occasionally sported for shock value. There was very little that could be called angelic about Reed. "At least you're good eye candy."

Eve groaned. He winked.

As gorgeous as Reed was—and he looked especially fine with an apron tied over his usual elegant attire—he had some seriously rough edges. But she didn't want to smooth them away; she wanted to understand them. She knew firsthand that he was the type of man who could lure a woman to sin with just a look. Charm wasn't a necessity. Still, Eve strongly suspected that some of the crudity that spilled from his mouth was due to his nervousness around her. It was oddly endearing that he would be so affected by her. She couldn't resist exploring the attraction further.

Sydney cleared her throat. "Tell me the whole story. From the beginning."

Eve looked at her. "Surely you've heard it too many times already."

"Not from the source. I want to hear it from you."

"All right." Eve leaned into the counter. "When I was a newbie, I stumbled across a tengu who didn't smell like shit and had no details. I told Cain. We told Gadara. Gadara told us to find out where the demon came from. Abel agreed and put the order through."

Sydney shot a quick glance at Reed. "I remember hearing that you were assigned to a hunt before training."

Reed's features took on a stony cast. As Eve's handler, he was the only person who could put her to work. Marks weren't supposed to hunt before they were fully trained.

Eve nodded. "In his defense, no one believed me. They thought I was in transition and my Mark senses hadn't fully kicked in yet."

"How green were you?" Montevista asked.

"A day or two."

Sydney whistled.

"Yeah. Rotten," Eve agreed. "Especially after I proved I wasn't nuts and we *still* had to track down the source of the tengu's abilities."

"The masking agent," Montevista offered. "Stuff that temporarily hides Infernal stench and details."

"That's what they started calling it. Cain and I discovered that they were producing and distributing the mask out of a masonry located less than an hour's drive from here."

"Ah." Sydney grinned. "Upland."

Eve nodded sheepishly. She was never going to live that down. "The masking agent was concocted from blood and bone meal made from Marks, animals, and Infernals. Plus spells and other stuff. Cain came up with the idea to destroy the mask ingredients in the masonry's giant roller kiln. I came up with the idea to toss the Nix in there and evaporate him, too. Abel came up with the idea to lock the Black Diamond Pack's heir in the kiln room. And it was God's idea of a joke to make the masking agent a life preserver when cooked at high heat. It kept the wolf and Nix alive when they should have been blown to smithereens. It's also what saved Montevista a few weeks later."

Sydney shot a concerned glance skyward. When lightning didn't strike Eve for her blasphemy, she said, "I heard the kiln explosion left a crater in the ground the size of a city block."

"At least." Reed snorted. "It was like a mini–atomic bomb."

Montevista grinned. "The stories aren't exaggerations."

"Wow." Sydney looked at Eve. "So, you killed the wolf a second time, but the Nix showed up today at the festival."

"Exactly." Eve's fingertips traced the veins within the granite countertop. "In fact, the police left a message on my voice mail this afternoon. I wish they would have called yesterday or even this morning. Then I would have been prepared for the Nix to pop up."

Pausing his stirring, Reed stared hard at her. "The same detectives who are investigating Mrs. Basso's death?"

"The ones from Anaheim, yes. Jones and Ingram. I haven't heard from the Huntington Beach Police since their initial interview."

"What do they want?"

"To talk to me. They didn't give any specifics. I'm guessing the Nix might be back to his old tricks. He'd already killed a dozen people before Mrs. Basso, so I can't see him stopping now." Her chest ached at the thought of her neighbor. "I don't understand why we weren't hunting him a long time ago. Isn't it our purpose to save lives?"

I'm sorry, babe. The sympathy in Reed's tone elicited a grateful smile from her.

Montevista gave her hand a commiserating squeeze. "No one knows what criteria the seraphim use to target Infernals."

Most demons kept a low profile. Being too obvious not only pissed off God, it pissed off Satan, too. Neither of the two was ready for Armageddon just yet. Satan wasn't powerful enough, and God liked things the way they were.

But the Nix was too cocky. He'd been killing women all over Orange County and leaving distinctive "calling cards" that caught the attention of the police—a water lily floating in a Crate & Barrel punch bowl. The death of Mrs. Basso had brought notice to Eve, too, who'd unfortunately had her own Nix calling card sitting in plain sight on the coffee table. Now, the detectives were looking at her for information she couldn't provide. Replying with, *There's a rogue demon on the loose, but don't worry because I'm a demon slayer for God,* wasn't the way to alleviate their concerns.

Alec suddenly appeared on her left side, shifting into her home without warning. "Let me guess: Kung Pao chicken."

"Good nose." Eve looked back and forth between the two brothers, noting the perpetual tension that filled a room when they were both in it. Alec should have knocked. Since he lived in Mrs. Basso's old condominium next door, it wouldn't have been a hardship. But a traditional entry wouldn't have the same irritate-Reed factor.

Alec set one hand on the countertop and the other on the back of Eve's stool. Leaning in, he pressed his lips to her temple. "If Abel's cooking for a girl," he murmured, "it's always Kung Pao."

"*Really?*" She looked at Reed with raised brows.

Montevista's dark eyes filled with amusement. Sydney glanced away with a half-smile.

Reed glared. "If you count 'always' as being a one-time thing in nineteenth-century China. We'd get more mileage talking about Cain's 'Hop on, baby, let me take you for a ride' spiel. You think I suck at pickup lines—"

"I've actually got something worth riding on," Alec drawled.

Reed's bamboo spoon hit the side of the wok with a clatter. "Saddle up and fuck off, then, shithead. No one invited you over."

Eve slid off the stool. "Enough. Satan's lackeys are after me and you two want to argue about who's more adept at getting laid?"

"He started it," Reed snapped.

"I'm finishing it." Eve wished a shot of liquor was an option. Unfortunately, mind-altering substances were ineffectual in her mark-enhanced body. She crossed her arms and asked Alec, "Did you come over because you have some news for us?"

He shook his head. "That's the problem. Not a word on the streets about this supposed bounty. We'd expect to hear *something* through an informant or an Infernal seeking shelter, but it's dead quiet."

"You had to barge in on our date to say you don't have anything to say?" Reed growled.

"No." Alec smirked. "I had to barge in because it pisses you off."

Eve snapped her fingers to bring their attention back to her. "The fact that we've been busier than usual can't be a coincidence, since you're always telling me there is no such thing."

Alec nodded. "Right. I'm still digging."

"Also . . . thinking about that night in Upland brings up something important that I forgot until just now."

Four pairs of eyes trained on her.

"The Nix said something to me," she went on, "just before I rolled him into the kiln. I asked, 'Why me?' and he answered, 'I do what I'm told.'"

"You didn't tell me this before," Alec accused.

"I'm sorry." And she meant it. Staying alive meant not dropping the ball. "He was dead and sent back to Hell. I was trying not to join him. The memory got lost in my brain."

"Shit. This is why you're not supposed to be able to shut us out."

Eve didn't know how or why she was sometimes able to circumvent the inherent connection between Marks and their superiors, but she was grateful. A woman had to have her secrets, especially while embroiled in a contentious relationship triangle.

She continued before they got off on a tangent. "I also noticed something new today—his details say he's now one of Asmodeus's lackeys."

Reed turned off the fire on the stove. "The Nix's details were courtesy of a lesser demon."

"They've changed since that first day you and I saw him," she insisted.

"Sammael *and* a king of Hell," Sydney breathed. "Yowza."

Eve could only give a lame nod. And to think she had once thought of herself as a lucky person. "Can I ask why Satan is a prince, but the demons under him are kings?"

"No!" Reed and Alec barked in unison.

She held up her hands in a defensive gesture. "Ooo-kay, then . . ."

Alec stared at her with narrowed eyes. "Damn it, angel."

Evangeline. Eve. Angel. A nickname only Alec had ever used. He still said it with the rumbling seductive purr that had gotten her into this marked mess to begin with.

Montevista gave her a wry look. "Only you would have multiple high-level contracts out on you, Hollis."

"Maybe the Nix and the wolf met after the explosion, and became friends. Maybe Asmodeus and Grimshaw were friends," Eve said, "and Asmodeus is trying to help his buddy out in the revenge department. Maybe the Nix jumped ship to Asmodeus so that he had a valid excuse to hunt me."

"There's a hell of a lot of 'maybes' in there," Alec bit out. "And friendship is relative to demons. Favors aren't free. Asmodeus would've had to be paying a debt or getting something in kind."

That didn't sound good to Eve.

"That would have to be a huge debt or gain to make Asmodeus go after someone important to Cain," Montevista pointed out. "Grimshaw came after Hollis in vengeance for the death of his son. Asmodeus has no excuse, and he knew he'd piss off Jehovah and Sammael at once."

Eve sighed. The battle between Heaven and Hell wasn't a free-for-all. For the most part, Celestials and Infernals lived alongside each other in a wary truce. Satan's minions were ordered to stay under the radar, so they could do the most damage. Marks were only assigned to take down rogue demons. Montevista was right. Something big had motivated Asmodeus to break the rules in such a major way.

"Unless Sammael told Asmodeus to do it," Sydney suggested quietly. When everyone stared at her, she shrugged.

Montevista broke the silence. "She's got a point."

"I hadn't run over his dog yet," Eve reminded.

Dog. Ha! Since the damn creature had been the size of a bus, Eve's mind could barely connect "dog" to her road kill in the same train of thought.

"This has to be about more than Sammael's damned hellhound," Reed insisted. "He doesn't care about anyone but himself. Everyone and everything else—including pets—is expendable."

"So he wants something? I don't have anything valuable." Her gaze darted between the two brothers. "Except for both of you."

Alec and Reed fell silent, both physically and mentally. They knew she was a liability to them.

Eve refused to stay that way.

Reed turned back to the stove. Alec began routing orders through the mental switchboard system each archangel had to everyone in their firm. She moved into the living room. She was still within seeing/hearing distance, but the space helped to give her mind a break. Tuning the others out, Eve settled onto her down-filled sofa and contemplated the mess that was her life.

The Nix and Grimshaw's kid hadn't been the only Infernals in the kiln room that disastrous night in Upland. There had also been a gaggle of tengu—Japanese gargoyle-type demons. Since the Nix and the wolf had both lived to be killed another day, it was reasonable to wonder if the tengu might have found second lives, too.

Alec shifted over to her and settled into a seated position on the edge of her glass-topped coffee table. The thick denim of his blue jeans did nothing to hide the fine form of his long, muscular legs.

"You're going to get in trouble for using your powers so much," she admonished.

For seven weeks a year, each archangel was given free rein to use his powers to facilitate in training new Marks, a duty they rotated between them. But the rest of the year using their gifts meant facing consequences. *Suggesting* they live secular lives was God's way of fostering empathy for mortals. Eve thought it was a recipe for resentment.

Smiling, Alec said, "I'm not a firm leader yet. The same rules don't apply to me."

"Isn't that always the case?"

He leaned forward and rested his forearms on his knees. "I've double checked the security measures we installed against the Nix the first time around, both in this building and in your parents' house. I've also assigned a security detail to guard the perimeter against any new threats."

"Can they get rid of that nut job on the corner?"

"What nut job?"

"Don't tell me you haven't seen him. The guy who looks like an evil Santa Claus? Preaching fire and brimstone with his acoustic guitar?"

He stared at her.

"The dude with the big sign that says YOU ARE GOING TO BURN IN HELL?" When he continued to gaze at her blankly, she shook her head. "Are you shifting around so much that you haven't checked out the neighborhood in a while?"

Alec was gone in a blink. A split second later he was back in the same spot.

"I see," he said. "He's harmless."

"He's annoying, and he's been there for days." She snapped her fingers. "Hey, maybe God will take a trade between him and me?"

Eve was only partially kidding. The whole marked system was jacked, in her opinion. There were millions of religious zealots around the world who killed in God's name every day, but they didn't get marked. Instead, the Almighty used the impious. It was like boot camp for sinners and nonbelievers. God seemed to be saying, *See who you shall hang out with if thou shalt not change thy blasphemous ways?*

"Not a fair exchange," he said, with a hint of a smile. "You're worth a hundred of that guy."

"That's your opinion."

"Clearly I'm not the only one who thinks so, since he's out there and you're with me. I'm also going to talk to Abel about lowering your caseload for a while."

Eve's brows rose. "Won't that put a burden on the other Marks in the area?"

"Somewhat."

"You can't ask me to do that and live with the consequences."

"I'm not asking you."

She considered that for a moment, her fingers drumming on the armrest. "Being an archangel suits you, I see."

"Don't," he warned.

"Infernals are swarming into Orange County—possibly because of me—and you want me to sit around while other Marks deal with the mess? They already don't like me."

"They'll get over it."

"Easy for you to say. No one hates you for working with me."

"You wouldn't do anyone any favors by getting yourself killed."

"Oh, I don't know about that." Her smile was grim. "I can think of a few people who want me dead."

"Not funny, angel."

She sighed. "You know me. I'm a big scaredy-cat. I don't *want* to jump into oncoming traffic, but I can't hang out here watching *Dexter* reruns and eating Ben & Jerry's while other people are facing a horde."

"Argue all you want, it's still not happening."

"Gadara would put me out there."

"He's not here."

"And what's being done about that?" she challenged. "Or are archangels more expendable than I thought?"

Alec reached out and touched her calf with his fingertips. "We're working on that, too."

"It's been two months. I can't imagine it's been a vacation for him in Hell."

"We can't charge in. It would be a suicide mission."

"So what do we do?"

"*You* are going to follow orders. *I'm* going to work on securing leverage."

Eve ignored the first part of his statement and concentrated on the last half. "Leverage. As in . . . something you have that Satan wants more than he wants to keep Gadara?"

"Yes. Sammael has to bring Raguel to us. That's the only way we're going to get him back."

"What does Satan want more than an archangel bargaining chip?"

His mouth twisted wryly. "That's the question, isn't it?"

He ducked without warning. Something small and white flew through the space his head had been occupying. If Eve hadn't been gifted with enhanced sight, she would have missed it.

"Watch it, prick!" he barked at Reed.

"Keep your hands to yourself," Reed shot back.

Eve watched the object hit the balcony screen door and bounce back into the room. It rolled to a stop by the leg of the coffee table. She glanced over her shoulder. "A water chestnut?"

"It was either that or this—" He waved one of her Ginsu knives.

"Thanks for showing a little restraint with your testosterone." Pushing to her bare feet, she set her hands on her hips. "Now knock it off."

"You can't expect us to like this situation," Alec said.

"I'm not liking it either."

When she was alone and contemplative, Eve acknowledged that her feelings of loneliness and separation were goading her to accept a situation she never would have in her normal life. Technically, she wasn't doing anything more than spending private time with both of them, but technicalities weren't much of a buffer against hurt feelings and possessiveness. She felt disloyal to Alec—even though he couldn't return her affections—and she was concerned for Reed, who was so edgy about the whole thing.

"Maybe sticking strictly to business is the only option," she said.

Both men quieted, their jaws taking on stubborn cants. Montevista and Sydney looked at each other with raised brows.

"This isn't working," Eve persisted, her foot tapping on the hardwood.

Reed went back to chopping vegetables.

Alec leaned forward again. "Are you going to stay put like I'm ordering you to?"

Eve crossed her arms. "What do you think?"

"Right." He stood. "So, starting with breakfast tomorrow, you're back to having a full-time mentor. No more of this shifting in only when you need me."

"You're going to be my baby-sitter?"

His dark gaze raked her from head to toe. "Only if I can take you over my knee when you're naughty."

I'm still holding the knife, dickhead, Reed bit out.

Eve dropped back onto the couch with a silent groan. The two brothers were going to be the death of her.

If the demons didn't kill her first.

CHAPTER 3

E ve held a protein shake aloft. "Want one?"

Alec eyed the green beverage with obvious wariness. Dressed in long shorts and a white sleeveless T-shirt with steel-toed boots, he had the bad-boy look down to a science. His shades were hung backward and rested against his nape, tangling with the overlong mane of dark hair that she loved to run her fingers through.

Behind him, early morning sunlight filtered into her living room. Sydney was asleep in the guest room after an all-night watch, and Montevista was outside getting reports from the guards on the street. Beyond her balcony, surfers called out to each other as they hit the waves before the workday.

"You've got that look in your eyes," Alec said, grinning. "You want me."

She turned her back to him. "I'll take that as a no."

"Yes. I want it." He approached. "I want whatever you're dishing out. Enough that if you don't hurry up and give it to me, I just might have to take it."

There was a dark undertone to his voice that set off alarms. The old, prearchangel Alec would never say such a threat to her, but the new Alec . . . Not only did he say things that were out of character, she half feared he wasn't entirely kidding when he said them.

Eve reached behind her and proffered the glass. His fingers curled around hers, warm compared to the chill of the shake. He kept coming until his every exhale disturbed the loose tendrils of hair that always escaped her ponytail. Through their connection, she sensed his pleasure in the smell of her shampoo and the way their bodies fit so well together. The sharing of information worked in reverse, too, so he knew damn well what he was doing to her. When he stepped back, she missed his body heat, but she didn't miss the darkness in him that chilled her.

There's something . . . in me, he'd told her recently, and she believed him. She sometimes felt it. It was ruthless and cold, and it took every opportunity to slither against her.

She poured another glass from the remains in the blender. Her hands shook slightly in response to his proximity. Desire—for sex and/or violence—was the only emotion that affected a Mark's nervous system. "Let's go back to the construction site where we first learned about Gehenna Masonry."

There was a pause, then he said, "Shit. I forgot about the tengu."

"Me, too, until last night." In the process of hunting down the initial masked tengu, she and Alec had ended up at a construction site for a new Gadara Enterprises building—Olivet Place. They'd killed the two tengu they found there, but . . . "The building has four corners. Since they like to pack together, I figure they'd want to regroup."

"Why not go back to Upland where they were created?"

Facing him, Eve leaned back into the edge of the counter. "Because we blew it up?"

"You know what I mean. Why Raguel's building? Why not one of the others on Gehenna Masonry's list?"

"Because I was invited to this one. Remember?"

"Right," he murmured. "The invitation."

"One of many dangling threads in my life."

She'd stumbled upon the building by accident in her search for the tengu, but later found an opening-day invite in her mailbox. It had been a mock-up of the final invitation and not yet ready for publication, but someone had addressed it to her and mailed it. Someone had wanted her to check it out.

"I looked into it," he told her. "You were invited because all local interior designers and architects were. I checked it out myself. Your name was definitely on the list. All of your old colleagues at the Weisenberg Group were."

"Were the other invitations going to be shipped to home addresses?"

He leaned into the island. The casual pose did nothing to hide his alertness. "Good point. It should have been mailed to your office."

"At the time, I asked you what the chances were that I would be lured to a demon-infested building at the exact same time I was marked. And you said—"

"—slim to none."

Eve nodded. "So what changed your mind?"

"My thoughts went along these lines: the invitations were ordered by Raguel, the infestation was in one of his buildings, and we eradicated the two tengu we found when we got here."

"So you thought it was the work of a divine hand?"

"Could be. The good guys benefited. Anyway, why would an Infernal deliberately set up something that could potentially expose the mask? Makes no sense."

"Is it possible that Gadara set it all up?" She wouldn't put it past him. The archangel had been making her job as difficult as possible from the very beginning. As a mentor and Mark pair, Alec and she were a package deal. Gadara was relishing the novel opportunity to have Cain—and Cain's prestige—attached to his firm. However, his coup didn't stop him from using Eve to assert his authority over Alec. By moving her around like a pawn, he forced Alec to toe the line or risk her paying the consequences.

"He's more direct, you know that."

"But if you believe the invitation was celestially motivated, someone had to know about the tengu. Who?"

"Angel, it could go as high as the seraphim."

"Why not use the established chain of command? Send the order to Gadara, he would assign it to a handler, a handler would assign it to a trained and capable Mark. Bringing it straight to me is ridiculous."

"Is it? You got the job done."

"Flattery will get you nowhere in this. Other times, maybe. But not this time."

He gave her an exasperated look. "I take it you're thinking this is part of a plot of some sort?"

"I don't know. That's why we're heading over there."

His dark eyes were amused. "You know, your brain turns me on."

"Everything turns you on."

"Everything about *you*."

"You're feeling punchy this morning."

"I like being out in the field. Especially with you. Your ability to attract disasters definitely keeps things interesting."

"Not funny." Eve drank deeply and tried to picture him at a desk job. After a minute, she gave up.

"This shake isn't bad," Alec noted, licking his lips.

"What a compliment." The shake was orange juice and banana with green tea protein powder. She thought it was delicious, plus it would keep her fueled for a few hours at least. Marks burned calories like mad. As Reed said, *Highly efficient machines use superior fuel.* Translation: she ate like a sumo wrestler.

"I thought I was making you One-Eyed Jacks."

"When we get back. I'm eager to get moving."

"To face a possible horde of tengu? Why?"

"Can't you read my mind?" she challenged, even as she shut a mental door in his face.

His gaze narrowed with concentration, then one dark brow rose. "We have to figure out how you do that."

"What's to figure out? My acclimation has been out of whack from the beginning." She rinsed her glass out in the sink. He came up beside her and shoved his under the running water. At the same moment, the thought of the Nix entered both of their heads. As one, they pushed the thought away. One demon at a time.

"I'm serious, angel. Our connection can save your life."

"Not my fault. My Novium happened way too soon. Let's face it: the mark and I don't mesh well."

The Novium was a physical and mental transition Marks suffered through to progress from trainee to full-fledged. Like puberty, it altered a Mark's physical makeup, enhancing already keen senses and instilling a devil-may-care confidence. Side effects were edginess and lowered inhibitions. It created a fever that strengthened a Mark's tie to her handler while cauterizing the connection to her mentor. In Eve's case, it had created a triumvirate communication pathway that she was pretty sure would drive her crazy one day.

"Don't blame this on the mark," he chastised. "You're closing me off on purpose."

"You don't need to know everything."

He caught her around the waist when she tried to pass and tugged her close. "I *want* to know you, inside and out."

"So figure me out the old-fashioned way. It's more interesting that way."

She'd been in love with him since she was eighteen years old. It sucked that while he was back in her life now, he could never stay in it permanently. Alec was a killer by nature. He didn't just excel at it, he loved it. Not the kind of guy a woman settled down and had kids with. Of course, Marks were physically incapable of bearing children, but that wasn't the point.

Alec pressed a kiss to the tip of her nose. "You ready to go?"

"Don't shift!" she said quickly. "Let's take the bike."

"Ha! Make you a moving target? No way."

"It's less than ten minutes away! Besides, you don't even know if the bounty is real."

"I'm not using you as bait to find out."

Eve reached around and cupped his ass, giving him a slow, firm squeeze.

"Not fair," he rumbled.

"Did you forget how to ride after all that shifting around you've been doing?"

"Hardly."

"I can drive," she purred, looking up at him from beneath heavy-lidded eyes. "You can shield my back. No Infernal is going to mess with badass Cain of Infamy."

"*You* better not mess with me either," he warned, his eyes dark, "unless you're prepared to deliver."

"Hanging on while I drive is a guaranteed way to cop a feel."

"With our clothes on," he retorted. "Not nearly as fun."

Despite his protests, he shifted them into the carport next to his Heritage Softail. It was a black and chrome beauty, boasting custom saddlebags and a well-worn seat.

"Well, look at that." Eve whistled. "I was half expecting it to be covered in dust."

Alec tossed her the keys. "Shut up and hop on, before I change my mind."

Five minutes later, they were roaring out of the subterranean garage. When the Bible-thumping Evil Santa on the corner screamed *"Jezebel!"* after her, she stuck her tongue out at him. Alec gave her a playful swat to the hip.

Told you, she muttered.

Behave.

Taking Hamilton to Magnolia, Eve weaved confidently among the massive sport utility vehicles, sleek Porsches, and hybrids. A variety of music filled the air from open windows—thumping bass, twanging guitars, and soulful ballads. For the first time in far too long, she didn't wonder how many of the drivers around her were lower-ranking demons. She forcibly shut out the world and concentrated on the joy of driving a Harley with the hottest man on the planet wrapped around her. As far as Heaven went, this was pretty close.

They reached the Gothic-inspired office building before she was ready. Eve considered driving on and circling back later, but a Jeep Liberty was pulling away from the metered curb just as they pulled up. Recognizing the celestial hint, Eve steered the hog into the spot and cut the engine.

"Got you here in one piece," she teased, pulling off her helmet.

The heated thoughts in his mind slipped into hers, telling her bluntly that the feel of her body so close to his was something he craved to a dangerous degree. She slid off the bike and kept her gaze on the building, her breathing altered by the depths of his arousal. There was nothing tender about it. It was pure ferocious lust.

"You can run . . ." he warned.

But she couldn't hide. Her head turned, her senses perking up and searching out any possible threats. The scent of rotting soul drifted on the balmy breeze, but not in a quantity that would alarm her. Infernals were everywhere, working every sort of job, living in every community. Their presence alone wasn't concerning, only the number, which seemed to be under control.

Unless some were masked.

"It wears off, remember?" Alec said, securing the helmets to the bike.

"There could be more."

"Doubtful, since we killed the creators. Regardless, Hank is working on an antidote."

Eve looked over her shoulder at him. "Really?"

"Would I lie to you?"

"Are you sure you want to go there?"

He held up both hands in a gesture of surrender, but the wicked curve of his lips ruined the image.

Shaking her head, she started toward the front door. The building wasn't yet fully operational, but the lobby area was completed and an office for the sales team and property manager was open for business. A perky blonde in a sleek gray suit rushed out when they entered, then laughed when Eve pulled out her Gadara Enterprises badge. "I was ready to give you my sales pitch."

"I'm already sold," Eve said. "Hostile takeover."

Angel . . .

There were two guards at the security desk, one mortal and one Mark. The mortal took her badge and ran it through a scanner to record their entry time.

Gadara's security measures weren't any more rigorous than the majority of corporations, but they were certainly monitored more closely. Instead of keeping watch on things with a celestially enhanced eye, the archangels were forced by the empathy-for-mortals rule to rely on modern mortal technology. They could choose to do otherwise, but there were consequences. That was one of many things that drove Eve nuts about the Almighty. He claimed to give people a "choice," but usually the ramifications of making the wrong choice ensured it wasn't much of a contest.

"Great bike," the mortal guard said to Eve.

"It's his." She gestured toward Alec with a tilt of her head.

"I should let my girl drive."

Alec raked Eve with a heated glance. "It definitely has its benefits."

She pushed the sign-in sheet back over. "Elevators working yet?"

"Yes. Finally." The relief in the guard's voice made her smile. Patrolling the three stories without a lift would be a breeze for the Mark, but for the mortal it was probably more of a workout than he wanted from his job.

"Thanks."

As Eve headed toward the elevators, she noted the limestone floors and pointed arch facades that surrounded the brass elevator doors. A rose window took prominence at the rear of the building just above the exit. She made a mental note to look into the identity of the architect. The building's style was incongruous among its modern glass-hulled neighbors, but not in a garish way. It provided an elegance that the surrounding area had been lacking.

The moment the elevator doors shut, Alec's presence overwhelmed the enclosed space. He stood opposite her with his hands wrapped around the handrail behind him, his biceps and pectorals prominently displayed by his stance. His dark gaze was slightly mocking and more than a little insolent in his appraisal. It turned her on, and she shifted her weight from one foot to the other.

The Novium was a pain in the ass.

It didn't help that sex was like breathing to Marks. The constant near-death experiences created tension that was best alleviated with extended hot sex. The need was designed to force Marks to seek out companionship and comfort from others, rather than retreating into themselves. Eve's platonic double-dating meant she didn't have the stress outlet she needed. Even if that wasn't the case, Alec was different. The softer emotions he used to have in his eyes when he looked at her were gone. He wanted her, and she believed him when he said that he would always want her, but great sex wasn't enough for her. Not after knowing what it was like to have more.

"What's the best thing about being an archangel?" she asked in an attempt to keep her mind out of the bedroom.

"Relief from the rising cost of transportation."

"Be serious."

"You want the Hallmark card answer? Making a difference." He straightened as the car came to a stop. "No one knows better than me how difficult it is to be a Mark. There are aspects of Gadara Enterprises that I can tweak to make things easier on those in the field."

There was no inflection in his voice, no passion. She wondered how he could function that way. God felt it was necessary for the archangels to be emotionally neutral, but Eve called 'em like she saw them—they were unfeeling—and she couldn't imagine that being anything but miserable.

I feel what you feel, Alec said, watching her intensely. *I feel what Abel feels, as well as echoes from every Mark under me.*

So he knew what it was like for her to love him and he knew what it was like for Abel to want her. Maybe that's where his uncustomary sexual aggression was coming from.

Or maybe it was coming from that dark place inside him . . .

Regardless, the whole thing was screwed six ways to Sunday.

Eve sighed and turned her attention to the opening elevator doors.

The third floor was a notable change from the lobby. Ceiling fixtures had yet to be installed, the walls needed paint, and the industrial pile burgundy carpet had yet to be trimmed along the missing baseboards.

"So," she began, leading the way to the roof staircase, "you wanted to know why I was eager to come here."

"Shoot."

"When I went through this building the first time, I had no idea what I was doing. I didn't know what to look for, where the threats were, what was out of place. I need to see it again. Retrace my steps. I feel like I missed something and it's driving me nuts."

Alec's hand wrapped around her elbow. She'd dressed in a pale pink sleeveless shell and well-worn jeans. The outfit was comfortable, feminine, and allowed for ease of movement.

"We don't get to decide when it's time for things to happen, angel. We just roll with the punches and have faith that everything happens for a reason."

"I don't have faith in a divine plan, you know that. I think life is what we make of it and God throws curveballs on a whim just to keep his days interesting."

"Watch it," he admonished, as if lightning might strike her in the enclosed space. Eve wouldn't be surprised. The Lord had yet to do her any favors.

They stepped into the stairwell. Warm, stagnant air rushed around them, in stark contrast to the cooler air-conditioning of the occupied areas. The heavy metal door thudded shut and images of Reed flooded her mind. He'd branded her with the Mark of Cain in the stairwell of Gadara Tower, a raw and violent coupling that would forever be burned in her memory.

If you don't stop thinking about that, Alec warned roughly, *I'll replace that memory with another one. Right now.*

She blanked her mind quickly.

The Alec she had once known would never have made such a threat. Seduce her, yes. Make love to her until she couldn't move or think, yes. But primal fucking was Reed's style. Alec had been a lover. Eve didn't know how to deal with the new version of him. He was more aggressive, less patient. More like the biblical Cain, she supposed. The side of him she had never seen. She knew she would enjoy whatever he did to her—he wouldn't tolerate otherwise—but she couldn't risk sinking deeper. She was already neck-deep as it was.

The roof door opened above them.

"Pretty Mark came back," a tengu singsonged, followed by a frenzied thumping as it jumped for joy. "And Cain, too. Time to play."

Tengu were mischievous creatures. They lacked initiative and ambition, so they fell pretty low on the "must-vanquish" scale. Reed likened them to mosquitoes—annoying and you wished they didn't exist, but not as disgusting as rats. They infiltrated establishments as decorations, then worked to cause distress and anxiety in the inhabitants. Buildings with tengu had higher suicide rates than those that didn't. Higher rates of business failures, extortion, eviction, embezzlement, and adultery. Tengu infestation was the cause of community decline, dead malls, and ghost towns. In packs, they could be deadly, or at the very least, seriously destructive.

The door slammed shut and a riotous banging resounded on the roof, the sound of little stone feet dancing. Lots of feet. Lots of dancing.

"Damn, you're good," Alec said.

Eve sighed. Sometimes, she hated being right.

CHAPTER 4

"What are you doing, *mon chéri*?"

Reed stiffened at the sound of the familiar purring voice. Glancing over his shoulder, he met the calculated gaze of Sarakiel, one of the seven earthbound archangels. She walked into Cain's office as if she owned it.

"That's none of your business," he drawled.

"I hear Cain has returned to the field with Evangeline. Perhaps that is why you are rummaging through his office? 'While the cat is away . . .' as they say."

The manner in which Sara said Eve's name spoke volumes. She still coveted Reed, even though they had split ages before Eve was born. The head of the European firm of Marks was often assumed by theologians to be a male. Their mistake was laughable. Sarakiel was a woman in every sense of the word, one who shared his penchant for rough sex and designer clothing.

He pushed the top drawer of Cain's filing cabinet shut. The archangels usually stayed within their own territory. They didn't like to defer to each other, which was expected when entering another firm's boundaries. It was also dangerous to have archangels in close proximity to one another. Infernals would love to cripple multiple firms with a single blow. But Sara was here because she had requested to assist Cain with his assumption of Raguel's firm. She'd been given her desire because it was her personal guards who had assisted Cain and Eve in Upland. She was lauded for being proactive, when the only reason she'd lent her team was because Reed had paid her with the use of his body. Now, her mentorship of his brother kept her uncomfortably near his business.

"What do you want, Sara?"

"What do I always want when I see you?"

A ripple of disquiet moved through him. "Not today, darling. I have a headache."

Her lips thinned at the blatant lie. *Mal'akhs* were impervious to mortal maladies. Still, the beauty of her features was unaffected by her anger. Tall, willowy yet fully curved, Sara was physically perfect in a way mortal women spent thousands of dollars to replicate. Her pale blonde hair and angelic features were so compelling, they were the impetus that funded her firm. Sara Kiel Cosmetics was a worldwide phenomenon, with sales inspired by the unequaled face of its owner. There had been a time when the mere sight of her could make Reed's blood heat dangerously, but no longer. Now his focus was narrowed to one particular brunette.

Sara stepped farther into the room with her distinctive sashay, her red silk pantsuit whispering seductively as she approached. She reminded him of a tigress—golden, lithe, predatory. "You have a dreadful way of showing gratitude."

"You haven't done a damn thing for me, Sara, aside from the occasional orgasm." Reed shrugged. "I can get that anywhere."

"You used to only want them from me."

"That was a long time ago." Knowing that appearances spoke volumes to her, he sank into Cain's large leather office chair and forced his frame to relax into the plush back.

"You want what he has," she taunted, sinking into the visitor's seat on the other side of the desk. A wave of her hand encompassed the entire room, a corner office that boasted two walls of windows, a private bathroom with closet and shower, and a glass and chrome desk with industrial styling. Leaning forward, she ran her fingertips over the silver picture frame that held a black and white photo of Evangeline. "You always have."

"I want what I deserve, what I've proven myself capable of handling."

"And Cain keeps getting it first."

"That works in my favor. He always fucks things up and makes me look good."

All of his life, Reed had been the one to follow the rules and surpass expectations. He was perfect, damn it. Perfect for advancement, perfect for heading a firm. It made no sense that his brother was the one promoted. Cain didn't want responsibility of any kind and he'd been a nomad for too long. He had never learned to play well with others.

Sara pouted. "I am trying to help you, and you are not giving me any credit. I sent Izzie here, did I not?"

"I'm supposed to thank you for that?" He had been indiscreet with the blonde and Eve had caught him at it. Now, every time she saw Izzie, the memory stung her and caused him to lose what little ground he gained in his attempts to win her.

"You should have stayed away from her."

"You knew what would happen," he bit out. "And you told Izzie to be around when it did."

"As a firm leader, it is my responsibility to prepare for every eventuality. There was a chance that desire for your brother's lover would drive you elsewhere. I had to make accommodations for that event, just in case."

Her crimson-painted fingertips drummed atop the armrests. "Do you think I wanted Cain's woman to affect you so strongly?"

Iselda Seiler had been one of Eve's classmates. A woman whose Goth sensibilities manifested in pale skin, kohl-rimmed eyes, and a fondness for purple lipstick. Izzie also had the distinction of having fucked Cain at some point in his past. One of thousands who'd serviced him over the centuries. His brother didn't remember her, but Izzie didn't care. She just wanted another go-round, both for the sex and because it was guaranteed to stir up trouble. She had lain in wait to sabotage Eve in any way she could, and she'd been ready and more than willing when Eve had pushed Reed too far to think clearly.

But why Sara would claim to want him in the same breath as she admitted sending another woman to service him made no sense.

"You're a real piece of work," he said. "I wonder, do you make Father proud?"

Sara gripped the ends of the chair arms with white-knuckled force, but her voice came with its customary whiskey smoothness. "You malign me without cause, *mon chéri*. You and I are two of a kind."

"Except you're an archangel, and I'm not." There had been a time when he'd been foolish enough to hope that she might help him achieve his own firm. Then he realized that she would never see him as equal to her. He provided stud service and nothing more. "You could have helped me, but you didn't."

"Obviously Jehovah is in agreement with me, since he has yet to promote you."

"Fuck you."

"Finally, a crack in your composure." Sara smiled. "Let me give you a tip: Evangeline is waiting for one of you to make the decision for her. She does not want to bear the responsibility of choosing one of you. With the right push, she will tumble from the tree like a ripe apple."

The allusion to temptation wasn't lost on him. Reed yawned, feigning boredom. "How would you know?"

"I am a woman. I know how women think." When silence stretched out between them, she asked, "Are you snooping in here because of her or not?"

"I want to know what we're doing about Raguel."

"Nothing."

"That's what I thought." What Eve thought, too, and it was niggling at her in a way that concerned him. When she focused on something, she was like a dog with a bone. She wouldn't let it go. And he had his own reasons for feeling similarly about Raguel.

"It is best to move when the time is right," Sara explained. "The seven firms are intact for the present. We can afford to move wisely and not rashly."

"Bullshit."

"What can we do, *mon chéri*? We have nothing with which to entice Sammael to start bargaining."

"You're not even trying."

"Cain is." Sara licked her lips. "Do you hope to win Evangeline's favor by playing the hero? Is your brother one step ahead of you again?"

"You know, Sara," he steepled his fingertips, "Cain isn't the only one who's accumulated favors over the years. If I wanted to, I could make your life far more difficult than it is."

The rage of angels gave her blue eyes a golden tinge. Her voice resonated with an archangel's command, "Do not threaten me, Abel."

"I won't." His mouth curved. "Just reminding you that I have teeth, and they do bite."

As quickly as it came, her rage was gone and in its place was arousal. Despite her claws, or maybe because of them, she craved a firm hand. His hand was firmer than most. But while Sara liked rough sex—regardless of who her partner was—Eve had been shocked by her enjoyment of his handling. She'd responded with complete abandon, in a way that Sara never could because the archangel was devoid of the ability to care deeply for anyone but God. Eve's helpless pleasure had added an edge to their encounter that he craved like a junkie.

But no one could ever know that, or how much he needed her now that Cain was an archangel. Through his connection to her, Reed could conceivably tap into his brother's knowledge and power. He could learn along with Cain, then surpass his brother as he always did.

If his tie to Eve was strong enough.

If she trusted him enough to let her guard down.

If they were lovers.

"Abel." Sara stood and rounded the desk. Her fingers went to the button of her coat and slipped it free, exposing a black camisole and hard nipples. "You look so lovesick when you are thinking of her, you know. But I would be happy to play surrogate . . . for now."

He lunged for her, vaulting from the chair and tackling her to the carpeted floor. Her cry was tinged with both pain and excitement. Bright-eyed and panting, she writhed beneath him. He settled between her spread legs and ground lewdly against her.

"You want it?" he whispered, his mouth hovering just above hers.

"No."

Reed smiled grimly at the familiar game. "Good. Because you're not going to get it until you help me get Raguel."

Sara stilled. "What?"

"You heard me." Shoving off of her, he pushed to his feet. "I get what I want, you get what you want."

She laughed, but it was a mirthless, bitter sound. "As you said earlier, you have nothing I cannot get elsewhere."

"Then get it elsewhere and leave me alone." He straightened his tie and ran a hand through his hair.

Sprawled on the floor and disheveled, she remained undiminished. "I can destroy you."

"Do it," he taunted. "It would benefit both of us. It's so clichéd, you know. This vixenish, sex-starved, femme fatale role you play. You need a makeover, Sara. Perhaps if I'm gone, you'll get one."

For a moment, Reed thought she might shred him to pieces. She could, if she desired. She was far more powerful than he was in every way. Then the moment passed. Her expressive face showed the transformation from furious indignation to sly consideration. She held her hand out to him for assistance. Catching her wrist, he pulled her to standing.

"Why such concern for Raguel?" she asked, righting her clothing.

Reed shook his head. What he wanted from Raguel was for him alone to know.

"I underestimated you." Her tone was thoughtful. She thrust her fingers into her shoulder-length tresses and shook them out. "Trust me on this point: Evangeline cannot be pulled to you. She must be pushed. Rescuing Raguel will not be enough to win her from Cain."

"Why are you so fixated on Eve? Get over it."

"I want *you* to get over *her*," Sara said without inflection. "And the surest way to do that is to let you have your fill."

He watched the way her gaze darted around the room. Cain's room. The seat of his new power. Understanding dawned. "Ah, I see. Clever girl. This doesn't have anything to do with me. Or sex. This is about my brother."

For once he wasn't needled by Cain's prominence. He was, instead, relieved Eve was not the focus.

Her chin lifted. "Must everything in your life be about him?"

"Don't put this on me," he admonished, amused by her chagrin. "You have to compete with a new archangel, one who retains Jehovah's favor no matter how fucked up he is. Giving Eve to me means getting her away from Cain. That might make him crazy enough to do something stupid. Maybe prompt a response that might prove him unworthy of the ascension"

"You are obsessed with—"

"I like the way you think, Sara," he interjected. "Don't ruin my moment of admiration with your bitching."

Her mouth snapped shut.

Reed moved to the desk and leaned against it. "I'm surprised you approached me with the Eve angle, though. Why not dangle Cain as the bait? Did you really believe she would be more of a draw than my brother?"

"I have never seen you so focused on a woman. I saw the tape. Of you and her in the stairwell. When you marked her."

A surge of fury moved through him. That was for him and Eve alone. The thought of someone else observing—especially Sara—made his gut and fists clench.

He uncurled his fingers one by one.

"Ah, but she's not just any woman, is she?" he murmured. As Sara's mouth curved in a smile, he knew he had her. "We want the same thing, and we're agreed on how best to get it."

Eyeing him warily, she returned to her seat. "So . . . ?"

"I don't think Izzie's enough to lure him away, or to drive Eve to me."

"Iselda had him once."

"When he thought he couldn't have Eve. That's not the case now."

"You spoke of favors owed. What favor would he have cashed in to be promoted?"

Reed stilled. "Maybe . . ." he murmured, "it's a favor he *promised*."

After a moment of silence, she began to applaud, each measured clap like a gunshot in the room. "Brilliant."

"Find out to whom," he ordered, "and—if you can—what the ante is."

"Well," she drawled, "that will only take me a few decades. I am not even certain how many seraphim and cherubim there are."

He knew she would find a way. She wouldn't be the last female archangel heading a firm, if she wasn't both ruthless and resourceful.

As for Raguel, Reed would have to seek alternate routes to reach him, and he would have to move cautiously and alone. No archangel would initiate an offensive maneuver against Sammael, which ensured that no *mal'akh* or Mark would help him either.

To whom did one turn when he wished to go where angels feared to tread?

He turned away from Sara.

To a demon, of course.

Another horde of tengu.

Alec looked at Eve and groaned inwardly. She attracted disasters. And it had nothing to do with her smelling like a Mark.

"Come here," he beckoned, his voice resonant with an archangel's command but lacking coercion. He wanted her to come freely.

She looked at him with wary eyes, sensing the turmoil within him. He wondered if she heard the stirrings in his head, the needs that hissed like serpents, prodding his temper and making him both irritable and mischievous.

If she only knew what that prim pink shirt of hers did to him. The snug fit made it hard for him to concentrate on the task at hand. He wanted her; the darkness in him pushed him to take her, while another part of him was far more fascinated by the little freckle on her nape and the small section of silky hair that was always falling out of her ponytail. The two halves were fighting all the time, exhausting him and leaving him confused.

Did all archangels suffer a similar duality? Or was he—Cain of Infamy—uniquely evil in a way he'd denied for centuries?

As an archangel, he had been stripped of the ability to love anyone but God, but his need for Eve was more urgent than ever. Malevolent voices had joined him with the ascension. They whispered deep within his breast, fueled by the connection he had to all the Infernals within the firm. As long as Eve was near, his control was tenuous. She was a beacon in the gloom and he craved her in a ferocious way, but he couldn't relinquish her, even for her own benefit. She was a direct line into Abel's head and all the knowledge his brother had gained in the centuries he'd been a handler. As a fledgling archangel, Alec needed that information to run the firm.

He couldn't keep his promise to help free her from the mark. Not yet. Maybe never.

"I can never read what you're thinking," she said, "when you have that particular expression."

"I can show you what I'm thinking . . ." He was unable to curb the edge to his words.

"You and your brother are more alike than you realize."

"Perhaps we're more alike than *you* realize," he warned. His smile felt cruel. He wouldn't be able to resist having her much longer, and when it happened, he doubted he could be as gentle with her as he'd once been.

A shadow passed over her features and through her mind. A sense of loss and melancholy.

Regret settled heavily over him, his humanity waxing and the recklessness waning in response to her withdrawal.

"Come here," he repeated, gentler this time, his hand extended to her.

With her chin lifted, Eve descended the few steps between them. Frustrated by that hint of reluctance, Alec caught her around the waist and pulled her flush against him. He shifted so quickly that she was still midgasp when they alighted on a nearby rooftop.

She smacked him on the shoulder. "You could have warned me!"

He nipped the end of her nose with a tiny love bite. "I could have. But this was more fun."

"For who?"

"For both of us. I know you, daredevil. You're the type of girl who'd take off with a stranger on a Harley just for the ride."

Her nose wrinkled. "Where's a stranger on a Harley when I need one?"

"What? And miss this party?" He gestured to the roof of Gadara's unfinished building.

A couple of dozen tengu danced excitedly around the massive ventilation and air-conditioning units dotting the shiny metal top. Each little gray stone beast was the size of a gallon of milk. They sported tiny wings and broad grins. Eve had once called them cute, although they were far from cuddly.

"Right," she said, hands going to her hips. "Figures it would have to be the roof again."

"Tengu were the original inspiration for gargoyles. What better place to hide than in plain sight?"

"I don't care about that. I care about my fear of heights not meshing well with running around on rooftops."

Alec looked at her. He knew she had a phobia about heights, but it didn't affect her decisiveness. Her features were set in her gearing-up-to-brawl look: pursed lips, narrowed eyes, and a stubborn jawline. He didn't like her being in the line of fire, but he sure liked her game face.

"Look at the little bastards," she muttered, sending his gaze back to the tengu. "They're trying to brain us."

Sure enough, the tengu had formed a ladder of sorts by standing on each other's shoulders. Other tengu climbed up the backs of their brethren to reach the top of the stairwell enclosure. They waited there for a chance to jump on whoever stepped onto the roof, their hands clasped over their mouths to stem their incessant giggling.

"Why do you think we're over here?" he said. "I wanted you to see what we're up against before you barreled headfirst out the door and into danger."

"I wouldn't have done that!"

"Would have been the first time you held back."

Eve faced him. "As a warm-up to kicking their asses, I'm about to kick *yours*. Why are you pushing me?"

"Because that's what mentors are supposed to do, angel."

She exhaled harshly. "Did you notice that it didn't stink when the door was open? And look, they don't have any details."

"I noticed."

"The mask is supposed to wear off. Maybe we didn't wipe out everyone who knew about the formula."

"Yep. Could be trouble."

"Or could be they were made with the masking stuff mixed into the cement."

Alec smiled.

She shot him a wry glance. "You already thought of that."

"Yes, but only a second before you did."

"We could also have a leak somewhere in the firm."

"It's possible," he conceded, "but that would be my last guess."

While most firms had Infernals working within their ranks, they were rarely trusted with sensitive information. Demons never fully acclimated to the celestial life and the rules that came with it. Many considered their "conversion" temporary. They secretly hoped to get their hands on valuable information or an object that would prompt Sammael to take them back into the fold. However, both Raguel and Alec trusted Hank—an oc-cultist who specialized in the magical arts—to oversee the investigation into the mask. Hank had been with the North American firm for so long that he was a fixture. He was still inherently evil, but he was content to be evil for the good guys.

"So how do we want to do this?" Eve asked, tightening her ponytail. "I suppose we should keep one of them to see what they're made of."

"If you can manage it this time." The last time they fought tengu on Gadara's roof, she'd vanquished both of them.

Shoving him playfully in the shoulder, Eve said, "Bring it on. Let's see which one of us can catch one."

"What's the ante?"

"Hmm . . ."

"Sex."

"With me? That's worth more than a tengu."

Alec laughed. "Agreed. But I'm hard up, I had to try."

"We'll just keep it on retainer."

"Works for me. Gives me time to come up with something really good."

"Ha! Assuming you'll win, which you won't."

He held out his hand to shake on it. "Bring it on."

Eve accepted the handshake with a mischievous gleam in her dark eyes. "I'll take the lower left corner."

"Upper right. Meet in the middle?"

She nodded.

He snatched her close and kissed her. A hot, wet, deep kiss that took advantage of her gasp to sneak inside and lick. At the same time, he shifted them to the tengu-infested roof, so it was over the moment it started. But it was great while it lasted. He dropped her off, then shifted to the corner on the diagonal.

"Pretty Mark!" an observant tengu cried, followed by excited squeals from the rest of the mob. The few on the stairwell jumped down, one breaking off a leg in the process. It collected its detached appendage and continued on with a one-legged hop.

"Hey," Alec roared as they all surged toward Eve.

"Cain!" several yelled gleefully, separating from the mass and chang-ing direction toward him.

Eve was already in motion, darting to the side and catching a tengu by the arm. Swinging in a wide arc, she gained velocity. She hurtled the de-mon into its brethren like a bowling ball into pins. Some crashed into those behind them, some leaped over the tumbling wave. She knocked one back with a roundhouse kick and feinted away from another one. Her grim de-termination and unwavering focus arrested Alec. When Marks were on a hunt, they were bolstered by the effects of the mark—adrenaline, aggres-sion, increased muscle mass. Fear was held at bay by those things. But Eve wasn't on a hunt, she was on her own. She managed it beautifully.

Two tengu launched a third one at Alec like a missile. He ducked. Like Eve, he used rapid kicks to keep his immediate perimeter clear, but maintenance wasn't the goal. Eradication was. A loud crash and high-pitched shouts of dismay on the other side of the roof told him Eve had just smashed one. Tengu were all for having a little evil fun, but not if it meant getting hurt.

Catching a tengu in each hand, he bashed them together. Debris exploded outward and turned to ash before hitting the ground. "Two down. Ten more to go."

"Cain can't save pretty Mark," a tengu sang, flapping its stone wings. "Sammael gets what Sammael wants."

"Sammael is going to get *me,*" he barked back, "if he doesn't keep his minions to himself."

Laughing, the tengu regrouped and rushed him. He waited until the last minute, then shifted away. The converging tengu collided. Two overzealous ones hit each other with enough force to wipe each other out. A cloud of ash plumed upward and dissipated in the gentle breeze.

The sound of thick metal sheeting bending in ways it shouldn't turned his head toward Eve. His gaze found little cement feet protruding from a hole in the air-conditioning unit. They'd already repaired the massive and expensive system once before, due to their last altercation with tengu on this roof.

Hang in there, he said, sensing Eve's strength was strained by the heavy beasts.

Don't worry about me. Take care of yourself.

Alec wondered if she knew that she was the only person in existence who worried over him. He stepped up his pace. He snatched up any tengu unfortunate enough to get too close and used them to crush their friends. As he worked, he crossed the roof, closing the distance between him and Eve. She was still several tengu deep, but seemed to be holding her own.

I'm winning, he taunted.

In response to his challenge, she became more aggressive, lunging and catching the little demons just like he was. Considering her much smaller size, he was impressed with her ability to keep up.

They should have backed off by now, she grunted.

Eve was right. Tengu liked to play, but when the tide turned against them, they ran.

They want you, he explained.

Huh?

I'm thinking the ice bitch wasn't kidding.

Fucking fabulous, she muttered, hefting a tengu overhead and braining another with it. Both burst into ash.

Alec grabbed two tengu by the backs of their skulls and pounded them together. Then he moved toward Eve.

Back off, hero, she said, kicking another into a ventilation turbine. *I've got this.*

Grinning, he stepped back and crossed his arms. *There's one to your left. Right. Left. Behind you. Ooh, great shot. Kick it again. Duck!*

I'm going to kill you next, she bit out, struggling to shake off a tengu clinging to her back.

You'd miss me. He rubbed at his chest and the swelling pride that made it ache.

Not right now. She snatched at the demon and yanked it over her head. She swung it like a golf club into the one wrapped around her leg, knocking both free and sending them flying. With arms splayed, Alec caught them in each hand and launched them discus-style into the heavy stairwell door. Stumbling from the blow to her leg, Eve faced the last tengu standing.

"Sammael wants you, pretty Mark," the Infernal said, hopping.

Eve regained her balance and pushed a few stray stands of hair back from her face. "He'll have to take a number."

"You can't run, you can't hide."

"You can't scare me," she sang back with a humorless smile.

"Sammael will."

He dashed toward her with a growl. Alec straightened abruptly, prepared to leap in. Eve feinted to the side, catching the demon's arm as he passed. She swung him up, then hammered him down into the rooftop. Ash mushroomed and hovered for a heartbeat in a pocket of still air, then burst free in a sudden breeze.

Alec applauded. He doubted many novices would have handled multiple opponents with as much aplomb.

It took her a moment to shake off the bloodlust brought on by the lingering effects of the Novium. But when she did, she smiled sheepishly and sketched a quick, exaggerated bow. He loved the bow and the strength of character that made it possible for her to dust herself off so quickly.

He glanced at the kicking feet of the tengu stuck in the side of the van-sized AC unit. "You win."

"Damn straight."

"Of course, you have a great mentor."

The wry look she shot him made him laugh, something he only ever did around her.

"That—" she pointed a finger at the writhing tengu, "—isn't going to fit on your bike."

"Right. Do you want to go back for the car? Or have me do it?" He could shift with mortals and Marks, but not with demons. "I'll have to drive back, so it won't be quick."

"Quicker than me. You can shift to the garage. I have to drive both ways."

"You sure?"

"Sure." Her gaze narrowed on the wriggling cement buttocks. "If it acts up, I'll spank it."

"Lucky tengu."

With a wink, he shifted away.

CHAPTER 5

Less than half an hour later, Eve and Alec were exiting the elevators on the lobby level of Olivet Place with the tengu tucked under Alec's arm. To mortal eyes the little beast appeared as rigid as its stone imitators, but it was in fact wriggling madly.

"Keep it up," Eve warned, "and we'll drop you to the bottom of the Mariana Trench and you'll have to hike back."

The tengu gasped, then stilled.

"Where are you going with that?" the mortal guard asked, but the Mark next to him touched his arm and shook his head.

"You won't miss him," Eve said, waving good-bye. "Trust me."

They stepped outside. She moved directly to the Harley and pulled her Oakley shades out of the leather pouch on the gas tank. "Where's the car?"

"Around the corner."

She gestured ahead with a wave of her hand. "I'll follow you."

Alec took the lead, shortening his long-legged stride to keep her close. Eve walked behind him and slightly to the left, allowing the tengu to be carried along the curb and away from other pedestrians. Her nose wrinkled as the scent of rotting soul roiled in the wind. She held her breath, but a hard bump to her shoulder by a passing pedestrian knocked her back and made her turn her head. She caught the culprit leering back at her. With fangs. His face was covered in writhing black details and his eyes glowed laser-green. With a chopping motion of his hand, he mouthed, *Head will roll.*

Despite an inner shiver, Eve flipped him the bird . . . and crashed into something rock solid.

"Watch it," Alec bit out.

When she looked up at him to explain, she found him staring down the fleeing vampire with the look of death. Coming from Cain of Infamy, it scared even Eve. Then his head turned, raking their surroundings with an examining gaze. She followed suit and froze. Infernals littered the sidewalks in unusually high concentration for the area, far more than had been present when they'd arrived. Having the headquarters of the North American firm here in Orange County discouraged Infernals from playing in the vicinity, but apparently not today.

Alec's growing fury filtered through her, chilling her with his cold aggression. A low, resonant snarl rumbled up from his chest and throbbed outward, visibly pushing every demon back. The power he exuded was dizzying for Eve, who felt it like a phantom limb. An archangel's power alone would be too much for her, but Alec's outburst contained an iciness that seized her lungs.

Alec . . .

The surge ebbed. She reached out to the nearby light post and sucked in deep breaths. That had been an act of possession and claiming, like a dog pissing on a hydrant. And every Infernal within a half-mile radius got the message loud and clear.

Eve studied Alec closely, slightly frightened by the look of mayhem in his dark eyes. "What the hell was that?"

"We need to get you out of here." He gripped her elbow and pulled her down the adjacent street.

The weight of dozens of eyes goaded her into faster steps. She had to jog to keep up, but it wasn't a struggle. Several feet away from her Chrysler 300, Alec hit the trunk release on the remote. He put the tengu in the back and tossed the keys to her. "Wait until I bring the bike around, and we'll head back together."

She nodded.

He shifted away. A moment later she heard the Harley rumble to life around the corner.

Eve closed the trunk, revealing a man standing directly beside her car. She jumped back with a squeak.

"Yeesh." She shook her head. "You scared me, Father."

"Sorry." Father Riesgo's smiling green eyes softened his rugged features. He looked so out of place in the priest's collar that it almost had the look of a costume. Frankly, he looked more renegade than missionary. His cheek was marred by a knife scar and his dark hair was overlong and slicked back in a short tail. Just shy of six feet and built like a tank, Riesgo wasn't handsome, but he was very charismatic and singularly compelling.

"How are you, Ms. Hollis?"

"I'm good." Thumping came from the trunk and Eve smacked her hand down on it.

Riesgo frowned. "What was that?"

"What was what?"

"That noise."

"I didn't hear anything." She glanced around warily, noting how the Infernals held back. Maybe due to Alec's unspoken threat, maybe due to the presence of a priest. "So . . . how are you?"

His gaze lifted from the trunk to meet hers. "Better now that I've seen you."

For some men, that would have been a pickup line. With Riesgo, it was her soul that interested him, not the package it came in.

"Have you been reading the Bible I gave you?" he asked.

"I did. Thank you. I've been meaning to bring it back to you, but work has been crazy lately."

"Do you have any questions?"

Alec could melt wax with his voice, but Riesgo was no slouch in the alluring department. His voice bore the deep sultriness of a phone sex operator. Not that she'd ever called a sex line, but she imagined that's what the men who worked them would sound like. Eve wondered if he was aware of how many women attended mass at St. Mary's just to hear him talk with that suave Spanish accent.

"No questions," she replied, listening to the rumble of the Harley fade as Alec circled the other side of the block.

"And you don't want to keep it for future reference?"

More pounding came from the trunk.

"No thanks," she said, careful not to raise her voice even though it was competing with the noise from the tengu. "I have a good memory."

"What is in your trunk, Ms. Hollis?" he shouted.

"Excuse me?" Her car was beginning to rock and she pushed down harder on the trunk with her superstrength to keep it still.

He leaned closer. "What. Is. That. *Noise?*"

"I don't hear anything."

A dark brow arched. Reaching out, his long fingers caught the keys held in her free hand and tugged them free of her grip. Not that she offered much resistance. She was too shocked by the way he took over. How could a man so clearly commanding in nature become a Catholic priest?

With his forearm, he pushed her back from the car. When it began to bounce violently, he shot her a challenging glance.

"You're pushy, Father."

Riesgo hit the trunk release and it popped open. The tengu froze. The car settled. With one hand on the lip of the trunk lid and the other holding the keys at his side, he stared down at what was a gargoyle statue to his eyes.

"Do you like it?" she asked.

The tengu's head shook violently.

"It's cute." Riesgo glanced at her. The tengu stuck his tongue out behind the priest's back. "What's the matter with your car?"

"Nothing. Runs like a dream. I recommend the 300 to everyone."

Alec's Harley rumbled to a stop beside them. From behind the shield of her sunglasses, her eyes ate him up as if he was dessert. Which was a fairly apt description, now that she thought of it. He'd hooked her the same way ten years ago. A hottie on a Harley.

He cut the engine and smiled at Riesgo. "Father."

The two men shook hands.

"You might want to take Ms. Hollis's car to the dealership," Riesgo suggested. "Her rear shocks are bad."

Alec looked at Eve, who jerked her chin toward the open trunk.

"I think it's due for regular maintenance," Alec conceded with a big smile, his teeth white against his tanned skin.

Riesgo turned back to Eve and held out the keys. "I look forward to seeing you again."

Beyond his shoulder, she saw the proliferation of demons lying in wait. "Be careful on the way back to the church, Father."

After another long look into the trunk, he shook his head and closed it again. With a wave, Eve hurried to the driver's side and slid behind the wheel. Alec shot off ahead of her and she pulled out behind him. The tengu began kicking the backseat.

"Dumping him in the ocean is a great idea," Reed drawled from the passenger seat.

Eve swerved like a drunk. "Damn it! Don't startle me like that!"

"You're jumpy." She felt his gaze move along the side of her face.

"Hell is breaking loose. Literally. I have good cause."

His hand settled on her knee. The warmth seeped through the worn denim and into the flesh beneath. *I won't let anything happen to you.*

In the enclosed confines of her car, the scent that was distinctly Reed's filled her nostrils—leather and starch, a hint of spice and heated male skin. Comforted by his proximity, she set one hand atop his and squeezed.

The tengu continued to bounce around in the trunk of her car.

"If you dent my car," she yelled over her shoulder, "you'll really piss me off!"

The intensity of the blows reduced, but the frequency didn't slow.

Alec passed through Brookhurst, confirming that he was headed for Gadara Tower. That worked for her. She didn't want the tengu in her house for any reason. The damn things were bad luck.

Sensing Reed's disquiet, she asked, "What's troubling you?"

"I've been looking into our Nix problem."

"Oh?"

"It's been two months since you blew him up, but there have been no new reports of murders with his calling card—until this past week."

"Maybe the police have kept it under wraps. They do that some-times."

His fingers linked with hers, then he moved their joined hands to his thigh. "You watch too much television. And quit feeling guilty for touch-ing me."

Her lips twisted wryly. "Burning a stick of dynamite at both ends makes me nervous."

An image of him covering a disheveled Sara on the floor entered his head, and subsequently hers. Her breath held as she absorbed the searing flash of jealousy she wasn't expecting.

Reed stared straight ahead. His Ray-Bans hid his gaze and his profile revealed nothing more than a ticcing muscle in his jaw. "It's not what you think," he bit out.

Eve blanked her mind. "You don't know what I think."

"You drive me nuts."

"That's not me. That's all the stuff you have rushing through your brain." There was a tremendous amount of information moving through him—kill orders flowing down from Alec, assignments meted out to the Marks under him, reports coming back in from them. The human mind could never handle such an influx and outpouring of information simultaneously, but *mal'akhs* dealt with it daily. The teeny bit she felt through him was cringe-worthy.

Eve tugged at the hand he held. He released it. "I think we need some distance between the three of us."

His lips thinned. "Why do women always pull this shit when they get jealous?"

"Fuck you, you conceited bastard."

"I'm not the bastard," he bit out.

"I'm a liability and you know it. This dating bullshit isn't worth the risk. Alec can't feel anything for me and you're not there yet. We've only been seeing each other a few weeks. Better sooner than later."

His head turned toward her. "Is Cain getting this little speech, too?"

She nodded. "He will."

"So . . . you're saying Cain is heartless, and you think I don't care enough yet. Where does that leave you? Still pining over him?"

"Not enough to hang on, obviously." Her gaze went back to the road. She merged into the left-hand turn lane at Harbor Boulevard, one car behind Alec. "Listen, the cons outweigh the pros here. I'm a vulnerability that neither of you can afford. And I feel guilty. I hate that."

Reed's fingers tapped his thigh. Because he was rock-hard muscle, the flesh was like a solid surface beneath his impatient touch.

You're gonna notice shit like that, he scoffed, *in the same breath that you're saying you don't want me?*

"I didn't say I don't want you. I just said this isn't going anywhere."

"Quit worrying about where it's going and focus on where it's at."

"I want to focus on staying alive."

"You need sex to do that. It's the way Marks are wired."

"I know."

The silence that filled the car was heavy enough to block out the cavorting of the trapped tengu.

Reed's voice came dangerously low, "Oh, hell no."

She made the turn onto Harbor, then glanced at him. "Excuse me?"

He pulled off his shades and stared at her with hard eyes. "I've played this game by your rules. Now you're telling me the board's getting put away before I score? Fuck that."

Eve gaped. "Don't tell me I *owe* you a screw."

"Damn straight. And I'm collecting."

"That is the most immature, chauvinistic—"

"Yeah, yeah. Save it."

"Give Sara a booty call if you're hard up enough to blackmail someone for sex," she snapped.

"I've been celibate for *you*. *You* owe me."

Celibate for her.

Didn't make up for him being an asshole. "From what I saw, Sara seems to miss your caveman side."

"So do you." He slipped his shades back on and crossed his arms. "That's where I'm blowing it. I should be listening to your body language and not the crap coming out of your mouth. I should toss your ass over the arm of your couch and nail you. Then you'd know this brush-off shit doesn't work with me."

"I wouldn't fuck you if you were the last man on earth."

Reed held a hand to his ear. "Did you hear that? That was the sound of the gloves coming off."

"Whatever. Grow up."

"I wanted you to make the first move. Now . . ." His head turned toward the window. "I just want you."

The last was said without the cockiness of the rest. It was softer. Resigned. There was more to his need than the physical. Outwardly, he didn't show it, but she felt it.

While it wasn't particularly common for Marks to connect romantically with their handlers, it wasn't unheard of either. The flow of assignments and field reports between the two created a sense of intimacy that sometimes blossomed into love.

"Even if wanting me is what's setting me up as a target for Satan?" she asked, hoping to goad him into lowering his mental guards.

"Even if."

Eve turned her head toward Reed, only to find that he'd left; shifted off to someplace else in the world. That ability to be here one second and gone the next reminded her of superheroes like Superman or Spider-Man.

"But I'm not playing the role of the always-a-hostage love interest," she insisted aloud. "You hear me?"

If he did, he didn't answer.

From his position at the head of a massive U-shaped table, Sammael relished the view of Raguel, the most arrogant of all the archangels, kneeling on the stone ground before him with head bent and fingers curled with white-knuckled force. The pure brightness of his brother's white wings was incongruous compared to the underlying wanness of his coffee-dark skin and the ragged appearance of his woolen shift.

Sammael leaned back into his chair with a smile. Pain. So beautiful and effective. Of all of Jehovah's creations, pain was his favorite. Terror and depression followed a goodly distance behind.

But pain alone would not be enough to break Raguel.

Despite over a month of hellfire burning, there was a lingering elegance to the set of his brother's shoulders, the sight of which Sammael welcomed. The archangel's display of his gold-tipped wings was an additional act of rebellion designed to inspire fear in the lesser demons. It inspired amusement in Sammael.

"Are you enjoying your accommodations?" he asked solicitously.

Raguel's head lifted, his dark eyes revealing a wealth of hatred and fury. He said nothing.

Perfect. There was no room for love of God when the soul was filled with viler emotions.

"Speechless? Ah, well . . . Are you hungry?" Sammael tossed a hunk of meat onto the floor. "It's quite good."

His brother's eyes never left his. No move was made to reach for the sustenance, despite the obvious signs of emaciation. Raguel wouldn't die of starvation, but he was suffering from it.

Smiling, Sammael raked his gaze over his surroundings. Both the Great Hall and the wooden table that filled it grew in proportion to its occupancy. So while it appeared that every seat was taken, in actuality the space was bereft of the number of minions that usually filled it. He hoped the absent ones were enjoying the lovely Southern California weather. Their vacation would soon be over.

"What do you want?" Raguel's voice was hoarse from endless days of screaming. He was kept suspended over hellfire in a metal cage, his flesh seared with every flare, then rebuilt by his angelic gifts. Drained by the need for constant healing, he lacked the strength to free himself. Even now he kneeled, not because he deferred to the Prince of Hell, but because his legs would not support him. He'd put too much effort into re-creating those magnificent wings.

Suddenly irritated by that display, Sammael stood. His wings snapped outward, blood red and tipped with black. The demons in attendance roared and raised their fists. Raguel's chin lifted. Ever defiant.

"Cain is helming your firm," Sammael purred, his hands clasped beneath his wings against the small of his back. "Our siblings do not seem to be in any hurry to bargain for you. Perhaps they do not miss you. The Seven is intact without you."

"I am not concerned."

"Cain has implemented some changes which have increased productivity and lowered Mark causalities. He has also exposed flaws within the existing system."

"Is he hitting you where it hurts?" his brother goaded.

Sammael laughed. He began to round the corner to his left, his cloven feet striking the floor in rhythmic clops. The massive ruby chandelier above them followed him as he moved. It was the fate of lessers to live in darkness, except for the light he brought them. "For a time it seemed as if his fascination with Evangeline Hollis had passed, but now he courts her again. What does he see in her? What is it about her that makes him cleave to her as he has not done with any woman since his wife, Awan?"

"I care not."

"Truly? Now I see why they have abandoned you. You have grown lazy." He brushed a hand across a succubus's cheek as he passed by. "After all these years, out of all the females in the world—all the Marks and Infernals, all the nephilim and mortals—he finally recommits to this one unremarkable woman. And you do not ask yourself why?"

Raguel's jaw tightened.

"I ask why," Sammael murmured, having no need to raise his voice since no one would dare to speak over or around him. "What distinguishes her? Would you like to know what I have decided?"

"Not especially, no."

The silence remained unbroken, but the shock of Raguel's disrespect rippled outward. It would spread like a cancer if allowed.

As Sammael passed a berserker, he touched him. A loving, gentle caress that made the demon smile . . . before he dissolved into a rancid puddle that splashed over the bench to pool on the floor. Fear spread through the room and tainted it with an acrid scent.

"I am feeling generous," Sammael said, smiling, "so I will tell you anyway. I think it is her lack of faith that fascinates him. I think he relates to her agnosticism and finds compelling similarities between them."

"Cain is pious," Raguel bit out.

"Is he? Can he be?"

"Has he not proven so?"

"He is God's primary enforcer. He kills as often as he breathes. Can such a creature carry love in his soul?"

"His love for Evangeline Hollis proves that to be true."

"*Does* he love her? Truly? Or does something more base and raw move him? Perhaps he has a hidden purpose. Or perhaps it is simply an incestuous fondness for her name. *Eve*. The Temptress. As fresh in my thoughts now as she was the day I met her."

"I pray her memory festers in your mind like an open sore."

Sammael's fists clenched beneath the concealment of his wings. "Cain running a firm. Who could have conceived of him reaching such heights? It must chafe you terribly."

"Do you have a point, Sammael?"

"I am just conversing, my brother. It has been so long since you and I were last together."

Raguel flapped his mighty wings, using the resulting updraft to push his worn body to its feet. "I have nothing to say. Send me back to my hell."

"Say please."

There was a protracted silence, then a snarled, "Please."

His brother's hatred was a writhing, burning thing.

Beautiful.

Pleased with the progressing state of affairs, Sammael sent Raguel back with a snap of his fingers while simultaneously shifting to his receiving room. Azazel appeared a moment later, taking a knee and bowing. Aside from similar height and form, his lieutenant was as different from him as Heaven and Hell. White hair and pale irises showcased skin like ivory, while garments of ice blue and silver emphasized Azazel's frosty demeanor. He could chill a room with his presence and was most useful in cooling Sammael's fiery temper.

"My liege," Azazel murmured.

"What was your impression of Raguel?"

The demon's gaze lifted. "He is unbroken, but soul-weary."

"Good. Exactly the way I want him. Now, tell me you have news."

"The *yuki-onna*, Harumi-san, betrayed us to Evangeline Hollis. Cain has returned to the field. It will be more difficult to reach her now."

Sammael smiled. "She has other vulnerabilities."

"Her best friend is backpacking in Europe, and her sister lives in Kentucky."

"Excellent."

"Her parents are local."

Sammael moved toward his throne. His lower limbs changed as he crossed the mosaic floor, turning from hindquarters to legs. His wings retracted, sinking into his spine as if they had never been. "Leave them."

"My liege, I think—"

"No, you do not." He adjusted his black velvet slacks before sinking into his seat and gesturing for Azazel to rise. "Take away her family, and you take away her reason to live."

"Why would that be a bad thing?"

"Her family keeps her mortal, which makes her weak. Why do you think the seraphim choose the unencumbered to be Marks? A soul is most dangerous when it has nothing to lose. We want her motivated, not a grief-stricken vigilante. She might even become an ally."

"An *ally*?"

"Why not?" He waved one hand carelessly. "She does not believe. It would seem likely that she wants to be free of the mark. Anyone who could assist her in that endeavor would be a friend."

"You seek to extort *and* befriend her?"

"Or kill her. Whatever purpose suits me best. Discover everyone who means anything to her but whose loss won't break her. Close coworkers. School friends. Neighbors."

Azazel snorted. "Ulrich took care of the neighbor already. She would have been perfect. As close as family."

"Ulrich? The Nix?" Sammael's gaze lifted to the mural of Michelangelo's *Fall of Man* on the domed ceiling. "Asmodeus oversteps his place again."

"He is ambitious."

"He is overzealous. He has already succeeded in killing her once by lending a dragon to Grimshaw." He looked at his lieutenant. "Watch him closely. He and I may soon have things to discuss."

A rare smile curved Azazel's mouth. "Yes, my liege."

Sammael leaned his head against the throne and closed his eyes. "And get someone to clean up the mess that berserker made in the Great Hall."

CHAPTER 6

Eve steered her car into her assigned spot next to Alec's and cut the engine. The subterranean parking lot of Gadara Tower was darker and cooler than the ground level. The temperature change was enough to silence the tengu in her trunk.

With her fingers wrapped around the steering wheel and her senses achingly aware of how pissed off Reed was, she stared at the single placard that displayed both "A. Cain" and "E. Hollis." Such privileges alienated her from the other Marks.

Her car door opened. Alec's large hand extended into her view. She pulled the keys out of the ignition and accepted his offer of help. She'd barely cleared the roofline when she found herself pinned to the rear door by six-plus feet of hard-bodied male.

"So I've been thinking . . ." Eve began.

The tengu resumed bouncing around in her trunk.

We need to tighten things up, he said, *keep information strictly between me and you. Got it?*

"Gotcha."

Alec's hands gripped her waist, his thumbs sliding across her hipbones, his sunglasses dangling from his fingers. "Did I hurt you?" he asked softly. "Earlier?"

Just the memory of his power surge at the tengu building made her shiver, but she shook her head. "I'm fine. You just took me by surprise."

"I didn't think about how it might hit you."

"Do you hear me complaining? I think you saved us from getting jumped."

His forehead dropped to hers. "You're too good for me."

"Alec . . ." Her throat tightened.

"But that Dear John speech you were talking to Abel about? It won't fly with me either, so save your breath."

Eve shoved at his shoulder. "Eavesdropper."

He backed away, laughing. "I'm ruthless."

Alec reached down through the driver's side door for the trunk release just as her cell phone began ringing from its spot in her cup holder. He tossed it to her. The caller ID said only *California,* so Eve answered with a brisk, "Hollis."

"Ms. Hollis. Detective Jones of the Anaheim Police Department."

She winced at the familiar voice. It held a bit of a twang, as if he had originated in the South, then migrated.

The mantra of California natives entered her mind unbidden, *Welcome to California. Now go home.*

As Alec gestured for her to go to the truck, Eve squeezed his arm and spoke with clear enunciation for his benefit. "Hello, Detective."

Alec paused.

"Did I catch you at a bad time?" Jones asked.

"I have a minute."

"My partner and I stopped by your condo an hour or so ago."

"I'm at work."

"No, you're not."

She rounded the rear of the car. "I'm not?"

As the tengu began pounding on the trunk lid, he asked, "What's that noise?"

"What noise? And why do you think I'm not at work?"

"Because we're sitting in your office right now." His voice rose in volume. "Can you hear me?"

Her gaze moved to Alec. He waited for her signal to open the trunk. "You're here?"

"Where are you, Ms. Hollis?"

"In the garage of Gadara Tower."

"We would like to speak with you, if you have a moment."

"Of course. I'll be up in ten." She disconnected.

Alec rested his forearms on the edge of the open door. "I have someone taking coffee and donuts to your office."

As convenient as the archangels' mental switchboard system was, Eve wasn't sure it was worth the headaches. Information flowed through Alec like a sieve, but not in the same manner as it did through Reed. Handlers were stopgaps designed to alleviate the firm leaders' burdens. They had only twenty-one Marks to concern them; the archangels were responsible for thousands.

"They might find the donuts stereotypical and insulting," she pointed out, shoving her phone into her pocket. She hunkered down in preparation of the trunk opening.

"Good. They should know better than to pick on my girl." He hit the truck release.

The tengu burst free with a squeal. Eve caught him with a grunt, but the force of the little beast's velocity knocked her on her ass.

"Pretty Mark!" he cried, snapping at her with his stone teeth.

She waited until Alec rounded the trunk. Then she threw the demon at him.

As usual, the vast lobby of Gadara Tower was congested with many business-minded Marks and mortals. The industrious whirring of the glass tube elevator motors and the steady hum of numerous conversations were now familiar and soothing to Eve. She felt safe here, cocooned from the world outside where demons ran amok.

Fifty floors above her, a massive skylight allowed natural illumination to flood the atrium. The gentle heat from the sun combined with the multitude of planters created a slight humidity. It emphasized the overwhelming scent of Marks to a near suffocating degree.

Beside her, Alec inhaled deeply, then exhaled in a sigh of pleasure. She felt echoes of the surge of power that hit him whenever he was in close proximity to multiple Marks. That charge was unique to him, the original and most badass Mark of them all. She wondered how he'd managed to remain autonomous for so long, considering how much strength he gained when around other Marks. There was a story there, but Alec wasn't telling it.

As they weaved through the crowd, Marks paused to gape at the tengu. It was their first sighting of a masked Infernal. The ripple of unease that followed in her and Alec's wake was tangible. Eve hoped the advent of the mask didn't foster too much doubt. The last thing they needed was for frightened Marks to target mortals by accident.

They'll be all right, Alec said, shaking the writhing tengu as admonishment to keep still. *I'll see to it.*

Eve knew he would. His strength of conviction was powerful. She glanced at his profile and was struck by thoughts of Batman's nemesis Two-Face and the dual sides of Alec's personality. Alec killed with one hand, but worked to preserve life with the other.

Since his ascension to archangel, the division within him felt soul-deep to her. But maybe he had always been so divided and she just hadn't known it. His promotion had come within hours of her Novium, which first established their connection. She hadn't had time to dig into the brain of the old Cain before he became the new one.

They moved to a hidden bank of elevators that descended into off-limits areas of the building. She rarely saw her office on the forty-fifth floor. The majority of her business in Gadara Tower was conducted in the subterranean labyrinth of floors and corridors that housed Infernals both friendly and not.

"Pretty Mark not so nice," the tengu complained as they stepped into the elevator car.

"You're one to talk," she scoffed. "You tried to brain me, tackle me, bite me—"

"Fun, fun!"

Eve flipped him the bird. He stuck his stone tongue out at her.

"Cut it out, kids," Alec said, his dark eyes laughing.

She glared at the speaker in the corner. "What's with the Barry Manilow? Every time I get in the elevator, it's Manilow."

"You're just lucky. By the way, I'm going up with you."

"The detectives don't know you work here."

"So? It's clear you're coming in off the clock. Tell 'em it's your day off and you forgot something."

She looked down and checked herself out. Her jeans were dirty, her boots were scuffed, and her shirt was torn at the hem.

Alec grinned. "Your hair needs help, too."

Turning, Eve looked at her reflection in the shiny brass of the elevator walls. Her ponytail was askew, odd loops of hair protruded all around the top of her head, and Infernal ash concealed its natural luster.

"Oh my god." She hissed as her mark burned in chastisement. "You let me go around looking like *this*?"

"You're still hot."

She glared at him over her shoulder. "You suck."

"Abel didn't say anything either."

"You both suck," she qualified, pulling out her hair band.

I'd still do you, Reed said.

Gee, you're a class act, she retorted.

The car came to a stop and the elevator doors opened with a ding. Immediately the stench of multiple Infernals filled her nostrils and made her nose wrinkle. A waiting area to the right was occupied with a dozen demons of various classes, all bitching about the wait. To the left a female werewolf sat at the receptionist's desk. She wore headphones and was busy filing her claws.

As Alec's presence became known, silence descended, but he paid them no mind. Eve, however, was totally aware of those around them. Marks and Infernals alike watched her warily. Sadly, it was her fellow Marks who looked at her with malice, while the Infernals were simply curious.

Following Alec down the hallway, Eve read the gilded lettering on the glass doors as they passed them. There was a thin layer of smoke in the air, which—combined with the overall decor of the place—created an old '50s film noir feel. Only the labels on the doors gave away the otherworldly purpose of the place.

When they paused before a door that read Forensic Wiccanology in gold lettering, Eve stepped up and knocked. The knob turned and the door swung inward, seemingly without assistance, since no one stood at the threshold. Inside the room, the overhead lights were out. Pendant lamps hung over various island stations, spotlighting specific work areas but leaving the rest of the space in deep shadow.

"Eve!" The coarse, raspy voice coming from the back of the room always reminded her of Larry King. Eve waited for the familiar black-clad figure to emerge from the stygian darkness.

"Hi, Hank," she greeted him in return. "We brought a present for you."

But the figure who appeared wasn't Hank. It was a young girl with hair as white as snow and yellow eyes like a wolf's. She was around five and a half feet tall, slender as a reed, and timid in the way she moved.

"Hello." The girl offered a shy smile. "I'm Fred."

Eve bit back a smile at the masculine name. Hank and Fred. She was pretty sure Fred was a girl. No one knew what sex Hank was, but Eve thought of him as a man, since he was always in male form when speaking to her.

"Nice to meet you, Fred," Eve said, extending her hand.

Fred shook hands with Eve, then looked at Alec. "Cain."

Alec acknowledged her with a quick, dismissive nod.

Hank stepped into the illuminated circle created by a hanging fixture. His black-clad form altered as he emerged from the darkness, changing from a hunchbacked crone to a tall, dapper gentleman with flame-red hair. Hank was a chameleon, changing form and sex to suit the client. The only things that were immutable were the red hair, masculine smoker's voice, and black attire.

"My new assistant," Hank explained. "It's been so busy around here lately, I needed the help. Fred is half lili/half werewolf. Gives her great eyes and a nose for research."

Lilin were the offspring of the seductress Lilith—first wife of Alec's father, Adam, and mother of innumerable demons. Eve had yet to run across the blonde she-bitch, and she hoped she never did.

"Her fault it's so hectic," Alec said, nudging Eve's shoulder.

She shoved him back.

Hank laughed. "Can't blame him for being right, my lovely Eve. I hear there are a large number of Infernals in town, possibly gunning for you."

"Because of him," she argued, stabbing a finger in Alec's direction.

"Good point." Hank stepped closer to examine the oddly quiet little demon under Alec's arm. "A tengu? Fascinating. The mask hasn't worn off. Or else they've managed to create more of it."

"That's what I need you to find out," Alec said. "Also why this one's so aggressive."

"Traitors," the tengu hissed, glaring at both Hank and Fred.

Fred snorted. Hank laughed. "My theory is that his behavior is a side effect of the mask. Over the course of my experiments, I've discovered that the infusion of Mark blood and bone doesn't sit well with Infernals over an extended period of time. I'll examine this fellow and see if I can prove it definitively."

"Keep me posted," Alec said.

"Of course." Hank looked at Eve. "It looks like he did a number on you."

"He had friends," she grumbled, dusting off her jeans with her hands.

Hank faced Alec and altered into a Jessica Rabbit look-alike in a Morticia Addams dress. "I have also been playing with reversing the mask."

Eve perked up. "Would it make Marks blend with mortals?"

"It should make Marks smell like demons."

"Eww . . ."

Hank shifted back into his masculine form. "However, so far I've only been able to make demons smell like Marks."

"Yikes."

"Destroy that recipe," Alec ordered.

"Already done."

Fred reached out to the tengu. The little beast hissed at her, but she seemed unconcerned. "I'll take him."

Alec handed him over. The demon snapped at Fred with his teeth. She snarled and bared deadly canines.

"My teeth are bigger," she growled.

The tengu whimpered and curled into a ball.

"Does it bother anyone else," Eve asked, "that the demons are so far ahead of us in regards to experiments and genetic mutations? The correct word is 'genetic,' right? Or is there something else I should call it?"

"Infernals don't lack research subjects," Hank explained. "Marks, on the other hand, are trained to kill. They rarely capture for torture or experimentation."

She looked at Alec. "We should work on that."

"We are."

No elaboration, but she was getting used to that.

"Hank," Alec went on. "Do you still have that punch bowl I brought you? The one the Nix gave to Eve?"

"Yes."

"Did you ever get anything from it?"

Hank frowned. "Nothing definitive. And once the Nix was dead, I put it away."

"I need you to dig it out. He's back."

"Back? Like Montevista? And Grimshaw's kid?"

"Exactly." Alec caught Eve's elbow. "We've got an appointment upstairs."

"I'll holler when I find something." Hank waved his hand along Eve's length and she suddenly felt cleaner.

Glancing down, she found her clothes in pristine condition. "You rock."

"Of course."

Eve yelled into the darkness where Fred had disappeared, "It was nice meeting you, Fred."

The lili shouted back from a seemingly great distance, "Bye, Eve. Bye, Cain."

Not for the first time, Eve wondered how big Hank's office was. She was about to ask Alec when she found herself standing in the reception area of her office.

"I hate when you do that," she complained, blinking past her disorientation.

"Don't want to be late."

Candace, the Mark who was her secretary, stood with a smile. "Good afternoon, Ms. Hollis. Cain. I took coffee in to the detectives, as you requested."

He nodded and pulled Eve toward her frosted glass office door. She took a deep breath while he turned the knob. He was cool and calm while she was neither. She'd only spoken with Jones and Ingram briefly a few months ago, but it had been enough to tell her that they were good men. Men who were fighting the good fight with only mortal skills. And she had to look them in the eyes and lie to them. The mark on her arm burned with the sin, which didn't make sense to her at all. It's not like she could tell them the truth.

Detective Jones pushed to his feet when she entered. He was a nondescript man clad in a dated suit dyed a shade of curry that hadn't been used for clothing in the last thirty years. His partner, Detective Ingram, stood at the window looking at the city below. His taste in garments was better, but the handlebar mustache he sported set him back a few decades, too.

"Nice view," Ingram said, eyeing her carefully. "But I was hoping to get a bird's-eye view of Disneyland."

She smiled. "There's a 2.2-square-mile zone around the amusement park that is designated as a resort district. When you're inside the park, there aren't any tall buildings to ruin the visitors' sight lines. They don't want to ruin the fantasy."

"Ah, well," Jones said. "Some of us have to live in the real world."

Eve moved to her desk and sank into her slim leather chair. "What can I do for you, Detectives?"

Jones glanced at Alec, who stood like a sentinel by the door with his wide-legged stance and crossed arms. The detective seemed prepared to protest Alec's presence, then he shrugged and sat. The way he moved caught Eve's attention. His stocky frame didn't show the stiffness of an older man, like his taller partner's did. With narrowed eyes she studied him and came to the conclusion that he was far younger than he appeared. She suspected the misconception was by design and she grew even more wary. Jones was a hunter, too, and the information she held was his prey.

He went straight to the point. "Do you have any further information regarding the death of your neighbor, Ms. Hollis?"

Eve shook her head. "If I had anything to share, I would call you. I still have your card."

"Do you know an Anthony Wynn? He graduated from your high school the year before you. Chinese American. About five foot—"

"Yes. I know him. We attended the same elementary and junior high, too."

"He's dead."

She froze. They had been no more than acquaintances, but she'd partied with him occasionally and thought fondly of him. "When? How?"

"Drowning. Same as the others," Jones said. "When was the last time you saw him?"

It took her a moment to reply. "A-a few years back. I passed him in a grocery store aisle."

"So you haven't kept in touch?"

"No. We weren't close. The only things I can say about him are that he was quiet at parties and drew really great pictures on napkins."

Ingram stepped up to her desk, taking one of her business cards from its beveled crystal holder. "You've only been with Gadara Enterprises for a short time, is that right?"

"A few months."

"You were hired just prior to the murder of your neighbor, Mrs. Basso."

"That's right." She resisted the urge to look at Alec. *Where is this leading?*

Not sure yet.

Ingram shoved her card into his pocket, then reached down for a briefcase resting against the leg of Jones's chair. He pulled out a photo and set it on her desk. It was a picture of one of her business cards surrounded by an L-square ruler. It had the wrinkled look that paper took on after it had been soaked with liquid, then air-dried.

Alec approached. He looked at the picture, then at Ingram. "You found this at the crime scene?"

Jones settled back into his chair, his forearms resting casually atop the leather armrests. "Do you have any idea why we would find your business card on the corpse of a man you haven't seen in years, Ms. Hollis?"

Eve stared at him, dismayed. The Nix was taunting her. "I have no idea."

Ingram reached into the briefcase again and pulled out an item just as familiar as the last—a photocopy of a sketch artist's uncanny rendering of the Nix. The detectives had shown the image to her before. A florist had described the customer who frequented her shop to purchase water lilies.

"We want you to look at this again," Ingram said, holding the image directly in front of her face.

She looked away, disgusted. "I've never seen him."

The mark heated at the lie.

Jones heaved out a frustrated breath. "Look harder, Ms. Hollis. *Think* harder. He has a German accent. He got his hands on your business card at some point. Did he come here to see you? Did you run into him somewhere?"

"I don't remember him." She rubbed at her burning arm. "I sent out letters that included my new business cards to all of my former associates, clients, college classmates, and friends. I mailed at least a thousand announcements about my move to Gadara Enterprises. I also frequently drop them into those fishbowls on restaurant counters, since you never know when you might get a lead."

"Was Wynn on that mailing list?" Ingram asked.

"No. I don't know where he lives. I told you, I don't know him that well."

"He lived on Beacon Street."

Fear formed a knot in Eve's gut. *That's next to my parents' house . . .*

Alec mentally transmitted orders to subordinates with such velocity, she was dizzied by it. Her fingers lifted to her brow and rubbed.

Jones straightened. "Can we get a copy of that list?"

"Of course." Eve reached for her phone.

"This could be personal."

The detective's low-voiced statement stopped her with her arm extended toward the handset. Her gaze met his. "You think this is about me?"

The detective glanced at Alec, then back at her. "This guy stuck around Anaheim for the last nine months. He stepped out of his comfort zone only once that we know of—"

"Mrs. Basso."

"*Your* neighbor. Then his next victim is an old acquaintance of yours and your business card is found floating in the punch bowl with the lily. Things like that are rarely coincidences."

Eve pushed back from her desk and stood, feeling too restless to sit. Jones rose when she did, then resumed his seat.

"What about the other victims?" She looked back and forth between the two detectives. "Did I know them, too? Were they connected to me in some way?"

Was it possible that the Nix had been circling her since *before* she was marked?

This time it was Jones who reached into the bag of horrors and withdrew a typewritten list of names, birthdates, addresses. She looked the column of information over carefully, wracking her brain.

"None of these names look familiar."

"We can't find a connection either," Ingram said. "Maybe you caught his eye just recently. It could have been something as simple as you cutting him off in traffic. Whatever the reason, we think he's stepping things up a notch by terrorizing both the victims he kills and you."

Eve looked at Alec. *I want him dead.*

He met her gaze. *Me, too.*

She crossed her arms. "Were all the victims found in their homes?"

"Yes."

"Then don't worry about me. Nothing unusual has happened in my life recently. Nothing that concerns me or gives me pause. Since Mrs. Basso's death, our homeowners' association authorized the hiring of an extra security guard in the building, so now we have two. One roaming, and one at the elevator on the lobby level. You just concentrate on finding this guy before he gets to someone else."

"It's our job to worry about you, Ms. Hollis."

"No, it isn't." The last thing she needed was to dodge the police while trying to bounce some bounty hunting demons back to Hell.

"Yes, it is," Ingram said dryly. "You see, Ms. Hollis. For the present, you're our strongest lead."

Jones stood with briefcase in hand. "In other words, get used to seeing us around."

CHAPTER 7

The detectives have left the building.

"Somehow," Eve said with a wry curve to her lips, "that doesn't have the same ring as Elvis's sign-off."

Alec sent a brief mental acknowledgment to the Marks monitoring the security feeds, then turned his attention to Eve. He knew she wasn't going to like what he had to say, but he hoped she wouldn't get overly pissy about it. He had too much shit on his plate, in addition to a simmering temper and a pressing need for a long, hard screw.

Being in Gadara Tower only made things worse. He'd always gained strength and power from other Marks, always relished the rush he felt when he entered a firm. But now the Mark in him wasn't the only thing that recharged. The dark place inside him responded similarly; it had even absorbed power from the Infernals loitering around Olivet Place. That the resulting explosion had nearly injured Eve terrified him.

"You have to let me handle this," he said grimly. "You need to stay home with Montevista and Sydney until we figure out what the hell is going on."

She gave him the "you're-smoking-crack" look. "You're funny."

"Don't cross me on this," he warned, his voice sharper than he intended. He knew a clusterfuck when he saw one and this one had Eve right in the center. As usual.

Her hands went to her hips. "What the hell did I go through training for?"

"Why do you think you have a mentor?" he shot back. "You can't learn everything you need to know in seven weeks. You're not up to a fight like this yet, Eve, and I can't do what needs to be done when I'm worried about you."

Cain. Sabrael's voice throbbed through his brain with the unalloyed power of a seraph. *You must speak with me.*

Alec was physically jolted by the violence with which the darkness inside him recoiled from Sabrael. *Not a good time,* he snapped.

You owe me. Have you forgotten so quickly?

Have you forgotten that I told you I'd get to you when I get to you?

Eve pressed on, unaware of the silent exchange. "So assign me to another mentor."

Alec's first urge was to hit her, which scared the shit out of him. He clasped his hands behind his back. "No."

"Why not? If you're too busy to do your job, you should assign me to someone else."

Fury battered his control. How had Raguel managed it? Alec was exhausted by the constant struggle.

"You're mine, angel," he said harshly. "Even if you don't act like it."

"This is business we're talking about." Her chin lifted. "Raguel threatened to reassign me, so I know it's possible. The mark system has a backup plan for everything."

"I'll back you up." He stalked forward. He felt himself move as if on autopilot, his mind disconnected from the seething emotions that drove his actions. "Against a wall. Nail you right to it."

Another couple of feet and she'd be cornered. Trapped. Nowhere to run . . .

Eve held her ground. "You sound like your brother."

Alec's brow arched. "You spit that out as if you don't want him. And we both know that you do."

Impatient, he shifted across the distance to her, catching her ponytail in a fist and a belt loop with his fingers. The loop ripped free, the tearing noise sparking a wave of heat between them.

"Alec . . ." Her voice was breathy and tremulous. He wanted it throaty and hoarse. Wanted her nails in his back and her sweat on his skin.

He closed his eyes and breathed deeply, relishing the feel of her slender body trembling against his. He felt the Infernals in the firm tapping into his lust and fury. He cut them off and heard the echoes of their protesting cries. Weakened by the loss of their power, Alec sucked the energy he needed from Eve, taking her mouth with a desperation that crawled over his skin.

She gasped her breath into his lungs, her lithe frame stiff at first, then a surging warmth against him. Her lush breasts pressed into his chest, her fingers tangled in his shirt, her legs intertwined with his.

Eve bit his lip. "Is this what you want? To take me down fighting?"

The taste of blood hardened his cock until it ached. He shook her. "I don't give a shit how I have you. I just want you to stop jerking me around and give up the goods."

Her hand fisted in his hair and yanked. "Who the fuck are you? Because you sure as hell aren't Alec Cain."

Shaking violently, he felt like a drunk in need of booze. The vestiges of Eve's Novium were leaching into his system, spurring his dark needs further. He changed tactics.

"Come on, angel," he coaxed. "You know you want it as bad as I do. You know how good it is between us. How hard you come when I'm fucking you . . . until you're begging me to stop . . ."

Her dark eyes were fever-bright, her lips slick and swollen. "You're pushing me like Robert," she said scornfully. "Remember him? My ex from high school who wanted to pop the cherry I saved for you?"

"Eve—" Bloodlust surged at the memory of the cocky blond kid who'd tried to hard-sell Eve into a screw in the back of a Mustang. Alec had known then that he couldn't allow anyone else to have her.

Don't let the thing inside you have her.

His grip ripped her jeans further. A second more and there would be nothing left.

She yanked his head down to hers, her mouth slanting across his, wet and hot. Fueled by anger and determination, the kiss punished him so thoroughly his throat clenched tight against it. He hated her like this, hated himself for making her like this.

I'm sorry, angel . . . sorry . . .

She changed at the sound of his voice. Gentled. A low moan vibrated in her chest, a sound of longing and surrender. The convulsive flexing of her fingers at his nape and the feel of her hand sliding up beneath his shirt conveyed a wealth of feeling. Her tongue pushed past his lips, licking deep and slow. Savoring. She loved him too much to stay mad at him.

And the part of him that had loved her before the ascension knew if he didn't get her away from his personal demons, they would break her.

He twisted his head away, gasping. *He* didn't want her in rushed brutality. He wanted her slow and long. Soft and pliant. It was the *thing* inside him that wanted to turn what they had into something . . . wrong.

"Alec." Eve pressed her forehead to his. "Something isn't right with you. Isn't right *in* you. I can feel it."

Take her, the voices urged.

"I need to fuck," he said coldly. Deliberately. "Take your clothes off before I rip them off."

She pushed away. The pain in her eyes made him desperate to take the words back. He didn't.

"Alec?"

He ripped open the button fly of his jeans, freeing his cock. "On your knees. I want your mouth first."

"Fuck you."

"I'm going to fuck *you* instead."

Her arms wrapped around her torso. She backed away a step at a time. He forcibly restrained himself from stalking her further.

A tear slipped down her cheek. "It's like there are two people inside you. The Alec I know, and a monster."

"You're starting to bore me, Eve." His mark burned at the lie.

"You're starting to scare me."

Alec struggled to remain upright, wracked by a pain in his chest that threatened to double him over. But she didn't seem to see it. No, she saw only the darkness inside him that wanted to do things to her Alec couldn't allow.

"I changed my mind." He rebuttoned the fly of his jeans with slow, leisurely movements.

Her gaze was wary, as if she was considering running. He hoped she didn't. He wasn't sure he could fight the urge to hunt her down.

"I've decided to accept your Dear John speech after all."

Her gasp was audible, as if he'd struck her.

"What?" he queried snidely. "Didn't you mean it?"

Alec turned his back to her, walking around her desk to put something substantial between them. "That's one of your problems, Eve. You're a tease. You were fun while we were fucking, but now—"

She reached out to Abel and an instant later was gone, shifted away by his brother before he could say more. Alec leaped over the desk, unable to fight the fury at her loss.

An unseen force restrained his pursuit. His feet were rooted to the carpeted floor, causing him to nearly topple when he attempted to lunge.

Sabrael's amused voice spoke behind him. "You broke her heart with laudable precision. You always did cut to the quick."

Alec stumbled as he was freed. He pivoted, flinching from a blinding brightness that put the sun to shame. Blinking rapidly, he engaged the thick layer of corneal lubrication that enabled him to see through the seraph's glow to the man within. Sabrael sat at Eve's desk, his six wings tucked away, his feet resting atop the edge of her desk. The wicked spikes that lined the outside edges of his black leather boots glinted in the glare of his luminescence. The brutal footwear was a stark contrast to the white, one-shouldered robe he wore. The visual dichotomy was a physical manifestation of the angel's temperament. Outwardly a model of his station, Sabrael hid a razor's edge of cruelty.

"I'm busy, Sabrael. You'll have to wait in line."

The seraph's eyes filled with the purest, bluest of flames and a hint of laughter that made Alec's hackles rise. "Relax. I am not here to cash in my chips, Cain. I am here on behalf of your mother."

"No." Alec shook his head, anticipating the question. "Not now."

"You keep delaying her. She is displeased."

Alec snorted. "Haven't you noticed the world's gone to shit? It's not safe."

"Gabriel disagrees." Sabrael's smile was both beautiful and frightening. "He is weary of her complaints, so you have a week to prepare for her. Besides, you have a home now. Surely this visit will be less hazardous than when you were roaming."

"You're pissing me off." The seraphim regularly withheld information from God, but the extent of their subterfuge never failed to astound. "Tell

Jehovah what's going on down here and he'll settle her. He won't risk her, you know that."

Sabrael crossed his massive arms. "You have everything under control, do you not? If you are incapable of the task you requested, simply let me know and I will relieve you of the burden."

Jaw clenching, Alec fought the urge to attack. With a seraph, it would be suicidal. "I've got a handle on things."

"Excellent. Then there should be no problem with your mother visiting." Sabrael brushed at his immaculate robe, as if he were not intensely focused on Alec like a hawk with its prey in sight. "Does Evangeline know that this promotion is what you wanted? Did you tell her that?"

"Does it matter now?"

Sabrael laughed softly. "I suppose not."

"Sara was with Abel for a long time," Alec said with a shrug, while inside, his discomposure grew. "Relationships aren't impossible."

Yes, he'd suspected he would lose his ability to love Eve—if only subconsciously—but he'd planned on her leaving him first. He'd intended for her to be mortal again and moved on with her life when his advancement came. The loss of his ability to love her would have been welcome then. How else would he survive her loss?

But Eve wouldn't understand. She would see only that his love for her had taken a back seat to his ambition.

"Sarakiel *toyed* with Abel," Sabrael argued, "and Abel used her in return. God created us to connect physically by design. But sex does not a true partnership make."

"I really don't care about Abel or our anatomy."

"And now, you do not care about Evangeline either. Life must be much simpler for you."

"Go away," Alec dismissed. "You're annoying me."

The seraph burst from the chair like a rocket. In a flaming trail of wings, leather, and spikes, he kicked Alec in the chest and ripped through to the other side. The gaping, smoldering hole Sabrael wrought was so wide it nearly severed Alec's torso in half.

Dropping to his knees with an agonized scream, Alec toppled to the floor, his cheek skinned by the harsh pile of the carpet.

You forget yourself, the seraph roared.

In torment, Alec tapped into the power of his beast and found the strength to extend a middle finger and flip Sabrael off.

There was a moment of terrible silence, when his pained gasps were the only sounds to fill the eerie quiet. Then Sabrael laughed—*laughed*— and hauled Alec to his feet, restoring him.

"You amuse me, Cain." The seraph brushed away Alec's tears with tender swipes of his thumbs. "Because I like you, I will not tell your precious Evangeline about your choice of ascension over her. Your secret is safe with me."

Alec slapped the scorching hands away. "Leave Eve out of this."

The seraph hovered over him with a broad smile. "Might I suggest you purchase new linens for your guest room? Something floral, perhaps? Your mother does love gardens."

As swiftly as he'd come, the seraph was gone.

Alec began to pace, his mind working judiciously. The seraph clearly needed something else to occupy him. But what?

Then there was Eve . . .

The time had passed when he could have laid everything out on the table for her. Now he had to find a way to get his shit together. He refused to believe that his brother had been right all those years ago, when he'd shouted the words that had goaded Alec to kill him.

The darkness in him smiled at the memory and his lips curved in a mirroring movement before he caught himself.

Who the fuck was running the show in his body?

He inhaled and exhaled, restoring a semblance of his usual equanimity.

One thing at a time. Sabrael. Eve. Himself.

Hand to his stomach, Alec still felt the tearing of the seraph's boots through his entrails.

Black leather. Spikes.

An idea formed.

He shifted to another part of the building and paused, eyeing the lone blonde on the indoor shooting range. Tucked away in the bowels of Gadara Tower, the range provided a convenient place for Marks to hone their marksmanship. Silver bullets were still the swiftest way to vanquish werewolves.

Sensing his perusal, Iselda Seiler—Izzie, as the other Marks called her—turned her head and met his gaze. She set her gun down and removed the glasses and hearing protection that was less critical for Marks than mortals, but still necessary. She studied him with a now familiar odd intensity that had taken him some time to become accustomed to. There was an air of expectation about her, a sense that she was searching for something in his speech or expression.

His gaze lowered from the kohl-rimmed blue eyes, to the purple-stained mouth, to the spiked leather collar around her neck.

Malice made him smile. "I have a task for you, Ms. Seiler."

Her eyes glittered. "I'm at your service."

Eve was drawing a supporting column in her preliminary sketch when Montevista shouted from her living room.

"Hey, Hollis! Wanna play?"

She finished the precise line before answering. "No, thanks. You two go ahead."

"Aww, man," Sydney complained. "I'm getting tired of kicking his ass at Wii tennis."

"Try the bowling."

She glanced at the clock on the wall. Staying focused for longer than fifteen minutes was impossible when she felt as if her world was falling apart. In her mortal life, her brain would have overridden everything and allowed her to lose herself in her design work. As a Mark, her body was a machine that no longer listened to her brain. The mark tapped into her roiling emotions and channeled them into a nearly overwhelming desire to run, hunt, kill . . .

Alec dismissed me as if I meant nothing to him.

Eve wished she could cry. As it was, she felt as if her heartbreak was bottled up inside her, building in strength until something exploded.

"Ugh." Abandoning the drawing table, Eve moved to the desk and woke her computer. She logged into the Gadara Enterprises system and opened the file that contained her report of the Upland incident. When she'd been told that the mark system kept secular records as well as celestial ones, she had been shocked at what she considered a security breach waiting to happen. But both Gadara and Alec had assured her that a divine hand protected the information. God liked the status quo.

As she refreshed her recollection of the report, she noted the sidebar with various links that ran along the right side of the main text. There were reports from Reed and Mariel—both handlers who'd lost Marks to the hellhounds—as well as the guards who'd been present, Alec, and Gadara himself. It was the latter she was most interested in, so Eve clicked on it. A password prompt box appeared and she frowned.

What would Gadara use as a password?

Archangel. God. Celestial. Mark. Christ. Jesus. Jehovah. Bounty hunter. Christmas.

Nothing worked. Eve growled. A warm breeze moved over her skin. Her eyes closed.

Reed.

She reached for him, into him, farther than was necessary, running the name "Raguel" through his mind to see what stirred.

He who inflicts punishment upon the world and the luminaries.

"That doesn't help," she muttered.

Quit digging, he admonished, with warm amusement. *I'll be there soon, and you can ask me what you want.*

Breathing deeply, Eve closed her eyes and reached out to Alec. She moved tentatively, furtively, like a blind person searching through an unfamiliar room.

Until she was snatched by thick, talon-tipped fingers and tossed into the darkness.

CHAPTER 8

Alec's mind was like an ocean in the midst of a hurricane. Eve was tossed, battered. Dunked beneath the surface, only to emerge gasping. How would she ever find anything inside him? She couldn't even find Alec.

What do you seek?

She ceased her thrashing. The voice was only vaguely familiar, yet alluring in a way only Alec's could be. Floating among the flotsam of his emotions, she waited with bated breath for another word from him that might reassure her.

Ah, pretty angel. You seek Raguel here?

Alec? she queried, still wary. The voice was Alec's, but the inflection was not.

Who else would it be? You want Raguel. One of the holy angels, who inflicts punishment on the world and the luminaries.

Yeah, I heard that already. Give me something new.

Luminaries, angel. Now come see me. Give me some gratitude.

You kicked me to the curb, she reminded, reaching out to Reed for the leverage to pull herself free.

Makeup sex is the hottest.

We haven't made up.

The sea of madness churning around her rose up like a tsunami, dragging her with it to the very peak.

Eve. Alec's voice at last, furious and frantic.

He threw her out of his mind like a bouncer would a drunk at a bar.

Startled upright, Eve opened her eyes. She punched out *luminaries* on her keyboard.

The computer screen flashed, "Good afternoon, Raguel."

"Luminaries, eh?" she muttered, hating that Gadara's sojourn in Hell was the reason she was able to snoop without fear of repercussion. The report opened and she leaned back in her chair to read, her hands rubbing at the goose bumps on her arms. How awful that Alec—the one man who had always made her hot—now left her cold.

Eve quickly scanned the brief text. It was only a few pages and focused more on Reed's uncustomary behavior than on the actual documentation of the events surrounding the discovery of the mask and tengu.

. . . argued extensively about assigning Evangeline Hollis before training . . .

. . . lack of objectivity . . .

. . . too emotionally attached . . .

. . . overreached his position and approached Sarakiel for use of her personal guards . . .

Eve's fingers dug into the flesh of her thighs. Reed. He'd made a deal just as Alec had. But for what purpose? For her? Or for Sara, who'd been his lover for many, many years? Sara had benefited from her team's support during the raid that night, with added prestige and expanded duties. Gadara believed Reed had done it for Eve.

The true dilemma in her relationships with both Alec and Reed wasn't monogamy or honesty, although she most often cited those. Really, it was trust. She didn't know how much of their wanting her was ambition and how much of it was desire. As long as the two brothers continued to clash over her, she was a valuable pawn to more than just Gadara.

The feel of firm lips pressed to her nape made Eve jump in her chair. The flick of a tongue sent a shiver along her spine. She hit the key on her keyboard that pulled up her e-mail screen and concealed Gadara's report.

"How are you doing?" Reed murmured, his breath a gentle caress over her moist skin.

"Fine."

"No, you're not." He spun her chair around. "You can't lie to me. I feel you. I'm sorry I bailed on you earlier."

Eve tilted her head back to look up at him. He'd shifted her home, then taken off immediately afterward. "Don't apologize. I know you have twenty other Marks to worry over. I'm just glad you came when you did."

"I'll always be here for you." Reed caught her wrist and tugged her up, pulling her toward the futon she kept against the wall. He sat and gestured for her to take a seat beside him. "Tell me what happened."

"Don't you know?"

"You shut me out."

"Really?" She twisted sideways to face him. "And I wasn't even trying."

He mimicked her pose, tucking his right leg onto the seat and tossing his arm over the back of the futon. Her gaze was caught by his Rolex, because of both the beauty of the white gold against his olive skin and the surprise of an immortal concerned with the passing of mortal time.

"Cain pissed you off." It was a statement, not a question.

She made a careless gesture with her hand. "No. He told me to get lost. Apparently I'm boring when I'm not putting out."

There was a beat of silence, then, "He *broke up* with you?"

"That's a kind way to say it."

Reed's gaze roamed the length of her and paused on her ripped waistband and belt loop. He grew dangerously still. "Did he hurt you?"

"Not in the physical sense, no."

"He breaks things, babe. That's what he's always done."

"There's something wrong with him."

"You're just now figuring that out?"

"Be serious."

Reed's fingertips touched her cheek. "I am."

Eve stared at him for a long moment, waiting for some sign that he was playing with her or being less than serious. There was none. All she saw were warm brown eyes filled with compassion. He wore a graphite gray shirt today, open at the collar with rolled-up sleeves, as usual. He was an impossibly handsome man, physically perfect. But it was his imperfections that really did a number on her.

She leaned into his touch. "What do you know about archangels?"

His hesitation was nearly imperceptible, but she was looking for it. "Are you digging for anything in particular?"

"Is there any part of the change that would make someone more aggressive than usual?"

"Cain. Is. A. Dick. Period."

"Listen to me. Don't judge."

"Fine." He couldn't have sounded more disgruntled.

"I know Alec Cain. But Cain the archangel . . . I don't know him at all. They're not the same guy."

Reed's lips thinned, then he exhaled harshly. "You've known Cain three months total, with a ten-year gap in between. Why won't you consider that he was on his best behavior for a while and now the effort is wearing thin?"

"Time has nothing to do with intimacy. You can be around someone for years but not really know them at all. The reverse is also true."

"I think he's fucked you into believing whatever he wants."

Eve bit back harsh words. Reed wasn't trying to be an asshole, he was simply tactlessly blunt. "You can learn a lot about a person when you're making love to them."

He snorted, and she realized he might not know anything about that.

"Making love is for girls," he said coldly, confirming her suspicions. "Guys fuck. We'll do whatever it takes to get into the pants of a woman we've got a hard-on for. Cain is no exception."

"Then do this for me. Dig into ascensions and see if any possible explanations jump out at you."

He froze, his nostrils flaring. "Damn, you've got balls."

"You can't tell me you don't feel the mess inside him. We're all connected. There's something in him that wasn't there before."

"He's the same as he always was," Reed bit out. "He just has more power and less reason to play nice."

"You talk a good game," she shot back, "but that's all it is. I want to know what's inside him."

"I don't think you do." He held up a hand when she opened her mouth. "Say no more. I'll ask around."

"Thank you." She put every ounce of gratitude she felt into the words, but his face remained impassive.

He stood and looked down at her with disdain. "Think about how screwed up you are, Eve. I'm right here trying to be what you want, and you're asking me to help you with a guy who can't love you."

She opened her mouth to argue, but he disappeared.

Sighing, she said, *Come back.*

Eve waited, hating the feeling that her life was spinning completely out of her control. Pushing to her feet, she reached out to him again. *I would do the same for you, Reed. I wouldn't let it rest, if I knew something was wrong.*

Silence.

"Ugh. I can't win for trying."

Exiting her office, she looked down the length of her hallway to the view of the ocean and sky beyond her living room balcony. She was so damn restless, she felt like she was going to crawl out of her skin.

The Novium was pushing her body to have some fun kicking demon ass. That lust for violence could be channeled into a lust for sex as a delaying tactic, but Eve wasn't getting any, which left her spoiling for a good brawl. Here she'd been bitching about how much hunting she was doing, when it had actually been really damned convenient as far as her Novium was concerned. It took being cooped up at home for a couple of hours to drive that point home.

Now, what to do about it? Playing Wii sports wasn't going to cut it. She'd suggest to Montevista that they go to Gadara Tower and use the gym, but she didn't want to risk seeing Alec right now. She would have to thicken her skin before she exposed herself to his barbs.

Eve turned away from the beckoning beach and headed toward her bedroom instead. The moment she entered, she spotted an unfinished task—the beautifully embroidered burgundy leather Bible Father Riesgo had lent her.

Perhaps Montevista wouldn't bitch too much about escorting her somewhere, if she was going to church. Not that a church was any safer than other buildings; nothing was sacred to demons. But worst-case scenario would be that they cross paths with some bounty-hunting Infernals and throw down, and she'd welcome that. The demons were in town because of her. They should be fighting her, not making life hell for the other Marks.

She'd rounded the bed and was reaching for the Bible when she heard the door shut and lock behind her. Tensing, she glanced over her shoulder. Her hand fell to her side.

"All right," Reed said gruffly. "I feel it, too. Happy?"

His hands were shoved into the pockets of his black slacks; his face was austere and somber.

Eve sensed how it pained him to make the admission and how hard he fought against his jealousy in order to be honest with her. He would have preferred for her to give up on Alec altogether. Instead, he gave her hope.

"Don't get too excited," he muttered. "He's still a prick. He knew what he was getting himself into when he went after the ascension."

She became very still. "You think he *wanted* this?"

"I think he pursued it." Reed looked at her. "There are many handlers who are better qualified. Cain was chosen because he secured an endorsement somewhere."

It felt so odd to be so composed on the outside when she was breaking into pieces on the inside. "H-he had to know that things would change between us in the process, right?"

His face took on a stony cast. "He knew archangels are incapable of romantic love, yes. But he might not have been thinking about that—or you—at the time."

More honesty, even though keeping that last sentence to himself might have helped his cause with her.

"Thank you," she said quietly, rounding the bed toward him. After Alec's Jekyll and Hyde complex, it was a relief to interact with someone who was bare and genuine. To his possible detriment, no less.

Perhaps Gadara was correct in his assumption about why Reed had approached Sarakiel for assistance.

For her, Abel gave Cain the benefit of the doubt. It was only fair to give the same to him in return.

When she reached him, Eve didn't think twice. She cupped the back of his neck and pulled his mouth down to hers.

Reed's arms wrapped around her so fast, they felt like a steel trap snapping shut. His head tilted to better fit his mouth to hers. His aggressive hunger stole her breath and melted the chilled place inside her.

His fervor was far different from Alec's. There was lust, yes. Passion in spades. But his desire lacked the bite of fury and shadowy darkness of Alec's. With Reed, she didn't feel as if she was a waterlogged life preserver for a drowning man.

Breaking the connection, he rested his forehead against hers. "Don't use me to punish Cain."

"No." She pressed more tightly against him. "No Cain. Just you."

He cupped her buttocks in his hand and lifted her feet from the floor.

Eve . . . want you . . .

His lips, so firm and sensually curved, were softer than she'd expected. The last time he kissed her, he'd been rough. Angry. This time, his tongue was velvety soft as it licked deep into her mouth. The plunging motion was so deeply sexual she grew hot and wet. Moaning, she rubbed against him.

Want you, Eve, want you . . .

Alec's challenge echoed—*"What's more important? When someone wants you because they can't help it? Or when they want you because they make the conscious decision to want you?"*

But Alec was wrong. He didn't want her—consciously or otherwise. He *needed* her, but this afternoon she'd come to realize that she couldn't keep him afloat. Not in that sea of madness inside him. He would pull her under with him, just as he nearly had when he ascended to archangel. A Mark couldn't survive that Change—Alec, a *mal'akh*, had barely survived it—yet, as his body had altered states, he'd dragged her down into the inky blackness of his agony. It was Reed who'd pulled her free and saved her from certain insanity.

Reed pivoted, pinning her to the door. *Want you.*

Her legs wrapped around his lean hips. Their chests heaved together, the sound of their labored breathing more potent for its rarity. Marks didn't sweat, didn't get winded, didn't have racing hearts . . . except when gripped by lust for blood or sex. Stress didn't affect them, nor did regular exercise. The rarity of physical reactions created a craving for them, part of the way God encouraged Marks to retain their humanity despite a life of killing.

He pulled back and pressed his hot cheek to hers. "Sometimes, I hate you."

Eve felt that resentment occasionally, when he watched her and thought she wasn't aware. *If it's any consolation, sometimes I hate myself.*

"You wanted me before he came back into the picture, then denied me afterward." His hand cupped her breast, his thumb stroking across her nipple. Hot, dark eyes watched her pant and arch into his touch. They challenged her, mocked her.

"You damned me."

Want me back.

His voice in her mind was different from the one that spoke aloud to her. It was rougher, deeper, his half-formed fleeting thoughts pushed away as quickly as they appeared.

"I want to walk away from you." He rolled his hips so his hard length stroked directly against where she ached. "I want to fuck someone else and let you know that I have. I want you to lie in bed at night and wish you were beneath me. But you don't."

"I wish it now."

"I'm here now."

He continued to grind into her. The seam of her jeans became an added stimulation that coaxed a whimper of pleasure from her. She hadn't been able to send him away the last time he had held her like this, that first day when she'd thought he looked so much like Alec Cain they could be brothers. Who knew? She'd trembled in his arms like she was doing now and begged for mercy, even as she craved more.

Want me back, Eve, want me . . .

She nuzzled her check against his. *I do.*

"Then let me stay. Now."

Eve pressed her lips to his ear and breathed, "Yes. Stay."

CHAPTER 9

Izzie's blue eyes were wide. "You want me to seduce a seraph?" she asked in a voice inflected with a German accent.

If Alec were to guess, he'd say Sabrael might like it.

"If you can get that far." He smiled at the way she bristled. "But I'd be happy if you can just keep him out of my hair for a while."

The Mark clearly thought her charms were irresistible, which was another reason he'd approached her. In order to manage Sabrael, he needed someone whose confidence was bulletproof and who wasn't afraid of a little pain. He suspected Izzie's tough-as-nails appearance was more than just a fashion style. The gleam in her eyes when she was exposed to violence was a recognizable one.

"Why?" she asked.

"The 'why' is my part. The 'how' is yours."

Keeping Sabrael busy would keep the seraph away from Eve and out of the way when Alec approached Jehovah about delaying his mother's visit. Better for her to skip a year, than to be vulnerable at one of the most tumultuous times in history.

With his hand at Izzie's back, Alec led her away from the shooting range.

"Can't he hear you plan this?" Izzie queried.

"He could, if he was listening, but he isn't."

"How do you know?"

"Because he's not here kicking my ass," Alec said dryly.

Her mouth curved.

Alec used to seek out women such as her for sex, women who weren't looking for more than a hot, hard rut. Only with Eve had he taken the time to savor the connection.

And look how messy that was. All that angst and grief . . . not worth the trouble.

Ignoring the voices in his head, he said, "We'll get things rolling after I speak with Mariel about borrowing you for a while."

Assigning the latest class of Marks to handlers had been one of his first archangel responsibilities. He'd placed Izzie with the easygoing Mariel for two reasons: One, Mariel had recently lost one of her Marks to a hell-hound. Two, he sensed Izzie would manipulate a male handler.

Like Eve does Abel?

Izzie's breast pressed against his arm. "How will I meet this ser-aph?"

Unwelcome heat flared across his skin. "I'll arrange it."

"Why do you think I can seduce him?" Her voice was a throaty invi-tation to compliment her. Hit on her.

The part of himself that he was beginning to hate was considering it when a surge of lust burned through him.

Eve. She was achy and still aroused from his earlier handling of her. As he and Izzie reached the elevators, he glanced at the clock on the wall. An hour later and Eve was hotter than ever.

She's yours. Go get her. She'll give in . . . eventually. And if she doesn't, you can make her like it anyway . . .

His fingers stroked Izzie's lower back. "Because you're hot, Ms. Seiler," he purred.

I might have something that would interest you, Hank rasped.

The interruption was irritating. Alec had other things on his mind. *How interesting?*

I think it's significant.

Significant wasn't a word Hank used lightly. Grumbling beneath his breath, Alec punched the button on the elevator. Eve's desire was goad-ing his, which had every instinct he possessed urging him to get to her and put them both out of their misery. She might think she was scared of him, but he could make her give in. He knew all the right buttons to push . . .

I'm on my way, Alec told Hank. *But you better make this quick.*

As the elevator doors closed, Izzie sidled up to him.

He arched a brow in silent inquiry.

"You are flushed," she noted.

Yeah, he was aroused. He felt Eve as if she were in his arms, pinned to a wall and writhing against him. He felt her breast in his hand, tasted her flavor on his tongue, smelled the scent of her heated skin. The sensations were so vivid and so completely focused in his viewpoint that they felt like a wet dream.

A slow smile curved Izzie's painted mouth. "You are either very angry, or very horny."

Alec leaned back against the handrail and crossed his arms. "Neither of those things concern you."

"Once, they did." She stepped closer. "In Münster, only a few years ago."

Arrested by surprise, he barely registered the delighted, semimaniacal laughter echoing through him. Sweat dotted his brow and nape. The feel of Eve's nipple rolling between his fingertips was so real he was slow to process what Izzie was saying.

Then the memories came rushing back, bringing with them an acrid taste in his mouth.

It had been only hours before dawn. The stinking blood of an Infernal coated his hands and pictures of hundreds of exploited children filled his mind. *How long had the Ho'ok demon been running the child porn ring? How many kids had suffered? Why had the seraphim waited so long to end it?* Disgusted, disheartened, and raging with bloodlust, he wandered the streets of Münster until a blonde whore with spikes at her throat and wrists stepped out of a shadowy doorway in front of him.

"Wollen Sie einen Begleiter?" she'd asked, licking her lower lip. *Do you want company?*

He'd pushed her back into the alcove, lifted her miniskirt, and fucked her until the thirst to kill had faded to a distant ache. Then he'd shoved a handful of euros her way and left her—and the memory—behind.

Take her.

Alec stood frozen as the darkness surged up within him, curling around the lust inspired by Eve and hardening the entire length of his body. The elevator doors opened on Hank's floor, but he remained rooted in place. The raucous arguments of the many Infernals in the waiting room intruded into the once quiet space. Then the doors closed again, leaving him and Izzie alone with his inner demons and an instrumental rendition of "Copacabana" drifting out of the speakers.

He felt the phantom sensation of Eve arching against him the same moment Izzie's hand cupped his erection.

"Is this for me?" she purred, stroking him.

Fuck her.

The gritting of his teeth was audible. "No."

She shrugged and reached for the fly of his jeans with her other hand. "I will only borrow it, then."

As the first button popped free, the elevator began to ascend.

Forget Eve. She wants your brother. She's denied you for him.

Alec caught Izzie's wrist, staying her hand. Her gaze lifted. For a moment he saw almond-shaped eyes of soft brown. Then he blinked and stared into eyes of cool Nordic blue.

"You don't want what I'm ready to dish out," he warned.

"I do. I have for months."

Want you, Eve's voice whispered.

He shifted to his office.

But it was the beast in him that pinned Izzie to the wall.

* * *

Reed tossed Eve to the bed. She bounced with a soft cry of surprise, then reached for the fly of her jeans. Her limbs were lithe and perfect, the lines of her body slender yet generously curved.

Temptress, he'd once called her. And she was. A trickle of sweat coursed down his spine.

"Hurry," she urged, kicking free of her pants. A sexy-as-hell black lace thong was wriggled off next.

He remembered the one time he'd had her. Sent to mark her, he'd expected to merely toy with the woman his brother had spent a decade pining for. Then he'd passed her in the Gadara Tower atrium and found himself wanting her regardless of Cain.

Her gaze had followed him, filled with such hunger he felt it lick across his skin. That look had made him so eager to fuck her, he'd ripped the clothes from her body. *Hurry,* he had growled. The encounter had been over almost as soon as it began, yet it haunted him to this day.

Shifting out of his clothes, he left them puddled on the floor. He loomed over her. Eve paused in the act of pulling up her shirt, staring at his body with a mixture of awe and desire that swelled his dick further. She licked her lower lip and he groaned, fisting himself to buy a little time.

Did she see Cain in him? He almost probed her thoughts to find out, but resisted the urge. How she viewed him now wouldn't be the way she viewed him when he was done with her.

Eve reclined, half dressed, her pupils dilated from the Novium. She'd been scorching hot as a mortal. How much more intense would it be with her mark-enhanced body?

Reed's lips twitched, incapable of a true smile with his mouth so dry. She was impatient to have him, to the point that she couldn't be bothered to finish undressing.

"I won't fuck you until you're naked," he warned.

With two hands, she caught the rounded collar of her pretty pink shirt and ripped it straight down the middle.

That single act hit him straight in the gut. His breath hissed out between clenched teeth. He cupped her knees and widened the spread of her legs, wanting to see what he'd coveted for the last few months. She trembled under his gaze, her lower lip caught nervously between her teeth as if she feared he would find fault with her.

He wished he could.

"Slide back," he said roughly, following her retreat with one knee on the mattress, then the other. He pursued her across the California king until she reached the headboard and had nowhere left to go.

"Reed." Her breathless voice dragged his gaze up to meet hers. "Don't wait."

She was panting, and he hadn't even begun. Pressing his lips to her thigh, he hummed in chastisement. "Relax. This is going to take awhile."

"I have people here!"

He licked at the back of her knee. She shivered. "I wouldn't care if all the archangels were here. I'm going to get my fill."

Hurry up, damn you. She sounded winded in his thoughts, which told him how hot for it she was. Hot for him.

He pushed his hands beneath her buttocks. *I'm going to do everything to you. Everything.* As he lifted her to his mouth, her back bowed. *I'm going to push so deep into you that you'll miss me when I'm not there.*

Her legs fell open, offering herself to him. His first lick was slow and soft. Deliberately teasing. She was slick and burning with need, writhing within his grasp.

She keened softly as he pierced her hard and fast. *Don't stop . . . don't stop . . .*

A quick flutter over her, then he stiffened his tongue and worked the tiny bundle of nerves at the apex, relishing her throaty pleas for more. *Don't stop . . .*

He groaned and ground his hips into the mattress, knowing that he had to get her off now, fearing that he was too far gone to be able to bring her to orgasm later. He was spurred by the knowledge that this was Eve, the woman he wanted for reasons unrelated to sex. Now she was right where he wanted her—spread and willing, mewling with helpless pleasure. They were in the moment together, connected body and mind. He hadn't known he was alone—an angel who stood apart—until he wasn't alone any longer.

Reed grew more fervent, fueled by gratitude and an odd . . . joy. Afraid to be too rough with her, he siphoned the surfeit of lust through Eve and out to Cain, where it could be disbursed to the others in the firm. The tactic bought him some control, allowing him to be gentle with her as he hadn't been before.

Eve climaxed with her hands fisted in her comforter, her thighs shaking, the tender pink flesh beneath his lips spasming with a greed that might equal his own.

He rose to his knees, grasping her legs when they threatened to fall to the bed. He wiped his wet mouth against a perfect calf and the feel of her skin stirred the need he'd denied for months. Denied for her.

"My turn," he bit out, shifting both of her legs to one shoulder and taking himself in hand.

Pliant and drowsy-eyed, she touched his thigh with gentle fingers. He froze, wondering if she'd changed her mind now that the Novium was appeased, and whether he could stop if she had.

The look on Reed's face made Eve's eyes sting with unshed tears. The hand gripping her ankles was flexing convulsively and his throat worked as if he wanted to speak, but couldn't.

"I want you," she whispered. *Inside me . . . with me.*

Take me, then. He lunged forward with a snarl.

Her resultant cry was both pained and pleasured. She had forgotten how he felt inside her, so thick and long, nearly too much. Before she could catch her breath, he launched into a pounding rhythm, surging into her with a force that shoved her into the headboard. Placing her hands above her head, she pushed back when he pumped, shoving him so deep it ached in just the way she needed.

Today, she was as greedy for him as he'd always been for her. He was raw, without artifice, with none of the steely control Alec usually displayed. Reed climaxed immediately and unabashedly—his head thrown back, his neck taut, his abdomen rippling with working muscles. He roared as he came, his wings bursting free in an explosion of white, his thighs straining as he took his pleasure in her willing body.

Eventually he slowed, his chest heaving. He spread her legs, wrapping them around his hips and settling over her. His mouth moved over her face, kissing her, his gusting breaths a separate caress over her damp skin. One arm slid beneath her shoulder, anchoring her. The other hand cupped her breast, kneading. Beneath her calves, she felt his steely buttocks clench and release as he propelled himself into her. Slow, steady, and deep.

Reed—the ferocious one, a man known for his penchant for rough sex—was making love to her. The relief and . . . *joy* of being connected to someone brought tears to her eyes, but she blinked them back.

"Mmm . . ." He purred like a contented panther. A drop of sweat dripped from his brow to her cheek and he licked it away, then nuzzled against her. "That was worth waiting for."

His luxuriant, leisurely thrusts made her moan and arch upward. "Reed," she gasped, shivering into a violent orgasm beneath him.

His smile held a hint of male triumph. His eyes were dark and intent, his biceps flexing as he rolled her nipple between talented fingertips. Against the backdrop of white feathers, Reed's skin was golden, glistening with a fine sheen of perspiration that told her just how aroused she'd made him.

He pressed his lips to hers and whispered, "Now we can get started."

Alec stood before the wall of windows in his office and ran an agitated hand through his sweat-soaked hair. The air smelled of sex and fury, as did his skin. His shirt was torn and wet. He yanked it over his head and tossed it aside, then shoved down the boxer briefs he'd lowered only enough to free his erection.

His stomach roiled and he found himself wishing he could vomit. He felt violated, as if he'd raped his own body.

Want you inside me . . . with me. Eve's breathless voice combined with the dark ones in his head to goad him into an act he regretted more than the first time he'd killed his brother.

He could barely stomach looking at the woman sprawled on the floor behind him, knowing he'd betrayed Eve with her. Izzie had started out by goading him, spurring his lust and anger, relishing his single-minded focus on rutting. She might have thought it similar to the way he'd been with her before.

That changed as the darkness overtook him. He'd merely been the vessel used to carry out the act and at some point, she realized that. Surprise had hit her first, then fear, followed by anger. In the end, the pleasure overwhelmed the rest, but Alec doubted she would seek him out for sex again. He prayed to God that he would be able to resist her if she did.

I have to gain control of whatever the ascension awakened in me.

Naked, he moved to where Izzie lay sleeping and bent to pick her up. She whimpered and rolled away from him, exhausted by the demands made on her body. He had the strength of an archangel and the needs of a multitude of voices in his head. For all intents and purposes, she'd been fucked by a dozen insatiable appetites. Her clothes were in tatters, her eye makeup and lipstick smeared.

Alec deposited her gently on the black leather sofa that rested against one wall, then moved to the bathroom and the shower that waited there. He'd practically lived in this office after his promotion. Knowing immediately that something was wrong with him, he had been determined to keep away from Eve. But the thought of her with Abel—or any another man—had been unbearable. He'd given in to the need to see her. He didn't have to be in love with her to want to keep her. Affection, admiration, respect, and desire . . . some marriages had far less.

Want you . . .

He was so exhausted that even Eve's voice couldn't rouse him, but he felt a soft humming in his gut that signaled an eventual recharge. He had to get out of the tower and away from the other Marks who made him so powerful.

What have I done?

As the scorching water beat down upon his head and the odor of sweat and sex dissipated in the steam, Alec placed his hand against the cool tile and stared at the water swirling down the drain. Just like his life—and his relationship with Eve.

The things he'd said to her . . . Now that he could think clearly, he knew the full extent of what he had done. His intentions had been right, but the approach was hideously wrong.

He thought of Izzie's exhaustion and his own stamina. He winced. While he didn't like the means, he was grateful the thing in him hadn't used Eve that way.

Cleaned and dressed in new clothes, Alec moved back into the main part of his office and collected Izzie. He shifted to her apartment and tucked her into bed.

He loathed himself in the brief moments that he hovered over her unmoving form. She had started out a willing participant and he'd pleasured her well, but too much of anything was too much. He'd been rougher with her than he had ever been with another female in his life.

He was exhausted when he shifted back to the hallway outside of Hank's office. So tired that knocking on the door was a chore, but an invitation was the only way to breach the occultist's inner sanctum. As it had earlier in the day when he'd come with Eve and the tengu, the door opened without tangible assistance and Alec entered the shadowy space.

"Took you long enough," Hank rasped, appearing out of the shadows in the familiar crone guise before altering into a voluptuous and lovely red-haired female. Alec used to wonder if the haggard witch guise was really a glamour at all, but later decided it was just a quirk. A ritual Hank performed to get in the mood to work his—or her—magic.

"Sorry." The simple word was incapable of relating the full depth of Alec's remorse.

Hank came to a stop just a few inches away. "You look like shit."

He felt like it, too. "What have you got for me?"

"Some advice." Hank crossed her arms beneath an ample bosom. "End whatever sort of relationship you have with Eve. You are weakening each other at a time when you both need to be the strongest."

"I've already broken it off with her."

"Ah . . ." Hank studied him with narrowed eyes. "You seem more affected by the loss than you should be as an archangel."

Alec almost snapped back—his temper was still sharp—but the last couple of hours had afforded him just enough control to fight the impulse. "What do you know about the ascension to archangel?"

"I know I've always believed that archangels were born, not made."

Hank turned and gestured for Alec to follow. As they moved, a circle of light, like a spotlight, moved with them. Alec got the sense that the room extended infinitely beyond the shadows, which wasn't possible according to the limitations of mortal structures. But he'd learned to just accept that Hank was a demon of unknown power and origins, and to appreciate the fact that the Infernal was on his side and not on Sammael's.

"Any guess as to why more haven't been created?" Alec asked.

"Because the Seven have remained intact."

"The Seven. You say that as if it were an entity and not just a number."

A small, rough-hewn wooden table came into view and Hank settled daintily into a matching chair, gesturing for Alec to do the same. In all of the years he'd worked with Hank, this was the first time he'd ventured more than a few feet inside the occultist's domain. The air was hotter back here and smelled of sulfur.

Alec sat. The tengu waddled out of the darkness carrying a tray, as docile as a well-trained butler. He set a pitcher of amber-colored liquid and two crystal tumblers on the table, then bowed and scampered away. The stench of his rotting soul lingered.

"What the hell?" Alec barked. "It stinks. And it's . . . well behaved."

"We'll get to that in a minute. Of the many other archangels, only Michael, Raphael, and Gabriel have retained their foothold. Metatron, Ariel, Izidkiel . . . and all the others, where are they now?"

"With God."

"Because they were not able to manage firms and a secular life as well as the others?" Hank queried, referencing the widely spread belief. "With all the power and knowledge at an archangel's disposal, only *seven* were able to remain on Earth? God didn't want to create more in the hopes that they might be able to handle it? And no *mal'akh* has proven capable of taking on the task in the interim? Until you?"

Lifting his glass, Alec sniffed the contents and asked, "What is this?"

"Iced chamomile tea."

Alec set the glass back down. "I was promoted because Raguel was taken." And because he'd promised Sabrael an as-yet-unknown favor, but that was a matter best kept between him and Sabrael.

Hank filled her glass to the rim and downed the contents in one audible gulp. "Which effectively kept the number of archangels on earth at seven."

"You think the number is deliberate? Like a cap?"

"That, or the change is so difficult it is the very rare *mal'akh* who can manage it. I like you quite well, Cain, but you and I both know that there are others who are better qualified for the advancement than you are."

Exhaling harshly, Alec leaned into the seat despite its creaking protests. Hank had a generous expense account and could easily afford to upgrade the furnishings, but appearance was everything to the occultist. The rickety table and chairs were meant to convey something that Alec didn't yet grasp. And he couldn't waste time thinking about it now. "No one is more knowledgeable than I am about saving Mark lives."

Hank flicked a lock of long red hair back over her shoulder. "Since when is that an archangel's purpose?"

The subtle challenge caused Alec's lips to pull back from his teeth in a snarl.

"Look at you," Hank rasped. "Like a rabid dog on the edge of attack. Yet you found the will to break up with Eve, when I'm certain that's the last thing you wanted to do. You're not supposed to be able to love her."

"It's not the same as before."

"Diminished, but not gone. Why isn't it gone? Is it because you were in love when the ascension happened?"

"I don't need more questions," Alec bit out. "I need answers."

Hank shrugged. "I'm a scientist. It's in my nature to question things."

"Find the damn answers! What the hell is wrong with me?"

"What's wrong is your belief that something is wrong."

Alec's fists clenched. "I don't like hitting women, but you're pushing me."

The occultist altered shape into a young girl of around six or seven years old, but spoke in the eternally present gruff voice. "Every celestial believes that demons choose to be evil. None will consider that we're created the way we are. We couldn't see the world as you do, even if we wanted to. Just like you can't see our point of view."

But Alec could now. That was the problem. He saw the appeal. Worse, the urges he felt seemed an inherent part of him, not an addition. "So you think I'm supposed to be this way? That I've always been this way. Is that what you're saying?"

"Perhaps you're fighting the change." Hank picked up Alec's untouched glass and downed the contents. "Perhaps the ambitious part of your soul, the part that yearns to be closer to God, is what's rebelling in you. It's becoming feral because it isn't getting what it wants."

"Maybe it's the part of me that wants Eve," he said, just to be contrary.

"Personally, I think it might be that other, darker part of your soul asserting itself. That part you ignore and everyone pretends doesn't exist."

Alec growled at Hank's perceptiveness, the sound more animal than angel. "It doesn't exist. It's a myth."

"A lie from an archangel, instead of mere evasion. That has to be a first." Hank smiled. "Regardless, my concern was for Eve and you've seen to that. Cain of Infamy can take care of himself. I suggest you ask one of the other archangels what to expect. Why come to an Infernal when Sarakiel is here to assist you?"

"Because I'm in competition with the other archangels now."

Similar to children, archangels curried the favor of their Father. They competed with their siblings in the hopes of outshining them. He was now a threat. They'd be sabotaging themselves in order to help him. No archangel was that selfless.

Altering back into the sex kitten form, Hank stood and gestured for Alec to follow suit. "Come on. Let me show you why I called you down here. It might cheer you up."

CHAPTER 10

The soft trill of an incoming text message pulled Reed from a doze. "Can I smash your phone?" he murmured, nuzzling his lips against the crown of Eve's head. "I'll buy you a new one."

She wriggled against his side, her body a warm weight he was reluctant to lose. "Some of us have to communicate the hard way," she teased. As she pushed up on one elbow, the thick curtain of her hair tickled his chest.

He felt a shadow of unease cross her mind, followed quickly by a stab of guilt. Rolling, he pinned her beneath him and took her mouth in a hard, hot kiss. She softened, her hands sliding into his hair to hold him close.

Pulling back, he touched his nose to hers, somewhat bemused by his need to be tender. "If you start thinking of this as a mistake, I'll bend you over my knee and spank you."

Eve laughed, but her gaze was somber. "You're going to have to be patient with me. I'm not in the best shape to jump into something serious. I told you that before."

"I'm not in any shape to jump into anything. You know that. I have no idea what the hell I'm doing."

"Or if you're going to want to keep doing it," she added.

Reed winked. "I definitely want to keep doing it."

"Fine. We'll keep it sexual."

"That's not what I meant."

"Yes, it is." She wrapped a leg around his, rolled him back over, and kept on going. She continued alone until she rolled to the edge of the mattress, then slid off of it.

"Babe . . ."

She moved over to the dresser and unplugged her cell phone from its charger. A few button pushes later, she said, "Sara is looking for you."

Closing his eyes, he bit back a frustrated groan. He had a cell phone, but he kept it off 90 percent of the time for just this reason. Anyone he wanted to talk to could do so without secular means. Everyone else could damn well wait until he got to them.

"How bad is it that she knew she'd find you with me?" As she talked, Eve's voice grew distant.

Slitting his eyes open, Reed caught her hot little ass disappearing into the bathroom. Shamelessly naked, which he found very appealing.

She probably contacted all of my Marks, he replied privately, knowing that calling after her would be heard by the two Marks in the living room.

The shower came on. Eve's room was large, with vaulted ceilings and a door-less entry to the bathroom that was several feet wide.

How long were you with her? she asked.

Reed slid out of bed and followed her into the bathroom. "I know what you're thinking, and it wasn't like that."

He found Eve standing with eyes closed and head tilted back beneath a massive showerhead. The shower stall had been built with no door and only a slender floating glass partition, which afforded him an unobstructed view of every inch of her.

What was *it like, then?* she rejoined.

"A waste of time."

Eve straightened and wiped the water from her eyelashes. "Some relationships end with feelings like that, but they rarely begin with them."

"I wouldn't know. I don't do relationships."

"Was she that good in the sack?" She posed the question casually, but he sensed that her interest in the answer was far from it.

"She was convenient. No dating, no wooing, no foreplay. The less I cared about her pleasure, the more she liked it."

"Maybe because she cares about you."

Reed laughed. "She's an archangel, remember? There's barely enough room in her heart for God."

"I'm not kidding. I've seen the way she looks at you."

"She wants my cock. That's not caring by any definition."

Eve squirted apple-scented soap into her palm and shot him a wry glance. "I know some men have fantasies about penis-starved women, but that's a bit much."

He leaned his hip into the counter and crossed his arms, watching her shampooing her long hair with avid interest. "That's not what you were moaning thirty minutes ago."

She paused long enough to throw a loofah at him. Catching it neatly, he straightened and approached her.

"I asked Sara to do something for me," he told her. "She strung me along for years before admitting that she wasn't going to follow through."

"Maybe she *couldn't* follow through."

Reed tossed the loofah back at her, then caught her hips and spun her out of the shower spray.

"Hey!" she protested, as he stepped under the water.

"The point is that she knew she wasn't going to help me. She just led me to believe otherwise." Shaking out his wet hair, he ceded the shower back to her and reached for her shampoo.

"I thought archangels didn't lie."

He paused a second, as if considering that, then began scrubbing his hair. "Why are we talking about this?"

"I want to learn more about you." Shrugging, she began scrubbing at her skin, turning it a lovely shade of soft pink.

"Then why are you asking questions about someone else?"

"Fine. I'll ask a question about you: what did you want her to do for you?"

His hands moved from his chest to hers. The look she gave him said she wouldn't be distracted.

"It's not important now," he said.

Suddenly, she smacked him on the shoulder. "I was right," she crowed. "You *do* want to be an archangel."

Reed growled and tugged her soapy body against his. "I stayed out of your brain. You have no business digging around in mine."

"*You* thought of it. It just popped into my head."

It hit him that their newfound intimacy might open pathways he'd prefer stay closed.

As if she caught his reluctance, Eve frowned. "What's the big deal anyway?"

He felt her begin to pull back, both physically and emotionally. His fingers flexed into her buttocks.

"It's a lofty ambition," he explained tightly, knowing that he was going to have to open up at least a little if he hoped to keep her. "Not one you want to advertise."

"I can understand that. But you trusted Sara with it. When I asked you about it before, you blew me off."

Bending at the knees, Reed fit his frame more perfectly to hers. "You share thoughts with my brother, babe."

"Why would he care if you want to be promoted?"

His jaw clenched. Talking about himself was one of his least favorite things to do. "In the past," he said carefully, "if Cain knew I wanted something, he would usually get it first."

"Oh." Her arms came around him and the loofah in her hand scratched his back deliciously.

"Scrub my back?" he asked, kissing her forehead.

"Keep talking?" she dickered.

"There are more enjoyable ways to pay you in kind."

"Deal or no deal?"

Grumbling at his inability to tell her no, he altered their positions so that she could stay warm beneath the water while he stood outside of it.

As she ran the loofah over his skin, she asked, "Do you think Alec will interfere with your advancement now? He's already been promoted."

"Yes, I think he'd get in the way. He's better at killing things, but that's the only thing he's better at. He knows I'd surpass him."

Eve's movements slowed, then stopped altogether. He waited, then looked over his shoulder.

Her gaze met his. "You said you think he secured the endorsement he needed with a bargain."

"I do. Hasn't he proven that's the way he works? He bargained with God to mentor you. He bargained with Grimshaw to get to you at the masonry. He bargained to resurrect you after Asmodeus's dragon killed you. Cain will break any rule, and he's in demand. Others barter with him to accomplish tasks they're afraid to do themselves."

"The way you bargained with Sara to get her guards to help me in Upland?"

Reed froze. *How much did she know about that transaction?* "Is that what you were digging around for earlier?"

Her gaze lowered. "Did I get it wrong? Did you do it for her?"

He swallowed hard, relieved by her apparent ignorance of his prostitution and terrified by the sudden expectation between them. It felt like a turning point and he wasn't ready for it yet. Didn't know how to get ready for it. "Not for her," he managed, finally.

The grateful kiss she pressed to the wet skin of his biceps made him look away before she saw whatever his face might reveal. She could bring him to his knees with a look. It would be best if she didn't know that.

She cleared her throat. "It would have to be a seraph who helped your brother, right? They're the only ones who have the ear of God."

"Not the only ones, no. The cherubim and thrones are also near Him. But the thrones are humble angels. They lack the ambition to strike a devil's bargain with Cain."

Eve held up both hands in a gesture of surrender. "I'm not in the right frame of mind to have a lesson on the hierarchy of angels."

"Good." He gestured at his back and gave her his best smile. "Please?"

As Eve resumed scrubbing, Reed faced forward.

"I'm really worried about Gadara," she murmured. "It's driving me crazy that everyone seems to have written him off. I want people running around, pushing for answers, hitting the pavement . . . something."

He nodded.

"I have an idea."

Reed tensed at Eve's tone, which held a note of reluctance, as if she knew in advance that what she was going to say would cause an unpleasant reaction. "What?"

"We want Gadara. Satan wants me. Why don't we offer a trade?"

He froze. His chest lifted and fell in normal rhythm, but his heart raced. It shouldn't. He wasn't aroused; he was horrified. "Are you insane?"

"Maybe. Probably."

Facing her, he caught her by the hips. "No fucking way."

"Come on." Her gaze was forthright and earnest. "If we put our heads together we can figure out a way to pull it off without one of us getting killed."

"Helllloooo? Earth to Eve. This is Sammael we're taking about. Aside from Jehovah, nothing exists that can defeat him."

Her jaw took on a stubborn cant. "I'm not talking about defeating him. I'm talking about tricking him."

He shook her. "And what do you think he's going to do when all is said and done? He's already set a bounty on your head!"

"If he really wanted me dead, I'd be dead."

Convoluted logic or not, she had a point. Still, the risk she was willing to take made Reed's gut churn. "He likes to play with his kills," he bit out. "That's all."

"Just think about it."

"No."

"It's the only option we've got!"

"Bullshit." He had a much better trade in mind, but she wasn't going to like the terms. "It's not an option at all."

Eve opened her mouth to argue, but he sealed his lips over hers and shut her up.

"I'll cook dinner tonight," Reed offered. "And no, it won't be Kung Pao chicken."

Eve finished pulling a T-shirt over her head, then glanced at him. His head was down, his eyes on his belt buckle as he fastened it. Perfectly polished, as usual. She took a good long look at him, appreciating his elegance even more for its artlessness. He hadn't primped when he exited the shower; didn't even glance at the mirror. A quick run of his hands through his hair was all that was needed due to the precision of his cut.

This was what she'd once thought her married life would be like. Great sex. Showering together before work. A man she couldn't get enough of looking at. She was turned on by the dichotomy of Reed's present composure contrasted against his fervency in bed and the heat with which he'd rejected her suggestion of a trade for Gadara.

Even knowing that he wanted to advance to archangel and lose whatever feelings he had for her, she still wanted him.

Eve sighed. It had been clear from the beginning that she'd never be able to keep either brother. Their purpose was infinite, hers was finite. She didn't want to hold either of them back and she wasn't willing to give up her own dreams of normalcy, which meant it was up to her to keep her heart out of it.

Reed was reaching for his watch on the nightstand when he caught her staring. He paused, his previously absorbed expression changing to one of bemusement. He really had no idea what to make of her, and that told her that whatever she was to him, it was unique.

She licked her lower lip and watched his breathing quicken.

"Got a minute?" she asked breathlessly.

His slow smile made her toes curl. "I've got all the time you need."

"What the hell am I looking at?" Alec asked, straightening from the microscope.

Hank smiled. "The reason for your tengu friend's docile behavior."

"Explain."

"The mask suppresses aspects of Infernal genetic makeup, hence the reason for the change in their scent and skin. I just adjusted the spell they used to alter emotions instead. Think of it as Valium for demons."

"But it requires the same materials?"

"Yes."

Alec made an aggravated noise. The masking agent had been made with Mark blood and bone. They had a limited stockpile that they'd confiscated from the masonry in Upland, but once it was gone, there was no way to get more aside from killing Marks. "Does it wear off?"

"Don't know yet, but I would be surprised if it didn't." Hank gestured to the right and a sudden light illuminated a kennel that contained the tengu. "I chipped a piece off his heel and ran some tests. The masking agent was mixed with the cement. That might have been the inspiration for the creation of the hellhounds."

"But even though the mask was built into the tengu, you could still change its purpose?"

"The materials in the tengu are immutable, but the magic isn't. The damned creature was a nuisance, so I cast a spell on it and—" Hank pointed at the tengu, "—that's what happened. So I began playing with the formula to see what variations I could come up with."

A movement by the cage drew Alec's gaze. Fred stood to the side, taking notes.

"It's interesting," Alec conceded, looking back at Hank. "And Valium for demons could come in handy, but considering the limited quantities of supplies, I don't see it being viable."

"It's the first time anyone has subdued an Infernal's base nature," Hank huffed, clearly affronted.

Alec patted her on the shoulder. "Great job. Now . . . can you make me something I can use? An antidote to the mask? A mask for Marks that uses Infernal ash instead of Mark blood? Something along those lines?"

"Those are not the same lines. They are two very different things."

"You know what I mean." Irritation and impatience crawled through him, making him eager to get away. Whatever endorphins his recent orgasms had afforded him were rapidly diminishing. "You've had the masking ingredients for months. I expected more from you by this point."

Fred whistled and sidestepped out of the light.

Hank's beautiful features hardened. "Go away now, Cain," she said with dangerous softness. "Before one of us says or does something that we both regret."

Knowing that Hank was right, Alec shifted away.

"Hey."

Sara smiled at the cocky young man who called out to her. As she passed the volleyball court in the open courtyard of Izzie's apartment complex, he watched her with avid interest. Dressed in only board shorts and a pair of sunglasses, he was handsome enough and boasted a well-muscled physique. She briefly considered dallying with him just for the sport, but the notion quickly soured. His leer told her he lacked the experience to properly satisfy her.

Dismissing him, she climbed the steps to the second floor and knocked. She had to knock again before the door opened and Izzie was revealed. Fresh from a shower and makeup free, the blonde looked impossibly young. Fragile and wary as only a child could be.

Sara pushed her way inside when the door didn't open fast enough for her. The apartment was expansive and bilevel, with vaulted ceilings and steps up to the open dining area and kitchen, as well as a guest bath and bedroom. The master suite was on the same level as the living room and steam from the shower brought humidity into the lower half of the space.

"What happened to you?" Sarakiel demanded, eyeing the Mark critically.

"Cain."

"Really? You look worse for wear. Not that I am surprised. Cain is Cain, after all."

"I am not so sure about that," Izzie said wearily. Bundled inside a thick terry-cloth robe with wet hair hanging around her shoulders and wan face, she padded over to a red velvet sofa and sat.

Sara joined her. "Tell me."

When the tale was finished, Sara settled into the crook of the sofa arm and considered the possibilities. "Did Cain give a name to the seraph?"

"No."

"Can you get it out of him?"

"You don't understand." Izzie's slender fingers played with the loops of cotton. "He was reluctant at first, and later, like a . . . machine. There was nothing in his face . . . in his eyes. Nothing. He spoke in a language I couldn't understand."

"Hmm . . . I will see for myself."

Izzie's head cocked to the side. "How?"

"There are video feeds all over the tower."

"He is not the same man I met before. Something isn't right with him."

Sara pulled out her cell phone. She tried Abel again, knowing she would only reach his voice mail but needing to make the attempt regardless. On a whim, she texted a message to Evangeline.

How would the Mark handle the news of Cain's infidelity? And how far would Cain go to keep the knowledge from her?

A seraph. She hid an inner smile. That limited the scope of her search considerably. Whomever it was, he'd paid a visit to Cain recently enough to spark the ludicrous plan he'd presented to Izzie. Perhaps the meeting had taken place in the tower. While the divine radiance of the seraphim was undetectable to mortal technology such as the video cameras used in Gadara Tower, perhaps Cain had spoken the seraph's name in the course of their discussion. It was a lead, however faint.

"What do you want me to do now?" Izzie asked.

"Mariel will not assign you once Cain speaks with her, so enjoy some time to yourself."

"I'm here if you need me."

Sara brushed the back of her fingers across Izzie's pale cheek. "You will go far, Iselda."

The Mark curled deeper into the couch with a weary sigh. "As long as I go to Heaven. Having seen the alternative, I will do whatever it takes to go the other way."

"Anyone up for tacos?" Eve entered the living room and noted the setting sun just beyond her balcony window. The sky was multihued, telling her that she'd spent hours in bed with Reed. Long enough for Sydney to give up on the Wii and switch to her laptop. Montevista was nowhere to be seen.

"I am." Sydney snapped her computer closed and stood, stretching. "Montevista went to check on the perimeter guards again."

"Great. We can catch him downstairs and save him the trip back up."

Sydney rounded the coffee table. Eve once again marveled at how different the Mark looked in street clothes versus her work attire. Dressed in a dark pink Juicy Couture jogging suit, she didn't look anywhere near her centuries-old age.

"Are you okay?" Sydney looked her over. "You look sad."

Eve was taken aback a moment, then realized that while she might not consciously acknowledge her feelings of loss over Alec, that didn't mean they weren't visible. "I'm fine."

And she would be. Eventually. She didn't regret her afternoon with Reed, even though she'd further complicated her already messy love life.

After grabbing some cash from her purse, Eve followed Sydney out the

door and locked the many dead bolts she'd had installed for protection
back when she was Unmarked. Then they set off, passing the door to Alec's
condo. He'd made it clear on more than one occasion that he would prefer
to be living with Eve and not beside her, but the Hollises were Southern
Baptists and shacking up before marriage was a serious no-no in her family.
Even the next-door neighbor thing was a little too close for comfort.

The ride down to the lobby level was quick and they moved onto the
marble-lined entryway with light steps.

"I'd kill for a place like this," Sydney said.

"Don't you?" Eve quipped, glancing at her. "You should check with
someone about moving, if you're not happy where you live."

"I'm okay. But I could be happier in a place like this." Sydney smiled.
"Not worth it for me to hit up Ishamel about it, though. He freaks me
out."

Frowning, Eve asked, "Who's Ishamel?"

They crossed through the parking garage and exited out a self-locking
iron gate. Eve glanced to her left, searching out the corner where Evil Santa
missionary usually hung out. He was there and talking to Montevista.
Luckily, the nut job was facing away from her, while the Mark looked directly at her.

"Heading to El Gordito," she said, in her normal conversational tone,
knowing his mark-enhanced ears would easily allow him to hear. He gave
a surreptitious thumbs-up.

"Ishamel is Gadara's factotum."

"The secretary?" The man who kept Gadara's office running like clock-
work was white-haired and slightly stooped at the shoulders, with a penchant for sleeveless sweater vests and bow ties. Whenever Eve crossed his
path, she wondered what he could have done to get marked. Since the mark
arrested aging, he'd been old from the get-go.

"No, that's Spencer. He handles everything inside Gadara Tower."
Pushing sunglasses onto her face, Sydney turned toward the beach.
"Ishamel is the off-site guy. I'm sure you've seen him around. He dresses
in gray from head to toe. Rides around in a limousine."

Eve's stride faltered. Gray Man. She'd met him back when she was a
brand-spanking-new Mark. He'd picked her up in a limo and driven her
to Gadara Tower. "He's creepy."

They hit the sand and turned left. The restaurant was within sight, a
casual Mexican cantina with a Plexiglas-framed patio.

Eve considered whether or not it had been a mistake to forget about
Ishamel. If he was Gadara's right-hand man, he would know how archangels functioned. Maybe he could help her figure out what was happening to Alec.

"I get the willies just thinking about his grin," Sydney went on.

"It's really more like a constipation-induced grimace." Eve tried to
recall other details about him, but without much luck. "What is he? I

don't remember him smelling like anything—Mark or Infernal—but I was really green at the time."

"Ishamel is a *mal'akh*, but not a handler like the others. His sole purpose to make life easier for Gadara, handling all the pesky little details that are beneath an archangel but too important for Marks."

"Arranging housing is too important for Marks?"

"Moving into more expensive digs would take authorization a mere Mark couldn't give. Especially in this crappy economy. All the firms are taking a hit."

"I didn't think about that." Eve's nose wrinkled. "I hate to admit it, but I guess I've come to see the firms as solid. Invincible. But you're right. We're based in California—the epicenter of the housing market collapse. And Gadara specializes in real estate."

They reached the patio and took an empty table with an unimpeded view of the beach. Trays and trash littered the surface due to an inconsiderate patron, but they tossed the mess in a nearby trash can and waited for a busboy to wipe the table down with a rag.

Montevista walked up just as the waiter approached.

"Three taco plates, please," Eve ordered. "Extra pico de gallo and sour cream." She looked at her companions. "What are you having?"

Sydney laughed. "I had no idea interior design worked up such an appetite."

Eve was grateful the mark prevented blushing.

After the orders were in, drinks were on the table, and they were relatively alone, Montevista leaned back in his plastic patio chair and said, "The reverend on the corner is really gunning for you, Hollis."

"Reverend?"

Montevista smiled. "Presbyterian."

Eve reached for her iced tea. "He's a whack job. Zealots like that should be marked. They're clearly devoted. If the seraphim sent enough of them after Satan, he'd give up quick."

"He thinks you're a call girl."

"What the hell?"

"Because of the number of men you have visiting you."

"Maybe I'm holding Bible study. Did he ever think of that?"

Montevista's eyes twinkled behind his dark shades. "He says you have a body built for sin."

"Gee, thanks. Did you straighten him out?"

"I fought the good fight, but he says I'm bewitched. I don't think anyone short of God will get him to change his mind."

"Great." Eve crossed her arms.

Sydney smiled. "Hey, look on the bright side. I wish someone said I had a body built for sin."

"You do have a body built for sin," Montevista said with a soft purr that made Eve look twice.

Sydney stared at her partner for a long moment, then gulped down her soda. Eve's brows rose. How long had Montevista had the hots for Sydney? And why did Sydney seem so surprised? After they'd worked together for decades, any sort of attraction shouldn't have gone unnoticed.

"Anyone short of God, eh?" Eve repeated, considering. "You just gave me an idea."

"Uh-oh." Montevista looked at her with brows raised above the top edge of his sunglasses.

Eve gave him a mock glare. "I have to return a Bible to Father Riesgo. I'll ask him to come over and put in a good word for me."

"Tossing a priest into the line of fire?" Sydney asked dryly.

"Have you seen Riesgo? That man can take care of himself. Besides, he seems determined to save me." Eve sat back as the waiter returned with a tray overflowing with plastic plates. "He can start with Evil Santa."

CHAPTER 11

Alec sat on the steps of the old Masada fortress for nearly an hour before the power he gained from proximity to the firm waned and he felt remotely like himself again. He breathed slowly and deeply, battling against his new nature until he reestablished enough control to consider associating with others. He needed help, but he wouldn't get it if he kept being an asshole.

Where could he turn? Uriel was his first choice, but if the archangel suspected that Alec was a danger to himself or others, he would tell Michael and Gabriel. They would kill him, Alec had no doubt. But who else had answers? Who would protect him if they discovered his secret?

There was only one place he could go where he would be accepted as he was. Whether that was also the place where he would find answers was something he'd determine when he got there.

Shifting before he could change his mind, Alec entered Shamayim—the First Heaven, abode of his parents. His booted feet hit the dirt with a thud and he took a deep breath to regain his bearings. The neatly tilled rows stretching out in front of him caused a pang in his chest. There had been a time when he couldn't imagine his life being anything other than that of a farmer.

He wasn't that guy anymore.

So a man will leave his father and mother and be united with his woman . . .

"Cain!"

Alec turned his head and found his father at the far end of the field. Adam dug the plow tip into the dirt and tied the reins of his mule around a handle to keep the beast in place.

Shifting to a spot just a few feet away, Alec offered a wary smile and spoke in Hebrew by habit. *"Shalom,* Abba."

"Your mother has been missing you," Adam said gruffly, pushing his hat back from a sweat-slick forehead. His dark eyes were assessing, watchful.

Alec resisted the urge to bristle at the thinly veiled chastisement. "I miss you both, too," he replied tersely. "It's crazy down there. There's not enough time in the day, even when the days are endless."

He'd learned to include his father in his replies, but Alec resented the fact that Adam couldn't say anything remotely supportive or appreciative. Abel had always accepted their father's distance without issue, but it ate at Alec. When he'd been younger and more hotheaded, he would pick fights to ease some of the sting.

"How is Evangeline?"

The question startled Alec. He hadn't been aware that his father knew, or cared, about the details of his life. "She's perfect. I'm the one who's fucking everything up, as usual."

"Something wrong?"

"What do you know about the archangels?"

"I know you're one now. Who would've thought, eh?"

Alec bit back harsh words. Of course his father wouldn't expect him to attain such heights. "Yeah. Would Mom know more about them?"

A fond smile curved Adam's mouth. "She's a woman and a mother, she knows everything. Plus she took a bigger bite of the apple."

"Right." Alec turned to face the large cottage shielded from the sun by a copse of trees. As an afterthought before departing, he tossed over his shoulder, "Good seeing you, Abba."

"Are you staying for dinner?"

"I might. Depends."

"Not enough time in the day," Adam parroted with a mocking tone.

Alec shifted to the cottage, pausing outside of it. Behind him, the bare field was hot. Here in the shade, the temperature was ideal. The home had been built like a fairy-tale cottage, a whimsical request from his mother that his father had spent years seeing to fruition.

A familiar and beloved figure filled the top half of the Dutch front door.

"You just going to stand there gawking?" his mother asked, pulling open the bottom section. She dried her hands on an apron wrapped around her waist and held her arms out to him. "You look like shit."

"While you look beautiful, Ima." He stepped into her embrace and pulled her close. His nostrils filled with her unique scent and some of the vibrating anxiety inside him calmed.

Withdrawing, he smiled down at her. The phrase "you haven't aged a day" applied to both of his parents. They were arrested in time with the appearance of mortals in their late forties.

"Don't jest," she chided, examining his features with narrowed eyes. "You look sick. You're pale, and the skin around your eyes looks bruised."

A mirror wasn't necessary to confirm her words. He felt wrung out. The fact that it showed was alarming. He was an archangel, damn it. He should be healthier and more powerful than he'd ever been in his life.

Her cool hands brushed over his face, pushing his hair back from his forehead and smoothing his brow. "You need looking after. It's been too long since I visited you."

"I have questions," he said grimly.

She nodded. "Come in and sit."

Alec followed her inside. She untied her apron while moving toward the kitchen in the back. The scent of a cooking meal soothed something inside him. He settled on a sofa in the family room and watched as his mother grabbed a half-filled pitcher from the counter. By the time she reached the seating area, two glasses had materialized on the coffee table in front of him. The darkness within him was irritated by the offering, which made him feel like a visitor rather than a member of the household.

Ridiculous, he knew, but his brain wasn't running the show.

The interior of his parents' home was a mix of primitive and modern. Contemporary sofas rested on a dirt floor and trendy glass tiles decorated the walls of a kitchen that boasted a water pump at the sink. Both his *abba* and his *ima* were blessed with an odd amalgamation of gifts. His mother could chill liquids with a touch and heat them just as easily. Prey came to them willingly, but they skinned and filleted their catch by mortal means. God had made their lives convenient in some ways, while still grounding them in the world they'd known since Creation.

His mother sat across from him, her long dark hair pooling on the seat behind her. She was as lovely as she'd always been, inside and out. Her concern for him was reflected in her brown eyes and the way she worried her bottom lip with her teeth.

"You should have come home sooner," she admonished. "Is there any news about Raguel?"

Alec shook his head. "Nothing. At this point, Sammael hasn't even acknowledged that he has him. Shows how powerful he's become to keep his minions quiet about something of such magnitude."

"He's always been powerful. Don't let mortal gossip cloud your mind. You know better."

Leaning against the overstuffed sofa, he looked out the shaded window at the swaying branches and asked, "Do you know what happened to the other archangels? Sandalphon, Jophiel, and the rest?"

His mother reached for a glass. "No."

"It was suggested to me that there are only seven archangels by design."

"Why? It places an added burden on all of them."

"I wonder if that's the point," he murmured. "Like mischievous children, if you keep them busy, they don't get into trouble."

"What kind of trouble could they get into?"

Alec exhaled harshly. "They control *mal'akhs* and Marks. If they found a way to work together, think of all they could accomplish."

His mother stilled with her glass to her lips. "Are you talking about a coup against Jehovah?"

"A revolt maybe. A bid for more power. Added privileges."

The glass returned to the table with a sharp click. "You shouldn't say such things. You shouldn't even think them."

"I should have faith," he bit out. "Right?"

Her arms crossed. "When I heard that you'd been promoted, I assumed you must have found a deeper communion with God and this advancement was your reward."

The voices inside him laughed at the notion and prodded him to say bitterly, "Nothing so edifying, I'm afraid. I do the dirty work, Ima. That hasn't changed."

She sighed. Then her shoulders went back, a sign of her determination to ignore his faults and tackle the problems they created. The attitude reminded him so much of Eve that his jaw tightened.

"So someone made you an archangel for a price?" Her fingertips strummed silently atop the padded arm of her wingback chair. "Who?"

"What does it matter?"

"You are now the most powerful weapon ever created." Her dark eyes stared into his. "I want to know who had the balls to pull that off. And why."

"It's like a ghost town around here," Rosa mumbled around a bite of double-cheeseburger. "Brentwood is boring."

Reed set his soda down and lounged in the restaurant booth they occupied. "Maybe that's the way Grimshaw's Beta is assuming control of the pack, by keeping them tied down until they adjust."

"No. It's because the population of Infernals in the area has dropped considerably in the last couple of weeks. They're all migrating to the southern half of the state."

Hunting Eve. Reed reached out—*Babe?*—and was reassured when she nudged him back.

Don't worry about me, she scolded.

Yeah, right. He returned his attention to his charge. "You did a smokin' job on this latest hunt," he praised. "I think you set a new record for killing a gwyllion."

"I kicked that *corno* back to Hell and I'm ready to roll." She smiled. "Wouldn't mind seeing Disneyland."

"Is that why you wanted to meet with me face-to-face? You want a vacation?"

"I want to be where the action is."

Rosa resumed eating. The burger was almost too big for her to hold. A lovely Venezuelan with snapping hazel eyes and short, spiky black hair, she'd been in her midtwenties when she'd been marked about five years ago and her youth stood her in good stead. She was fast and nimble, with a fiery temper and staunch Catholic faith. Her father had been abusive to both her and her mother. One day, she'd had enough and she put a stop to it. Permanently.

He reached for a french fry, grinning inside at the cause of his unusual hunger. The second go-round with Eve had taken things between them to a whole nother level. He wondered if she knew that. If not, he planned to bring her up to speed, pronto. "There's plenty of action here."

"Not right now there isn't."

"You know something that's got you fired up," he said, sensing it through the connection between them. "Spill it."

Setting the burger down, Rosa met his gaze. "If this is the start of Armageddon, I want to be in the thick of it."

Reed's brows rose. "Is that what's being said? That it's the end of days?"

Marks gossiped madly. Some of what they made up was entertaining. Some of it was dangerous.

"It's obvious. Satan is breeding hellhounds, Grimshaw was planning a revolt of some sort, and every Infernal within three hundred miles has a hard-on to kill Cain's girl. What the—"

"No." The denial was out before he could censor himself.

"No?" Rosa studied him. "Are you living in a different world than I am?"

Exhaling slowly, he worked to suppress his jealousy. To call his response "possessive" would be an understatement. Eve was no longer Cain's. But for Reed to stake his claim now would only make things more difficult for her. Many of the other Marks resented her for the advantages they assumed she gained from Cain's mentorship. If they learned that she'd moved on and with whom, those resentments might intensify, and right now she needed all the help she could get.

"I meant," he began, "that what is going on now doesn't necessarily signify that it's the beginning of the end. There are signs that would warn us. For one, the Rapture has yet to happen."

"Whatever." She shrugged dismissively. "Just send me down there."

Reed nodded. "All right."

"Yes!" Her eyes lit with both triumph and bloodlust.

"But if I need you somewhere else, don't give me a hard time."

She rolled her eyes and grabbed her burger. "By the way, Sarakiel is trying to get a hold of you."

"I'll touch bases with her when we're done here."

But he didn't.

After he watched Rosa's Prius pull out of the parking lot and head toward the freeway, he went to Charleston Estates. The gated community was the home of the Black Diamond Pack, which had recently suffered the loss of its Alpha, Charles Grimshaw.

Its Beta—now Alpha—was Devon Chaney. If Chaney followed precedent, he would be eager to establish himself as stronger and more powerful than his predecessor. Reed was counting on that impetus to make his plan work.

A guard station stood at the entrance and the exit, and a tall stucco wall surrounded the perimeter. Affluence and privilege were two of the words that came to mind when one saw the exterior. But beyond the crescent moon emblem embedded in the circular cobblestone driveway, there was nothing to betray the fact that every single resident was a werewolf.

He walked up to the guard station with one hand in his pocket and the other twirling his sunglasses. He glanced up casually, a smile curving his mouth as the guard realized what and *who* he was.

"Call your new Alpha," Reed said smoothly, "and tell him I want to chat."

"Repent, Jezebel! Repent or you'll roast in *Hell*!"

Eve fought the urge to roll down her window and sock Evil Santa in the mouth. Instead, she sat impatiently at the stoplight while the zealot stood at her window, strumming his guitar and screaming at her through the glass.

When he didn't get a rise out of her, he moved to the driver's side passenger window and yelled at Sydney. "Save yourself from lust of the flesh and the claws of this heathen woman! Save yourself, before you burn in the lake of fire!"

Montevista cleared his throat, drawing Eve's gaze to where he sat in the front passenger seat. "Okay," he said. "I'm liking your priest idea more and more."

"Yep." Eve hit the gas pedal the moment the light changed. Thankfully, when she'd called the church after dinner, Riesgo had been there, and he had agreed to see her right away. They were heading to Glover Stadium in Anaheim, where he was filling in as a coach for a Little League practice for one of his parishioners.

"Do you think Father Riesgo will help?" Sydney asked. "You're not a member of his congregation."

"I hope he'll play along, but at this point, he could definitely resort to extortion. I'd actually attend one of his services, if it would get that nut out of my hair."

Montevista shook his head. "I've never worked with a Mark who had no faith. Your parents are pious, right? What happened with you?"

Eve held up a hand. "You and I are friends. That means we can never talk about politics or religion."

He started to retort, then glanced at her. His mouth shut. "All right."

"I know that tone," she said, fingertips tapping against the steering wheel. "You think I'm pissed off at God and irreverence is my retaliation. But I'm not mad. I just think that many of the stories in the Bible show a God who has the same faults we do. He has pride and a temper, and he plays with humans like we're toys. It'll take a damn sight more than the promise of an unseen heaven for me to worship someone like that."

"Yeesh," Sydney breathed.

"Sorry I asked," Montevista agreed.

No one said anything else the rest of the short drive. Not because of the discussion about religion, but because of the number of laser-bright eyes that followed them as they progressed. The sidewalks were only slightly more crowded than usual, but the number of Infernals was clearly elevated by a tremendous degree.

"When we get to the stadium," Montevista said, "just idle by the entrance while I see if the priest has arrived. If shit hits the fan, you punch the gas and get the hell out of there."

Sydney leaned forward. "I can run in. If it comes down to it, you're the best one to protect her."

He made an aggravated noise, then spoke harshly, "No. You stick with Hollis."

In the rearview mirror, Eve watched Sydney's brows rise. The Mark settled back into the seat and caught Eve's gaze.

PMS? Eve mouthed.

A wry smile curved Sydney's lips, but it didn't reach her eyes. Montevista was a bit off kilter this afternoon.

They pulled into the tiny parking lot adjacent to the stadium. The place was familiar to her. Although her high school was a few miles away, Glover Stadium was the official home of Loara High School football.

Montevista had the door open and was unfolding from the car when Riesgo appeared from between two vehicles. The moment he saw her, a grin lit his blunt but arresting features. He was dressed in black sweats and athletic shoes, and he had a baseball bat bag slung over one shoulder and a mesh bag filled with mitts in his other hand. She hit the button to lower her window.

"Hey," he said.

"Hey to you, too. I brought your Bible back."

Even with the dangerous scar that marred his cheek, the amusement that lit his features made him look boyish. "You could have mailed it."

"Yeah," she conceded, returning his smile, "but I have a favor to ask, too."

"Really." His gaze moved to Sydney, then to Montevista, who stood next to the open passenger door. "Hello. I'm Father Riesgo."

Montevista introduced himself. Sydney stepped out and followed suit. Riesgo looked back at Eve. "What kind of trouble are you in?"

"Who said I'm in trouble?"

"You have bodyguards."

She blinked, startled by his perceptiveness.

He jerked his head to the left. "I charge for favors. Park your car and come with me."

Eve looked at where he gestured and saw an open parking spot at the end. She glanced at Montevista, who clearly wasn't keen on the idea of her being out in the open. Despite it being a very public place, Infernals would come for her if they thought they could get away with it.

"Close the doors, guys," she said. After a brief pause, both Montevista and Sydney did as she said, joining Riesgo outside. She pulled into the empty spot, exited, and hit the lock button on her remote. She was lucky there'd been a space available. The alternative would have been to park in the larger lot on the other side of La Palma.

Riesgo was waiting nearby. Montevista was saying something to the priest that had both men looking absorbed. Sydney, on the other hand, was scanning the area. Eve followed her lead and noted the stragglers that loitered around the perimeter of the stadium. There were only a few Infernals, for now. They had to be working in packs, reporting her whereabouts in a chain that led from her house to here. She flipped them off, encompassing them all with a wide arc of her hand. One of them flicked his forked tongue at her, reminding her of her first run-in with the Nix.

Another problem to deal with some other time.

As a group, Eve and the others traversed the curving cement path that led from the lot to the stadium bleachers.

Ahead of them, a group of kids played on the dirt near the pitcher's mound. They appeared to be in the eight to ten year range. Their laughter drifted on the early evening breeze and made Eve tense. They were so young, and innocent of the proliferation of demons she had brought to their doorstep.

"What happened to the coach?" she queried, wondering at the man inside the priest. Physically, he was big and powerful, although not in the way of Alec or Reed. Riesgo was barrel-chested, with thick biceps and thighs. A juggernaut.

"He's having an emergency root canal. So I'm helping out."

"Yuck."

"You're helping out, too," he said. "You can pitch."

"No, I can't."

He glanced at her.

"I'm not kidding," she insisted. "I can't throw worth a damn. I never hit what I'm aiming for."

Of course, Riesgo didn't believe her until he actually saw her in action. Some of her pitches didn't even make the distance to home plate. Others were skewed to the left or right. He thought she was pretending at first.

"Gimme that," he said finally, approaching her from his position as catcher. "You take first base."

She plopped the dusty ball into the palm of his extended hand. "I told you."

"Yeah, yeah."

In short order, Riesgo replaced her with Sydney, who threw like a professional. Montevista took second base. Practice took an hour. The bright field lights came on, turning dusk into day. Like vermin, the Infernals in the area encroached to the edge where light met night. Parents eventually started showing up to reclaim their kids. The team's coach appeared just in time to close shop, mumbling instructions through numbed lips. Montevista and Sydney took opposite positions on the field, staring down the Infernals that the mortals couldn't see in the oppressive darkness.

Riesgo came up beside her. "So, what's with the protection detail?"

She shrugged and told him the truth. "I pissed someone off."

He glanced at the two Marks. "Must be a pretty dangerous someone."

"You could say that."

His mouth tilted up in a mysterious half-smile. "So, how can I help?"

"There's this vagrant on my street. He's a bit of a nut."

As he started toward home base, Riesgo gestured for her to follow him. He picked up discarded mitts and balls as he went along and she helped, finding an odd comfort in his presence. She'd shortchanged him by crediting his charisma and velvet-smooth Spanish accent for the size of his congregation. He had an air of confidence; a rock-solidness that was soothing. He clearly found strength in being devout, yet Eve didn't chalk that up to naïveté as she did with most pious people.

"You want me to find him a shelter?" he asked.

"Uh . . ." She hadn't thought of that. Some days the guy was on the corner, some days he wasn't. He was rarely there past dark. She'd just assumed he had a place to live and chose to haunt her corner for the hell of it. "Well, I'm not really sure he's homeless. He claims to be a reverend. One of those wrath-of-God, hell-and-damnation types."

Riegso glanced over his shoulder at her. "Does he wear the same clothes every day?"

Eve shoved a mitt into the mesh bag. "I really haven't paid attention. He wears jeans and a T-shirt, but whether or not they're the same daily? Couldn't tell ya. I have a good excuse though. It's hard to pay attention to clothing when you're getting screamed at."

"He screams at you?" The priest stilled.

Explaining the situation only took a moment. The silence that followed lasted longer.

"Why," he said slowly, "does he think you're a jezebel?"

"There's a lot of foot traffic around my place. But I'm not a prostitute."

"The bullet catchers are the traffic." It was a statement, not a question.

"Bullet catchers? Oh, the guards! Yes. They're nice people," Eve defended. "The good guys."

Riesgo caught her elbow and led her to the aluminum bleachers. "Who are the bad guys?"

This was the part where things got tricky. "That really doesn't have anything to do with Evil Santa."

"Sure it does. The guards attracted the zealot to you, you came to me; they're connected."

"In a six-degrees-of-separation kind of way, maybe." She sat next to him.

The field was now silent and the sound of numerous cars on Harbor Boulevard was only a distant roar. Above them, the sky was a charcoal blanket with few stars. Metropolitan light pollution vastly reduced the visibility of celestial bodies, which made her feel somber and lonely. Before she could stop herself, she reached out to Alec. Where the warm light of his soul used to be, she felt only roiling darkness. She withdrew, feeling even more melancholy.

Reed.

He touched her briefly, like a quick kiss to the forehead that was distracted and hurried. She pulled back when he did, resenting her own clinginess. Regardless of the numerous Infernal eyes watching her with tangible malevolence, she would take care of herself. This was *her* calling—for now—whether she wanted it or not. Damned if she wouldn't own it while it was hers.

Pivoting at the waist, Eve faced Riesgo. "Do you believe in demons, Father?"

"Yes," he said carefully, warily.

"Do you believe they walk among us? Live among us? Work alongside us?"

His brown eyes were watchful and alert. "Did you hire bodyguards to protect you from demons, Ms. Hollis?"

Eve exhaled audibly. "What would you say if I said yes?"

CHAPTER 12

Alec stared across the small table at his mother and wanted to reach out to her. She had always loved and accepted him just as he was. She had forgiven him when no one else would, and pleaded his case along with his brother Seth to turn his sin into his salvation. But the darkness inside him clenched his throat tight, preventing him from finding solace where he could.

"It doesn't matter who helped me," he managed finally.

"Helped you?" Ima scoffed. "Helped themselves is more like it."

"Whatever." He reached for the juice on the table just to have something to do. He drank it, but tasted nothing.

"What about Evangeline?"

Exhaling harshly, he snapped, "What about her?"

"Oh my." His mother sank back into the chair. "What have you done?"

What had to be done. "I came here to talk about the archangels, not about me."

"Are you no longer together?"

At that moment, he felt Eve gently prodding through the connection between them. Her sadness was a salve, soothing the voices inside him that were irritated by the relief he found by being with his mother. They wanted anarchy and chaos, not peace. He closed his eyes and willed himself to be still inside, a sleeper not yet awakened.

She will turn to Abel, they whispered, fighting his restraint. *Let us have her, before it is too late and she no longer wants you.*

Alec mentally bared his teeth. *Fuck off.*

Eve pulled away. His hands fisted as he held back the part of himself that wanted to snatch her close and use her. Instead, he shut a door between them, a thick barrier that took great energy to erect and maintain. He had no choice but to trust that Abel would keep her safe for now. There was too much inside him that could hurt her, not the least of which were his most recent memories—

"Cain."

His mother's voice brought him back to the world around him. He opened his eyes.

"Your eyes," she breathed, with a hand to her throat. "They're *gold*."

A prickling chill swept over him, like the shock of jumping into an icy lake.

She stood. "You still live next door to Evangeline, don't you?"

Alec nodded.

"Good. I'll talk with her while I'm staying with you, see if we can salvage things."

"Ima . . ." His tone was a warning. "You are *not* coming to visit now. It's the worst possible time."

"Bullshit." She caught up her hair and twisted it into a knotted bun. "It's the perfect time. Have you considered that things might be so crappy because I haven't visited in a while?"

His brows rose. In every myth and fable, there was a grain of truth. In his mother's case, the tale of Persephone's journey between Hades's underworld and Demeter's Earth had been inspired by his mother. She didn't make flowers bloom or increase crops, but she did seem to have the ability to rejuvenate Marks. For many, her existence established the veracity of the Bible in a way that not even he or Abel could.

"There are rumors that Sammael has set a bounty on Eve's head," he explained. "Demons from all over the world are flooding the area where we live. You're a prime target. You always have been."

"Like Evangeline is?" she rejoined. "And now she doesn't have you to lean on."

His teeth ground audibly, his temper barely checked. "Abel will keep her safe. That's his job. Not that he's been doing it so far—"

"Then, he can keep me safe, too."

Alec pushed to his feet. "For fuck's sake, Ima! She's a Mark. She is trained to kill demons. You can't compare the two of you."

"Don't use that tone with me!" Her hands went to her hips. "You need me. Evangeline needs me. I'm sure your home is a veritable fortress in order to protect her. It can protect me, too."

"Not like Shamayim. Nothing can get to you here." He ran an aggravated hand through his hair. "I can't deal with worrying about you right now, okay? I can't."

"I'm coming along to worry about *you,* not the other way around." His mother left the room, heading toward the back of the house and her bedroom.

He followed, but stopped when he found his father filling the front doorway with his broad-shouldered frame.

Adam shrugged. "Her mind is hard to change once it's been set. I've never been able to do it."

"She could be killed," Alec bit out. "It's as dangerous now as it's ever been."

"I heard."

Which meant that after Alec had come inside, his father had left the field to make inquiries and get brought up to speed on events. Since Jehovah was probably unaware of the full extent of the story, either Adam still didn't know everything or he had a source of information within the ranks of the seraphim.

The seraphim didn't give anything for free.

Alec was beginning to wonder if his entire family was a pawn in a bigger game he couldn't see because he was in the thick of it.

"How much were you told?" he asked.

As Adam stepped inside, he pulled off his hat and met Alec's gaze squarely. "Enough to know that your mother isn't going anywhere without me. So you better have enough room for both of us."

The new Alpha of the Black Diamond Pack met Reed outside the gates of the Charleston Estates community and together they began walking toward a nearby public park. Although the Alpha appeared to be alone, Reed knew wolves followed them. If Chaney was an idiot, he'd try an attack. Taking Abel down could be seen as a way to firmly establish his new position. But if Chaney was smart, he would consider a long-term alliance more valuable than a quick strike that would bring the wrath of God upon his pack.

California had three Brentwoods—one in Northern California, where Reed presently was; one near Victorville; and one in Los Angeles. This particular Brentwood had once been a farming community, but it was becoming increasingly residential as the years passed. The sidewalk they traversed framed a wide street. Around them, the youth of the buildings was evidenced by their modern architecture.

As they walked, Reed worked judiciously to keep his connection to Eve at bay. At the moment, the less she knew, the safer she'd be. He had no choice but to trust that Cain and the guards would keep her safe for now. Cain was a prick, but he wasn't idiotic enough to jeopardize her life over personal issues.

"To say I'm surprised you came to see me would be an understatement," Chaney said, after they'd walked a couple of blocks. "Are you here about the breeding operation?"

"No. I'm well aware that Grimshaw's hellhound-whispering days are done." Reed had moved on to the next problem in line.

"So, then." Chaney glanced at him. "What do you want?"

"I think we'd better start off with what *you* want. Are you taking part in the bounty hunt for Evangeline Hollis?"

The Alpha's stride faltered, a mistake Grimshaw would never have made. "I don't know what you're talking about."

It didn't matter that Reed had no intention of following through with his plan. Just discussing it aloud—especially to an Infernal—scared the shit out of him, but he needed a bargaining chip to get things rolling. Later, he could work on the logistics of the double cross. There were a lot of bigger fish in the pond than Eve, even with her ties to him and Cain.

"Well, you're still up here," Reed continued. "So I could take that as a sign that you're not interested in collecting the prize. But it's such a rare opportunity to participate in the kind of free-for-all we're seeing in Orange County now." Reed kept his gaze straight ahead. "I thought every ambitious demon was pursuing it."

"Like you said," Chaney muttered tightly, "I'm still here and I've got enough on my plate at the moment. Besides, I have no idea what you're talking about."

"Right."

They reached the park and turned into it, taking a winding cement path toward a cluster of sheltered picnic tables. The night air was temperate, the breeze light and pleasant. Around them, Reed could sense wolves watching, moving, even though he couldn't hear them. They kept upwind and he wondered if they thought he was stupid, or if they were just poorly trained.

Stopping abruptly, Reed said, "Then we're done here."

Chaney rounded on him, slightly hunched as if prepared to pounce. His lip curled back, revealing pointed canines. "You didn't step out of your comfort zone for nothing," he growled. "What do you want?"

Reed shoved his hands in his trouser pockets. "I want Raguel back."

"What the fuck? Since when is he gone?"

It was clear the Alpha was clueless about the archangel, as evidenced by the strength of his reaction compared to the one he'd had to the mention of the bounty hunt. Sammael was cunning enough to know that the knowledge would be more valuable to upper-level demons when kept a secret; whereas for lesser demons, sharing would be of greater benefit.

Chaney straightened, his eyes glowing yellow in the moonlight. "Whatever it is, I want in."

Reed hid his satisfaction behind a bored mien. "It will take more than enthusiasm to get the job done."

"And it'll take more than vague references to missing archangels to get the rest of what you need from me."

So . . . the Alpha had a little bite to go along with his bark.

Rocking back on his heels, Reed asked, "Were you privy to the discussions Charles had with Asmodeus?"

"I was privy to everything."

"Excellent. Let's get him involved again." The overly-ambitious king of Hell needed to be dealt with as well.

Chaney's head cocked to one side. "I take it you're offering your brother's whore in trade? I'm not sure that's fair. An archangel for a green Mark."

"Sammael clearly thinks she's valuable."

"But you don't?"

"Like you said, she's Cain's whore," Reed drawled, fists clenching in his pockets.

"You two still haven't gotten over yourselves?" Chaney laughed, the yellow of his eyes softening. "His promotion must really sting."

"You assume I couldn't have prevented it, had I wished."

The narrowing of Chaney's eyes betrayed his renewed unease. It was best if the Alpha didn't get too comfortable around Reed.

Clearing his throat, Chaney said, "Ah, well . . . Works in my favor, doesn't it?"

"I'm also willing to discuss sweetening the deal, but first, I need to know that Raguel is alive."

"I'll get to work on that."

Reed extended his hand to the Alpha. When the gesture was accepted, his mouth curved.

The Alpha began to scream, then howl, his knees giving way so that he kneeled before Reed like a supplicant. As dark forms rushed out of the bushes and leaped over backyard fences, Reed released him. Chaney held his injured hand in the palm of the other, gasping.

"You should memorize that," Reed suggested, gesturing to his cell phone number now seared into the Alpha's palm, "before it heals."

Chaney's head tipped up toward the moon and his true visage shimmered just beneath his mortal guise. As his pack bounded toward them, his mouth widened into a terrible maw, his yellow eyes glowing from pain and the resulting bloodlust.

Reed sketched a quick bow, then shifted to Gadara Tower.

"You hired bodyguards to protect you from . . . demons?" Riesgo asked carefully.

"Um . . ." Eve's mark heated, even though she hadn't yet voiced the lie.

"Do you believe the reverend is a demon?"

"No! He's a pain in my ass, but he's not a demon."

He shook his head, as if she were a troublesome and frustrating child. "Those two are guarding you like they expect something to run onto the field and tackle you."

"How do you know so much about guards?" She shifted in an effort to get more comfortable on the cold metal bleachers. Mark or not, a hard seat was a hard seat.

He bent forward, putting his forearms to his thighs. "I was born in Inglewood, raised in Compton, and nearly killed in a knife fight when I was fifteen."

"Gangs?"

"Sureño."

"Wow. Is that how . . . ?" Eve touched her cheek in echo of his.

"No. Got the scar in the Rangers."

She nodded to herself. That made sense. Military service explained the confident, capable, yet dangerous vibe he gave off as well as the knowledge hinted at by his comments.

Eve wondered if he'd joined the priesthood as a way to save his life. Most gangs were "blood in, blood out"—you killed someone to get in and you had to be dead to get out. But a priest's robes would be a hard barrier for a would-be killer to get past. Fact was, the majority of the United States population believed in a higher power.

He steepled his fingertips. "The Army gave me a way out of South Central. God gave me a way out of the Mexican Mafia. Okay, so I've told you mine. Now, you tell me yours."

"It's a long story, and one you wouldn't believe anyway." She reached up and tightened her loosened ponytail.

"Try me." He bumped shoulders with her. "The Lord keeps bringing you back my way. There's a reason for that."

"Father . . . Trust me. If the Lord is deliberately pushing me into your life, that's not a good thing. Not for either one of us."

"We won't know until all is said and done, oh ye of little faith."

"You don't understand me, Father. And I sure as hell don't understand you. Don't you read that Bible you preach from? God isn't perfect. He's just like everyone else. Have you read the Book of Job? First, God brags to Satan about how loyal Job is. Then, when Satan bets him that Job will turn against him if they make him miserable enough, God takes the bet."

Riesgo's gaze was on Montevista as the Mark abandoned his position on the lower right infield to head toward Sydney. "Do you have any idea how many times the Book of Job is tossed out as an argument, Ms. Hollis?"

"Eve," she corrected.

"I expect you to be more original, Eve."

She smiled without humor. "Have you ever considered that Job's story might be a piece of a larger whole? Maybe Job is a construct that represents the entirety of man. Maybe his tale is a parable and not absolute truth. Maybe Satan and God are still trying to win that bet."

The priest turned his head to look at her. "You're attributing mortal qualities to God, like the Greeks did with their gods. The One True God is above those frailties."

"Really? I don't get that from the Bible," she muttered. "What I get out of the Bible is a God so high on himself that he has minions running the show while he lounges around listening to cherubs sing his praises endlessly."

"I can put up with a lot, Eve." There was an edge to Riesgo's voice. "But disrespect and blasphemy aren't on the list."

She blew out her breath in a rush, suddenly feeling very weary. "I'm sorry, Father. I don't mean to belittle your beliefs. It's just that I'm never going to see God the way you do. It's like we're looking at different sides of the same coin. Please don't ask me to come around to your side."

"That's my job," he said gruffly, looking obliquely at her. "I bring God into the lives of others."

"God is in my life, Father." Eve looked him at him squarely, willing him to see the truth of her words in her gaze. "We're working out our issues in our own way. But, in the meantime, that dude on my corner is seriously driving me insane."

"What do you suggest I do about that?"

"You can come and vouch for me."

"Vouch for you." Riesgo's half-smile returned. "For all I know, he could be right about you."

"Ouch." Crossing her arms, she straightened. "Okay, how about I take you to my office first? Have you been to Gadara Tower? It was voted Anaheim's most beautiful property a couple of years ago."

He reached over and patted her on the knee. It was a grandfatherly gesture, but his touch was so hot it surprised her. The contact was brief, over as soon as it began, but the heat lingered. "Give me directions to your place. I'll run by there in the next couple of days and talk to him."

"Thank you." She returned his earlier bump to the shoulder before standing. "I owe you one."

"Yes, you do." He rose in an economical, yet graceful movement. Power leashed with an iron fist. "We're having a potluck picnic at the church in three weeks. I expect you to come. Bring your boyfriend and those two—" He looked toward the field and frowned. "Where did they go?"

Eve's gaze followed his. Montevista and Sydney were nowhere to be seen. She engaged her mark-enhanced vision, but delving into the darkness beyond the reach of the powerful field lights was impossible without the nictitating lenses that engaged only when she, too, stood in the dark. "I don't know."

She started down the bleacher steps with growing apprehension. The moment her foot hit the dirt, a flash of white caught the periphery of her vision. Too fast to be mortal. Lightning-quick, Eve darted after it. It was faster than she was, feinting to the left and right. Several seconds later, she found herself on the pitcher's mound again. She ran back to Riesgo. The priest was presently rubbing at his eyes with his fists.

"I must be wiped out," he said. "My vision's getting blurry. One second, it looked like you were over there. Then the next, you were right here."

Catching his elbow, she tugged him toward home base. It was rarely good to be cornered, but at least she'd have one less side—their rear—to worry about defending.

"What are you—" He quieted, sensing her preoccupation. Without another word, he bent and picked up a metal baseball bat. Sans the collar and dressed in black sweats, he looked like someone you didn't want to fuck with . . . if you were mortal.

Eve's brows rose, but she put her back to his and tried angling him to face the corner. He, being the chivalrous type, tried to maneuver her the same way.

The flash of white came again, but this time it stopped in front of her. An Infernal such as she'd never seen, with white hair and eyes. He was wearing an ice-blue and silver Halloween costume that included a doublet and bombastic hose.

Her connection with Reed allowed her to recognize the demon inside the getup.

"Azazel," she greeted grimly.

"Hello, Evangeline."

Riesgo positioned himself shoulder to shoulder with her. "Is this the guy that's after you?"

"One of them." Eve sent up a request for a flaming sword. She wasn't too surprised when nothing happened. She widened her stance and raised her fists. The demon laughed, a sound made more maddening for its rich, deep tone.

This Infernal was clearly confident about his skills.

"*Stand easy, Evangeline.*" The unknown voice rumbled through the air from no discernable source.

The ground shook and a fissure opened. Blood rushed upward from the depths like a geyser before settling into the shape of a man with massive, beautiful crimson wings.

Satan. Eve knew who it was without any help.

"Holy Mary, Mother of God," Riesgo breathed. He made the sign of the cross with his free hand.

"Mary can't save you, priest," Azazel said, with a malicious smile. "God won't save you either."

Fear blossomed in Eve's chest like a spreading stain. The Prince of Hell was impossibly beautiful, far more so than even Sabrael. His skin shimmered as if coated with gold dust. Shiny black hair fell halfway down his back, rippling and writhing with a life of its own. The silky tresses moved sinuously, covetously; caressing him as a lover would, framing a face that could not have been more perfect. His irises flickered like flames, while his mouth curved in a smile that was terrifying for its seductiveness. The urge to undress and spread her legs for him was strong enough to tug Eve forward one step. She jerked herself to a halt by clinging to Reed in her mind, like a snapping flag anchored to a pole.

"Ah," Satan murmured, circling from a distance with a smooth alluring gait. Sex incarnate. "I see why they want you. Looking at you makes a man hard and ready to fuck."

Eve flipped him the bird.

With a careless wave of his hand, he snapped the digit, bending it backward until her knuckle touched the back of her hand. She dropped to her knees, screaming.

Riesgo stepped forward, but she caught him with her left hand around his ankle. As a mortal, she would never have been able to stop him. As a Mark, she nearly toppled him.

"Don't," she ordered in a richly nuanced rumble.

He stilled instantly, frozen.

Persuasion. A gift given to Marks that she likened to the Jedi mind trick. Why it would kick in—for the first time—*now,* when what she really needed was a weapon, was a gripe she would add to her long list . . . later. And while she was bitching, she'd mention the failure of her mark to kick in and give her some ass-whupping mojo.

Where was Reed? Alec? *Anyone?*

She released the priest and reached for her broken finger, groaning through gritted teeth as she wrestled it back into place.

Azazel tsked. "They teach less and less respect as the years pass, my liege."

Satan came to her, looking down at her with gorgeous, emotionless eyes. His clawed fingertips lifted her chin and moved her head from side to side. His touch was cool, almost tender. She was riveted as much by that tenderness as by horror. Deep inside her, something trembled in paralyzing fear.

With proximity, the full effect of the Devil's allure was undeniable. He wore a three-piece suit that reminded her of Reed, but the overlong hair and Dr. Martens were Alec's. Even his features and build resembled her lovers, as did his scent—smoky, exotic, and deeply male. She wondered if he wore a guise to disorient her, or if she and God just had the same idea of what constituted a hot guy.

"Get away from her," Riesgo growled.

Satan shot him a bored but dangerous look.

Eve caught the Devil's wrists, wincing at the throb of her injured hand. It would heal with time, but would hurt like hell in the interim. "It's me you want. I'm the one who ran over your dog. Let the priest go."

The Devil's sleek head turned back to her. He looked amused. "But the priest is the means by which I will force your hand."

She quivered inside. "No. You don't need him. Deal with me."

"You do not yet know what I want," he crooned, cupping her face in his hands. His touch was so invasively cold it seeped into the very marrow of her bones, making her shiver violently. "Perhaps I want to defile you, lovely Evangeline. Perhaps I want to do things to you that will break your mind and spirit. Perhaps I want to watch while others do those same things to you. Listen to the melody of your screams until there is no fight left in you."

She wished she could laugh at his drama, but really, she feared pissing herself instead.

Where were Montevista and Sydney? Were they battling Infernals somewhere? Were they dead?

"Please. L-let him g-go," she managed through chattering teeth. She might as well be dunked in a frozen lake for all the warmth she felt.

Riesgo growled and began to speak. "I command you, unclean spirit, whoever you are, along with all your minions now attacking this servant of God, by the mysteries of the—"

"Shut him up," Satan snapped.

Azazel flew like a bullet across the yardage that separated him from Riesgo. The priest was in the middle of a retaliatory lunge at impact, the crashing of the two bodies thudding violently. The ground opened as they fell, swallowing them whole. As the chasm closed as if it had never existed, the earth shuddered like a child who'd swallowed particularly nasty medicine.

"Oh my god," Eve breathed, so shocked and frozen that she barely felt the burning of her mark. "What the fuck are you doing?"

Satan smiled, his thumbs brushing across her trembling lips. "Such a lovely mouth. You really should be working for me. I would appreciate your cynicism. I certainly appreciate how readily you discount Jehovah's lies."

Somehow she managed to wrench free, tumbling to her side and crawling with what strength she could muster. He followed her with leisurely steps, his hands clasped behind his back.

She stopped after progressing only a few feet. "What d-do you w-want?"

"Poor Evangeline," he murmured, reaching for her. "You are chilled to the bone. Let me warm you."

The moment his hand touched her skin, warmth coursed over her body like a hot summer breeze. So startled was she by the change that it took a moment before the sudden softness of the ground beneath her registered.

Satan straightened. Eve's head turned slowly.

It was now the middle of the day, and they were far from the baseball field. Warm sand cushioned her side and the sun blazed in the cloudless sky above her. It was a desert of some sort, barren except for golden sand and large monolithic outcroppings. The chill in her blood began to fade. She struggled to her feet, ignoring the hand that the Devil held out to assist her.

Eve faced him with shoulders back and chin lifted.

"Some of your mannerisms are so like hers," he murmured, with a mysterious smile.

"So like whom?"

"Your namesake." His gorgeous blood-red feathers fluttered in the oven-hot breeze. "Otherwise known as the ransom you will bring to me in return for the priest. And Raguel."

CHAPTER 13

W hat?" Eve hoped she was having a nightmare. "Where are we?"

"Come now," he chastised, "your marked hearing works well enough to have heard me."

He ignored her other question. Was she in Hell? Or some other plane of existence? Her mind whirled with the possibilities.

She turned slowly, keeping pace with him as he circled her so that he never had her back. "You want *Eve?*"

He applauded as if she was slow-witted and finally catching on. "Very good."

Eve hated that he moved so elegantly. Hated that he was so beautiful, so seductive, so much more of both qualities in the light of the desert sun than he'd been under the artificial brightness of the stadium lights. She was mesmerized by him, enough that she sometimes lost touch with how terrified she was. It was a trick of some sort, an illusion.

"She's dead," she managed finally, her voice raspy from the dry air.

"And what is death, Evangeline?" Satan continued his slow, steady walk around her perimeter with hands clasped beneath his wings. "Mortals think of it as the end, like an extinguished flame. But that is not the way of it. The worthy come to me, the unworthy go to Jehovah. They all continue to exist, just in different places."

"Don't you have that 'worthy' thing backward?"

He shook his head. "I expected better of you. You are too intelligent to buy into Jehovah's lies. In fact, I was quite impressed with your argument regarding the wager. How astute you are."

Eve didn't know what to say. In her mind, she imagined that God must be every bit as frightening as Satan. Who was the good guy? Were there any good guys in this mess?

The Devil watched her with a predatory intensity. "I confess, I regret that I was not the first to get my hands on you."

"I don't feel the same," she muttered. "And I don't see how I can help you."

"You have everything you need in that eager flesh between your legs." His words were crude, but his tone was conversational. "Spread them well enough, moan loud enough, beg sweetly enough . . . Cain and Abel will give you whatever you want."

"They're not going to give me their mother!"

Why were they so damn silent? Had Satan cut her off from them? Was he powerful enough to impede a God-given connection?

He gave an offhanded shrug. "They can lead you to her, and you can lead her to me."

"What do you want with her?"

"That is none of your concern."

"You're asking the impossible."

"I will give her back," he said solicitously. "I just want to borrow her for a short time."

Eve's eyes stung. Riesgo had been taken because of her. She couldn't abandon him and she couldn't turn down an opportunity to get close to Gadara. She also couldn't do what Satan wanted in return. Either way, she was seriously fucked. "I can't trust you."

"Can you trust anyone?"

He had a point.

"Evangeline, I have no need for lies. The truth works well enough. Remember that I am not the one who created man and wanted to keep him ignorant. I am not the one who commanded Abraham to kill his only son to prove his devotion. I am not the one who burned, drowned, and buried alive hundreds of thousands of mortals. I am not the one who demanded a man be stoned to death because he collected wood on the day set aside for slavish worship." His head tilted slightly. "Did you know Jehovah almost killed Moses because his son was not circumcised? Yet *I* am the monster?"

Because she was becoming disoriented, she stopped turning. Even after she stilled, the desert around her tipped and tilted. It was too hot now. Arid.

Satan smiled. There was a wealth of promise in the curve of his lips. Temptation. He was infamous for it.

Eve's hand went to her throat, massaging it as if that would create the moisture she craved.

"Jehovah is the original spin doctor," he continued, his voice lifting and falling in a soothing, lulling cadence. "I give him credit for his brilliance. Somehow, he became revered despite his cruelty. I, on the other hand, am reviled for my honesty."

How the hell was she going to spin this to work in her favor? There had to be a way, but it was hard to think. Her mouth and throat were dry. She'd give anything for a drink of water . . .

"Call off your minions," she said gruffly. "They're complicating things."

"Someone must earn the bounty," he reminded, finally drawing to a halt. The spinning stopped along with him. "As I said, I always keep my promises."

"How much am I worth?"

"Immunity. One get-out-of-Hell-free card."

"Hmm . . ." She wouldn't have thought she'd be worth that much. When Infernals were killed, they stayed in Hell a few centuries. A rapid turnaround could make a demon pretty damn cocky and reckless, she'd guess. "Give the credit to Azazel. He's the one who made the first move."

Satan's nose wrinkled slightly, which—insanely enough—humanized him. "Most would find that unfair. Azazel has always moved around freely."

Her hands went to her hips. "I don't give a shit if it's fair or not. I'm a prisoner in my own house right now. Not very conducive to getting things done."

"Fine. I will think of something suitable." He was definitely amused now. She could see it in his eyes. "In return, you will say nothing of our bargain to anyone. You break your word, I am free to break mine . . . including keeping the priest and Raguel. Anything else?"

In hindsight, she realized she'd played right into his hands. He clearly wanted to keep her off-kilter by confusing everything in her head.

"Yeah, actually." Eve began to circle him in a vain attempt to fight the feeling of a noose circling her neck. She felt manipulated and outmaneuvered. "I also have a Nix problem."

She braced herself for whatever demand he would make in return.

"Ah, yes. You do."

"Suck him back down with you when you go."

"But Ulrich is doing so well." There was a teasing note in the Devil's voice. Again, it softened him.

It's all a trick, she reminded herself.

Eve came to an abrupt stop, frustration riding her hard. "If he kills me, I won't be of any use to you."

Satan grinned. "I would have you full-time, then."

"Cain and Abel would have me no-time," she pointed out while fighting the urge to scream. Why was everyone betting that she'd go to Hell when she died?

"True." He extended one hand to her. Nestled in his palm was a golden chain with a charm—an open circle with various lines and circles within it. "Wear this to protect yourself from the Nix. Put it around him to prevent him from shape-shifting into water."

She stared at the necklace. *Beware of demons bearing gifts.* The thought of having something around her neck that came from Satan gave her the willies. "Isn't there another way? Gold doesn't look good on me."

His brow arched, then he walked toward her. Eve wanted to back away, but was rooted in place by an unseen force. His fingers encircled the wrist of her injured hand and the lingering pain faded. "If you do what I say," he murmured, "we can both get what we want."

Satan released her arm, then draped the charm carefully around her neck. He tucked it inside her shirt with a humming sound of satisfaction. "There. Nix problem solved."

He backed away. Her pent-up breath left her in a rush.

"You will have to kill him yourself, of course," he added. "But without the ability to shift, he should be a much easier target for you. He can be mortally wounded then."

"Gee, thanks," she groused.

Their gazes met and held. Eve wondered if he truly believed that she would hand over Alec and Reed's mother to him. If so, why did he believe that the priest and Gadara were so valuable to her? Worth enough to betray the men she loved.

She had to figure out what Satan was seeing that she was missing. Maybe he thought she'd be grateful to have him call off the bounty and help her with the Nix? He couldn't be that vain. It was more convenient for her, yes. But no matter what, she would have dealt with the Nix and the bounty anyway.

"Are we clear about the terms, Evangeline?"

"Let me get this straight: you want Eve temporarily, in exchange for permanently returning Father Riesgo and Raguel?"

He nodded. "I will call off the bounty and in return, you agree to keep this matter private. I will know if you err. Unlike Jehovah, I keep my finger on the pulse."

"What do you want for giving me the Nix on a silver platter?" she asked, suspicious.

"I will get my reward in the entertainment value. The odds are being evened out, but he may kill you anyway. How can I take recompense for so little?"

With an offhand flick of his wrist, she was back on the baseball field and he was gone.

Eve spun, looking around, finding herself alone.

She set off at a run toward the darkness beyond the athletic field lights, searching for Montevista and Sydney with a sickening feeling of dread.

"Is that where Evangeline lives?"

As Alec pushed his rarely used key into the lock of his front door, his head turned to follow the direction of his mother's finger. It had been awhile since he'd used secular means to enter his condo, but his parents weren't *mal'akhs* and what little gifts they had in Shamayim were stripped from them on Earth. They were mortal in every way but their age. "Yes."

Before he could stop her, his mother was striding down the hall and knocking on Eve's door. He steeled himself to see Eve again. Everything knotted up inside him, except for the voices that relished chaos.

No one answered Eve's door.

His mother frowned at him. "I thought you said it wasn't safe for her to be out."

His father stood at her back, hovering and watchful.

Alec unlocked his dead bolt for his parents, then shifted into Eve's house. It was dark and quiet as a tomb. Standing in her living room, he reached out to her and was met with an eerie silence.

Eve. Where are you?

She hit him in a rush, a full-throttle blindside of fear and worry that knocked him back a step. He growled and shifted to her.

She screamed when he arrived beside her, recoiling from his sudden appearance. Alec caught her by the back of the neck and clasped her to him. "Shh . . . I'm here."

As she trembled against him, a rapid-fire series of images hit his brain. Montevista. Sydney. The priest. Azazel.

Fury churned inside him.

Abel!

His brother's name was a roar. Once again, Abel had left Eve hanging in the wind.

It would be the last time.

Setting Eve away from him, Alec's fingers linked with hers. He pulled her along the length of the chain link fence, searching for any signs of blood, torn clothing, or a scuffle.

Then he felt the Marks. Faint, but nearby. He shifted Eve to the parking lot on the other side of La Palma. The open space was poorly lit, but his enhanced vision picked up two forms crumpled atop each other in the distance.

He shifted again, moving them closer more swiftly. He stabilized Eve when she stumbled from disorientation.

"Oh my god," she breathed. Her hand tightened on his, then she released him and knelt beside the fallen guards.

Montevista sprawled atop his partner, almost as if he'd shielded her body with his own. Eve reached out and brushed her fingers across his cheek. He groaned, then stirred.

"They're alive," she said.

As their firm leader, Alec knew that, but he didn't belabor the point. Instead, he stood behind Eve, wondering why it had taken a few moments for their connection to be reestablished.

Abel appeared on the other side of the two prone figures on the ground. "What the hell happened?"

"If you'd been doing your job," Alec snapped, "you would know."

Eve growled. "If you two start fighting—"

"Where the fuck were *you*?" Abel challenged.

"With Ima and Abba."

His brother's eyes widened. "Why?"

"Don't worry about my business. Worry about hers—" Alec jerked his chin toward Eve, "—and how Azazel snatched the priest right in front of her."

"I can see that." Abel stared at Eve with a frown, getting caught up to speed by sifting through her thoughts.

"You both suck," she groused. "These two are hurt and you're going to stand there bitching at each other?"

Alec ran a hand through his hair. "Get her out of here."

Abel stood and shifted to her side. He glanced at Alec. "You got these two?"

"Yeah. Go."

Eve shook her head. "I'm not going to—"

She was shifted away midsentence by a touch of Abel's fingertips to her crown.

The silence that followed their departure was brief. Montevista groaned and rolled to his side. Sydney gasped and lifted her head.

"Where's Hollis?" she asked.

Alec knelt beside them. "Safe."

But for how long? The assault on the priest had been too bold. Why not just take Eve?

He placed a hand on both Marks, and shifted with them to Gadara Tower.

"—leave them here like . . . What the hell?" Eve snapped, lurching as Reed returned her to her living room. "I hate when you do that with no warning!"

"Sorry, babe." Reed steadied her with gentle hands. "But you had to know we weren't going to leave you out there."

She glared at him. "And you have to know that I'm going to be worried sick until I know they're all right."

"I'll find out for you." He pressed his lips to her forehead. The moment they connected, the realization of how close he'd come to losing her hit him right between the eyes. His hands tightened on her biceps. She made a soft noise of protest and he released her hastily.

He stepped back, retreating to a safe distance.

"Hey," Eve said softly. "It's okay."

But it wasn't. Not for him.

She tapped her temple with her finger. "Keep me in the loop."

He managed a smile. *Of course,* he assured her. "Get comfortable. When I get back, I'll start that dinner I promised."

Eve opened her mouth to say something, but he shifted away quickly. He went to the subterranean floors of the tower and leaned heavily against the wall. As Marks and Infernals rushed past him in the busy hallway, he took a moment to pull himself together.

Jerk, she scolded. *I was going to ask if I should get anything ready for you.*

Just yourself. I'll manage the rest.

"Abel."

Reed's gaze lifted to watch Hank—guised in the Jessica Rabbit/Morticia Addams getup—approach with a sex-kittenish sway to her hips. "Hey, Hank."

"How are you?" The note of elation in the occultist's gruff voice was unmistakable.

"Not nearly as good as you, sounds like." Reed straightened. "What's up?"

"I've been experimenting with the mask. I think I'm on to something."

"Oh?"

Hank grinned. "When you're free, stop by and I'll show you."

"Will do."

Shaking off his lingering disquiet, Reed set off toward the main reception area where he could inquire about the location of Montevista and Sydney. He was several feet away from the end of the hallway when Sara rounded the corner. He almost shifted away, but she spotted him and delayed him with an extension of her hand.

"*Mon chéri.*" She smiled. "Do not rush off just yet. I have good news for you."

Reed stood stiffly as she lifted to her tiptoes and pressed her lips to his.

"Take us to my office," she murmured.

He conceded to her request only because he didn't want any interaction between them to be witnessed. As soon as they arrived, he pushed her away. "Make it quick."

"You never answer your cell phone," she complained, with an affected pout. "If you did, I would not have to waylay you in this manner."

The excitement on her face kept him around when he would have shifted. His arms crossed. "You've got my attention now."

"I was right. About Iselda and Cain."

He stilled. "Go on."

As she backed up toward her desk, her smile was wide and girlish. "Let me show you instead."

Picking up the remote that waited there, she activated the screen that lowered over the lone window. Her office was much smaller than Cain's but more elegant. Sara preferred damask over leather and multihued over monochromatic.

The lights dimmed and the show began. Reed looked away halfway through. By the time it was over, he was sitting with his back to the screen in one of the chairs positioned in front of the desk.

Sara took a seat with a rapacious gleam in her blue eyes. She turned off the feed with the remote. The screen retracted and the lights came back on. "I saved a copy on a jump drive for you. All you have to do is find a way for Evangeline to see it. Then sit back and watch the sparks fly."

"I'm not showing that to her," he said tightly.

Her smile faded. "Why not?"

Reed's foot tapped a silent but rapid staccato on the carpet. If Eve saw that tape . . . His jaw tightened. It hurt *him* to watch it, and he could give a shit about Cain or Izzie. Physically, they'd looked to be having a good time. Mentally . . . the depth of anguish on his brother's face would be painful for anyone to watch. Considering how deeply Eve cared for Cain, it would kill her.

"Damn you," she breathed. "You are protecting her."

"It would hinder our cause."

Her gaze narrowed. "How so?"

He considered the best way to answer. "She came to me this afternoon, insisting that something's wrong with Cain. She asked me to look into it and see if the ascension is responsible for his behavior. If she gets a look at that video, she'll be sympathetic and even more determined. It'll have the opposite effect."

Sara's manicured fingertips drummed atop the carved wooden chair arms. "You think you know her so well?"

"She's my charge. Of course I know her. Besides, it's no longer necessary to split them up. Cain did the deed himself earlier today."

"*C'est des conneries!* Cain's reactions are separate from hers. *She* needs to cooperate. He will want her back eventually and when that happens, we have to be sure that she will refuse him. That will be his breaking point. Not this—" she gestured to where the screen had been "—temporary insanity."

"So," he murmured, "you see it, too."

"He is fine now. I saw him a few moments ago when he brought the two guards in."

"Did we just watch the same video?"

"Perhaps that is just the way he likes to fuck."

"Now who's talking bullshit? What the hell is wrong with him? Is Eve right? Did the ascension screw him up?"

"How would I know?" she said crossly. "The rest of us were created as we are. Stop worrying about Cain, and give me a better reason for why Evangeline should not see that tape."

"You know . . ." Reed lounged, but stayed watchful. "Despite your animosity toward her, Eve spoke on your behalf today."

"*Vraiment?*" Sara tried to sound nonchalant, but failed.

"I told her you were a lying, self-centered bitch."

Rage shimmered in her eyes. "I have never lied to you."

"You knew I wanted to advance. You let me believe that you would help me do that."

"You used me, too."

He heard the bitterness in her tone and stood, rounding the desk with a deliberate stride. "Eve suggested that maybe you didn't help me not because you *wouldn't,* but because you *couldn't.*"

"I do not need her to speak for me." Sara swiveled her chair to face him and crossed her long legs. The red pantsuit gave her a seductive, wicked edge. The wary look she wore softened the image and reminded him that at one time he'd thought they were perfect for one another.

Placing his hands atop hers, Reed bent over her. She licked her lower lip and stared at his throat.

"At first," he went on, "I thought she was being overly kind by attributing qualities to you that you don't have. But I have considered it a little more, and you know what conclusion I've come to? I think you'd rather lose me than admit there's something you can't do."

Her shoulders pressed more firmly against the seat back. "Did I ever really have you, *mon chéri*?"

"For a while there, you did. Because of that, you owe me the truth, Sara. If you'd wanted to help me ascend . . . could you have? Or was it impossible?"

She swallowed, then answered, "I wanted to help you."

The knot in his gut loosened. "Why didn't you just point me in the right direction? Tell me to go higher?"

"I went higher," she snapped. "I spoke with Jehovah himself. I had to hide the request from the others. If Gabriel or Michael knew, they would stop me. But in the end, it was pointless."

"Why?" Reed straightened. Running his hands through his hair, he asked, "Why was it possible for Cain, but not for me?"

He moved away, needing space, and heard her stand behind him.

"Think of that game," she said softly. "The one where you try and spot the things that are missing from a second picture that were in the first. What is missing now, that was here before?"

"Raguel." Rounding on her, he said, "He's dead, isn't he? That's why none of you are actively pursuing him."

"Look on the bright side," she evaded. "Would you want to suffer like Cain is?"

"Cain's issues might be unique to him and you know it. And what if you're all wrong? What if Raguel is alive and we can get him back?"

Sara's knuckles whitened. "Then one of us would have to cede territory for the establishment of a new firm."

Reed moved to the window. He stared out at the nocturnal cityscape, but didn't register the view.

Cede territory. For the first time, he wondered if the archangels had cannibalized their numbers. Survival of the fittest, perhaps. Could they be affecting Cain in some way? Corrupting him? Pushing him into madness? Sara was supposed to be mentoring him, yet she was actively working to sabotage him.

Even though Reed had turned away from the screen when the video was on, he'd still heard everything. Cain had spoken in tongues. They both knew every language ever created, so that was not a surprise. It was the words themselves that chilled him.

I command you, unclean spirit, whoever you are, along with all your minions now attacking this servant of God—

The Rite of Exorcism. While *fucking*? It was perverse, and so bizarre Reed couldn't begin to guess why the words were spoken.

Why did Azazel take Riesgo and not Eve? Why would Cain break up with Eve—then turn to Izzie of all people?

Cursing inwardly, Reed knew that he could trust only a handful of people now. They all had something they wanted, and were all ruthless about getting it.

Who could Cain trust since he'd alienated Eve?

Reed smiled grimly. *Their parents.*

He was surprisingly soothed by the thought. If Cain was aware of what was happening to himself, he'd be working to fix it.

Fixing it . . . Alienating Eve . . .

"Shit," he breathed, considering that Cain might have pushed Eve away not because he didn't care about her anymore, but because the reverse was true.

Reed looked over his shoulder and met Sara's gaze dead-on. "Find out who helped Cain ascend. I don't care how you do it, but make it quick."

Sara nodded. "What does this mean for us? You and me? Anything?"

She couldn't love him. He wasn't sure why she bothered to act as if she cared.

"Not now." Withdrawing his cell phone from his pocket, he prepared to shift. "My phone is on. Call me when you know something."

He left to search for his brother.

Sara stared at the spot where Abel had been. There was something different about him, a change profound enough to make a noticeable difference since she'd spoken to him in Cain's office that morning.

Suspecting it was connected to Evangeline Hollis, she woke her computer and tapped out a rapid series of keystrokes, pulling up the recorded feeds from the Mark's home made earlier in the day. She stiffened when she found what she'd been desperately hoping she wouldn't.

"Abel," she whispered, hating him with a passion that equaled her lust for him.

She forwarded the video to Cain's e-mail account. For good measure, she sent a copy of Cain's video to Evangeline.

Then, smiling, Sara left her office to set her back-up plan in motion. If Abel didn't have balls enough to get things back to normal, she would simply have to do it herself.

CHAPTER 14

Eve flipped through Riesgo's Bible while making a mental list of all the things she needed to accomplish. She was on her couch, legs curled up, a glass of soda on the coffee table in front of her. Gavin Rossdale's gorgeous voice was singing "Love Remains the Same," and the History Channel was muted on the television in the hopes that a biblical documentary might air.

Going through the motions as if everything was normal was one of the ways she'd learned to cope with chaos. It didn't always work—sometimes screaming was better—but in this case, she couldn't risk freaking out and alerting Alec or Reed to her problem. Losing Riesgo and Gadara was too great a price to pay for breaking her deal with the Devil.

She needed answers, but without being able to discuss her problem with anyone, how would she get them? The archives in the Gadara system went back so far it would be like looking for a needle in a *field* of hay. The only solution she could come up with was to visit Hank, who could read her mind. If she managed to let something slip . . .

If she had the means, she would go to Hank now, but her car was still at the stadium, and asking one of the exterior guards for a ride would arouse suspicions she wasn't sure she could deflect. She supposed she could call Hank through a landline and ask for a house call. . . .

Alec's front door opened.

Eve stiffened at the familiar, unmistakable sound. For a moment, déjà vu was so strong it was heartbreaking. She couldn't help but think of her old neighbor, Mrs. Basso, and how much simpler life had been just a few months ago. Eve missed the words of wisdom and support her neighbor used to share with her, and she missed having her best friend Janice—presently on sabbatical—around to commiserate and laugh with.

When the knock came at her door, Eve forcibly tamped down her apprehension. For Alec to come to her the secular way had to mean something. Whether he wanted to talk about Riesgo and the guards or what had happened between them personally, it would be taxing for both of them. She breathed carefully, trying to attain a semblance of composure.

"Evangeline? Are you home?"

The soft, feminine voice froze Eve midstride. Frowning, she became more cautious, sidestepping to avoid being directly in front of the door. She considered grabbing the gun she kept in a padded case in the console drawer—clearly God was done giving her swords when she needed them—but she was concerned about what she might do with it. Jealousy was eating at her, goaded by the volatility of the Novium. What the hell was a woman doing at Alec's place?

"Who is it?" Eve called out.

"I'm safe, I promise."

Eve kept the chain on, but unlocked the series of dead bolts. She pulled the door open and peeked out the opening. The woman on her doorstep was so beautiful, she had to blink a few times to process it.

"Hi," her visitor said with a friendly smile. "I'm Cain's mother."

Her mouth fell open and her grip on the doorknob tightened. *Holy shit.*

Lightning quick, she freed the chain and yanked the original Eve inside. She glanced up and down the hallway, then slammed the door shut and locked it. Spinning around, she faced Alec's mom with her back pressed to the door.

She swallowed hard. "Hi."

"You're just as beautiful as I imagined you would be," Alec's mother said with a warm smile. She approached Eve with arms wide and embraced her. "I'm so happy to meet you, Evangeline."

"It's a p-pleasure to meet you, too . . . Eve," she managed, while alarms were clanging in her mind.

Satan wanted this woman enough to give up Gadara for her. Why? And how had he known she would soon be within reach?

"I would like it if you'd call me Ima," Alec's mother said, stepping back to study her.

They were of a height and similarly colored, but the biblical Eve was more exotic, with almond-shaped brown eyes and a luxuriously voluptuous figure.

She wore a simple linen dress that looked to be handmade, and she appeared to be somewhere in her midforties, which certainly could not be the case. She definitely didn't look old enough to be Alec and Reed's mother.

"Ima," Eve repeated, her brain reeling over the fact that the mother of all humanity was standing in her living room.

"What a lovely place you have." Ima walked deeper into the room, her head tilting back to take in the vaulted ceilings. "Cain says you're an interior designer."

"Yes." Eve followed after her. "Would you like a drink? I have water and tea. Soda, too, if you like that sort of thing."

Eve didn't know whether the woman standing in her living room was a ghost or real. Did she eat and drink? Sleep?

"What are you having?" Ima asked, gesturing at the drinking glass sweating condensation onto the coffee table.

"Diet Dr Pepper."

"Diet?" Ima smiled over her shoulder. "You don't need to diet."

"Yeah. The whole mark thing . . ."

"Not because of that. You're gorgeous just the way you are."

"Thank you." Eve passed her on the way to the kitchen. She hit the light switch on the wall and grabbed a cup from the cupboard. The barely there weight of the necklace felt like a yoke around her neck.

Alec's mother pulled out a bar stool and sat at the kitchen island. "I'm making you uncomfortable."

Pausing with the cup in hand, Eve sighed and offered a rueful smile. "No, it's not you. I'm just surprised. I'm still getting used to meeting people I always thought were . . . mythological."

"Didn't Cain tell you I'm real?" The grin that accompanied the question had a touch of mischievousness that was endearing. "I saw that you're reading the Bible. Is there anything in particular that you're researching?"

For a moment, the rattling of the ice maker prevented speech. Then, Eve pulled a can of soda out of the fridge and turned to face Ima. She was debating whether she should talk about the whole Garden of Eden, apple, Satan incident so soon after meeting the pivotal figure in the tale, but time was short. Who knew what Father Riesgo and Gadara were going through right now? And how long could the priest be a missing person before his life was irrevocably changed?

Eve set the glass in front of Alec's mom and popped open the can. "I was reading Genesis, actually."

"Don't believe everything you read." Ima picked up the can and poured some soda into the glass. She sat with spine straight and shoulders back, elegant and delicate. Her hair was a deep chestnut curtain that fell to the seat cushion. There was a fine cluster of silver strands at her right temple, almost too faint to be noticed.

"Really?" Eve set her elbow on the island and rested her chin in her hand. "What shouldn't I believe?"

"Well, you won't find it in that version you have there, but that ridiculous story about my husband only liking the missionary position? Ridiculous. He's a man. He'll take it any way he can get it and the less work he has to put into it, the more he enjoys it. Lilith spread that tale because she's bitter."

Eve bit back a smile. Then a knock came at the door and she straightened abruptly.

"Stay here," she said, rounding the back of Ima's chair. "If something happens, run to one of the rooms down the hall and lock the door."

A grip on her biceps stopped her.

"Unless you're expecting someone," Ima said, "it's probably Adam."

Eve blinked. *Adam.* The knock came again, louder and more insistent.

"Isha?" a masculine voice called.

"Isha?" Eve repeated.

"Wife." Ima slid off the chair and moved toward the door. "He'll be so excited to meet you."

Eve's brain took a moment to catch up, then she rushed forward protectively. If something happened to Reed and Alec's mother on her watch . . .

When Adam entered her home a moment later, Eve was dumbstruck. The resemblance to his sons was disconcerting. He was gorgeous. There was a quiet dignity to his bearing, distinguishing him in the way some men achieved with age.

As Eve stood beside the doorway, staring, Adam perused her from head to toe. His face was austere, giving nothing away. Eve squirmed inside, wondering what he thought of her, whether it was good or bad.

She was surprised when he hugged her, so much so that she stood rigidly for a moment before she hugged him back.

"I can see why Cain thinks she was worth waiting for," Ima said, smiling as Adam straightened and adjusted his rough-hewn vest with an awkward tug. Public displays of affection seemed to be uncomfortable for him.

Eve jumped as Reed appeared beside her with a plastic bag in his hand.

"Don't shoot me, but I brought takeout." He spotted his parents, and his eyes widened. "I didn't know you were visiting!"

"Surprise!" his mother said, dark eyes sparkling.

"Sorry about dinner," he murmured to Eve. "It's almost ten o'clock. I figured it was too late to cook. You didn't eat without me?"

Feeling the heavy weight of his parents' stares, she could only manage to shake her head.

"Good." He pressed a kiss to her forehead, then smiled at his parents. "Luckily, I couldn't make up my mind and bought an excessive amount of food. We can all eat together. Hope you're in the mood for Italian."

He moved toward the kitchen. Eve followed with heavy footsteps.

She heard his mother speak quietly behind her.

"Dear God. Not again."

Reed massaged Eve's shoulders as they stood in the common area hallway and watched his parents disappear into Alec's condo. "Relax. If this place is safe enough for you, it's equally safe for them."

When she heard Alec's dead bolt slide into place, Eve pulled out of Reed's grip and returned to her own home. She'd spent the last two hours wondering if Alec was going to show up. She was both relieved and disappointed that he hadn't.

"They like you," Reed said, closing her door and locking it.

Eve wasn't so sure about that. They'd had a decent time together once the food had been served, but there was an underlying awkwardness that Reed seemed impervious to.

"How are Montevista and Sydney?" she asked.

"They were sleeping in the infirmary when I got to them, but the witch doctor said they're stable and in no danger."

Frowning, Eve settled onto the sofa.

He sat beside her and tossed one arm over the back of the couch. There was something in his face, a hint of strain.

She reached out and set her hand over his knee. "Is everything all right?"

"No. Everything is far from all right." He laced his fingers with hers. "Obviously Azazel knocked the guards out of commission before going after the priest. The question is: why didn't he come after you instead? He must want something from you in return—guilt, recklessness, anger . . . something. But then why not take your parents? Or your sister? The move was both really bold and too restrained. Makes no sense."

Her grip tightened on his. "I would have lost it if he'd gone after my family."

"Exactly. So he's playing with you. Why? Why not go all the way and hit you where it really hurts?"

Because Satan was clever. He wanted her pushed into a corner where she'd be desperate, but not wild with it. He wanted her levelheaded so that she could do his dirty work. Perhaps he even wanted to seem reasonable. She didn't see how, but then she didn't understand how any of these people worked.

Eve shrugged in reply. "Maybe the bounty isn't for killing me, but for fucking with me? Putting the screws to me because of the whole hellhound thing?"

"Is that what the *yuki-onna* told you?"

"She was under duress at the time," Eve reminded him dryly.

"Why were you out there with the priest to begin with?"

Eve explained the chain of events, wincing inwardly as his face darkened with every sentence.

"So let me get this straight," he said tightly when she finished. "You're supposed to stay in the house. Instead, you left to talk to the priest about a nut job who wouldn't bother you if you stayed in the house like you're supposed to?"

"I guess. But—"

"But nothing. What the hell were you thinking?"

"You know what I was thinking! The demons want me. We want Gadara. Hiding here isn't going to help move things along. I don't need more guilt, Reed. I'm aware that Father Riesgo's abduction is entirely my fault."

Her eyes stung and her vision blurred. She scrubbed at her lashes with impatient fingers. She hated crying in front of other people, but it was worse with Reed, who fidgeted uncomfortably in reaction. Much like his father. So unlike Alec, who felt too much and was open about it.

Reed looked down at their joined hands. "Raguel is probably dead."

Eve froze. It was a good thing her heart worked like a machine, considering how many times she'd been surprised today. "What would make you say that?"

"The impression I got from Sara is that Cain wouldn't have been promoted if Raguel was still alive."

"Do you believe her?"

"I don't know. It makes sense. There have only been seven firms forever. Maybe that number is immutable." His gaze lifted to meet hers. "I have to look into it."

If Gadara was dead, then Riesgo might be, too. She supposed she'd rather take the word of an archangel over Satan. But she had never been a blind-faith sort of person. She couldn't believe anything without proof. Which meant that somehow she had to get Satan to provide some evidence that he had the goods.

She had a long day ahead of her tomorrow.

"I need to crash," she said. The sooner she fell asleep, the sooner she could get up and get to work.

"Yeah." He watched her with dark, slumberous eyes. Waiting.

"I don't want to be alone tonight."

In answer, he stood and pulled her to her feet, then carried her to bed.

A ringing phone woke Eve.

Turning her head, she peeked at the nightstand clock with one eye. It was just before eleven in the morning.

"Oh man . . ." she groaned. "We overslept."

Reed pinned her in place with a heavy leg thrown over hers. "Ignore it."

"The world is going to hell," she argued, "and we're in bed."

"Anywhere else you'd rather be when the world ends?"

He had a point. She lifted the arm he had draped over her torso and kissed the back of his hand. "I have to answer that."

He rolled onto his back with a growl, freeing her. By the time Eve picked up the receiver, voicemail had intercepted, but a quick scan of the caller ID told her the call had originated from Gadara Tower. She was about to dial her office line when the phone started ringing again.

She sat up. "Hello?"

"*Ms. Hollis.*" Her secretary, Candace, spoke in a whisper and sounded slightly panicked. "*The police are here for you.*"

Eve brushed her hair back from her forehead. Beneath the oversized T-shirt she wore, Satan's necklace throbbed between her breasts. "Yikes."

"I told them you were out to lunch and that you would call them when you returned, but they insisted they'd wait for you to come back."

"Double yikes."

Reed sat up.

"Okay," Eve said. "I'll get there as fast as I can."

"Thank you."

"No, no. Thank you. You're doing a great job. Be there soon." She hung up and winced at Reed. "Cops."

"I heard," he murmured.

Eve stared at him, unable to look away. As a *mal'akh*, he suffered none of the aftereffects of sleep that mortals did. His eyes weren't puffy and he had no morning breath. He was simply gorgeous. Relaxed in a way she'd never seen before, bare-chested with slightly mussed hair that looked as thick and soft as it felt.

Sighing, she tossed the covers back and climbed out of bed. "I have to go."

"I'll take you there."

Right. She had no car. "Forgot about that."

Half an hour later, she was dressed in a pencil skirt and silk blouse with her damp hair restrained in a sleek chignon and three-inch heels on her feet that still left her shorter than Reed.

He'd showered with her, then shifted home to change. While he was gone, she thought about how little she knew of him. She'd never been to where he lived, so she had no idea what his taste in furniture and design was like. As a designer, knowing those things would give her a lot of insight into who he was. As would the selection of books he owned or the lack thereof, his MP3 playlists, DVD collection . . .

"Ready?" he asked.

Eve nodded. "What about your parents?"

"I checked on them on the way back from my place. They're fine. Dad is snoring on Cain's couch. Mom's watching the news and catching up on the soap operas she likes to watch. She says she can miss a year and still not miss anything." Gripping her biceps, he smiled. "Damn, you clean up nice, babe."

"You're never anything *but* dressed up," she said, looking at the perfect knot of his tie. No one wore a three-piece suit like Reed.

"Complaining?"

"No way I could when you look so fine. But you know that."

"Just need you to know it, too. Hang on."

A few minutes later, Eve's heels were tapping out a rapid beat down the hallway to her office. She slowed before entering, grateful that her breathing and heart rate remained steady and even.

"Detectives," she said in greeting as she spotted the two familiar figures waiting in the receptionist's area of her office. "What a surprise."

Ingram and Jones stood, Jones with the dreaded worn briefcase in his hand. "Ms. Hollis."

She gestured for them to follow her into her office. Taking a seat behind the desk, she reached for her phone. "Can I get you something to drink? Coffee or tea, perhaps? Or water?"

"Nothing, thank you," Jones said, with an edge to his tone that told her he was done tiptoeing around her.

"Okay." Eve clasped her hands atop her desk calendar. "Please don't tell me there's been another death."

"Not yet," Ingram answered, stroking the end of one side of his mustache as he studied her. "Do you know Father Miguel Riesgo?"

Eve wished she had a good poker face, but knew that she didn't. The two detectives watched her avidly. Jones leaned forward.

"Yes, I know him," she answered.

Ingram nodded. "When's the last time you saw him?"

"Last night. Why?"

"A missing persons report on Riesgo was filed this morning by a Father Ralph Simmons."

"A little premature, isn't it?" she asked.

"There is no waiting time in the state of California," Jones said. "Father Riesgo didn't show up at the church this morning and his car was found at Glover Stadium here in Anaheim. So was yours."

"Yes. My boyfriend picked me up for an impromptu dinner." She cursed inwardly when her mark burned. *Give me a break,* she thought. *It's pretty damn close to the truth.*

Jones withdrew a notepad from his pocket. "Alec Cain?"

"No. Reed Abel."

"Cain and Abel?" Ingram's brow rose.

She shrugged lamely.

A knock came at the door just before it opened. Gray Man walked in. He was dressed in a three-piece suit of dark gray, his tall and slender frame moving with an easy grace. His hair and eyes were a lighter shade of gray than his garments, and his thin lips were curved in the vaguest hint of a smile that never seemed to reach his eyes. Eve's gaze moved past Ishamel to her secretary. Candace offered a reassuring smile.

"Excuse us," Jones said, pushing heavily to his feet. "Can you please wait outside until we're done here?"

"I represent Ms. Hollis," Ishamel said smoothly, approaching and extending his hand. "Ishamel Abramson."

"Do you feel the need for counsel?" Ingram asked Eve, eyeing her.

"I am here at the request of Gadara Enterprises," Ishamel explained, taking a seat on the sofa near the door. "Ms. Hollis is pivotal in the redesign of the Mondego Hotel and Casino in Las Vegas. We want to be certain that nothing interferes with the completion of the project."

Jones stood motionless for a long moment, then he hummed a doubtful sound and sank back into his chair. He proceeded to ignore Ishamel in favor of focusing more heavily on Eve.

She cleared her throat. "I'm confused as to why homicide detectives would take an interest in a missing persons case."

Ingram dug into the briefcase. "Once your name was brought into it, we followed a hunch."

Great. "A hunch?"

Once again, photographs were pushed across her desk toward her. This time, it was a stack half an inch thick. She flipped through the uppermost layer.

The photos were black and white, and very grainy. Eve looked them over, quickly deducing from the quality and angles that they were stills taken from security cameras around the athletic field and nearby traffic lights. She was relieved to see that neither Satan nor Azazel were visible to the cameras, although in some shots she looked ridiculous because it seemed she was talking to dead air.

"See what we see?" Ingram asked, scooting to the edge of his seat and leaning over her desk.

Eve frowned, not sure what he was referring to.

"Here." He pushed the photos around, revealing the ones that sat beneath the few she'd glimpsed on top.

Her breath caught at a blown-up image of the chain-link fence behind her. The Nix stood there, fingers linked through the chain, an odd smile on his face. She glanced at Ishamel, who stood and came forward.

"That looks like the guy in the drawing you showed me," she said to the detectives, sitting back to put distance between her and the image. "The sketch artist's rendering."

"Right," Jones said. "The man we're looking for in conjunction with the Punch Bowl Murders. We've got him on a traffic light camera a block away. He was standing alone on the sidewalk, but he might have an accomplice who managed the abduction."

"Punch Bowl Murders?" she repeated, finding it horrifying that something so heinous would bear such a ridiculous name.

Ingram's fingers tapped the stack of pictures. "Unfortunately, the quality of the security cameras around the stadium is poor. They have blind spots and record in intervals, so there are times when neither you nor Riesgo are on film, followed by times when you are."

Eve silently thanked whoever had the foresight to take care of that.

"So here's what we've got," Jones said, straightening his tie over straining shirt buttons. "Your neighbor, Mona Basso; your school chum, Anthony Wynn; your priest, Miguel Riesgo; your car at a possible abduction scene, and a serial killer. You're smack dab in the middle of everything, Ms. Hollis. I've been at this long enough to know that you're withholding valuable information. Which doesn't make sense, considering this guy clearly has it out for you. Tell us who he is, before Father Riesgo pays the price. You don't want the death of a priest on your conscience."

Eve's gaze moved between both detectives. "I have no idea," she said fervently. "Believe me, if there was some way I could help Father Riesgo, I would. Even though he isn't 'my' priest."

"What business did you have with him, then?" Ingram asked.

She explained, leaving out why she wanted a Bible in the first place. "The last time I saw Father Riesgo, he was picking up bats and mitts."

Not exactly the truth, but . . .

"Would you let us take a look at your car?" Jones asked.

"Of course."

"We also need you to come down to the station and give us a statement about last night. We might have your car finished by then."

"Can I come by after work? Say around five o'clock?"

"Fine. We'll send a squad car around to pick you up."

"That won't be necessary," Ishamel assured. "I'll bring her in. Which station?"

"The one on Harbor. By the way." Jones's pen hovered over his notepad. "Which route home did you take with your boyfriend and what does he drive? We'll want to check the cameras and see if this guy was following you home."

"Reed drives a silver Lamborghini Gallardo Spyder. And we took Harbor to Brookhurst." She glanced at Ishamel, who somehow conveyed reassurance without any alteration in his stance. He would find a way to make her fictitious trip home happen for the detectives.

"Lamborghini, eh? Must be nice. Thank you."

The detectives rose to their feet. Ingram collected the photos. His gaze lifted and locked with hers. "Think about what happened last night. Every detail. Every word spoken. Anything that might strike you as odd in hindsight. The smallest detail can sometimes break a case."

"Of course." She stood along with them. "I'm eager to help."

Ishamel walked the detectives out. Eve expected him to return, so she waited for him. But he didn't come back.

Knowing she'd see him on the way to the police station, she set off to find Hank instead.

CHAPTER 15

Raguel smelled the scent of ripe mortal terror before the door to his cell opened. Using what little strength he had left, he altered his appearance, tucking away the wings that kept him warm and altering his features to those of a teenager. He *would* get out of Hell, and when he did, he couldn't risk being recognized as the real estate mogul who was so widely known.

The new arrival was pushed into Raguel's stone enclosure with such force, he stumbled. Shock had already begun to set in. The man's eyes were dilated and his breathing was too quick.

It took a moment before recognition hit Raguel. *Evangeline's priest.* The one to whom she had turned, which had in turn prompted an investigation into the tengu infestation at Olivet Place. She must be the reason why the priest was here.

"Have a seat, Padre," Raguel said, gesturing to the wide expanse of stone floor. "As you can see, there is plenty of room."

Like Jehovah, Sammael employed drama for effect. In this instance the allusion was to the Spanish Inquisition, a time when atrocities had been committed in God's name. Manacles hung from the wall, and distant screams kept nerves on edge and prevented restful slumber.

"Where are we?" the priest asked, sinking to a crouch with unfocused eyes.

"I think you know."

In a rush, the man stood and moved to the door. He gripped the rough iron bars and tried to see outside. There was nothing out there but fire and heat. No ground below, no sky above. Sammael could choose to make it the most gorgeous of spaces, but that would be too kind. This way, the feeling of safety came from their imprisonment.

"There was someone else with me," the priest said roughly. "A young woman."

"Evangeline is fine. For now."

"How do you know?"

Raguel wrapped his arms around his knees. His soul was cold when separated from God. "You would be dead otherwise, or not here at all."

"Who are you?"

"A prisoner like you. Leverage to force those on earth to do a demon's bidding."

"Are you one of them?"

"No. I am a servant of God, just as you are."

"How can I believe you? How do you know Evangeline?"

"You will have to take it on faith, Padre."

The priest's knees lost strength and he dropped to the floor. His lips moved in what was likely a silent prayer. Raguel didn't see the point in telling him that Jehovah couldn't hear him here. Hope was something neither of them could afford to lose. They had time enough to talk after circumstances sunk in through the shock. There was no point in questioning the man when his brain wasn't running at full speed.

A long time passed. Raguel had begun to doze when the priest spoke again.

"She asked me if I believed in demons."

Raguel scrubbed his hands over his face, hating the smell that coated his skin. "What was your answer?"

"I'm not sure I gave her one."

"Understandable. Even those with faith have their limits."

The priest looked at him. "She claims to have no faith, yet she believed. She even hired bodyguards to protect her."

With narrowed eyes, Raguel asked, "Did you meet these guards?"

"Yes."

"What were their names? Do you recall?"

"Montevista and Sydney. Why do you ask?"

She was in danger. Somehow, Cain or Abel had known she was at risk before the priest's abduction. What was happening? Why would Sammael want Evangeline?

"How long have you been here?" the priest asked. "Are you the reason she believes in demons?"

Raguel leaned forward. "You and I have much to talk about if we are to find a way out of here alive."

"*Can* we get out?"

"We must." *At the very least, I must.*

Cain would have to relinquish the position he'd stolen. Somehow, Raguel would find the tools he needed to make that happen. The priest was all he had to work with and time was short. A prolonged stay in Hell was like a cancer that ate its way in from the outside. The longer the mortal was here, the less of his soul and sanity would remain. Raguel was already feeling the effects and he was far stronger.

"Get comfortable, Padre," Raguel murmured. "I will need you to be as precise in your recollections as possible."

* * *

Eve had just raised her hand to knock on Hank's door when it swung open of its own accord. It was dark inside, as usual, with only strategically placed lighting over counters littered with petri dishes and glass tubes. Unlike usual was the racket resounding from the depths of the room. It was the first time she'd visited Hank's domain when it wasn't deathly quiet.

"Hank?" she yelled.

He stepped out of the darkness as a man, dressed in black slacks and dress shirt. The somberness of his garments allowed the brilliant red of his hair to take center stage. Eve was slightly envious of that color.

"Eve." He held out his hands to her. "What brings you to me?"

"What the hell is that noise?"

"Your tengu friend."

In the distance, she could hear Fred cursing and growling.

"What's the problem?" she asked.

"I've been experimenting with the fellow, using him as a guinea pig for my masking agent trials. This most recent test involved a higher Mark-to-Infernal ratio and the demon in him is rebelling."

She winced. "How long will he be like that?"

"Another couple hours, at least."

"I don't think I can shout that long!"

His smile was charming. "Should we go somewhere else?"

"If you don't mind."

They were about to exit when the rapid thudding of cement feet betrayed the approach of the escaped tengu.

"Watch out!" Fred yelled.

"Pretty Mark!" the tengu screeched, before launching like a missile toward Eve.

"Oomph!" She hit the floor on her back, her teeth snapping together painfully.

Her arms wrapped around the heavy beast and she rolled, knowing from experience that it was best to avoid taking the bottom position with a tengu.

They grappled like wrestlers. Eve's stilettos made it difficult to gain purchase on the polished cement floor. The Infernal took advantage, cackling in a manner she'd never heard before. Less mischievous, more maniacal. With a resonance that sounded almost as if there were multiple beings laughing instead of just the one.

Fred bounded out of the darkness in wolf form, barking.

"*Enough,*" Hank roared, reaching down to free Eve.

But the tengu caught a fistful of her chignon and held fast. Eve screamed as he pulled. In the violent jostling, the necklace fell from the V of her neckline. The moment it touched the tengu's forearm, the demon stilled.

His mouth opened in a surprised O, then he blinked as if waking. The hand in her hair loosened and the arm fell to the floor with a heavy thud.

"Pretty Mark," he said in a soft whisper, appearing dazed.

She yelped as she was hauled upward by Hank.

The occultist grabbed her necklace and stared hard at it. "Where did you get this?"

Eve blinked as rapidly as the tengu had. She thought of Satan and hoped that Hank would read her mind as he often did. Instead he glared at her. When the tengu began to stir and rumble low in his throat, Hank pulled the necklace over her head and dropped it around the tengu's neck. The Infernal quieted, sitting with hands in his lap and his head cocked to the side. His cement fingers caressed the charm reverently.

"Sammael," Hank murmured, setting Eve on her feet and straightening her collar.

"I need that," she said, pointing at the necklace.

"I can't read you when you're wearing it."

"Oh."

"And you can't hear me when your friend is having fits. We kill two birds with one stone this way. You can recover the piece later."

"Gotcha."

Fred altered shape, shifting back into her lili form. Since she was naked, Eve looked away, but she heard Fred pick up the tengu and pad back into the darkness.

"You're in deep shit," Hank said, gripping Eve's elbow and pulling her deeper into the room.

She was startled by the sudden appearance of a wooden table and chairs. Hank sat and she followed suit, once again wondering at the lack of gentlemanly manners.

He studied her intently. "It's clear that neither Cain nor Abel know. If they did, you'd be locked away. Pointless as that would be."

"I can't say anything."

"And your memories of Sammael are like static on a television." Hank sighed. "Very well, then. I'll do the talking. You just have to ask the right questions."

Eve nodded. She had no idea how old Hank was, but there was no doubt that he held a staggering amount of information inside him. But did that information extend back to the beginning of time?

"Do you know," she began, "exactly how much of the Eve and the apple story is true, and how much of it isn't?"

"Ah, Genesis . . . Interesting." Hank's lips pursed momentarily. "The tale varies depending on who you ask. Some say the Bible is as accurate as can be expected. Others say it's more of a fable, with hidden meanings."

"Such as?"

"Such as Sammael's serpent being a phallic allusion and the Tree of Knowledge referring to female sexual awakening."

She whistled. "Holy shit."

"There are those who go so far as to say that Cain is the son of Sammael and not Adam, and that is why he's so good at killing."

Eve heaved out a shuddering breath. If Satan wanted some reunion nooky, they were all fucked. Talk about disasters.

"He's a good-looking demon," she said. "He wouldn't secretly pine for her, would he? He's got endless choices."

"You have to understand the layers that exist." Hank rubbed the back of his neck, one of very few times that Eve had ever seen signs of stress on him.

"Go on," she coaxed.

"It's a misconception to say that Sammael rules over a place called Hell. Sammael rules the earth. He was banished from Heaven, but given domain here. He isn't roasting in some fiery pit."

"He isn't?"

"No. He can create that visual effect and often does because we've been trained to fear it, but it's just window dressing. There are layers to Heaven and there are layers to earth. Like an onion. Sammael can strip or combine layers in order to create the desired effect."

Fred appeared from the darkness dressed in a lab coat and bearing a slight smile. Carrying a tray with a pitcher and half-filled glasses, she looked more harmless geek than killer demon.

Eve leaned back to make room for the refreshments. "Will you join us?" she asked the lili.

"I can't, but thank you."

Hank's gaze followed his assistant as she retreated. "She's worried that she'll die at any moment. She never relaxes because of it."

One hundred lilin died every day. Eve couldn't imagine living with that hanging over her head.

"Okay, back to the layers," she redirected.

"The layer that you and I occupy most of the time is tricky to navigate for both Jehovah and Sammael. As you know, they don't play well together. So when they want to function here with the full range of movement that mortals have—to touch, to taste, to lust—they need emissaries."

Understanding hit her right between the eyes. "Like Jesus Christ."

"And the Antichrist. You may feel the hand of God or the claws of Sammael in a figurative sense or through secondary beings such as demons and *mal'akhs,* but you can only feel them literally if they gain access to this earthly layer through an emissary."

"So let's say—hypothetically—that Satan wanted to give me a gift. Not a power, but an actual *thing,* like a necklace, he would have to do so through an emissary?"

Hank wrapped a hand around his drinking glass, but didn't pick it up. "Or he would use an emissary as a gateway to do it himself. If the emissary was strong enough, perhaps Sammael could even manifest separately and the two could occupy the same plane at the same time."

If the emissary was strong enough . . .

Eve wondered why the room didn't spin. She thought it should, considering how shaky she felt on the inside. "Is Cain the gateway?"

How else could Sammael have known that the original Eve would be visiting this layer?

Hank's gaze lifted from watching his thumb draw lines in the condensation on his glass. "Now, you're starting to ask the right questions."

"Why won't anyone give me a straight answer?" Alec rolled his shoulders back, fighting fatigue when he shouldn't be tired to begin with. "You've kept me cooling my heels for hours, then you talk in circles. It's a simple yes-or-no question."

Uriel handed him a bottle of chilled water and sat in the wicker chair opposite him. The head of the Australian firm was shirtless and barefooted. His long, sun-bleached hair fluttered gently in the ocean breeze coming through the open French doors of his office. He was considered one of the foremost yacht builders in the world, but had recently diversified into wine making. The world economy was unhealthy, curtailing luxury purchases.

"Yes, there are only seven of us," the archangel finally answered, after twenty minutes of evasion. "And yes, it might be by design. Is that better?"

Alec snatched up the water and downed the contents in a few greedy gulps. His body grew more feverish by the hour, leaving him with a dry throat and perspiration-damp skin.

"You really don't want to fuck with me now," he growled, returning the empty bottle to the glass-topped wicker coffee table with a hollow thud.

"I hope, for your sake, that you do not think we are evenly matched," Uriel warned. "Or assume that my easygoing nature gives you an edge."

Alec took deep, measured breaths, carefully reining back his temper.

Why can't I feel Eve?

He hadn't been able to feel her since they'd found the two guards. As the archangel responsible for Abel, he could sense that his brother wasn't alarmed, but that only spurred Alec's envy. The damned thing inside him was costing him the only thing that mattered to him anymore.

"Whose design?" he bit out, returning to his previous question. "Did you and the others practice a little sibling winnowing to get to a manageable number?"

Uriel's brilliant blue gaze narrowed. "You tread dangerous ground with your accusations."

"How did you convince Jehovah that seven of you were enough?"

"We have no control over Jehovah. You know that. As with anything, the pros and cons were weighed."

Alec couldn't help but wonder if he was experiencing the cons. Despite the cool evening air gusting in from the balcony, he was sweating. There was no doubt the chaos within him was escalating. "I'm not . . . well."

"I can see that," the archangel murmured, his casual pose unchanged.

"Did the others—the archangels who aren't here anymore—experience similar . . . problems?"

"What problems are you experiencing?"

"Let me rephrase," Alec said tightly. "Have you ever had to put down another archangel because he was out of control?"

Uriel brushed his hair back with a rough swipe of his hand. "No. We seven were created as we are, Cain. You are an aberration. An unknown. Perhaps your once-mortal body is incapable of handling an archangel's power."

"I was *changed*," he argued. "It felt like I was being ripped apart. The pain was indescribable."

Uriel's mouth quirked on one side. "I bet. That doesn't mean you are now one of us. For Abel to become a *mal'akh,* he had to die. For Christ to achieve his aims, he had to die. It is quite possible that your transformation cannot be completed without shedding every vestige of your former self."

"If I'm an aberration, is it possible that Raguel's still alive and that's why my ascension is fucked up?"

The sudden stillness that gripped the archangel didn't go unnoticed. "I suppose."

Well, that explained why none of them were actively searching for their brother. They assumed he was dead.

Restless, Alec stood and prowled. If there could be only seven archangels, he was in an untenable position. He would first have to ascertain whether or not Raguel was alive. Then, he would have to decide whether to kill, or be killed.

How badly do I want this?

The darkness in him roiled in protest. Power was like a drug, one not easily relinquished.

He moved toward the window and stood on the threshold, his damp skin chilling in the gentle gusts of wind.

Uriel's voice came soft and coaxing behind him. "What ails you?"

"There's something *in* me. It's angry. Violent. Very strong."

"Too strong?"

"Not yet." Alec looked at the ocean. At night, one beach looked like another. He couldn't help but think of nights spent with Eve. The selfish part of him wished he could share this mess he was in with her. "But I want better control over it."

"Perhaps the ascension freed a . . . *repressed* part of your personality?"

"Do you believe everything you hear?"

The wicker creaked as the archangel rose to his feet. Although his approach was silent, Alec sensed Uriel coming. The rush of power he felt around a single archangel was of equal force to the rush he felt when entering a firm.

"Depends on who is doing the talking," Uriel murmured.

Did Jehovah know the truth behind the rumors?

Alec's heart rate kicked up in response to his panic. Something was overriding the safeguards of his mark and the unexpected physical response caused a slight disorientation.

His hand rubbed at his chest through his thin cotton T-shirt. "Who did the talking to you?"

"Does it matter? The point is that perhaps the problem is in your blood." There was a length of silence, then Uriel touched his shoulder. "You should direct your questions to Jehovah."

"And fail my first challenge as an archangel?" Alec scoffed. "No way."

"You think this is a test?"

"Isn't everything? My entire life has been a trial." He faced Uriel. "That isn't a complaint, just a fact."

"I understand. We all face trials, saints and sinners alike. I wish I could help you with this one."

Alec's brow arched. "Are you sure you can't? You haven't offered me much of anything."

Uriel smiled, but the gesture didn't reach his eyes. "The best advice I can give you is to look elsewhere. You speak of anger and violence inside you, yet you do not approach the one of us known for those traits? Why?"

"Michael?"

"Commander of the Lord's army. Who knows darkness better than he? He has defeated Sammael himself."

Alec stepped farther outside. Uriel followed. Together, they stood at the railing and watched the moonlight shimmer over the water.

"You fear him," the archangel noted, still looking forward. "You should. But if anyone can help you, it would be him."

"Thank you."

"Do not thank me yet, Cain." Uriel glanced at him. "If you become a danger, I will hunt you myself."

Inside Alec, the thrill of prospective battle quickened his blood.

Uriel's gaze hardened. "I smell it on you. Perhaps you should go, before I decide not to let you."

Cursing inwardly, Alec shifted away.

Reed was preoccupied with his thoughts. So much so that it took him a moment to register that the beer he'd ordered was sitting in front of him. The waitress who'd brought it was waiting patiently.

"I'm sorry," he murmured. "I missed what you said."

"Would you like anything else?" The pretty brunette smiled wide. Her name tag said she was "Sara," which was an unfortunate moniker but not her fault.

"No. I'm good, thanks." He picked up the bottle, ignoring the frozen glass beside it. For mortals, it was perhaps a bit early in the day for booze. For a *mal'akh,* it wasn't any different from drinking sparkling water.

"I'll check on you in a few minutes," she said. "But if you need anything in the meantime, just gimme a wave."

"Got it."

Sara winked before sashaying back into the restaurant. The invitation to flirt with her was clear and brought Reed some amusement, but he hadn't the time to indulge in such games now. There was far too much at stake.

Alone again, Reed appreciated his status as sole occupant of the House of Blues patio. Music drifted from the interior—of sufficient volume to identify the songs, but not so loud as to impede conversation. Despite the sluggish economy, foot traffic through Downtown Disney was steady. A mixture of trolling teenagers and tourist families window-shopped, ate, and commingled with a large proliferation of Infernals. The mortals had no clue, their open and happy faces betraying their ignorance of the danger. What would they say if they knew the vendor hawking caricature drawings was an incubus? Or that the woman filling popcorn buckets was a *djinni*?

"Abel?"

Turning his head with studious nonchalance, Reed watched as Chaney and Asmodeus approached. The new Alpha was dressed in casual Dockers pants and an oversized polo shirt. His companion, one of the seven kings of Hell, was dressed similarly to Reed—Armani suit, pristinely pressed shirt, and gleaming leather dress shoes. The glamour he wore was impressive. He'd chosen a muscular build and angular features to hide the multiheaded monstrosity he was in reality.

As the demons came around the short metal patio fence and joined him, Reed remained seated. He drank his beer and watched the pedestrians pass.

"Raguel is alive," Asmodeus said without preamble. "Presently enjoying the hospitality of the second level of Hell."

The level that Asmodeus ruled. Of course. The demon must have pleased Sammael in some way to be given such an honor.

"Even better than I expected," Reed returned. "We both have access to what the other wants."

He watched both Infernals through his sunglasses. Neither met his gaze. The Alpha turned his head to people watch and Asmodeus peered into the doorway of the restaurant, making eye contact with Sara.

The two demons ordered food and drink. Reed asked for a second round. When they were settled, Asmodeus pushed up his sunglasses and revealed laser-bright red irises.

"I want more," the demon king said smoothly.

Reed picked at the edge of the beer bottle label, but kept his eyes on his companions. "Do you?"

"I don't see how it benefits me to share a bounty with a lower-level demon. I get a better boon from having Raguel under my watch."

"Ah . . . I see."

"You're not surprised," Chaney noted.

"Of course he's not." Asmodeus laughed. "He knows me well enough."

"I was hoping you would insist," Reed said easily. "I want more, too. I want the priest."

"Done. We don't have any need for him, beyond getting our hands on Cain's woman."

Fingers tensing, Reed drawled, "Right."

The waitress returned with the drinks, promising to be right out with the food. Reed couldn't even imagine eating at this point, and suspected their order was a ruse to appear more in control than they were.

Regardless, they had more control than he did.

"So what more do you want?" he asked, when the silence stretched out.

"What can you get?" Chaney asked.

Reed laughed. "I don't work that way. Let's start with you telling me what I'm bidding against, and I'll see if I can beat it."

The Alpha tried to look innocent. Asmodeus didn't bother. He tossed his head back and laughed.

"I've always liked you, Abel." He grinned. His teeth were a hideous shade of yellow, incongruous within the beauty of his glamour. "How did you know?"

"I didn't," Reed confessed, his mind spinning with the possibilities. "I suspected, you confirmed. I figured someone else besides me would want Raguel back. I couldn't be the only one who'd bargain with a demon to do it."

Cain, maybe? Someone sent by Sabrael? Ishamel?

"I'm under a vow of secrecy," the king said. "Can't tell you who it is."

"I don't care about *who*." He'd tackle that next on his own. "I care about *what*. They're offering you something, but you think you can get more out of me or you wouldn't have shown up today. What are they proposing, and how much more do you want?"

Asmodeus glanced at the Alpha, then back at Reed. "They're offering to widen the Black Diamond Pack's territory by thinning the ranks of the perimeter packs."

"Okay." Reed waited a moment, then, "Come on. You already said that sharing the spoils with Chaney doesn't work for you. So, what are *you* getting out of it?"

The king slouched in his chair and smiled. "A handler. One who's been a pain in my ass for too long."

Reed staved off his horror and launched into his bid. "I can top that. Easily."

"Oh?" The Infernal smiled. "Whatcha got?"

"An archangel to replace the one you're giving to me."

Chaney whistled. "Which one?"

Asmodeus laughed. "Who do you think?" His eyes brightened to the point that Reed appreciated his sunglasses. "He's going to give us Cain."

CHAPTER 16

Azazel stood with hands clasped behind his back, separate from the mass of celebrants around him. "You gave her the amulet, my liege?"

Sammael shrugged. "Doing so serves many purposes, not the least of which is that she will be marginally safer until news of the successful bounty reaches everyone."

"If you say that I took part in the hunt, it will lower my status. I am above such games."

"Are you?" Reclining more fully on the divan, Sammael watched the revelers through the filmy sheers that surrounded his pallet. Between his spread legs, a succubus worked, her mouth gliding up and down the length of his cock with laudable skill. "How odd. I thought your place was where I put you."

His lieutenant bowed. "I meant no offense, my liege. I simply point out that my ability to perform the tasks you set for me is enhanced when others fear me. That fear is more easily invoked when I am seen as separate from the masses."

Sammael hissed in pleasure at the fervent tongue stroking the underside of his cock. "Worry not, Azazel. I told Evangeline that I would think of something. I did not say I would use her suggestion."

"Thank you."

Sammael turned his gaze back to his subjects who danced and fucked with abandon just beyond the edge of the divan. Unfortunately, his lieutenant's continued agitation affected his enjoyment of the debauchery. "You still have questions."

"Just one."

"Well, spit it out. I resent how readily everyone believes in a divine plan, yet I am always questioned."

"You've given a convenience to someone who is a pawn of our enemies. I just want to understand why."

"Convenience," Sammael repeated slowly. "Yes. I suppose the amulet is convenient. It certainly evens the odds between a powerless Mark and a gifted demon."

"Yes. You could have ended the bounty without making things easy for her."

Lifting his hand in a delaying gesture to his lieutenant, Sammael rolled his hips, screwing into the eager mouth that serviced him. Taking his cue, the succubus increased the pressure and tempo of her suckling. He came with a low groan, shuddering with the welcome release of tension.

"Excellent." He pushed his fingers into the demon's hair and yanked her head back. She stared up at him with heavy-lidded, worshipful eyes. The Asian glamour she wore had been her idea, but he'd taken a perverse enjoyment in it after meeting Cain's woman.

"Azazel is too grim," he murmured, caressing her cheek. "Help him relax."

"With honor, my liege." She crawled over on her hands and knees, the awkward movement made sensual by the leisure with which she crossed the distance.

"I'm not grim," Azazel protested. "Just curious."

Sammael yawned, dangerously bored and only slightly mellowed by his recent orgasm. "Convenience works both ways," he said. "Now loosen up. The priest is our next entertainment, and I want you to enjoy the show."

Eve pushed aside her doubts and trusted her instincts. "I don't believe Cain has anything to do with this. He's not well, but he isn't a portal to a Hell-layer either. He's got too much good inside him."

"He doesn't understand what's happening to him," Hank argued. "How can we rule anything out?"

"He understands enough to push me away." Her head turned to look into the darkened depths of the room. Compared to the racket the tengu had been making before, he was now eerily silent. "I was too hurt to see it at first, but he's trying to protect me from himself. He proved he still cares last night when he showed up at the stadium. The Cain we know is still in there somewhere. He's not completely possessed."

She looked back at Hank. "He would need to be possessed, right?"

"So I assume, but Cain is a loose cannon right now. There's never been anything like him. We're all learning as we go when it comes to him."

As Eve considered the best way to handle the situation, long moments passed. Her fingers drummed atop the wooden table and her lips pursed. Alec hadn't come to her for help and clearly didn't want it, but she wouldn't let that hold her back. If he came apart at the seams, it would be bad for everyone. Especially for him. She had no doubt the other archangels would kill him.

"Hey." She perked up. "You said he doesn't understand what's happening to him. He came to see you, didn't he? He wanted your help."

"Everyone comes to me for help." He shrugged. "I don't always have the answers, but I appreciate being kept in the loop."

"What answers was he looking for today?"

"Actually, I called him down here to talk about your tengu friend. But we also talked about his unsuitability for the position of archangel."

Eve frowned. "Unsuitability? I think he's perfect for the job. He always takes command of the situations he walks into and he knows this job better than anyone."

His mouth curved. "Cain is a hands-on sort of Mark. He's best in the trenches. There are others who would have been better suited to give interviews to the press and sit in an office."

"Maybe that's his problem," she suggested. "Maybe he just can't handle all the periphery stuff. Just listening to the amount of information flowing through Abel's brain makes my head hurt. It's like standing at the base of Niagara Falls. I can't bear more than a few seconds of it. And Cain skipped right over that section of the information superhighway and jumped headfirst into the part where he's getting a gazillion times more info than that. That could drive a person crazy."

"I suppose. Although I've met other archangels who've disliked it and they didn't fall off the deep end."

Eve thought of the archangels—Sarakiel, Raguel, Michael, Gabriel, Raphael, Uriel, and Remiel. They'd all seemed very comfortable with their jobs. "Which ones? How did they get over it?"

"Chamuel had a hell of a time. I don't think he ever got over it. There were others, but their names escape me now."

Leaning over the table, she asked urgently, "There were more than the seven I've met? Abel has a theory about a possible cap on their number. If he's right, we need to know what happened to the others."

"Your guess is as good as mine." Hank's voice remained raspy and steady. "All I know is that shortly after the firms were created the number of archangels rapidly diminished until only seven remained."

"Why? We need to— *Ow!*" Eve caught her head in her hands. "Shit . . . migraine."

But she didn't get migraines. Hank stood and came up behind her, touching her shoulders. As the pain bore deep, she curled over the table. Then, as suddenly as it had struck, it disappeared. Leaving behind Alec, who was searching through her brain like a spreading flame, licking along the surfaces of her memories.

Alec.

Where have you been?

He sounded just as angry as he'd been before. It had to be exhausting, carrying around all that fury.

Searching for you, she gasped, still reeling from the force of his entry.

Don't. Not safe.

Let me help you!

He began to withdraw in a rush. Eve caught him with both hands, but it was hopeless. He moved too quickly, like smoke sucked out by a vacuum. In an instant, he was gone.

Eve bolted upright. The back of her head cracked into Hank's chin. He cursed and stumbled back.

"Sorry," she cried, jumping to her feet so quickly the chair fell back and hit the floor. "Jeez, Hank. I'm sorry!"

"Bloody H. Christ!" he snapped, holding his chin. "Don't apologize to me. Are you all right?"

She almost ran a hand over her face, then remembered that she was wearing makeup. "It was Alec—*Cain*—digging around in my brain."

"He hurt you?"

Hank's tone alarmed her, so she quickly explained. "He was trying to share information. The other archangels believe that Raguel is dead, but Cain doesn't. He thinks Raguel is alive and that's why he's so messed up. He believes that the number seven is an absolute when it comes to archangels."

"You were in great pain," he insisted, releasing his chin to grip hers. He turned her head from side to side. He snapped his fingers and a handkerchief appeared. He pressed it to her right nostril. "Your nose is bleeding."

"It was like 'e 'ad to punch 'is way in," she mumbled through the cloth.

"He's your firm leader. He shouldn't have to 'punch his way in' to you . . . Ah!" A look of discovery crossed over his face.

"What?"

"Try reaching him again." Hank rushed into the darkness. He shouted over his shoulder as he retreated. "See if you can make contact."

Eve reached out to Alec. Against her nose, the cloth grew warm with blood. She found him, swirling like a hurricane, furious and destructive.

She reached out to his humanity. *I have so much I want to tell you. I want to . . . lean on you.*

The cyclone slowed marginally, then swayed. Alec didn't say a word, but she could feel him softening.

You owe me, she prodded, *after the shitty way you treated me yesterday.*

I did you a favor.

She snorted. *Bite me.*

Watch out. His voice changed, taking on a singsong note of madness that gave her chills. *I just might.*

"Here." Hank appeared out of nowhere, tossing the necklace at her. It whipped through the air and she ducked, avoiding a lash to the face. But when it neared her, it opened, lassoing her neck in a way that would be impossible without some preternatural means.

And like a dropped cell phone signal, her line to Alec died abruptly.

She blinked at Hank. The mark had done its job and healed the injury to her nose, but the deeper ramifications lingered.

Dropping the hand holding the handkerchief, she asked, "What happened?"

The occultist crossed his arms and looked thoughtful. "That piece of jewelry appears to put a damper on an Infernal's powers."

"I thought it only worked on the Nix."

He shrugged. In the back of the room, the tengu began to screech and bang against something metallic. A cage perhaps.

"Why would a charm against Infernals work against Cain?"

"We're circling back to my theory now, aren't we?"

"But I don't—"

The tengu continued his tirade.

"Can you shut that thing up?" she yelled. Bending down, Eve righted the fallen chair.

Hank nodded and gestured for her to follow. The spot of illumination followed them, a trick she wished she knew how to pull off herself.

As she'd suspected, the tengu was caged in what looked to be a large dog kennel. He clung from the top with fingers and toes, shaking and shouting violently.

Fred stood nearby, taking notes on a clipboard. She glanced up at Hank and nodded at whatever cue he'd given her. Turning, she set the clipboard on a lab counter, then grabbed a canister that had a nozzle like a fire extinguisher. She aimed it at the tengu and sprayed a reddish cloud of fine mist at him. He sputtered and coughed, causing him to lose his grip and crash to the bottom. He lay there for a spell, shaking his head and appearing nearly as dazed as he had while wearing the necklace. The red liquid was quickly absorbed into his cement shell, leaving him looking the same as always. Hank spoke a lyrical incantation, and the tengu sat up and looked at Eve.

"Pretty Mark," he said, hopping to his feet.

"You're a noisy fellow," she replied.

He moved his gaze to glare at Hank. "Traitor."

Eve leaned toward the occultist and whispered, "What was in the can?"

"Infernal blood."

She almost asked where he got it, but decided she didn't want to know. "Demons find demon blood soothing? We could win the war with that. Kill some, spray the others."

"It wouldn't have any effect on a healthy Infernal. In this case, it's just canceling out the overdose of Mark blood I gave him earlier. I doubt you want to try your scenario with Mark blood."

"Right." Moving closer to the cage, Eve studied the little stone beast. "That was a very ferocious reaction this guy had."

"Oil and water," Fred said. "Infernal and Mark don't mix."

"No kidding."

"About the Nix." Hank walked over to the counter where Fred had set down the clipboard.

"Yes?"

"I dug out that punch bowl you brought me before. I know Cain wanted me to scry for the Nix through any residuals that might be on it, but I'm afraid that isn't possible."

"Oh." Her nose wrinkled. "Would have made things easier, but since he's after me, we'll see him again regardless."

Thanks to the necklace, the Nix was the least of her problems at the moment. She pushed thoughts of him aside for more pressing problems.

"Right, but using a combination of bits and pieces of the mask, I was thinking I could create a repellent of some sort."

Her brows rose. "Unless it's a permanent repellant, I think I'd rather just kill the sucker and be done with it."

"Well, I didn't know about the necklace at the time." Hank leaned into the counter with one hand and set the other on his hip. It was a very feminine pose and made her smile. "Now that I do, I'm thinking I might be able to tweak it in the reverse."

"Reverse?"

"Make you more attractive. Irresistible."

"She doesn't need any help being irresistible."

Alec's low, deep voice hit her ears just before she registered the sound of his boots thudding rhythmically onto the cement floor. He appeared out of the darkness, wild-eyed and dangerous, the veins in his forearms and biceps thick and visible. She might have swooned if she was the type and Unmarked. As it was, she licked her lips. She'd always had a thing for his bad boy vibe, but this . . . yowza.

"You resisted me well enough earlier," she managed.

He kept on coming, a raging force of nature that pinned her against the cage holding the tengu.

His hand caught the back of her neck. "Don't you *ever* hang up on me."

Her shoulders went back. "What are you going to do about it if I do?"

As she'd thought he might, he yanked her closer and kissed her, his lips mashing hers without any semblance of finesse.

His hand at her nape moved, sliding around in a quest for her breast, focused solely on his animal urges despite their audience. Reaching up, she caught the necklace chain. She pulled it up and over her head, then dropped it around his neck.

Alec froze. There was an awkward moment when they stood like statues with their lips pressed together.

What the hell?

Eve pushed him back and moved away from the cage where the mischievous tengu had been poking her in the butt with his stubby fingers. She studied Alec, noting the drastic change in his eyes and stance.

Sucking in a deep breath, she greeted the Alec she knew. "Hi."

He frowned at her.

"How do you feel?" she asked.

Hank sidled closer. "Yes. How do you feel, Cain?"

"How the fuck am I supposed to feel?" he barked, but it lacked bite. He scrubbed both hands over his face, as he did when first waking up in the morning.

"Not angry?" Eve suggested. "In control?"

Alec lifted the amulet and stared at it. "What is this?"

"A lucky charm."

"Lucky for whom?" His gaze lifted and met hers. A pained look crossed his face. Guilt settled like a heavy stone in her gut. Not hers. His.

"Lucky for us," she said. They'd deal with guilt later. "We need you on top of your game now. If decking you out in a pimp chain does the trick, I'm all for it."

"Where did you get this?"

"I tossed it to her," Hank improvised. "It's something I'm working on." Eve shot him a grateful glance.

"Whatever it is," Alec said, "it's perfect. Glad something is working out for us in the experimental department."

His head tilted to the side as if hearing something she couldn't, then, "Montevista woke up. I need to talk to him."

Hoping the guard would be able to tell Alec what she couldn't, Eve said, "Go check it out."

"You're coming with me." He gave her a stern look. "I need to talk to you, too. Best to get you, Sydney, and Montevista together, and see if we can figure out what happened last night."

"I still have some business with Hank," she protested.

He looked at the occultist. "He's not making you anything to attract the Nix. That's an order."

Hank lifted his hands in a gesture of surrender. "I have no idea if I can pull it off, but if I could, it can help you set the time and place of the showdown to your liking."

"That could come in handy," Eve pointed out.

"Like you don't have enough Infernal trouble with the bounty?" Alec scoffed, tugging her toward the door.

She waved bye to Hank before they moved too far away and he was lost in the darkness.

If I could get Gadara back, she wondered, *what would happen to Alec?*

She'd like to ask whoever endorsed Alec's promotion, but that could run the risk of them killing him. If Alec was the emissary, they wouldn't hesitate.

He's not the emissary, she scolded herself. Besides, she didn't have a clue about who was responsible.

A sudden image of eyes the color of blue flame filled her mind. She almost set the thought aside, telling herself that of course she would think of him. He was the only seraph she'd ever met.

Then, she realized the thought came from Reed.

Chaney slumped back into the plastic chair, clearly taken aback. "I knew you hated your brother, but this . . . Aren't you going to get in trouble for this?"

"Actually," Reed picked up his beer, "I'm sanctioned."

"Someone gave you the authority to get rid of Cain?" Asmodeus was clearly disbelieving.

Reed considered how much to reveal. "Something went wrong with the ascension. He's a danger to himself and to others."

"We could use a man like him."

"He'll be fatally wounded by the absence of God in his soul, I suspect. Worthless to everyone." Reed looked at the increasing number of tourists as the amount of Infernals grew in proportion. Casting a glance into the dark interior of the restaurant, he regretted his decision to sit outside. The same exposure that gave him a modicum of safety around Asmodeus also bared him to any of the dozens of Marks policing the overabundance of demons in the area. They were too visible out here.

"A fate worse than death for you guys, eh?" Chaney cut into his rare steak and bit into a piece with relish. "Hope I never get on your bad side."

"Then don't fuck up this exchange."

"How do you propose we do this?" Asmodeus asked, poking at his VooDoo Shrimp appetizer with his fork.

"I need you to bring the Nix," Reed murmured, twisting his beer bottle to catch the sunlight. "But rein him in. He needs to be a threat, nothing more. Cain will come to the rescue and I'll make sure there's no one around to get in the way."

"What about Raguel and the priest?" Chaney licked blood off his lips. "Who's going to play the hero? You?"

"No. Let them escape."

"What are you getting out of this, then?"

"The seraph who endorsed Cain wants his mess disposed of," he lied. "That's a favor I can call in later. And without Cain, Evangeline Hollis serves no purpose. Raguel will appreciate both the loss of his replacement and the end of the bounty. Again, another favor to call in at a later date."

"Lose one, save many."

Asmodeus's fork tapped against the edge of his plate. "I'll need help to pull down Cain."

"That's your problem," Reed dismissed. "Not mine. However you go about doing it, just show up the day after tomorrow at Hollis's condominium complex. The Nix knows where she lives, if you don't. Say . . . midafternoon? We'll be out by the pool. I'll open the water lines so the

Nix can get in. He can be the distraction while you do whatever you have to do."

"That place is a fortress," Asmodeus growled. "It will be an all-out bloodbath."

"Which is why you better make damn sure that Raguel and the priest are already on the move, if you want to avoid pegging yourself with a Vanquish Me sign."

"Pick a different place," Chaney said.

"Can't," Reed retorted curtly. "After the way the priest was snatched, Hollis is locked up tight. It's either her home or work, and there's no way you're getting into Gadara Tower. We all know that."

"Shit."

"No," Asmodeus said. "I'll wait until things settle down, then I'll go after her when it's more convenient."

Reed's foot tapped silently beneath the table. He'd prefer to wait, too, but the priest wouldn't make it that long. And if the priest died, Eve would never forgive herself. "She and the priest might be dead by then."

"I would rather lose them," Asmodeus snapped, "than me."

"You might lose Cain, too, if he doesn't get his shit together." Standing, Reed pulled his money clip from his pocket and tossed a couple of twenty-dollar bills onto the table. "You know where I'll be, if you change your mind."

"I don't like being played with, Abel."

Reed's mouth curved. "You won't know if I'm playing with you, unless you show up."

"Mariel? Are you all right?"

Mariel pulled her gaze away from the party sitting on the patio of the House of Blues and returned it to her companion. The balcony of Ralph Brennan's Jazz Kitchen was across the busy promenade from the other restaurant, but Mariel's *mal'akh* hearing had no trouble picking up the treasonous conversation taking place there. Even from this distance, she could see the laser brightness of the demon's eyes and hear the malevolence in his voice.

"No," she replied in her Mark's native Zulu. "I'm far from all right."

"What—"

"Don't." She stayed Kobe Denner from turning his head with her hand atop his. "What you don't know can save your life."

Kobe frowned at her, his dark eyes concerned. One of her best Marks, he'd been with her for years. "What can I do?"

"I think we're going to have to end our lunch early."

He pushed his half-finished meal away. "Of course. Go, if you must."

Mariel bunched up the napkin in her lap and set it on the table. "I'm going to shift you out of here. I don't want you to be seen."

Her urgency was conveyed in her tone. He stood quickly. She dug into her purse and left some cash on the table. They gave a quick explanation to the startled waiter before making their way down to the lower floor.

Ducking into the hallway that led to the bathrooms, Mariel quickly shifted them back to the tower.

Alec dragged Eve down the hall and around the corner. There was an alcove with a water fountain and he crowded her into it, pressing her into a corner and cupping her face in his hands.

"I'm fucked up," he said bluntly.

"I'm not exactly prime goods either." Her tone was dry, but her dark eyes glistened in the shadowy hallway.

"We need to talk about the personal stuff later." He touched his forehead to hers, feeling as thrashed as he did after a particularly nasty vanquishing. "It's ugly and painful, but we have something worth fighting for, if you give me a chance to fix this mess."

He felt her fingers hook into the belt loops of his jeans. "Yes. We need to talk."

Alec sensed a shiver of wariness move across her mind, but he couldn't read the details. Still, that shiver was more than he'd been able to get out of her the last couple of days.

"Are you blocking me?" he asked harshly. "Or is my . . . *condition* causing a poor signal between us?"

"A little of both, maybe," she confessed, tucking the necklace into his shirt. "When I tell you something, I want to do it the mortal way. You and me. Talking out loud. Unhurried and in private."

"Okay. As soon as we get done here." He tugged her out of the alcove with him.

"I have to go to the police station after this."

As they hurried down the hallway, she filled him in.

"Okay." His fingers tightened on hers. "We'll go together."

"Ishamel is going to take me. Part of his lawyer act. It might look weird if you came along."

"Why?"

"Uh . . ." Eve glanced aside at him and winced. "I kinda told them that we broke up."

Alec was grateful his step didn't falter, since he felt like he'd been punched in the gut. He exhaled harshly. "That was quick."

"Cut me some slack. Things are flying at me from all sides. I said what I needed to say at the time."

He didn't have a firm foundation to stand on, since he was the one who'd pushed her away. But that didn't make things easier. "As long as you weren't serious."

She squeezed his hand back. "One thing at a time."

His hand was on the knob to the infirmary when he heard Eve's name being called. He looked around and saw Mariel approaching with an unusually brisk stride.

"Evangeline," the handler called out. "Can you spare a minute of your time?"

Alec released the knob. "What do you need, Mariel?"

"Just Hollis." Her smile was so slight it was more of a grimace. "Girl stuff, Cain. You know?"

"No, I don't." He glanced at Eve. "Come in as soon as you're done."

She nodded. "Of course."

Feeling like something precious was slipping through his fingers, Alec left her in the hallway.

Eve didn't need the ability to read minds to know that the *mal'akh* was terribly upset. The fact that Alec didn't fully pick up on his handler's agitation was further proof that he was still seriously out of whack. Mariel knew it, too. Her gaze remained on the door until it closed with a firm click.

"He's not well," Eve said softly. "I'm guessing you feel it through the connection between handler and firm leader."

"I'm hoping he adjusts soon, but right now, his inability to read us is a blessing in disguise." Mariel turned her attention to Eve. "We have a serious problem. I fear for his safety and Abel's. You're the only one I can trust to find a solution that keeps them both alive."

"What's going on?"

"Something isn't right with Abel. He's not himself. You're not going to believe it when I tell you."

Not himself . . .

Gripping Mariel's elbow, Eve pulled her a short distance down the hall. "Tell me everything . . ."

CHAPTER 17

I don't remember much of anything," Sydney said with a turned-down mouth and averted gaze. "I was eyeing some movement under the bleachers when Montevista tackled me. I must have been knocked out by the impact. The next thing I knew, you were waking me up, Cain."

Alec turned his attention to Montevista, who looked as miserable as Sydney.

"I've got nothing," the Mark said. "I don't even remember *that* much. I was standing along the fence, mad dogging some Infernals. Then I was here in the tower."

Both guards sat at a metal table dressed in pale blue hospital scrubs. Alec sat across from them, hyperaware of the pendant heating the skin between his pectorals. Something had to give, and fast. Lack of sleep was taking its toll, but he needed to be available to help Eve during the day and he had inquiries to make about his condition when she was sleeping at night.

He glanced at the witch doctor who ran the infirmary. The woman was short, no more than three feet tall, with cropped blonde curls, and a child's features. "Any idea what happened to those two?"

"They both check out," she said. "In Sydney's case, I think she lost consciousness on impact, as she suggested. In Montevista's . . . I'm not sure. I'm inclined to think he jumped in the way of a direct hit. Maybe an energy blast aimed at her. An impact to the back of the head would have knocked him out and caused him to crash into her. Something like that would explain the memory loss, especially if Azazel was the one attacking."

"What are the aftereffects? Are there any?"

"Fatigue. Otherwise, no."

"I'd like to get back to duty," Montevista said.

"Me, too," Sydney concurred.

"Are you sure you don't want some time off?" Alec asked, probing their minds for any traces of trauma.

The search was difficult, mostly because of the suppression of the voices inside his head. Their absence left an odd quiet within him; not a departure, more an anticipation. He knew something wasn't right. He was just waiting for the explosion to prove it.

Montevista nodded and spoke for both of them. "We're sure."

A brief knock came at the door, then it opened and Eve stepped in. She moved straight to the two guards with arms open. They stood, hugging her in return. It was her way. She was so open, so willing to connect to others. Eve let people in from the get-go and hoped they would turn out to be worthy friends. So opposite from him, who had learned to keep people at arm's length until they proved they deserved otherwise.

She asked about their health and how they were feeling. When they requested to resume guarding her, she accepted readily. No recriminations, no guilt trips. The two Marks were clearly relieved.

Looking over her shoulder at Alec, she said, "Is that okay?"

For a second he tensed, expecting the compulsion to say something unkind. He'd begun to feel the way he imagined Tourette's syndrome patients felt, spewing out words before his brain registered them. When the voices remained silent, he grinned.

"Whoa," Sydney murmured.

"Yeah, sucker punches me, too," Eve muttered.

As long as he could still get to her, all wasn't lost.

"I have no objections, if you're all okay with it," he said. "But I want to keep you two out of the field for a couple days, at least."

"Works for me," Eve agreed. "After I hit the police station, I'm going home and staying there. How about they head over there with you now? They can rest in my place while you catch up on some downtime with your folks."

"My folks?" He rose to his feet.

The knowing look in her eyes answered his unspoken question.

Alec looked at the Marks. "Get dressed. I'll be back in a few."

"We'll be ready," Montevista said gruffly.

Heading toward the door, Alec gestured with a jerk of his chin for Eve to come along. He caught her elbow at the threshold and urged her out ahead of him. They passed neat rows of hospital beds, most of which were empty, and exited back out to the smoky hallway.

"You met my parents."

"Yep. Your mom and dad came over last night."

His jaw clenched. He'd known Ima wouldn't let it go until she'd met Eve face to face. His mother wasn't the type to wait until he was nearby to alleviate her curiosity. "Did you like them?"

He saw the right corner of her mouth lift in a slight smile. "Love them. They're both very charming. I think they might like me, too. They seemed as if they did. It was hard to read your dad. But you've met mine, he's really reserved, too. I didn't take it personally."

She stopped beside the alcove he'd caught her in before, and faced him.

He loved her like this, all prim and proper in her business attire. He couldn't help but note the changes the years had wrought in her, turning her into a formidable woman. Freed momentarily from his personal demons, his chest swelled with affection and pride.

"Forgetting you and me for the moment," she began, knocking his ass back into the present, "you need to decide how badly you want this archangel gig."

She pressed her fingers to his lips when he started to speak. "Think about it. Running with the theory that seven archangels is the limit—what's going to happen when we get Gadara back? Are you going to take him on? Step aside? Take out one of the others? How will you feel if God decides he likes things the way they were and knocks you back down to Mark?"

The determined glint in her dark eyes told him that he'd better keep his silence for now and pretend that he was still undecided. He'd learned long ago that women wanted men to overthink things like they did.

"And," she continued, backing up, "I don't mean to heap added pressure on your decision, but I won't invest myself in a relationship with someone who can't love me."

"Angel—"

"Hey." Her voice was husky. "No hard feelings, if it works out that way. I haven't forgotten that we were always going to be temporary."

As Alec started toward her, a familiar figure rounded the corner behind her. Alec's fists clenched.

"*Eve.*"

She turned around at the sound of Abel's greeting. To Alec's surprise, her fists clenched, too. "What?"

Abel's eyes narrowed at her tone. "You ready to go home?"

"I have to go to the police station and give a report."

"Okay." Abel's gaze lifted to Alec's, but he continued to speak to Eve. "I'll give you a lift."

"That's not necessary. I'm riding with Ishamel."

"Why?"

So . . . Abel couldn't read her either. She was like a radio station with static. A problem they'd have to look into.

The tempo of her walk changed, the click of her heels betraying agitation.

Go home, she told Alec sternly. *Park Montevista and Sydney in front of my Wii and don't let your parents out of your sight for even a minute until I get there.*

And here I thought I was running the show.

After I get back, you can go do whatever you want, she offered.

Whatever I want, huh?

But if you take that necklace off, I'll kick your ass.

What do I get if I keep it on?

She stalked right past Abel. *Keep the necklace on, keep a lid on your parents, and it'll keep you on my good side.*

After yesterday, he couldn't ask for more. But she didn't know about that . . . yet. *I've got shit to do, angel.*

After your personality transplant yesterday, I still trust you, she argued. *You owe me a little trust in return.*

I trust you.

Good. Then do as I say. I'll see you later.

He wasn't used to following orders from anyone but Jehovah. But she was right, he owed her. And he was exhausted. He hadn't slept in almost two days. That was too long even for an archangel. He'd take a nap, then track down Sabrael when Eve returned.

Abel pivoted and followed her around the corner. Alec had no idea what his brother had done to piss her off, but he was glad they were both on the outs with her.

He tried to tell her that he'd have dinner waiting, but the connection was static again.

They'd *really* have to talk about that when she got back.

"Let me guess," Reed drawled. "You're mad at me."

Eve reached the elevators and stabbed the call button with her finger. "I don't have time to play games with you now."

He moved in front of her, forcing her to look at him. As with Alec, the sight of him made her a bit weak in the knees, despite what an asshole he could be. "How many times do I have to tell you, Eve? I'm not playing with you."

Her lips pursed. "You know 'The Gift of the Magi'?" Not the biblical story; the one by O. Henry."

"Who doesn't?" His dark eyes narrowed.

"You and I are working at cross purposes now, Reed. I know what I'm doing, you don't. Take my advice and take a trip somewhere. Come back in a few days."

"Eve." He caught her hand. "What are you talking about?"

He had a great game face, but she knew him well enough to sense that his guard was up. Guilty as charged, apparently. But she believed he was trying to do the right thing—to get Gadara and the priest back, and save her from the Nix. However, she didn't doubt for a minute that Reed was willing to let Alec be collateral damage. Fratricide was ingrained in them, but damned if she'd be the cause of either of their deaths.

She felt him trying to probe her mind. She pulled away, breaking the physical contact between them. "I have to run. Think about that story. Tack an unhappy ending onto it and that's what you'll get if you don't back off."

The elevator dinged and the doors opened.

"*Abel.*"

They both turned their heads to see Sara approaching. Eve ducked into the car while Reed was distracted, and hit the button for the lobby.

"Hey." He caught the door before it closed. "What the hell?"

Eve pushed his hand out of the way. "Your brother isn't expendable to me, Reed."

He stared at her with a hard gaze until the doors shut.

Once she reached the lobby, she switched elevators to catch the one that would take her up to her office on the forty-fifth floor. The number of Marks in the tower was declining steadily as the workday winded down, allowing the sickly sweet scent of their souls to settle down to a manageable level.

As Eve entered the reception area, Candace stood and offered a slight wave. Eve smiled in greeting.

"Ishamel said he'd be here at four-thirty," the secretary reported, rounding her desk with message pad in hand.

"Perfect." Eve headed toward her office.

"You have an e-mail from your sister, and also one from Sarakiel that's marked urgent."

Eve paused and Candace almost ran into her from behind. "If it's urgent, why didn't she just call and tell me? She's got my number."

"There's an attachment, so that might be why. Want something to drink?"

"No, thank you. You can go home now."

Eve went to her desk and sat before her computer. She accessed her e-mail and read her sister Sophia's note first. Pictures of Eve's niece and nephew filled the screen and caused her a pang of envy. She was the eldest, but Sophia was years ahead of her when it came to settling down. And as long as Eve had the mark, she would remain behind. Marks were sterile.

She typed out a quick "as soon as I can" reply to Sophie's query about when she'd be coming to visit. Then, she reclined into her chair and took a moment to push past unwelcome feelings of resentment.

As she often did at times like these, she glanced around her office, taking in the mixture of traditional modern and Asian-inspired bamboo pieces that made up the décor. Most of the furnishings had been moved from her previous, much smaller office at the Weisenberg Group. Part of the effort to blend her old life with her new. That's what she remembered when she felt down—that she'd been allowed to blend her two lives together. None of the other Marks were so lucky.

Refocused, she straightened and clicked open Sara's e-mail. The name of the attachment that came with it gave her pause, since it was clearly a recording of a video feed from "CainOffice" made yesterday. Had Sara become aware of Alec's problems? How much danger was he in if she had?

Eve double-clicked on the video and waited for it to load.

Once the replay began, it took her a minute to comprehend what she was watching. It took a bit longer to break the stillness caused by horror, freeing her to kick the computer's power cord out of the outlet in the floor. The monitor turned black and the computer's cooling fan stopped, leaving behind an empty silence.

Breathing in and out deliberately, Eve leaned into her desk and tried to forget what she'd seen.

"T-that wasn't Alec," she told herself. "That wasn't him. You know it."

It's ugly and painful, but we have something worth fighting for . . .

He meant to tell her. She knew it. Lay it all out there and hope she'd understand. But she was still jealous and pissed off.

Standing, Eve began to pace. Her emotions wanted an outlet and there wasn't one. From the expression on Alec's face, he had been as much of a victim as Izzie. Whatever comeuppance the German bitch deserved for making a play at another woman's man had been served during the act.

Which left only Sara.

Eve stopped at the window and leaned against the console positioned in front of it. What the hell had the archangel hoped to gain by sending that video to her? Sara wanted her away from Reed, so why send her something that was troubling enough to push her right into his arms? Hell hath no fury like a woman scorned, right? Sara had to know that if Eve was pissed at Alec, the best way to pay him back in kind was to hook up with Reed.

"What do you want, Sara?" Eve wondered aloud, her fingers digging into lip of the console. "What do you stand to gain?"

Hell hath no fury—

Her eyes widened, her mind jumping to the conversation she'd had with Mariel . . .

"Are you ready to go, Ms. Hollis?"

Turning her attention to the door, she found Ishamel standing there.

"What are you to Raguel Gadara?" she asked, straightening.

His gray brows rose. "I beg your pardon?"

"You're his lieutenant, right? His right-hand man?"

"Something like that."

Eve nodded. "Is it just a job to you, or do you genuinely care about him?"

There was a slight hesitation, then, "Raguel is a friend to me."

"Is. Present tense." She stopped in front of him. "You think he's alive, too."

He gave a brief nod.

"Do you have access to everything? Can you authorize investigations?"

"What do you want, Ms. Hollis?"

She caught his arm and directed him toward the door. "Call me Eve, please. And don't shift us downstairs. Makes me dizzy. Let's do things the mortal way, if you don't mind."

Again, the terse nod of his head.

"Now," she continued, "I don't know if you'll believe me or not, but I want Gadara back, too."

They moved out to the hallway and turned toward the elevators.

"And how do you plan to get him back . . . Eve?"

"I'm afraid I can't tell you that."

Ishamel stared at her intensely the entire length of the descent to the lobby level. Despite her determination, it still made her squirm. He had the eyes of a shark. Dark and dead.

They exited to the circular driveway. Idling near the center fountain, the requisite limousine waited. At least it was requisite for Ishamel. Eve was more interested in Reed's Lamborghini, which he'd arrogantly left parked directly in front of the entrance. The convertible was a silver beauty, as sleek and dangerous as its owner. She pictured him driving over from his meeting with the demons at Downtown Disney and her jaw clenched. Instead of shifting from location to location, he'd used the car for effect. Maybe as a way to humanize himself, to seem at ease and unconcerned when meeting with a king of Hell. Bravado was a necessary tool of the trade when dealing with demons.

She glanced at the valet booth and pointed to the Lamborghini. "Do you have the keys for this?"

One of the three valets nodded but looked wary.

Ishamel snapped his fingers and the valet kicked into gear, ducking inside the booth to pull keys off one of the many hooks on the wall. He ran over to them and Eve held out her hand.

"Thanks," she said when he dropped the key ring into her palm.

She pulled open the passenger door for Ishamel before running around to the driver's side. Sliding behind the wheel, she adjusted the seat forward, then gripped the steering wheel with both hands.

"Wish I hadn't left my sunglasses at home," she murmured, half afraid to borrow Reed's car without permission. He might find it amusing, or he might be furious.

Ishamel held his hand out and she found her sunglasses clasped between his fingers. With a wry smile, she accepted them. It sure would be handy to be able to shift anywhere and back in the blink of an eye. She pushed the key into the ignition and turned the engine over. It roared to life, then purred deliciously.

"Seat belt," she said, while securing her own.

Then they were off, gliding around the center fountain and exiting onto Harbor Boulevard. The police station was on the same street just a few miles down. Eve told herself that Reed shouldn't get too pissy, since she was just taking a straight shot up the road.

"What do you need from me?" Ishamel asked.

"Can you . . ." She hesitated, then glanced over at him. "Would you be open to spying on an archangel? Do you have people who'd be capable and willing to do it?"

"Cain?"

She sucked in a deep breath and hoped that she wasn't screwing herself royally. "Sarakiel."

"Ah . . ." In the periphery of her vision, she saw his fingertips drum silently on the seat. "And you need this information for use in retrieving Raguel? Are you certain you don't have personal considerations?"

"You don't have to tell me what you find," she said. "Just look into it and if something strikes you as off, deal with it as you see fit."

"An odd request," he murmured.

"Trust me, if you find what I suspect you might, there won't be any doubt that it isn't personal."

He didn't say anything. Eve hoped that he was thinking it over.

A few minutes later they pulled into the parking lot of the police station and she slid the car into a diagonal space that had empty spots on either side. She didn't want to have to explain a door ding to Reed on top of the grand-theft auto.

They entered the station and shortly after, Ingram joined them from somewhere in the back. He led them to a room with a beat-up table and a large two-way mirror. A form and a pen waited there. He directed her to sit and give her statement regarding what she remembered in as much detail as possible.

Eve sat and began to write. Ishamel moved to the far corner and sat in a chair with his eyes closed. He looked as if he was napping, but she suspected he was sending orders to whoever fell under his purview.

She was halfway through her second page when the door opened. The stench of Infernal assaulted her nose and her head snapped up. A uniformed officer entered the room with a bottle of water in his hand. She watched, wide-eyed, as he set it on the table. His mouth curved in a malevolent smile. His detail crawled up from beneath his shirt, coming to rest over his Adam's apple. It was an insignificant design as suited a lesser demon.

"Thought you might like something to drink," the demon said in a friendly voice designed to fool those who might be watching through the glass. Eve got a different show from the front. His lip curled back, revealing the pointed canines of a vampire. "Holler if you'd like anything else. There are plenty of us out there."

Sitting back slowly, she glanced at Ishamel. He hadn't moved, but his eyes were open. The Infernal didn't pay him any mind. Eve didn't know if that was because he was stupid and couldn't pick out a celestial without a Mark's scent, or if he was so cocky he didn't view a *mal'akh* as a threat.

"Thanks," she said aloud. Then, she spoke through her smile. "The bounty's over."

"I ain't heard that," he hissed back. "Lying bitch."

The Infernal departed, but his stench lingered, capping off what had been a brief but crappy day. She set her pen down.

Either the demon was seriously out of the loop, or Sammael had reneged on his end of the deal. She wished she knew which one was true.

"We should go," Ishamel said. His lips moved without sound, *Before too many of his friends arrive.*

I'll finish this later. Eve wrote a quick "to be continued . . ." on the page, then stood.

Ingram was at the door the moment she opened it. "Are you done? Before you leave, I'd like to go over your statement with you."

"No, not done yet," she said, glancing to the left and right, highly conscious of the number of eyes watching her.

It wasn't safe for her to be out anywhere with a price tag stapled to her forehead. Not that she could tell Ingram that. What could be safer than a police station, right?

"We need that report, Ms. Hollis," he said sternly, his mustache twitching in a way that hinted at impatience. "It's vital to our getting a clear picture of what happened."

"I'm sorry. I didn't realize it would take this long." She touched his arm, but pulled back when he tensed. "I borrowed my friend's car—since you have mine—and I have to get it back to him."

"It's only been thirty minutes," he pointed out.

"My client is very busy," Ishamel said smoothly.

"Can you come by the tower for the rest?" Eve asked, regretting that she was taking up the detectives' precious time. They should be working on crimes they could solve, not dicking around with her. "Do I *have* to fill it out here?"

He frowned.

Jones appeared behind him. Shorter and lighter than his partner, he'd approached stealthily. "I'll give you a call in the morning and set up a time."

"Good. Thanks." Eve shook both their hands quickly. "I'm sorry for the inconvenience."

Ishamel caught her arm and steered her toward the door. "When we get outside the front doors, I'll shift us back to the tower."

"I can't leave another car behind. You'll have to come back and get it."

"I don't drive. Abel will have to do it."

"You *don't*—"

They'd barely put their hands on the handle of the double doors when they were ambushed. Bold as you please. Shoved outside with hurricane force.

Ishamel sailed into the landscaping on the right side of the door. Eve was sent spinning like a top on the ball of one foot, making a few revolutions before she stumbled to halt.

"Ms. Hollis."

She looked at the door and saw Jones standing on the threshold, holding it open. She brushed flyaway tendrils of hair back from her face. "Yes?"

He looked around her. She did, too, trying to see where Ishamel might have gone. The only evidence of the tackle was some broken branches on one of the bushes and some fine ash that bore witness to the death of an Infernal. The *mal'akh* himself was gone, most likely shifted away to avoid being seen.

"Where did your lawyer go?" the detective asked.

"Bathroom."

Jones frowned, but nodded. "I was wondering. The car you borrowed . . ." He looked beyond her to the parking lot and whistled. "It *is* the Lamborghini."

"Uh . . . yes."

"Mind if I check it out?"

"Uh . . ." Shit. Her gaze darted around the lot again. It looked peaceful enough, but she didn't want to risk the cop, too. Infernals had already proven that they'd take anyone, anywhere, anytime.

The door opened again and Ishamel stepped out, looking none the worse for wear. She breathed a sigh of relief.

Jones was already walking toward Reed's car. Eve rushed to catch up. Ishamel followed at a more discreet pace.

It would be safer to shift, the *mal'akh* said. *But it appears we have no choice.*

She disengaged the car locks and alarm with the remote, and Jones opened the driver's-side door. He glanced over his shoulder at her. "No scissor doors?"

Eve gave a clueless shrug.

The detective stood in the V of the open door and looked at the interior. With the top down, he had an unobstructed view. She glanced at Ishamel, who stood guard on the other side. The feel of Infernal eyes was strong.

If they could just get in the car . . .

"Very nice," Jones said. "How does it drive?"

"Like a dream," she said, with a smile that felt strained. "Detective, I'm sorry. I really do have to run."

"Right." He backed out of the way. "I'll give your office a call tomorrow."

"Great."

Eve hopped into the car and got it started. Ishamel waited until she put the transmission in reverse before climbing in beside her.

Jones stood nearby, watching them with an eagle eye. The detective didn't trust her as far as he could throw her.

Backing out of the spot, she hit the road.

It was hard driving while trying to keep an eye on any possible threats. Eve relaxed slightly when they reached the intersection of Katella and Harbor, feeling somewhat safer in a crowd. The sidewalks were clogged with tourists and business-attired pedestrians leaving the convention center. The excited screams of riders on the various California Adventure amusement park attractions competed with the thumping bass of a nearby car radio. There was a tiny souvenir shop next to the 7-Eleven on the corner; its wares spilling over into its equally tiny parking lot. Customers picked through racks of Disney- and California-themed T-shirts, while a postcard display stand reminded Eve of unfinished business.

"Would you investigate a postcard I received right after I was marked?" she asked, returning her attention to the road. "It came from Gadara Enterprises, so someone there has to be responsible for it."

"What do you want to know?"

The tower was only a short distance away but from the looks of things, Eve was pretty sure Ishamel had already called in reinforcements. There seemed to be an inordinate number of white Chevrolet Suburbans around them.

"Well, for starters," she said, "who sent it. I want to ask them why."

A police car flashed its lights and chirped its sirens until it maneuvered into position directly behind her.

"Jesus," she breathed, wincing at the burn of her mark. "Is he trying to pull me over?"

Ishamel looked over his shoulder. "I sent it."

"*What?* Why?" She eyed the cop through the rearview mirror. The Infernal revved his engine and grinned beneath his shades. The vamp again. Her hands fisted on the wheel.

The Lamborghini was at the light, first one on the line, but in the middle of the multilane road. She was stuck until the signal changed.

"Divine compulsion, perhaps?" Ishamel replied. "I saw the postcard on Raguel's desk and thought it might pique your interest. The building wasn't done and it needed a designer."

"If you're trying to say that it had nothing to do with turning me into a Mark, I don't believe you."

He looked at her, then resumed staring at the squad car behind them. "It had everything to do with the Change. You were agnostic. Appealing to your secular talents was a substitution for appealing to your faith, which is why Raguel scheduled a job interview with you. The postcard was meant to be a follow-up, an added lure. But Raguel was called away and Abel was . . . *impatient*. You were marked before it reached you."

The opposing traffic light changed, turning yellow. Eve prepared to hit the gas. "What about the tengu?"

"I didn't know about the tengu. As I said, perhaps it was a divine compulsion. Not all coincidences are bad, after all."

An eighteen-wheeler barreled west down Katella. As the pedestrian countdown timer began to flash red, the semi's front tires crossed over the line.

The demon revved his engine again. She pretended to run her hand over her chignon to disguise flipping him the bird. He slammed into her, shoving her forward into the middle of the intersection.

The semi hit its horn. Eve saw her reflection in the chrome grill and screamed.

CHAPTER 18

"Look at that car, Adam. There's nothing left of it."

Alec kept his eyes closed and pretended he was sleeping. His mother's fascination with the news and daytime drama programming was beyond his understanding. Why couldn't she watch chick flicks or the action movies Eve favored? Instead, she'd been surfing through cable news stations since the soap operas had ended, switching channels whenever a commercial popped up.

A soft snore from the opposite couch told Alec that his dad had managed to crash. Alec couldn't, and not just because his mother insisted he hang out in the living room with them. His hand kept straying to his chest, rubbing at the amulet even as his mind pondered how the thing worked. Good luck charm? Bullshit. It was designed to repress something, and he wanted to know what it was. What was in him that was affected by the amulet, and how did Hank create the suppressant?

"Those expensive sports cars fall apart when they get hit," his mother continued. "If Abel wasn't a *mal'akh,* I'd make him get rid of that car of his. The one on TV is just like his and look at it now, you can't even tell it used to be a car. I can't believe a police officer was responsible for such a horrible accident."

Alec opened one eye and glanced at the TV. The reporter stood on the corner, pointing at the vehicle splattered like a bug against the grill of an eighteen-wheeler truck.

". . . there are said to have been several repair requests on file for the police cruiser—a Ford Crown Victoria—involved in this accident. It is not yet known whether the patrol car malfunctioned or if driver error played a part in this tragedy. The name of the officer involved and the identities of the occupants of the Lamborghini convertible have not yet been released."

Alec froze, realizing that the twisted and charred metal on the screen was silver not due to chipped paint, but because silver had been the color of the car.

He bolted upright. *Abel!*

What? his brother snapped in reply.

Leaping out of the recliner, Alec startled his mother into a screech, which in turn caused his dad to roll off the sofa.

Where is your car? he asked carefully.

In the driveway of the tower.

His eyes squeezed shut, along with his throat. *Where is Eve?*

She's at—

The sudden silence was ominous. Broken by a sudden banging on his front door.

"*Cain.*"

Recognizing Ishamel's voice, Alec shifted out to the hallway, pushing the *mal'akh* aside to look left and right. When he didn't see Eve, he set off toward her condo. "Where is she?"

"I don't know."

Alec spun about. "Say that again."

"I had her wrist in my hand before I shifted out of the car." Ishamel's voice had a slight, uncustomary rasp. "But when I reached the tower, she wasn't with me."

Beyond closing his eyes, Raguel hadn't moved since a pair of Infernals had taken the priest out of their cell. He barely had the energy to reopen them when Riesgo was returned. Maintaining the guise of a mortal was draining. Unfortunately, he didn't need his eyesight to see that the priest was badly shaken.

Still, he watched Riesgo retreat to a corner and sit. The priest's arms wrapped around his knees and he curled into a ball. It was alarming to sense such vulnerability in so proud and strong a man. Sammael intended to break them both, and this was a way to accomplish that task with one blow. Raguel was deeply affected by Riesgo's tangible shock and desolation.

"Are you hurt, Padre?" Raguel asked gently, pushing up from his prone position.

There was a drawn-out silence, then, "No."

"You were not gone long."

"Really? It seemed like forever." Riesgo sighed heavily. "I thank God something called him away. I'm not sure I could have borne a moment longer in that place."

"Want to talk about what happened?"

Riesgo set his cheek on his knee. "I'm not sure I know."

Leaning back against the stone wall, Raguel waited patiently. The deeper the silence, the stronger the urge to fill it.

"He wasn't what I expected," the priest said finally. "Satan, I mean."

"He is always what you need him to be. That is his gift."

"He was . . . paternal."

"Because you seek God in this Hell, he tries to fill that role for you. Did he meet with you alone?"

Riesgo stared at him almost blankly. "No. There was some sort of celebration. An orgy. Sex, dancing and . . . other acts that don't bear repeating. There was blood . . . so much . . ."

"He plays the role of an anchor in the storm. A stalwart presence in a world gone mad."

"Like God in the world above, offering peace amid the chaos."

Raguel was impressed by the priest's perceptiveness. "Did that disturb you, Padre? Did it shake your faith as he intended it to?"

"I-I don't know." Riesgo shrugged lamely. "He was reasoned. Quiet. His confidence frightened me more than anything."

"You imagined him to be volatile."

"Yes. Wild and out of control. Someone with a hair-trigger temper. Someone I could see arguing with God enough to get kicked out of Heaven."

"Instead, you found someone cool and calculating. Sammael does not get angry. He gets even."

Riesgo's fingers dug restlessly into his knees. "He had me sit with him on a pallet in the middle of the room. He offered me something to eat and drink. I was so thirsty, but I didn't take anything from him."

"It would not have harmed you if you had," Raguel said, knowing the mortal wouldn't survive long without sustenance. The priest wasn't the only fragile one. After weeks in solitary, Raguel wasn't certain he'd survive the loss of his only companion.

If they could somehow manage to get beyond the void they hovered in, Raguel thought he might be able to get them out. They were in the second level of Hell. He might be able to break into the first, despite his growing weakness, then bargain their way out from that point.

"He had a woman there," Riesgo continued in a whisper. "He told her to m-massage my shoulders."

"A lure, enhanced by powers you cannot expect to resist."

Riesgo stiffened and spoke tightly, "God expects me to resist."

"You did nothing wrong."

"You don't know that!" The priest leaped to his feet. "She changed, while she was touching me. Her appearance . . . *morphed*."

"Did she show you her true face? The rot beneath the glamour?"

"I wish she had." Riesgo ran both hands through his hair and groaned.

The priest's restlessness was so pronounced it penetrated Raguel's weariness and arrested his attention.

"She became Eve," Riesgo bit out. "Evangeline."

Raguel frowned. Then his brows rose as understanding dawned. "It was a cruel trick," he soothed. "It means nothing."

"It means *something*! I was irritated by the woman—until she changed.

Then . . ." Riesgo moved to the door and fisted the bars. "Then, my reaction to her changed."

"You are speaking of the Devil himself," Raguel argued, struggling to stand. "He has ways of making you see things that are not there. He can make you believe a lie as if it were gospel. It is no reflection on you or your faith."

"Isn't there a grain of truth in every lie?" Rattling the bars, Riesgo craned his neck to see outside. "I have to get out of here. Now. I have to get out."

Raguel moved carefully over to the priest and touched his shoulder. "You feel drawn to Evangeline because God has a purpose for you in her life. Sammael has twisted that in your mind to circumvent God's will."

"You don't know that." Riesgo looked at Raguel with wild eyes.

A guttural, yet amused voice intruded. "I was going to let you out. But what's the point when you two are so damned loud?"

Turning his head, Raguel found Asmodeus at the door.

Riesgo retreated with a horrified gasp.

Raguel's shoulders went back. He, too, was disgusted by the multi-headed demon, but he would not show it.

Glamourless, Asmodeus was a squat, wide, lumbering monstrosity. A creature both demon and beast. The king leered with his many mouths and stepped back, gesturing at the cell with a wave of a cloven hand.

The lock bent of its own accord, shrieking as the metal was distorted beyond use. The door fell open.

"Go that way." The king pointed to the left. A cobblestone path appeared, floating over the endless void and seemingly without end. "You'll find a pond a ways down. Swim to the bottom and you'll find a cave. Take that to its end and you'll be back on the surface. The portal won't be open long. You'll have to make a run for it. If you're able."

Raguel hesitated. If Sammael had truly decided to free them, he would do so himself. That way, he could boast of his largesse.

Asmodeus laughed. "Hurry, Raguel. Before the distraction I created runs its course."

"Distraction?" Glancing at Riesgo, Raguel found the priest to be deathly pale but nodding slowly.

"When Satan was called away," Riesgo said. "It seemed urgent."

"That's why they sent you back so soon."

"Yes."

Raguel turned back to Asmodeus, but the king was gone.

"Let's go," he said, gesturing for Riesgo to precede him out.

They didn't look back.

Reed shifted into the hallway outside of Cain's condo. He ignored Ishamel in favor of his brother. "What the hell is going on? Where is my car?"

"Abel."

His mother's voice drew his attention to Cain's open doorway. She stood there wide-eyed, with a trembling mouth. "Is that *your* car on the television? Was Eve in it?"

"My car is on television?" Irritated by the distress everyone was displaying, he brushed past his mother and entered the living room.

He found his father sitting on the couch facing the TV. He turned to look, watching as a camera zoomed in on firemen using the Jaws of Life to pry open what remained of his car.

"Holy shit." He shifted back to the hallway, landing directly in front of Ishamel. "Where. Is. Eve?"

The *mal'akh* met his gaze directly, unresisting yet defiant. "I don't know."

Catching him by the lapels of his gray suit, Reed slammed him into the wall. "Wrong answer."

Cain grabbed him by the shoulder and yanked him around. Ishamel's feet hit the carpet with a thud, but he didn't stumble.

"You are such a monumental fuck-up, Abel. You have one job. *One* fucking job, and you can't get it right."

"Cain . . ." their father warned.

"No, Abba." Cain made a slashing gesture with his hand. "Your precious Abel fucked up, whether you want to hear about it or not. He's supposed to be keeping his charges safe, but in the last two days Eve was ambushed by Azazel and now—"

Cain's voice broke, which nearly broke Reed. Was Eve still in the accordion-like remains of his car? Nothing could survive a collision like that. Nothing.

"*You're* her fucking mentor, asshole," Reed tossed back, fists clenching at the brutal understanding of his own culpability. He hadn't wanted Rosa in the vicinity, yet he'd allowed Eve free rein because . . . Fuck.

Because she was mad at him and he wanted to pacify her? Because he couldn't read her and took it personally? Because he felt like he was hanging on to her by his fingernails and was afraid to fight with her?

"She was driving *your* car!" Cain bit out.

"I didn't know! I thought she was riding in the limo with Ishamel."

Cain's face took on an ugly, twisted cast. "Betcha left the Lamborghini out front, right? Smack dab in the entryway so everyone would see it. 'Look at my awesome car, which I drive to stroke my massive fucking ego and compensate for my minuscule prick.'"

"Cain!" their mother snapped. "That was completely—"

Reed didn't wait for the rest. He lunged across the space between them, tackling Cain halfway down the hall. They hit the carpet and skid, grappling. Weeks of frustration, jealousy, and anger poured out through his fists. He didn't feel his brother returning blows. He didn't feel fear at challenging an angel far more powerful than himself. All he felt was good. Really damned good.

Arms and hands intruded too swiftly; his father and Ishamel digging between them to rip them apart. With his wrists restrained behind his back, Reed was pulled off Cain and yanked upright. He continued to kick with his legs—once while his brother was still on the floor and again as Cain managed to regain his footing.

"Enough!" their mother shouted, slapping Reed in the face, then Cain. "Why can't you work together for once? Is your feud more powerful than your feelings for Evangel—"

The sudden halting of her tirade arrested everyone in the hallway.

She moved closer to Cain, her fingers finding and lifting the necklace that had fallen out of his shirt. "W-where did you get this?"

Cain looked down at her hand, his irises still flickering with the lingering rage of angels. "Eve gave it to me."

Reed's teeth ground together. Eve had given a gift to his brother?

Doors opened along the hallway and residents poked their heads out. Sydney, too, appeared from Eve's condo.

"What's going on out there?" one woman asked crossly. "I'm calling the police."

"That won't be necessary." Ishamel released Reed and moved away to address the concerns of the onlookers. Sydney joined him in working damage control.

"Where did Evangeline get it?" their mother persisted, sounding formidable despite her petite stature.

"An Infernal in the firm made it," Cain answered.

Their father stood still and watchful. "No, he didn't."

Tugging at it, she said, "Give it to me."

Cain's head tilted. His gaze narrowed. "I can't. I promised Eve I wouldn't take it off."

"She could be dead!" she snapped, chilling Reed with her callousness. "Give it to me."

Then she gasped and covered her mouth as her careless words registered. "I'm s-sorry. I didn't mean that."

"What is this, Ima?" Cain asked with dangerous softness, watching her like the predator he was. "What does it do?"

"It doesn't *do* anything."

"How do you know?"

Adam stepped forward and caught her wrist. "Leave it."

"I can't just—"

"Leave it," their father repeated harshly. He pulled her back down the hall to Cain's condo.

Reed turned his attention back to his brother. "What the fuck is going on around here? Where's Eve?"

"Missing." Cain shoved the necklace back inside his T-shirt, then pointed an accusing finger. "Find her. If she was in your car . . ." His throat worked. "Just find her."

Agreeing that Eve came first and killing his brother could come later, Reed shifted to the men's restroom of the 7-Eleven on the corner of Katella and Harbor. As he exited to the street, he saw the crowds and heard the sickening grind of metal being ripped apart. His gut knotted.

Eve.

"You are not wearing the chain I gave you," Satan said smoothly, snapping his fingers and conjuring a throne in the center of the yellow desert. He sank into the seat and stretched out his long legs. His crimson wings were tucked away, leaving behind a frighteningly normal vision of a breathtakingly handsome man. What was worse was his resemblance to Cain. And Abel.

Eve would really like to hear the explanation for that one.

"We really have to stop meeting like this," she muttered, tugging one of her heels out of a crack in the hardened ground.

"I just saved your life."

"I'm sure Ishamel would have done the same, if you hadn't beaten him to it. And by the way, I have to point out that my life isn't supposed to be in danger. You agreed to call off the bounty."

As if wounded, he set an elegant hand over his heart. "I did."

"The vamp that rammed me into traffic didn't seem to know that!"

"Sometimes it can take awhile for word to spread. However, you are none the worse for wear."

"The car I was driving can't say the same."

There was something off about the nonchalance the Devil displayed. If he'd done as he said—and she believed he spoke at least in half-truths—then he'd been openly defied. It was hard to believe he would take such an offense so easily.

"Where is the necklace, Evangeline?"

The way he used her full name gave him a paternalistic air that chilled her blood as surely as his touch did. She wished that she'd gone to the ladies' room at the police station. "Somewhere safe."

"Hmm." His head cocked to one side, allowing a curtain of silky black hair to fall over his shoulder. "What do you consider *safe,* I wonder? Your parents'?"

"As if I would drag them into this. It's not a big deal, okay? It's fine."

"Maybe I want it back, if it is of no use to you."

"You can have it back once I kill the Nix. That was the deal." Eve had no idea how she sounded so calm and in control when she was far from either, but she was grateful. "Now, why did you bring me here? It's only been one day since we made our little arrangement. You'll have to give me more time."

"Abel?" he persisted. "Sarakiel? Cain?"

Her brow arched, but her fingers were digging into her biceps through her silk shirt. "What. Do. You. *Want?*"

"Perhaps you asked Eve to watch it for you?" he purred.

"No."

One second he was in the chair; the next he was directly in front of her. He gripped her head in his hands, his palms pressing into her temples. He tipped her head back. Looking into her eyes, he held her captive with his icy touch and his burning stare. She couldn't blink, couldn't back away.

His mouth moved, as if he was speaking, but all she could hear was her own blood rushing through her brain at a breakneck pace. Then she realized it was *him* in her mind, sliding in and around everything. Touching Alec. Then Reed. Through her. As if he *was* her.

A smile curved his mouth. His head lowered to hers. Slow. Impossibly slow. When his lips touched hers, she whimpered but couldn't pull away. The kiss he gave her was Alec's. The touch, taste, and texture. The possession and passion; the love and the lust. It was a deep, lush melding of their mouths and she found herself participating with ardor. Tears leaked out of the corners of her eyes and dried in the arid breeze, but whether they were happy or sad tears, she couldn't say.

He groaned softly and pulled away. "You kiss like a woman in love," he murmured, his thumb brushing across her bottom lip in the way Alec's did. "Thank you."

Eve blinked up at him, dazed.

Satan released her and walked away. "That will have to tide me over, I suppose, since you have completed the task I set for myself. Indirectly, of course, and in doing so you have denied me a pleasure I anticipated with relish. But I will consider your part of our agreement met. Regardless of the fact that I was not the messenger, the message was still delivered. You are free."

"Huh?" She kicked herself mentally. If he said she was done, great. Even if it didn't make a damn bit of sense. "What about Riesgo and Raguel? Are they free, too?"

"According to your memories, someone has already made arrangements for their *escape.*" He walked back to his throne. "I cannot release that which I no longer possess."

Settling into the seat, Satan smiled at her. "You will just have to hope that one of those other bargains is successful."

"That's not fair!"

"Why? Because now you have to decide who to save and who to sacrifice? Maybe you will decide to do nothing at all and leave the matter in the hands of Jehovah. I am curious to see which way you lean."

He snapped his fingers.

Eve found herself in the living room of her condo, directly between the television and Montevista. The Mark was sleeping on her couch.

Kicking off her heels, she sat next to him and set her hand on his shoulder. He was cold to the touch, and it took a couple hard shakes to bring him back to the land of the living.

"Hey," he murmured huskily, scrubbing a hand over his face.

"How are you feeling?"

"Like I should have shut the sliding glass door before napping. It's starting to get cold at night." He moved to sit up. "How'd it go?"

"To shit." She slid over to the coffee table. "I'm going to need your help."

"Tell me what you want me to do."

CHAPTER 19

In search of privacy, Eve took the elevator down to the marble-lined foyer of her condominium complex.

Alec.

She'd barely managed the silent summons before he was in front of her, gripping her by the arms and giving her a not-so-gentle shake.

"Where have you been?" he demanded, before crushing her face into his cotton-covered chest.

She mumbled into his pecs. He fisted her chignon and pulled her head back.

"Not funny." But there was a hint of amusement in his eyes. "You scared the shit out of me."

"Does Abel know?"

"All of Orange County knows. It's on the news."

"Man . . ."

Eve sent a silent apology to Reed. He appeared as swiftly as Alec had, his gaze just as haunted. Poor guys, they'd been worried sick about her. She loved them for that.

Despite Alec's rumbling protest, she pushed away from him, putting equal distance between the three of them so that they formed a V-shaped formation. Through the glass door behind Alec, she could see the nut-job reverend singing on the corner.

She turned her attention back to the two brothers. "We're racing against the clock here."

Both men's brows rose.

Eve pointed at Alec. "You need to figure out what's going to happen to you when Gadara comes back. I'm guessing you have less than twenty-four hours."

His arms crossed. "What have you done?"

She pointed at Reed. "And your secret plan is fucked in so many ways, not the least of which is that it's not a secret anymore. Satan knows about it."

Reed scowled. "I don't know what you're—"

"Yes, you do." She looked back at Alec. "What are you still doing here?"

"Well, *bossy,* I'm waiting for my parents to finish packing so I can escort them back home. After I do that, I'll follow your orders."

Eve's head tilted in concern. "But they just got here."

"Cain caused another fight," Reed said.

"*I* didn't," Alec corrected with a fulminating glare. He pulled the necklace out of his shirt. "*This* did."

Reed nodded. "Ima took one look and lost it."

"Lost what?" Eve asked.

"Her temper. Her mind. Everything."

"Did she say why it bothered her so much?"

"Nope." Alec eyed her suspiciously. "But she did say that Hank didn't make it."

"Actually, Abba said that," Reed amended, eyeing her with the same expression.

"No one said Hank made it," she corrected.

"Where did you get this, angel?"

Eve knew that silky tone all too well. Alec always used it right before she got into trouble. "Would you believe a Cracker Jack box?"

"This is serious, babe," Reed murmured.

What could she say? She didn't want to start shit between Alec and his parents. If their mom hadn't told them about Sammael and the necklace after all these years, Eve wasn't going to be the one to do it.

Something in the periphery of her vision caught her eye. She turned her head to find Evil Santa at the bottom of the steps leading to the locked door of the foyer. He was giving her the death stare from the sidewalk, singing loudly and off-key to the strumming of his guitar. The light of the street lamp circled him in a yellow glow that only made him creepier.

"Can one of you *please* do something about that guy?" she groused.

Alec and Reed looked over their shoulder.

"Do what?" Alec asked.

"I don't know. Take him around the corner and flash your wings. Send him on a mission for God, or at the very least tell him I'm one of the good guys."

Alec gestured toward the door with a flourish. "That's all you, bro."

"Fuck you," Reed shot back. "You do it."

"Somehow, I don't think my black wings will go over well with that guy."

Reed glared at his brother, than glanced at Eve.

You owe me, she reminded, *for bargaining me for Gadara.*

Babe . . . He sounded frustrated. *Do you trust me?*

She did or else she'd have decked him by now and told one of the archangels what he was up to. Still, she wasn't willing to give an inch at this point. As far as she was concerned, he was due for some serious groveling.

Eve set one hand on her hip. *You're kidding, right? You're asking me that after you offered me up on a silver platter to a king of Hell?*

Yes, damn you, I am. You owe me, too. You wrecked my car.

Whatever. There's no comparison.

He shot her the dark look that she thought was hot; the one where he looked hard and dangerous, primitive despite the urbanity of his clothing. *You have no idea what I've been through waiting for the fire department to cut open my car . . . waiting to see what they'd find in there.*

She softened. *I'm sorry.*

Then she noticed how rumpled he was. A quick glance at Alec revealed that his T-shirt was stretched in places.

Sighing inwardly, she waved Reed toward the door. *Take care of wacko out there and I'll get back to you about the trust issue.*

He went, but with a clearly aggravated stride.

When she was alone with Alec, she said, "We need answers. Go to the source if you have to, just find them."

He leaned into one of the metal mailboxes built into the wall. "You sound as if you know for a fact that Raguel will be back."

"Maybe I do."

"You need to talk to me, angel."

"I can't. You're connected to everyone in the firm in an unpredictable way. We can't risk a leak like that. You'll just have to hang on for the ride."

He exhaled harshly. "I've been doing that since I met you."

"It's not so bad, is it?"

"Can you at least tell me *why* you have this necklace?"

"To kill the Nix. It, uh, apparently suppresses Infernal tendencies."

Alec grew very still.

"Yes," she answered his silent question. "Something is in you that shouldn't be. But I think you knew that already."

"I didn't know it was Infernal. I thought it was just . . . me." He reached out and caught her hand, his fingers playing with hers. "Angel. I have to tell you something."

"No, you don't."

"Yeah, I do."

"No, really." She squeezed his hand. "I know about Izzie. I know that wasn't you."

He looked shell-shocked, then relieved. His entire frame visibly deflated from the release of tension. "I don't deserve you, you know? I never have."

"Well." The toe of her shoe followed a grout line in the marble. "I have something to tell you, too."

"No, you don't."

"Yeah, I do."

"I don't want to hear it. And when I saw the name of Sarakiel's e-mail attachment, I didn't want to see it either. So I deleted it."

Her shoulders went back. "Because you feel guilty over something you're not responsible for. You think this makes us even, but it doesn't, Alec. I knew damn well what I was doing; you didn't."

"I don't care," he said stubbornly.

She laid it all out there. "I would do it again; you wouldn't."

"I'm not going to give you a reason to do it again." Alec straightened. "Let's go check on my parents and see if they're ready to go. I need to hit the road."

"Fine." There was no point in talking to him about it now. He wasn't listening. She'd revisit the subject later. She had to. Everything was different. Ignoring those differences wasn't going to help any of them. "But I'll need you back here before noon. You and that necklace. Got it?"

"Got it." Alec shifted them up to his apartment.

His mother sat on the black leather couch in the living room. His father was apparently in one of the back bedrooms. When Eve jerked her chin down the hall, Alec took the hint and joined his dad, leaving her alone with his mom.

Ima looked up at her with reddened eyes and nose. She looked years older than she had the night before, with deep grooves around her pretty mouth and slumped shoulders. Eve took a seat beside her and offered her a commiserating smile.

Setting a hand on Eve's knee, Ima asked in a whisper, "How did you get the necklace?"

"Satan lent it to me."

"Why?"

"It wards off Infernals."

"Does it?" Ima looked away. Her tone grew distant. "I didn't know. It didn't do that for me."

Eve looked down the hall, making sure that Alec was still occupied with helping his father. Then she leaned in and queried softly, "It's yours, isn't it?"

Nodding, Ima explained, "When I married Adam, Jehovah gave it to me, along with twenty-three other pieces of jewelry."

Was the piece around Alec's neck the only one that was charmed? Perhaps they all had a unique gift. "How did Satan get his hands on it?"

"I gave it to him. In a way, it's fitting that you would give it to Cain."

A sentimental gesture. A gift of some meaning, apparently. *A message delivered*, as Satan had said.

"You shouldn't say any more," Eve murmured. "Cain shares my thoughts and memories. Whatever I know, he eventually finds out about."

"Ah, I see." Ima gave her knee a gentle squeeze. "Thank you for the warning."

"Will you be okay?"

"Adam and I have been together forever. That's not going to change now."

"I hope I see you again. A longer visit, perhaps."

"I would like that."

Ima hugged her. A few moments later, Adam did the same, albeit with some awkwardness. Then Alec shifted away with them. The parting was bittersweet for Eve. She'd spent only enough time with them to learn that she wanted to spend more.

Knowing there was much to be done before the morning dawned, Eve returned to her condo. Sydney was cooking chili in the kitchen, Reed was on the phone with his insurance company, and Montevista was in the shower. Once again, Eve kicked off her heels, hoping it would be for the last time tonight. She was beat. She pushed them under the console table by the front door and padded down the hallway to her office.

Ishamel was there, sitting at her desk and staring intently at the computer monitor. He leaned back when she entered and sighed. That sound softened him in her eyes, as did the sight of him sans jacket and waistcoat.

"Hi," she said.

"How are you?"

She hummed a noncommittal sound. "I've been better."

"I found what I think you were looking for."

"Oh?"

The *mal'akh* gestured at her monitor. She rounded the desk to see what he was referring to.

Frozen on the screen was a grainy image of Sarakiel in sunglasses, sitting at a picnic table in what looked to be a public park. Across from her sat another blonde woman and a large dark-haired man.

Eve asked, "What am I looking at?"

"Sarakiel." Ishamel pointed at the familiar figure. "This is Asmodeus. And this is Lilith."

Eve's mouth formed an O. She leaned in closer. Unfortunately, not much was distinguishable aside from body type and hair color. She couldn't get a good idea of what Adam's first wife looked like, much to her disappointment. "That can't be good. How did you get this?"

"Raguel is gone. Two archangels are on his turf. I thought it'd be wise to keep a close eye on things in his absence."

She straightened. "You rock."

"Now it's your turn," he said. "Tell me what this means."

Moving over to the futon, Eve sat with her legs tucked beneath her and explained what Mariel had told her.

She finished with, "Trading a handler would knock twenty-one Marks off their game, but only temporarily. I can't see that being worth trading Gadara for. Unless the handler was Abel."

"That ups the ante considerably," Ishamel agreed.

"Exactly. And leave it to a demon to tell Abel to his face that he was being traded."

"How did you narrow the culprit down to Sarakiel?"

Eve shrugged. "It's a woman thing, I guess. We can be vindictive when slighted."

"You're taking a risk telling me this," he pointed out. "You are all expendable to me, if that's what it takes to get Raguel back."

"Right."

"So you must have a plan."

"I guess you could call it that." She smiled. "Clusterfuck also works."

Ishamel nodded. "Count me in. What do you need from me?"

"An odd location for a meet, Cain," Sabrael murmured. "The most popular place to commit suicide in the United States. Is this a message of some sort?"

"Nothing so morbid." Alec blinked and engaged thick tears, protecting his eyes from the seraph's brilliance. "Eve pointed it out while watching a television show about witches."

"Far from morbid," the seraph said wryly, "I think that qualifies as romantic."

The view from the top of a Golden Gate Bridge tower was unrivaled. The waters of San Francisco Bay shimmered with the city lights and the sea breeze was cold, damp, and brisk. It kept Alec's head clear, which he appreciated.

Sabrael took a seat beside him, his powerful legs dangling over the edge. "Are you enjoying your ascension?"

"For the most part."

"Am I here to be thanked?"

Alec's mouth curved. "I have a few questions, if you don't mind."

"Hmm."

"What would happen to me if Raguel came back?"

"Ah . . . Excellent question." Sabrael turned his flame-blue gaze on Alec. "I was not expecting something so thoughtful."

"Glad I could surprise you."

"What do you think will happen?"

"I don't know. Will I die?"

Sabrael laughed. It was a gorgeous, heavenly sound. Unique to the seraphim. "My dear Cain. I doubt Jehovah could afford to lose a Mark of your talents. You are irreplaceable, I would say."

"Good to know."

"However, you would lose the North American firm and all that comes with it."

"Everything, then," Alec clarified. "Would I return to the way I was before? Would I at least be restored to a full *mal'akh*?"

"You misunderstand me. I would see to it that you retained your arch-angel gifts, despite the lack of responsibilities that usually accompany them." The seraph's voice took on a biting edge. "Do not forget that you owe me, Cain. No matter what task I decide upon, having you as an arch-angel is of greater benefit to me."

"I've never failed you, and that was while I had no gifts beyond those of an average Mark."

"What are you saying? Have you decided that the life of an archangel is not to your liking?"

"I haven't gotten that far yet. But my goal was to head a firm, not ac-quire more gifts. Without the one, I have no need for the other."

"*I* have need of it, and I will not give it up simply because you miss your Evangeline."

"She isn't gone." Alec's fingers curled around the red-painted ironwork. Despite the chilly temperature and the soothing necklace, his skin was growing as hot as his rising temper. "If I can get my shit together, her and I will be okay."

"You have come to the wrong place to ask for sympathy." The seraph's tone lacked all inflection. "She weakens you, and Abel. She is a mediocre Mark, barely sufficient in the practical applications, and prone to blas-phemy and irreverence. You are a fool if you think I will sacrifice *you*—the greatest killing machine ever created—for *her*."

Alec's grip tightened to the point of pain.

I won't invest in a relationship with someone who can't love me, she'd said, and he knew it was true.

Which made Abel a greater threat now than ever before. He'd become the go-to guy when she couldn't turn to Alec.

Sabrael levitated until his feet were once again level with the top of the tower. "You will remain an archangel until I decide you are no longer use-ful in that capacity. I find that possibility very slim indeed."

The seraph left.

Alec lingered, hoping that time would present the solution he searched for.

Once Sydney and Montevista were settled for the night—Sydney in the guest room and Montevista on the couch in the living room—Eve had Ishamel shift with her to the subterranean floors of the tower. Together they knocked on Hank's door.

"It's late," Eve said. "Are you sure he's still here?"

"He lives here." Ishamel set a hand at the small of her back and urged her through the opening door.

"Welcome back," Hank said, appearing out of the darkness. "You've had an interesting afternoon since you left me."

"You could call it that," she agreed dryly.

He must have noted Eve's velour jogging suit and Ishamel's casual state, because he changed from dress slacks and shirt to a black sweat suit that reminded Eve of Riesgo's, although the priest was considerably more muscular.

Her resolve strengthened further. A lot of people were depending on her to not screw everything up. "I have a couple of questions for you."

"Let's sit." Hank led the way to the now-familiar rough-hewn table. Immediately afterward, Fred approached in a tight patent leather and metal bodysuit. Her face was heavily made-up and her long white hair was teased big. She set a tray down bearing a pitcher of Hank's favored iced tea and three glasses, then sashayed away, revealing a horsetail-thing swaying from the rear of her outfit.

Eve stared. Ishamel looked away.

"Hot damn, Fred," Eve called after her.

Hank gave an elegant shrug. "Note that the tengu is quiet. Seems he's become enamored with Fred. The dominatrix guise keeps him distracted."

Since Eve herself had been rendered speechless for a moment, she could see how well the getup worked. She returned her attention to Hank. "Do you have something or some way to keep Infernals from disintegrating when killed?"

One red brow rose. "Why?"

"I need a body."

"The masking agent seems to preserve bodies."

"It also restores them." She shook her head. "I don't need any more recurring kills. I want the vanquished to stay dead, but I need some remains. At least until cremation."

"Hmm. The necklace might do the trick."

Eve sat back. "You think?"

"It's a possibility."

"Okay, next question. What happens to mortals who see things they shouldn't?"

Hank's fingertips rubbed back and forth along a deep groove in the table. "Depends on how credible the witness is and what proof they have, if any. It's impossible to say until it happens. You'll have to take your chances."

Ishamel picked up a glass and swallowed tea in great big gulps. When he finished, he wiped his mouth with the back of his hand and asked, "It just so happens that I might have a use for a Nix attractant. You wouldn't happen to have one, would you?"

"Why, yes." Hank smiled wide. "I have one. Glad you can use it, since our firm leader ordered me not to give it to Evangeline."

Fred reappeared with a lovely green glass atomizer bottle, which she set down in front of Ishamel. Eve studied the lili while she was close, looking beneath the cosmetics to the delicate features beneath. Eve wondered how closely Fred resembled her mother. She was a very pretty girl, with a delicate deportment that effectively hid the nature of the beast within.

"Thank you," Ishamel said.

Eve's lips pursed.

"What troubles you?" Hank asked.

"Would Lilith have a reason for wanting to get her hands on Abel?"

Ishamel stared hard at her. "You assume she is interested in him. Why not assume her motivation is the resulting gain? I see him as a means to an end."

"Perhaps it's *you* she wants," Hank suggested, catching up on the conversation by reading Eve's thoughts. "Perhaps she views you as a surrogate Eve, beloved wife of Adam. She hates both of them with a passion."

"Let's skip that avenue for now," Eve said. "It's a dead end. Lilith would either kill me or torture me. Either way, end of story. But if she had Abel, what would she do with him? Keep him or trade him, right? If she kept him, why? And if she traded him, what would she trade him for? What does Satan have that she might want?"

Ishamel laughed, a rusty unused sound. "Lilith wants everything. And she's had pretty much everything in Hell in her bed at some point or another. The earth is a playground to her."

Eve looked at Hank, who tossed up his hands in a clueless gesture. "Ishamel's right. Lilith wants everything."

"My mother," Fred said, lingering at the edge of the circle of light that hung over the table, "is motivated by boredom. She does things for odd reasons and oftentimes for no reason at all. I gave up trying to figure her out."

"All right." Eve stood and yawned. "Thank you both for your help."

Ishamel stood along with her. Hank remained seated.

"You're determined to jump the gun and set this off tomorrow?" the occultist asked.

"I'm just setting the stage." Her smile was grim. "Whether the show starts or not . . . We'll have to wait and see."

"Don't get yourself killed. I want to see you again."

Eve gave him a mock salute.

"Good luck," Fred said.

"Thanks. We're going to need it."

CHAPTER 20

It was a little past seven in the morning when Eve left her bedroom and moved down the hallway to the living room. She checked on Montevista, usually the first one awake while on watch, but presently the last one still sleeping. Sydney sat at the kitchen island in a pale blue bathrobe and red slippers reading the newspaper report of the Lamborghini wreck.

"Coffee?" Eve asked, as she opened the freezer to grab the beans.

"Sure." The Mark smiled. "I love how normal you are."

Eve snorted. "This is normal? Shoot me now."

Sydney abandoned the newspaper. "When I was first marked, I didn't know how to take it. It seemed like such a huge responsibility to be a warrior for God. And everything was so different. I used to love coffee. I drank it all day. But I gave it up, thinking there was no point anymore since I couldn't feel the buzz from the caffeine. Because I changed so many things about my life, I felt like a stranger in my own skin for a long time."

Knowing that feeling all too well, Eve nodded. "Look on the bright side, that dedication makes you a much better Mark than I am. I want to be you when I grow up."

Sydney slid off the stool and moved to the cupboard. She grabbed three mugs. "I'm hoping to be more like you."

"Bad with a sword and accident prone?"

"Shut up. Killing things is just *part* of the job, not *all* of it. I actually think your agnosticism gives you an advantage. You don't take anything at face value, so you see things the rest of us don't. Since I met you, I've been trying to reconnect with the things that used to define me. I bought bookshelves last weekend and an outrageously expensive coffee station the week before that. Sounds like nothing, I know—"

"No, I get it. You're building a future instead of living day to day. And you're letting yourself have fun with your life. Good for you."

"Thanks." Sydney set the mugs on the counter. "I'm much happier now that you've rubbed off on me."

Eve bumped shoulders with her. "Here's to hoping some of your kick-ass qualities rub off on *me*."

There was a beat of silence as Eve poured the beans into the grinder, then Sydney whispered, "I guess the new me is more attractive, too. I've been working with Diego a long time and he's never paid any attention to me as a woman. In fact, he once said I wasn't his type."

"I'd say that's changed."

"You noticed it, too?" Sydney's eyes had a sparkle that warmed Eve's heart. She liked both Marks, and wanted them to be happy.

"Totally. He's got it bad." Eve decided it was as good a time as any to broach a sensitive topic. "Hey, do me a favor. Keep an especially close eye on him. I think he's too proud to admit that he's not up to full speed yet."

"Already on it."

"Of course you would be. You rock."

Pressing on the lid of the grinder, Eve turned the beans into fresh grounds. When she let go and the racket died down, Montevista was clearly heard stirring on the couch.

"Time to get up, sleepyhead," Sydney called out, moving toward the living room. "We have to clear the residents out of the building."

Eve turned the coffeepot on and washed her hands. Part of the plan she'd passed on to Montevista included informing all the condo residents of a suspected (and fictitious) gas leak. The Marks who'd been running guard duty around the perimeter were gearing up to pose as local utility inspectors and firemen. In order to keep the complaints down, Ishamel had arranged for Gadara Enterprises to foot the bill for a local hotel stay and two-hour gondola rides. The last thing any of them wanted was to catch some mortals in the crosshairs. Better to be safe than sorry.

Moving to her office, Eve sent an e-mail to her secretary, telling Candace that she wouldn't be coming in today. She would wait another hour, then call the detectives and let them know. With her schedule set, she leaned back in her chair and stared up at the ceiling.

What would Gadara be like when he returned? He'd been gone so long . . . And Riesgo. How would he be? Her heart ached for the both of them and what they must have endured.

"So . . ."

Eve lifted her head and discovered Reed in the doorway. "Hi."

"I'm still trying to decide how I should feel about sleeping alone last night."

"We don't live together."

He entered and took a seat on the futon. His shirt was a deep red, perfectly pressed and left open at the throat. Paired with black slacks and his dark hair, it was edgy in a way that made her toes curl.

"So Cain calms down a bit," he said tightly, "and you throw me over, is that it?"

"No. That's not it."

"Am I your dirty little secret now, babe?" His dark eyes were hard and cold. "Are you going to pretend that we didn't happen?"

"I'm going to pretend that you're not insulting me now. I'm going to convince myself that it's because you like me so much that you're being an asshole."

"Are you going to tell Cain about us?"

"I already did. Well, I tried to," she amended. "He didn't want to hear it, but he knows."

Reed's entire mien changed, softening to the point that it made her breath catch. He was as vulnerable in that moment as he'd been with her in bed. It was somehow more intimate with them both fully clothed and a room's length away from each other.

"Is it over between you?" he asked.

"Honestly?" She rubbed her palms over the arms of her chair. "I don't think it'll ever be over. I'm in love with him. I've been in love with him forever."

As he nodded slowly, Reed's gaze remained on her but it was distant. Unfocused.

"Thing is," she continued, "I'm pretty sure that I'm halfway in love with you, too."

He stiffened, now tensely alert. "Go on."

"I have no idea how that's even possible, but there it is. I know you're not good for me. You're needy and self-centered—"

"Eve . . ."

"—but I crave you like chocolate."

"And what do you think Cain is?" he snapped. "Healthy for you? Gimme a fucking break."

"He's *healthier,* but I have a sweet tooth. That doesn't mean you're my guilty pleasure, so don't take it that way."

"You don't know what you're doing."

"I know I can't have both of you. And I can't choose between you. I guess that leaves me with having neither of you."

"Fuck that," he retorted without heat. "I've got you right where I want you now."

"Is that so?" Eve tried to hold back a smile, but felt her lips twitching anyway.

"Oh, yeah." Standing, Reed came toward her. He leaned over her and pressed his lips to her forehead. "Thank you."

"For what?"

He retreated enough to meet her gaze. "For everything, really. Most especially for not castrating me for offering to send you to Hell. You say you don't trust me, but you couldn't prove more clearly that you do."

"What's your plan anyway? Get everyone here tomorrow, then what? The way I understand it, you'd have to go into the trade assuming they let Riesgo and Gadara escape. You know better than to trust a demon."

Reed's mouth curved in a slow, smug smile. "Ah, but they don't know better than to trust me. That's the beauty of it. Asmodeus is worth a lot to Sammael. He's one of only seven kings in Hell. Once Asmodeus makes sure you and Cain are here on the premises, he won't be able to resist trying to nab you. He can only see things from his perspective, and to him it must be a potent temptation to get rid of Cain. It won't even enter his head to think I'll double-cross him and take him prisoner instead."

"And if things go to shit, then what?"

"Cain would be with you to protect you. For all his fuck-ups, I'm sure that when push comes to shove, he's got your back. And I'm confident that Sammael won't kill him."

"That is *not* what you were thinking when you offered him."

Reed winked. "Prove it."

"Well, if Sarakiel has her way, you'll be there to protect me, too."

He straightened abruptly. "Sara?"

Eve explained about the tape of Sarakiel's meeting with Asmodeus. "My guess is, Asmodeus is gambling that he can take all three of us at once. With Sara's help, why not?"

"One day, you're telling me you think she loves me. The next, you say she wants me burning in Hell."

"It's because she loves you that she wants you to burn in Hell."

Snorting, he said, "That's female logic if I ever heard it."

"What can I say? We're twisted."

"Don't lump yourself in with Sara." He licked the tip of her nose. "I'm going to deal with her today. Right now, actually."

"Then I need you to round up Asmodeus."

His gaze narrowed. "Tomorrow. I need time to get things together."

"I've already got things together. Ishamel helped. You know how thorough he is."

"Do you have any idea of what kind of manpower we're going to need to nab Asmodeus?"

"We're not going to nab him. We just want him here."

Reed sank to a crouch in front of her, leveling their gazes. "Spit it out. All of it."

"You're right, Asmodeus is valuable to Satan, but not for the reason you think. Satan knows your plan. He tried to act nonchalant about it, but I read between the lines. He's pissed, and he's going to take Asmodeus down."

"Good. Let him."

"Sure," Eve agreed. She opened her mind to him, allowing him to see her conversations with the Devil. "But not now. You've been bargaining with Asmodeus but really, the deal is between me and Satan."

"Babe . . ." He made an exasperated sound and dropped his head into her lap. "You're a walking disaster," he mumbled.

"Listen." She lifted his head with her hands. "He promised me something, then reneged."

"And that's a surprise to you? Come on, Eve—"

"He wouldn't renege with me, Reed," she insisted. "For whatever reason, he wants me to trust him. He's going to fulfill his end of our agreement."

"That's not what he said to you!"

"What he said was that I'll have to let the moves you and Sara made play out."

"What he said," he retorted, "was that he can't release what he doesn't possess. A melodramatic way to say he got what he wanted, and you're on your own."

"Or it's a roundabout way of saying someone stole from him." Eve shot him a wry glance. "Do you really think he's just going to let that go?"

"He doesn't need *you* to put Asmodeus in line."

"Right. He just needs to fulfill his end of the bargain. He gave me two choices—help you or Sara with your plans, or leave the whole thing in the hands of God. But—" she wagged a finger at him "—he knows I'm not a believer. He made a big deal out of my agnosticism being one of the reasons he likes me. He appreciates my cynicism."

"He's always trying to lure Marks to the dark side. He doesn't *like* you. He doesn't give a shit about you, other than the fact that fucking with you fucks with a lot of other people, too."

She pressed on. "I think his question was incomplete. I think what he was really saying was, 'Will you leave it in the hands of God . . . or *me*.' That was the basis of our previous conversations. He says God isn't going to give me what I need, but *he* will. This is his chance to prove it. I think he's going to take it, if only because he wants to knock Asmodeus down a notch in a major way."

He gripped her hands painfully tight. "You know . . . Marks spend their entire careers hoping they never meet Sammael. But not you. No, you lack the self-preservation gene."

She could feel his fear for her in the connection between them. She was freaked out, too, but things were getting out of hand—Gadara, the priest, Cain, the Nix, and Satan running around as he pleased. It was time to set the world to rights.

Eve squeezed his fingers. "Hank told me Satan's using an emissary to be able to meet with me face-to-face. We need to know who it is. I have a theory, and this is the way to prove it."

"What theory?"

"It's too dangerous to share until I know for sure."

Reed's jaw tensed. "It's Cain, isn't it?"

"Just trust me, okay. You get Asmodeus to show up, and we'll see if the emissary passes the news onto Satan so that *he* can show up."

"You're not going to rest until I'm insane, right?" Tilting his head, Reed pressed his lips to hers. The kiss started out short and sweet, but swiftly heated. When he straightened, she made a small sound of protest.

"You owe me," he said. "Dinner. Hot dress. No underwear. High heels."

"You're a pig."

"Can't help it. I think I'm in love. Why else would I agree to this shit?"

He shifted away before she could reply. She sat there for a moment, considering. Another tall, dark figure filled the doorway to her office.

Alec came in with a mug of hot coffee and set it on her desk. From the café au lait appearance, she knew he'd fixed it perfectly. From the look on his face, she knew he'd heard Reed's declaration.

"Good morning," he said.

"To you, too." She lifted the mug. "Thank you."

"Anytime." He managed a ghost of a smile. "I thought I'd come over early. Get the day started."

"You're always welcome here."

He moved to the futon. "I followed your orders. Looks like I'm too valuable to kill."

"I could have told you that." She smiled against the rim of her cup.

"But I would lose the firm."

Eve swallowed a mouthful of perfectly creamed coffee, then set her mug down. "I'm sorry. I know how much you wanted it."

Alec sat back and crossed his arms. "I want you, too. Can't have both, so something's got to give."

She knew what that was like.

He sat with widespread legs, his booted feet resting flat on the carpeted floor. His jeans were worn in all the right places and the arms of his T-shirt stretched around gorgeous biceps. He hadn't aged a day in the ten years since she'd first seen him.

"You're not upset?" She studied him for hints of underlying disappointment or frustration.

"You know I'm not doing well with it," he said gruffly. "I have to be collared like a dog to get a grip on myself."

"Did you talk about that to whoever you went to see last night?"

Alec shook his head.

"Why not?"

"I thought he might change his mind and decide to knock me out of commission after all."

Eve stood and moved to sit beside him. She set her hand on his thigh. "What is it with men not wanting to ask for help?"

"I've been asking for years, angel. No one's talking." His foot tapped restlessly atop the carpet. "For a long time there's been speculation that my mother was unfaithful and the result was me."

"Do you believe that?"

He glanced aside at her. "You won't tell me about the necklace, and I couldn't get anything out of my parents either. It's never good when you can't get answers. If there was nothing to worry about, there'd be nothing to hide."

"Alec." She squeezed his leg, which was like stone beneath her hand. "What are you thinking?"

"You said this necklace suppresses Infernal traits, and the ugliness inside me shuts up when I wear it. What does that tell you?"

"That you think you're half-demon?"

"It's not like my mom had a lot of choice in men back then," he said dryly. He leaned into her. "Maybe the ascension triggered some repressed asshole genetics. What if they can't be locked up again? Like Pandora's Box or something. I'd be too great a threat to keep around."

Wrapping her arms around him, Eve pressed her lips to his forehead. The scent of his skin and the feel of him beside her was familiar and beloved. "I don't know the answer to your question."

"I can see that," he said, reminding her that if she didn't work actively to keep him out of her mind he had free access to everything.

She pushed him out, gently but firmly. "If there's a story there, it's not mine to tell. And I don't want secrets like that between us."

Alec slid an arm between her and the futon, then tugged her into his lap. "I don't want *anything* between us. I want to fix us. You and me."

"Are we broken?"

"Abel slipped into a crack, so we must be."

"You wanted this promotion. My understanding is that you had to bargain for it, probably with unfavorable terms for you. Don't give it up for me. I want you to be happy."

"I'm unhappy without you. We'll get Raguel back, and life will return to the way it was before and I'll be okay with that. More than okay."

"Are you sure?"

"Completely."

The phone rang. Eve scrambled off his lap and returned to her desk, picking up the cordless handset. "Hello?"

"Ms. Hollis. Detective Ingram here."

"Good morning, Detective."

"Your secretary told me you wouldn't be in the office today. It was your boyfriend's car that was in that big wreck yesterday on Harbor, right? Shortly after you left the station?"

"His car was in a wreck, yes. Fortunately, neither of us was in it and he has good insurance." She rushed forward, waylaying any further questions on the matter. "I know you need the rest of my statement, but you still have my car."

"If you're up to it, we'll come to you. The first forty-eight hours after a disappearance are crucial, Ms. Hollis. You might have information we can use and not realize it."

"When would be a good time for you?"

"My partner and I could come by in about an hour and a half, if that's okay."

"That's fine. See you then." She hung up and returned the receiver to its base. She looked at Alec. "Visitors in ninety minutes."

"You couldn't put them off?"

"They're all over me. If I delay any longer, it might get ugly."

Asmodeus had already stated his desire for the cleanest extraction possible. If he was coming, he'd wait until the coast was clear.

"Angel—"

Eve stood. "You'll know what to do when the time comes."

"I hate this," he growled, rising in a fluid ripple of power. "I hate not knowing when to duck."

"You love it," she retorted, stepping close enough to set one hand on the taut muscles of his abdomen. "Unpredictability is your forte."

"I've had enough of that the last few weeks." Alec caught her hand and moved it over his heart. "I'm ready for stability."

"Haven't you noticed that I'm normalcy-challenged? Chaos reigns in my life. If I'm your best shot at stability, you're in trouble."

He grinned. "Don't I know it."

The police arrived before an hour had passed. Eve suspected they'd done so as a way to keep her unnerved.

Montevista and Sydney rode the elevator down with her and Alec, but they separated on the ground floor. The guards headed toward the open-air courtyard where the pool was. Eve and Alec went to the glass entrance door and let the detectives in.

"I hope you don't mind that we're early," Jones said as they stepped into the foyer. He was sporting an avocado green suit and the grimly assessing gaze she was getting too familiar with. "We were in the neighborhood."

Ingram shook Eve's hand with a palm made cold and wet by the chilled water bottle he carried. He shot a sidelong glance at her when he greeted Alec the same way, betraying his dubious view of her dual boyfriend situation.

"I see firemen around the building," Jones noted. "What's going on?"

"Suspected gas leak on one of the floors," she lied, becoming irritated when her mark burned.

Is that really necessary? she complained, with a glare sent skyward. *It's a white lie.*

"Should we go somewhere else?" Ingram asked.

"My floor is clear, but we can sit in the courtyard." She gestured in that direction and they moved ahead of her. She and Alec exchanged glances.

They gathered around a circular glass patio table, one of the few that lacked an umbrella, since the temperature was cool and the sun warm. The pool was being topped off. A small spigot released a stream of tap water, raising the water level. The tinkling sound created a tranquil atmosphere. Eve deliberately chose a seat that kept her back to a planter bordering a wall. Montevista and Sydney, professionals that they were, were inconspicuous.

Jones was lugging around the briefcase Eve had come to dread. He set it on the pebbled cement and withdrew her unfinished statement. After pushing it across the table toward her, he leaned back in the cushioned metal chair.

"I've been going over our previous discussions," he said.

Eve picked up the pen he provided. "Yes?"

"And I think—"

A burst of crimson. A scattering of black feathers. Alec's chair rocked back onto its rear legs before toppling him completely. The gun's report echoed.

He was sprawled across the patio before anyone registered the ambush.

Reed was waiting at Sara's desk when she came in. Her dangerously short pinstriped skirt was paired with a fitted white dress shirt and four-inch stilettos that matched her red lipstick. The length of leg exposed and the lack of a bra weren't lost on him, but neither did they impress.

She paused just inside the threshold, eyeing him warily. "Abel. What are you doing?"

He smiled. The chair he occupied was angled parallel to the length of the desk. His right arm draped along it, his fingers drumming into the stained walnut top. "Didn't I tell you that showing that video to Evangeline would be counterproductive?"

She stepped closer, her gaze moving to the computer monitor. She saw that the "sent" folder of her e-mail client was on display and murmured, "You go too far."

"You think so? But I haven't gone nearly as far as you have. For example, I haven't yet offered to trade you to a king of Hell to be rid of you."

Reed had to give her credit, she didn't even blink.

"We match today, *mon chéri*. We look so good together. Perfect for one another." Sara reached him and settled into his lap, her slim arms encircling his shoulders. "I would never wish to be rid of you."

He caught her close and whispered, "I can't say the same about you."

An instant later, they occupied a sofa in Michael's office. It was after six in the evening in Jerusalem, and the head of the Asian firm was literally on his way out the door when he spotted his visitors.

"Abel. Sarakiel." The archangel paused and pushed his hands into the pockets of his Western business slacks. His voice was deeply resonant, powerful in a way even some seraphs never achieved. "I suggest you find another place to play your games."

Reed pushed Sara unceremoniously onto the couch beside him and stood. He withdrew the jump drive he'd brought with him and tossed it. "Sara's latest game is one you may not want her to continue playing."

Michael caught the drive with a fluid outstretching of his arm. He looked at the item in his palm, then back at Reed. One dark brow arched in silent inquiry.

"It seems," Reed explained, "that our lovely Sarakiel has taken to making deals with demons."

Michael's eyes shimmered with blue flame. He looked at Sara, who tilted her chin defiantly while tugging her skirt back into place.

Reed crossed his arms and prepared to enjoy the show. Then Eve hit him like a freight train. He stumbled from the blow.

"Gotta run," he said.

Sara straightened. "You cannot leave me here! It will take at least a day to get back—"

He shifted away before she finished her sentence.

As Alec rolled out of his chair, Ingram yelled and reached into his jacket for his holstered gun. A bullet caught him in the back, exploding through his right shoulder in a shower of flesh and blood. His chair tumbled to the left. His arms flailed, then his skull hit the edge of a stucco planter with a sickening thud. He crumpled to the ground, still as death.

Eve slid under the table in a limbolike glide. Arching over the metal legs, she scrambled for Ingram's gun. Her hand circled the grip and she yanked the weapon free of its shoulder holster. Another shot rang out and Jones jerked violently. He crashed headfirst into the tabletop, shattering the glass on impact. The slivers rained down on her, prickling across her bare arms and skittering along the patio.

A battle cry preceded the snapping deployment of Alec's wings. He launched from the courtyard floor in a streak of ebony, his ascent propelled with such force that the downdraft shoved Eve into the planter.

As he targeted a marksman in an open third-floor window, she struggled to her knees. He disappeared into the building and a moment later, a horrendous scream cut off abruptly.

Sydney appeared at the end of the courtyard. She darted toward Eve, weaving around the obstacles between them. Bursts of green hellfire dotted the ground behind her, mimicking her footsteps and urging her to a faster pace. Montevista shouted and ran the length of the opposite side of the pool, deliberately drawing fire away from both Eve and his partner.

Eve scrambled out and upright, slipping in the blood pooling beneath

Detective Jones. His body hung over the broken table, folded at the waist with his arms, torso, and head inverted inside the empty frame.

She hopped into the planter behind her and took cover behind a mature palm tree. Hugging the trunk, she aimed Ingram's gun around it. Windows along the upper floor were dotted with demons. She and the two Mark guards were in a fishbowl, with enemies positioned all around the rim.

By clearing out the building to protect the mortals, they'd opened the entire complex to an Infernal infestation. Eve didn't wonder how they'd gotten past the perimeter guards. She'd made it possible, after all.

Sydney jumped into the planter behind Eve, shielding her back with a flame-covered sword. Montevista was pinned behind a trash can, crouched low and holding two flameless daggers in his hands. He popped up occasionally, hurtling the weapons at strategic windows, then ducking to summon replacements for the next salvo.

"He's covering us," Eve bit out. "So we can get to the lobby."

"On your count," Sydney said. "We'll make a run for it."

Eve fought off the emotions she didn't have time to feel and revealed the whole of her plan to her handler in one powerful surge of thought.

A massive shadow swept over the courtyard. *Alec.* Flying across the expanse from one window to another. Another scream rent the morning calm, followed by another trail of black as he darted back to the other side. Creating a canopy of sorts with his body, a barrier between her and the Infernals above.

As the Marks who'd been on watch on the street joined the fray, flickers of flame could be seen behind many of the windows. Eve's mark began to burn, pumping adrenaline and aggression like a cocktail through her veins. Her gaze met Sydney's. On the silent count of three, they leaped out of the planter in unison.

"Not so fast."

Eve turned. A three-headed . . . *thing* galloped toward her on mismatched animal limbs. She aimed and squeezed the trigger. It feinted fast as lightning, dodging the bullet before lunging. Eve was propelled into the pool, striking the water on her back. The massive demon pushed her beneath the surface, weighting her down in a rapid descent to the bottom.

The shock of the water caused Eve to drop the gun. The weapon hit the bottom with a muffled thud and skittered away. She couldn't retrieve it while pinned nine feet down.

The necklace.

The moment the thought entered her mind, a shadow blotted the sun. An object struck the water and sank quickly. As Alec moved out of the way of the light, the gold chain glittered, catching a ray of sunshine. The necklace arrowed its way toward Eve as if she were a magnet.

The demon released her in a panicked scramble that tore flesh from her thigh, bolting from the pool like a missile. The amulet settled around her neck and she clawed her way upward, breaking through the surface with great, burning gasps.

"Hollis!"

Sydney stood at the pool edge, one shirt sleeve bloodied but the other arm extended. With a mark-fueled kick, Eve surged up and toward her, catching Sydney's hand and gripping it tightly. The Mark hauled her out with a violent yank, dropping her on the ground in a bleeding, sputtering pile.

Eve gained her hands and knees, then ducked as a flame-covered dagger flew over her head. Her gaze lifted to Sydney's, but the Mark was looking beyond her, tossing blades in a barrage.

Eve looked over her shoulder. A massive man stalked toward her, wet and naked, with dripping black hair and laser-bright red eyes.

One by one, he gripped the dagger hilts from where they protruded from his chest and ripped them free, stomping forward with a ferocious, relentless stride.

Alec swept down in a potent gust of wind, alighting on the path between them and roaring like a beast. Many beasts. A sound so fearsome the walls shook with it and the pool water sloshed up and over the rim in a wave.

She had the necklace. There was nothing reining him back now.

His thirty-foot wingspan refolded into his back as if it had never been. The demon hunkered down before quickening into a full-bore run, fisting bloodied daggers with upraised arms, blades leading the way.

His forward momentum was awesome, each footfall shaking the ground like aftershocks. Alec crouched, visibly braced for the impact.

"Cain!" the demon bellowed, leaping high and hurtling downward.

He was directly above Alec when he stopped abruptly, momentarily hovering before snapping backward as if retrieved by a rubber band.

The demon's flight was halted by a brutal collision with something on the walkway. His body slid down, revealing Satan standing rigidly behind him. Claws formed from the Devil's hands and dug deep into the demon's torso, arresting the downward slide in a vicious semblance of an embrace.

Eve glanced at the detectives, but they lay unmoving. Were they both dead? Casualties of a war they didn't know was being waged?

She looked back at Satan and found him staring at her.

"Took you long enough to step in," she muttered.

Alec backed up in deliberate steps, forcing Eve to clamber to her feet to get out of his way. She was behind him one second, then tossed over Reed's shoulder the next. "*This* was your plan?" he bit out.

He shifted her near a body lying prone on the ground.

Montevista. Felled like a cut tree with his eyes open and sightless. The whites swallowed by black.

"Damn it," she breathed, hating that she'd been right. She grabbed the Mark's shoulder and rolled him into her lap on his back. She brushed his dark hair back from his forehead and hunched over him protectively, linking her fingers with his and holding his hand to her chest. Alec shifted Sydney over a split-second later.

From their position on the opposite side of the pool, she watched in horror as Satan reaffirmed his dominance.

"You want what's mine, Asmodeus?" the Devil hissed. His claws rent through the demon's torso, eliciting screams so agonized tears came to Eve's eyes. Through the lacerations in his mortal skin, Asmodeus's true shape could be seen. The monstrous many-limbed body writhed and sizzled within the torn flesh. Smoke poured from the widening cavity and filled the air with the stench of rotten soul.

"It will cost you," Satan crooned with his lips to the demon's ear as if they were lovers.

The Prince of Hell threw the decimated body into the swimming pool like rubbish. The water shuddered in response, bubbling red and churning, boiling and hissing steam. A geyser erupted from the center, spewing into the air in a twenty-foot tower.

Eve looked at Satan, who smiled his gorgeous smile. Dressed in black velvet vest and pants, he was classically and elegantly beautiful.

Something flitted across his features. A wince, then widened eyes. He clutched at his chest, hunching over with a groan.

Montevista's hand tightened on hers with a pained gasp. *"Eve."*

She jolted in surprise, then looked down at her friend. Montevista's powerful body began to shudder. His eyes were his own, no longer black.

"Only way," he wheezed.

The necklace draped inadvertently over their clasped hands, awakening the Mark in him and freeing him to summon the dagger now impaling his heart.

"No!" Reaching up, Eve caught Reed's wrist.

His gaze moved from Satan and settled on Montevista. "Oh shit . . ."

"Take him to the tower. Hurry."

Reed hefted the Mark into his arms and shifted, disappearing in the blink of an eye.

"Eve," Satan snarled. His arm snapped out toward the pool, the veins bulging along the rigid muscles.

The earth shuddered and groaned. The water in the center of the pool twisted into rope and arced onto the cement, forming the outline of a man whose endless arms extended in a desperate grasp for Alec.

The Devil's form flickered, his face contorting with savage rage and frustration. Then he faded completely. There one moment, gone the next.

Eve lunged into the Nix's path. He caught her, laughing, hauling her across the pool and up against his chest.

"Fuck you," she bit out, ripping the amulet from her neck and shoving it fist first into his torso. He instantly gained form, materializing into a man as nude as the others had been. Her hand pulled free of the closing flesh, leaving the necklace behind inside him. He fell on her, writhing. She drew back her fist and decked him, sending him rearing upward with a violent arching of his back.

"Freeze! Police!"

The Nix clawed wildly into his mortal chest, struggling to excise the necklace.

A gunshot reverberated in the semienclosed space. Followed by another. The Nix jerked with each impact, screaming an inhuman sound as two holes appeared in his torso. Blood spurted onto Eve. He fell to his side, convulsing before shuddering into stillness.

Eve twisted to look behind her.

Detective Ingram kneeled beside his fallen partner with Jones's gun in hand. As his gaze met hers, his pistol arm fell to his side. A trail of blood marred his temple and the side of his neck.

"Are you okay?" he asked, swaying.

"Detective . . ."

His eyes rolled back in his head. He slipped into unconsciousness, slumping to the ground before she could reply.

"Holy shit." Eve rolled painfully to her stomach.

As she regained her feet, the pool continued its roiling boil. She stared at it, unblinking.

When Gadara burst from the depths in a flurry of dirty and tattered wings with Riesgo cradled in his arms, she was too numb to be surprised. The archangel landed on both feet, then fell to one knee. Riesgo lay in his embrace with arms splayed wide and head lolled back, breathing shallowly. The picture they presented—that of wounded angel protecting frail humanity—struck her with a message of faith and benevolence as nothing else in her life had ever done.

"Alec," she croaked.

He shifted beside her and caught her close.

CHAPTER 21

E ve tried not to look disgruntled as Reed pushed her through the hospital room doorway in a wheelchair.

I feel ridiculous in this thing, she muttered.

You looked ridiculous trying to maneuver on crutches, he retorted, softening the sting of his words with a squeeze of her shoulder. "Good afternoon, Detective."

Ingram offered a slight wave that jostled the IV tube connected to the back of his hand. The detective's other arm was in a cast. He looked soul-weary, the pale blue of the hospital gown only emphasizing how wan he was. The other bed in the room was closed off by a curtain, leaving the detective alone with a uniformed female officer whom he introduced as his daughter.

"Nice to meet you," Eve said, extending her hand as Officer Ingram stood. The younger Ingram was trim and fit, with pretty features and dishwater blonde hair cropped super short.

"Are you okay?" the officer asked.

"Yes. I'm fine. Healing nicely, they tell me."

Eve didn't really need the wheelchair. The mark had healed the deep gash to her thigh over the last forty-eight hours and only a little redness remained. Still, the subterfuge was necessary since the wound had been nasty enough to take weeks for an Unmarked body to heal.

"You're a popular guy, Detective." She gestured at the profusion of flowers and balloons.

"They should be sending these flowers to the funeral home," Ingram said bitterly.

Reed's fingers caressed the side of her neck in a silent offer of comfort.

"I'm sorry for your loss," she said quietly.

"We all lost." Ingram sighed heavily. "Jones was a great cop. I was honored to w-work with him."

Her eyes stung when the detective's voice broke. "I need to thank you, Detective. You saved my life."

He flushed. "I was just doing my job."

"You're a great cop, too, something I'm profoundly grateful for." Changing the subject, as she'd learned to do when her dad became uncomfortable with sentimentality, she asked, "How long will you be in the hospital?"

"I'll be released tomorrow. Thank God."

She nodded and managed a smile. "I'm going to check on Father Riesgo now, but I'll stop back by before I go home."

Ingram looked at his daughter. "The priest is back?"

"Popped up yesterday," she confirmed. "Said he decided to walk home."

"From Anaheim to Huntington Beach?" Ingram was clearly dubious. "What's he doing in the hospital?"

"Severe dehydration."

"From the trek home? No, don't answer." Ingram heaved out a sigh. "I swear this world is going to hell in a handbasket."

Reed turned Eve's wheelchair around and pushed her back out to the hallway. As he steered her in the direction of Riesgo's room, he murmured, "Well, they'll be out of your hair now."

"See? It all worked out."

"Oh, no, babe. You're not getting off the hook that easily. Your plan was more fucked up than mine."

"No way," she argued, tilting her head back to look up at him. "Everything's wrapped up perfectly—the mask is contained, the wolf and Nix are finally dead, so are the hellhounds, the police are off my back, and the tengu are eradicated from Olivet Place. I finally feel like I can get started with a clean slate, like every other Mark does."

"If the way this shit has gone down is your idea of perfect," he said dryly, "we have a lot to talk about."

Reed slowed, then turned into a room. There were two beds—one occupied, the other freshly made. The patient in the far bed was sleeping. And he wasn't Riesgo.

"Wrong room," Eve said.

Backing up, Reed looked at the number by the door. "No. This is the number they gave us at the desk."

He hailed a passing nurse and asked, "Do you know which room Miguel Riesgo is in?"

"I believe he was discharged," she said briskly. "Just a short while ago."

Eve frowned. "Thank you."

The nurse moved away.

Reed's hand settled on her shoulder. "Didn't you leave a message that you were coming?"

"Yes, this morning." She reached up to link her fingers with his. "I'm really worried about him."

Riesgo had looked so broken when he'd returned. Half-dead. She could only hope that his emotional state was better than his physical one. She wouldn't relax until she saw for herself.

"We'll track him down when we leave here," Reed promised, giving her hand a reassuring squeeze. "We'll make sure he's okay."

Eve wished it was possible to fade into the woodwork while staring straight into a satellite feed. Alas, there was no way to hide from the many eyes that rested heavily on her.

"How is it that no one recognized what happened to Diego Montevista?" Gabriel asked. "He worked directly with all of you. You saw him every day."

Five beautiful faces frowned in unison from the massive LCD screen hanging on the wall directly opposite Eve. The feed was divided into six equal sized boxes, with one box left blank because Sarakiel was present at one end of the table. Gadara sat across from her, separated by several feet. Hank, Alec, Reed, Sydney, and Eve rounded out the room's occupants. A shade had been lowered over the wall of windows, dimming the light from the midmorning sun.

Hank leaned forward and all eyes moved to him. "It appears that Montevista could be left dormant at times and activated at others."

"But you suspected him, Evangeline?" Remiel asked. Like most of the other archangels, he was dark-haired. Unlike the others, his eyes were almond shaped and his features tinged with a decidedly Asian cast.

Eve cleared her throat. "I didn't at first, no. But when Hank told me about his experiments with the tengu and I saw how violently it reacted to the mask mixture, I started thinking about Montevista and his resurrection from the hellhound blood. The only other known . . . *resurrectees*—is that a word?—were the wolf and the Nix, both of whom acted erratically after they came back to life. It seemed reasonable to assume Montevista wouldn't be the only one unaffected."

"That is a considerable leap," Michael said, in a voice that was both deeply seductive and highly terrifying. There was power in that voice. It underlined every word he said with a threat. The fact that he was gorgeous only made him more frightening. "To decide that he was Sammael's emissary because of the behavior of two lesser demons."

"I *guessed*," she corrected. "And it wasn't just because the wolf and Nix seemed to have lost all sense of self-preservation after cooking in the masking agent." She looked at Alec. "Cain became erratic, too. He wasn't himself. Since all of you have the same setup at your firms that he had—the connection to Marks and Infernals working beneath you—I looked at the differences between his situation and yours."

"Everything about his situation is unique," Uriel said.

"Including Montevista," she finished. "I figured that if he was connected to Sammael by the mask, some of that evil would filter into Cain. It would explain a lot of Cain's behavior if that was the case."

"There were other possible explanations for that."

She met the archangel's gaze directly, understanding that he was referring to the paternity gossip that pained Alec so greatly. "I'm not one to rule anything out. The mask, Cain's problems, the way Montevista would lose consciousness every time Satan manifested—there were a lot of considerations involved. But since I didn't know for sure, I wasn't going to accuse him outright. It was too dangerous for Montevista. I hoped that if I turned out to be right, Hank could save him somehow."

"I am concerned," Remiel said, "at how often you work alone. You have a mentor for a reason. We cannot afford to have these types of large-scale battles waged in public places."

"And I," Gadara said dryly, "cannot afford to replace every luxury car that has the misfortune of crossing paths with her."

"I didn't have much choice," Eve protested. "In this case, Montevista was a wild card. I guessed he was involved in some way, so how could I share information with Cain, knowing it might leak to Montevista? If Satan knew we were on to him, what would he do? That was my concern."

"You should have approached your handler."

"She did." Reed leaned forward to set his elbows on the table. "She asked me to touch base with Asmodeus, and when everything blew up, she called me in to keep one eye on Montevista. When he blacked out, it proved her theory. She also kept Ishamel and Hank in the loop. She doesn't have a savior complex, if that's what you're inferring. She knows her limits."

Don't piss them off, she protested, knowing he was already taking heat for his deal with Asmodeus.

They're pissing me *off,* he shot back.

Raphael rocked back in his office chair. "And Sarakiel made herself a threat with her association with Asmodeus, so you could not turn to her. But you must understand, Ms. Hollis. You are consorting and conspiring with Sammael by your own admission. You say that he deliberately summoned the Nix for you to vanquish before he lost contact with Montevista. His offering to you concerns us, of course."

Okay, they're pissing me off, too, Eve groused.

"Is there news of the priest?" Uriel asked.

Gadara leaned forward. There was nothing about his posture or features that bore witness to his ordeal, but it was there in his eyes. Especially when he looked at Alec. "Nothing," he replied. "He has not been seen or heard from since he recovered enough to leave the tower. He has left the church and broken his residential lease. I *will* find him. It is only a matter of time."

There was a length of silence as the archangels flipped through copies of the various reports in search of unasked questions. Eve waited for queries about Ima or the necklace, but they didn't come.

Sydney raised her hand, which raised one of Gadara's brows.

"Yes, Ms. Sydney?"

She cleared her throat. "Montevista . . . Did he get in?"

"He committed suicide," Sarakiel said.

"I *know* that. What does that mean?" Sydney's gaze darted across the screen, then shot to Gadara. "Diego did it for us. To save us. To save us all."

"I testified highly for him, Ms. Sydney," Gadara murmured.

"As did I," Alec said.

"That's it?" She looked at Eve and tears welled. "That's all?"

"I think we are finished here," Michael said. "If we have further questions, we can revisit this discussion."

Eve quickly found herself in the hallway outside the conference room. Sydney hurried off, her shoulders tight and her posture defensive. Sarakiel, Gadara, and Reed lingered behind, speaking in harsh tones.

Hank was walking up to Eve when Alec appeared beside her. He caught her elbow and asked, "Can it wait, Hank?"

"Certainly." The occultist smiled. "Good to have you back, Cain."

Alec grinned. One blink later, Eve found herself standing in the midst of a city at night. The sights, sounds, and smells were foreign and exotic. Her disorientation lasted a moment, then she tugged free of Alec's grip and smacked him in the arm. "Don't do that without telling me first!"

He caught her about the waist. "Have you ever been to Cairo before?"

"Cairo," she repeated. "No, I can't say I have."

"There's a first time for everything." The glint in his eyes told her he was thinking of a more intimate first time between them. "Are you hungry?"

"When am I not these days?"

"Good." He held her hand and tugged her out of the shadows. "There's a great restaurant up the street I've been dying to take you to . . ."

Lilith stood in front of the window with her back to him, dressed in white from head to toe—turtleneck, slacks, and high-heeled boots. Her waist-length hair was so pale that it blended in with the rest. As a whole, her sleek alabaster form was a stark contrast to the greens and blues Sammael had determined would showcase her to perfection.

The same snap of his fingers that had wrought the instantaneous change in the color palette also urged her to turn around. She spotted him and her entire demeanor changed. Her shoulders went back and her stance widened. Defensively aggressive.

"Lilith," Sammael murmured. "How good of you to come so quickly."

"As if I had a choice," she retorted, but her breathless tone gave her away.

He terrified her. He could make her tremble and cry, cower and beg.

And she loved it, which gave him power she'd rather not cede. She'd been grateful when he tired of her so many, many centuries ago.

Which begged the question: what had possessed her to incite his wrath, when even his amusement was a horror to her?

"You did have a choice." He moved to the chaise by the fire and sprawled across it. "You chose to barter something of mine for your own gain. Which is why you are here now. Had you chosen to barter something of your own, you would not be."

Her chin lifted. "You have something that belongs to me. I needed something of yours to entice you to give it back."

"Hmm." His mouth curved. "You speak in near riddle. I need to punish you soon, so hurry up and tell me what you wanted."

Lilith hesitated, her gaze darting about as if she was trapped, which she was. He couldn't allow anyone to steal from him. Such offenses had to be dealt with harshly and swiftly, as he'd proven to Asmodeus.

"I want Awan."

Surprise reverberated through him, followed by a growing delight. "I had forgotten about her."

"I haven't."

"You could have just asked me."

She clasped her hands behind her back. "I knew you wouldn't give her to me."

"Did you? And you reached that conclusion how?"

"Because," she pouted. "You've always made certain that I never get what I want."

Sammael propped his head on one hand and looked into the fire. "You think too highly of yourself, if you believe I deny you for the simple pleasure of it."

"Prove me wrong."

He raked her with an insolent glance. "Nothing about you gives me pleasure . . . except this request."

Lilith stood frozen, then a look of wonder crossed her beautiful face. "You'll recycle her?"

"Yes, but you will not be seeing her for a while." He breathed on his claws, then buffed them across the settee's velvet. "You see, a prison cell that has recently become vacant must be filled."

She inhaled sharply.

"Come now," Sammael crooned. "You have been missed around here. You should have many visitors. Most will be very eager to reacquaint themselves with you. And have no fear, I will not be one of them."

He waved her away. Two demons emerged from the shadows to take her by the arms.

"I hate you," she spat.

"My dear Lilith." Sammael laughed. "I really would not have it any other way."

* * *

"Are you okay?"

Eve glanced up as Reed straddled the picnic bench beside her. The ocean breeze ruffled his hair, giving him the deliciously disarrayed look of a man fresh out of bed. She'd only seen that look on him a few times, but it was a look she loved.

"I miss Montevista," she admitted. "And I'm angry about it. It's not fair."

"Babe . . ." The frown on display above his Armani sunglasses betrayed his concern. "He's in a better place. Trust me."

"Look at Sydney." She jerked her chin toward the sullen Mark who sat at a table near the grill where Alec flipped burgers. "She was just starting to get her mojo back. Now she's back to square one."

"This job is rough." Reed surreptitiously stroked the side of her pinky finger. "I worry about what it'll do to you."

Eve worried, too, which was why she'd brought her parents along today. They kept her grounded. Her dad sat at a table with Kobe Denner and Ken Callaghan, one of her marked training classmates. Her mom was working her way through the gathering with a tray of mini sushi and her shockingly naughty sense of humor. If some of the Marks were jealous that Eve still had her folks in her life, they weren't showing it today. Montevista was on everyone's mind and grief trumped envy every time.

"I'm going to go sit with her," Eve said, climbing off the bench. Reed came with her.

Sydney was accepting a plate from Alec when they joined her. The grill he manned was massive; large enough to cook hamburgers for a dozen oversized Mark appetites at a time. It had taken a trailer to get it out here—a tailgate party done on a Gadara Enterprises scale. Eve had mentioned her desire to do something for the Marks who'd come under fire because of the bounty, and Ishamel had swiftly taken it to the next level.

"Hey, you." Alec leaned over and gave her a quick peck on the forehead. "You feeling medium, or medium-well today?"

She was about to reply when the distant rumble of a Harley gave her pause. Pulling tendrils of windblown hair out of her lip gloss, she watched through her sunglasses as a platinum blonde on a hog maneuvered into the parking lot. Dressed in a black leather halter vest and chaps, the rider drew every eye except for Alec's.

The bike rolled to a halt beside the trailer as Alec turned his head. The pretty blonde winked at Eve, then blew a kiss at Alec.

The spatula in his hand clattered onto the cement.

Eve looked at Reed. "Who's that?"

"Awan." He grinned like the Cheshire Cat. "Cain's wife."

"Ex-wife," Alec correctly swiftly.

Awan licked her lips and purred, "Hi, honey. I'm home."

She was a lili. The demonic green eyes gave her away. They were laser-bright and filled with mischief.

Eve stood. This was the mother of Alec's children; the only progeny he would ever have. She had a piece of him that no one else ever would.

Eve's turmoil must have reached Alec, because his fists clenched. Awan laughed. With a saucy wave, the lili roared off as quickly as she'd appeared.

For a long moment, no one said a word.

Then, Sydney broke the tense silence. "Uh . . . I thought your wife was your sister."

Alec snatched the spatula off the ground and threw it into the back of the trailer. "My father kicked Lilith to the curb long before I was born. There's no relation between me and her kids."

Eve cleared her throat. "Your c-children were half demon?"

His shoved his hands through his thick hair. "One quarter demon."

What could she say to that?

Her mom walked up with an empty tray and a bright smile. "What a great party!"

Reed tapped his steepled fingertips together and kept on grinning.

Tossing her bath towel over the hamper, Eve left her bathroom. A quick glance at the clock told her it was nearing eight o'clock in the evening. She pulled on her favorite pajamas and shook out her damp hair, contemplating how best to spend her evening. A feel-good movie while curled up on the couch sounded like heaven to her. She usually preferred blow-'em-up action flicks, but she'd had enough explosions for a while. Maybe *Becoming Jane* would do the trick or something stupidly funny like *Blades of Glory*.

She moved down the hallway toward the kitchen, seeking comfort food. Hot coffee, maybe. And something sweet. She deserved it after today.

Straight ahead, the balcony door was closed. It was starting to get cold at night. Summer slowly turning into autumn. What a year it had been so far. Last Christmas she'd grumbled at RSVPing to the Weisenberg Group's company party without a date. Now, she had her dream job at Gadara Enterprises and two determined men she couldn't resist.

Admittedly, the dream job was more of a nightmare and the two men were both in the off stage of the on-and-off relationships she had with each of them, but she wasn't going to think about that now.

Eve was turning into the kitchen when Stevie Nicks's beautiful "Crystal" replaced the silence. She stopped midstride. Then cautiously started forward again, continuing to where the hall emptied into the living room.

On the coffee table, a silver champagne bucket held a napkin-wrapped bottle next to two half-full flutes. The man at her entertainment center felt her gaze and turned to face her. Although he appeared casual and relaxed, his dark gaze was avid. "Hi."

"Hi, yourself."

He approached, picking up the glasses along the way. "I hope you don't mind that I popped in."

"You're always welcome. Nothing is going to change that."

A cool flute was pressed into her hand. She looked down, catching sight of something circular glittering at the bottom. Her breath caught.

"I'm glad to hear that," he murmured with his warm fingers wrapped around hers. "Because I have a question to ask you . . ."

APPENDIX

The Seven Archangels

These are the names of the angels who watch.

1. Uriel, one of the holy angels, who presides over clamor and terror.

2. Raphael, one of the holy angels, who presides over the spirits of men.

3. Raguel, one of the holy angels, who takes vengeance on the world of the luminaries.

4. Michael, one of the holy angels, to wit, he that is set over the best part of mankind and over chaos.

5. Sarakiel, one of the holy angels, who is set over the spirits, who sin in the spirit.

6. Gabriel, one of the holy angels, who is over Paradise and the serpents and the Cherubim.

7. Remiel, one of the holy angels, whom God set over those who rise.

—THE BOOK OF ENOCH 20:1–8

The Christian Hierarchy of Angels

First Sphere: Angels who function as guardians of God's throne.
- Seraphim
- Cherubim
- Ophanim/Thrones/Wheels *(Erelim)*

Second Sphere: Angels who function as governors.
- Dominions/Leaders *(Hashmallim)*
- Virtues
- Powers/Authorities

Third Sphere: Angels who function as messengers and soldiers.
- Principalities/Rules
- Archangels
- Angels *(Malakhim)*

Abbreviated Playlist *(in no particular order)*

- "Killing in the Name Of"—Rage Against the Machine
- "Blasphemous Rumours"—Depeche Mode
- "California Love"—Tupac
- "Carry On Wayward Son"—Kansas
- "Wanted Dead or Alive"—Bon Jovi
- "Blitzkrieg"—Metallica
- "Symphony of Destruction"—Metallica
- "Like a Dog Chasing Cars"—Hans Zimmer and James Newton Howard
- "Voodoo"—Godsmack
- "Ghost Riders in the Sky"—Spiderbait
- "The Judas Kiss"—Metallica
- "Dare You to Move"—Switchfoot
- "Love Remains the Same"—Gavin Rossdale
- "Broken, Beat & Scarred"—Metallica
- "Crystal"—Stevie Nicks

MORE EXTRAS AT WWW.SYLVIADAY.COM

ABOUT THE AUTHOR

SYLVIA DAY is the #1 *New York Times* and #1 international bestselling author of more than a dozen award-winning novels translated into over three dozen languages. She has been nominated for the Goodreads Choice Award for Best Author and her work has been honored as Amazon's Best of the Year in Romance. She has won the *RT Book Reviews* Reviewers' Choice Award and been nominated for Romance Writers of America's prestigious RITA award twice. Visit the author at www.sylviaday.com, facebook.com/authorsylviaday, and twitter.com/sylday.